THE STEEL WAVE

THE STEEL WAVE

A NOVEL OF
WORLD WAR II

JEFF SHAARA

BALLANTINE BOOKS

New York

Copyright © 2008 by Jeffrey M. Shaara
Maps © 2008 Mapping Specialists, Ltd.,
Madison, WI, U.S.A.

Published in the United States by Ballantine Books,
an imprint of The Random House Publishing Group,
a division of Random House, Inc., New York.

BALLANTINE and colophon are registered trademarks of Random House, Inc.

LIBRARY OF CONGRESS CATALOGING-IN-PUBLICATION DATA
Shaara, Jeff
The steel wave: a novel of World War II / Jeff Shaara.
p.   cm.
ISBN 978-0-345-46142-1
1. World War, 1939–1945—Campaigns—France—Normandy—Fiction. I. Title.
PS3569.H18S74 2008   813'.54—dc22   2008004813

Printed in the United States of America on acid-free paper

www.ballantinebooks.com

2 4 6 8 9 7 5 3 1

First Edition

Book design by Mary A. Wirth

FOR LISA

TO THE READER

This book is the second volume of a trilogy, focusing primarily on America's involvement in World War Two in Europe. In each book I've written, I've felt I should add the disclaimer that, no, this is not a blow-by-blow history, it is not a comprehensive collection of facts and figures. That kind of book certainly has its appeal, and professional historians are far better qualified to tackle that task than I am. This is a novel, and though I am careful to "get it right," by definition the dialogue and inner thoughts of the characters have to be described as fiction. My research relies almost exclusively on original histories, memoirs, diaries, collections of letters, and photographs, as well as interviews with living veterans. This choice of sources reflects my attempt to get into the minds of these characters, to tell their story as they would tell it themselves. The events are true, the history accurate.

Pearl Harbor, Iwo Jima, Stalingrad, Hiroshima. Those names are familiar even if, often, the real story is not. But no event in the history of the Second World War has inspired more popular attention than what we call D-Day, the invasion of Normandy. Hollywood alone has offered dozens of films and countless documentaries that explore the events that we know by the date every schoolchild is taught: June 6, 1944. As I began the research for this book, I was deeply concerned that I would be telling you a story you already knew too well, but as my research progressed and I dug more deeply, my fears abated. I was surprised to find a story that spreads out with a far greater scope than what Hollywood (or your high school history textbook) typically offers us. As the characters became more familiar to me, I realized that the greatest drama here is not the event but the raw and frightening uncertainty for everyone involved. It is easy to view history in hindsight, as though it were a foregone conclusion how the war, or this particular piece of it, would turn out. But for those men whose deeds and accomplishments created this history, there were no foregone conclusions at all.

I also discovered that the story of D-Day is not merely the story of what happens on June 6. For most of us, our familiarity with the Normandy invasion comes from the few existing film clips of that one horrific day, used countless times in documentaries, dramas, and various historical features. Memoirs abound and accounts have been written from every perspective imaginable, many focusing on one awful place called Omaha Beach. Some of these accounts are familiar to any fan of John Wayne or Tom Hanks or Stephen Ambrose. But there is more to this story than one amphibious invasion across one stretch of sand. (Most Americans have heard of Omaha, and with good reason, but how many can name the other four beaches?)

Every war has its share of both glory and horror. I try not to succumb to the temptation to embellish history, to offer morality tales or lessons in hindsight. I make no snide winks toward the reader, subtle scolding that we should compare lessons learned then to lessons we should be learning today. That might make for a fine civics lecture or play into someone's political agenda, but it has no place here.

My goal is to tell you a good story by taking you into the minds of several of the key participants, the men who made this history, to show you the events as they saw them, to hear their words and their thoughts as this extraordinary drama unfolds. From conflicts and strategy sessions between the men at the top to the grinding endurance of the young soldiers who face the enemy, this book is based on the accounts of the men who were *there*. The most gratifying parts of my research were the surprises I found, the voices I hadn't heard before. I hope, by the end of this book, you are surprised as well.

My trilogy on the Second World War (of which this is the centerpiece) is the first time I have had the privilege of speaking to living veterans. Those soldiers are fewer in number every day, and in every instance, when

I interviewed a veteran, he mentioned that fact. I feel strongly that this story has to be told with respect and accuracy. Tribute must be paid. To those soldiers, this is my respectful offering.

JEFF SHAARA,
May 2008

CONTENTS

LIST OF MAPS

RESEARCH SOURCES

I am frequently asked for the sources I have relied upon. The following is a *partial* list of those whose firsthand accounts and overall historical perspectives proved invaluable to me in writing this book.

THE AMERICANS

General Omar Bradley
Captain Harry Butcher
Lieutenant William H. Callaway
General Joseph Lawton Collins
Historian (Lieutenant Colonel) Carlo D'Este
President Dwight D. Eisenhower
Lieutenant General James Gavin
Chaplain Raymond S. Hall (101st Airborne)
Historian Robert Leckie
Secretary of State George C. Marshall
Private John Nowak (First Infantry Division)
Lieutenant General George S. Patton
Journalist Ernie Pyle
General Matthew Ridgway
Private Douglas C. Saum

THE BRITISH

Prime Minister Winston Churchill
Historian (General) David Fraser
Historian (Captain) Sir Basil Liddell Hart

Field Marshal Bernard Montgomery
General Sir Frederick Morgan
Air Marshal Sir Arthur Tedder
Brigadier General Desmond Young

THE GERMANS

Corporal Paul Carell
Colonel Hans von Luck
Field Marshal Erwin Rommel
Admiral Friedrich Ruge
Field Marshal Karl Rudolf Gerd von Rundstedt
Major Heinz Schmidt
Lieutenant General (Dr.) Hans Speidel
General Siegfried Westphal

The following have generously provided me with an astounding variety of research materials. I am enormously grateful to them all.

Fred Alexander, Franklin, North Carolina
Bruce Breeding, Lexington, Kentucky
Curtis Callaway, Danville, Virginia
Andrew Carroll, Washington, D.C.
Tony Collins, Washington, D.C.
Bert Conroy, Prospect, Kentucky
Colonel Keith Gibson, Lexington, Virginia
Major Daniel Hall, U.S.A.
W. D. Hardy, Hardin, Montana
V. F. Henderson, Fort George G. Meade, Maryland
Rocky Hoagland, Marysville, Washington
Phoebe Hunter, Missoula, Montana
Jack Ingram, Columbia, Maryland
Ira Jacobson, New York, New York
Bruce Ladd, Chapel Hill, North Carolina
Bruce Novak, Needham, Massachusetts
John Tiley, Half Moon Bay, California
Kay Whitlock, Missoula, Montana
Michael Wicklein, Baltimore, Maryland

INTRODUCTION

I n December 1941, only days after the Japanese launch their devastating surprise attack on the United States at Pearl Harbor, Hawaii, Japan's ally Germany declares war on the United States. Americans quickly unite behind President Franklin D. Roosevelt's call for action against the infamy inflicted upon our forces, and to most Americans the primary enemy is clearly the Japanese. But Roosevelt and most of his military strategists, including Chief of Staff George C. Marshall, recognize that America's interests are threatened from two directions. Despite the outrage many Americans direct toward the Japanese, the military's first priority must be to confront Adolf Hitler. Though the navy and the Marines will focus most of their energy in the Pacific, Roosevelt and Marshall plan at the same time for America's ground forces to make their first strike across the Atlantic.

Well before the Japanese attack on Pearl Harbor, Roosevelt had taken a stand against German aggressiveness in Europe by not-so-discreetly backing the British war effort. The Lend-Lease Act opened a floodgate of equipment and raw materials, food, and basic necessities that flowed in a continuous stream to the British. Despite some support for Hitler in the States, including angry opposition to Roosevelt from celebrities like Charles Lindbergh, the president unabashedly has referred to England as our most important ally.

Germany's diplomatic outrage is entirely predictable, but even before war is declared, the German navy launches a devastating undersea campaign to destroy Allied shipping. Throughout the first three years of the war, German U-boats are nearly unstoppable. Hundreds of Allied merchant ships are sunk, including some within sight of the American coastline, spectacular displays of destruction that shock Americans from New York to Miami. It is a poignant reminder that Hitler's ambitious claw does indeed reach the borders of the United States.

By 1941, Hitler's war machine has washed over most of Europe. The armies of Poland, France, the Low Countries, Denmark, and Norway have been crushed. The British have been driven completely off the European mainland, their army nearly destroyed in the process. The British military and their American counterparts fully expect the Germans to invade the British Isles, a logical and strategically sound move. If the British are conquered, Hitler will control all he has sought in western Europe. His next step will very likely be a strike across the Atlantic, and Roosevelt knows that America's armed forces are woefully ill-prepared for confrontation.

As the German military commanders prepare for their powerful surge across the English Channel, Hitler suddenly vacillates. To the enormous frustration of his key generals, nearly all of whom believe an invasion of England will succeed, Hitler's order never comes. Instead, he orders his Luftwaffe to bomb British cities, killing civilians at random. Hitler believes this assault on civilian morale will bring the British to their knees. His generals can only watch as thousands of German bombers are confronted by a thin defensive line of British fighter planes. In 1940, in what becomes known as the Battle of Britain, British pilots engage the Luftwaffe with extraordinary gallantry and effectiveness. Hundreds of German aircraft are shot from the sky, and Hitler's dreams for an easy conquest of England go down with them. Strategically and militarily, it is Hitler's first catastrophic mistake.

In June 1941, Hitler makes his second huge miscalculation. Though he has signed a nonaggression pact with the Soviet Union, Hitler surprises the Russians by launching a massive invasion that nearly succeeds in conquering that enormous land and its vast resources. But like Napoleon before him, Hitler finds his army cannot maintain an offensive through the brutal Russian winter, which proves as challenging an adversary as the enormous Russian army. Though German troops close on Stalingrad and reach the gates of Moscow, they cannot finish the job. For the remainder of the war, the Russian campaign will become an enormously costly drain on German manpower and resources. Hitler's most capable field generals begin to wonder whether their Führer's fanatical ambitions can succeed.

While German forces obliterate their opposition on the European mainland, in the Pacific, Hitler's ally the Japanese share similar success, wiping American defenders from the Philippines and occupying nearly every chain of islands in the South Pacific. Though Pearl Harbor is a devastating strike at the U.S. Pacific Fleet, an enormous rebuilding effort begins, with some of the damaged ships from Pearl Harbor made seaworthy in a matter of months. The nation is now energized for war. American forces under General Douglas MacArthur swell in number and effectiveness and begin to push back at the Japanese. With fierce determination, American naval and air defenses hold the line in the central Pacific at the island of Midway, and American and British forces stem the Japanese tide that threatens to wash over Australia and India. As the war progresses, the Japanese military leaders learn that they are not quite as invincible as their emperor has told them. In Europe, that is a lesson Hitler's generals learn as well. But like Emperor Hirohito, Hitler sees neither his own flaws nor the flaws of those sycophantic military planners around him who shelter him from reality.

Despite the increasing irrationality of their Führer, the German generals are for the most part the finest military minds of the war, and German commanders in the field understand what they must do to win their campaigns. But Hitler makes another monumental mistake, one he repeats often; he thwarts his most talented commanders by appointing himself Germany's chief strategist. Yet Hitler never visits frontline positions, never sees for himself what his decisions and his meddling are costing his army.

I n 1941, in North Africa, a German campaign to support Hitler's ally Italian dictator Benito Mussolini becomes a theater of war all its own. The British, based in Egypt, engage in furious battles to prevent conquest of the Suez Canal and the oil fields of the Middle East. Their adversary is Erwin Rommel, a German commander whose energy and audacity have made him a legend. But Rommel's reputation alone cannot bring a German victory. After enormous success against variously inept British commanders, Rommel is finally stopped. Early in November 1942, his army suffers a major defeat in western Egypt at a village called El Alamein. His

British adversary, newly in command, is Bernard Law Montgomery. Monty is a brash and disagreeable man who is no one's first choice for the job. But when his predeccesor is killed unexpectedly in a plane crash, Winston Churchill reluctantly approves Montgomery for the command. Montgomery's stunning defeat of Rommel gives the British a much-needed hero and launches Montgomery into the spotlight as England's most accomplished field commander. Rommel is unimpressed with Montgomery, believing him too slow and methodical. As Rommel retreats westward across Libya, land he had once taken from the British, he is painfully aware that had Hitler responded to his general's repeated cries for supplies and manpower, guns and gasoline, the Germans would never have been turned back. It is a bitter pill for Rommel, who continues to plague the German High Command with incessant calls for support. As the British bolster Montgomery with a steady flow of crucial supplies, Rommel's army is increasingly ill fed and ill equipped. Instead of opening Hitler's eyes to the importance of the North Africa campaign, Rommel has become a pariah, seen by Hitler's henchmen as a bothersome defeatist.

During most of 1942, as the British wage their seesaw war back and forth against the tanks of Rommel's formidable Afrika Korps, the American military pours into Britain with the energy and resources to launch their own ground campaign against Hitler's Fortress Europe. George Marshall vigorously insists that the British agree to an American plan to attack straight across the English Channel, an invasion onto the coast of France. But the British are skeptical. They have already suffered humiliating and costly defeats and have endured far more casualties than the British people can accept. Memories of the First World War are too vivid, and Winston Churchill and his chief of staff, Sir Alan Brooke, are in no hurry to repeat that kind of disaster. The British insist that Hitler's fortifications on the French coast are far too formidable to breach and the cost of such an invasion is far too high. Marshall and the Americans, helpless against British intransigence, know they cannot wage war against Hitler alone. Churchill convinces the Americans instead to join the British in a new strike into North Africa, finally to destroy Rommel's army and begin a campaign to clear the Germans out of the Mediterranean. After much rancor and debate, the Americans agree to put off their plans for an invasion of France. With the British supplying most of the sea and air power for the North African assault, the Americans will provide the vast majority of the ground forces. After much political wrangling, the decision is made to place an American in overall command. The man chosen for the job is General Dwight David Eisenhower.

Eisenhower comes to command after long years in service as an exceptional administrator, a man known for a sharp organizational mind. To the field generals who have faced the enemy, however, Eisenhower is a complete unknown, and there are grave doubts about his abilities on both sides of the Atlantic. But George Marshall has known Eisenhower for many years, considers him far more than just a capable subordinate, and convinces Roosevelt that "Ike" is the man for the job. In the late spring of 1942, Eisenhower arrives in England, where he faces the daunting challenge of uniting the armies, navies, and air forces of two separate countries into one cohesive and cooperative fighting force. Eisenhower faces another challenge as well. He is only a major general, and thus he is outranked by every one of his key British subordinates.

On November 8, 1942, as Montgomery slowly pursues Rommel's bloodied army, the Allies launch Operation Torch, the largest amphibious landing ever attempted. It will become America's first land-based operation of the war and results in a relatively easy conquest of ports and territories in Morocco and Algeria, which are defended mostly by weak Hitler-dominated French forces. The victory emboldens the Americans, who begin to believe that the war will be a rapid affair, brought to a close by their superior arms and cocky enthusiasm. To Rommel, the successful invasion means that he is now squeezed between pressure from Montgomery, to the east, and the hard thrust from American and British troops closing on him from the west. With characteristic speed, Rommel reassembles his army from their lengthy retreat and strikes at the Americans, who he believes are not yet prepared for a serious fight. The Americans first meet Rommel at Kasserine Pass, Tunisia, where inept and unprepared American commanders discover that Rommel's reputation is well earned. Kasserine Pass is an American disaster, and panicked troops and their commanders fall back to safe havens in Algeria. Despite his success, Rommel is virtually ignored by the German High Command. Though he has become a hero to the German populace, Rommel cannot convince Hitler of how inadequately his army is being supplied. As he tours the battlefield, he ruefully observes the enormity of the raw materials and tools of war the Americans have brought to the fight. No matter how often and how successfully he strikes at the enemy closing around him, defeat in North Africa is inevitable.

By the spring of 1943, his pessimism strikes one too many nerves in Berlin, and Rommel is recalled from North Africa. Eisenhower makes a purge of his own, removing several Allied commanders who are not up to the task. As he scrambles to put the best army he can into line against the experienced German opposition, capable U.S. officers begin to emerge. To bolster the sagging spirits and ineffectiveness of the American infantry, Eisenhower names George S. Patton to command the American ground forces. Patton is a fiery and profane man, who shows every indication that he will go only forward on a battlefield. Under Patton, Eisenhower assigns command to another rising star, a West Point classmate whom Eisenhower knows well. His name is Omar Bradley.

Within weeks, Montgomery's forces are united with Eisenhower's, and the Germans in Tunisia are utterly defeated. Their presence in North Africa is eliminated entirely.

But Eisenhower does not rest on his laurels. Immediately, the Allies plan for their next assault, to strike directly into Europe. Still thwarted by the stubbornness of Winston Churchill, the Americans agree to a plan for the invasion of Sicily, to confront the powerful German armor and Italian infantry that have made the island a fascist stronghold. If successful, the conquest of Sicily will open the door for the Allies to invade the Italian mainland.

In July 1943, the invasion is launched: the British under Montgomery, the Americans now led by Patton. Within weeks, Sicily falls, though Patton and Montgomery clash repeatedly over tactics and matters of ego—a feud that will plague Eisenhower for the rest of the war.

With Sicily secure, the Americans continue to accept Winston Churchill's philosophy that the best way to defeat Hitler is to strike hard at his "soft underbelly." In September 1943, the British, again led by Montgomery, and the Americans, led by General Mark W. Clark, invade the Italian mainland. Though the invasion succeeds in driving Mussolini from power, there is no clear military victory. The Italian campaign will drag on for nearly two more years.

Having satisfied Winston Churchill's inflexible insistence on attacking Hitler from below, the Americans begin again to promote their concept of a cross-channel invasion of France. Despite Churchill's stubbornness and the power of his personality, the British realize that if there is to be a victory in Europe, it is American productivity and American manpower that will enable the Allies to continue the fight. Across the Atlantic, American factories are pouring out aircraft, tanks, and military vehicles at an astonishing rate, equipment that is flowing mostly into England. The German U-boat war has been blunted significantly by the use of Allied convoys, enormous numbers of merchant ships traveling in clusters, protected by numerous submarine-destroying ships and planes. There are technological advances as well, such as radar and sonar. As the number of German U-boats declines, the amount of aid and matériel flowing into England dramatically increases. The British have become enormously dependent on American industrial and agricultural production. Finally, despite his misgivings, Churchill accepts the American strategy. There will be an invasion of France.

Throughout the summer and fall of 1943, staff officers in England labor in obscurity, executing the logistical and tactical preparations required for what will be a massive operation. Command of the planning is given to the British general Frederick Morgan. Morgan's title, Chief of Staff to the Supreme Allied Commander, provides the name now given this stage of the operation: COSSAC. In the winter of 1943, Morgan's plan is presented and is amended considerably by those who will carry it out, notably, Bernard Montgomery, who will command the Allied ground forces. But the basics of the plan remain. It is Morgan who suggests that any invasion of France should avoid the Pas de Calais, which is the logical and most predictable place for the invasion to occur. Calais is the closest point to Britain on the French coast, and the Germans have fortified that region to the extreme. Morgan assumes that if the Allies see Calais as the likeliest invasion point, the Germans will do so as well. Morgan chooses instead the less-well-fortified beaches on the northern coast of Normandy.

In early 1944, Morgan's job is complete and COSSAC ceases to exist, replaced by a far larger and more complex command system. The operation is controlled and organized from a vast infrastructure of offices, named Supreme Headquarters, Allied Expeditionary Force, or SHAEF. The invasion plan is given a name: Operation Overlord.

In Washington, General Marshall and President Roosevelt discuss the leadership options for such an enormous and dangerous undertaking. Though Marshall puts his own name up for consideration, Roosevelt realizes that his chief of staff is far too valuable in his current position. Though disappointed, Marshall turns again to the only man who has yet demonstrated the ability to manage such a large-scale organizational nightmare: Dwight Eisenhower. Despite more grumblings from the British, notably Alan Brooke, Winston Churchill begins to champion Eisenhower as the only logical choice to command Overlord. In January 1944, Ike leaves his command in the Mediterranean and returns to London.

Having made too many enemies in the German High Command, Erwin Rommel sits in bored obscurity in a meaningless post in northern Italy, hoping that Hitler will once again come to rely on him for some significant duty in the field. Instead, in late 1943, Rommel receives word that he is being assigned the position of inspector for Army Group West, under the thumb of one of Germany's grand old soldiers, Gerd von Rundstedt, headquartered in Paris. A dismayed Rommel is appointed commander of Army Group B, with the responsibility to fortify and protect the French coastline. Rommel views the position with disgust, believing, with most other German officers, that he has been placed in a backwater of the war. But he attacks his job with the same fervor he has shown throughout his long career and begins to light fires under the complacent commanders who are staring idly out to sea. Despite no indication of an impending invasion, he recognizes that such an attack is inevitable and begins his inspections along the coast, examining what Berlin has labeled Hitler's Atlantic Wall. Rommel is deeply disheartened at what he finds. Should the Allies come, he knows the German defenses are woefully inadequate. He observes firsthand that the defenses along much of the French coast are more fantasy than fact and that the fortresslike barriers exist only in Hitler's mind. Since Rommel has been given a job to do, he decides to do it correctly. If Hitler insists on an impregnable defense along the coast of France, Rommel will do all he can to provide it.

PART ONE

We Germans have a far greater and more urgent duty towards civilization to perform. . . . We, like the Japanese, can only fulfill it by the sword. War is a biological necessity.

FRIEDRICH VON BERNHARDI (1849–1930)

We are determined that before the sun sets on this terrible struggle, our flag will be recognized throughout the world as a symbol of freedom on the one hand, of overwhelming power on the other.

GENERAL GEORGE C. MARSHALL, 1942

1. THE COMMANDO

AT SEA, BAY OF THE SEINE
JANUARY 25, 1944

The air underwater was foul and wet, five men pulling against the thinning oxygen. He sat erect, his back painfully pressed against a coil of wire, part of the electrical system of the craft. She was an X-5 class midget submarine, designed to deliver a magnetic mine or similar explosive device, something to be attached to the bottom of an enemy ship. They were stealthy, of course, no blip on anyone's radar screen, so the British navy had used them on raids all along the coastline, from Norway to the Mediterranean, usually with enormous risk to both the subs and their small crews. But tonight the sub was not armed, and where explosives had once been stored she now carried three passengers and their equipment.

He tried to stretch his back—no room—and twisted his shoulders instead, working out the kinks. The air was growing worse, thin and acrid, bitter smells of oil and wet cloth. There were no dry places in the small sub, every surface had a slick coating of oily grease or water, mostly condensation. The engine made a low hum, deadened by the steel of the bulkhead, the sub lurching slowly from side to side, held now by long low waves that rolled silently toward the beaches.

"Suit up, lads."

The voice was low, a croak from the lieutenant. He knew the order was coming, yanked hard at his small duffel bag, and retrieved it from the tight gap beneath his feet. Inside were all the tools he would need for the mission. The first priority was unrolling the tight spool of the rubber suit, a single piece, zipped open down the front. There was little room to stand, and he fought to slide the thin rubber over his legs, working his feet downward, pushing. He slid the suit beneath his bottom, pushed his arms into the narrow sleeves, freed his fingers, gave one loud grunt, and pulled the suit up over his shoulders. The others were grunting as he was, straining in the tight space, backs and arms bent low, each man forcing himself into his taut suit. He tried to relax, leaning back against the bulkhead, and took a breath, sour air filling his mouth, took another, felt his chest heave in a futile gasp. He was sweating, worse inside the suit, and the air was growing fouler still. No matter how the air cleaners strained, they were not designed to handle the nervous breathing of five men.

He leaned forward again, pulled the zipper tight against his neck, then tugged at the headpiece, sliding it over his ears, snug, only his face revealed. He reached again into the bag, found a small tube of grease, black and oily, squeezed a thick stream onto his fingers, and rubbed it on his face, coating any part that would reflect moonlight. The duffel was nearly empty now, but he found his knife, his only weapon, and strapped it to his leg, tight and secure, then went into the bag again for a small bundle, a cloth pouch attached to a thin belt, and slid it around his waist. The man beside him gave him a nudge with his elbow.

"All set here. You all right, Dundee?"

"Yep. You tight in? Ready?"

The man slapped his hands on Dundee's leg. "Ready as I'll ever be."

Dundee leaned forward, looked past, and said to the third man, "Lieutenant? You set, then?"

The lieutenant scanned both men. Dundee could see his face sweating, a dull wet mask, lit by the yellow glow from the sub's instrument panel. Then the officer began to smear his face with the black grease.

"Don't concern yourselves with me. My job is to worry about you. And right now I'm ready to get this little show moving."

From the main control seat, the sub's commander turned around toward them.

"We'll be on the surface in half a minute. On my command, Mr. Higgins will open the hatch, and out you go. Make it quick. I'll not chance there's some Jerry lookout who's good at his job. This tub won't take pleasantly to incoming fire, and the sooner I can drop us out of sight, the better I like it." He looked at his watch. "Orders say two hours. I'll wait for three if I have to, but that's it. I'm not about to sit out here and wait for the damned sun to come up. Sitting ducks, all of us. You got that?"

The lieutenant pointed at his own watch. "I know my orders, Captain. We'll be back in two hours. Don't go off sightseeing. You've got a periscope—keep an eye in it. I don't plan to tread water any more than I have to."

"I know my tub, Lieutenant. And we're lucky tonight. The surface is pretty smooth right now. A dicky bird swims within a hundred yards of me, I'll spot her. You just do the swimming; I'll see you."

Swimming. Dundee swallowed the word silently. Most of the commando operations were launched from surface crafts, LCNs, small and rugged navigation boats. The LCNs slipped in close to shore, depositing their commandos in folbots, folding canvas boats, flimsy canoes the men would paddle hard to the beach. But there was too much tide and too much current along this stretch of the French coastline, and a folbot might swamp and drown the men before they could even reach the shore. It was a painful lesson; several men had been lost already in earlier operations. Besides being a danger to her crew, a folbot had to be hidden from German patrols, patrols that were growing vigilant. And so, tonight, they would swim.

The captain turned toward his instruments and pulled a lever, the sub tilting upward, the bow rising. Dundee pushed his hands into the narrow metal seat, his back leaning hard against the tight coils, and tried to distract himself, thought suddenly of the captain's boast. What the hell is a dicky bird? The sub swayed, rolling to one side, then upright again, and Dundee's stomach rolled, the stink in the air filling his head with a dull pain, now growing worse. He heard the splashing of water against the bulkheads; the sub was level again, and the captain's lone crewman stood, his hands pressed upward against the narrow hatch, and stared forward toward his captain.

"On your order, sir."

"Steady, Higgins. Not quite on the deck. Wait for it."

They sat quietly, feeling the low hum of the engine and, now, silence, the captain shutting down the engine. Dundee took a long breath, tried to

ignore the sickening smell, his head pounding, a quiver in his hands. He
shook his head, thought, All right, Henry, hold on to yourself. They taught
you this. It's all about lack of oxygen. We'll be out of this damned can in a
few—

"Now, Higgins."

The crewman pulled hard on a round crank: The hatch was suddenly
open, cold air filling the cabin, a splash of water. The lieutenant stood,
hunched over by the overhead close above him, moved toward the hatch,
slapped the captain on the shoulder, said nothing. Dundee waited for the
man beside him, Henley, up and moving, the well-rehearsed routine,
Dundee close behind him. The air was cold and delicious; a blast against
Dundee's face and the headache had vanished. He pressed forward, following the other two toward the blessed opening, watched the lieutenant pull
himself up through the hatch, now just his legs and then gone. Henley followed quickly, up and out of the way, and Dundee grabbed the edges of
the hatch and pulled himself up, his head clear of the dismal space. He was
outside now, in cold darkness, and he pulled his knees up between his
arms, thrust out his feet, sat on the edge of the hatchway, the deck of the
sub narrow and flat. The water was black and silent, long low swells. Now
came the splashes, the other two already swimming, the lieutenant leading
the way, long strokes of his arms, already distancing himself from the sub,
Henley trailing behind him. Dundee looked out that way, saw the shoreline, a vast shadow against the night sky. The sub suddenly rocked, caught
by a swell, and Dundee released his hands, slid down, let the motion of the
sub push him away, pressed his feet against the steel hull, and gave one
sharp push, his arms and legs working the water, the training taking over.
He moved with precise rhythm, his face bathed by the cold. He was a
strong swimmer, essential for this job, slicing quickly through the water,
lifted by more swells, the cold gone now, the strength returning, the power
taking over: so many miles of swimming and running, months of lifting
and climbing, all condensed into these long moments.

His brain kept count of the number of strokes, an exercise that might
have no meaning at all. But in the dark, they would make this swim again,
and if the captain was wrong, if the waves picked up or the surface became
choppy, at least the men could swim out to within yards of where they had
left the sub. It had always seemed to be a foolish gamble, but here, in the
black water, it might be the only chance they had to be picked up again.

His brain ticked past three hundred strokes, and he paused, raised his head, scanned the shoreline, fought for a glimpse of the others, but there was nothing to see, dull blackness, new sounds in his ears, surf, gentle waves rolling forward. He swam again, pushed out sharp breaths, felt aching in his arms, his legs growing stiff, his chest heaving with each breath. Something rose up in front of him, a thin black shape, a man, standing and then dropping down again, crouched low, one hand pointed toward him, a signal, more of the training. *Stand up.*

Dundee eased his legs downward, his feet stopping on hard sand. He was breathing heavily, felt giddy, stupid, thought of the lieutenant, the man's face invisible in the darkness, laughing at him. Every time, he thought, every damned swimming drill, so many times before. Every officer had teased him about it: Dundee, the man who swims until the sand bumps his chin. He knew what the lieutenant was thinking, had heard it too many times. Yes, you can stop swimming, you idiot. It's three feet deep.

The three men moved close together, and Dundee stared at the beach, a wide stretch of flat sand, saw a fence row, posts, odd, his brain trying to understand. Fences? The lieutenant moved away, low in the water, crawling, moving up onto the sand, seeming to ignore the others, and Dundee followed, feeling his way with his hands. They were clear of the shallow surf, and the lieutenant kept himself low, began to run, heavy deliberate steps. There were no orders now, the training so familiar, and the others followed automatically. Dundee felt the sand hard beneath his feet, his footsteps echoing in small thumps, shallow puddles. He passed one of the fence posts, glanced up, saw it tilting outward, toward the open water, a small round hat on top. He understood from the briefings, drawings they had seen. They're not fence posts. It's low tide, and they're shore obstacles. And the hat on top? It's a mine.

The sand began to slope upward, the men climbing, the sand softer, beyond the high-water line, and Dundee kept running, felt the strength in his legs, his breaths heavy and sharp. The lieutenant stopped and knelt low, ducking behind a long low mound of rocks, something else from the briefings, another landmark. Then he pulled a small bundle from the pouch around his own waist, and Dundee understood. It was the tape, the fluorescent stringer that would guide their return, the only way they would ever find their way back to this point on the beach. Dundee watched him unroll it and anchor one end in the sand with a small metal spike. The lieutenant seemed to pause. All three men were breathing heavily, and Dundee heard a whisper.

"Time to go to work, gents. Welcome to Omaha Beach."

They were one squad of the Combined Operations Assault Pilotage Party, a mouthful of description for the men who were sent ashore to find out just what the Allies might be facing on the beaches that had been designated for Operation Overlord. The training had begun months before at the enormous facility at Achnacarry, Scotland. Nearly every commando unit in the British army had received training at Achnacarry, and the Americans had gone as well, Darby's Rangers, men who had already been through the bloodiest days of the fights in the Mediterranean. Many of the commandos had been designated to make armed raids, landing in fleets of rubber rafts, attacking the enemy's seaside installations, ammo and supply dumps. Some of the raids were launched against various ports, other midget submarines slipping into the harbors to target German ships. Few of the raids had been terribly successful, and many of the Royal Navy's higher-ups considered the midget subs a dangerous waste of machines and good men. The X-5 class midgets had no defenses and could barely escape the enemy's spotter planes and fast-moving E-boats, but in the dark the subs could bring their commandos close to the shore, close enough for the folbots and, tonight, close enough for the men to swim.

Their mission was absurdly simple: Gather samples of the sand and rock on Omaha Beach. The beach itself was cut by four draws, deep ravines, passageways that led inland, dividing the high bluff into sections that the mapmakers had designated by various code names. But those ravines interested not just the infantry commanders but the engineers as well. Over the centuries, streams and floodwater had flowed into the sea, and with it had come tons of silt. If that silt was too soft to support the weight of trucks, tanks, and other armored vehicles, an amphibious landing on Omaha Beach simply wouldn't work. The entire motorized portion of the invasion would grind to a halt, embedded in a mire that would make them stationary targets for the German artillery above.

The engineers had another concern as well, so more commandos had gone ashore on other nights with other objectives. Behind the bluffs, around the seaside villages of Colleville-sur-Mer and Saint-Laurent-sur-

Mer, the land was rich in history, a countryside once occupied by the Romans. But the Romans had left a mystery and, possibly, a deadly problem. The land along the Normandy coastline had often been used to farm and gather peat, thick layers of sod used for fuel and building material. The question had to be answered: Had the two-thousand-year-old peat bogs become vast pits of soft mud? For now, though, that wasn't Dundee's problem. His problem was keeping up with his lieutenant.

On this night, Dundee's mission had much more to do with engineering than combat, the men armed only with their knives, since any weapons fire was certain suicide. On the bluffs high above what the planners had named Omaha Beach, German gun emplacements, artillery pillboxes, and machine-gun nests covered the open sands below in what would certainly be interlocking fields of fire. Among the various outposts, German infantry had also been positioned, the Allied aerial reconnaissance showing miles of trench works. Any lookout who heard movement on the beach would know to fire a star shell or a Very light, which would bathe the beach in the glow of man-made sunshine for deadly seconds. As much as Dundee felt the itch to have his pistol handy, tonight there could be no firefight. Just do the job and then find that precious line of tape and make your way back into the surf, all the while praying the midget sub's captain could find you in the black water.

They moved across the sand in total silence, even the gentle surf too far away. Dundee knew the timetable, the tide expected to rise well before dawn, but to a level he found hard to believe. The training taught them that the tide here rose eight feet or more, and in a few short hours, the flat plain of hard sand they had run across would be completely submerged. The high tide would provide a fatal disguise, submerging the posts, the steel girders and wooden poles capped by the mines. As the tide came in, the distance they had to swim would lengthen by hundreds of yards. But it would be far worse to make that swim over and around the hidden obstacles. There was danger enough from the enemy lookouts, without risking a single kick of the leg that could blow you to pieces.

He followed the shadows, the lieutenant leading the way, Henley between them. The ground above them seemed to fall away, a deep cut opening up in the hillside, a wide draw: their objective. Dundee was counting to himself, more training, each step forward ticking off how far they had come, and as the lieutenant stopped, Dundee's mind locked on the number of steps: *Two hundred eighty-six.*

They remained still. Dundee, staring at the dark form in front of him, thought, What is it? I don't hear anything. Sure as hell nobody out here tonight. We in the right place? Looks like the draw we're supposed to find, for sure.

And then he heard the voices.

The men moved along the rocky ledge, a few feet above the commandos, the sounds of footsteps on loose rock. Dundee took a long breath, put a hand slowly down, slid it along his leg, and touched the small leather strap that clamped around his knife. The men above them moved closer, low voices, now one man talking aloud, clear and sharp, the words bursting into Dundee's brain. He didn't know much German, only what the training had taught him: the right questions to ask if he was captured, the right responses to give. The loud German began to laugh, right above them, more steady footsteps, moving past. Dundee wrapped his fingers around the knife, stared ahead, fought the aching need to look up: *No, keep your face down.* He held his breathing in, soft and low, his brain focused on the sounds above and the feel of the knife in his hand. *Where the hell is my pistol?*

The Germans were past them now, the talk continuing, and now one voice rang out from above.

"Hauptmann Schlieben!"

The men stopped, one man close by responding to the call, more words flowing down from high up on the hill. Dundee listened to the words, his brain screaming at his own ignorance: Dammit, teach us German next time! What they hell are they saying? The Germans began to move quickly, away from the rocky wall, climbing, moving into the draw, their footsteps fading. And then they were gone.

He felt himself sag, released the grip on the knife, saw the lieutenant turn and sit down slowly in the sand; audible breathing. Dundee wanted to say something about his pistol: Who the hell thought of that? Send us in here without a bloody firearm? He knew the answer, of course. We're not here to kill Germans. And, we're expendable, after all. Part of the stinking job.

The lieutenant began to move again, pulled himself up, grabbed Henley by the shoulder, pushed him away. Dundee knew the message: The time had come for the men to spread out, go to work. He felt for the pouch at his waist, the small zipper, felt inside, the cloth sack he was supposed to fill. Henley was scampering silently up the ravine, staying close to the left side. Dundee waited, and the lieutenant reached back, touched his shoulder. All right, sir. I got it.

He felt his way silently over the small rocky ledge, hard flat ground above it. He pushed out to the right, focusing on that side of the draw, his brain still counting steps. Won't get lost now. Those rocks behind me are what matters, just so I can find that damned tape. He thought of the Germans, moving up this same direction: Bloody swell, that is. One of them stops to drain a kidney, and I'll run right up his fanny. Of course, if they went this way, it means there's no booby traps, no mines. Keep a good thought, mate.

He glanced to the left, tried to see Henley, fought the urge—Nope, stay on course. He knows what to do. The ground was softer under his feet, and he stayed low, his knees beginning to ache, thought of crawling. Slowly, mate. It's here, don't break your damned neck. His eyes probed the dark, the lightness of the sand, and he saw now the wide yawning ditch, what the reconnaissance maps had shown to be a tank trap, a wide trench dug along the mouth of the ravine. He probed with his foot, slid down the side of the ditch, the bottom hard and wet, and climbed quickly up the other side, a spray of sand in his eyes. Dammit! He was up again, past the tank trap, and his brain began to count the steps, methodical, a steady rhythm, the orders matching the cadence of his steps.

Find . . . some . . . damned . . . rocks . . . small . . . ones. The count continued, the steps slowing, the hill growing more steep, his brain clicking off numbers: *One hundred.* He paused and took a long low breath. One hell of a mission: finding something for the engineers to play with. You'd think, if this place was full of rocks, that's all they'd want to know. Hell, you could see them from a damned plane. He thought of the briefing the night before, the colonel, those two engineers.

"We have to know what kind of rocks are on this beach, what kind of ground we will have to deal with in these draws."

So here I am. Bloody hell.

He saw movement out in the open center of the draw and froze, a cold shiver in his chest. The shape was hunched low, as he was, and he thought, It's the lieutenant, you stupid idiot. He's got the happy job after all, waltz right up the wide open middle of this damned ravine and scoop up a pail of dirt. Dundee moved forward again, his brain still counting: *Two hundred*. All right, time to do the job.

He pulled the cloth bag from the pouch, settled down on his knees, ran his hand across the ground. He felt a rock, smaller than his palm, let out a breath. Good, that's one. Eleven more, and we can go home. He stuffed the rock into the bag and reached out again, his hand sliding over the rough dirt. Another rock? No, hell, too large. Keep looking, mate. He crawled to his right, closer to the high wall of the draw, felt soft dirt with his hands. All right, now we're getting into it. He felt another rock, the size of an egg: Perfect, stick that one away. The ground was still soft, and his fingers pushed through, probing, and now he felt something hard, thought, No, too big . . . and then he froze. His brain snapped into focus, his breathing stopped. It wasn't a rock at all. It was steel and curved, buried slightly beneath the soft dirt. He knew the shape, had drilled and studied, and on one terrible day during training he had watched one blow off a man's legs. It was a land mine.

He pulled his hand away, felt his fingers twitching, his heart pouding. That's why the ground is so damned soft, you bloody moron. You're in a minefield. He looked to the side, saw no one, no motion, thought, *Two hundred steps*. That was the drill, where I'm supposed to be, and that's where I am. No one said anything about a minefield. But those damned Jerries came up here. . . . Well, hell, they knew the trail, even in the dark. Something about land mines makes you pay attention to that sort of thing. He backed away now, retraced his knee prints. The ground was harder, and he let out a breath, closed his eyes, thought, The lieutenant won't mind if I just . . . take a bit of a break. He felt the cold again, a breeze on his face, clenched his fist around the top of the cloth bag. A dozen. All right, mate, keep looking.

The bag began to fill, and Dundee raised up, searching, saw the shadow of the lieutenant again, the man huddled low, watching him. He began to back slowly down the flat draw, his mind locked on the number of rocks in the bag, and now his hand gripped one more, perfect and round. Bloody hell. That's twelve. He slipped silently toward the lieutenant, saw the man's hand come up, Yes, all right then. Slow it down. He thought of the timetable, how long has it been? Well, that's his job. Mine's done.

He was beside the officer now, heard the soft whisper.

"Bag full?"

"Yes, sir."

"Let's go, back down to the rocky ledge. Henley might be there already."

Dundee followed the lieutenant, both men crouched low, soft steps. They slipped down into the tank trap, then up again, and he could see the rock ledge, lining the shore, remembered the lecture, some geologist, so many years of pounding surf, the ocean spitting out these small bits, pressing them up on the sand. The lieutenant went over the ledge, dropped down, still silent, waited, Dundee doing the same. He felt his breathing again, relief, the bag of rocks heavy at his waist. Bloody engineers. Ought to keep one for myself, a souvenir.

Above them, up in the draw, there was a sudden flash of blinding light, the sharp echo of a blast. He looked up, over the rocks, saw nothing, heard a tumble of rocks, the low voice of the lieutenant.

"Land mine. Henley. *Son of a bitch.*"

And now, loud voices, up high, straight above them. Dundee felt a hard hand on his arm, steel grip, low voice:

"Go! Now!"

The lieutenant was up and moving, and Dundee followed, jelly in his legs, quick steps, realized he could see the tape. He stared down, ran in step with the lieutenant, his brain taking over, counting, one hundred, but the thoughts were swept away now, no need to count, the tape visible even in darkness, some toy invented by some engineer, the stupid joke from training: *Your line of bread crumbs.* His chest was burning, hard breathing, and now there were shots, blasts of machine-gun fire, arcing lights streaking over the beach. He wanted to stop, to lie behind the cover of the rocky ledge, but the lieutenant kept moving, and Dundee knew to follow, could not forget the training. *Never stop.* The streaks of tracer fire popped close overhead, a shattering of rock behind him, fire well out in front of them. His brain screamed at him, They don't know where we are! Firing blind! Thank God! The lieutenant suddenly turned, ran toward the water, and Dundee saw now, the tape had ended. He followed, felt the soft sand, glue-like on his feet, slowing him down. Behind him, at the draw, men were calling out, the rattle of machine guns filling the darkness, more tracers arcing into the open water. The lieutenant was leaving him behind, a faster runner, and Dundee focused on the man's back, lit by the tracers, the sand harder, splashes of water. The water was up to his knees now, and still they ran, louder splashes, water in his face, the beach behind him suddenly bright with daylight, the pop of a star shell. The lieutenant dove down, was gone, and Dundee took a hard breath, couldn't hold it, gasped for air, tried again, filled his lungs, felt the water at his waist. He dove as well, streaks of light past his head, pops and splashes of machine-gun fire, zips in the water. He could hear nothing but his own swimming, gasped for breath, rolling over in the water, a quick glance back, the flare extinguished. His feet couldn't touch the bottom, and he began to swim again, his arms and legs leaden, searing pain. He had forgotten to count, vicious anger in his brain, stupid orders, useless. He pushed himself through the water, ignored the burning, Find the rhythm, one arm, turn, the other, steady kick. He couldn't hear the machine guns, the sky black again, his shoulders on fire, numbness in his legs, a quick look up, straight away from the beach, Yes, keep going. Thank God for swimming. No damned folbot, not tonight. We'd be staring at bayonets, or worse.

He kept swimming, peered up every few seconds, felt himself rise up on a swell, scanned the smooth surface, no sign of the lieutenant, dammit! What the hell do I do, swim to Dover? He looked back toward the beach again, saw a searchlight, the sound of a truck, Yep, you go right ahead, search that whole damned beach. He let his legs drop, treading water, thought of Henley, the man's big laugh, always a slap of the hand on your back. Swim, you idiot. He turned in the water, began to kick again, the motion steady, thought now of the submarine, where the hell are you? And now he heard a quick shout, raised his head up, a huge hulking mass. Oh, God! Thank God! He gulped a bellyful of salt water, pushed himself that way, his legs useless now, no strength at all, and there was a hand, grabbing his, pulling him clear of the water, the submarine already moving, submerging, and he dropped down, inside, the hatch closing above him.

He gasped for air, felt a lurch, the submarine rolling to one side, the captain at the controls, no words, the crewman close to Dundee, looking at his face.

"We ha'nt seen your mate! You sure he's not coming? Captain, ought'n we wait for him?"

"Can't do it, Mr. Higgins. All hell's opening up on that beach. They'll spot us in a flash."

Dundee realized now the lieutenant was lying on the narrow deck beside him. The officer rolled over, said, "No. Get moving. Henley's gone."

Dundee tried to sit, the sub tilting, rolling him forward, and he reached out, felt the lieutenant grab his hand.

"Thought you were gonna swim straight home, Dundee. You passed me like a damned fish."

He looked at the lieutenant's face, saw the man's head go down. Dundee, still gasping, spit salt water. "A land mine. There were minefields. It had to be. Henley . . ."

"Yeah. Never knew what hit him, most likely. A blessing in that. We were damned lucky to get out of there." The lieutenant looked down toward his own belt, raised the pouch. "Mission accomplished. Got what we came for. They'll test this sand, see what it can hold."

Dundee nodded slowly, tried to see Henley's face, gone now, as though he never existed. The word came to him again, the word they all understood: *expendable.* He put his hand on his waist, felt for the pouch, the rocks. He pulled the pouch around in front of him, unfastened the strap, held it up. Mission accomplished. Those bloody engineers had better make some use of this. We lost a good man . . . for a bag of rocks.

2. ROMMEL

They brought the body up the draw on a stretcher, four men whose faces showed no taste for the job they were doing. Rommel watched from above, turned away now, said, "British?"

"Yes, sir. About one this morning. We sent out patrols along the beach in both directions, searched every possible hiding place. This body was all we found."

Rommel turned toward the water again, pointed out. "Do we have any idea how many there were?"

"No, sir. This one is wearing fatigue clothing, beneath a rubber suit. No firearm, no demolition equipment. There had to be more than one of them. This one apparently tripped a land mine. Along the beach, there are tracks in the sand, men running, toward the east, and we found a strip of some sort of marking ribbon. They must certainly have escaped in a boat."

"But you saw no boat?"

"No, Field Marshal."

"And no equipment? His friends may have been able to carry it away." Rommel stared out along the wide beach, scanned down into the sandy draw, the wide cut in the cliffs. "Where is the barbed wire I ordered?"

"It has not yet arrived, sir."

Rommel rolled his hand tightly around his baton, slapped it into his palm.

"No, of course it has not arrived. Never mind. I will make some calls. Again."

Below them, the tide had fallen quickly, and men were filing out onto the flat beach, a wide plain of wet sand. Rommel saw the pattern of steel and wood stakes, other barriers, more elaborate, crisscrossed steel beams, what the soldiers were calling *hedgehogs*. The columns of men began to move past the rows of stakes, some carrying poles, others in pairs hauling more steel, some with tools, shovels, one small bulldozer following behind. He watched them for a moment, spreading out over the exposed sand. Yes, he thought, move *more* slowly. Go about your job as though you have an eternity to complete it. He was angry, knew the feeling too well, slapped the baton into his hand again.

"Colonel Heckner, I want more men on that job. You have four companies of infantry within a kilometer of here. Call upon them, under my authority. I did not order these works to be constructed to provide these men a holiday at the beach." He watched for a response, saw a slight nod, weary obedience. "Are you paying *attention,* Colonel?"

The man seemed to wake up, snapped his heels together. "Yes, certainly, Field Marshal. I will see that more men are put to work on the barriers."

Rommel could see there was more, the man hesitating with his words.

"You have something to say, Colonel?"

The man glanced down. "Well, yes, sir. There are reports. . . . I have heard that the enemy is planning an invasion of Norway. It seems to me, sir, that our energies should be directed to where we know he is coming. Forgive me, Field Marshal, but is that not reasonable?"

"Colonel Heckner, I will not waste your time with a discussion about matters of strategy, of which you know nothing at all." He felt his voice rising, the control slipping away. "You have orders. *My orders!* You will construct a strong line of obstacles to prepare against an invasion along this portion of this beach in which you hold command! In both directions, commanders have been ordered to perform the same task. What might occur in Norway is none of your concern. It is none of your concern what might occur anywhere along this entire front, except in your specific zone of command. Should I be explaining this to you, Colonel?"

The man remained stiff, staring ahead, past Rommel. "Certainly not, Field Marshal."

Rommel turned away, fingered the binoculars at his chest, took a long breath, calmed himself. How much of this can be blamed on one colonel? These are soldiers, after all, and we put them to work beside laborers, so they begin to think like laborers. He stared out to sea, raised the binoculars, stared at the empty horizon: old habit.

"What did they want here, Colonel?"

"I have considered that, sir. The guns, perhaps. The shore batteries. All would make good targets."

"What shore batteries, Colonel? Most of them are not yet constructed. The largest piece I see here is a 105, not what I would call a target to inspire a commando attack. You said the man carried no demolition equipment. Would they risk a team of commandos just to see how our construction work is progressing? They can do that from the air."

"We have first-class antiaircraft personnel, here, sir. The British know that. They would not dare—"

"Do not tell me what the British would do. They *dare,* Colonel. Those commandos came here for a specific mission. They have been coming in all along this coast for weeks now. We capture some, kill some, and we cannot know how many more complete their missions and return home."

"Yes, sir. Of course, sir."

Rommel looked at the man, thought, An empty mind, telling me only what I want to hear, so I will leave him in peace. He thought a moment. All right, here's some peace for you, Colonel. "It occurs to me, Colonel Heckner . . . perhaps, it was *you* they were after, an assassination squad, targeting senior officers. Your minefield might have saved your life."

The man seemed to soak up his words, pondering the thought with growing alarm. Rommel had planted as much of a seed as his patience would allow, thought, Maybe tonight you will be more vigilant. He turned away, moving toward the staff officers, who waited beside his car. They stiffened as he approached, and he looked past them, saw a cluster of soldiers gathered around the dead commando, could see the man's black bloody clothes, shreds of rubber on the man's blasted legs. All eyes were on Rommel now, the men moving slowly to attention. He scanned them. Yes, they look like common laborers. What has happened to my soldiers? He turned and looked back toward Heckner, who stiffened again.

"I will have your barbed wire here as soon as possible. I want it deployed in depth across every access point at the base of this bluff. I will also send you more land mines, a great many more. Those barricades in the tidal area must be increased, made far more numerous. Take advantage of the lowest tides and add another row, farther out. And, for God's sake, widen that tank trap. The enemy has engineers, Colonel. They will find a way to bridge your little ditch. Put land mines in the bottom."

"It will be done, sir."

"It will be done *immediately,* Colonel."

T he staff car bounced along the pockmarked farm lane, past open fields hemmed in by tall ridges of brush. The roads were mostly hard, gravel or packed dirt, and Rommel kept his eye in front of the car, thinking of tanks, the road's surface more than adequate to support a panzer division. In the front seat, his aide said, "Sir, we are approaching zone fourteen. Colonel Sasser's headquarters."

Rommel thought of Sasser, a small thin man, capable. "Yes, very well. Let us visit Colonel Sasser."

"He will probably be out with his men, you know. He does that sort of thing."

The voice came from beside him, the tall man in the dark uniform of the German navy. Rommel nodded. "Yes, Friedrich, I know. Sasser is a colonel who uses a shovel. If we had more like him, we might be winning this war."

The naval officer did not respond, and Rommel thought of the ears in the front seat, the staff officer, the driver. He glanced at the man beside him, nodded. Yes, I know. I should not make the staff uncomfortable. Some thoughts are best kept quiet. He spoke silently in his mind, apologizing to the man beside him.

Vice Admiral Friedrich Ruge had been assigned to Rommel's command as a liaison for the navy, to coordinate naval strategies and activities along the French coast, that vast stretch of territory that Rommel controlled as commander of Army Group B. Both men had come to France from Italy. While Rommel had chafed in the northern mountains with virtually nothing to do, Ruge had been effective as head of naval operations in the one theater of the war that might still favor the Germans. Rommel knew Ruge had spent most of his life on the water and was one of the most capable seamen in the Kriegsmarine. He was three years younger than

Rommel, their ages close enough that each man knew the various daily challenges of rising up from a hard bed. Besides Ruge's expertise and clear-headed grasp of naval tactics, Rommel had been surprised to find that, unlike most of Hitler's naval commanders, Ruge understood the army's side of the war as well, and thus was perfect for the job as Rommel's liaison. Rommel had become far too accustomed to commanders and their subordinates who seemed to be fighting a war to serve their own glory. Others were fighting only for survival, to find a way to endure the inevitable, a war going badly, men making discreet preparations to protect their families should Hitler's Reich collapse. Ruge seemed to have none of that, no pretense, no mindless pride, none of the conspirator's slipperiness, and no need to curry favor with anyone. After working alongside the man for a few short weeks, Rommel had come to regard Admiral Ruge not only as a valuable colleague but also as a trusted friend, something Rommel had not experienced since his days in North Africa.

They stepped from the staff car, and Rommel saw the salutes, the troops quickly aware of his presence. He began to move, stopped on instinct, heard a low hum, the men close to him staring up, searching the sky. The sounds grew, a low steady drone, very high and far away, the sound of bombers. It was commonplace now, American B-17s making their daylight raids far behind Rommel's Atlantic Wall, into Germany itself. All throughout Germany the raids had grown more numerous and more intense, the bombers seeking industrial and military targets around every major city. It had become well known that the Americans came only in daylight and the British at night, a peculiar division of labor Rommel had never understood. He avoided the skyward stares of the troops—there was nothing to see and certainly no danger here, so close to the coastline. Behind him, Ruge emerged from the car, a second car rolling to a halt, discharging more staff officers.

Along the edge of a wide field, tents were scattered, a field headquarters, sheltered by sheets of camouflaged netting. The officers were emerging now, word reaching them that Rommel had arrived.

"Welcome, sir!"

Rommel recognized the face, a young captain, Sasser's aide. "Where is Colonel Sasser?"

The man stood at attention, saluted, then pointed.

"He is to be found on the bluff, sir, at the sea. They are constructing a large artillery emplacement, largest one in this sector, sir."

"Yes, I know, Captain. You may lead the way."

"I am honored, Field Marshal."

Rommel glanced at Ruge, saw a smile. The young captain did not hesitate but moved away along a wide graveled trail. Ruge, now beside Rommel, said, "I never received any reception like this, not on any ship in my command. It's true, all that talk I've been hearing. You are nothing less than their hero."

"Silence that, please. I am their worst terror, and they know it. Until they hear the enemy shooting at them, they know they have nothing more to fear than me. I shall continue to accommodate them."

They followed the young officer, climbing a short rise, a cold stiff wind in Rommel's face, the ground falling away to the open sea. Below, along the beach, a swarm of men were hauling and digging, more pieces of the same barricades Rommel had ordered all along the coast. To one side of him, the ground rose to a fat knob, made fatter by a vast wall of concrete. Above, a crane holding a large spiderweb of reinforcing steel began to lower it into place, one more piece of the great wall, shirtless men shoveling wet concrete into a vast pit below. Rommel heard shouts, commands, a half dozen men responding, moving in one motion toward the descending web of steel, hands going up, turning, guiding, as the steel settled into the waiting concrete. Rommel clamped the baton under one arm, clenched his fists. Yes, by God, that is strength! That is what this ridiculous Atlantic Wall is *supposed* to be.

"Sir! Field Marshal! Forgive me!"

Rommel saw him now, the short man scampering up the bluff. Sasser's shirt was open, a gray smear across his white undershirt. He drew himself up, saluted, said, "Welcome, sir! I did not know when you would arrive."

"And you never will, Colonel. You may compose yourself."

The man seemed aware of his uniform now, a slight panic, buttoned his shirt, tugged at his jacket, the image of the officer replacing the manual laborer.

"Please forgive me, Field Marshal. I have found that our productivity increases—the men respond better to orders if I show them I am not above the work. It . . . inspires them, sir."

Rommel thought of Africa, riding a tank straight into the chaos of a fight, seeing it for himself, the inspiration the men drew from that, and the

enjoyment Rommel felt from the startled looks on the faces of his young
lieutenants who thought *they* were in command. Where was Sasser when I
needed this kind of man in Egypt?

"May I see your hands, Colonel?"

Sasser seemed puzzled, turned his palms up, glanced at them, then jut-
ted them out toward Rommel.

"Certainly, sir. I do not understand—"

Rommel grabbed the man's hands, looked at Ruge.

"Look at this. An officer who is not afraid to get his hands dirty. Or
better yet, who raises blisters." He released Sasser's hands and turned
toward an aide. "Go to the car. Retrieve a concertina."

"Right away, sir."

Rommel looked at Sasser again, the man still puzzled, and said, "Colonel, as you know, I have been inspecting the Führer's impenetrable Atlantic
Wall for some months now. When I arrived here, I was shocked by what I
saw: the complete lack of urgency, the utter disregard for our Führer's orders. I was given the responsibility, and the very specific instructions, that
this coastline be made invulnerable to any assault the enemy could attempt. I have made every effort to carry out that order, to instill and inspire a sense of mission in these men. In *you*, Colonel."

"Of course, sir."

The aide had returned, handed Rommel a small accordion. Rommel
held it out toward Sasser.

"You have done your duty, Colonel, and so this is for you. My gift. It
is my way of showing you respect."

Sasser took the accordion, squeezed the sides together, the sharp whine
emerging. He looked at Rommel now, a broad beaming smile, then snapped
himself again to attention.

"Thank you, Field Marshal! I shall treasure it always."

"It is my hope that one day, when this war has concluded, the officers
who have received these gifts might gather at some place and share their accomplishments. I would be very proud to be a part of that."

"By all means. We shall make that happen, Field Marshal!"

Rommel paused, looked past Sasser, saw the work ongoing.

"You may return to your efforts, Colonel." He glanced at Ruge, saw a
slight smile. "I must resume my inspection."

Rommel spun around, Ruge and the aide following, the men moving
quickly along the path to the camouflaged tents. More of his staff were

gathering at the cars, the rear doors of his car pulled open. In seconds, the two officers were in the car, the driver moving them back out into the countryside.

Ruge seemed energized beside him, and Rommel, knowing the man's mood, waited for him to speak. After a short moment, Ruge said, "How many of those concertinas do you have?"

"More than enough, unfortunately."

Ruge chuckled. "They would probably prefer medals."

Surprised, Rommel looked at Ruge and shook his head. "I do not agree. Have you seen how many medals we are awarding now? Berlin is minting them faster than we produce artillery shells. Every officer on this front expects to receive one for his outstanding service to the Reich. Our officers have come to believe that loyalty to the Führer is the most valuable skill they can demonstrate. It is a deadly mistake. It will destroy this army."

Ruge said nothing and stared out toward the fields, the car bouncing on the rough road. Rommel felt a familiar pain in his side, rubbed his hand inside his heavy coat, and looked at the two men in the front seat.

"Captain Lang, you are well aware that I value your discretion, is that not true?"

The man turned. "Most certainly, Field Marshal. Sergeant Daniel and I are occupied with other thoughts, always."

Rommel smiled and tapped his driver on the shoulder. "I am not concerned about you, Sergeant." He turned to Ruge. "The sergeant has proven himself to me on many occasions. Sometimes, I am not even certain he is capable of hearing anything at all. Are you deaf, Sergeant Daniel?"

"Yes, Field Marshal."

Ruge laughed. "All right. My caution is unfounded. I meant no insult to your staff. But . . . concertinas?"

Rommel probed his side again, a nagging ailment from the misery of the African desert, never quite letting him forget.

"I promise you, Friedrich, when all of this has past, when medals and decorations hang over every fireplace in Germany, those concertinas will occupy a special place. Those men will not forget that I chose them to receive a gift so . . . unmilitary. They might even learn to play the thing."

There was silence, the car breaking out into open ground, a village in the distance and, to one side, a railroad track, a line of heavy railcars. Rommel strained to see, and his driver seemed to feel the movement.

"Shall I stop, sir?"

"No. We have much ground to cover. I was just observing. Those rail-cars were carrying a shipment of eighty-eights. Very good. We will need enormous quantities of those along every open beach, especially the Pas-de-Calais. The enemy knows already that we have no better weapon to destroy his armor." He glanced at Ruge again. "I have tried to explain that to von Rundstedt ever since I arrived here. I have asked that batteries of eighty-eights be interspersed among every one of the larger shore guns."

"Will the shore guns not be enough?" Ruge said. "Heavy batteries of three-hundred-millimeter cannon will provide all the firepower we would need against enemy ships."

"Guns that big are too visible from the air. The enemy will send their bombers to target every installation. Despite Colonel Sasser's good work, we do not have enough concrete to protect every battery, and our *outstanding* engineering corps seems to believe that we can make do in those casements with half the thickness I have specified. In any invasion, we could lose our most effective shore batteries before the enemy even attempts to land. The eighty-eights are mobile, can be hidden from the bombers, and, should the enemy attempt to land his armor, they can be moved quickly to the greatest point of attack."

"As usual, Field Marshal, I bow to your experience."

Rommel saw the familiar smile, felt his own good humor fading away. "It so distresses me. For every Sasser there are ten Colonel Heckners. The British land a squad of commandos right under his feet, and the only way we find out about it is when one of them blows himself up."

"How dangerous can they truly be? The British are scouting us, determining what kind of strength we have put into place. There was no evidence that the raid this morning had any other intent than to observe. Somewhere in London, mapmakers are drawing furiously, mapping out every meter of our coastline. You and I would do the same thing. And if they come, you know as well as I do that they will come at a place that makes the most strategic sense. If they come, you will know where and when. You are as capable of knowing the mind of the enemy as any British or American strategist."

"But, Friedrich, I do not make the decisions. No matter what I may believe, I am subject to orders." He paused. "You saw Colonel Sasser, the man's hands. He *works,* he is a soldier's soldier, *he* will do his job. Behind us, old men and sycophants hold our future in hands that are fragile and soft, hands that have never held the steel. We are losing this war because of Russia. We have drained Germany of the strength and the power that could so easily have prevailed. The Russians are savages, led by subhuman Bolsheviks. But their numbers are too many and their land is too vast, and they have bled us dry. The British and the Americans know this with complete certainty, so what will they do? It is a question any schoolchild could understand. We are weakened now, and so they will come. They will come here, somewhere on this coastline, and if we do not meet them at the point of attack, if we do not destroy them on the beaches, they will keep coming."

"Von Rundstedt disagrees with you."

"They all disagree with me. I know what they believe. We should allow the enemy to land: Then our mighty Luftwaffe and our mighty panzers will strike them and destroy them. Yes, yes. I have heard that too many times. It is wrong. Damn them all, it is *wrong*. If we allow the enemy to plant his feet in the sand, we will never get him out. Last autumn, we held every advantage in Italy, the Bay of Salerno. *Kesselring will destroy them on the beaches*. Yes, I heard that. Now where is Kesselring? His back is pushed north and north again."

"Kesselring has forced a stalemate, Erwin. Let us not forget that. He has held the enemy below Rome."

"A *stalemate*? Are we so desperate that we now believe that a stalemate is a *victory*? There can be no stalemate here, Friedrich. I have seen what the Americans bring to this war. I have seen the tanks and guns and trucks. And one day soon, how many millions of those Americans will push their way into France? Von Rundstedt insists that the most brilliant strategy is simply to allow that to happen, then, once they are ashore, we can attack them and drive them into the sea. It is fantasy. No, worse, it is suicide. And men like Colonel Sasser deserve better."

3. EISENHOWER

"The war could very well be over by April. In fact, should our plans continue unimpeded, I am quite certain of it."

Eisenhower leaned back in his chair, already exhausted by Air Chief Marshal Harris's bluster. He glanced at Smith, stroking his chin, could see that his chief of staff was itching to reply. It was Bedell Smith's way to hold nothing back, a trait that had endeared him to no one but his boss. Eisenhower had always known that "Beetle" inspired a chorus of grumbling from the British, mostly deserved. He had a clumsiness to him; his attempts at diplomacy always fell short. But now, an indiscreet missile launched at the arrogance of this British air marshal would have been perfectly appropriate.

Harris, oblivious to the frowns, continued. "We have quite perfected the art of the massed bombing attack, you know. The Hun tried it against us, and, dare I say, it was only the stiff backbone of the British people that prevented it from working." He paused, a professorial tilt to his head, speaking to inattentive students. "In 1940, you know. Our splendid resolve in the face of certain disaster. What we of course refer to as the Battle for Britain." Eisenhower nodded, forced himself to hide a screaming need for sarcasm.

"Yes, I am familiar with the term. I have made it a point to study the history of the past four years."

Harris seemed satisfied that his lesson had taken hold. "Well, yes, of course. Naturally, the Germans have no such pride, and thus, by widespread destruction of their cities, we shall achieve what Mr. Hitler could not. We shall utterly destroy the enemy's will to fight. It is a grand spectacle, you know. One simply cannot imagine the power, the pure delight at seeing a thousand heavy bombers letting loose their loads to deliver what could only . . . well, I daresay the Almighty Himself would be impressed. Every one of these missions produces a rain of fire of biblical proportions. And, as I said, it will end this war. All this nonsense about land forces, amphibious invasion . . . such a waste."

Eisenhower could feel Smith twisting in his chair and glanced at him again, the silent order: No, keep quiet, not now. This jackass is, after all, our ally.

Air Marshal Arthur "Bomber" Harris was a thick-chested bull of a man whose credentials included combat hours in a fighter plane in World War I. Now, he commanded the Allies' strategic bombing campaigns. Harris had worked hard to gain approval for his strategies and was in part responsible for the plans that had nearly obliterated the German city of Cologne in 1942, a devastating attack that had impressed even Winston Churchill. Harris's was the loudest voice among many of the air commanders, including several Americans, whose faith in the heavy bombers had convinced them that Operation Overlord was not only a waste of time but would cost far more than it would gain. It was one more argument that Eisenhower didn't need.

"Marshal Harris, I appreciate your input. I believe your statement is a bit optimistic."

Harris seemed wounded. "But you must understand. Even your president has stated that absolute destruction of the enemy is our most desired alternative."

Eisenhower closed his eyes for a brief moment. He knew exactly what Harris was referring to. "What President Roosevelt said was that we should accept only unconditional surrender from the enemy. I believe now, as I believed then, that the president's choice of words was an unfortunate error. It is not my place to correct anything the president says, but now we must all live with the consequences of that . . . um . . . policy."

"A good policy, I assure you. In fact, the only policy we should aspire to."

"No, Marshal Harris, it is not. What we have done is unite the German people behind the fanatical ravings of their oppressive leaders. Their propaganda ministry has made great play of this, you know. The German people are being told that our only goal is to wipe their nation off the map. Instead of taking away their will to fight, we have given them a cause to fight us even harder. Destroying their cities will only convince the German people that what the president said is accurate. That plays directly into the ranting of Hitler and his goons." He stopped. Griping about the president was a bad idea, especially to a senior British commander. Harris wore the smirk of a man who has failed to enlighten the uneducated, but Eisenhower had endured all he could. "I must ask you to excuse us, Marshal Harris. I have many appointments still to attend to. I'm sure a man in your position understands."

Harris seemed to ponder the message. "Yes, of course. But be assured, despite all this enthusiasm for your land invasion, if allowed the opportunity, the Allied air forces can end this war. End it absolutely, with minimal casualties. Is that not our common goal?"

"Certainly. Thank you for your reminder."

Harris was up now, a short bow toward Eisenhower. He seemed to ignore Smith, spun around, and was quickly out the door. Eisenhower felt the air flow out of the room, a great deflating balloon. Smith put both hands on his head, smoothed back his hair.

"Good God, Ike. That man's insufferable."

"Yep." Eisenhower thought a moment. "You ever do a jigsaw puzzle?"

Smith seemed caught off guard by the question. "Uh, no."

"Pain in the ass. Ten thousand pieces, all of them the same, supposed to fit neatly together. But then, you find out they're not cut the same: little differences, no matching parts. You spend a damned hour finding two pieces that work, and you're no better off than you were before. That's what this is, a big damned jigsaw puzzle. Ten thousand generals, plus a few civilians thrown in just to make it interesting. No, check that. Just to make it impossible. FDR makes one damned statement without asking anybody if it's a good idea and changes this whole war. *Unconditional surrender.* Can you believe that? Dammit, Beetle, not one of these people who are bellyaching about Overlord have any idea what the German soldier is like. I guarantee you, every damned Kraut private has been told about Unconditional Surrender. Every damned one of them now thinks we're out to destroy his country. And these air people, like this jackass Harris, keep insisting that if we destroy their cities, the Germans will just quit. All we're doing is making them fight harder."

Smith seemed to measure Eisenhower's mood. He chose his words carefully. "They're right about one thing, Ike. We're blasting their factories. That's already making a difference. We keep targeting them—"

"The Brits bomb at night, Beetle. Almost no chance of precision. Sure, they might wipe out a few factories, but the worst job is ours. The damned B-17s make their runs in the daylight, and we're getting our asses chewed up by the Kraut fighters. For every target we eliminate, we lose too many of our own pilots. We can't ask the air boys to do all the damned work while the rest of us sit back and watch. And, it won't work anyway, no matter what that blowhard Harris says. End the war by April, for God's sake. *April*."

Eisenhower saw the blue uniform at the door, the one smiling face in the entire headquarters. It was his naval aide, Harry Butcher.

"What the hell do you want?"

Butcher looked at Smith but knew not to ask questions. He had seen too many of Eisenhower's bad moods. "Sorry to interrupt, chief, but General Patton has been waiting for a while."

Smith laughed. "Killed anybody yet? Old George isn't the most patient man in this army."

"Shut up, Beetle. Let me talk to George alone. This day is only going to get worse."

Smith started toward the door. "Sure thing, Ike. I have to meet with some of Monty's people in a half hour. Some bitching about gasoline."

"Don't tell me about it until the problem is solved."

Eisenhower was alone now, a brief gasp of calm. He leaned his head back and stared up through the dull white of the ceiling. You know, he thought, if this ever ends, I think I'll go grow corn in Kansas.

"I saw Bomber Harris outside. Not such a pleasant sort. Okay for a Brit."

Eisenhower knew Patton would have plenty to say, no matter what the topic. He looked at the man's belt and saw the two pistols. "George, why in hell are you armed? I haven't seen a single damned German in these offices yet."

Patton shrugged, unfazed. "Good for the men, Ike. Those guards out there, they understand. All these damned staffers, clerks, secretaries. Inspires them, lets them know what we're about. Makes every one of them want to join the fight, find out what it really takes to win this thing."

"Where the hell did you get the pearl handles?"

Patton seemed to inflate, his eyes wide. "Dammit, Ike, not you too! Who in hell would carry a pearl-handled revolver? Pimps in whorehouses and tinhorn gamblers! They're ivory! The real stuff, finest around. I'd have killed the elephant myself if I had to."

Eisenhower had no energy for this. "Wouldn't have had to, George. He'd have rolled over at your feet for the honor of giving you the damned tusks."

Patton calmed, stuck out his chin, and nodded. "Damn right. Some Kraut bastard sticks his head out, and I'll show him why."

Eisenhower looked down toward his desk drawer. Whatever you say, George, he thought. Just keep those damned things holstered for now. He reached into a drawer and pulled out a folder of papers.

"You've been briefed on your new assignment? Beetle fill you in?"

Patton seemed to grunt at the mention of the name, and Eisenhower knew it was one more cross he had to bear. Patton might have harsh opinions for every officer in the war, but he especially seemed to hate Bedell Smith. Patton squared himself in the chair. "I know my job. The Third Army will make you proud, Ike. I told you. I always knew if you just had faith, I'd come through."

"You don't make it easy."

Patton seemed suddenly subdued, a transparent show of humility that Eisenhower saw through. He knew what was coming.

"I owe you, Ike. Always will. You stuck behind me, you and Marshall both. When I heard you had been put in command of this whole operation, I told . . . well, everyone. No better man. None. You're going down as one of the best in history, better than Napoleon. The enemy hasn't got a prayer in hell with you at the wheel. I won't let you down, I promise you that, Ike."

Eisenhower held up his hand. He felt buried in molasses. "Stop! Look George, just keep your mouth shut, all right? No talking to the press, no speeches, no big damned tours. And stay the hell out of hospitals."

"Absolutely, Ike. You can count on me."

"We're all counting on you." The words were useless, Eisenhower falling into Patton's trap. Yes, we all count on everyone. We're all one big damned football team. Rah, rah.

"Bradley's a fine choice, Ike. First class. Always thought highly of him. He'll come through. It's a pleasure to be in his command."

It was a gesture from Patton. Eisenhower looked hard at him and thought, Is it really?

"How about Monty?"

Patton sniffed, shrugged. "Monty's okay. You'll have to prod him though, keep on his ass. Too damned methodical for my taste. Waits until every damned duck is in a row before he moves. I could have nailed down Sicily by myself, you know, if you'd let me."

"Knock it off, George. I didn't bring you here to lecture me or hear your opinions. Your HQ all set up?"

Patton seemed to calm himself, an effort to become the good subordinate. "Met them last night. Not too happy about that, Ike. My troops aren't scheduled to arrive for weeks yet. No one's giving me a straight answer. Beetle wouldn't tell me how long it would take for the first divisions to ship in."

"Not weeks, months. Beetle didn't tell you any more than that because those were my orders. I need to talk to you about the plan myself."

Patton seemed to sag. "What's going on, Ike? You changing your mind? Some stinking goddam senator put a bug up Marshall's ass? Am I still in command of the Third Army?"

Eisenhower let out a long breath. He could see Patton's face turning red. "Relax, George. Yes, you are in command of the Third Army. But you won't hit France until the beachheads are well in hand. That's for Monty to do, and Bradley. You will go in after them, try like hell to punch a hole, drive the enemy back to Germany. Nobody I'd rather have in charge of that kind of job than you. You got that?"

Patton looked at the floor for a moment. "Not really. You don't want me to lead the assault? I did a damned fine job of that in Sicily. Is this Monty's crap? He still pissed about Messina? Hell, if he'd gotten off his ass and shoved his people where they needed to be—"

"Stop!"

Patton was leaning forward, clearly angry; Eisenhower pointed a finger at him.

"*That's* why, George. Some jobs require thought and planning before the shooting starts. Monty's a thinker, Brad is a thinker. You . . . you lead with your fists. Fine, that's a good thing. I'm counting on you for that . . . when the time comes. But I have a much more important job for you right here."

Patton's mood changed abruptly. Eisenhower saw he was curious. "What kind of job?"

"The enemy knows very well what you mean to us, how you inspire the troops, what the newspapers say about you, all of that. Despite everything we've done to keep word of your whereabouts secret, the enemy's intelligence knows you're here."

Patton seemed to puff up again, and Eisenhower thought, Of course, he's proud they keep track of him.

"I'll keep my head down, Ike. We find any Kraut spies, I'll string 'em up myself."

"Actually, George, we've already found a few spies. The Brits have done one hell of a job nailing Hitler's intelligence people here. Better than that, we've been able to turn them around."

"You're asking Kraut spies to work for us?"

"*Asking* isn't the word I'd use. They either work for us or they're executed. It's called a strong bargaining position. Point is, so far, it's worked out well. We've been feeding the enemy false information; then we sit back to see if they respond. Stupid little tests, like information about some raid we're going to launch on a weather station or some fortified gun battery. It's worked. The Germans have responded just like we wanted them to. They still believe their agents are doing their job. What they don't know is that their communications are being monitored by our people."

"How long do you think this is going to work? Sooner or later, one of these turncoats is going to remember his beloved Führer and stick someone in the back."

"Could happen. The Brits are all over this. Double and triple cover. A lot of stuff I don't even want to know about, details I don't need to know."

"Don't like this, Ike. A Kraut is a Kraut."

"I don't care if you like it or not, George. I need you to follow orders. And this is a beauty. We plan to let it leak that you've arrived in London, for one very specific command."

"They'll learn about that sooner or later, Ike. You can't hide a whole damned army."

"We don't plan to hide one. We plan to create one. The plans are being put into place. The First United States Army Group, commanded by General George Patton."

He had never seen Patton so confused. "A fake army? What the hell for?"

"To convince the enemy that we're going to make our landing at Calais. That *you* are going to make our landing at Calais. We're still figuring out some of the details, but the plan we're putting together calls for you to become visible in every place where it makes sense for an army group commander to be. The Brits are jumping on this like flies on a dead mule, George. They've already got construction people lining up to build fake wharves, shipping depots, tank and truck parks. Churchill loves it, wishes he had thought of it himself. He's pushed like hell to get British factories to turn out all kinds of tricks. The G-2 people are talking about rubber tanks, plywood trucks, artillery pieces made out of plumbing."

"Rubber tanks?"

"It sounds bizarre, George, I know. But if this works, if the enemy swallows it and believes we are landing at Calais, he will reinforce his position there. It could tie down entire divisions, panzers, artillery. It could mean the difference between success and failure at Normandy. It's that damned simple. Your headquarters has already been established. It will be fully staffed and there will be considerable communication flowing in and out, just what the enemy would expect to hear."

"But . . . the troops. Where are the troops coming from?"

"There are no troops. That's the point, George. We're training like hell to put our people across the beaches at Normandy, along the Cotentin Peninsula. Every effort has to go to carrying out that operation. But the enemy needs to believe that we are coming in at Calais. Hell, he *should* believe it. It's the most logical place, the closest point to Dover, good beaches, a straight shot into Germany. The Germans read maps as well as we do, George. They'll *want* to believe this."

Patton stared at him and shook his head slowly. "This is the stupidest damned plan I've ever heard."

"Correction. This is *the* plan. It's *your* plan, *your* mission, *your* orders. And you will damned sure make it work."

Patton was scowling, a look Eisenhower had seen before. "But the Third Army . . . is that real?"

"Yep. But that comes later. We need this first. Otherwise, when we hit those beaches at Normandy, our people might get chucked right back into the damned sea. If that happens, it could be a year or more before we could even try to do something like this again. The Brits . . . they've just about had enough, George. They can't absorb another kick in the ass, another Dunkirk. If Overlord doesn't work, the Germans will gain more than a victory. Every Kraut will know they chewed up the best we could give. Churchill? Hell, I don't know what he'd do. He's fought this plan from the beginning. And FDR? He'd have to bend to the pressure from MacArthur and put our best strength in the Pacific. And he'd be right."

Eisenhower paused. Patton was staring at him, serious. He knew what he should say, what would mean more to Patton than politics and grand strategies.

"George, if this thing falls apart, if we don't put our people across those beaches and hold on . . . it won't matter much to you and me. We'll spend the rest of this war pushing pencils in some closet in Washington."

4. EISENHOWER

"I had hoped we would land a wildcat that would tear out the bowels of the Boche, but it appears we have instead landed a vast whale, with its tail flopping about in the water. I am not at all pleased with this operation. Not at all." Churchill took a long drink from a crystal tumbler, set it down in front of him, and glared at the men around the table. "What are we planning to do here? Is there a plan at all?"

Eisenhower had grown used to Churchill's bellowing his displeasure at any campaign that floundered, any single officer who did not perform. This time the campaign was Italy, the particular operation the invasion at Anzio. The entire operation had in fact been Churchill's idea from the beginning. The amphibious landing was inspired by the Allies' lack of success in driving the Germans northward through the Italian peninsula. In fact, Field Marshal Kesselring's Germans had anchored themselves solidly into a defensive line that made considerable use of the mountainous terrain across central Italy. The battles there had become slugfests, with little progress and little movement on either side. Churchill was enthusiastic for what Allied planners described as an American end run around Kesselring's western flank, though it had amused Eisenhower that Churchill required an explanation as to just what an *end run* actually meant. It had not occurred to the Americans that Winston Churchill would have no grasp of a term that applied to American football. But Churchill recognized that the plan was clear cut in its simplicity and could be the least costly way to break what was becoming a miserable stalemate.

The plan called for the American Sixth Corps, under Major General John Lucas, to land on the beach at Anzio, only thirty-five miles south of Rome, well behind the German defensive line. Establishing their beachhead, the Americans would quickly drive inland, severing the link between the German positions and Rome itself. If the plan worked, Kesselring's forces would be pressed from two sides and possibly surrounded. At the very least, American troops might sweep northward into Rome, which would be an enormous boost of morale for the Allies and the beleaguered Italians, who still feared that the Germans might destroy their ancient city. If the Germans somehow escaped the pincer, Kesselring would have no choice but to pull his forces northward, farther up the Italian peninsula and away from the mountainous defenses that had given the Allies such difficulty. Faced with such a crisis, it was unlikely that any German troops could be stripped away from Kesselring and sent to reinforce the defense of the beaches in France. A successful landing at Anzio could very well shorten the war.

On January 22, Lucas's thirty-six thousand men and a massive supply of trucks and armor landed with virtually no opposition; the Germans seemed caught completely by surprise. But then the plan broke down. Though the beachhead was secured, Lucas delayed his push inland, choosing instead to reinforce his already formidable strength, resupplying and consolidating his position along the coast. The delay gave Kesselring's Germans all the time they needed to mount a brutal counterattack, and now the Americans were pinned against the Anzio beachhead in what had become a desperate fight for survival. Within two weeks of the landings, Allied optimism for a quick burst into Rome had dissolved, and Anzio was now a raw nerve for the prime minister. Eisenhower understood that the operation now bogging down so badly was too reminiscent of the British disaster at Gallipoli, the amphibious operation in the First World War that had nearly cost Churchill his career. Whether or not Churchill was overreacting to the American failure, Eisenhower knew, as did Marshall, that if the Germans crushed the Allied effort in Italy, it would seriously dampen the tentative enthusiasm the British were showing for Operation Overlord. Instead of shortening the war, it could lengthen it considerably. Thus far, the only thing shortened was General Lucas's career.

Eisenhower scanned the long table. Sir Alan Brooke, the British chief of staff, was staring sourly into his cup of tea.

"There is responsibility here," Brooke said. "Jumbo Wilson knows this. Despite our best efforts, we have underestimated the enemy's will to resist. It was perhaps premature to remove some of our best people from the Mediterranean before conditions there were more secure."

It was a familiar refrain, the British seeming always to dwell solely on the difficulties of any operation, an annoying tendency Eisenhower had to deal with carefully. He knew the reasons, an ingrained dread that had come from the disasters at Dunkirk and Tobruk. There were successes, of course, but the British could not escape their memories of the Great War, the awful carnage born of stalemate, the years of unending death that had cost England, and Europe, a generation of young men. It had infected the British throughout the planning for Overlord, fears that even a success-ful invasion of Normandy would result in that same kind of stalemate, in the same part of France that had once been the awful no-man's-land of the Western Front, places like the Somme and Ypres. Across England, the mood of the people had begun to affect the mood of Parliament, a growl-ing discontent that perhaps enough was enough. The mood had spread throughout the British high command, Churchill himself knowing that the war could not go on for years to come, that the British could not ab-sorb the loss of another generation of young men. Eisenhower knew that, without the fresh energy of the Americans, the fear of another catastrophe would overwhelm the British spirit.

There was silence for a few moments. Eisenhower knew he had to say something to break the gloom. Bradley was looking at him from across the table, a hopeful expression with just a hint of anxiety. Eisenhower nodded toward him—*Yes, I know*—and said, "Sir, I believe matters in Italy will re-solve themselves. General Marshall has already suggested that General Lucas be replaced in the field by Lucian Truscott. As you know, General Truscott served as my deputy in North Africa, and he has already been pro-moted as Lucas's number-two man." He looked at Brooke now. "I do not agree, sir, that removing some of our key people from Italy was premature. I know that General Wilson would agree, as would General Alexander.

They have the resources and the skill. Despite the difficulties, they will get the job done. I would add that General Marshall has absolute faith in our people in that theater."

Churchill jabbed the air with his cigar. "Yes, dammit, we do as well. Jumbo Wilson was not given command of the Mediterranean because he was pretty. He'll kick the proper backsides. Let the matter rest, for now. If General Marshall believes Truscott is the man, so be it."

At the far end of the table, Montgomery slowly rose, claiming the floor. Churchill looked that way, the others as well, and Eisenhower knew it was Montgomery's design, a curtain rising on some dramatic show. Montgomery smoothed his sweater, the strange turtleneck he almost always wore.

"I concur. Jumbo Wilson will not be denied, and with our allies put on the right track, the enemy will not resist for long. My concerns are those facing us right here. I am wondering what sort of progress has been made regarding the transport of the gasoline booster xylidine. I have heard no reports yet of any shipments reaching our air boys."

It was pure theater. Glancing at Air Marshal Tedder, Eisenhower saw the man clench his jaw. "I have received assurances from General Marshall that supplies of the gasoline booster are being produced as we speak. Shipments will be forthcoming beginning in early March."

He paused. Montgomery was eyeing him, as though seeking more formal assurance. Eisenhower heard the words in his own mind: No, don't swallow the hook. Keep it simple.

"Since we have made it a point at this meeting to express our combined faith in those people who are on the job in Italy, perhaps we should do the same for the men right here. I am assured by my supply and ordnance people that when supplies of all kinds reach these shores, they will be efficiently distributed. No one needs to be reminded of his job."

Montgomery seemed satisfied and sat down; Bradley was looking at Eisenhower again, a slight smile. Yes, Brad, get used to this. Monty is going to let us know how well every one of us is doing *our* jobs. I just hope he does *his*.

SHAEF, BUSHEY PARK, OUTSIDE LONDON
FEBRUARY 16, 1944

"Right now, our best estimate for the target date is early June, the fifth, sixth, or seventh. Good moon, the tide is low at dawn. The original plan suggested May, but with the operation now so much larger, we need another month for preparation. The air boys are happier too, thinking the extra warm weather will give them a few more days of bombing. We'll take all that we can get. As for the date and hour of the assault—well, the chiefs have left that in my hands, thank God. All they sent me was this."

Eisenhower handed the order to Bradley, who read for a moment. "Brief and to the point. Nice, for a change." Bradley read aloud: "*You will enter the continent of Europe and, in conjunction with the other Allied Nations, undertake operations aimed at the heart of Germany and the destruction of her armed forces.* Not much to argue about there."

Bradley returned the paper to Eisenhower.

"Wrong, Brad. Plenty to argue about. I never saw so many mother hens trying to keep their own eggs in the basket. Hell, I don't have to explain that to you. At least we're all in agreement about the infantry. Morgan's original plan didn't call for enough people, enough power. Not his fault. Nobody could have done as good a job putting this thing together. But he underestimated what we'd need to get ashore and hold the beachheads. No one would commit to giving him any landing craft, so he had to assume we couldn't get more than three divisions ashore. It was Monty who pushed the idea that we need five beachheads and a hell of a lot more people. He's right on that one, for sure."

Eisenhower paused.

"I have no problems with the navy, not yet anyway. Admiral Ramsay has committed the British to as much support as we could ask for. I like the man, Brad. I worried that when Cunningham was moved up to First Sea Lord, we lost the best friend we had. I expected it would cause us some problems working with the navy that we never had before. But Ramsay is top notch. Tedder too, of course. Always liked him. The Joint Chiefs have agreed with me that he'll be my number two here, and not just command the air forces."

He paused again.

"I'm getting some bitching from our side about this, that this is just North Africa all over again. All my principal subordinates are British, and there are still some people who choke on that. The smart ones know to keep their choking quiet, but I know it's there. Annoys the hell out of me, Brad. There has to be some political reality here. We're trying to build a team, and I've got to have the full support of our people *and* theirs. Churchill understands that. He knows the value of what I've tried to do."

"No objection from me, Ike. I'll do what Monty needs me to do, until you tell me otherwise."

Eisenhower had no doubts about Bradley's ability to follow orders. "I don't need to hear that, but thanks. I wish . . . hell, it's not like I'm happy with everybody. This isn't some pleasant little social club, and I can't tell everybody how I want them to act. Too much out of my control. All those British air commanders—so damned ritualistic. Every damn operation falls under some kind of textbook rules. I can't get them to understand that Overlord isn't just another normal tactical operation, but I don't have the authority to tell them what to do. I keep yelling at them that we're going to need bombers on the beaches, and they keep saying, no, we'll just keep bombing Germany, and we won't need the beaches at all. The fighter people, Leigh-Mallory and his bunch, keep reassuring me that their fighter planes can get the job done and we don't need the bombers at all. He's been chosen to head the combined air assault. The man has never worked with ground commanders before. Never. It surprised hell out of me that Brooke would push him for the job. All I know about Leigh-Mallory is that he's a man who makes enemies, and in the British air force he has quite a few. The bomber people despise him. Doesn't bode well for cooperation. They're in some kind of damned contest with each other over who gets the glory, while the infantry is supposed to wade ashore hoping somebody's paying attention—somebody besides the damned Germans."

Bradley said nothing. Eisenhower appreciated the silence. Enough damned ranting, he thought. He looked through Bradley's ever-present eyeglasses, no change of expression on the man's face. "You talked to Monty today?"

The expression changed, a slight frown.

"This morning. He called to tell me he had been out to the Twenty-ninth Division. Checking on the progress of the training."

Eisenhower sagged in the chair. "He's touring *our* divisions? Without you?"

Bradley shrugged. "Sure. I have no problem with that. The men seem to like the attention. I know Monty does."

Eisenhower felt cautious. Don't say too much about Monty. Things like that have a way of biting you in the ass. But dammit, he should have stayed in the Mediterranean. His troops are down there, and he's up here making headlines.

Bradley shifted in his chair. "I have no problem with Monty, Ike. I really don't."

"Dammit, Brad, you're not supposed to read my mind. You know I wanted Alexander, definitely thought he'd be the best man for the job. Churchill thought so too. But Brooke pushed hard for Monty. I understand that, I suppose. Morale is crucial to this operation, and the Brits need a hero, someone who looks good in the newspapers. Right now Monty's the best one they have. After all, he's the man who whipped Rommel. It doesn't matter much who else was in that fight, or that Rommel might have whipped himself. Like you say, Monty likes the attention, and he's done a hell of a job promoting his own legend. Even our people cheer for him. That can't hurt a damned thing."

He paused, the caution slipping away.

"If Churchill hadn't been so sick, we'd probably have gotten Alexander anyway. It was pretty scary for a while, that damned pneumonia he caught in Africa or wherever the hell it was. If Churchill keeled over, it would cost us a hell of a lot more than a little chaos in the British government. It would be a disaster of morale for everyone involved. But I have to hand it to Brooke. I have no idea why he's such a fan of Monty, but he picked a good time to push him down Churchill's throat."

"Monty will be fine, Ike. He's a leader. We get along."

Eisenhower couldn't stifle a laugh. "You'll be the first. Patton would just as soon shoot him."

Bradley didn't smile. "Patton might want to shoot *me* before this is over," he said. "Don't worry about George."

Eisenhower was still smiling. "You amaze me, Brad. You're the calmest man in this army."

Bradley shrugged again. "I'm nervous as all hell, Ike. Can't think about that. Got a job to do."

"I hope it's that simple. Just . . . do the job. I thought Clark would do the job in Italy, and listen to the bitching. That damn AP reporter, Wes Gallagher, is making himself a real pain in the ass about Anzio. Gallagher's a good guy, always liked him, been around the HQ since North Africa, but now he's raising hell: I should still be down there; I should have taken command instead of Wilson; Alexander and Clark aren't up to the job. Makes good press, I suppose. But it's too easy to bellyache about things you don't understand, especially when you have an audience who eats up anything you tell them from the front lines. The Germans aren't just pushovers, and I told Gallagher that. Reminded him we got our butts kicked in Tunisia before things turned around. We have nothing to apologize for in Italy." He squinted at Bradley, stared again through the man's glasses, saw he had Bradley's full attention. "We're all scared as hell, Brad. But I need you to keep it locked up. Deal with Monty, handle Patton. Do the damned job."

"Count on it, Ike. June fifth, you think?"

"That's the plan right now, but it could change. Weather makes all the difference. The maps are still being drawn, and those will change too. The air boys might be right. Who the hell knows what's going to happen?"

Bradley felt his jacket pocket. "Oh, I forgot. Something to show you." He pulled out a small glass vial, uncorked it, and poured the contents on Eisenhower's desk.

"What the hell is that, sand?"

"Not just sand. The engineers have a fancier name for it, silicate something-or-other. Came from Omaha Beach."

"So? There's fancy sand on Omaha Beach?"

"There's *good* sand on Omaha Beach. The engineers say it means we can land tanks there, heavy equipment, no bogging down. I was sweating this one, Ike. Could have caused us some serious problems."

Eisenhower sat back, staring at the small pile of sand, and suddenly recalled the quote—Ben Franklin—and thought, Good God, this is a perfect example. *For want of a nail . . .* For want of good hard sand.

"Chief?" The voice was Butcher's. Eisenhower looked past Bradley. "What is it, Harry?"

"We just got a note from the European Advisory Council."

"Who?"

"Hell, I don't know, sir. A group that's working on treaties and stuff. This just came from Ambassador Winant. They insist you be informed that they've come up with the list of terms for Germany's unconditional surrender: occupation and subjugation, changes to German laws, boundaries, all that kind of stuff."

Eisenhower blinked and looked again at Bradley, felt no energy, his strength drained away.

"Leave it to the damned civilians. They put it on paper, and I guess that means the war's over. What the hell do they think this will accomplish? Does anyone believe the Germans are ready to agree to this stupidity?"

"That's what Beetle said, sir. Thinks they're counting chickens before they hatch."

"Does Beetle have any thoughts on what we should say in response to Ambassador Winant?"

"Not really, Chief."

Eisenhower saw a smile on Butcher's face. Yep, he can read my mind too, he thought.

"Maybe give Patton a call. Tell him I have someone he can shoot."

5. ROMMEL

"I was promised that we would have two thousand tanks per month, seven thousand aircraft. I was promised all the concrete and steel I required. In the past two weeks, I have not been given enough barbed wire to encircle this château."

Von Rundstedt looked up at him with tired eyes, shrugged his shoulders. "So the little corporal tells you everything you want to hear, and you believe him. Whose fault is that?"

Little corporal. Rommel had heard that insult before; von Rundstedt never referred to Hitler with any respect. Rommel could not help feeling uncomfortable, no matter how little regard he had for Hitler's strategies. The man was after all still the Führer and still very much in control of his officers and his army. Since he had come home from North Africa, Rommel had tried to guard his comments, to keep his lack of respect for Hitler hidden. It was the great value of a man like Ruge, a confidant Rommel knew he could trust. But von Rundstedt seemed not to care about any of that. He was growing old, sixty-eight now, seemed to have no fear of Hitler's dangerous tentacles, seemed not to care what might happen if word of his insulting arrogance reached the ears of any Gestapo officer.

The command structure in France and the Low Countries was a symptom, just one more hint of the great disease that had infected the army. Von Rundstedt suffered from it as much as any other officer in the Wehrmacht. No matter how much authority any senior commander was given, he still had to answer to Hitler's whims and erratic strategies. In France, the command structure was as fractured and illogical as any theater of the war. Army Group West was von Rundstedt's command, which included all of France, Belgium, and Holland. Rommel was his immediate subordinate, commanding Army Group B, which included the northern half of von Rundstedt's theater of the war, from Denmark to as far south as the Loire River. Farther south, von Rundstedt also held rein over Army Group G, under the command of General Johannes Blaskowitz, who controlled all of southern France. Blaskowitz was an old friend to Rommel and had commanded an army in the Polish campaign in 1939. But he had been outspoken about the severe butchery of the Polish people, so Blaskowitz had made enemies. To Hitler's staff, Army Group G seemed as far from the war as any German commander could find himself, far from any glory that would come from the great victory that the Propaganda Ministry continued to trumpet. Rommel knew that to many of those same detractors, his own Army Group B was not much closer.

To make matters worse, Rommel did not have authority over the troops stationed in his sphere of command. The SS troops were under separate authority, those more fanatical units that were thoroughly loyal to Hitler, men whose indoctrination made them feared not only by the enemy but by many in the German army as well. But the worst pill for Rommel concerned his beloved panzers, the powerful armored divisions still commanded by many of the exceptional officers Rommel had cultivated in North Africa. The panzers stationed in Rommel's arena were now separate and autonomous. The armor was commanded by Baron Leo Geyr von Schweppenburg, a man Rommel despised. The feeling was mutual.

Though all these mixed commands fell under von Rundstedt's umbrella, the old man himself seemed unwilling to keep a tight grip on any of his subordinates. It was a curse Rommel had suffered through in North Africa: divided authority, boundaries determined by the forces of personality and politics and ego, with little regard for sound military strategy. Rommel knew this had cost the Germans the North African campaign, and it certainly led to continuing disaster in Russia.

Throughout all the frustrations of the diluted authority, Rommel still had Hitler's ear, had been instructed to report directly to Hitler if there were concerns Rommel felt an urgent need to address. Whether von Rundstedt resented the obvious slight, he showed little concern, one more sign that the old man was merely biding his time until he finally slipped into retirement.

Rommel had always had a strange and unpredictable connection to Hitler. Despite the failures in North Africa, Hitler still seemed willing to refer to Rommel as Germany's great warrior, and the Propaganda Ministry was well aware that the German people still regarded Rommel as a genuine hero. Since the defeat in North Africa, Rommel had been very much the outcast in Berlin and had fallen completely out of Hitler's favor, but now the bruised relationship seemed to be healing. Rommel had seen that the Führer's grasp of the reality of the war was shaky at best. Hitler had personally given Rommel assurances that the Atlantic Wall had become a high priority. Within a few short weeks, Rommel knew better.

"Have you completed your inspections?" von Rundstedt asked.

"I have inspected most of the entire coastline, from Copenhagen to the Pyrenees. I thought you might have read my reports."

Von Rundstedt didn't flinch at Rommel's barb, but there was a silent pause. Rommel regretted the small indiscretion and glanced around the room, unable to avoid the opulent luxury, artwork and antique furniture in every corner. Von Rundstedt had planted himself in a château that bristled with finery, too close to Paris, too close to distractions that would tempt anyone to lose focus on his priorities. Rommel had always been disgusted by this spectacle, and though he found von Rundstedt to be charming and generally pleasant to be around, it was one more reason why he knew the old man was simply wrong for the job.

"So, what are your recommendations?" von Rundstedt said.

Rommel swallowed the word, had already made too many recommendations. He had notes in his pocket, brought them always to any meeting with von Rundstedt, prepared always to answer the question.

"Besides the numerous requests I have made for barbed wire, steel posts, and concrete, I have now determined that we require as many as twenty million land mines. In time I should like that number increased ten times."

Von Rundstedt laughed. "Two hundred million land mines? Ah, yes, I understand. You request a ridiculous number, hoping you might get what you really want. But really, Erwin, twenty million? Do you expect anyone in Berlin to take you seriously?"

"I expect *you* to take me seriously. We must create a coastal barrier no army can cross. And we require much more. I have already begun to install aircraft barriers to the west, in the bocage country in Normandy, tall posts in a random pattern in the open fields. Any airborne units attempting to land will be broken to pieces."

"Ah, yes. *Rommelspargel,* Rommel's asparagus. I have heard talk, of course. Quite amusing, actually."

"I do not find it amusing at all. When the Allies come, they will come with enormous strength, including quite probably airborne landings. They have learned from their failures and their successes. We must prevent a successful landing at all costs. It has been enormously frustrating to me that I cannot get the quantity of railcars promised me, that the larger artillery pieces are unfinished in their factories, that the tanks I was promised do not seem to exist. And where is the Luftwaffe? None of the airfields I have visited has any sizable number of fighters. Is Göring hoarding them somewhere?"

Von Rundstedt sat up straight now, a hard frown on his face. "Enough of your demands, and enough complaining. You are the one who speaks to the sympathies of the little corporal. Speak to him now. I can get nowhere. You have been given more than anyone else in my command, and I do not hear such complaining from the others."

Rommel felt the old rage returning; he could never keep it hidden for long. "Perhaps it is because no one else is facing an enemy invasion."

"How do you know that? How do you know where they will come, or when, or even if? There are no intelligence reports I am aware of that reveal any plans to attack Holland or Calais or Normandy or Brittany."

"There are no intelligence reports because there is no intelligence."

Von Rundstedt slapped the table. "You will stop this!"

Rommel leaned back in his chair. There were boundaries he could not cross with the old man.

"Erwin, there is considerable discontent among your subordinates. Several of your generals are critical of how hard you are working the men."

"Salmuth." Rommel felt his stomach tighten.

"Well, perhaps, but there are others."

Rommel had heard the griping before, and was suddenly furious that von Salmuth had gone over his head. Hans von Salmuth commanded the Fifteenth Army. Along with the Seventh, it comprised the bulk of Rommel's troops. Von Rundstedt continued.

"General von Salmuth is one of those who believes you are asking too much of the men, that by employing so many soldiers as construction workers you will exhaust them. Should there be an invasion, the army might be too worn out to resist it. The officers are often working as hard as their men."

Rommel stood suddenly, fighting to control his temper. Von Rundstedt seemed to know he had primed the explosion.

"I have already had this discussion with General von Salmuth. I will have it again, if necessary. I work the men too hard? Perhaps, sir, you should go out in the field yourself and *look* at these men. We have entire regiments made up of prisoners of war, foreigners who now fight for us so they do not have to go to a prison camp. Russians!"

"They are not prisoners, Erwin, they are refugees. They are grateful to be fighting against our shared enemies."

"In Russia, perhaps! Any Russian soldier worth a rifle should have the opportunity to turn that rifle against the communists. But here? Who is their enemy here? What will happen when we ask them to face the guns of the Americans and die for us? How much loyalty will they show for *our* Führer?"

There was no answer from von Rundstedt. Rommel continued.

"The Western Front has become one enormous recuperation center. I have entire divisions that are at half strength, bled down by the fighting in the east, and so they are sent here to rest and refit, although refit with *what*, I do not know. Now, we must tell them to conclude their pleasant seaside vacation and prepare to fight again, this time against the Americans. How many fights do these men have left?"

"You have merely repeated the complaints of your generals, Erwin. Why must you work these men so hard?"

"Because if we do not, if our Führer's mythical Atlantic Wall is not reinforced and strengthened and made as invincible as the German people have been led to believe, this war is over right now. We have one hope: to meet an attack with a more powerful attack of our own. Keep the enemy on the beaches and prevent him from establishing a landing."

Von Rundstedt held up his hands. "Stop it. I have heard too much of this from you. Every other commander here believes we can trap the Allies into a landing that will serve us perfectly. We have the mobility to move panzer divisions as quickly as they are needed. If we keep our troops prepared . . . and rested . . . they can be put into any threatened area in short order. You know as well as anyone the power of a swiftly executed counterattack. Allow the enemy to come, give him false confidence. No invasion, no matter where it comes, can be without chaos for the invader. That is our advantage. We are here, and we will be prepared. That is your job after all: *Prepare us!*"

Rommel felt the words roll around inside him and stifled his arguments. Too many arguments. He knew there would be nothing to gain, not now, not while there was so much still to do. If his generals would cooperate, he would continue the inspections, continue to lecture them, continue to prod and energize and inspire them. Though they might not agree, sooner or later they might actually obey his orders to put some power behind that ridiculous Atlantic Wall.

The inspection tours had continued, endless days of visits to officers who dreaded his arrival. The progress along the beaches was painfully slow, but after so many weeks, there *was* progress, and many of the line officers and their superiors had begun to accept Rommel's vision, had responded to his criticism by pushing their men a bit harder. There was energy in his words, and the men were always inspired by his presence. He was, after all, still Rommel.

Since his first days in command of the French coastline, Rommel had hoped to hear something specific from German intelligence. He had to believe that, sooner or later, one good spy would send some definitive word on where and when the attack would come. But so far the German intelligence network had been nearly useless in determining anything, no reports had any solid reliability.

Rumors ran rampant, but his own instincts were failing him, his gut feeling for the mind of the enemy, an innate sense that had served him so well in North Africa. There were many options for the Allies, and Rommel was not helped by the resistance and foot-dragging of those officers who, amazingly, didn't believe an invasion would come at all. It was maddening to him, this blind faith in the ongoing propaganda from Berlin, how Germany's power was unflagging and no army, no matter how powerful, could shatter Hitler's Fortress Europe—a fortress that Rommel was trying desperately to construct. But his old ailments were returning, the hard reality that he could no longer drive himself without a breath. The suffering inflicted on him by the African deserts had mostly faded away, but with the work had come new sickness, mostly from exhaustion. Maybe, with so much work now going on all along his coastline, he would make time to see his home, to walk in the Swabian hills, to nest in his wife's softness, to find a little peace.

HERRLINGEN, SOUTHERN GERMANY
FEBRUARY 23, 1944

He had made a momentous decision, encouraged by his staff. He had allowed himself a brief leave, a quick visit to see Lucie, to rest his spirit.

It was very cold, and he tugged at his coat, blew out a thick breath of soft fog, studied the tracks in the snow. It had been too long since he had gone hunting, and the tracks inspired him, his mind working, estimating the size of what was surely a magnificent wild boar. The animal had betrayed himself in the deep snow, the tracks a clear trail to his hideaway, and Rommel stood up straight and stared into the trees, suddenly wishing he had a rifle. He let out another breath, felt a shiver, his feet growing wet, and thought, No, not today. There is no time for such things. But surely you can make the time. You are on *leave,* for God's sake. He had heard that already from Lucie, more than once, her scolding reminders to take advantage of these precious few days. He had even secured a leave for his son, made possible only because Manfred's father was the great Rommel.

He held Lucie's voice in his head, saw the smile, heard the words now: *You are a stubborn man.* It was no insult, just her playful teasing. But she was right. He knew, too well, that his stubbornness had made him enemies. Kesselring understood me better than most of them, he thought. Just like von Rundstedt. He knew I was right, that every complaint was legitimate, and he knew I won every debate. And yet, not much had changed.

By God, it did not have to be! We were winning this war, should have won it two years ago! But we squandered away the victory, on . . . what? Russia? Yes, surely. One mistake among so many. Hitler surrounds himself with imbeciles, men who make him feel good because he controls them so completely.

He kicked through the snow, moved away from the animal tracks, saw smoke above the trees, the fireplace warming his home. He pushed hard at the thoughts, the doubts, the cracks in his armor. If we had crushed the

Russians, truly crushed them, what would we have won? No, that cannot be a question for soldiers, not for this soldier, anyway. I have one job to do, and if I am *stubborn* about it—well, perhaps I will get the job completed.

He had a flash of light in his brain and thought of the fields in the bocage, the hedgerow country, where aircraft barriers had been installed. He smiled, enjoying the description from the troops: Rommel's asparagus. Fine, if that inspires you, make all the jokes you want. But his mind would not rest. Even here, in the soft snow above his home, he could not escape the vision of those fields. Aerial reconnaissance over England had revealed the existence of gliders, and the clarity of that information had energized him even more. Rommel had begun to consider how to confront an airborne assault. Ideas blossomed in his mind as to how the poles could be made more effective. Of course, I should have thought of this in the beginning. The posts should be tied together, cable perhaps, steel wire. Every open field could become a spiderweb, destroying any craft that tries to land there. Deadly for paratroopers too. And install mines on those posts, or small artillery shells, detonating on impact, just like the beach obstacles. Tie the whole thing together, one giant bomb . . .

He forced his mind to quiet. Yes, another request, send me thousands of artillery shells, so that I may attach them to fence posts in open fields. One more reason for them to dismiss my concerns. I cannot get them to send me artillery pieces, why should I expect them to send shells? He had already suffered the infuriating bafflement from Berlin about the beach barriers, all the variety of methods he had devised to disrupt an invasion. Even von Rundstedt didn't understand. The old man had questioned him why others before him had not suggested such plans, constructing barricades in the sand, mined poles, steel hedgehogs. Von Rundstedt had answered his own question with an observation that perhaps it was because, before Rommel, no one had ever thought of doing this before. The idea seemed to amuse von Rundstedt, but to Rommel it was only one more frustration and produced yet another question in his own mind. Why? Why had no one ever thought to protect the beaches, to *prevent* a landing instead of responding to one?

He was walking quickly, energized by the idea, lists of materials forming in his mind, numbers he would add to the pile of notes on his desk. He stepped down through the snowy trees, breathing hard, saw the house in front of him—and in front there was a car, unfamiliar. He kept moving, shook his head; he had no patience for visitors now. Damn. Can they not

leave me alone? He studied the car, long and black, civilian. He tried to recall his schedule. Have I forgotten about some appointment? Well, we
shall see.

The man stood, a hat in one hand, and to one side Manfred was standing too, the boy's uniform starched, his back straight. Rommel knew
the civilian well.

"Dr. Strölin! I did not expect—"

The man held up his hands. "I apologize deeply, Field Marshal. I have
a matter of some importance to discuss with you, and I only learned yesterday that you had come home. I hope you do not mind; I have been con-
versing with your son. He is already quite the soldier, I hear."

Rommel was distracted for a moment. "Yes, Luftwaffe Auxiliary. He
was inducted only a few months ago."

"Yes, yes, so he tells me. Fine lad. They are teaching him to shoot
down enemy planes! Quite amazing for one so young."

Rommel saw a proud smile on his boy's face, but the news that Manfred had been summoned to service had left Rommel with very mixed feelings. He was only fourteen.

Rommel had served with Strölin in the Great War and knew him to be
a dignified and honorable man, a man who would waste no one's time.
Concerned about the brutality of the Gestapo, Strölin had visited Rommel
months before, with deeply disturbing reports that the relocation of the
Jews and other minorities had in fact become mass exterminations. Rommel had heard rumors of such things, even Lucie had brought him suspi-
cions that the Jews were not simply being moved to new settlements. But
he was deeply skeptical that there was so much blood on the hands of the
Gestapo, on SS officers who were said to have performed unspeakable
atrocities. In North Africa, Rommel was far removed from such talk, but
now the rumors had been given substance, details Rommel still found hard
to believe. To a soldier's mind, such things had nothing to do with duty.

Manfred spoke now, holding himself at attention. "Father, did you
know that Dr. Strölin is the mayor of Stuttgart?"

Rommel tried to smile. "Yes, I am aware of that. We are honored to
have such a visitor. And such an old friend."

There was silence now, awkward. "Is there something I can do for you,
Doctor?"

Strölin glanced at Manfred. "May we speak in your office, Field Marshal?"

Strölin was strangely formal, and Rommel felt suddenly cautious. "No, we may speak here. In this house we do not have secrets."

Strölin nodded and pointed toward a chair. "Very well. May I sit?"

"I will join you. Manfred, sit there."

The boy moved silently, obedient. Strölin sat gingerly, seeming to pause, seeking the right opening.

"There are a great many men of influence and substance in Germany who have become distressed by what we see as the destruction of our country."

"The war hurts everyone, Doctor."

"I am not talking about the war. Not entirely. I came to you a while ago, with the purpose of revealing things . . . events I knew you might not be aware of. I took a great risk that I might anger you, that our friendship would be destroyed. But I had to know that you are still the decent man that I knew you to be before . . . before all of this. The tragedies are ongoing and cannot be washed away. Our Führer has shown himself to be no friend of Germany. Indeed, there is a growing concern across this land that he is our enemy."

Rommel stood now, forced himself to be angry. "I will not have you slander our Führer's name in front of my son."

He saw pain in Strölin's face, unexpected. "Then please allow me to speak to you alone. I did not come here to promote rumor or to slander anyone. Please. It is most important."

Rommel looked at Manfred, saw disappointment. Yes, you understand, don't you? "Let us retire to my office, Doctor. Manfred, I will speak to you later. You may check the rifles; be sure they are clean. There is a large boar roaming the hill up above us here. Perhaps we should pursue him later this afternoon."

Manfred seemed to perk up, could not hide his enthusiasm. "Yes, Father!"

The two men moved to the office. Rommel waited for Strölin to sit, then he closed the door. "Now, Doctor, you may speak to me about anything you wish. But I cannot promise I will agree with you. Or even listen."

"Do you no longer call me Karl? All right, I understand your caution. And I understand a soldier's duty. That is part of my dilemma. I must not anger you by what I have to say. I do not speak to you today for myself alone. I am but one voice among many hundreds . . . thousands, perhaps. It is well known that your—um, enthusiasm for the Führer is not what it once was." Rommel started to object, and Strölin held up a hand. "Please, Erwin. Let me speak. There need be no pretense here. I have come here to reveal to you things for which I could be imprisoned. But I cannot be intimidated by that. As I said, I am only one voice of many. And despite what you may believe, I am still your friend."

Rommel felt his head spinning, the room growing warmer. He gripped the sides of his tall chair. "I do not wish to talk about politics, Doctor. What do you want?"

"There is great energy behind a plan to remove Hitler from power."

Rommel leaned forward, felt the words cutting into him, cold in his gut.

"Whose great energy?"

"Men you know, Erwin. Names you know. There is no specific plan, not yet. There is fear that if Hitler is simply . . . captured, forcibly removed, it could ignite a conflict within Germany that is more costly than the war. Our country might never recover. If there is suddenly a vacuum at the top, those most loyal to him . . . the Gestapo, certainly . . . well, everything could be destroyed."

"How could you possibly believe this kind of plan could succeed?"

Strölin smiled, and Rommel suddenly realized why. "Thank you, Erwin. You have just revealed what I had to know. You are at least sympathetic enough to listen to what we have to say. I admit, I was not completely certain."

Rommel felt sweat in his clothes. "I should probably have you arrested."

"Probably. But you won't. Because you know we are on the right path. You know we have lost this war. No matter what happens now, Germany has been too weakened by too many disasters of leadership to prevail over either the Russians or the Americans. You know that, don't you?"

Rommel did not answer, felt his breathing quick and sharp in his chest.

"We believe that if Hitler is removed from power, the British—and the Americans in particular—will open their arms to us and accept our calls for an armistice and for assistance inside of Germany. No one wants to see the Russians marching into Berlin. No civilized German wants to see Bolsheviks determining our future. So we must make a powerful overture to the West, to show them that Germany still has a meaningful national identity, that we are—well, that we are worth saving. That is why I came to see you."

Rommel was puzzled now. "You want me to . . . what? Surrender? You cannot be serious."

Strölin shook his head. "No, not surrender. Not yet, anyway. First things first. If Hitler is removed, there must be a single voice to replace him, someone whose influence will carry weight not only with our enemies but with the German people. We need a strong man to step into the void and assume command. It will be a delicate situation, to say the least. But we believe that man is—"

"Me? You want me to become the leader of Germany?" He realized he had shouted the words and glanced toward the door, his stomach locked in a twisting turmoil.

"You are the one man who can draw the respect of both the West and our own people. There simply is no one else. You are a Hero of the Fatherland and the finest general in our army."

"Stop! I have heard enough! You are committing treason, Doctor!"

"Listen to yourself! Treason against what? A madman who slaughters his own people? A madman who is so diabolical he will only leave this world if he takes our entire nation with him? The war is *lost,* but he will never surrender, you know that. If Hitler remains in power, Germany will be carved up from outside like a side of meat. You know I'm right, Field Marshal! You know what our future must be. You know what action we must take!"

Strölin was sweating, red-faced; he wiped at his brow with a white handkerchief. Rommel tried to calm himself, felt sick, tried to stand, could not. Strölin leaned forward, calmer now.

"Think about what I am saying, Erwin. Think hard. I speak truth, a truth you know only too well. Your son is on a path to join the Luftwaffe . . . to serve under that monster Hermann Göring! Is that what you want for your son? For Germany's sons?"

Rommel stared at the desk in front of him, the pile of paper, his notes, troop counts, and the tonnage of supplies, construction materials, and tools of war that didn't exist. He let out a long breath, closed his eyes, then blinked hard, sat in silence for a long moment, Strölin's words blistering inside of him, one word—*truth.* He said slowly, a low voice, "I am proud of my son, and I was proud when I heard he had been called up for service.

Then, I realized: They are drafting fourteen-year-olds. On the Western Front, I command thousands of men who can't even speak German. I can't make myself call them soldiers. Even von Rundstedt labels them what they are: refugees. They are already defeated men, and now they stand side by side with what is left of the German army. It is an illusion and it is my job to believe that illusion, and to make it work." He took a breath, looked at Strölin. "If they had allowed me to do my job, we would have defeated the enemy in North Africa. I would be in Cairo now, or Baghdad or Stalingrad, commanding a victorious army where the strength of Germany was the strength that inspired the entire world. Power and dignity for all of mankind, prosperity—"

"Was that ever real? Now it is you who are creating the illusion! Hitler has slaughtered hundreds of thousands of people in concentration camps all over this land. Civilians, many of them German citizens! I know you are skeptical of that, of the numbers, of the reasons. But how many soldiers have died, some in your own command, killed in a hopeless fight, killed because of insane orders you had to obey? Is your fight not hopeless now? In the east, the Russians have every advantage. Don't ask me how I know. It is a fact. It is only a matter of time before they cross the Polish frontier and their forces reach our own borders. That was unthinkable four years ago—three years—but it is truth now. Can you keep the Americans and the British out of France? Can your friend Kesselring prevail in Italy? How many enemies can we fight at one time, on how many battlefields? How many wars?"

Rommel felt himself weakening, felt his strength giving way. Damn you. Damn *them*. I am only a soldier. He looked down for a long moment, then raised his head and stared at Strölin.

"What is your plan?"

Strölin shook his head. "It has not yet advanced to that. There are many among us who are in disagreement."

"Whether or not you should murder him."

"I cannot speak of that. All I ask of you is that you offer us your name, let us be encouraged by your endorsement."

Rommel tried to sort through the thoughts in his brain, but the heat in the closed room was overwhelming him.

"I will not support any effort to assassinate the Führer. No soldier will allow that. The army would never support you. Remember that, Karl. It would be a catastrophic mistake."

"There is no plan to kill him. That is all I can say."

Rommel stared again at the desk, thought of von Rundstedt, his generals, the griping about his orders. I am a soldier, I will always be a soldier, and when the enemy comes, I must fight him, and if I can I will destroy him. I *must* destroy him. This must be the only thing that matters.

"Karl, I cannot put myself at the head of some kind of conspiracy. I love my country, and I love the army, and I will do what I believe to be the best for Germany. I am not even certain what that might be, not now, not with all you have said. I cannot dismiss you, I cannot ignore what you say. No matter what you do now, you must use great caution. I do not want to hear anything of your movements or who you talk to. I cannot support such a plan, not now, perhaps not ever. No matter what you say, I am still a loyal officer of the Reich, and I will obey the orders I am given. And right now I have to fight a war."

PART TWO

Gashed with honourable scars, low in glory's lap they lie,
Though they fell like stars, streaming splendor through
the sky.

James Montgomery (1771—1854)

In war, there is no prize for runner-up.

General Omar Bradley

6. ADAMS

He was one of the few enlisted men who stood with the officers, the reviewing stand dotted with uniforms of various colors: Sergeant Jesse Adams, on the highest row, the very back, just behind General Gavin, who in turn was behind those men who outranked him, the most senior officers placed along the front row. There was no mistaking the importance of this show, more brass gathered in one place than Adams had seen since he came to England. He had grown more comfortable around gatherings of officers, more comfortable keeping his mouth closed, knew that Gavin brought him to these assemblies for one reason: to pay attention, particularly to what the air force people had to say, especially the Brits. It had been more than four months since Gavin had come to England, to serve as senior airborne advisor to General Sir Frederick Morgan. Morgan's COSSAC plan had become the backbone of what was now Overlord, and Gavin's role, with Adams serving as one of his staff, had been to push forward any plan that would involve the airborne forces, the paratroopers and glider troops that Gavin and the more senior airborne commanders believed would be essential to the Normandy invasion. From the first meetings he had attended, clipboard in hand, a silent witness, Adams had seen the patronizing cloud of superiority that the air commanders had blown toward Gavin—indeed toward anyone who advocated the paratroopers' mission. Despite their ultimate success during the Sicily invasion, many among the bomber and fighter commands placed no value in the men who jumped out of airplanes. Fortunately for the airborne divisions, Omar Bradley had been one of their primary champions.

Following orders, Sergeant Adams had stayed close to Gavin throughout the endless days of meetings and conferences, map studies and engineering lectures, all those ingredients that now comprised Operation Overlord. Hundreds of officers and specialists were still contributing, defining what it was that Eisenhower would actually command, what would actually occur sometime around the end of May. Adams had witnessed Gavin's remarkable endurance in arguments, hot disputes with all levels of strategists and tacticians, especially those who had no concept of fighting any war that did not involve enormous numbers of troops marching forward in massed attacks. But it was the air commanders who most infuriated the young sergeant, as they had infuriated General Gavin. Gavin could speak out, but Adams was just one more anonymous aide, silent in front of these colonels and generals spouting their tactics.

Despite the clean uniforms, good food, and close quarters with the high brass, Adams had been frustrated by much of his job. In Sicily and Italy, Adams had toted a Thompson submachine gun. Now his weapon was the pen, his duties involving taking notes and recording appointments, all those jobs that would normally be done by some nameless secretary. But Gavin had made it clear that Sergeant Adams was *involved* and would accompany him as a silent aide—or silent witness. For reasons Adams still did not completely understand, Gavin trusted him, respected him, and even, on occasion, used him as a sounding board. It was the greatest compliment of Adams's life.

The men on the viewing platform all stared toward the far horizon, toward the growing hum, the planes hidden by a gray pregnant sky that hovered close overhead. Adams scanned the crowd, more interested in the ranks around him than in the drone of four dozen C-47s. Close in front of Gavin was the Eighty-second Airborne's commander, Matthew Ridgway, chewing the ever-present cigar, his face a permanent scowl. Ridgway was in his late forties, but his relative youthfulness among the division commanders didn't prevent every man in his command from referring to him as the old man, though no one would dare let Ridgway hear it. Down that same row was Maxwell Taylor, new in command of the 101st Airborne, the man whose appointment had surprised everyone, especially the officers of the 101st. The 101st had been commanded by Bill Lee, who had been the energetic force behind the creation of America's first airborne units and Jim Gavin's first airborne commander. But after a massive heart attack in early February, Lee had been sent home.

Lee's sudden collapse had devastated the morale of the 101st, and those men had every reason to expect one of their own would rise to fill Lee's shoes. Taylor had been the Eight-second Airborne's chief of artillery, but in Washington, his name outshined many of the candidates from the 101st, mainly because Taylor had considerably more experience in combat zones than anyone else on the list of prospective commanders in the division. Adams knew enough of loyalty among the enlisted men to wonder if Taylor would ever be accepted by his new command.

Down the row in front of Ridgway were the British, and Adams focused on the blue coat of Trafford Leigh-Mallory, the dapper square-jawed commander of the Allied tactical air forces. Adams knew Leigh-Mallory was Gavin's nemesis; he had made it clear that he considered paratroop and glider operations to be far too costly and a gigantic waste of time. Now, with the drone of the C-47s growing louder, Leigh-Mallory stood in the thickening chill, staring up toward the sound, and Adams could only believe that as the squadrons of transport planes drew closer, Leigh-Mallory was expecting some kind of debacle.

Down below a shout rose up, hands pointing. Looking that way, Adams caught the first glimpse of the formations, the C-47s barely visible in the low-slung clouds. Behind each plane were two gliders, attached by invisible tow lines. Adams watched intently. Gavin had said that this exhibition had one useless purpose: to convince everyone what the Americans already believed. If the gliders landed successfully, the proponents of the airborne operation, men like Taylor and Ridgway, would confirm what they already knew, that gliders were an asset and would be an essential part of the landing operation. If there were problems, it would only give ammunition to those who were still fighting to keep the airborne out of the Overlord plan altogether.

As the planes roared overhead, Adams measured the altitude in his head: five hundred feet, too low probably. But those damned clouds. The glider pilots had to be able to see the field. He was surprised to feel a hard pounding in his chest, the excitement spreading through all of them, the twin engines on each plane drowning out anyone's comments. What the hell are you so nervous about? You've bailed out of those damned planes a hundred times. But still he focused, stared at the lead squadron, waited for the telltale sign. It came now, the two gliders suddenly veering away, the towlines released from the C-47 that pulled them along. The others began doing the same. Adams didn't count them; he knew there were forty-eight.

The small American Waco CG-4A was the glider that would primarily carry the infantry or a single artillery piece. Behind would come the larger, heavier British Horsas, capable of hauling both men and a great deal more equipment, including a pair of cannon or jeeps. As each glider was released from its tow, it began to circle, the pilots focusing on the wide airfield, just another drill they had practiced dozens of times before. Adams shivered and shook his head, unable to avoid a strange fear. No damned way they're getting me in one of those gliders, he thought, no matter how well they're supposed to fly. Give me a chute and a plane I can leave behind. I'd a whole lot rather be a one-man target than stuck inside some big floating box.

He heard a cracking sound, an audible gasp from the men around him, looked out to one side, and saw two gliders locked in a shattering embrace. They had crashed together and tumbled downward, a sickening sound of cracking timbers, crushed metal—and men. What the hell happened? Adams stared at the heap of wreckage, bits of metal and wood still drifting to the ground and heard Gavin in front of him:

"Dammit! Dammit to hell!"

Men were shouting, one jeep moving quickly, men running, and now there were new sounds, a rumble of wheels on the smooth grass, gliders landing all across the open ground. Adams heard another crash, saw one glider standing on its nose, the tail straight in the air, the fuselage cracking, the tail section collapsing, men tumbling out onto the ground. Another came in low in front of the reviewing stand, one wing dipping, the tip catching the ground, the glider in a half cartwheel. In front of him, officers began moving away, more jeeps coming out from behind the platform, medics, shouting men. Adams waited for Gavin to move too, so he could follow his commander, but Gavin waited, seeming to absorb the scene: more gliders coming in, many more landing without any problems at all. All across the field, the attention was on the wreckage, some men pulling themselves out from the carcasses of their gliders, some retrieving the injured, medics scrambling into the chaos, officers close behind them. Adams wanted to say something to Gavin, thought, We have to help, but Gavin lowered his head, removed his hat, slapped it hard against his leg. Adams looked below, at another man not moving at all, the blue uniform of Trafford Leigh-Mallory. The British air marshal looked back toward Gavin with a grim stare.

"I would anticipate fifty percent casualties, and that is optimistic. No commander I know would subject his men to such a certain calamity. I truly do not believe this sort of operation is possible."

Adams, sitting close behind Gavin, knew what was coming.

"We just did precisely this kind of operation in Sicily!" Gavin said. "With considerable success! There is nothing impossible about it! Dangerous? I have no doubt there are dangers, there are dangers to the infantry who are going to cross those beaches, dangers to the navy men driving the landing craft, danger to every man engaged in this operation."

Gavin took a breath. Adams watched Leigh-Mallory and saw no change of expression. To one side, a new voice joined the argument. It was Bradley.

"Gentlemen, I agree that this operation carries risk, but the greatest risk is to the enemy. We must not forget that the purpose of the airborne operation is to disrupt and destroy the enemy behind his beachfront fortifications. Once our paratroopers and glider troops are on the ground, their orders are quite specific; they will patrol aggressively. General Gavin is quite correct. Our success in Sicily owed a great deal to the paratroop drops, most specifically in the American sector. Our experience there and at Salerno demonstrated that a nighttime drop will cause complete havoc in the enemy's position, his communication, and his ability to mobilize an organized front. General Eisenhower has granted his full approval of the airborne assault. I do not see what can be gained by further pessimism."

Leigh-Mallory seemed unaffected by Bradley's encouragement. "I cannot in good conscience support this part of the Overlord plan. The disaster during the glider demonstration only strengthens my resolve."

Bradley stood. "Marshal Leigh-Mallory, you may certainly exercise whatever resolve you feel is necessary, but my orders are to include two American airborne divisions in my planning, and Monty has included the British Sixth Airborne in his. We are depending on your tactical air support, and I know of no reason why that should not be forthcoming."

Leigh-Mallory stood, slipped his hat beneath his arm. "Gentlemen, I must return to my headquarters. I would only ask that you consider that there are other historical lessons besides the campaign in Sicily. Recall if you will the enemy's disaster in Crete. Our boys there destroyed most of Hitler's paratroop forces, and only by a series of unfortunate command decisions was the enemy allowed to drive us away. Only the Nazis would consider their excessive losses in that campaign a worthwhile price to pay for such a victory. Good day, gentlemen."

Leigh-Mallory moved out the door, his aide following. Adams felt an almost overwhelming need to follow him and plant a fist into the man's smug face. There was a momentary hush in the room.

"He has a rather loose grip on history," Bradley said. "The German paratroop drop in Crete was launched directly into the teeth of the British defensive position. I intend that you gentlemen drop your people *behind* the lines, not *into* them. Or is that too much common sense?"

HQ, EIGHTY-SECOND AIRBORNE DIVISION,
BRAUNSTONE PARK, LEICESTER
MARCH 24, 1944

"When was your last jump, Sergeant?"

Adams hated to answer, hesitated. Gavin nodded.

"Yeah, I know. Last year sometime. Me too. Ridiculous. Never expected I'd be away from the airfields as much as this. Even if we had the time to join the men in their training jumps, the weather here is so bad we can't put anybody into a regular schedule. Never saw so much damned rain."

"I'd be happy to jump in the rain, sir."

Gavin laughed, sat back in his chair, pointed across the office. "Maybe. Until you jumped blind into some Brit's barn. Grab that chair. Sit down."

Adams obeyed, his pen in one hand and pad of paper in the other, ready to write, the routine every morning. He gripped the pen and waited.

"Hate this place, don't you?" Gavin said.

Adams hesitated again. "Not always, sir. It has been an education."

"An education in what, how much bull there is in every HQ? How many morons are running this show?"

Adams didn't respond. He had seen Gavin in this kind of foul mood before and knew when to shut up. Gavin pushed a folder toward him.

"Here, look at this. Latest recon photo of the drop zones behind Utah Beach. Our drop zones."

Adams slid the photo from the folder. Short dark lines were scattered in blocks of gray fields. Gavin continued.

"The air recon people wait until late in the day to let the sun create shadows, so we can see what the enemy is doing. We couldn't figure out what those were until they started to grow in number. Those little specks are shadows cast by some kind of posts or poles, which the intelligence people believe are designed to disrupt our airborne landings. Could play hell with the gliders. One more can of gasoline for Leigh-Mallory's fire. Damn that pessimistic son of a bitch." Gavin stopped and looked at Adams, a sharp glare. "You didn't hear that. Ike is pretty touchy on anyone bitching about the Brits. We have a good plan, Sergeant, a damned good plan."

Adams studied the photograph. Pretty damned smart of the recon people to wait for the shadows to come. I guess that's why I'm in this office, and not out taking pictures. Gavin continued.

"Bradley impresses hell out of me, and General Ridgway—well, he's the best man to run this division. They should have given tactical air command to someone who knows what's really happening on the ground. Ridgway would have been perfect. Too many high-ranking Brits ahead of him, though."

Adams looked up. "Yes, sir. I agree, sir."

Gavin smiled. "I see you've been properly indoctrinated. I've had my share of arguments with General Ridgway, which is pretty rare in this outfit. It's best to keep your conversations with the general short. You disagree with him, tell him why as carefully as you can, then shut the hell up while he tells *you* why you're wrong. He doesn't tolerate much discussion about anything. Tough bird. Difficult. Believes he knows what's best, and most of the time it's hard to disagree. In this outfit there's the right way, the wrong way, and the Ridgway."

"Yes, sir. I've heard that often, sir."

"You didn't answer my question, Sergeant. You hate this place, right?

It's all right, I do too. That photo, pretty interesting stuff. But all it shows me is where I want to be. I miss those damned C-47s; I miss strapping on a chute. Nothing I can do about that, not yet anyway. Pretty proud of this job, Sergeant. Never thought a kid like me would get to shout at generals to their faces. Learned that from Ridgway. He's good at it too. But, dammit, I need to see a chute over my head, jerk some risers, feel the grease of a carbine. I see those damned green jump lights in my sleep."

Adams couldn't help a laugh, stifled it.

"What?"

"Me too, sir. Can't stop thinking about Sicily, the dark, trying like hell to find someone who didn't want to kill me."

Gavin stared at him for a long moment, said nothing. Adams waited for orders, straightened the pad of paper, the pen ready. There was little chatting with Gavin.

"I've been giving this some thought, Sergeant. Damned selfish of me, pulling you off the line."

"Oh, no, sir. I was honored. Surprised you even knew who I was."

"Knock it off, Sergeant. Every man in the Five-oh-five knew who you were. There's probably a silver star somewhere with your name on it."

Adams let the words flow past him. What the hell is going on here?

"I doubt that, sir. Begging your pardon."

"Answer my damned question, Sergeant. You hate this place?"

Adams stiffened, had a sudden flash of memory: a week ago, some British general ordering him to get coffee, Gavin standing up for him, no, he's not a mess orderly. Adams was grateful for the chance Gavin had given him, an honor indeed, even if the job was more clerical than anything he ever expected. He took a breath.

"Sir, I feel like I'm suffocating here."

"So do I, Sergeant, so do I. Problem is, I still have work to do here. You've been an enormous help. Good work, fine work. But we've got replacements coming into the Eighty-second who don't know a damned thing about the enemy, who are going to be a part of this operation when the only jumps they've made are at Benning or Bragg. We're going to get our asses shot off if we're not ready, and right now we're a long way from ready." Gavin reached into a desk drawer, pulled out a single sheet of paper. "Had this here for a couple days. Debated like hell telling you."

"Sir?"

"Read it."

Adams took the paper, saw the insignia of the Eighty-second Airborne, General Ridgway's official letterhead.

Sergeant Jesse Adams is hereby ordered to report to Colonel William Ekman, Commanding Officer, 505th Parachute Infantry Regiment, where Sergeant Adams will resume his post as jump instructor, with full seniority over the regiment's other noncommissioned instructors.

"I wanted to make you a first sergeant, but that will have to wait. Ekman suggested we give you a commission, make you a damned lieutenant. He thought it might be a good bribe to get you out of this place and back into jump boots. Told him you wouldn't need that. The last thing I want anyone to say about you is that you're a ninety-day wonder. And I don't really think you're officer material, Sergeant. That's not an insult, I promise you. Just look around this place."

Adams felt his brain swimming. "No, sir. I understand, sir." He read the orders again, could not hold the smile, and looked up at Gavin, who smiled as well. "Thank you, sir."

"You might not thank me when this is over. This isn't Sicily we're going after. But dammit, we need the best people out there, people who know what the enemy looks like. I'll be out there too, eventually. I feel like I'm turning into corn mush in this office, my belly's as soft as Jell-O. So there's no way in hell you're going into France without me. Ridgway will be there too, count on that. When I get back out there, when I can finally get my ass into a C-47, I want to see you at the end of the line, and I want every damned one of those troopers to be more afraid of you than they are of the Krauts. Now get the hell out of here."

Gavin had stopped smiling. Adams, still hesitant, stood slowly, stiff and straight, and stared at the wall over Gavin's head.

"Thank you, sir. I'll be waiting for you."

He turned, felt like running out of the office but held tightly to his composure, moved out through the door, and passed slowly through the outer office, the staff at work, low hum of voices, men watching him, curious, someone calling his name. He moved out into the chill, glanced up at gray skies, heard the soft drizzle of rain, and stopped on a narrow porch, steps in front of him, soft green grass between many, many buildings. He tried to hear Gavin's words again, the compliments, the duty in front of him, felt the old burn returning, a smoldering fire, wanted to run, to feel the churning in his legs, the hard breaths. He had no idea where he would go, just out, away from the dead air and stifling work. He realized he had the pen and notepad still in his hand, the fixtures attached to him for so many months. He moved to one side toward a fat green garbage can, tossed the pad in, gripped the pen and threw it across the open grass like a small spear, held the energy inside, and walked out into the perfect rain.

7. ADAMS

He stared at the rain, thick and gray, shrouding the C-47s in a ghostly haze. The gloom was complete, another frustrating day, little to do but drill the men once more on their preparations, packing their chutes, stuffing backpacks and belts and pants pockets with their equipment. It had been this way for a week now, either rain or a misty fog so heavy that every training jump had to be canceled. Outside, long rows of C-47s sat empty, silent, mostly under camouflage netting, someone's attempt to disguise them from German fighters and recon planes.

Adams glanced up. Who in hell do they think is flying in this stuff? he thought. I haven't seen a German fighter since I've been here. How hard would it be to figure out this is an airfield, anyway? If I saw a clump of bushes anywhere near a runway, I'd bomb hell out of it.

His boredom was blossoming into raw frustration. Adams had never been good at clamping his feelings down. During the months as Gavin's aide, it had been Gavin himself who had intimidated Adams into silence. The message from Gavin had been clear and brutal: I have to put up with this, so you have to put up with this. Adams had no trouble obeying Gavin. He had an instinctive feeling that he never wanted to be on the receiving end of the man's temper. Gavin felt the same way about Ridgway; everyone in headquarters knew the commanding general's fury was a spectacle to behold, as long as it was directed elsewhere. Adams had begun to suspect that, above them all, Eisenhower probably commanded the same kind of fear, maybe more so. *Maybe Ridgway is as scared of Ike as I am of Gavin. And I'm supposed to make these logheads scared of* me. Hell of a way to run an army. He backed away from the wide opening of the hangar and turned toward the rows of long tables: several hundred men, dutifully packing their chutes. He focused on his own squad, his corporal moving among them, coaching, cursing, but, most important, allowing each man to complete the job on his own. It had been the most basic of lessons, begun at jump school at Fort Benning: Each man packs his own parachute. It was the one part of the classroom experience you could count on to get the full attention of the men. No one shirked, no one fell asleep. Every man understood that packing your chute incorrectly would most likely kill you.

Adams tried to ignore the dull throb in his temples, the wet chill that soaked his bones. He walked toward the men, the corporal eyeing him. Adams didn't particularly like the man, a skinny runt named Nusbaum from somewhere in northern California. Nusbaum had only been there a few weeks, but runt or no he had earned his second stripe by good work at Benning, something Adams had to accept. The man had an annoying whine to his voice, an attitude that spoke of privilege. There was nothing specific to Adams's dislike of the man, nothing Nusbaum had said or done. And Adams knew very well that any man who emerged from training at Benning had already proven himself as much as anyone could without actual combat. If you survived the training there, you had to have that peculiar brand of courage that allows a man to jump from an airplane, as well as physical stamina and enough brains to learn the basic techniques of the jump and, more important, the landing. Nusbaum had accomplished his training with that something extra that had caught the eye of the captain, so Nusbaum was now Adams's corporal, his second voice. But Adams still didn't like him.

The lieutenant was a different story. His name was Pullman, and Adams guessed him to be the youngest officer in the entire division. Pullman commanded the platoon, sixty men, of which Adams commanded one of the four squads. Gavin's order had given Adams seniority over every other sergeant in the 505th, but Adams knew it was a symbolic gesture. He would rarely have any contact with the other squad leaders. If the issue ever arose at all, it would probably be in some crisis situation, the worst kind of chaos on the battlefield, the possibility of two sergeants suddenly butting heads over the next move they should make. Adams couldn't think about that; there was no kind of planning or drill that would prepare a man to face such a ridiculous scenario. You don't shove your orders into the face of another soldier when the machine guns are firing. You make a decision, you hope it's the right one, and if the men respect you they accept your control. But you damn well better be right. I wonder if Lieutenant Pullman knows that?

Monroe Pullman had come to Benning from the Virginia Military Institute and never hesitated to mention that General George Marshall had passed through the same historic hallways. The men in the platoon weren't nearly as impressed by that as Pullman himself. Adams knew that Pullman was barely his own age, twenty-two, and the fact that he had made lieutenant was an eyebrow-raising surprise. The lieutenants were the most unpredictable group in the army, some earning the label *ninety-day wonders* and never rising past it. Adams scanned the hangar, searched for Pullman, didn't see him. Probably getting coffee. Man drinks more damned coffee than anyone I've ever seen. Not sure what that means about his leadership, but if he does that in combat, at least he'll be awake.

He moved close to one of the long tables, scanning the rows of packs, the chutes mostly secured, a few of the men still struggling with the folds. He had no patience for the slow ones. How many times had they done this? And they still can't do it right?

"Speed it up! It's almost time for chow, and no one in this squad goes to the mess until every chute passes inspection!"

One man spoke, unfamiliar, from the far end of the table.

"Hey, Sarge, I didn't come all the way over here just to stand in the rain. Does it ever stop? I heard them planes out there are just fakes. I coulda stayed home if all we was gonna do was go swimming."

Adams stepped that way. One of the new men, Dexter something. He saw the man's chute still on the table, saw the smart-assed smile as the man turned away from him. Adams felt the anger rising. I have no patience for this, he thought. No patience for anyone's bitching, no patience for anything at all.

"Who the hell are you?"

"Private Dexter Marley, Sarge."

"Marley. You're new."

"Yes, Sarge."

"Look at me, girlie."

The man turned toward him. Adams ignored the others, knew they were all watching.

"Name's Marley, Sarge."

"Not in this outfit. Not until you learn to get your chute packed as quick as the rest of us. And not until you learn that bitching about the weather just pisses people off. You ever actually jump out of a C-47, girlie?"

Adams saw the man inflate, preparing for an argument, the man's pride taking over. Beside him, a hand gripped Marley's arm.

"He's OK, Sarge. Dex doesn't know the drill yet."

Adams knew the voice: Unger, the kid, pimples and all.

"Shut up, Unger."

Marley was looking at him now, and Adams saw the glint of defiance, a big man who believed he could stand up to his short stocky sergeant. It was another spurt of fuel on Adams's fire.

"So, girlie, you've made some friends here. Well, right now you don't have any friends. I think you're a screwup, and in this company, we handle screwups one way." He was pulsing mad, saw a hint of fear on Marley's face, more fuel. "You listen to me, Private. The next time we jump, you'll be right next to me, I'll be the one checking your gear. I'll be the one who shoves you out the door of that damned plane, and I'll be the one who might accidentally unhook your line."

He stopped, hollow silence in the massive hangar, felt himself sweating, knew he was being abominably stupid. Marley's defiance was gone, replaced by blinking fear, and Adams held his stare, the man several inches taller, broad-chested, thick arms. Adams felt the fight coming, felt his hands balling up, focused on the man's chin, the target.

"Morning, Sergeant. Everything all right here?"

The voice punched him from behind, firm and unpleasant. He let out a breath, unclenched his fists, turned, and saw two men, Lieutenant Pullman and a face he had not seen since he had been back with the division, the familiar face of Ed Scofield.

"Captain . . . sir."

Adams threw up the salute, could see Scofield's hard stare, softening now.

"We have a problem here, Sergeant?" Pullman said.

"No, sir. Just trying to get the men to pack their chutes with a little more . . . efficiency."

He knew Pullman wouldn't buy it, but the lieutenant eased past him, close to Marley.

"Private, you having trouble remembering how to pack your chute?"

"No, sir."

"Then pack the damned chute!"

"Yes, sir."

Marley began to work on the fabric, the folds. Men were murmuring now, the ones who were farther away going back to their business. Pullman always seemed to be careful around Adams, had never chewed him out for anything, and Adams knew he wouldn't do it now. He noticed the man's coffee cup. Of course.

"Sergeant," Pullman said, "Captain Scofield tells me you have some history together."

Adams saw a smile on Scofield's face. "Yes, sir. That we do."

Scofield said, "Lieutenant, do you mind if Sergeant Adams walks with me a bit? Things seem to be under control here."

"He's all yours, sir."

Scofield looked past Adams, scanning the tables, the rows of men. "You men had better listen to Sergeant Adams, every damned word. You want to survive this war, he's the man who will keep your butts in one piece. You hear me?"

There was a sharp chorus. *"Yes, sir!"*

Scofield continued to examine the men and their equipment, then looked at Adams again. "Let's go, Sergeant."

Scofield walked away and Adams followed, moving toward the wide opening of the hangar. He felt a strange energy. He had not seen Scofield since Italy, since the day General Gavin had chosen Adams to go to England. Scofield was the company commander, and Adams had served with him throughout the fights in Sicily and after. There was no uncertainty about Scofield, no need for guessing whether or not the man was a leader. In Sicily, Scofield had been everything a soldier needed to see, and Adams had learned to trust him with a loyalty many veterans knew was rare.

The captain led him out into the rain, lighter now, more of a thick mist. As Adams followed, Scofield moved close to one of the C-47s, its camouflage netting pulled away. Adams saw the cockpit: Two pilots were in place, unexpected. Scofield turned to him.

"We're going up. The entire damned division. General Ridgway is sick of sitting on his ass, so the word came down a half hour ago. The weather is better, supposed to clear up a good bit more, give us some chances at a jump or two. Have your men recheck their chutes, load up their packs. I don't trust weathermen, and I'm not sure why General Ridgway feels any different, but orders are orders."

Scofield was looking at him, and Adams saw a smile.

"It's good to see you too, sir."

Scofield put a hand on his shoulder, a hard grip. "This is eating you alive, isn't it, Sergeant?"

"Not sure what you mean, sir."

Scofield looked up, squinted through the wetness on his face. "I feel it too. Every veteran I've spoken to is chewing nails to get on with it. Most of us thought we were done after Italy. Figured someone else would pick up the slack. But, hell, I knew better than that. We're the best this army's got. And from what I hear, that's what we're going to need." He paused, removing the hand from Adams's shoulder. "I had a feeling you'd go crazy as a staff sergeant. Gavin never changed your designation, you know. Did that on purpose, left it so you could come back to the company. I suspect you know more about our mission than I do, and that's fine with me. I'll learn what we're supposed to do when Colonel Ekman decides to tells me."

"Yes, sir."

Scofield looked at him, hard in the eyes.

"Good. Keep your damned mouth shut. I was hoping you wouldn't spill your guts. Hell, I knew you wouldn't. You've been drinking tea with British generals, and we've been out here fielding rumors. Lots of rumors. All bull. Well, hell, you know that. But those replacements, they'll listen to anything." He paused. "Now that you're back, you see what we've got here. We're not ready, are we?"

Adams hesitated, then shook his head, wiped a hand through wet hair. "They're fit, sir, but they're not combat ready. The last group of replacements, those fellows that came in a week or so ago: plenty of hotshots, big-mouths. It's a mystery to me where the hell we're getting these guys. But if we don't get some jumps in soon—"

"We will. Starting today. I'm a little concerned about the big-mouths too. One in particular."

Adams understood. Scofield had heard too much of his idiotic attack on Private Marley.

"Sorry, sir. Just trying to put some steel in the new ones."

"That's crap, Jesse. Those men aren't raw recruits, they're fully trained. You know what it takes to get through jump school, and every man in this outfit is here because he earned it. Steel? They've got plenty. What they need is *experience*. You're just pissed off, and you're taking it out on the men. Save some of that for the enemy."

Adams looked down. "I haven't made a jump in six months, sir. I feel like a damned rubber tire, all gut."

"None of us have jumped, Sergeant. But you and me—the veterans— we have to lead the way. We know what the enemy looks like, and what it feels like when our buddies die. That's the one thing missing from these new men."

"I can't teach them that, sir."

Scofield put his hands on his hips and stared up at the clouds. Adams could feel the mist growing lighter, saw a sliver of blue in the distance.

"The weather boys might be right," Scofield said. "Guess we'll find out soon enough. Get your men ready to load up."

Adams saw a jeep in the distance, three officers, moving out through the formations of parked planes.

"The get-rich-quick boys," Scofield said. "Major Turner, Captain Fishman. Don't know the other one. They're trying to get their five jumps in so they can be ready for the mission. Scares hell out of me, Sergeant. We've got officers in this division who've never seen combat at all. General Ridgway can't be happy about that, but we've got no choice. I'd trade a dozen of those guys for one Jim Gavin." He looked at Adams. "Get those boys ready. You want to beat hell out of some smart-mouth private, I'll look the other way, and Lieutenant Pullman will do the same, as long as you don't make a habit of it. But you don't have to show them how tough you are. Hell, they're already afraid of you. I can see it in their faces. I need you to show them why they should *follow* you."

"I understand, sir."

Far across the field, lines of men began to emerge from the rows of hangars, filing toward the waiting planes. In the distance, C-47s began to wake up, clouds of black smoke rising, the cough and sputter of engines.

"That's the Five-oh-eight. They're first to get moving. We'll follow the Five-oh-seven. Double time, Sergeant. Time to knock off the rust."

There was no hint of blue sky. Adams was jumpmaster, sat farthest from the cockpit, kept his eyes on the eighteen men, two rows, facing each other. The plane bounced once, a sharp drop, the familiar groan from those with the weaker stomachs. He knew some of them were struggling, no one wanting to be the first to show the sickness, to be responsible for stinking up the plane. As Adams had promised, Private Marley was closest to him. The man was silent, subdued, obviously surprised that Adams had been serious. Adams ignored him, knew that by now, Marley had developed a perfect fear of his sergeant. At Benning, silencing the big-mouths had been fun, and later, when the men had been in combat, the mouthing off had mostly stopped. These replacements had brought a new wave of talk, all that cheerleading about what they were going to do to the enemy. The veterans mostly ignored it. Adams looked across at Unger, small and skinny, relaxed, no sign of nervousness. Yeah, Unger, you're Marley's friend, aren't you? Probably told him not to screw with the sergeant. Good advice.

Wallace Unger had been with the squad since Sicily. Adams was certain he was well underage, must have lied to sign up. But the files showed Unger to be eighteen, and whether or not Adams believed it, Unger had endured every challenge and faced the enemy as well as Adams himself. More, Unger had shown himself to be a natural marksman. With the M-1 or even the Thompson, Unger could shoot as well as any man in the squad. Adams stared and caught a look from Unger: sharp bright eyes, a quick smile. Damn you, you're sixteen. I know it.

The plane banked, and Adams looked out through the wide opening beside him, still nothing but gray. He could feel the plane descending, saw motion along the rows of men, the plane dropping to the jump altitude. Adams tried to turn in his seat, to see farther out the wide jump door, but there was too much gear, every man carrying exactly what he would if this were the real thing. Dammit! How the hell are we supposed to jump if we can't see what's below us?

The plane continued to descend, and suddenly the red signal light came on. Adams stood quickly. "Stand up! Hook up!"

The men obeyed, automatic, each man hooking the static lines from his chute to the cable above their heads.

"Check equipment!"

It was the routine order, each man checking the gear on the man in front of him, no dangling straps or buckles that had come loose. Adams watched carefully, then turned and looked out the doorway; solid gray, wet mist soaking the inside of the plane. What the hell is going on? The weather isn't better, it's worse, and if I can't see the ground, neither can the damned pilots. Dammit! He focused on the men again, the red light still glaring above him.

"Count off!"

Marley, close in front of him, staring past him, shouted, "Eighteen! Okay!"

Behind him, each man followed suit, counting down, until the last man closest to the cockpit shouted, "One! Okay!"

Adams looked at the signal light, still red, and glanced outside again, a low curse growling through his brain. Wonderful. Just wonderful. He tried to see past the row of men to the cockpit. What the hell are you jackasses thinking? Now the light turned green, the answer to his question, and there was no thought, just the training. Marley moved to the doorway, quickly out and gone, the next man a second behind him. They moved past him quickly, no one slowing, no hesitation. Adams waited for the last man and followed him out into the gray mist.

The ground came up quickly, a house, fence lines, and he jerked the riser, tried to spin to one side, saw a small rooftop, a low stone wall, round, a *well*. He dropped close beside the roof, hit the ground hard, crumpled sideways, awkward, tried to roll to ease the shock, but his back slapped into the stone, stopping him cold, his helmet popping off his head. The chute came down around him, no wind, thank God, no jerking him across the ground. He felt a sharp pain in his side and lay still for a few seconds, his own routine, testing, checking each bone. There were pains all along his legs, but the worst jolt came from his ribs. He kept the pain inside, no sound—the training—and thought, What the hell did you do? His legs were moving now, and he tried to push forward, away from the stone, his face rolling into muddy water, a puddle, dammit! The chute was on top of him, draping the well itself, a soft white tent, and now he heard voices.

"I say! What have we here? Oh, my God! Henry!"

There were more sounds now, a woman shouting, footsteps on the muddy ground. He tried to stand, grabbed at the chute, to pull it away, to see, but there was something in his back now, pushing him down into the mud.

"Bloody Nazi bastard!"

Adams spit water from his mouth, couldn't see, put his hands down, the pressure in his back stabbing him. He thought of the well, the house: These were farmers, the sharp point was . . . a pitchfork?

"Hey! American! I'm American!"

The chute was pulled away, and he saw legs, moving closer, one man still pushing him into the mud.

"Oy, Nigel, he's not a Nazi. Look here. Helmet's all wrong."

"You sure? Been expectin' this. Bloody sneak attack!"

"I'm an American, dammit!" The pressure in his back grew lighter and Adams took a breath, spit more mud from his mouth, pushed himself over onto his back. "I'm an American! Damn you!"

"Curses like one. Ugly bloke too. Look at all the thingies. Grenades and whatnot."

Hands were on him now, and Adams felt resigned, let them pull him upright. He sat, the pain in his side curling him, and pushed the hands away. "Give me a second. I hit pretty hard, might have busted some ribs."

He looked at them now, four men, two women standing behind them. His eye caught the point of the pitchfork.

"You could have killed me."

"Tried to, at that. Been lookin' for Nazi buggers to come droppin' in 'ere. Robert's got a shotgun, but he's off in the town. Good thing for you, eh?"

The man laughed, and Adams saw brown teeth, thick dark skin, realized they were all older, sixties, more.

"Excuse me, but can you tell me . . . did you see any more parachutes?"

"Sarge!"

The farmers close above him backed away, and Adams saw two men coming quickly, Unger and another familiar face, Conley, more behind them. Oh, thank God!

Behind him, a woman said, "Henry, there's a bloomin' wad of them. Why in blazes are the Americans invadin' us?"

Adams pulled himself to his feet, Unger's hands under his arms. "I'm okay. I hit this damned well. Everybody else all right?"

"Think so, Sarge. Most of us came down in a field, out past those trees."

Adams looked at the man with the pitchfork again. "Look, I'm sorry we surprised you. We're on a training jump. It seems we were dropped a little off course."

The farmers gathered closer again, curious eyes examining the gear, the dirty uniforms, one man reaching out with a careful finger to touch the Thompson strapped to Adams's hip. The man laughed.

"I know that one. You're lost. I spent two weeks in the mud in Ypres, back in the last war. Hadn't a glint where in blazes I was. The generals didn't know either." The man rubbed a round belly. "Training, eh? You know General Patton, then? He's been through here, a while back. All glory and commotion, sirens and lights. Bugger woke up the damned cows and scared Eloise."

A woman spoke now, confirming the old man's story. "Scared me half to death, that he did. Handsome bloke, though. All fancy with his silver helmet. He was lost too. Wouldn't admit it. Had his driver ask us where the road to Hargrove was. Poor young man was scared witless. Your General Patton lit him up with some mighty colorful language. Made me blush."

"Nothing can make you blush, woman," the farmer said. "But General Patton, he's not as friendly as you chaps, I give you that. You hurt, then?"

Adams tried to ignore the pain in his side. "I'm all right. So, we're near Hargrove? Are you sure?"

He knew it was a stupid question, and the man laughed. "You've no bloody idea where you're at, have you? They can't even put you chaps in the right piece of countryside, and you're still in merry old England. Doesn't bode well, does it?"

Adams saw more of his men coming past the house, looked up, the sky a solid gray, and said a low curse to every weatherman in the army. The farmer was more serious now, and Adams saw the look, the eyes of a veteran, a man who knows what a screwup is and what it can cost an army.

"No, sir. It doesn't bode well at all."

8. ROMMEL

He had relocated in early March to a new headquarters that seemed more of a medieval fortress than a modern facility for a German army commander. The castle was perched against a rocky hillside, with a sweeping view of the river, a natural barrier to any invader who happened to come by land. But these days the greatest threat was from the air, so the castle had been ringed by a tight cordon of antiaircraft batteries, along with a company of highly trained troops whose sole priority was to protect Field Marshal Rommel.

The tall windows of his office opened onto a magnificent rose garden, and he watched the French groundskeepers working diligently, as though nothing had changed, no disruption to their routine, tireless efforts to carve a small swath of beauty from the rocky soil. Above him, in the high floors of the castle, the occupants remained, French aristocrats, the duc de La Rochefoucauld, a man whose lineage could be traced back through centuries of French history. The duke accepted his new tenant without any vigorous protest, the man's family keeping mostly out of sight, resigned, as best as Rommel could tell, to the inevitabilities of war. Even the desk Rommel had commandeered had a history. It was massively heavy and ornate, centuries old, and Rommel, hesitant to tamper with this gracious display of French pride, would not clutter the walls and shelves with his own history—no photographs, no official memorabilia. It was a temporary home at best, and no matter how much of himself he devoted to the job at hand, Rommel knew that one day, the duke would return to his rightful place at the head of his own table. Rommel had no illusions that any part of the occupation of France was permanent.

E ffective April 15, his chief of staff, General Alfred Gause, was replaced by General Hans Speidel. Gause had been Rommel's dutiful staff officer from the days in North Africa, but Rommel had grown tired of the man's surliness. Speidel's availability had made the decision to remove Gause that much simpler. Speidel shared considerable history with Rommel, having served alongside him in the First Great War. The man brought another comfort Rommel appreciated: He was Swabian, his family from the hill country of Württemberg, so he shared Rommel's own distinctive accent, which marked them both as southern Germans, so different from the Prussians to the north. That distinction had far more meaning to the Prussians, who considered themselves Germany's elite. The Prussians brought a snobbishness to the officer corps that had always dug at Rommel, and their disparaging remarks about the peasants of Württemberg had followed him from his first days in the army. Rommel had never measured his respect for anyone based on what part of Germany they were from.

Speidel had been a welcome choice for Rommel, his request passing through the hands of Hitler's chief of staff, Alfred Jodl. Speidel had been one of the few bright spots for the German High Command during the Russian campaigns, having served several primary commanders in the field exceptionally well. Beyond his qualifications, Rommel appreciated Speidel's civilian education, the man having long ago earned a PhD in history. Though Berlin rarely paid much attention to intellectual accomplishments, Rommel was the son of a teacher, and Speidel's rank in the army had much less meaning for Rommel than did the title of *Doctor*.

S peidel sat across the desk from him, sifting through papers, and Rommel, watching him, suddenly smiled. "You truly look like a professor, you know. Have you never thought about a more flattering pair of eye-glasses?"

Speidel seemed surprised and put a hand to his face. "What's wrong with my glasses? They allow me to see. I never paid much attention to . . . fashion."

"Nonsense."

Rommel stood now, walked toward the window, felt the thick lushness of the Persian rug beneath his feet. The entire castle was ripe with this sort of luxury, tapestries on the wall, great colorful portraits of the duke and his ancestors. It was an odd setting for Rommel, softness beneath his boots. There was a heavy mist outdoors, the tall glass panes glistening, the view of the Seine distorted. He was suddenly in no mood to work but felt a strange detachment as he watched the boats and barges on the river, slid-ing past, hauling all manner of goods, most of it destined for his army.

"Is something bothering you, sir?"

Rommel brought himself back into the office and tried to clear his mind, his eyes still fixed on the watery windowpane. "We have a remark-able sense of fashion in this army, Hans. Every uniform on every officer: perfect fit, the medals arranged just so, the polish on the boots. It has al-ways been that way, I suppose, something about being—well, German. Don't you agree?"

Speidel hesitated. "I had never really thought about it. I joined the army, and they gave me a uniform. It fit."

"In Berlin or Berchtesgaden, all those gray birds that flutter around Hitler . . . you know very well that before they ever dare to preen and pose for the Führer, they check themselves very carefully in the mirror."

"Wouldn't you?"

Rommel put his hands on his hips, focused on the rose garden below the window where a one-armed man knelt, pulling a small strand of muddy weeds.

"I have in the past. Too many photographers following me around. I would send them away, and they would scatter like pigeons, only to light around me minutes later. That damned Berndt."

"I'm sorry, sir. Who?"

"Captain Alfred Berndt, a Gestapo officer assigned to me in Libya. He was supposed to be in charge of the publicity that surrounded my camp." He shook his head. "It was all propaganda, of course. He would send a steady stream of photographs and news releases home to Goebbels, all for public consumption. All the while, I wasn't supposed to notice that Berndt wore a Gestapo uniform. It was Berlin's clumsy way of keeping an eye on me." He paused, looked at Speidel. "You are aware that there is no Berndt pecking his way around here? I wouldn't allow it. Berlin was very . . . gracious about it, actually. I suppose, with von Rundstedt watching over me, I am not as likely to disturb their version of events. It isn't necessary to observe my every indiscretion. Or did they tell you otherwise?"

"To be honest, sir, General Jodl told me that you are often capable of a defeatist attitude. I have seen nothing of the sort."

Rommel studied Speidel, the small hawkish face, the face of a professor.

"I am a defeatist in Berlin because I see this war for what it has become." He stopped but saw no change in Speidel's expression. He expected a protest from Speidel, was surprised the man did not object to his indiscreet comment.

Speidel pretended to busy himself with some bit of paperwork, nervous now, and did not look at him, but said, "There are many who agree with your sentiments, sir. Many of . . . us. I am greatly disturbed by events as they are now."

Rommel was surprised, felt an odd tug inside of him, that same caution he had felt with Dr. Strölin. Speidel looked at him.

"I believe you are acquainted with Dr. Karl Strölin?" Speidel said.

"Why do you ask?"

"He is a good friend. To all of us. Especially to Germany. He is a man with an optimistic view of the future."

Rommel hesitated, the familiar caution spreading through him. He stepped slowly to the chair, sat, and began drumming his fingers on the desk, tension rising up inside of him, his heart beginning to pound.

"Tell me, Hans, are you as optimistic as Dr. Strölin?"

The hint of a smile appeared on Speidel's face. "We are all fighting for what is best for our country, sir. I prefer to believe that Germany has a prosperous future. No matter the outcome of this war, the German people must not suffer as they did after the last one. The German people have enemies within our borders who must be removed. To put it bluntly, this war has made Germany an enemy to the civilized world. We are hated, in fact. No decent German should be willing to accept that. Wouldn't you agree, sir?"

Rommel understood now, with perfect clarity. His chief of staff was

not only acquainted with Dr. Strölin, he was part of the movement to remove the Führer from power.

"I do not wish to continue this conversation, Hans."

"My apologies, sir. I would never attempt to involve you in matters
that are objectionable to you."

"I didn't say it was objectionable." He didn't know what else to say, no
clever euphemisms came to mind; he was not as talented as Speidel at dis-
guising his words. They sat quietly for a moment, Speidel busying himself
with the papers again. Rommel still tapped his fingers on the desk, saw
Speidel glancing at the sound, at Rommel's hands. It had been a long time
since Rommel felt intimidated by anyone, certainly anyone he outranked.
But he was intimidated now. The questions rose in his mind: What do you
know, Hans? How deep is this conspiracy? Is there a conspiracy at all, or
just a group of malcontented friends whose conversations could get them
arrested? No, don't be naïve. It is more than simple conversation. These are
educated men, men who understand politics, men who . . . yes, men who
love their country. He moved in his chair, feeling strangely uncomfortable. I chose you to be my chief of staff, he thought. It was my decision to
bring you here. Now I wonder, is that truly how it happened? Or did you
choose me?

He sat back in the chair, his eyes closed for a moment. Dammit, I am
only a soldier. He blinked hard, looked again at Speidel, the man seeming
to avoid his gaze, the shuffle of paper continuing. Rommel could not stop
the questions in his mind. How many are you? Who shares these *conversations*? How many are generals? He thought of von Rundstedt and his ever-
ready insult, *the little corporal.* Is he a part of this? He was growing angry at
himself now. Enough of this. He wanted so much to know more but could
not ask, pushed hard against the questions, fought for words, something to
ease his own tension. He could not avoid a feeling of affection for Speidel;
he was more comfortable with him than he had ever been with any subordinate before.

His fingers stopped their nervous dance, and after a long moment he
said, "Tell me, Hans, what will you do? When all this is over."

Speidel tilted his head to one side, eyeing Rommel. "I would like to
teach, I suppose. I love history, you know that, sir."

"Yes, of course. You would be good at it. I hope you have the opportunity."

"If I may ask, sir . . . what about you? This war will end, and perhaps there will be the opportunity for you to do many things for Germany in the peacetime."

Rommel rubbed the dull pain in his side, forgotten for a moment but always there. He pondered Speidel's word, *peacetime.* It seemed odd, foreign. Was there ever peace? Well, of course, for twenty years. Rommel stared down, searching his mind for flickers of memories. It is so hard to recall anything from those days, he thought. Two entire decades when there was no war. Everything is *now.* He stared toward the window, saw nothing beyond the glass, his mind beginning to flood with thoughts of Lucie, his son, their home, the hills, hard winters and snow, and then spring and flowers. He was suddenly homesick, a throbbing ache in his brain. God, how I miss it all, he thought, holding her, walking in the gardens. . . .

"Sir, are you all right? Forgive me, but you concern me. If you wish to be alone, we can go through these numbers later. Perhaps you should take a walk. The rain is not so bad. I can summon the bodyguards."

Rommel focused, pleased by Speidel's concern.

"You are . . . how old?"

"Forty-seven, sir."

"Yes, that's right. Plenty of time for you. Make good use of it, Hans."

"You as well, sir. We are not so different in age."

Rommel stood again, moved toward the window. "We shall see. I'm not certain there would be a place for me . . . in that world."

Speidel said nothing, and Rommel stared outside, a loud voice in his brain. What is wrong with you? Get control of yourself. There is no room for this kind of self-pity, for moaning about your future. There is no past either, no usefulness in pondering what used to be. What there is . . . is now. He took a long breath, looked at Speidel, ignored the schoolmaster's glasses.

"We have work to do. When is Guderian coming?"

"He should arrive early this evening. General Geyr will accompany him, of course."

"Of course. Geyr would not miss any opportunity to drive his inane strategies down anyone's throat, even Guderian's."

Rommel put his hands up, felt the cool of the window glass. "I have no choice, do I? I must plead my case one more time. Heinz Guderian is a good man, one of the best in the army at understanding tactics. He invented the blitzkrieg, for God's sake. Every success of our panzers belongs to his ingenuity. I should not have to convince *him* that I am right."

"It will not be like that, sir. Surely."

"Why not? And tell me, Hans, why is it that General Guderian, this brilliant man, no longer sits on Hitler's knee?"

"It is not for me to say, sir."

"Because he did not win in Russia. He suffered defeat and disappointed the Führer. And so his career stagnates. I outrank him, you outrank him, half the generals in this army outrank him. Instead of leading his panzers on the battlefield, one of our finest generals has become an errand boy, a minion of the High Command."

"He is still influential, sir. That's why they are sending him here. The High Command knows there are conflicts of opinion among Field Marshal von Rundstedt's generals. He is a good man to sort through all that, make the best decisions. You should trust General Guderian, sir."

He studied Speidel again and stifled a small laugh. The only man I trust around here might be *you.*

General Baron Leo Geyr von Schweppenburg seemed to Rommel to personify the annoying Prussian aristocrat. Geyr was five years Rommel's senior, ruggedly handsome, wore the self-satisfied expression of a man utterly sure of himself. Like so many of the Prussians, he had come up first through the cavalry, the expected posting for Germany's most elite young officers. Geyr had served as a subordinate to Heinz Guderian during the blitzkrieg that crushed Poland and shared in the accolades that Guderian earned. Eventually, Geyr followed Guderian to Russia, performing as well as any panzer commander could be expected to. Yet, despite his many accomplishments, Geyr, like Guderian, was mildly distrusted by Hitler. It was something Rommel shared with the Führer. Neither man liked Prussians. Like Rommel, Geyr answered to von Rundstedt, but Geyr paid very little attention to anything von Rundstedt had to say. And he cared even less for Rommel.

Geyr held up a rolled map. "I will not compromise the fate of my panzers. We must maintain a strong mobile reserve far back of the coastline. *Mobile* reserve! No matter where or when the attack comes, from the sea or from the skies, we can move our strongest forces into line quickly and surround the problem. I cannot put all my concerns on the coastline. What of the enemy's paratroopers? Surely, Herr Rommel, that was a lesson we all learned from the disaster in Sicily. My armor must be prepared to confront a sizable force of paratroopers, and if they come it will be inland, away from the beaches. How many times must I paint this portrait?" He turned to Guderian. "What must I do? The proper strategy is brutally simple! Herr Rommel has a basic lack of understanding of the principles of armored tactics!"

Rommel raised his eyes, met Geyr's, stared hard, Rommel speaking to Geyr in his head: *You, sir, are an idiot.* He fought the urge to stand and spoke slowly and precisely.

"Do not dare to insult me, General Geyr. All you know of armor is what you learned in Russia, fighting a brutally stupid enemy who threw himself against your guns with blind charges. Even with tanks, you could not kill enough of them to prevent their victories. But to believe that the British and the Americans will fight the same way is a display of shameful ignorance. I am very much aware of the need for mobility, General Geyr. But what of the enemy's air power?"

Geyr sniffed. "The Luftwaffe has shown they are the equal of any air force they meet in the skies."

"What Luftwaffe?" Rommel glanced at Guderian and saw a hard frown. He flexed his fingers, trying to calm himself. "I learned in North Africa that when the enemy has dominance over the skies, mobility must be confined to the darkness. If you fail to heed that warning, the enemy's air power will destroy you. The enemy we will face in France is already superior to us because they dominate the air. I do not care what Reichsmarschall Göring tells you! These are the facts. The enemy's dominance of the skies will prevent us from being as mobile as we would like to be. We must not put the armor so far from the coastline. It will be a fatal mistake."

Guderian spoke now, rubbing his forehead. "Gentlemen, please refrain from these displays of temper. Herr Rommel, I do not agree with you. Certainly, the enemy is powerful, and his air power is not to be taken lightly, but we have always shown the ability to move our forces as required. Yes, I agree that this enemy is not to be confused with the Russians. But here, our armor is unmatched. If the enemy is strong, our best advantage is in our ability to counterattack. You learned that in North Africa, Herr Rommel."

Rommel leaned back in his chair. There was little else he could say. He struggled through the plans and the maps in his own brain and said softly,

"If we allow the enemy to make his landings in France, we will never dislodge him."

Geyr began to speak but Guderian held up a hand. "The Führer has been very clear about my purpose here. I am to analyze the various viewpoints and make recommendations on the best manner in which to meet and destroy what he understands to be the inevitable invasion of France. I believe we have the proper troop strength in position, though of course I will suggest we move up as many reserves as can safely be drawn from other sectors of the fighting. Field Marshal von Rundstedt insists that we divide the main panzer forces, so that they are dispersed both north and south of Paris, and he is most clear that he believes they must be held back, away from the coastline. I am not completely in agreement with dividing the armor in that way, but it is a compromise I feel we must all accept. Field Marshal von Rundstedt agrees with me—and with you, General Geyr— that once the enemy makes his intentions clear, a swift first action, an immediate counterattack, should be our highest priority. I admire you, Herr Rommel, but in this instance I believe you are wrong. Mobility and power are our two most valuable assets. We will prevail."

CHÂTEAU, LA ROCHE-GUYON
APRIL 23, 1944

The rains had stopped, and Rommel watched the groundskeepers, the men with muddy boots, shovels and rakes working the soft brown earth. The others had gone, Geyr returning to his headquarters, Guderian to Paris to visit von Rundstedt. Rommel's breakfast lay untouched on his desk. He stood for a long moment, hearing noises in the corridor, low voices; they were being quiet and would not disturb him until he gave permission. He turned and looked toward the grand doorway.

"You may enter!"

The door opened silently. It was Ruge, Speidel behind him. Rommel smiled, always smiled when he saw Ruge.

"Good morning, Admiral. Please, sit."

Ruge was not smiling. He moved slowly into the room, Speidel lagging behind. Rommel nodded toward his chief of staff.

"Come in, Hans. The two of you might enjoy sharing what remains of my breakfast."

It was a weak attempt at lightheartedness, but Ruge seemed lost in thought.

"Is there a problem, Admiral?"

Ruge sat and looked at him, one hand now rubbing his jaw as though nursing a toothache. "I have spoken to Admiral Krancke. He does not share your concerns that we should deploy minefields in strength along the coastline. He has refused my requests to deploy the mine-laying ships at all. He is concerned they will come under enemy attack. Therefore, he does not wish to risk the loss of what he refers to as his limited resources."

Rommel moved to the chair, sat heavily. "He does not wish to take a risk? Can you go past Krancke and contact Admiral Dönitz directly? This is an essential part of our coastal defenses."

"Admiral Krancke has already conferred with Admiral Dönitz regarding this request. Admiral Dönitz has placed his full confidence in the wisdom of Admiral Krancke. The matter has been decided."

"The navy has determined that they cannot be a part of our defensive strategies, because it might involve engaging the enemy? What in God's name do they think a navy is for?"

Ruge took a long breath. "I am sorry, Erwin. I made every effort, every argument—"

"Stop. I am already too familiar with the kind of wisdom that infects our generals. Admirals, it now seems, are not immune."

There was a soft knock at the open door; it was a staff officer, an envelope in his hand.

"Yes, Colonel, what is it?"

The man entered quickly, placed the envelope in front of Rommel, backed away. "Sir, this just came for you. Highest priority."

"You are dismissed, Colonel. Thank you."

Rommel saw the seal, *OB West*, waited for the officer to leave, and said, "It seems that von Rundstedt is up early this morning. So, what do you think? Am I being relieved? Perhaps they have had enough of my nagging." He glanced at Speidel. "Or perhaps they feel I am being a defeatist again."

He opened the envelope, unable to avoid an annoying stir in his stomach, and read, his eyes growing wide.

"I may have underestimated our intelligence agents. It has been discovered that American general George Patton has established his headquarters in Kent, England, in command of the Allied First Army. It seems that our agents have confirmed beyond all doubt that the enemy is planning to launch his offensive at the Pas-de-Calais, with Patton in command." He read the dispatch again and handed it to Ruge. "This is most impressive, but it fits with my own expectations. Calais is the closest point across the English Channel, providing the enemy with the shortest straight line into the heart of Germany. And Patton is the best man for the assignment."

He watched as Ruge read, then as Ruge passed the paper to Speidel.

"This is good news, Erwin."

"Indeed it is. Patton is a formidable enemy, but he is predictable. He will come at us hard and he will not be deterred from making large-scale frontal assaults. That will play into our hands. Von Rundstedt wants us to play a chess game with the enemy, maneuver and outmaneuver. Patton should not only make that possible, it might be the best strategy to defeat him."

Rommel stood, moved to the window, felt the old energy returning, punched one fist into an open palm, stared into sunshine. He flexed his ribs—no pain—the sun warming his face. The view of the river was magnificent, a glistening pathway, leading the ever-present barges to the seaside fortifications, where his men were working still. Could it be? he thought. Could this still work? He had too many reasons to doubt Hitler's instincts, had no confidence in von Rundstedt's leadership, no faith that Geyr and the rest of them would perform as he needed them to perform. And yet . . .

He thought of Dr. Strölin. Yes, I love my country, and yes, I know what Hitler has done to it. If there is to be any peace for Germany, we must make that peace with the West. And the only way the British and the Americans will stop and listen to us, the only way they will be compelled to offer us a just end to this war, is if we bloody them, show them we can still *win.*

He could feel it swelling inside of him, a glorious feeling he had not enjoyed in a very long time: hope. He brought his thoughts back into the office and turned toward the others.

"Yes, this is very good. Now we know *who* and we know *where,* and we may plan our movements and deploy our defensive strengths accordingly. My greatest enemy now is time. If the enemy will just allow me sufficient weeks to strengthen, even complete the fortifications, we shall await them on the beaches at Calais and throw them back into the sea."

9. PATTON

He stared at the rows of tents, new white canvas spread out across an open field. To one side, another field intersected, the open ground divided by a thin row of trees. He walked that way, sucked hard on the cigar, spit out the smoke, saw a half dozen black tanks, a scattering of trucks and other vehicles. The men followed close behind him, one man speaking up now, too eager.

"General Montgomery was just here, sir. So very sorry you missed him. He ladled on the praise, if I do say so. We're mighty proud of our work here."

Patton didn't look at the man, couldn't remember his name, major something. Idiot. "You're proud of this?"

"Oh, quite, sir. We've given Jerry a tough banger to chew on, that's for certain. They can't observe any of this and not be convinced."

Patton heard the familiar whine of airplane engines, a formation of four British Spitfires, coming in low over the trees. He could feel the major flinching beside him, a common instinct. Patton ignored it. "What the hell are they doing here?"

To one side, another man moved closer, an older man, the one Patton was actually supposed to talk to. "Patrolling regularly, sir. We're doing the same thing in Scotland. The idea is to keep the Jerries at high altitude, give their observers only a rough look. Can't have anyone dipping in too close, so the RAF boys stay down here, making a good show of prowling low altitudes."

It made sense. Patton glanced at him, saw a brief smile, Patton's own lips twitched, the man's joviality reaching him despite his best efforts to keep it away. "Sounds like they've thought of just about everything, Colonel."

"Just about, sir."

The older man was Rory MacLeod, and where Patton's fictitious command encompassed southeastern England, MacLeod held a similar fictitious post in Scotland. The deception plan had a name now, Operation Fortitude, and British intelligence officers were already aware that the details they had planted of Patton's new "army" had become well known in Germany. To add to the legitimacy of the deception, Colonel MacLeod had been named to command the northern wing of Fortitude, one more part of the show, designed to convince the Germans that while Patton would invade France at Calais, MacLeod would deliver the massive British Fourth Army into Norway. Just like Patton's First U.S. Army Group, MacLeod's Fourth Army didn't really exist.

Patton moved toward the tanks, studied them, shook his head. "What are they, rubber? Looks like something at a county fair."

The major came close again. Patton could feel the man's annoying burst of energy. "Oh, they're quite convincing from the air, sir. Would you care to touch one up close? They're really not much more than large balloons."

The word stabbed Patton. Good God, I command a field of balloons! "Inflated no doubt by a flock of your politicians."

"Oh, yes, jolly good, sir."

"Skip it, Major. Those trucks out there, they look more substantial. Can't be steel. What are they, plywood?"

He didn't wait for the response but moved into the field, the others scampering to keep up with him. He walked quickly past the tanks—couldn't bear to look at them, poor fakes of the armor he so loved. The trucks were in a short row, others beyond, scattered; when he looked down he was surprised to see tank tracks in the soft dirt.

The annoying major was there again. "Amazing, isn't it, sir? They thought of everything. Tracks all across the field, the illusion of constant movement. Any Jerry flying above would see those tracks, one more reason to believe these are the genuine article."

Patton tried to ignore the major completely, saw motion along the far row of trees, a line of cows emerging. They ambled into the field, a ragged line working through the artificial trucks. Patton watched them coming. What would the Jerries think they were, armored cars? One cow stopped, moved away from the others, and Patton could see it was not a cow at all but a large bull. The major began to talk again, annoyingly cheerful, and Patton, still ignoring him, watched as the bull began to paw the ground. Patton put a hand on one of his pistols, thought, All right, Ferdinand, you decide you want to take a closer look at me, you better think again. The bull made an audible snort and lunged forward, the major suddenly aware.

"Oh, my word!"

The bull rammed into the side of a plywood truck, sheets of wood and timbers coming apart and falling all around him, the counterfeit truck now unrecognizable. Oblivious, the bull stumbled his way through the wreckage, and Patton began to laugh, high and hard, his hands resting on his pistols. "Well, now. Seems this damned army has been exposed for what it is."

There was only a scattering of laughter behind him.

Patton laughed for a long moment, but the humor was sliding away, so he wiped a tear from one eye and looked toward MacLeod. "A mighty fine show, eh, Colonel? We're in command of the most idiotic plan ever devised. Hell of a way to waste your career."

The scowl returned, the humor gone completely. Patton turned away. "I've had enough of this. What moron thinks anyone will be fooled by this stupidity? Tanks you can bust up with a BB gun? Empty tents? The only one deceived is that damned bull. Excuse me, gentlemen, but I've not known many cattle that possessed vastly superior intellect."

He walked quickly away from the others, back toward the one solid building on the grounds, realizing MacLeod was keeping pace with him.

The colonel said in a low voice, "If I may speak with you privately, General?"

Patton stared straight ahead, would not look at the rubber tanks, the long rows of tents. He knew MacLeod to be a good man and could not just ignore him. Glancing over his shoulder, he said, "They have lunch around here, or is that fake too?"

"The radio traffic out of my headquarters has been steady, and frankly, sir, we're pretty impressed with the results. We know Jerry is listening, and there has already been one air raid against one of our transmitting stations. That was a very pleasing result, especially since no one was injured."

Patton listened, took a bite from a sandwich, tried to find some flavor in the nondescript meat. MacLeod continued.

"We've been broadcasting all manner of innocuous snippets, including requisitions for cold-weather gear, ski fittings, snow boots, everything an army would need to prepare for a landing in Norway."

Patton swallowed. "You really think it's working, don't you?"

"Yes, sir, I do. With all respect, sir, there is one enormous advantage in our favor. The Jerries *want* to believe this. They want to believe we are going into Norway and Calais. It makes logical strategic sense. We know Hitler has kept Norway occupied by more than a quarter million troops, and every indication is that they're staying put. That's a stunning accomplishment, sir, stunning. Consider if those troops were suddenly moved to Normandy, how events might be turned, the scale be tipped. They believe they have discovered our real intentions because it fits with what they want us to do. That's why Fortitude will work. If I didn't believe that, I would feel very much as you do. I don't especially relish wasting what remains of my career commanding ghosts."

Patton finished the sandwich and swirled cold coffee in his mouth. He knew MacLeod was a veteran of the First World War and had been heavily decorated, something Patton had to respect. He pointed to the man's head. "I hear you carry some metal around with you."

MacLeod seemed frustrated at the distraction. "Yes, sir. Steel plate in my skull. Pretty extensive actually, a rather serious wound."

"This is a hell of a way to reward a hero. You don't feel they're just sticking you out to pasture?" Patton thought of the bull. "So to speak."

"I was already out to pasture. There wasn't much for a beat-up old soldier to do. Frankly, I thought they had forgotten about me. This assignment is an honor. If it works, it may change the entire war."

"If it works."

"Dammit, General!"

Patton was surprised, MacLeod showing a flash of temper. The colonel calmed himself, and Patton thought, He's sticking up for himself. Good. He saw that MacLeod had ignored his lunch and pushed his own plate away.

"Listen, Colonel. I thought Ike brought me to England so I could kick some Kraut asses. Every day I hear promises about, yeah, well, all that will come later. First I have to stand in a field watching bulls hump phony trucks. Ike knows I should have stayed in Italy. I could have done a whole lot more at Salerno or Anzio than Clark or anyone else. So instead we're stuck in molasses down there, getting chewed up every day because no one knows how to take a fight *to* the enemy! But I can't bitch too much about that because I know Ike's out on a limb for me. There's a bunch of Brits and a few Americans who'd love to see my ass hanging in the breeze. All right, fine. I know how to follow orders, so here I am, following them. But I don't have to like it. And I don't. I have no idea if this plan will work."

He paused, saw a grim angry stare on MacLeod's face, felt suddenly scolded. Dammit, he thought, I can't just bellyache like this, not to this man. He's seen more combat than I have, and he's paid a hell of a lot greater price for it. Steel in his skull, for God's sake.

Patton looked down, a moment of quiet between them, then said, "You really think this is working, Colonel?"

"I am certain of it, sir. So far, anyway. There is always the danger that the enemy will discover the deception. A great many things can go wrong. But when is that not the case? Consider Overlord. My God, if the invasion fails, we may lose this war. I have been given an opportunity to help, and by damn, I'm helping. You have the same opportunity, sir. I should think—with all respect, sir—I should think you would show some enthusiasm for that. We'd all like to be killing Jerries, and for you anyway, that time could come. For me—well, my combat days have passed." He paused. "Napoleon said it: *Glory is fleeting, but obscurity is forever.* I've had my glory on the battlefield, but I'm not ready to disappear into obscurity. This is the best war I can fight, and, forgive me, sir, but if it turns out it's the best war *you* can fight, why not give it a go?"

"Leave it alone, Colonel. I still hate this. But we'll make it work."

KNUTSFORD
APRIL 25, 1944

Patton sat in silence, the car passing small farms, bare brown fields, some just planted. He could not help thinking of MacLeod. He'd been curious about the man's wound, how the doctors knew to put steel in a man's skull, how much, where, how it was fastened. Have to watch that sometime, he thought. Find a surgeon who will let me have a look. Hell, if he's one of mine, I'll just order him to let me watch. They put screws in or what? Maybe they use a regular old screwdriver. Damn strange stuff.

MacLeod had returned to Scotland, to his counterfeit headquarters beneath Edinburgh Castle. Patton had appreciated the man's frankness. MacLeod had given him far more details about the northern half of the operation than Patton had known before. Despite MacLeod's seriousness and his optimism, Patton still believed it was pure stupidity. This had to be a British idea, he thought. Ike going along full tilt because he loves them, thinks they know everything about fighting a war. All they've done so far is lose. If we hadn't shown up, they'd still be in North Africa: Montgomery, that loud-mouthed jerk; Brooke; all of them. Ike's crawling into bed with them, and why? Marshall tell him to? Can't be, just can't. Maybe it's MacArthur. There has to be one major tug-of-war in Washington, MacArthur leaning hard on every senator he knows to get us to send everything to the Pacific. Damned stupid mistake, if that happens. So, all right, go along with the damned Brits, lick the Krauts first. Blow Hitler all to hell, and then keep the Russians from taking over Europe. God, I hate politics. There's a hell of a lot of problems in this world that could be fixed with a couple of tank divisions. But don't anybody ask me about that.

He stared out the window, saw children, a village, larger homes, a cluster of shops. Ike knows I scare hell out of the Germans, he thought, so they find a way to make sure I don't actually *fight* them. Third Army, sure. I'll believe that when it happens. If Monty gets tossed back into the ocean, the Third Army will be guarding our asses as we limp back to New Jersey. His mind wandered, absorbing the signs: a small bake shop, another beside it, a large sign that said simply SHOES. I wonder, he thought, if I'm as good as people think I am. He smiled, shook his head. Or as good as *I* think I am. Damn it all, I may never get a chance to find out.

The car was slowing to a stop. He saw a crowd, a large banner: WELCOME AMERICANS. He grimaced, had not wanted to be here at all, had turned down the official invitation to speak. But his appearance was at the special request of the Ministry of Information, and Patton appreciated the flattery. The gathering was a celebration for the opening of an official welcome station for American troops, a gesture of thanks as well as a morale booster for any units stationed in the area around Knutsford.

He leaned forward. "We late, Sergeant?"

His aide checked his watch. "Just a few minutes, sir."

He tapped the driver on the shoulder. "Good going. But you could have gone slower still. Maybe it will take me a few minutes to get out of the damned car. Sergeant, hold up some papers or something, let's make it look like we're busy as hell in here. Take your damned time about it, then come around and open the door. Gotta make a good show."

"Yes, sir."

Patton sat back, forced himself not to look at the waiting throng, focused on his aide. You're a good man, Alex, damned good man. I'd love to see a bar full of British drunks try to corner you. He had chosen Sergeant Alex Stiller to serve on his staff in Sicily, primarily as his bodyguard. Stiller, an unpolished and rugged stick of a man, had come through the service in Patton's tanks. Now he traveled everywhere Patton went, whether the job was dangerous or not. Patton couldn't help looking at the gathering civilians, saw photographers, made a silent groan, thought, What could be more dangerous than this bunch?

"Okay, Alex. Lemme at 'em."

He waited for Stiller to open the door, took his time, stood tall, pulled at his jacket. The photographers pressed toward him, and he held up his hands.

"Hang on, boys," he said in a loud voice, "I'm not here officially. You can't print anything I say or do, and no pictures for the papers. You got that?"

There was nothing friendly in his voice, and they lowered the cameras, seemed utterly dejected.

"Well, all right, look. Take a few pictures if you want. But hang on to them. Nothing can be published. At least not yet. You got that?"

They eagerly agreed. Patton posed briefly, then looked past them, saw the entrance to the soldiers' club and a large elderly woman waving to him. Oh, dear God, save me.

He scanned the program, saw a blank line where his name would go, noticed they had made a hasty edit, changing the description of his visit, replacing their wishful thinking for his official role, replacing the description with "offers his blessing." Damn it, I told them I couldn't officiate, no damned speech. That sort of thing makes Ike's kidneys bleed. Just be pleasant to everybody, be polite. He forced himself to smile and stared out at the crowd, several dozen civilians, mostly women in bright dresses and hats. Many were smiling back at him, and he nodded, showed dutiful appreciation, tried to avoid the drone of the speaker, a woman he now knew as Mrs. Smith, the chairman of the committee that had organized whatever details had been required to open the club. Beside him, a woman suddenly stood, and Patton realized she had been introduced, caught her name, Jeffery, and watched as the woman strode daintily toward the microphone, hefty applause from the audience. She turned toward him now.

"Before we complete the program, I know we should be ever so grateful if the general flatters us with a few words. We are certainly aware that you are not here officially, sir, and of course your presence will not be disclosed. I assure you, no one will repeat anything you say. Would you please, sir, just a few friendly words?"

Patton held the smile, the crowd applauding far louder now, his brain firing a tank gun into the woman's irritating smile. Now the Smith woman was standing, egging on the crowd, more generous compliments, his name called out. He stood, waved weakly to the noisy throng, moved toward the microphone. His gut was turning over, ice in his chest, and he steadied himself on the podium, thinking, Short, keep it short. Friendly. Then get the hell out of here.

"I am grateful for the efforts you ladies have put into creating a welcome club for our soldiers. Previous to today, my only experience in welcoming anyone has been to welcome Germans and Italians to the Infernal Regions. In this I have been quite successful."

There was a burst of applause, entirely expected, and he smiled, waved, waited for the noise to quiet.

"I feel that such clubs as these are a real value, because I believe with Mr. Bernard Shaw—I think it was he—that the British and Americans are two people separated by a common language, and since it is the evident destiny of the British and the Americans"—he paused, an alarm in his head—"and of course the Russians, to rule the world, the better we know each other, the better the job we will do. A club like this is an ideal place for making such acquaintances and for promoting mutual understanding. Also, as soon as our soldiers meet and know the English ladies, and write home and tell our women how truly lovely you are, the sooner the American ladies will get jealous and force this war to a quick termination, and I will get a chance to go and kill Japanese."

The applause followed him back to his seat, and he kept the smile, held it painfully through the rest of the speeches.

After a long hour, the gathering had concluded, and Patton moved back to his car with as much purpose as he could politely muster. The aides were waiting, Stiller holding the door, and behind him the ladies called out, waving hands and handkerchiefs, calls of flirtatious gratitude. He sank into the seat and waited desperate seconds for Stiller to put himself into the front seat.

"Go, dammit!"

The car began to move, the voices of the crowd drifting away behind him. Stiller turned toward him.

"Did it go well, sir?"

"Very well. They loved me." Patton let out a breath. "I'm just glad it's over."

10. EISENHOWER

"Rule the world? He told them we're going to *rule the world*?"

"Apparently so, sir."

Eisenhower stared up at the ceiling, felt crushed into the chair. "What the hell is the matter with that man? Is he just thick-headed, or is this some plot of his to drive me insane so he can take over running the damned war!"

Beetle Smith said nothing. Butcher was at the door now.

"Chief, two more. Papers from Leeds and Buckingham."

"Keep them the hell out of here. Five are enough. I doubt if every one of them misquoted the dumb son of a bitch. Harry, send one of the secretaries in here. Make it Captain Pinette. I need to cable Marshall. If we're lucky, this can be contained right here, maybe no one back home will hear about it."

"I doubt that," Smith said. "This will go off like a bomb in the States. George has too many enemies, and there's a lot of pressure on the president as it is. There are a few senators who will jump all over this."

"You're a fountain of cheer, Beetle."

The secretary came in, a young woman who had been on Eisenhower's staff since Algeria.

"Sit down, Mattie. We need to put out a fire."

She sat, pad of paper in hand, with a questioning glance toward Smith. Eisenhower said, "You'll know everything soon enough, Captain. This is a cable to be sent immediately to General Marshall." He thought a moment. "All right, take this down:

It seems that General Patton has broken out again. I regret that the man is unable to use reasonably good sense in all those matters where senior commanders must appreciate the effects of their own action upon public opinion."

He paused, watched as she wrote furiously, catching up to him.

"I have serious doubts at this juncture as to the wisdom of retaining him in high command despite his demonstrated capacity in battlefield leadership. I have grown so damned weary—no, strike that—I have grown so weary of the trouble he constantly causes you and the war department, to say nothing of myself, that I am seriously contemplating the most drastic action. I would prefer some comment from you before any final decision is made."

He waited for her to stop writing.

"Finished, sir. Should I read it back?"

"Just show the typed cable to General Smith and make sure it goes out right away."

He saw Butcher lurking in the doorway.

"What the hell am I supposed to do, Harry? How much hot water can this man plunge into? He's not satisfied just slapping his own troops. . . . Are we certain these newspaper quotes are accurate?"

"Let me grab the other papers, Chief. They seem pretty consistent."

Butcher disappeared briefly, returned with a thick wad of newspaper, scanned, shuffling the papers in his hand.

"This one says he mentions the Russians. That could be more accurate. Yep, here, again, he mentions the Russians. 'The British and the Americans and the Russians will rule the world.' That's not as bad, is it, Chief?"

"Thank God for small favors. But it could still hang him. I don't know how many Americans relish the thought of the Russians ruling the world. Damn it all! How in hell are we going to blunt this?"

He saw the young woman at the door again.

"The cable has been sent, sir."

"Thank you, Mattie. What time is it in Washington, five A.M.? If they haven't heard of this by now, that cable ought to wake somebody up."

W ord had crossed the ocean far more quickly than Eisenhower had imagined, and within hours the wire services had relayed Patton's comments to newspapers all over the country. The outcry was predictable and deafening, and within hours Eisenhower received Marshall's reply.

> Like you, I have considered the matter purely on a business basis. I am weary as well, but his relentless abilities on the battlefield must be considered. The final judgment as to his usefulness to this army rests in your hands.

He put the paper down. Empty, the office seemed cavernous, the stark silence revealing the thunder in his brain. So it's *my* problem? Well, I suppose that's appropriate. If we kick Patton out the door, there is one alternative for command of the Third Army. Courtney Hodges can get the job done. I think. But he doesn't have Patton's experience, and, unless he's kept it well hidden, he doesn't have Patton's bulldog drive. If I toss George to the wolves, it could cost us in terms that no bitching senator or newspaperman could understand. Isn't that the priority, after all? No, George, I can't fire you. Not yet anyway. But how many more times will this happen?

He focused, stared at the doorway, heard a burst of chatter from the offices beyond. He thought of calling out, knew that Smith was probably in his office. No, don't just holler your brains out. Show some decorum. He reached for the black phone.

"Put General Smith on the phone." He waited, knew he had been gruff, thought, Dammit, I can't always be nice to people. I'm the boss, after all. He heard Smith's voice.

"Sir?"

"Beetle, I want you to tell Patton to get his ass up here. He might not like what I have to say, but at least he'll still have a job."

SHAEF, Bushey Park
May 1, 1944

"George, you have gotten yourself into a very serious fix. What the hell were you thinking?"

Patton said nothing, just kept himself at attention, helmet and pistols, a show Eisenhower didn't need. He stared hard at Patton, saw no flinch in the man's expression.

"I've told you before: You talk too damned much! You can't just shoot off your mouth about anything you want, especially when it concerns politics. You spend too much time posing for cameras and crowds, and for reasons I do not understand, you insist on breaking out in these tantrums . . . at the worst possible time. Sit down! At ease, for God's sake."

Patton moved to the chair, eyeing him intently, Eisenhower trying to avoid Patton's piercing stare. Finally Patton cleared his throat.

"Sir, I want you to understand that I am very well aware that your job is more important than mine. If, in trying to save me, you are hurting yourself, then throw me out."

Eisenhower frowned. Theatrics, he thought. When was the last time he called me *sir*?

"Look, George, I have all the headaches this army can give me. This has nothing to do with hurting *me*. You've put me in the position of having to choose whether or not I must deprive myself of a fight-ing army commander! I've already gotten several cables about this from General Marshall. You have seriously hurt yourself at the War De-partment. Your permanent promotion has been put on hold, and might never be reconsidered. There's a whole flock of people in Washington who think you're unfit to command. Tell me how I'm supposed to disagree with that."

"I disagree with that most vigorously, sir. I believe I am the most capa-ble and most experienced American battlefield commander in this theater of the war."

Eisenhower thought, Yes, I'm sure that's exactly what you believe. And you may be right, dammit.

"General Marshall has left the matter in my hands. He is fighting like hell for you in Congress, George. You've called in every favor you ever had. What do I do here? Can you convince me this won't happen again? You've been told to keep your mouth shut, and still—off you go!" Patton seemed to sag, his shoulders drooping. "If I keep you here, how can I be sure this won't happen again?"

Patton stood suddenly and moved around the side of the desk. Eisenhower was amazed to see tears. He couldn't help himself but stood as well, amazed that Patton kept coming, his arms out, wrapping them around Eisenhower's shoulders.

"Dammit, Ike, I am so sorry about this."

He put his head on Eisenhower's shoulder, the silver helmet rolling off his head, tumbling with a loud clatter onto the floor. Patton was sobbing noisily now, and Eisenhower felt helpless, had no idea what to do. Then Patton stood back, red-eyed, wetness on his cheeks.

"I will not let you down, sir. If you allow me to keep my place in Operation Fortitude and my command of the Third Army, I will give every effort to the job. I am grateful to you and to General Marshall for standing behind me. There are forces at work around us, forces that would undermine our good efforts—" Patton stopped short, seeming to know he had taken it too far.

Eisenhower thought, That's right, George. Shut the hell up. But there still were the tears, Patton's amazing show of contrition. This is *bull,* Eisenhower suddenly realized. All of it. This is pure drama, a well-rehearsed speech. He put a hand on his own shoulder, felt the wetness, saw Patton composing himself, the helmet still conspicuously on the floor.

"Control yourself, dammit. The fact is I need you. There are too many weak links, too many variables in this operation that could destroy it. I'm worn out from wrestling with the Bomber Barons, and I've got to go see Churchill about God knows what. For now, you've kept your job. But don't get comfortable. The vultures are circling, and for all I know the president might find the need to toss you out anyway. It's an election year, you know."

Patton stood straight. "Yes, sir. I will do what I am called upon to do."

"Yes, you had damned well better do exactly that. Now pick up your damned helmet and go back to work."

After long weeks of debates and absurd haggling with the Allied chiefs of staff, Eisenhower was finally given command over the tactical and strategic air forces, at least those forces that would be directly involved in the bombardments that affected Overlord. But a new debate arose, which had far greater consequences. There had been two primary schools of thought on how best to wage the ongoing air campaign. One side, led primarily by American general Carl "Tooey" Spaatz, called for the bombers to concentrate in an all-out effort to destroy Germany's capacity to produce oil and gasoline, any petrochemicals that fueled the German military. Spaatz's argument was that if Germany's refineries and fuel plants were destroyed, the German army would grind to a halt. For Overlord, this meant that reinforcements would not reach key battlefields in time to prevent a solid Allied foothold.

The second argument focused on enemy transportation hubs and mobile facilities. This argument, championed by Eisenhower's assistant commander, British air marshall Arthur Tedder, called for all-out destruction of rail lines, bridges, and key roadways, especially those routes that led from German industrial depots to the coastline. Tedder believed this kind of disruption would be far more effective in stopping the Germans from bringing their forces into play.

Eisenhower realized that both plans had considerable merit, though it was highly likely that the Germans had stockpiled enough fuel and oil to move the bulk of their armor and mobile weapons into an effective confrontation with the Allied landing forces. Though Spaatz's plan was certainly an effective long-term strategy, Eisenhower realized that, for Overlord, a short-term plan was far more desirable. The most important priority was to secure beachheads on the French coast, and the best way to achieve that would be to keep any sizable German armor and infantry units away. If the transportation links were cut, the Germans would be slowed down considerably.

Tedder's argument had prevailed, but Eisenhower was suddenly confronted with political reality. Though Tedder's plan seemed to be of greater benefit to the Overlord operation, bombing the French rail hubs and transportation centers, including major traffic intersections, meant that Allied bombers would dump their loads on or near French towns. The certain result would be the killing of French civilians, quite possibly in enormous numbers. The cost could be catastrophic, and not just in terms of human life. The French underground had been enormously helpful in sabotaging German installations, and their assistance would continue to be a vital asset to Allied plans. By bombing targets without regard for civilian casualties, the Allies risked creating a new enemy: the French themselves. The argument raged, with Churchill and the British cabinet coming down hard against the plan. But Eisenhower received support from an unlikely source. Even Churchill was stunned to receive word from French general Pierre Joseph Koenig, Charles de Gaulle's liaison in London. Koenig seemed to grasp what every military commander had to accept.

> This is war, and it must be expected that there will be deaths. We will accept great loss to be rid of the Germans.

Within days, Tedder's Transportation Plan went into effect and Allied bombers began their work. Because of the urgent need to maintain the integrity of Operation Fortitude, Patton's phantom invasion, the bombers focused far more on the Calais area than they did on the transportation lines behind the Normandy beaches. Despite the diversion, Allied bomber strength had become so overwhelming that even with a fraction of the air power focused on Normandy, the devastation there was quickly apparent. Though the increased level of bombings could certainly give the Germans a major clue that an invasion was imminent, Eisenhower knew that British intelligence was continuing to do everything in its power to convince the German High Command that Calais, and not Normandy, was the target.

Throughout the spring, Allied fighter planes had accompanied the bombers, the normal procedure to protect the vulnerable bombers. As the range of the Allied fighters increased, so too did the number of opportunities to confront the Luftwaffe's devastating screen of Messerschmitts and Focke-Wulf fighters. By filling the skies with greater numbers of planes, the Allies were hoping to confront the Luftwaffe whenever possible. Intelligence had shown that German munitions factories were already stretched thin and the pace of replacing fighters had slowed considerably. On the Allied side, the situation was exactly the opposite. Enormous numbers of new and better planes were being introduced into action every week. The mathematics was obvious to everyone. The Luftwaffe had begun to withdraw many of its squadrons closer to home, to protect crucial industrial sites within Germany itself. The result was a lack of German air power along the French coast, something Eisenhower knew he couldn't take for granted. The benefits of air superiority had already proven itself in both North Africa and Sicily. There, the inability of the Luftwaffe to dominate the skies had done much to ensure Allied victories.

With a clear understanding of the value of their increasing air superiority, Allied commanders ordered their pilots to do whatever they could to bait more German fighters into a brawl. But the air forces' enthusiasm for increasing the number of dogfights had resulted in one enormously difficult moral dilemma for Eisenhower, a dilemma he had to discuss with Churchill.

TEN DOWNING STREET, LONDON
MAY 8, 1944

"You knew about this?"

Churchill pulled hard on the cigar, smoke billowing around him. "Of course I did."

"You knew your intelligence people were telling the Germans where we were going to hit them next? We gave them dates and times?"

"That we did. Damned effective, those intelligence boys. They have an entire network of German agents working for us. Remarkable, that. But from time to time we have to ensure that the enemy still believes the information we're giving them is accurate. The Nazis are a crafty bunch, and unless we toss them a biscuit to chew on, the whole thing might blow up."

Eisenhower shook his head and stared at the cup of coffee in front of him.

Churchill leaned forward. "Dammit, Ike, have some brandy. You can't run your motor on that swill."

"Not now, thank you. It's hard to fathom. We tell the enemy where and when we're going to strike, so he can prepare to meet us."

"Worked too. Bloody marvelous. Nuremberg must have been lit up like a festival."

"How many planes did we lose?"

"Don't like that question, and you shouldn't ask it. We shot down a goodly number of Jerry fighters." Churchill took the cigar from his mouth, raised his glass, tossed back the remnants of his drink. "It's war, Ike. How many lives have we saved by convincing the Germans that the intelligence network is still in their pocket? Isn't that the point? It's war!"

Eisenhower knew it was an argument he couldn't make; Dammit, he thought, he's right. He stirred in his chair, driven by the caffeine, watching as Churchill reached for the squat black bottle and refilled his glass.

"May I?" Eisenhower said.

Churchill smiled, pulled himself out of his chair, moved thickly toward a cabinet, withdrew a glass.

"I knew you'd come around." Churchill returned to the table and poured too much brandy into the glass.

"It's damned tough, that's all," Eisenhower said. "Damned tough. I can't help thinking about our pilots, sent to do a job, with no idea that back here somebody's given them up. It's criminal."

"It's war. And it worked. You want to lose sleep about men dying, you shouldn't—"

"Yes, I know. I accepted that a long time ago. Part of the damned job."

Eisenhower swirled the brandy in the glass, stared into the golden warmth, caught a whiff of the sharp smell. The room was empty, no one else attending the dinner, unusual. He had been concerned about Churchill's health; the man was close to seventy now, and Eisenhower knew that he pushed himself hard—too hard, perhaps, especially with all the travel. Within the last few months there had been conferences and meetings from Quebec to Teheran, and Churchill never seemed to stop, even when pounded by a vicious case of pneumonia. Eisenhower took a sip of the brandy. It's not just politics, he thought. He wants to win this thing, maybe all by himself. I just wish he wasn't so damned negative about Overlord.

Churchill emptied the bottle into his own glass. "Joe Stalin's been crowing like the feathered cock he is."

Eisenhower saw a smile. He knew Churchill too well and appreciated the change of topic. "The Russians are doing well," he said.

"You're a bloody master of the understatement, Ike. I admit I was just a wee bit uncomfortable telling Uncle Joe about the invasion dates. Had to, though. Didn't tell him anything about the actual landings of course, the locations. I knew you'd have indigestion about that. But if this is going to work at all, we need them to hit the Jerries hard, help take the pressure off. They've done a hell of a job all along the Eastern Front. Never thought that would have happened. Hitler was so close to Moscow, he could smell their sewers, and then he botched it up. Now, the Russians are damned near Poland."

If this is going to work . . .

Eisenhower closed his eyes, took a long breath. Dammit. He felt the same annoyance returning, so many arguments, so much pessimism.

"Overlord is going to work. We've put every gear into motion, every commander knows his role—"

Churchill pushed his glass aside, cut him off. "I know all that. I know how much effort you're putting into this, how much effort every damned officer in this country is putting into this. You know where I stand. There are some pretty damned smart people who think this entire operation is a crock, people I respect, people I rely upon. But I listen to you, and to Marshall, and to your president, and others of my own people, and everyone agrees we have to hit the Nazis hard. I still think it could be done with less pain if we went into the Balkans, but you don't agree. Fine."

Churchill stood. Eisenhower knew the look, knew the prime minister would hold nothing back. Churchill began to pace, then stopped and pointed the cigar toward Eisenhower's face.

"Do you know what I go through every damned night? I wake up at five o'clock in the morning, and I see bodies floating in the English Channel. The cream of our youth gone, washed out to sea. That's what I see! You tell me it's going to work, and I can't just accept it. I see the cost!" Churchill paused. "I know. All that drivel about generals accepting casualties. Sounds good, the stuff of textbooks. *You* have to think that way. It's your orders that send men to die. I'm just the . . . what? I'm the one who has to answer to the people. I have to look English mothers in the eye and tell them why their boys aren't coming home, why it was a good idea to send them into France. Again! How many Englishmen are going to die trying to save Frenchmen? Dammit! Tell me again it's going to work! Tell me!"

Eisenhower heard genuine emotion in Churchill's voice and realized Churchill expected an answer.

"It's going to work. I know there are people against this; I know you have doubts. But we've done the organizing, we've put good people in the right places. Next week—"

"Yes, yes, I know all about next week. St. Paul's School, the briefing. Yes, I'll be there. Everyone will be there. Everyone will be on his best behavior, all sticking up for the cause, showing support. There's a time for bitching and a time for shutting up. I know it's time to shut up. But I can still have my doubts, can't I?"

Churchill seemed much calmer now, and Eisenhower took the cue, tasted the brandy, watched Churchill light another cigar. The smoke covered Churchill's face, the room filling with the powerful smell. The lights were dim, the room warm, the chair beneath him soft, and Eisenhower, feeling a glow from the brandy, fought against sadness, the gut-churning anxiety he could never escape. No matter how good the planning, he thought, there is always the chance it will all go wrong. God help us.

Churchill said, "I've gotten more reports about their secret weapon, you know."

The words were jarring.

"*More* reports?"

"Stronger confirmation. Rockets of some kind. Hitler's telling his people the entire war is about to change."

"All I know is what the air people have said about Calais," Eisenhower said. "We started seeing what looked like ski jumps or something, scattered all over the place. We've been hitting them hard, but they're easy to rebuild, apparently."

"Scares hell out of me, Ike. What's that damned Nazi cooked up?"

"Could be fabrication. Just propaganda."

Churchill put the cigar down. "Could be. Can't assume that. If there really is some kind of weapon, it could be very bad here. I'm not sure how much more people can take. It's one thing to rally them around our boys in the sky, all of that. Worked miracles four years ago. Show them a fight in the air, blow some Jerry pilot to hell right over their heads. But rockets? We talking about explosives? Poison gas? What the hell does it mean?"

Eisenhower had heard the reports too, word coming through the Ultra intercepts, the system that had broken the German Enigma communication codes. But the reports weren't specific, nothing about *when,* only loud talk of Hitler's new secret weapon, and then those strange platforms suddenly appearing on the northern French and Belgian coastlines. Eisenhower had kept his focus on the impact some kind of new weapon would have on the invasion, the possibility of a major disruption at the gathering fields, the marshaling yards, the ports, anywhere troops and equipment might be assembled. It was obvious that Churchill was more concerned about the British civilians. As far as anyone knew, the schedule for Overlord's D-Day was still a secret.

Churchill shuffled back and forth, slow nervous pacing. "I know Roosevelt told you about his atom bomb."

Eisenhower nodded. "Yep. I know we're working on something. Weapon of incredible power. That's about all I know. There's a lot of physics involved, not my strong subject."

"Mine either. Supposed to be a big damned blast, though. I have to wonder if Hitler hasn't come up with something similar, something that could destroy half of London."

"Washington is being pretty closemouthed about the whole thing. I don't know anything more than that."

Churchill picked up the cigar again, eyed him. "Whatever you say.

Just keep your fingers crossed that Hitler hasn't got better physicists than we do. They were doing some work in Norway, all that business about heavy water. Have no idea how anyone makes water *heavy,* or what the hell it's for."

Eisenhower said nothing. The German heavy-water plant in Norway had been a key target for a long time. But the Germans had become nervous—Norway was too ripe for Allied invasion—and in November 1943, word had come through the Ultra intercepts that the Germans were moving their stockpile of heavy water to Germany. One part of the move would be to transport the water on board a ferry across Lake Tinn. On February 20, 1944, in a perfectly executed operation, agents of the Norwegian underground had boarded the ferry, and in hours the ferry and the entire stockpile of heavy water had disappeared into the deepest part of the lake. The Allies had to believe that whatever progress the Germans had made harnessing nuclear fission had been set back significantly.

Eisenhower knew there was something still on the prime minister's mind.

"We can't always be sure of secrets, you know," Churchill said, rubbing his chin.

"Not sure what you mean."

"As I said before, they're crafty bastards. You think they knew about the rehearsal?"

Eisenhower was still learning details of the mess at Slapton Sands, only a few days before.

"From what I hear, it was dumb luck. Bradley was there, said it could have been much worse. Just a few torpedo boats. Probably on patrol in the channel and stumbled right into us. Hated like hell to lose those landing craft."

Churchill cocked his head to one side. "What about the men? The casualties? See, you're better at this than you think."

"I don't have the casualty counts yet."

He took another drink of the brandy, felt like Churchill was playing with him. The disaster at Slapton Sands was one glaring hint that even the most careful plans could suddenly come apart. It had been a simple drill, a night landing by the American Fourth Division on the British coastline, an area that mimicked the conditions they would find in France, on what was designated as Utah Beach. But the calm precision of the rehearsal had been shattered by a sudden blast from German torpedoes, the surprise appearance of a squadron of German E-boats, small fast gunboats that had, by a simple quirk of chance, stumbled right into the maneuver. Hundreds of men had died, mostly Americans, but the greatest concern was keeping the entire debacle secret. Any word of the rehearsal itself would confirm German fears about the imminence of the invasion, so not even the families of the victims had been notified.

Churchill said nothing, and Eisenhower had kept it away until now, Churchill's nightmarish image of bodies floating in the channel. Churchill paced again.

"There will be time for truth later on. I've learned that, you know. People always assume politicians lie, that it's part of the job, part of our bloody makeup. But this isn't just politics. We're all keeping secrets now, all of us. Sooner or later, a lot of truth will come out. That should keep us on our toes. Slapton Sands or Ultra, whatever the hell kind of weapon Hitler has, whatever the hell an atom bomb is. It's all just . . . truth. Difficult, that. Should make us do the right thing, I suppose. We'll be judged for it, by history or by God, if you believe that sort of thing."

He stopped, looked down into his empty glass, sniffed. He sat heavily and stared across the table at Eisenhower.

"In 1940, people died from a Nazi air raid in Coventry, people we could have warned. Because of Ultra, we knew the planes were coming and which city they were going to bomb. But the secret was more valuable to us than people's lives. And so we let the bombers come. We didn't warn anyone."

"Yes, I know about that."

"I suppose you do. So now we send pilots over Nuremberg, after we tell the enemy they're coming. We sacrifice our own, our good trained men, just so we can hold on to our secrets."

Eisenhower didn't want this conversation. He knew the answers already, knew Churchill did as well.

"Your General Patton. Caused a big damned row, all over the place. His crime? He said we were destined to rule the world, you, me, and the Russians. Bloody gigantic mistake. But not because he was *wrong*. His crime was, he told the truth. Stupid bastard."

11. EISENHOWER

As the Overlord plan evolved, the Americans had pushed one more plan as well, George Marshall in particular championing a strategy that called for a large-scale invasion of southern France, codenamed Anvil, to coincide with the Allied invasion of the French coast at Normandy. As adamant as Marshall had been, the British had been just as adamant that the plan be shelved. Churchill had long been an advocate for an invasion of the Balkans, pressing hard that such a strategy would threaten Hitler's hold on all of southern Europe. Churchill also believed that such a plan would offer a serious threat to those German forces still engaging the Russians, by jamming a spear up toward Austria that would threaten the Eastern Front from behind. But the Americans had never accepted Churchill's logic, preferring to aim their thrusts into France.

Joseph Stalin had been warm to both strategies, long insisting that the British and Americans should launch a vigorous attack in the west, rather than consuming so many months talking about their various options. Both Churchill and Marshall understood clearly that Stalin was in favor of any plan that would relieve pressure on his army, and possibly draw German strength away from the horrifying slaughter that had consumed both German and Russian troops for three years.

Eisenhower had appreciated the value of Marshall's strategy. Operation Anvil could produce either one of two extremely positive results. If the Germans chose to confront the invasion on the Mediterranean coast, it could seriously reduce their ability to reinforce Rommel's forces in Normandy. Or if German strength in the south was weak, it would allow the Allies to punch a strong advance northward, which might threaten Rommel from behind or, possibly, allow the Allies to drive into southern Germany.

There were two primary arguments against Anvil, arguments Churchill and the other British chiefs made at every opportunity. The Allied troops that would participate would most likely come from Italy, where the Allies were already suffering a grinding war of attrition, caused by a lack of superiority in numbers. To draw off entire divisions from the Italian front would almost certainly guarantee that momentum would be handed back to Kesselring's Germans. The second problem was the availability of landing craft for both troops and equipment, a struggle Eisenhower had dealt with since North Africa. The craft, both large and small, were a hotly contested commodity that had never been available in sufficient numbers. Most were produced at plants in the United States, and for reasons Eisenhower could not fathom the production lines had been painfully slow. With ongoing pressure from the British, and faced with the realities of the lack of adequate numbers of landing craft, Marshall and Eisenhower had been forced to concede to the British objections to Operation Anvil. Though the Americans continued to insist that Anvil should and would take place, they finally accepted that this kind of operation in southern France could not happen until many weeks after the Overlord invasion. Ultimately, the debate had been one more cross Eisenhower had to bear, one more source of unrelenting aggravation that took precious energy away from the primary issue at hand. After so many months of meetings, the logistics and strategies for the Allied invasion of Normandy had finally jelled into a coherent plan, the machinery rolling inexorably forward. With only short weeks remaining until the D-Day that Eisenhower had chosen, it was finally time to reveal the strategy that so many Allied commanders had given so much to create.

ST. PAUL'S SCHOOL, HAMMERSMITH, LONDON
MAY 15, 1944

They filed in slowly, some in dress uniforms, some fresh from their offices in far more casual dress. They'll regret that, Eisenhower thought. But it couldn't be helped. No one could advertise the fact that King George himself would be here.

It was bitterly cold, unusual this late in the spring; most of the men were wrapped in coats and jackets, the vast lecture hall offering little warmth. The room itself was a dark and dismal place, built for function, not ceremony. But the cavernous size was necessary to accommodate the throng of officers and officials. He watched them carefully, mostly familiar faces, some officers he didn't know. The men of higher rank moved forward, toward a single row of armchairs at the front of the room, close to the stage. Behind them, the protocol was less severe, men filing down the rows of seats, some finding friends and casual conversation, others holding themselves silently inside the warmth of their coats, focused on the large map that stood on the stage, colorful and detailed. A map of Normandy.

Eisenhower saw men focusing on him, some offering a smile, others acknowledging his rank with a curt nod of respect. He stood close to the stage, beside a chair he would occupy, knowing the most important people had not yet arrived. He stared toward the back of the lecture hall, the crowd swelling even more, low voices increasing, a hum of chatter. From the far side of the stage, Montgomery appeared, nattily dressed in his battle uniform, unusual, and Eisenhower acknowledged him with a single word: "General."

Montgomery was unsmiling and formal, as he walked up onto the stage. Eisenhower turned again toward the back of the room, watched the open doorway and thought of Monty's uniform, no sign today of the beret or the ridiculous turtleneck sweater. He couldn't help thinking of Patton— yep, George would be happy that Monty dressed for the occasion. Eisenhower had heard the grumbling before, Montgomery's casual dress a particular thorn to Patton, who had often punished men in his command who failed to wear a tie. Monty probably has no idea, he thought; if he did, he'd wear his damned turtleneck on purpose. Stand out in a group by being too casual. Amazing. Never saw a man who so loved the spotlight. Except for Patton himself, of course. God help us.

The show would be Eisenhower's to start, but the briefings would come from a long list of senior officers and, of course, the two most notable civilians: Churchill and King George. The venue had been chosen by Montgomery. St. Paul's School was in fact Montgomery's headquarters, so the gathering here was a subtle hint of his own critical importance to the overall plan. Montgomery had always demonstrated an amazing talent for annoying every officer around him, yet despite claims that Montgomery had ridden hard on the backs of more deserving commanders, in North Africa, he had ultimately accomplished what no one else could do: He had defeated Rommel. As the senior ground commander, Montgomery would hold the rein over both Bradley's Americans and the British forces under General Sir Miles Dempsey, a wonderfully capable veteran of Montgomery's campaigns in North Africa, Sicily, and Italy. Long criticized for embracing details over action, Montgomery had impressed Eisenhower with his attention to detail, and despite Eisenhower's own misgivings about Montgomery, he had to believe that, in the end, ability and not personality would prevail.

The proceedings at St. Paul's were to begin promptly at 9 A.M., and the briefings were expected to last all afternoon. The purpose of the gathering was very specific: to explain the invasion plan, with various commanders from each branch of the service offering their viewpoints and outlining their specific contributions, timetables, and variables, so many precious secrets finally revealed. To some, it would be the first time the details of every aspect of the operation would be explained. The conflicts were still there, disagreements about specific tactics, mostly minor points now, but Eisenhower was comfortable that the major differences had been put to bed. If there was not perfect clarity in everyone's mind, this day would offer the opportunity for anyone to ask questions and speak out, on what might be the last opportunity to air concerns and grievances. He had always encouraged dissent and had encouraged the various specialists to critique whatever failings the plan contained. There is room for that still, he thought, but not much. He had felt it for some time, the momentum of Overlord slowly overwhelming the men who created it. I don't see what else we can do at this point to change things, he thought. D-Day is just three weeks away.

He saw Bradley moving toward the front of the room, purposeful, staring downward. There was no smile, no informal greeting, Bradley seeking only to find his seat, moving close to Eisenhower now, seeming not to notice him.

"Brad. Everything okay?"

Bradley looked at him, seemed surprised. "Sorry, Ike. Good to see you. You looked at the map?"

There was a hard grumpiness in Bradley that was unusual. Eisenhower looked up at the stage.

"Haven't gone over this one too closely. Monty's people drew it up. Is there a problem?"

Bradley glanced around, self-conscious, uncomfortable, and lowered his voice.

"Not the best time to talk about it. I had a few words with Monty. Not a pleasant way to begin this thing. But dammit, Ike, take a look. He's drawn in those idiotic phase lines. Told him I won't have that, not in my sector anyway. You can't lay out this campaign like some dance lesson. Worthless exercise. I won't impose that on my people." He stopped, waiting for more men to move past, Tedder and Ramsay, cordial nods to Eisenhower. Bradley was obviously upset. Eisenhower, looking toward the stage again, saw Montgomery standing on the far side, arms crossed, staring out at the growing audience with a look of patient satisfaction.

"It's not the time, Ike. Sorry I mentioned it."

Eisenhower studied the map and saw what Bradley was referring to, crooked lines of tape marking rows of boundaries that expanded away from the beaches, spreading out like so many ripples in a pond. Oh, for God's sake. That's pure Monty, planning out every last detail. He's predicting the future, telling his men where he expects them to be every step of the way. Nothing wrong with that, I guess, as long as he pulls it off. But Monty knows there's no hard and fast timetable to a campaign, no matter how carefully he designs one. We can't assume that every part of this operation is a well-oiled machine, no matter how much preparation Monty makes. The quote echoed through Eisenhower's brain, a cliché now, one of those Teutonic truisms they toss around at West Point. *No paper plan ever survives in practice.* Who was that, Clausewitz? Von Moltke maybe. But then, Monty didn't go to West Point.

Churchill appeared at the back of the room, a hum of activity flowing around him. He wore a heavy frock coat, held a cigar tightly in his teeth, and moved quickly through the officers: brief words, small greetings. He saw Eisenhower and removed his hat.

"Morning. Good time for some of that damned coffee you like so much. This place is an icebox. We getting started soon?"

Eisenhower saw the king approaching, all smiles and pleasantries. "I would say yes."

All the men were standing, obligatory respect. Churchill said nothing and moved toward a chair, dead center in the front row, seemed impatient for King George to make his way down the aisle. Eisenhower had met with the king on several occasions, had been surprised at first that George was so personable, a calm soft-spoken man who showed obvious respect for the officers who had earned their rank.

"Good morning, General," the king said. "Quite exciting, this, wouldn't you say?"

"Your Majesty. Welcome. I would hope we can save the excitement for the enemy."

"Ah, yes, good one, that! I quite agree!"

Eisenhower saw Churchill watching them, the king moving that way now, a brief greeting between them. The king was ushered to the center-most seat, the seat Churchill had seemed to choose for himself; Churchill sat one seat away, leaving a gap between him and his monarch. Churchill had not removed the cigar from his mouth, and Eisenhower looked away, thought, What now? More intrigue? Some spat between them? Is everyone in this damned war twelve years old? He scanned the faces throughout the room, and scolded himself. Stop that. You have a job to do, and so do they. As long as everyone knows that, nothing else matters.

The front row was filling quickly, the arrival of the king the signal for everyone to find a seat. Eisenhower nodded to more familiar faces: the South African, Field Marshal Smuts; the British chief of staff, Lord Brooke; so many generals, admirals, air commanders. He felt a stir inside him. Good God, he thought. Hell of a time for the Krauts to make a lucky air strike. I hope word has gone out to the antiaircraft boys to pay a little more attention today.

The talk quieted. Up on the stage, Montgomery pointed toward the back of the room. "Security, you will lock the door and man your posts outside. As of now, no one may enter."

At the rear of the room, two American military policemen stood tall in white helmets, white holsters holding their sidearms. Eisenhower knew they had been chosen for the job for one reason: They were both huge men, enormously intimidating. They obeyed Montgomery's order with silent precision, exited through the door, pulled it shut. Montgomery looked toward Eisenhower, who would give the first presentation, but

Eisenhower knew he would have to wait for Montgomery's own formal greeting, offering as host a show of ceremony that he was entitled to. Montgomery moved across the stage.

"I wish to welcome Your Majesty to these proceedings. Mr. Prime Minister—" There was a loud banging on the door, and Montgomery stopped, clearly annoyed. "What in blazes . . . ?"

Eisenhower rose, saw heads turning toward the back of the room, saw the door open with a loud clatter, a white-helmeted MP staring in, silently apologetic. Eisenhower thought, Who the hell would be late? An officer strode past the MP, silver helmet glistening, moving quickly down the aisle, silently finding a seat. It was Patton.

All eyes were on Eisenhower. He glanced at the king, who looked up at him with a benevolent smile, Churchill as well watching him with polite expectation. I'm not an orator, dammit. Don't look at me like I'm supposed to win the war on this stage. He glanced toward Montgomery, Bradley, Tedder, more faces, the division and corps commanders, naval officers, and airmen. There were no glimpses of the derision he had heard so much about, no one showing hints of their discontent either with Eisenhower's style or with his orders. It was there, of course, too many annoying reports of sneers and insults from some of these same men, spewed about in back rooms. No matter how much I insist we work together, we are two different people. No matter what I say or how much cooperation we've worked for, we can still spit at each other like alley cats.

But the faces that watched him showed none of that now, every man in the room seeming to recognize why they were there and how important the briefings would be. He drew energy from that, could feel a sense of cooperation, the backbiting and rivalry suspended, at least for a few hours. This will never happen again, he suddenly realized, not like this, not all of us in one place. He felt himself straining to hear outside, some telltale sign of an air raid, a siren, or the gut-churning drone of German bombers. But there was nothing, only silence, the men watching, waiting, each one there because he was a part of something much larger than these men themselves, much more significant than any of them could ever have imagined. He felt a strong confidence now, so many of the faces familiar in a way that suddenly inspired him. All right then. Let's get on with it.

"We are on the eve of a great battle. We have come here in this assem-

bly to deliver to you the various plans made by the different force commanders. I would emphasize that I consider it to be the duty of everyone
in this room who sees a flaw, in any part of this plan, to speak up. There
must be no hesitation. I have no sympathy with anyone, whatever his rank
or position, who will not accept criticism of what he considers to be his
own perfect strategy. We are here to get the best possible results, and those
results rely on every man in this room.

"This briefing will start with the three principal commanders, ground,
sea, and air, beginning with General Montgomery."

Eisenhower stepped down from the stage—full of nervous energy, his
heart pounding—moved to his seat, studied the map again and heard
Montgomery begin his presentation.

"This is an excellent plan. We have a sufficiency of troops, we have all
the necessary tackle. We will confront a man, Field Marshal Rommel, with
whom I am familiar. He is an energetic and determined commander and
has created a formidable obstacle for us to breach. But breach it we will.
He will do his level best to Dunkirk us. He will try to force us from the
beaches, and he will defend the towns of Caen, Bayeux, and Carentan with
his usual vigor. But he is too impulsive for the set-piece battle. His method
is disruption. He is best at the spoiling attack. We will instead do what we
can to spoil *him*."

After three brutal hours, they adjourned for lunch and then resumed
the meeting, the presentations and discussions lasting all afternoon.
Every senior commander offered details of the plan, some capturing the attention of the throng more effectively than others. Through it all, the commanders had given out a variety of details: the timetable for the amphibious landings, the troop movements beyond the landings, the goals that
Montgomery's staff had illustrated on the great map.

On June 5, the paratroopers would go in first, just after midnight, the
British 6th Airborne on the far left flank, the American 82nd and 101st on
the right. If the drops were effective, the paratroopers would seriously disrupt German movements behind the beaches by capturing bridges and key
intersections at various small villages.

Immediately after dawn, the amphibious landings would begin on five
designated beaches. Two, Omaha and Utah, fell into the American zone to
the west. Farther east, the British would land at beaches labeled Gold

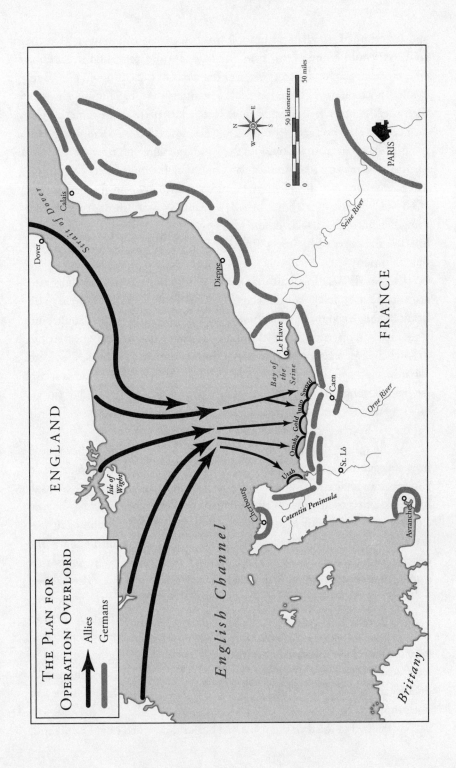

THE PLAN FOR
OPERATION OVERLORD

Allies

Germans

ENGLAND

Dover

Strait of Dover

Calais

Isle of
Wight

Dieppe

Le Havre

Bay of
the Seine

Caen

Sword
Juno
Gold
Omaha

Orne River

St. Lô

Utah

Cherbourg

Cotentin Peninsula

Avranches

English Channel

Brittany

FRANCE

Seine River

PARIS

N
W   E
S

50 kilometers

50 miles

0

0

and Sword, the Canadians at Juno. It had been a surprise to many that the landings would come at low tide, the troops to be deposited by landing craft far from the high-water line. But the work of the commandos and reconnaissance planes had convinced the planners that the landing craft and their cargoes of men and equipment would fare better if Rommel's enormous barriers of underwater obstacles were exposed. The disadvantage for the first waves of troops would be the wide-open ground they would have to cross, several hundred yards of wet sand, which would surely be a shooting gallery for German machine gunners and riflemen in the heights beyond the beaches. The choice of a dawn landing had been hotly debated, some believing the attack should come well before daylight, offering the infantry the cover of darkness. But the navy and the air forces had swayed that argument.

Even as the landing craft made their way to the beaches, an enormous armada of naval power would be called upon to blanket the German fortifications that faced the sea with a devastating barrage of fire that could suppress German opposition. In addition, vast waves of Allied bombers would drop their payloads on German positions along the beaches. To avoid friendly fire, the bombers and air gunners would require at least minimal daylight. Though the ground troops would be visible from shore, if the attacks by the air and naval forces were effective, there might be very little left on the beaches to oppose them.

As the infantry and engineers made their initial landings, they would be accompanied by armor, dozens of self-propelled amphibious tanks, odd contraptions that still inspired some skepticism, tanks surrounded by tall inflatable skirts to keep them afloat while a propeller drive pushed them to shore. The timetable of the landings had been designed carefully and methodically, additional waves of men and equipment pouring onto the beaches in a rhythm that would ensure that foot soldiers were supported immediately by additional manpower, as well as armor and artillery, allowing them to push inland as rapidly as possible.

Throughout the day at St. Paul's School, the details poured forth to the assembled mass of officers and officials, most of it matter-of-fact and specific, with only occasional bursts of hyperbole. The king had spoken as well, an effective display of encouragement and temperament, more subdued than most of the military men, but a positive message of hope and optimism.

By the end of the day, the plans had been fully spelled out. Throughout

it all, there were no cheers, only a few laughs, no applause, and no ceremony. At four-thirty in the afternoon, Eisenhower rose to speak again, the
day complete, the nagging fear that had gripped him all day finally releas-
ing itself.

"In one half hour, we shall have vacated this place. It is apparent to me
that Hitler will have missed his one and only chance of destroying, with a
single well-aimed bomb, the entire high command of the Allied forces."

As the room emptied, the collective exhaustion kept the conversation
to a minimum. Eisenhower knew that each man carried away from this extraordinary gathering much of the knowledge and planning of the others.
The parts had given way to the whole. Late in the day, as the speakers completed their tasks, Churchill had come forward. His speech had been fiery
and eloquent, with his usual flare for dramatic language. But Churchill
had offered one brief phrase that had driven into Eisenhower with sharp
meaning. For so many months there had been wrangling and argument,
debate and disagreement, what Eisenhower believed were fundamental
doubts among so many of his superiors, that Operation Overlord might
not work at all.

Now Churchill looked directly at him. *"I am hardening toward this en-
terprise."*

It wasn't gratuitous, no mindless optimism, no political grandstanding
or patriotic cheerleading. Eisenhower didn't know if the prime minister
had absorbed something new from the meeting itself, some clarity about
pieces of the puzzle he hadn't understood before. But it was perfectly clear
to Eisenhower that, finally, after so much rancor and so many disagreements, Churchill was offering a message to the Americans and to the rest
of the British high command. There was one goal now, one purpose: to de-
vote themselves fully to the success of Operation Overlord.

12. ADAMS

"All leaves are canceled and, effective immediately, all officers and enlisted men are confined to base. MPs will be patrolling the perimeter of this compound and will be regulating all vehicle traffic both in and out of base." Colonel Ekman looked up from the paper, seemed to dare a response. "Good. I don't want to hear any griping about this. You have a problem, tell it to your sergeant. Should you feel that need, he has my permission to slap hell out of you." He paused again, and Adams saw his eyes dart across the sea of faces. "This is the real thing, boys. There will be no further practice jumps. Those of you who are injured will have a few days to recuperate. And you *will* recuperate. I don't believe there is a single man in the Five-oh-five who will shirk from this duty. General Ridgway is counting on me, and I am counting on all of you. I have promised General Ridgway that we will deliver . . . and I'll be damned if anyone is going to make a liar out of me. You are dismissed."

Ekman stepped down from the makeshift platform, seemed to vanish behind a flock of officers. The hum began now, the inevitable questions, and Adams moved away from the crowd, staring out toward the distant rows of C-47s. He felt a strange coldness and clenched his fists, a chill in his hands. We're really going. Again. Son of a bitch.

The others were moving past him, the entire regiment pouring out of the hangar, the voices coming, loud calls, a few whoops, the sounds digging into him. He wanted silence, but there was nowhere to find it now, nowhere to go to escape the idiotic loudmouths, the men who truly had no idea what was about to happen. The veterans streamed past him as well, silent and subdued. Most of them were familiar to him, the faces if not the names. He had learned, they had all learned, that names didn't matter. Even the men in his own platoon could be no more to him than a rifle or a submachine gun, a grenade, a radio, and those precious few, a Browning Automatic Rifle, what everyone knew as simply the BAR. No matter the weapon, if one went down, another would follow, and every step they took along the way was one step closer to the unthinkable.

He thought of walking out, far into the field, but aircraft were in motion. Keep your ass inside, he thought. Nothing for you to do out there but get in the way. He glanced up at the thick gray sky, the inevitable rain. Too damned cold for this. No need to stick my boots into some muddy hole.

He had feared his ribs had been broken, the pain more severe than any injury he had suffered before. The lieutenant had ordered him to report to the doctor, an older grouch of a man, whose name seemed only to be Doc. Adams had been surprised by his own reaction to the examination, pure panic that a busted rib might actually send him home, take him right out of the war. But the doctor had dismissed him with a casual wave, said it was nothing more than a heavy bruise, had even complimented Adams on the exceptionally colorful results, a saucer-shaped patch of blue below his heart. The bruise was nearly gone now, a faint yellow stain, and he ignored it. Dammit, he thought, if I'm going to get hurt, it's not going to be from some useless practice jump. The voices were still swarming all around him, and he tried to avoid them, so many of the men spilling out their stupidity or their fear. Adams couldn't help his anger; he had felt this way with every wave of replacements. He hated them for their inexperience.

Over the past few weeks, the Eighty-second had made several practice jumps, good weather and bad, more screwups, more injuries. With every jump, he had grown more impatient, every hard landing reminding him that this was just play, artificial, meaningless. The men didn't need more lessons. They had all become proficient at packing their chutes, and they didn't need him to shove them out the gaping door of the C-47. The shirkers and malcontents were long gone. It was the same throughout the army. Every unit that had seen combat had the old and the new, and the untested would always harass the veterans for pieces of wisdom, what it was like, what the enemy would do, how it *felt*. It was happening again, all through the hangar, the new men jabbering nervously, responding to the hints of urgency from Colonel Ekman.

"Sergeant Adams!"

He knew the voice and turned, his hand twitching from instinct, prepared to raise the salute. There was a cluster of officers; Scofield, with more of the company commanders. He saw Lieutenant Pullman moving through them, and now the tall thin man, no smile, the man pointing his finger toward Adams. It was Gavin.

"Over here, Sergeant," Pullman said.

Adams moved that way, the salute coming up, Gavin motioning to the other officers. "Dismissed. I'll be back around tomorrow."

"Sir."

"Yes, sir."

Pullman seemed to linger, and Gavin said, "If you don't mind, Lieutenant, I'd like a word with your sergeant."

"Of course, sir. Sergeant, I'll speak to you later."

Adams threw the salute toward Pullman, said, "Yes, sir."

He looked at Gavin, none of the warmth, Gavin pointing toward the offices at the far end of the hangar.

"The Five-oh-five still make the worst coffee in England?"

"I believe so, General."

"Good. I could use some. Follow me."

They moved to a metal door. Adams saw two men emerging, lieutenants who seemed surprised to see Gavin. They passed with quick salutes and sharp glances at Adams. Wonderful, he thought. They either think I'm teacher's pet or I'm about to be court-martialed. He could smell the coffee, a small hot plate in one corner, saw a staff sergeant sitting at a desk, writing on a pile of papers, seemingly oblivious to the sudden appearance of a one-star general.

Gavin moved toward the coffeepot. "Take a break, Sergeant. You know how to stand up?"

The man rose with a clatter of his chair. "Certainly, sir. The coffee's fresh, just made it a couple hours ago, sir."

The man hurried out. The office now empty, Gavin handed Adams a cup.

"I wouldn't drink this stuff alone. Chances are one of us could end up poisoned. We'll need a witness."

He moved to the lone chair, sat, scanned the papers on the desk, pushed them to one side: no expression. Adams filled his cup halfway, stopped pouring. Fresh . . . two hours ago? he thought. It's paint thinner by now.

"I'm guessing the boys will be pretty pissed off about the order to close the base," Gavin said. "Those pubs in town are already dead empty. Probably break the hearts of half the damned women in England. Hard to believe how well these boys have done with the fairer sex. I expect the British have every reason to bitch about us. I've heard too damned much of that; we're overpaid, oversexed, and over here. Not sure what we've got that their men are lacking. Don't want to know, now that I think about it."

Adams knew not to speak. He had heard these monologues from Gavin before.

There was silence for a long moment, and then Gavin said, "You heard that the Five-oh-four finally got here, right?"

"I've heard rumors, yes, sir."

"You know that Ridgway and I had been begging General Clark to turn them loose, get them the hell out of Italy. But Clark wouldn't do it, said he needed them at Anzio, so they got chewed all to hell. I had hoped they'd be ready for this mission, but Ridgway says they're too shot up. He's grounded them. You know what that means?"

Adams knew the answer already, the one word in his mind: *veterans.* How much more do those boys need to go through? He knew, as they all did, that the 504th had been the victims of the horrific friendly fire incident off the Sicilian coast, nervous naval gunners ignoring their orders not to fire on the slow-moving transports that flew over them in the darkness. It had been a disaster for everyone involved, the 504th suffering more than two hundred casualties. Despite serious misgivings about the effectiveness of airborne drops, the 504th had been called on again, a crucial drop into Italy, which Adams and the 505th had followed. Then the 505th had been ordered to England, but the 504th stayed put and for several miserable months had been bogged down at Anzio.

Gavin didn't wait for him to speak. "It means, Sergeant, that we're going into France with one hand behind our backs. It means that right now, the Eighty-second will count, as its parachute regiments, the Five-oh-five, plus the Five-oh-seven and Five-oh-eight. So two-thirds of us are green, not a lick of combat experience. I bitched like hell to Ridgway—well, as much as anyone can bitch to Ridgway—but he wouldn't budge. Colonel Tucker's screaming like hell, and I bet every man in that outfit is pretty upset, but, hopefully, they'll get into this thing before it's over. Meanwhile, the Eighty-second is going to jump into the enemy's latrine with only one tested regiment."

Adams was uncomfortable now; it was not like Gavin to complain about anything. He waited through more silence. *Why is he telling me this?*

Gavin looked at the coffee in his cup, set it to one side. "Keep this stuff away from the gasoline tanks." He stood, moved to the one small window, stared out. "You know damned well not to repeat this, right?"

"Of course, sir."

"We had a hell of a fight at HQ a while back. You missed a good one. Word came from Washington that General Marshall wanted us to jump close to Paris, that we ought to raise hell with German installations, bridges, all of that. A hundred miles behind the lines. Apparently, General Marshall forgot that the Germans have tanks, and that a flock of paratroopers don't fare too well against armored vehicles. Thank God someone talked him out of it, Ike probably. I've got a lot of respect for General Marshall, but sometimes, these damned armchair types—"

Gavin turned around.

"This make you nervous, Sergeant?"

"No, sir."

"It ought to. It'd be awfully good for someone in your position to believe that those folks up the ladder know what the hell they're doing. I know what the hell *I'm* doing, and Ridgway knows what the hell *he's* doing. I suppose Ike does too. But some of those others fellows—I just found out they changed the mission on us. New jump zones. You know the mission?"

"No, sir."

"Hell, no, of course you don't. That'll come later. You'll be briefed when SHAEF says it's time. But it's gonna be hot. That's Rommel over there, and you can bet he's waiting for us. You still remember how to use that Thompson?"

"Definitely, sir."

Gavin nodded, still no smile. Adams could feel the weight in the room, the smell of dust and burnt coffee.

"This is important, Sergeant. Most important damned thing we've ever done. You understand that?"

"Yes, sir. I believe so, sir."

Gavin seemed mystified now, looked at Adams with a tilt of his head. "You recall why I wanted to see you?"

"No, sir. I assumed . . . maybe you wanted to talk to me about my work, something I screwed up."

Gavin smiled. "Nope. As much as I miss you on my staff, I'm not about to yank you out of here again. These boys would miss you a hell of a lot more than those paper pushers at St. Paul's." He paused, looked down, put a hand on the papers. "Damn. My brain's mush, Sergeant. I need this war to end so I can get a real night's sleep. I've told Ekman the Five-oh-five has some good people to carry the load. He knows that, of course, and it probably pisses him off when I tell him his business. No commander listens to advice from his predecessor. Even if he should." Gavin looked at his watch, shook his head. "Have to meet with Ridgway in an hour."

He looked at Adams now, moved around the desk, close to him, suddenly held out a hand. Adams took it, his own hand engulfed by the hard thin fingers.

"Once this thing starts," Gavin said, "I expect you to kill some Germans. Not sure where I'll be when D-Day comes, but you can damn well bet I'll be jumping somewhere close by. Try to find me if you can. I want a good point man in front of me. If I don't see you again—well, I expect—I expect both of us to get home in one piece."

BRAUNSTONE PARK, NEAR LEICESTER
MAY 30, 1944

They sat in a semicircle, braced against the hard chill, the wind whipping across the open ground. In the center, the doctor dropped to one knee, held up one arm of the man lying flat beside him on a wool blanket.

"Now, listen up. You insert the sharp tip of the syrette directly into a prominent vein." He looked down at his patient, held up one of the skinny arms. "You ready, Private Unger?"

"I think so, sir."

"Roll up your sleeve. This won't hurt."

Unger obeyed. Quickly, the doctor jabbed the syrette into the crease of Unger's elbow and continued his lecture.

"Like that. The morphine should be effective immediately. Even if you cannot readily dress the man's wounds, this should keep him calm and free of pain. For the most part."

Adams watched the others, no one laughing now. The doctor stood, holding the syrette in front of him.

"Use it all, every bit. Nothing wasted. It'll do a man far more good in his veins than on the ground. Any questions? Good. Now, on to the last matter. The division is issuing every one of you a prophylactic. At least one, though I'd like to see you each carry a dozen. We've been dealing with enough cases of venereal disease that you'd think someone upstairs would appreciate the need for the damned things. They will be included with your other equipment."

"Hey, Doc, we won't be needing those things anymore. They locked the gates, and all the Red Cross girls went home. There's not a gal anywhere around here. You know when they're coming back?"

Adams looked toward the voice; Marley, a broad smile on the big man's face. Beside him, another man spoke.

"You chased them all away, Dex. They get one look at the size of those boots and run like hell."

Adams was in no mood for this kind of fun. "All right, shut the hell up. Doc's got a lot to do. He can't waste his time listening to you morons."

"Actually, Sergeant, your man asks a good question. The Red Cross has withdrawn their personnel from this base and, as I understand it, other bases as well. The ladies did brighten the place up. I doubt they'll return before—um—before we receive our assignment."

There was no response.

"You get that?" Adams said. "The girls are gone. You should be paying attention to that. Same reason no one's going to town anymore. You idiots think this is a game? Put your mind on one thing and one thing only. We're getting orders soon, and when those orders come you'll find out what all this training has been for."

"Hey, Sarge, is that why they're feeding us better?"

Adams looked at Marley and thought about the food. I'll be damned. He's right.

"Could be. I figure the officers were getting pretty sick of cabbage and brussels sprouts. But maybe they think we need fattening up."

There were more laughs, and another man spoke: Buford, one of the newer replacements.

"Sounds like they're treating us like hogs going to slaughter, Sarge."

"All right, shut up. Let the doc finish."

The doctor was leaning low, close to Unger. "Oh, dear me. Private, are you conscious?"

Adams moved closer, saw Unger's mouth open, heard slow breathing, the hint of a snore. The doctor looked up at him.

"This happens every now and then. The morphine affects some people more severely than others. It appears Private Unger will be sleeping for a while." He stood up, stretched his back, rubbed a hand through the short gray beard. "I didn't realize he was so thin. My mistake. Very sorry."

Adams saw Unger's eyes twitch, heard a low grunt. He looked at his watch. "All right, it's close to chow time. Hit your quarters for ten minutes. I'll take care of this idiot."

The men were up and running, the usual routine, a double-timed jog everywhere they went. Adams bent low. With the doctor helping from the other side, Unger was hoisted up and over Adams's shoulder. He began to move away, Unger's head flopping against his back, the words of the doctor behind him.

"Truly sorry. Actually, he looks a bit young."

They stood in the usual chow line, a crackling chatter of music from a radio, some bouncy tune Adams didn't know. He didn't pay much attention to the popular songs, heard the names tossed around, Tommy Dorsey, Glenn Miller, the men speaking lustfully about the girl singers. Their posters draped the walls of the mess hall, movie stars as well: the leggy Betty Grable, a sultry stare from Rita Hayworth. Adams ignored most of that, didn't attend the occasional films, tried not to pay attention to the noisy speculation that Bob Hope would come. No one is coming now, he thought. The gates are locked. No time for dance parties.

The kitchen staff was lined up behind large steel bins, spooning out what seemed to be some sort of green vegetable, beside a large bucket of what Adams guessed to be creamed corn. But every man had picked up the new smell and stood in reverent silence, watching the last server digging a long fork into a huge pile of thick steaming meat. Each man in turn had a piece dropped onto his plate, each one then hurrying toward a place to sit, the silence replaced by joyous sounds of men eating beef. Adams brought up the rear of the line, had deposited Unger on the floor, propped up against the wall in a corner of the mess hall. He picked up two trays, then glanced back at the sleeping man. Yeah, fine, he thought. I'll get you some chow, stick one of those steaks under your nose. That ought to wake you up sooner or later.

Adams watched as the pile of meat grew smaller, a fork hoisting up the dark slabs, wet thuds on the trays. He couldn't help staring at the steaks, the smells filling him with memories. How long has it been, anyway? More than a year, I guess. Some cookout back home, somebody's father drinking too much beer. What the hell did we do to deserve steak? The question hung in his brain. In front of him, the new man, Buford, moved away with a full plate. Adams stared at his back, Buford's words punching clear and cold in his mind. Hogs to the slaughter.

13. EISENHOWER

He nursed the eye with a warm cloth, pressed gently against the swollen redness. He glanced at the tube of ointment, something the doctor had given him, thought, To hell with that. If warm water won't fix this thing, I'll just put on an eye patch. Pirate Ike. *Arrggh.*

The eye had been bothering him for several days now, coming as so many other afflictions had come, erupting from the overwhelming exhaustion of mind and body. He had been plagued by this kind of thing before, during the Sicilian operation and after; he knew the reasons then, as he understood them now. Eisenhower had driven himself to the point of utter collapse.

He sat on the narrow bed, the brief flash of humor wiped away. It was easier to be angry at himself, to curse this new plague, the eye tormenting him with burning misery. It's your own fault, he thought. You don't sleep enough, that's for sure. The staff has given up nagging you about it, Harry especially. They don't know what this is like, what kind of—he searched his brain for a word—swamp? Cesspool? Up to my knees in mud, trying to run a marathon. All right, stop this. You're doing the job, just like the rest of them. Well, most of them. No one expects this to be a piece of cake.

You wanted command, now you've got it. You know damn well how miserable you'd be if you were stuck back in Washington. Stop whining, for God's sake.

He dabbed at the eye again with the cloth. Don't even look in the mirror. It looks bad enough to the staff, no need to remind yourself you're not invincible. It'll pass in a day or two.

He tried to relax, find some kind of calm, and heard a soft breeze blowing against the wide canvas around him. He put both hands down beside him, propped up his slumping shoulders, and felt the nagging pain in his right arm. Another ailment. What the hell is this? You're falling to pieces. Hang on, old boy. You're the man at the top. No time for this crap.

The tent was Eisenhower's home, at least for now. Several weeks earlier he had ordered a command post to be set up in the far south of England, mobile, a large boxlike room hoisted up on the bed of a deuce-and-a-half, the reliable two-and-a-half-ton truck the Allies now used for so much of their ground transport. He called it his circus wagon. With his office perched on a truck, his command center could be hauled quickly to any point he needed to be. Close beside the truck were tents, makeshift offices and sleeping quarters for his key staff. It was far from anyone's notion of quarters for a supreme commander, but Eisenhower never paid much attention to the griping of anyone who thought war should be comfortable. Back at Bushey Park, Bedell Smith was dealing with the ongoing barrage of administrative matters, the offices there a constant rush of activity. Smith continued to ruffle feathers, especially among the British. Eisenhower enjoyed having a bulldog as his chief of staff, but Beetle had trouble reining it in, and both men knew he might end up causing some kind of diplomatic flap that might require too much of his boss's energy to unravel, energy Eisenhower simply didn't have. Marshall doesn't get along with people either, he thought. He wants to come across as a soldier, all that stiff-backed stuff, the thing that made Black Jack Pershing stand out in Washington. That works pretty well with congressmen and reporters, I suppose. Eisenhower recalled the story, how, in some meeting, the president had actually addressed Marshall as George. Marshall had responded that he preferred to be called General Marshall, pointing out the importance of chain of command. That took some brass, Eisenhower thought. Even Churchill calls me Ike. But it's Marshall's way. Fortunately for him, Roosevelt doesn't have a raw nerve about it.

He set the wet cloth aside, tested the eye, blinked hard several times.

The tent flaps were billowing inward, pushed by the wind, and he looked that way and blinked again, relieved that the swelling had not impaired his vision. But the itchiness was still there, the constant tears. Live with it, dammit.

He knew it would be dark soon and glanced at the small pillow. You came here to take a nap, he thought. So, take a nap. Just a few minutes maybe. But the wind was picking up now, the tent shaking, another spear thrust into this one quiet moment. The weather briefings were scheduled regularly: 9:30 each night, 4:30 in the morning. They're terrified of me, he thought, seem to think that if they bring me bad news, someone's going to get blistered for it. But they're meteorologists, after all, and right now I need them to spend every minute studying . . . whatever it is they study. I don't need them to tell me how their best estimates are only guesswork or some kind of intuition. Rather not hear that. There has to be some science at work here.

He looked again at the pillow, thought, Just a few minutes—

"Sir."

He looked toward the tent flap, saw one of his MPs, the telltale white helmet, the men Butcher called Eisenhower's snowballs.

"What is it, Corporal?"

"Air Marshal Leigh-Mallory has arrived, sir. He insists on seeing you. I didn't want to bother you, sir, but Commander Butcher is not here at the moment."

"Don't worry about it, Corporal. I'll see him in here. No need for both of us to traipse out into this weather."

The MP disappeared, and Eisenhower felt the chill of the wind. Dammit. Has the sun forgotten how to shine in this place? The man's face poked through the tent flaps, the neat mustache: Leigh-Mallory, his coat glistening from the rain.

"Ah, there you are. Very sorry to intrude, sir."

"Pull up a chair, if you don't mind getting your butt pinched. I decided the cushions could stay at home."

Leigh-Mallory seemed to take him seriously and sat slowly, testing the hard slatted surface of the small folding chair. Leigh-Mallory rarely engaged in useless small talk, and Eisenhower waited, knowing he'd go right to the point. Leigh-Mallory made a hard frown, looked down for a moment.

"Something wrong?"

"Well, yes, I'm afraid. I feel the need to go on the record, as it were. You know I have always had deep misgivings about the plans for the airborne assault. I must state officially that my feelings have not changed. I have studied this matter in detail and have concluded that your paratroopers will suffer a casualty rate as high as fifty percent, and a loss of glider strength as high as seventy percent. You have more than a thousand transport aircraft that must traverse the waters occupied by a portion of the invasion fleet. The danger of catastrophe from friendly fire is significant. There will be full moonlight, and once the first waves of transports reach land, the German searchlights and antiaircraft batteries will certainly gain accuracy in locating them. You know, sir, that the C-47, for all its marvelous advantages, has been described by some of its pilots as a flying bomb. There is no shielding, no armor to protect the fuel tanks. My analysis of the maps has indicated that the landing grounds are completely unsuitable, and the enemy's opposing forces will present a formidable hazard that your troops cannot overcome. Should this occur, those units will lose their tactical power, and their effective role in this operation will be negated completely. I cannot allow this operation to go unchallenged, when I feel you are risking the futile slaughter of two fine fighting divisions."

Eisenhower studied the man's dour expression and absorbed the message. "You didn't mention the British paratroopers. Is this just an American problem?"

"Oh, my, no. I mean no slight to Americans. The British operation will take place on far better ground, with objectives that are far more practical to achieve. I do not anticipate such difficulty there."

Eisenhower believed him. He ran a hand over his scalp, the eye itching more than before. "I respect your views. But if the Eighty-second and Hundred-and-first do not attempt their operations behind Utah Beach, the landing on that beach itself could become a disaster. At this point, we are committed to the plans. Why in hell would you bring this up now?"

"I have mentioned this previously to General Ridgway and General Taylor. They did not respond with . . . appreciation. I understand their need to protect the prestige of their divisions—"

"This isn't about prestige! This plan has been ripped up, shredded, chewed, spit out, ground up, stomped on, and ripped up again. The finest strategists in both armies have spent months—hell, a year!—going over every last detail. I don't expect this operation to go perfectly, but I expect it to *go*. We all have doubts! We're all concerned about losses, and I for one am damn well concerned that the Krauts might roll us right back into the ocean! Those paratroopers know what we're asking them to do, and regardless of Ridgway and Taylor, regardless of their *pride,* this strategy is the best we've come up with. We need those paratroopers behind Utah Beach. Bradley supports this, Montgomery supports this, this is the plan, and this is what we're going to do!"

He stopped, felt too angry, tried to hold it in. Leigh-Mallory looked down again, a slow nod.

"I could not, in clear conscience, allow this operation to go forward without expressing—"

"Fine. Put it on paper. Write me a letter. You want it on the record, that's on the record. I know you're sincere, I know it's what you believe, so do what you have to do. When this is over, your position will be documented. If there is a slaughter, you can say you warned me."

"I assure you, sir, I would never use this as a means to embarrass this command. I am deeply worried, that's all."

"Good God, man, we're all deeply worried. No army in history has ever attempted this before. This whole damned island is one giant military base. No, correct that—it's one giant parking lot. I've never seen so much equipment and armor. I didn't know it was possible to assemble so many bulldozers, railroad engines, and coils of barbed wire. Every damned open field is a supply dump. Some lieutenant told me his men had seen so many barrage balloons floating over this damned place, they figured it was the only thing keeping England from sinking into the ocean. Every day, I wonder how in hell the Germans don't know exactly what we're planning to do, how we've kept any secrets at all." He paused. "I haven't studied a single map in any planning center or anyone's headquarters without knowing that all those lines and dots and colored flags—those are soldiers. Men are going to die, possibly a great many men. Right now, I can't be concerned that your conscience is bothering you. My conscience bothers me every time I lie on this damned bed, every time I think about what's about to happen. But I believe in the plan, in what we have to do, and I believe in the people who will carry it out. Go write your letter. I won't advertise your views to anyone else. This command requires unity of purpose right now, and you'll understand if I don't air your concerns. But you'll be on record. I'll respond with a letter of my own. You already know what it's going to say."

"That is certainly acceptable, sir. I hope to God I am wrong. But I would not be doing my duty if I did not share my doubts. May I take my leave, sir?"

"Fine. Get some sleep. While you're at it, get some for me."

Leigh-Mallory moved out of the tent. Eisenhower lowered his head and held the cloth against his eye. The greatest amphibious operation in history, he thought, and I have generals who care first and foremost about covering their asses. The rain was falling harder now, a rattle on the tent. He heard a low voice outside, knew it too well.

"What the hell do you want, Harry?"

Butcher appeared, wearing a raincoat, dripping wet. "Sorry, Chief. Just got back. Couldn't help hearing the hubbub in here. I kept the guards at a distance, thought you'd not want anyone to hear what you were saying. I spoke to the air marshal briefly, but he's gone now. How's the eye?"

"Forget the damned eye. I was that loud?"

"Afraid so. I'm sure the air marshal had it coming. No one around here cares much for that man."

"I'm not sure he had it coming at all. He has doubts and felt he should let me know. His timing wasn't the best. Guess I blew up at him."

"Well, Chief, you might blow up at this too."

Eisenhower set the cloth aside, looked up at Butcher, saw a scowl. Unusual, he thought. Has everybody around here forgotten how to smile?

"What's happened now?"

"Uh . . . it seems a London newspaper has a crossword puzzle, pretty popular actually."

"What the hell are you talking about?"

"Yesterday, one of the answers—uh, fourteen down—was OVERLORD."

Eisenhower felt a stab of cold. *"What?"*

"Might not mean anything, Chief. It didn't say *code name for the Allied invasion of Europe,* nothing like that. Just the actual meaning of the term. Could be a coincidence. An amazingly bad coincidence."

Eisenhower felt for the pillow, lay back on the narrow bed. "Or some code sent to German agents." He put his hands across his chest—could feel his heart beating—and closed his eyes. "So, do we start arresting newspaper editors as spies?"

"It could be nothing, Chief."

"Nothing is *nothing,* Harry. There's meaning in everything that's happening now. I can't even ignore a stupid crossword puzzle. All we can do is hope to God you're right and it's just a coincidence."

"I spoke to some reporters earlier, Chief. Thought you might enjoy this. Word is circulating among the press people that all this talk of invasion is just a hoax."

Eisenhower opened his eyes. "A hoax?"

"That's what they're saying. They think there have been too many hints that something big is up, so they're starting not to believe it."

"Are you telling me that our nose-to-the-ground newspapermen are so bad at their jobs they can't smell all the machinery on this damned island?"

Butcher shrugged. "I heard it first from Howard Whitman. *New York Daily News.* He says word is spreading. Some of 'em figuring we're pouring on the propaganda so Hitler will get scared and give up."

Eisenhower put his hands behind his head and stared up at the canvas above him. "Best news I've heard all day, Harry. If we can keep this big a secret from our own reporters, what chance do the Germans have?"

"Oh, there's one more thing, Chief. The reason I came here in the first place. Sorry."

Eisenhower heard the change in Butcher's voice, more serious now.

"I have a feeling I should sit up."

"I'd stay lying down for this, Chief. I just spoke to Beetle, and he said the prime minister's office has informed us that once you've made your final decision about the timetable for the invasion, we should seriously consider revealing that information to Charles de Gaulle. Beetle says the prime minister thinks there will be some kind of diplomatic stink if the invasion goes off and de Gaulle doesn't know about it in advance. The French have been making noises about de Gaulle flying up to England, to be an active part of whatever plans we're making."

Eisenhower sat up. "An active part? I know what that means, Harry. It means de Gaulle will come waltzing in here and expect to take charge. He's still in Algiers, right?"

"That's what Beetle says."

It was a diplomatic quagmire Eisenhower had tried to avoid since the campaign in North Africa. After the collapse of the French army four years earlier, Charles de Gaulle had anointed himself leader of the Free French struggle against German occupation, first in London and then in his newly established administrative center in Algeria. The self-promotion had come as a surprise to everyone, including many of the French commanders who held station in Algeria. De Gaulle had been a faint blip on the French radar, a low-level general. But the sheer force of his personality and ego had swept most of the remaining French leaders aside, and now his people pulled most of the strings that coordinated the activities of the Maquis, the French underground. For the most part, the Maquis had been effective, a serious thorn in the Germans' side, sabotaging installations, destroying facilities, attacking supply lines and convoys. The Allied planners knew that once the Normandy invasion began, de Gaulle would most likely order the Maquis to launch their own full-scale military campaign throughout occupied France. It was hard to fault French enthusiasm for liberating their own country, but despite de Gaulle's bluster, the Maquis had never been equipped to stand up to German forces. No matter what might happen in Normandy, should the Maquis attempt to confront the Germans face-to-face they would most likely be slaughtered. Eisenhower had successfully convinced several French generals that the Maquis needed to be kept on a leash, but ultimately those men answered to de Gaulle, and no one expected de Gaulle to sit idly by while the Allies invaded *his* country. But regardless of any role the French underground might play, Eisenhower knew that informing de Gaulle of the timetable for Overlord had one serious drawback. Algiers was already well-known as a hotbed of German spy activity, and de Gaulle's own offices were described by Allied intelligence as little more than a wet sponge: Squeeze it and it dripped information.

Eisenhower swung his feet onto the wooden floor of the tent, trying to ignore the itching torment in his eye. "Tell Beetle to contact Churchill directly, and have a cable sent to the president as well. I'm not making any decisions about this without hearing from the top. As far as I'm concerned, de Gaulle can stay put in Algiers, but I know that's not going to fly. If we can hold off giving him any information until the last possible minute, that has to be the best course. I've been avoiding this, but I know damn well that we need him to issue a broadcast to the French people, telling them . . . well, hell, I don't know, telling them to stay calm. How the hell does anybody stay calm when your country's being invaded? But we can't have the underground running all over hell shooting things up, especially anywhere near Normandy. We'll have enough confusion out there as it is. That's all Leigh-Mallory needs to hear, that a bunch of our paratroopers got shot up by trigger-happy Frenchmen. I'm not saying anything to de Gaulle until I get orders. So get me some orders."

"Right away, Chief."

Butcher slipped back outside and Eisenhower stood, energized now, and moved to a small mirror hanging on a tent post above a small washbasin. He leaned close, the eye still bad, and dipped the cloth into the basin. To hell with this, he thought. I've had enough of a nap. He looked again toward the tent flaps, heard the roar of the rain close overhead. Not much of anything is going to matter unless this weather changes. He moved toward the tent flaps, a cold stiff breeze pushing them open, a pool of rainwater spreading out on the wooden floor. Just wonderful, he thought. We have a three-day window to launch this operation. If we don't make that, we're looking at two weeks or longer. To hell with de Gaulle. I can't think about that jackass right now. I have a million men on this island—no, hell, two million—waiting for me to kick this army into gear. And a hundred fifty thousand soldiers who need me to tell them when to oil their rifles and load up their transports. We're one big damned coiled spring, and I'm holding the trigger. He reached for his raincoat. Let's send word to all those damned weathermen, he thought. I need them right next to me. This is May thirty-first. Five days for this mess to move past, and that's it. There's a big beautiful blue sky up there somewhere, and if we don't see some sign of it very soon, we're in serious trouble.

14. EISENHOWER

Churchill chewed furiously on his cigar. "I have extended the invitation for Mr. de Gaulle to return to London. Gave me indigestion, but I did it anyway. I have been assured by the Foreign Office that he will be most willing to record the appropriate message for broadcast. Too many optimists in the Foreign Office. I have my doubts."

Eisenhower said nothing but glanced at Jan Smuts, the South African nodding in agreement.

"General, do you have your own text prepared?" Smuts said. "The wording must be chosen carefully."

"Not yet. I think it should be pretty straightforward, just telling the French people that we're launching a massive military operation to drive the Germans out of their country. I'll leave the embellishments to de Gaulle."

Churchill held the cigar out, examined it with a scowl, spit a small piece of something dark to one side, and stuffed the cigar back into his mouth. "He thinks he's bloody Joan of Arc. Maybe we should round up a few Catholic bishops who are handy with a bonfire."

Eisenhower heard a small chuckle from Smuts. He stared out the large window, a dull haze of fog spreading out on the water, the same gray skies he had cursed for days.

Churchill seemed to follow his gaze, rose, and padded toward the window, his hands resting on his hips. "Not that our own clerics are particularly helpful. You hear about the Archbishop of Canterbury?"

Eisenhower knew what Churchill was referring to, but Smuts said, "My word. You having some sort of row with him? What on earth did you do . . . this time?"

Churchill turned and looked at Smuts with mock annoyance. "You assume it was my fault? Wrong, old chap. The archbishop is a fine man, nothing but good intentions. Unfortunately, those intentions have caused something of a problem. Apparently, someone in our circle of privileged information thought it was acceptable to fill the archbishop in on the date for D-Day. He responded as all good clerics would respond. Thought it would be a jolly swell idea that, with so much at stake, we should designate June fifth as a national day of prayer."

"Not the best idea I ever heard," Eisenhower said. "Might just give the enemy a slight heads-up as to our plans."

Smuts shook his head. "I would say so. Someone . . . er . . . shut him up, as it were?"

Churchill laughed. "Well put, sir. I certainly wouldn't object to anyone offering their prayers at a time like this. After all, if there's a God up there to listen, I would suspect He'd pay a great deal more attention to the archbishop than He would, say, to me. We advised the archbishop to pray all he wants to but, for the time being, to keep it to himself. I phrased it a bit more delicately than that, of course." Churchill turned again toward the window for a silent moment. "Your next weather briefing is . . . when, Ike?"

"Tonight. Group Captain Stagg has been in constant contact with the whole lot of weather experts. I'm going to have them all here, have them speak to me face-to-face. Things are . . . tightening up. They keep telling me weather is *neutral,* as though it absolves them of any responsibility. I corrected that baloney in a hurry. I've drilled it into them how much is riding on what they can tell us. All those boys out in remote weather stations—Nova Scotia, Greenland—they suddenly found out we're looking over their damned shoulders. I want them to get it right."

Churchill turned and looked at him, the man's round shape outlined in the soft glow from the window. "I'm going along, you know."

Eisenhower was confused by the change of topic. "Going along . . . where?"

Churchill held his hands on his hips, his words flowing out in a pronouncement. "The invasion, of course. I insist upon it. I have informed Admiral Ramsay to place me aboard the appropriate vessel. I should like to fire a few rounds into the Jerries myself, once we're in position."

Eisenhower had heard rumors of this but had thought it was Churchill's usual brand of playful humor. But the man seemed serious. "You're not joking."

Churchill seemed bruised. "I am bloody well not joking! I have been looking forward to this for some time! I shall demonstrate to our boys that there is no place we will order them to go that their prime minister will not accompany them. I sense disapproval. Both of you." He motioned toward Smuts. "The field marshal here has been on my backside about this for two days. But I don't care. There are no decisions in my charge that cannot be made aboard ship. By damn, I'm going to watch our boys cross those beaches!"

There was a solid tone of defiance in Churchill's voice, and Eisenhower knew it was not an argument he could win. Churchill turned toward the window again. He seemed to sway, rocking front to back on his feet.

"I should point out to you, Ike, that even the supreme commander of this operation has no authority over the complement of a British naval vessel."

Eisenhower kept his protests quiet. Churchill was far too eloquent. If there was a debate, Eisenhower wouldn't stand a chance.

Within hours after Churchill had left Eisenhower's company, a phone call was made from Eisenhower's headquarters, the case presented, and the decision made by the one authority Churchill could not ignore, the one man who could sway him. Almost immediately, Churchill received a call. The order was firm and direct. King George told his prime minister that if it was too dangerous for the king to accompany his troops, it was too dangerous for Churchill. Despite Churchill's unbounded enthusiasm for the mission, his king instructed him to stay put. It was one more headache put aside, one more battle Eisenhower was thankful he did not have to fight.

SOUTHWICK PARK, NEAR PORTSMOUTH
JUNE 4, 1944

They sat scattered about the large dark room, men in soft chairs or sunk into the wide sofa. To one side, facing the sea, a thick curtain had been drawn over the wide window. Outside, the number of Eisenhower's so-called snowballs had been increased, white-helmeted MPs patrolling the predawn darkness close to the house; farther away, more troops patrolled the lanes and quiet roadways beyond the grounds of the estate. It was a necessary precaution. Word was coming through Ultra intercepts and British intelligence that German agents were on the prowl, seeking to learn where the supreme commander was having his high-level meetings. For the first time he could recall, Eisenhower had ordered his staff to carry sidearms, something no one had objected to.

All eyes were on one single officer, Group Captain Stagg, a grouchy Scot standing in front of a large map, displayed on an easel.

"The weather stations have reported appalling conditions, as far west as Greenland. The cold front is intensifying, and by midnight on June fifth, there will be a significant increase in seas, possibly as high as ten to twelve feet. Winds will reach—well, sirs, they will likely be gale force. Cloud cover will remain heavy. This system has all the signs of a typical December depression."

Eisenhower waited for the others to respond, heard mumbles around the room. Stagg seemed to anticipate the response.

"Yes, I am aware it is June. But the patterns as they are developing are exactly what one would expect to see in this part of the world during winter. I have no better explanation for it."

Eisenhower scanned the faces, Tedder gripping tightly to the ever-present pipe, Montgomery sitting back in his chair, expressionless. Across from Eisenhower, Ramsay and Leigh-Mallory sat side by side on the sofa, arms folded, staring at the weather map, sharing the same gloom.

"If your forecasts are accurate, tactical air operations will not be possible," Leigh-Mallory said.

Tedder nodded, both airmen perfectly aware of what this weather would mean for bomber support. If the bombardiers couldn't see the ground, they couldn't aim at their targets.

"Quite right, I'm afraid," Eisenhower said. "Admiral, what is your appraisal in terms of landing craft?"

Bertram Ramsay, the oldest man in the room, seemed far older now. He shook his head. "Landing craft will suffer severely in those kinds of seas. The response from the enemy's batteries above the beaches will be brutal, since we cannot hope to drop accurate offshore fire on them. Even our largest ships will be inefficient in such rough water. The smaller ships . . . I do not see how any ship can maneuver effectively in those conditions. We could put landing craft on the beaches to some extent, but I'm not certain I would recommend that. There is considerable danger of floundering, and we could lose a sizable percentage of our landing forces before they reached the shallows. Very distressing, if you ask me."

Montgomery stood, moved around behind the map, and leaned in close, Stagg making way for him. Montgomery seemed to scan the map carefully, then turned to the others, crossed his arms in front of his chest.

"Delay is too costly. If we do not put our boys ashore, the entire operation will be jeopardized. Time is critical, gentlemen. We have suffered difficult conditions before, and we can do so again."

Eisenhower felt Montgomery's fiery enthusiasm but knew that no one else in the room shared it. Tedder, who had been silent, spoke next.

"I do not agree. We have some options for this timetable." He looked at Eisenhower and removed the pipe from his mouth. "We have options."

Eisenhower appreciated the man's calm. Tedder, who despised Montgomery, was certainly exercising a major dose of self-control. Eisenhower looked past Stagg and his map toward the other weather experts sitting in scattered chairs against the far wall. "Do you have some estimate of how long these conditions will last?"

Stagg glanced back at the others, and one man spoke up. "Our best estimate, sir, is that this system will be in place for several days. There is a chance the intensity could lessen, but only a chance."

"To answer that question with specifics would make any of us a guesser, sir, not a meteorologist," Stagg said.

Eisenhower felt the others staring at him; no one moved. Montgomery still stood beside the map, and Eisenhower could not ignore him. The man was pulsing with energy. Montgomery said, "I should point out that, even as we speak, a significant portion of the invasion forces have sailed from their ports. We have already put into motion a very large wheel, and to reverse course now would have serious logistical consequences. These plans were decided upon with one very strict eye on the timing of the low tide. If we do not launch this operation within the next seventy-two hours, we will have no alternative but to delay for a fortnight, possibly longer. You are all aware of the risks that will bring. The enemy is no doubt at this moment in full detection of the movement of so many of our ships. No secret can be kept forever, and a delay could very well cost us the element of surprise. The cost to the morale of our army could be catastrophic."

Eisenhower saw a frown on Tedder's face, but the air marshal stayed silent.

"I'm afraid that morale will be the least of our problems if we do not postpone the landings," Eisenhower said. He looked at Ramsay, then Leigh-Mallory, then Tedder, each man returning the gaze. None of them are bellyaching about their authority now, he thought. They've said all they want to say, and this is my decision. He took a long breath, felt a hard churning in his stomach. "I see no alternative. We will postpone D-Day for twenty-four hours. H-Hour will remain the same. We will meet again at four tomorrow morning. Let us pray like mad that these gentlemen will bring us some better news."

SOUTHWICK PARK, NEAR PORTSMOUTH
JUNE 5, 1944

It was barely 4 A.M., and he had already spoken to several of the meteorologists alone, to hear their views untainted by the others. Now they gathered again, the storm above their heads lashing the house with driving rain and furious winds. He knew the weathermen would take a perverse pride in the strength of the blast, the enormous weight of their accurate forecast possibly averting complete disaster to the invasion force. Eisenhower could only assume that the sudden turnabout in plans had been a serious strain on the troops, so many men huddled in tight quarters on the transport ships. Montgomery had been correct that even as their meeting took place on June 4, a great many of the ships from ports farthest from the French coast had already begun their journey. But every ship had been successfully recalled.

Eisenhower glanced at his watch: 4 A.M., every man seated, expectant. "You may begin, Captain. Tell these gentlemen what you told me . . . what all of you told me."

Stagg stood erect beside the map. "As you can tell from the conditions outside, our predictions were on the mark. Though these current conditions are not expected to change a great deal today, it now appears that for June sixth conditions might become more favorable. It will continue to be windy, but not as severe, fewer than twenty knots, and by midday tomorrow there is a chance that even those winds will decrease considerably. The cloud cover will likely lessen somewhat, offering a slightly higher ceiling. Seas will continue to be rough, but not as bad as they are right now. I . . . we are pessimistic that this improvement will last for much more than thirty-six hours. By the seventh, conditions will most likely worsen."

Eisenhower felt the churning in his stomach again, but it was excitement now, the gloom fading from all of them. He clenched his fists and scanned the faces. "Admiral Ramsay, Marshal Leigh-Mallory, your operations are more dependent on weather conditions than the ground forces. I would like your most optimistic opinions."

Leigh-Mallory seemed to share Eisenhower's excitement. "By George, I think we should give this a go. It is a gamble, certainly, and I would rather appreciate these weather chaps offering us a bit more in the way of certainty."

"There is no certainty," Eisenhower said. "Captain Stagg has been very clear, as have they all, that this is, at best, guesswork."

Ramsay rolled his hand into a fist and began to pound the arm of his chair, light hammer blows. "Guesswork be damned. If the air can do it, then, by God, the navy can as well."

Eisenhower looked at Montgomery, who sat back, his arms folded, and said, "You know my position. I have one thought and one thought only. It's time to go."

They were all staring at Eisenhower now, a silent moment, broken by the wind billowing against the house. He thought of Marshall, of Roosevelt; they had put him here for this moment, this one decision. The planning was complete, the maps drawn, the troops as well rehearsed for this operation as any troops could be. Now, the great power of the army was poised in their transport ships, waiting for one order, the order that could be given by no one else.

"All right. It's time to move. D-Day is tomorrow, June sixth. H-Hour for the five beaches is unchanged. I have been informed that the Archbishop of Canterbury has offered to lead us all in prayer. I think you weather boys would agree: That's a fine idea."

NEAR PORTSMOUTH
JUNE 5, 1944

De Gaulle had come, finally, and the anticipated diplomatic flap had been perfectly realized. Eisenhower had accepted Churchill's logic that the French only be informed that the operation was set to begin, no more than that. Worse for Eisenhower's own efforts at diplomacy, de Gaulle rejected the request that the two men issue a joint communication to the French people. De Gaulle recognized no one's authority but his own, and he expected the French people to do the same. Regardless of what Eisenhower would broadcast, de Gaulle seemed to want the Maquis to stage an all-out uprising. Eisenhower could only hope that de Gaulle's appeal to French patriotism didn't result in a bloodbath for French civilians.

With so much swirling around him, Eisenhower did not expect that, on the day before the invasion was scheduled to begin, he would receive news from an unexpected source that would inspire every man in the Allied command. Nearly a month before, on May 12, a large-scale operation had begun across the boot of Italy, a bold attempt by Jumbo Wilson, Harold Alexander, and Mark Clark to break the stalemate against Kesselring's stubborn defenses. Finally, after so much effort and so much cost, the city of Rome had been liberated. It was far more of a symbolic victory than a strategic one—Rome itself was never an essential military objective—but the news that Rome was finally in Allied hands was an enormous shot of confidence for everyone at SHAEF. To the Italian people, it was a glimpse of salvation.

HQ 101ST AIRBORNE DIVISION, NEWBURY
JUNE 5, 1944

Eisenhower had toured one of the port facilities, observing masses of troops marching onto the transports, the incredible flow of men and machines boarding naval craft of a variety that amazed him even now. He knew that, far offshore, the minesweepers had begun their work, clearing specified sea lanes of any German explosives. The warships were already steaming toward their designated beaches, battleships, cruisers, and destroyers, the gunners readying themselves for the first bombardment of targets they had seen only on maps or clay models. By now, the infantry and armored troops sealed on board the ships knew something of their missions, details that could not have been revealed before. Their specific missions were passed down from senior officers to their engineers and to their company and platoon commanders. The junior officers in turn would brief their riflemen, radiomen, and medics, tank drivers and gunners, the men whose sole job would be to find their way across the beaches, to confront the enemy any way they could. Among them were American Rangers and British commandos, whose jobs were more specific, targeting the heavier German installations and artillery batteries.

But before any of that would happen, the airborne would have begun their own mission, massive formations of C-47s pushing skyward barely after midnight. With so few hours before it all began, it was the paratroopers Eisenhower had wanted to see, some final word of encouragement for those men who would lead the assault, who would be the first to touch the soil of France.

Butcher rode beside him, the long car rolling over a wide hill, open ground spreading out on all sides. They could see the transport planes now, rows of C-47s, standing in the open, no more camouflage, nothing to hide them or hold them back. From his first weeks in England, Eisenhower had made it a point to visit the troops, touring the various fighting divisions, British, Canadian, and American. His visits were never formal, none of the stiff inspections or speech-filled pep rallies that Patton and Montgomery seemed to prefer. Eisenhower made every effort to speak to the soldiers on their level, hear them voice their views, concerns, opinions. It wasn't completely realistic, of course. No enlisted man could regard the supreme commander as a pal. But now, with the first wave of combat troops already on their transport ships, he felt himself drawn to the airborne, those men whose journey would be the briefest but whose mission might decide the fate of the entire operation.

Eisenhower stared out across the open airfields, couldn't shake Patton from his mind, a conversation he had endured a few days before. Patton was not scheduled to mobilize his newly created Third Army for the trip to France for at least a month, maybe two. He would move into France only when the beachheads had expanded safely inland, when the enemy had been pushed away and was ripe for a hard shocking thrust that might break the Germans altogether. No one disputed that Patton was the most appropriate man for that job, but for now he wore two hats, supervising the training of his Third Army as well as continuing to sit atop the fictitious First Army Group. According to the Ultra intercepts, the Germans had swallowed that bait completely. Fully one-half of Rommel's command, the powerful Fifteenth Army, continued to hold their positions along the coast near the Pas de Calais. The Ultra code breakers had become one of the Allies' most valuable weapons, the Germans still unaware that every detail of their transmissions was being monitored. Ultra was far from perfect, though, and Eisenhower had been frustrated by gaps of information, days passing with no word at all. There were other inefficiencies as well; Eisenhower understood that even such a sophisticated intelligence system was subject to the failings of the humans who operated it. Too often, pertinent messages were not passed along to those who might need them the most. But one message had come through quite clearly. The Germans still believed Pas-de-Calais was the intended landing target.

The car began to slow, a stout wire gate, MPs peering in, well aware he was coming, waving the car past. Eisenhower looked out across the open fields again. He could see the paratroopers gathering near their planes, saw the equipment, bundles of dark canvas, already strapped beneath the wings. The men began to point, expectant, knowing from their officers who their visitor would be. The car stopped and Eisenhower prepared himself, more nervous than he had ever been before.

He had done this so many times, so many soldiers, so many meaningless chats, self-conscious conversation. Every time, the words had come naturally, the simple farewell, appropriate and expected: Good luck!

He realized suddenly, I cannot say that to these men. There is no luck here, no champagne toast to good fortune. Some of these men will die because of the job we need them to do. I have to speak to them, look them in the eye, but I cannot toss them a mindless *good luck*. In the end, whether we win this thing or whether we get our asses shoved into the sea, I owe them more than some meaningless platitude. He paused, paralyzed, his aide standing outside the car door, waiting for his signal to pull it open. Beside him, Butcher waited as well, to let Eisenhower be first out of the car.

"These men . . . they're jumping into France tonight, Harry. What do I say to them?"

Butcher hesitated, then said, "Tell them you're proud of them, Chief. Tell them . . . they're the best soldiers in the world."

"Is that true? Are they?"

"Doesn't matter, Chief. As long as *they* believe it."

15. ROMMEL

JUNE 3, 1944

Despite continuing assurances that the Allied attack would come ashore at Calais, Rommel understood that his preparations must allow for every contingency, every threat. There were a great many possibilities, and Rommel knew that secondary attacks could follow at several locations within his sphere of authority, including the Cotentin Peninsula, Brittany, and the ports of Cherbourg and Antwerp. Rommel thought that the ports themselves were unlikely targets, far too fortified against an amphibious attack, far too protected from a paratroop assault from behind. If the enemy was to put an army ashore, Rommel believed they would most likely choose one of several stretches of open beach. Though Hitler claimed to support Rommel's efforts along the entire Atlantic Wall, it was clear to Rommel that Hitler believed the Allies would strike at the cities themselves. Despite Rommel's attempts at persuasion, Hitler insisted that any invasion would immediately require the enemy to capture a major port, through which they could funnel supplies. Rommel tried to ignore Hitler's second-guessing of every command decision and pushed harder along the coast for the work to continue. There were renewed efforts to extend the beach barricades, to mine the passageways inland, to improve artillery bunkers and gun emplacements. Strategically, there had been no change in the disagreements between Rommel and the others, so Rommel had to make do with the resources he had been given. He had faith in his men and utter confidence as to how the enemy should be confronted, but again, as in North Africa, his power had been drained away by the inability or un-willingness of his superiors to see things his way and to provide the sup-plies and troops he needed to get the job done.

As much as he counted on the fighting spirit of his soldiers, Rommel had become alarmed by the ongoing flow of invalid troops pouring in from the Russian front, often ending up as replacements for healthier men, who were abruptly pulled away from his infantry. It was maddening that the High Command had no hesitation about draining the best manpower from France, so that Hitler could feed the great gaping disaster to the east. It was small comfort to those troops headed east that the dismal reports from Russia had grown less urgent, reflecting a lull of sorts. Throughout the spring there had as yet been no major attacks by either side, but Rom-mel knew, as did they all, that with summer the Russians would certainly launch another offensive. It was simple and straightforward strategy. Rus-sia was another of the Allies, after all, and it made perfect sense to Rommel that the Russians would support an Allied invasion by opening a new cam-paign of their own, holding German troops in the east to prevent Hitler from shifting strength to France.

Rommel also understood that he could expect no reinforcements from Italy. Kesselring's army had been weakened so much that the only way he could prevent an all-out disaster was to make a slow fighting withdrawal, using the natural defensive barriers provided by the Italian countryside. The best Kesselring could accomplish in that kind of campaign was to in-flict a bloody price on the Allies for every sliver of territory they gained. Ultimately, the outcome was predictable. There were no illusions in Berlin that Italy would somehow be swept clear of Allied forces; even Kesselring knew he was being given low priority by the German High Command.

Throughout France, the Allied bombers had intensified their attacks, striking hard at railways and supply terminals. At first, Rommel had been mystified by the randomness of the attacks, but as more and more valuable transportation links were obliterated, the tactic made sense. Though the targets were scattered throughout northern France, they all had one thing in common: Every one was an avenue, a means to transport crucial supplies to the German forces who would confront the invasion. As the number of bombing raids increased, Rommel understood exactly what the Allies were doing. However, there was no discernible pattern to the strikes, no hint that the bombing campaign was designed to give support to one invasion site or another. Rommel was still confident that the landings were coming at Calais, and nearly every German general in the theater agreed with that. But Hitler had surprised them all. Despite the pure logic of an attack at Calais, and despite intelligence data confirming that location, Hitler suddenly announced that the attack was certain to come in the Cotentin Peninsula, most likely at the beaches along the northern Normandy coast. Rommel was surprised by Hitler's sudden change of heart, and nearly every high-ranking commander continued quietly to believe Calais was the place. Though Rommel had already done much to prepare the Normandy beaches, and the hedgerow country inland was bristling with German defenses, Rommel had responded to Hitler's new concerns. The construction and placement of barriers was increased as much as possible, and once again Rommel made inspection trips to the outposts and fortifications that faced the sea.

NEAR COLLEVILLE-SUR-MER
JUNE 3, 1944

He rode with Ruge, the two men passing between heavy rows of tall dense brush, the same bocage country he had driven through a dozen times before. The car bounced hard, splashing into deep pools of muddy water, the rain incessant, turning many of the farm roads into soft ooze. He stared to the side, searching the occasional gaps in the brush for a glimpse of the larger fields. Along many of the hedgerows, his men had dug deep trenches and placed heavily disguised machine-gun nests and mortar positions. Out in the open fields, more men continued to plant the upright poles, his asparagus, the men then connecting them together with long clotheslines of steel wire. To add to their effectiveness, Rommel had requested that the ordnance depots furnish him with a supply of otherwise useless artillery shells, even obsolete calibers, and captured French munitions, anything that still had the ability to explode on contact. For an incoming glider or other small aircraft, the asparagus would be made even more deadly by attaching an artillery shell to the pole, the tip protruding upward, so anything descending onto it would detonate the explosive. But no one in the ordnance sections seemed to take him seriously, so the shells were slow in coming. It was one more frustration. Rommel knew that thousands of tons of French ammunition had been captured in the campaigns of 1940, piled uselessly in some warehouse or stacked in some long-forgotten supply dump. Every time it rains like this, he thought, the shells rust a little more, deteriorate a little more, when I could be putting them to marvelous use right here. Idiots.

They continued to move past his troops, some stopping their work to stare and wave, others saluting, officers mostly, men who recognized the pair of armored staff cars. They passed again into a narrow ribbon of road-way, squeezed on both sides by the wetness, the dark dense hedges. Rommel wiped a coat sleeve on the foggy glass of the car's window and stared into the brush: nothing to see, no sign that on the far side his men were making all manner of preparation for an enemy they might never see. The rain seemed to slow, and after a long moment, the hedgerow to one side fell away. The field beyond was revealed, a small green rectangle, and Rommel was surprised to see a single farmer standing among a scattering of cows. The man waved, oblivious to the weather, a casual show of cordiality. It was no surprise, most of the French farmers seeming not to care what was happening around them as long as the Germans did not interfere with what Rommel had to believe were excruciatingly boring lives. The car slowed and Rommel looked forward; the road ahead was partially blocked by a team of four horses and a carriage, towing something Rommel could not see.

Ruge said, "Those are our troops. What are they doing?"

"Sergeant Daniel, halt the car."

The man obeyed silently, the vehicle rolling to a stop. Behind him, the second staff car did the same, both easing slightly to the side of the narrow road. The horses plodded forward, just in front of them now, and Rommel could see that Ruge was right: two German soldiers huddled in rain gear, up on the seat of a small farm carriage, one man holding the reins. The men seemed to recognize him and pulled up sharply, halting the horses. Both men stood up high on the jostling carriage and saluted, unsmiling. Rommel opened the car door and stepped out toward them, catching the musky smell of wet horses. Behind the carriage trailed a decrepit artillery piece, which he stared at for a brief moment, mystified, unable to identify it. It was like no cannon he had ever seen.

The men held their salute, the horses jerking them slightly, and Rommel said, "You may be at ease. There is no need for you to fall off that thing and break your necks. What is your unit?"

One man spoke, a sergeant. "Division Seven-oh-nine, Field Marshal. Reserve artillery battalion."

Rommel continued to stare at the cannon they were towing. "What in God's name is that?"

The sergeant kept his gaze to the front. "That is a one-hundred-millimeter artillery piece, sir."

Rommel saw rust stains, a wet barrel green with corrosion, rubber tires barely in evidence.

"*Whose* artillery piece? We don't make a one-hundred-millimeter gun! Where did you get it?"

The man seemed to relax a bit. "Forgive me, sir, but it is definitely ours now. It is Czechoslovakian. We have a few more like it. Also, they have sent us pieces from Romania, Greece, and of course Russia, sir."

The man seemed surprisingly proud.

"*They?* Who? Ordnance supply?"

"Yes, sir."

Rommel stared at the cannon. "Have you fired it?"

"Um—well, no, sir. The ammunition has not yet arrived. Captain Riese said to expect it at any time."

Rommel heard Ruge emerge, saw him squeezing along the wet hedgerow on the far side of the car, also fixated on the odd cannon.

Rommel pointed down the road and said to the soldiers, "You may proceed."

Both soldiers stiffened as well as the moving carriage would allow, saluted him, and said in unison, *"Heil Hitler!"*

Ruge responded with the straight-armed salute, Rommel holding up his hand. The carriage moved away now, the horses' hooves splashing through more of the puddles. Ruge laughed.

"I admit I don't know much about field artillery, but that appeared to be an antique. Where did they find it?"

Rommel leaned against the hood of the car. "They didn't find it, they were *issued* it. It will most likely explode in their faces, if they ever get a shell that will fit the damned thing. It seems that, on top of every other war I must wage with the supply people, I must accept that they have provided us a veritable museum of artillery pieces." He paused and shook his head. "Does no one understand that we are fighting a war here?"

"Fine horses, I thought," Ruge said. "Don't know much about those either, I suppose. Not many horses in the navy."

Rommel knew Ruge well, knew it was his way of taking Rommel's mind away from the daily aggravations they confronted on every inspection. It had not even occurred to Rommel to think about the horses, something he was growing accustomed to now. All along the coastal defenses, the poor quality of so many of the troops had been equaled by the quality of their transportation. Trucks were becoming far too scarce. There were shortages of gasoline and oil, tires, and spare parts. Now, a sizable percentage of the German supplies and even the men themselves were being transported by horse cart.

He heard the familiar drone, glanced skyward. "Another bombing raid. That's the reason, you know. It must be better weather inland. The enemy has targeted our factories back home too often; now they are hitting us in France as well, rail centers and bridges. The raids have grown more frequent. It is logical, of course, just one more piece of the puzzle. It is the preparation for their assault."

Ruge stared up too. "I spoke to General Sperrle in Paris yesterday. He says our fighter planes have taken an enormous toll of the enemy's bombers. He insists the raids will soon stop because the Luftwaffe has made it too costly for the enemy to continue them."

Rommel sniffed, staring up into the thick gray sky. "And yet there they go. Who would you believe? General Sperrle is Göring's man, and he will only say what Göring tells him to say. It is daylight, so those are American bombers. Tonight it will be the British, like clockwork. And no matter their targets, we cannot stop them. And out here in the mud, our most powerful army, the most modern army in the world, is issuing its men artillery pieces suitable for the Crimean War, drawn by horses we have no doubt stolen from French farmers. You may believe Sperrle if you wish. I believe what I see and what I hear above those clouds."

CHÂTEAU LA ROCHE-GUYON
JUNE 4, 1944

The rain was steady, soaking the gardens, keeping the groundskeepers out of sight. It had come again during the night, and he welcomed the chance to stay indoors. There were disadvantages to the bad weather of course, so much more difficult for the teams of construction workers to do their jobs. But they will work still, he thought. A man can still sweat in the rain. What no one can do is drop bombs on a target you cannot see.

Speidel sat on the far side of the desk, making lists on a pad of the officers Rommel had not visited in a while, places where inspections were a high priority. The room was mostly silent, just Speidel's pen on the pad and the soft feathery brush of rain on the windows.

Rommel put his hands on the glass, wiped at the cold film of moisture, rubbed the wetness between his fingers. For the first time in many days, the pains were not with him, his mood buoyed by reports he had seen from the weather stations. This rain would continue, possibly several days if not longer, gloomy patterns of rain, fog, and dense cloud cover that had surprised the experts, a weather front rolling across the Atlantic seemingly more suited to winter than late spring. Even better, along with the rains, the weathermen had reported that the tides along the beaches were wrong for any kind of amphibious landings. Rommel agreed with von Rundstedt—with all of them—that when the Allies came they would most certainly come at high tide, the high water allowing landing craft to deposit their troops closer to the enemy they would have to combat. It was precisely the reason he had built the beach barriers as he had, to be hidden in high water, so the enemy's boats would be struck and ripped from below. A landing at low tide simply made no sense, especially along the shallow coastline of northern France. Low tide meant several hundred yards of flat open sand, a far more deadly obstacle for infantry to confront and a perfect shooting gallery for Rommel's riflemen and machine gunners.

Despite the misery the weather inflicted on his troops, there were those who loved the rain—French farmers, certainly, anxious that their fields be lush and green—and on this day Rommel shared their joy. He continued to stare out the tall window, an unusual peacefulness in his mind. He could see bits of the building around him, marveled at the architecture, tried to imagine when it had been built, the craft, the labor required to bring to life this medieval castle on the Seine. He locked his hands behind his back, rocked slowly on his heels, enjoyed the gray gloom that blanketed the sky, and thought, Thank you, thank you.

"I have never seen such beauty in bad weather, Hans."

"Sir?"

"Rain, Hans! There could be days and days of rain! Weeks, perhaps. Surely, you know what this means."

Speidel smiled, resumed his work. "Yes, sir. It means we can get some work done here."

Rommel turned to him. "You know as well as I do that it means much more than that. We have been given a reprieve. Right now, while I am enjoying the pure serenity of this day, across the English Channel, someone else is looking out at this sky and cursing his poor fortune. Our work can go on, yes, be certain of that, but over there, no matter their planning and their timetables, no one is about to launch an amphibious assault—or any kind of assault at all. It is the gift of time, Hans, the one gift I have asked for. We are stronger every day, and the more the enemy must delay, the more it will cost him."

He moved to his desk, opened a small notebook, flipped a page, smiled.

"This could be perfect timing, perfect. This will please her enormously."

"Sir?"

"Put that paperwork aside for the moment. I want you to arrange a trip for me. Official business, of course. With the weather this poor, I will take the opportunity to visit the Führer to discuss our progress. He continues to send me his heartiest compliments on our work here, so perhaps this time I can make use of his good spirits to convince him to listen to my strategies. But I want you to schedule the transportation to allow me a couple days in Herrlingen. I can leave even today. The Führer is presently at Berchtesgaden, which is but a short journey from my home. Yes, she will be greatly surprised and greatly pleased if I am there. This weather has opened the door. It is perfect timing."

"If I may ask, sir, is it a special occasion?"

"Quite special. I have been instructed not to reveal this, you understand."

Speidel smiled. "Anniversary, sir?"

"Not quite. Lucie is turning fifty. Her birthday is only two days away, on June sixth."

16. ADAMS

The day had passed with painful slowness, the natural letdown from so much adrenaline the night before. It was every veteran's nightmare, that once the call came, you geared yourself into that mindless mode, moving with precision, relying on the automatic memory from so much training, from having done it all before. But then the mission had been aborted. He had climbed out of the C-47 in a haze of despair, cursing as they all cursed, but the weather had turned truly awful, a hard blowing rain that soaked them through their jumpsuits.

The officers had hustled them quickly into the hangars, most of the men sleeping right there, on a vast sea of cots that had been set up days before. Spanhoe was the home for the 315th Troop Carrier Group, one part of the enormous armada of transports that would ferry the paratroopers and gliders into France. The paratroopers of the 505th had been hauled company by company to Spanhoe, one of several airfields where the C-47s would begin the mission, but this one was nothing like Adams had seen before. There were no sleeping quarters, no mess hall. What barracks there were at Spanhoe were already occupied by the huge number of ground and flight crews, so the paratroopers had slept in the hangars. The men groused, but only for a while, their attention caught more by the vast parade of C-47s that continued to land, coming in from airfields throughout England, great flocks of green birds, gathering in long rows along the various landing strips.

Their briefings had been more intimate this time, down to the company and platoon level, senior officers passing along detailed instructions to their subordinates, junior officers passing those details to the noncoms. Captain Scofield had gathered his company's lieutenants and noncoms into a cramped recreation room, the first time since Adams had served on Gavin's staff that he had been privy to a map of their part of the operation. It was the familiar shape of the Cotentin Peninsula, but now the map was marked in red: the angular, circuitous routes the transports would fly to sweep into France from the west, which Adams thought was someone's very good idea, staying far away from the naval ships along the invasion beaches. There were circles on the map as well, the drop zones, inland from where the American Fourth Division would push ashore, at the place someone had named Utah Beach.

Adams had seen these kinds of maps a year before, drop zones neatly circled on the maps of Sicily. Then, the perfectly precise plans on paper had become a disastrous comedy of bad weather and inept flying, green pilots scattering their paratroopers over a sixty mile swath of Sicilian countryside. But the paratroopers, led by men like Jim Gavin, had turned the disaster into victory: They had held the immense power of German armor back away from those landing beaches, allowing the infantry to come ashore and establish the critical beachheads. Now, the paratroopers had been asked to do it again, but this time, the numbers were immense. Instead of the three thousand who had made the first drop in Sicily, in Normandy the Americans would drop fourteen thousand men, two full divisions. Whether or not the pilots would do a better job of finding the drop zones was a question Adams tried not to think about.

The night before, they had gone through their usual preparation, blackening their faces and loading themselves down with more than a hundred pounds of equipment, from weapons to toilet paper. But first there had been another custom to observe: the evening meal, a spectacular bounty of fried chicken and gravy, fresh vegetables, and mashed potatoes that Adams swore had been drenched in butter, one of the rarest

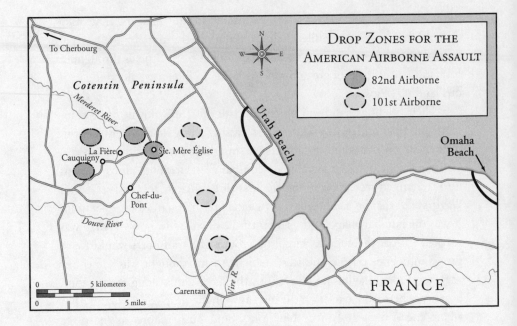

commodities of the war. The jokes had come, of course, their Last Supper, a final display of gratitude for men who were to begin an operation that would take them far from any kind of comforts.

When word came that the mission had been postponed, the mess officers had been as surprised as everyone else, and so one day later there was one more Last Supper, a chaotic affair tossed together by kitchen staffers at Spanhoe who scrambled and scrounged to find something for these two thousand men to eat, men who weren't supposed to be there. Stew, Adams thought. That's what they called it. They said it was beef, but who the hell knew? He rubbed a hand on his stomach, felt a rumble, but he couldn't fault the mess staff. I felt the same way last night, and it wasn't because I ate too much fried chicken. Nobody's guts are working too well right now.

"Line up here! If you can haul it, you need it!"

The men obeyed, Adams bringing up the rear of the line. In front of him, men pushed past tables and crates, loading up their pockets and belts, no one speaking except the ground crews, low voices, casual greetings, useless words of encouragement. The crews were handing out ammunition, grenades, and all the rest of the cumbersome gear the men would carry.

There was no talking, none of the raucous kidding around, much of that exhausted the night before. The first time, it had been something of a ridiculous party, so many frayed nerves betrayed by bad jokes and off-key singing, especially the new men, but tonight even they were quiet, absorbing the urgency and the fear. There had been some effort to get a card game going, but no one had enthusiasm for it, the poker players seeming to understand that luck was something best saved for what might happen in the morning.

The men were making slow progress in front of him, but Adams wouldn't be impatient, wouldn't gripe at anyone. Then, off to one side, he suddenly heard a voice, one man singing.

"Give me some men who are stout-hearted men,
who will fight for the right they adore.
Start me with ten who are stout-hearted men,
and I'll soon give you ten thousand mo-ore!"

Around him, his own men responded with puzzled annoyance, and Adams said aloud, "What the hell?"

He saw the singer now, slapping his buddies on the back, encouraging them to join in with him, some feeble voices rising, but not many.

"He's trying to organize a full-blown glee club," Adams said, to no one in particular. "Somebody needs to stuff a sock in his mouth. He must be one of the *brave ones,* all puffed up. Jackass."

The man gave up his efforts, no one in his squad seeming interested in his one-man attempt to rally their patriotic energy. In front of Adams, the men continued to press forward along the tables and crates of equipment, the only sounds the clanking of metal, equipment fastened and hooked and lashed to each man's jumpsuit. Adams looked out across the field, surprised he could still see, the darkness not yet complete. It was strange, something to do with British Double Summer Time, some odd way the British had of adjusting their clocks to make better use of daylight. Adams had never completely understood that; time was time. He looked at his watch. This late, it ought to be dark, he thought. I guess it makes sense to somebody who's smarter than I am. That's why I'm just a sergeant. He was suddenly aware of a voice tripping through his brain:

Give me some men who are stout-hearted men . . .

Oh, for God's sake! That idiot has me singing his damned song. Think of something else. What, another song? He tried to silence the music, then thought, No, just let it go. You have enough to think about. He ran a hand over the Thompson hanging off his shoulder. Think about that. Grab a ton of ammo. These guys think they need rations more than anything else. He called out ahead.

"All right, you morons. Fewer chocolate bars and more grenades. If you think it's too heavy, it's not. The army's not going to run out of this stuff."

Shoulder to shoulder, and bolder and bolder . . .

Dammit! Shut the hell up! If that jerk had been one of my guys, I'd stick a grenade in his jumpsuit. Ten thousand men! That's how many Krauts are waiting for us, at least. I wonder if the jackass who wrote the song thought of that.

"Keep moving!"

The words came from in front of him, Lieutenant Pullman, grim-faced, standing at one end of a large wooden box. Pullman would be jump-master of Adams's plane, the last man out. Adams would be crew chief, an unusual role for him. The crew chief was the last man to board the plane, stayed close to the wide doorway, and so would be the first man to jump. Adams wasn't used to that, was far more experienced being the thorn in the side of the hesitant jumpers, coming up from behind, pushing the man out the opening who might not be so eager to make the jump or, worse, yank-ing the man back, out of the way of the others. In training, if a man wouldn't go, you could urge him, prod him, yell at him, but ultimately no one was forced to jump. This time, there would be no one returning home with the plane. In combat, there was a different kind of urgency, the power of the entire stick overwhelming any one man's fear. If anyone froze, the surge of men behind him would solve the problem; no matter what terrors filled a man's thoughts, he would find himself rammed out through the door, his chute yanked open automatically by the static line above his head. Adams had seen it before, that strange paralysis that could infect even experienced jumpers, men who would suddenly lose their nerve. Adams scanned the men around him. That wouldn't be a problem, not with this bunch. He had an instinct for those men, one reason he had become such a good jumpmaster. You can tell who the problems are likely to be, he thought. Sometimes it's the quiet ones, but mostly it's the loudmouths, men like Marley. But he'll be okay, they'll all be okay tonight. He rubbed his stomach again, could taste the stew in his throat, cursed to himself. I hope that was beef. Damned English farmers. He recalled a lesson from Fort Benning, drilled into him from some textbook: *The anticipation of combat is far worse than the combat itself.*

That's a crock, but most of these boys don't know that yet. Scared is healthy, means you're paying attention. But nothing prepares a man for what he'll see on the ground. How many of these loudmouths know what they'll do when they see a Kraut pointing a bayonet at them? Like that moron over there, with his damned song?

And I'll soon give you ten thousand mo-ore. . . .

Dammit! That's what we should do: Sing that to the Krauts. Win the war by driving them nuts.

He reached the tables, looked at Pullman, could see the lieutenant sweating in the chill, making anxious motions with his hands. Pullman pointed into the crate closest to him.

"Grab a couple of these, Sergeant. Gammon grenades. Most of the men have no idea how to use the things, but I want you to carry them. We might run into some armor."

The grenades looked like bundles of socks, small black wads of cloth stuffed with pliable bricks of plastic explosive. To one side, Adams heard a voice: Marley, the big man already loaded up with a mountain of gear.

"Hey, Sarge, you ever use that stuff before?"

Adams stuffed one in a pocket on his pants leg. "Nope. Didn't have them in Sicily. You saw a tank, you either fired a bazooka or ran like hell. We did a little of both."

"You think we're gonna run into tanks, Sarge?"

Marley had lowered his voice, and Adams realized it was a serious question, the joking bluster of the man erased by the mood of the men around him. The lieutenant responded.

"We might, Private. If we do, these Gammon grenades are made to stick to their bellies."

"Sir, you mean . . . under? How do you get under a tank?"

Adams moved past Marley toward a box of magazines, ammunition for his Thompson.

Pullman said, "You let them come to you. If you're in a foxhole, they'll drive right over you. You just stay put and jab that thing up into the tank as it passes. It's supposed to wedge into whatever crack you can find."

Straight out of a training manual, Adams thought. He tried to respect Pullman, but the man had never seen combat. Adams had been in that exact situation in Sicily, a massive Tiger tank rolling up a hillside directly over a narrow foxhole. Then there were no Gammon grenades, nothing to stop the great steel monster. The only weapon was the bazooka, something most of the men had never fired or, worse, had never even seen. He glanced back at Pullman, saw him talking to Marley still, the tall heavy private seemingly eager to learn what he should already have learned in training. He can't have forgotten all that, he thought. No, he's just scared to death. Chattering. Maybe the lieutenant too. I wonder what either one of them will do if a tank drives over him?

He grabbed more of the magazines, stuffed a baggy pants pocket, moved along the rows of equipment, a routine he had repeated often. He wore the standard jumpsuit, heavy and stiff, the cloth impregnated with some kind of odd stinking chemical. It was said to prevent gas poisoning, though no one seemed to know how their jumpsuit would keep gas from finding its way inside. A gas mask was more comforting protection, and he hooked one to the pistol belt at his waist. The belt was a strap of thick canvas with eyelets that served as a tool belt for much of his equipment. The belt already held a .45-caliber pistol, and Adams had held on to his beloved Thompson submachine gun, even though most of the men now carried the M-1 Garand rifle. The M-1 could be broken down into pieces for the jump, the pieces held together in a tight cloth sack. That was one part of the training drilled into the men with as much precision as the jump itself: The M-1 could be assembled by every one of them in blind darkness.

Adams picked up a small hinged shovel and a canteen, already full of water, and hooked them to his belt alongside a small med kit. One of the crewmen handed him a soft cloth bag, issued one per man, packed with clean socks, a compass, rations, toothbrush, a small bar of soap, a safety razor. The bag also contained cigarettes, a thin billfold with some unknown amount of French currency, and water purification tablets. Adams chose a knife from several in a heavy wood box. He weighed one in his hand, felt the thick canvas scabbard, knew they were all the same, that no matter how sharp it might be, he would sharpen it anyway. He strapped that to a pants leg; easier access, should he need to cut his straps. That was every man's nightmare, his chute hanging him on some obstruction, a tree perhaps, high off the ground. Adams straightened his back, adjusting himself to the weight of the gear. Now it was time for the parachute, and he saw the shrinking pile of dark green bundles, the name tags, spotted the one marked with his particular drawing, black chevrons, his rank, easy to spot. He slid the chute up on his back, tightened the belly strap, reached for the straps under his crotch. Someone was helping him from behind now, the usual routine, and he said, "Thanks."

The man moved past him, toward the pile of reserve chutes, and Adams saw it was Unger. "Here you go, Sarge. Any particular one you want?"

The reserve chutes were more anonymous. Adams pointed. "Pick one that will open. Shouldn't need the damned thing anyway."

"I'm happy to have mine, Sarge. You never know. You gonna carry a Mae West?"

"We all carry a Mae West. You heard the orders. We're flying over water."

"Yeah, I know. Awful heavy, though."

Adams hooked the reserve chute at his chest and attached it to D rings from the main parachute pack. Unger was holding two Mae Wests, inflatable life vests, and Adams could see that Unger was fully loaded, was struggling to stay upright.

"How much longer we have to wait, Sarge?"

Adams took one of the life vests and clamped it under his arm. "No idea. They tell us to board up, then we'll know."

"You scared, Sarge?"

"Damned right. You know better than to ask that."

"Yeah, I guess so." Unger leaned closer to Adams, discreet. "Some of these boys, they talk a good game. Not so sure I believe all that rah-rah stuff. I heard Marley say he can't wait to get his hands on some French girl. Says they do things . . . well, *things.*"

Adams saw Marley to one side, still talking to the lieutenant. "You remember all the things those Sicilian girls did to you?"

Unger seemed mystified. "Uh, no, Sarge. Mostly they just waved as we went by."

"Right. I'm guessing the French girls are about as mysterious as that."

Unger laughed, surprising him. "That's a relief, Sarge. I wasn't sure how I'd . . . do that."

Adams shifted the weight of the pack, felt the gear dragging him down, an ache in his legs. Unger was still struggling to stand. Damn you, Adams thought, you ought to be dressing up to go to a prom.

"Let's move over there, take a load off. I need to sharpen this knife."

Unger followed him to a thick bundle. Adams knew they wouldn't sit for long, the ground crew would soon attach their seat to the underside of a wing. The bundles were like fat green sausages, holding more gear— bazookas, radios, or heavy machine guns. He sat, Unger beside him, both men staring out through the dimming light. Adams pulled the knife from its scabbard and slid the blade along a sharpening stone, something he always carried in a pants pocket. Around him, many of the men were doing as he did, some cleaning their already cleaned rifles, some examining the clips for their M-1s.

"You glad you signed up, Sarge? Would you do it again?"

Adams didn't want this conversation, but he couldn't avoid an affection for Unger, wide-eyed innocence, boyish stupidity.

"What do you think?"

"I figured you'd always be in charge here. I hated it when you got called away by General Gavin. Some of the guys said you'd never come back, that they'd make you an officer and you'd end up getting fat behind a desk. I told 'em you'd be back. I kinda expected you to be a lieutenant though."

"I like the stripes. If I was an officer, I couldn't bust you in the chops when you got out of line." He felt stupid making that kind of threat to Unger. The kid had never been a problem at all. He slid the knife blade along the stone, slow, even strokes. He glanced at the young man's smooth skin, almost no sign of a beard. He was curious now. "What about you? What made you want to jump out of a plane?"

"I didn't, Sarge. I'd never even seen a plane, except in Des Moines, at a big carnival. Everybody was all excited, said Amelia Earhart was coming. I saw the airplane, but that's about it. Didn't find out until later who she was." He paused. "I was drafted into the Fourth Division, those guys that are supposed to land on Utah Beach. We didn't know anything about that, not back then. One day a captain comes into the company mess, and I hear him say something about volunteering to become a *pair of troops*. A lot of the guys were cussing about that, and I thought that was pretty unsociable. Made me ashamed that my company was being rude to some captain we didn't even know. So I raised my hand, and the captain came toward me, patted me on the back, told the rest of the guys I was a good example. I thought that was all right, being a good example. Before that, nobody ever noticed me."

Adams lowered the knife—couldn't help a laugh—looked at Unger, and said, "A *pair of troops*?"

"Uh, well, yeah. I thought that's what he said. Sounded good to me, that I'd be teamed up with a buddy, might learn to be a better soldier by being in pairs. So, next thing I know I'm at Fort Benning, and the first couple days I keep asking who I'm being paired up with. Guess that was pretty stupid, huh?"

Adams saw the bright-eyed energy in the boy's face. "Yeah, kid, that was pretty stupid. You *are* a kid too, aren't you? I know it."

He tested the edge of the knife blade with his finger, felt satisfied, slid the knife into the scabbard again. His stomach was rumbling again; he didn't want to talk to Unger now—or to anyone. He stared out across the vast airfield. He had almost never seen so many C-47s in one place, not since before Sicily. He made a rough count: more than a hundred, huddled in neat rows. The body of each plane had been painted with alternating stripes, three white split by two black, to make sure every plane had the same identifying marks. It was someone's solution to the friendly-fire disaster in Sicily, to let the antiaircraft boys know that every Allied plane, whether transport or combat, would carry the same distinct markings. The stripes had been applied only a couple of days before. Adams had watched the crews working with their paintbrushes, had even volunteered his men to help, but there didn't seem to be enough brushes for everyone. It had raised only one question in his mind: Where did they find all that paint?

Adams was jolted by the sounds of jeeps, moving out past the hangars, and felt his heart jump. It was officers, the higher brass, coming to load up with gear of their own. Every one of the commanders would accompany their men, and that applied all the way to the top. In the Eighty-second Airborne, that meant Gavin and Ridgway as well. Adams had heard that Gavin was flying with the 508th, and understood why: Gavin's worry about untested regiments would keep the general close to them. No matter how cocky they might be, having Gavin close by would make them better soldiers. The 505th would be accompanied by its own senior officers, Colonel Ekman of course and the battalion commanders, Kellam, Vandervoort, and Krause. Adams had rarely spoken to any of them, had no reason to go any higher than Captain Scofield, who commanded the company. Most of the other sergeants reported only to their lieutenants, and Adams had no problem dealing with Pullman.

"Hey, Sarge, you heard anything about your brother?"

The question surprised him. "Not lately. Why the hell do you care?"

Unger shrugged. "Just wanted to know. Gotta be tough for your mom, having two sons in the war, scattered all over the earth like this."

"Don't worry about my mom."

Unger focused again on his equipment, and Adams thought of her last few letters, brief, pleasant, to the point. It's just her way, he thought. She writes me like I'm on a camping trip ten miles away. Probably writes the same stuff to Clay. Wonder what he's doing? He's gotta be okay. If something happened to him, the army would tell me that, for sure. Probably knee-deep in some swamp on some island in the middle of the Pacific. Why in hell would you join the Marines? He laughed quietly. Hey, you coulda jumped out of airplanes. Loads more fun.

"I'm sure he'll be okay," Unger said. "I heard that whoever kicks butt first, we'll all join up and finish the job."

"What?"

"Saw it in *Stars and Stripes*. We whip the Japs, those boys will come over here and help us. We get Hitler, we'll go over there and help them. You might see your brother yet, might even fight right beside him."

"You're as stupid as a bag of rocks. My brother's a Marine. Besides, I don't need him anywhere near where I'm fighting. Ever."

"Why? I think it'd be great to fight side by side with your brother. I like having friends in this unit, Sarge. Best friends I've ever had. Even . . . you."

"*Two* bags of rocks. I'm not your friend, Private. I'd expect that from these other idiots, but you're a veteran. You should know better. Don't make friends."

"If you say so, Sarge. But I thought you and Captain Scofield were good buddies. Always seemed that way."

"Check your damned equipment." Adams was annoyed with Unger because he was right. Adams had jumped with Scofield in Sicily and held on to the hope that it would happen again. Ed Scofield was far more than a capable company commander. He was an exceptional soldier, with perfect instincts on the battlefield, and the two men had survived the bloodiest days in Sicily by relying on each other to do the job. It was a dangerous exception to Adams's rule about friendships. Most of the men ignored the wisdom of that rule. There was a natural camaraderie among men who respected one another, a pride in knowing they shared the airborne's unique identity. Adams glanced at Unger. *He should know better, but still he follows me around like a puppy. If we get into some rough stuff, every one of these morons will find out that having your best friend beside you when you're under fire can be a costly mistake.*

Unger, busying himself with a strap on his chest, looked at Adams and smiled, toothy and infectious. Adams looked away. *Damn you! You're just too nice.*

Adams hadn't seen Scofield at all today, nothing unusual. It would take at least ten C-47s to haul just this one company. *I'll find him,* he thought, *somewhere. I think Pullman will do okay, but when we hit the ground, it'll be nice to know there's at least one man who has done this before.*

It was dark now, the distant rows of planes invisible. Close by, the low hum of voices was beginning to intensify, the brutal tension spreading through them all.

"Listen up!"

Adams turned. Pullman was climbing up on a thick bundle nearby. The lieutenant seemed nervous, still sweating in the hard chill, the man's face a soft glowing sheen.

"The crews are coming through with the face paint. Use enough to cover your skin, but save some for the next man. It's the same stuff as last night, greasepaint and burnt cork. It stunk like hell then, so I'm sure tonight it'll be even riper."

Adams saw a paint can appear, moving through the men, each man's fingers spreading the goop on his face. Pullman waited for a moment.

"All right, you remember what we said last night about the call signs? You had damned well better remember. First man says *Flash,* you respond *Thunder.* You got that? Flash and Thunder. I know some of you have heard about the metal crickets. The One-oh-one has been issued these little toys that click. That's fine for them, but General Ridgway has given orders that *we* make use of the call sign. All it takes is one dumb bastard to lose his cricket in the bushes, and instead of clicking the damned thing, he hollers out and draws fire from every Kraut around. I don't know how you got 'em, but I've heard a few of those clicks around here. Fine, I'm not going to search you. You want to carry a damned toy, you go ahead. But if you're near me and you don't use that call sign, I'll shoot you."

Adams scanned the faces, most of them darkened now, and saw one man, large, a beaming smile, holding up his hand, making a small *click-click* sound. Of course, if one jackass among us found a way to get one of those toys, it would be Marley.

The paint can had reached Adams, and he dipped two fingers in and smeared the greasepaint on his face, his nose filling with the smell of the burnt cork. Pullman was not yet through talking, and Adams looked back toward him, as the lieutenant went on.

"I've been ordered to make sure your canteens are filled with water, not beer or booze. Every one of you, open your canteen and let the man next to you have a smell. I'm going to trust you on this one, boys. But if you're stupid enough to carry alcohol instead of water, I don't want you in my platoon. If any of you let your buddy get away with that, just remember, he might be the one watching your back. One more thing. I've been hearing from some of the other officers, a few of them making a big show of telling their men that any one of you who doesn't jump tonight is subject to being shot. This platoon will fill three of these birds, and no one is coming back to England on any of *those*. General Ridgway might think threatening you is a good thing to do, but I won't have to. Because you're all going to jump."

There was a siren, far in the distance, and Adams knew the sound, felt it dig deep in his gut. Pullman eased himself down to the ground and stumbled under the weight of his equipment, two men steadying him. The others fell into line, silent, Adams letting them move past him, bringing up the rear. All across the field, the men were moving out in line, the lieutenants leading them to their planes. He tested himself for the idiotic song, but it had faded away, no sound in his head except the steady tramp of the boots.

They reached their plane, pilots already on board; Adams stepped out of line, moved to the front, and stood beside the door as one of the ground crew folded out a small ladder. The man backed away and Adams watched as the twenty-man stick stepped forward, Pullman in the lead, already at the ladder. The lieutenant reached out, tapped Adams on the arm, no words, and leaned over, put his hands on the deck of the plane, the weight of the gear dragging him down, and with one grunt propelled himself up into the cavernous hole. The others came forward, Adams helping those who needed it, boosting them up under their arms.

Inside the plane, the men were crawling forward, the only way they could move, rolling around into hard seats, pressed tightly together, each one making room for the man beside him. No one spoke, no laughter, no boasting, and Adams looked at each man as he passed, tried to catch the man's eyes, measure him. He saw the corporal, Nusbaum; the new men, Buford and Hovey; and some of the veterans, the small wiry frame of Unger nearly swallowed up by his gear. As Unger climbed into the plane, he said something to Adams, the words lost in the roar of tension in Adams's brain, and he couldn't respond, pushed Unger, a hard boost to help him climb the last step.

There were only a few now, and Adams saw the big man, Marley, leaning low, tugging at his equipment, head down. Adams heard a soft sound and realized Marley was crying. He wouldn't look—the crack in the armor—but cursed to himself: Damn you, there's no time for that! He wanted to shout at the man, but Marley was up and into the plane, the next man past as well, the last one, and now it was only Adams. He took a long breath, felt quivering in his hands, stared up into the plane, dark noises, equipment rustling and knocking, men breathing. He glanced back, across the open ground, silent ground crews attaching the last bundles under the wings. He clenched his hands, tried to stop the shaking, was breathing heavily.

Across the field, the engines began to fire, a growing roar, and he put a hand out against the cold metal of the plane, and put his foot on the bottom step of the ladder. The engines had filled every space in his brain, no room for voices, for music or fears. He looked up, high overhead, and realized the sky had filled with stars. He stared for a brief moment— cold perfection, vast emptiness—then took another breath, touched the Thompson again, pressed one hand against the reserve chute on his chest, and climbed up into the plane.

17. ADAMS

The pathfinders had gone before them, paratroopers armed with beacon lights and Eureka sets, designed to transmit a homing signal for the pilots, and Adams could only hope that those men were better trained and better equipped than they had been in Italy. Then, the technology was brand-new, untested, but it was a vast improvement over what had led the 505th the first time. In Sicily, the C-47s had been guided only by the ability of the flight crews to follow their instructions, searching a stormy darkness for landmarks that might or might not be there at all. Now the electronics would lead the way, but Adams knew that much would still depend on the skill of those pilots to put the pathfinders onto their drop zones with at least some accuracy. Otherwise, the pathfinders themselves would be lost, which would benefit no one at all.

With the pathfinders long on their way, the final order came from SHAEF for the airborne operation to begin. From nine British airfields, more than one thousand C-47s would climb into the sky, filled first with paratroopers, to be followed by hundreds more towing the gliders. When the order came, the first squadrons had gone aloft in slow arching circles, allowing more of their number to join them, gradually coming together into well-rehearsed V formations, three planes each. Each of those then formed larger Vs, and then, larger formations still. Once assembled in the air over southern England, the planes were directed southward, to a rendezvous point over Portland. From there, they would move over open water. As the enormous fleet of aircraft drew near to the island of Guernsey, they would receive a signal, transmitted by a British submarine, which would turn them eastward, on their direct course toward the coastline of the Cotentin Peninsula. Over the water, the planes would maintain an altitude of five hundred feet, but as they neared the coast, they would climb to fifteen hundred, better to avoid whatever antiaircraft batteries would respond to the unending roar of so many engines. Even in the darkness, the sheer number of planes would offer targets for gunners firing blind.

Once they reached the coastline, the planes would rely on the precise timetables the pilots had received, carefully plotted minutes of flying time over the invisible landscape below them. As they drew nearer their drop zones, the planes would descend again, down to five hundred feet, and slow their airspeed by a third, down close to one hundred knots. The slow speed made them exceptionally vulnerable to antiaircraft fire, but it was the only safe way for the paratroopers to make their jumps. Any faster, and the men could be severely injured by the brutal impact of the prop wash as they left the planes. If the pathfinders had been successful, the drop zones themselves would become visible, both electronically and to the eye, strings of blue lights arranged in a T shape.

The pilots would have one last duty to the troops they carried: flash the signal lights on a small electrical panel near the open door at the rear of the plane. The red light came first, alerting them that the jump was imminent. When the pilots were confident they had reached the actual drop zone, they would switch the signal to green. In less than a minute, the planes would empty, and the pilots would continue their course, out over the coastline and back to England. It was a plan that had been drawn up with precision and rehearsed many times over the British countryside. It gave Adams no comfort at all that a few of the rehearsals had actually worked.

For the 82nd Airborne, there would be another challenge that the planners could predict with grim certainty. The transports of the 101st Airborne would lead the way, so when those hundreds of C-47s reached the French coast, they would be a surprise to the enemy below. The men of the 101st would have a few precious seconds to move past the heaviest coastal batteries, before the German gunners could find the range. The planes carrying the 82nd would follow, passing over gunners who were by now fully alerted to the armada of slow lumbering aircraft.

JUNE 6, 1944, 2 A.M.

Adams sat huddled against the rear bulkhead, could not avoid the annoying quiver, the cold seeping into his boots, the numbness in his hands. He stared forward toward the rows of men facing each other in the tight space, knees in as tight as their equipment would allow, no tangling of feet. Far forward, he could see a glimpse of moonlight through the cockpit windshield and nothing else. The instrument panels were lit only by faint specks of red, one more precaution to keep any glimpse of light from escaping the plane.

There were low voices, nervous chatter, but none of the raucous blathering from the training runs. Adams knew that each man, every one of them, was deep into some private place, confronting his own emotions, even the veterans, struggling hard with the unanswerable questions: What would they see, what would the enemy do, and what kind of soldiers would they be? And the question that Adams had asked himself before, the question that drove anxious fear into the new men: When they found the enemy, what then?

The drone of the plane was soothing but no one was asleep. The churning in Adams's stomach was relentless. He tried not to think of the food, that strange unidentifiable stew. Would it matter anyway? You could have had caviar and steak and your gut would still be ripped to pieces. He had never been sick in a plane, but he knew that was no great accomplishment. No one got a medal for having a strong stomach. He had seen it too many times, some of the officers and even the toughest enlisted men losing that battle. Within minutes after they had moved over the water, the plane began to reek of the sour smell, unavoidable, inevitable, and no matter their disgust, no one complained. Every man knew that in the next minute it might be him.

The doorway at the rear of the plane had been closed on takeoff, which contributed mightily to the smells that engulfed them now. Adams had heard it from the pilot, instructions passed down from regimental. The C-47s were more than fully loaded and needed all the aerodynamic help they could get. The bundles under the wings were not only heavy, they provided drag. Adams knew his plane had taken an unusually long time to leave the runway. He didn't object to the door being closed, especially since he was the closest man, and tonight it was too cold for sightseeing.

The plane lurched upward suddenly, climbing, too sharply, the nose falling, then rising again, the tail bucking. Adams felt himself rise up, weightless for a brief second; then he dropped down hard. He cursed out loud, thought of the pilots. Only one of them was familiar, Murdock, a big-talking Texan, who had it fixed in his mind that being a pilot gave him some kind of elite distinction, even among paratroopers, something Murdock made sure no one forgot. Adams adjusted the straps that were crushing his groin, could feel the plane ascending again, at a more reasonable angle, and knew it meant they were approaching the coast. Good. Take it easy, Cowboy. I know you're as scared as the rest of us, but you're not on a damned horse. One of these days, we need to strap a parachute to you and show you what fun is.

He straightened his helmet, adjusted the chin strap, touched the greasepaint on his face, and rubbed it between his fingers: nervous motion. He glanced down, ran his hands over the pockets on his pants legs, stuffed full, and, touching the reserve chute, thought of Unger. You're right, kid, reserve chutes are good. All it takes is one time. The plane leveled out, the ride smoothing, and he felt his nervousness growing. We'll be over the coast pretty soon. He looked toward the others, small movements in the darkness, the glow of moonlight through the windows, thought, Enough of this. I need to see.

He slid closer to the door, gripped the handle, and eased it open a narrow crack, a blast of cold air watering his eyes. The sky was still clear and starry, out to the side he could see the plane closest to his own, one part of their small V. No more than fifty yards separated the wingtips. He strained to see more, pulled the door open farther, and realized the sky around him was a blanket of dull silhouettes, hundreds of C-47s, shadows in the moonlight. My God, he thought, here we are. All of us. He was truly excited now, foolish and childlike. Of course we're all together; it's too soon for us to be lost. His eyes squinted, and he scanned the immense fleet of planes, searching for any details, caught a hint of the black-and-white stripes on the closest ones. There was a flash now, toward the front, and he leaned out slightly, fought to see: streaks of light, bursts of fire. He leaned back from instinct and thought, Yep, that's the coast. The boys in front are attracting some attention. It won't take long, and that'll be us. Close the door, jackass.

He pulled the door almost closed, left a crack, a couple inches of precious fresh air and just a glimpse of the extraordinary sights. The bucking movement of the plane pushed him back into his seat again, and he felt his heart racing, the streaks of light closer, bright bursts, many more, the sounds reaching him, low rumbles. He leaned closer to the door, the blackness erupting into bright light, long snakes of red fire coming skyward, streaking far higher than the plane. He saw the first hint of land, a dull swatch of darkness at the edge of reflected moonlight. The antiaircraft fire was closer now, thunder, another flash, a hard pop in his ears. The plane rolled hard to one side, men falling forward to tumble into the men across from them, shouts and curses. Adams pulled himself up straight, shouted, "Hang on! Sit back!"

But the plane rolled again, and now he saw more flashes, heard an explosion much closer, a shattering rattle against the plane. The men were calling out, terror in some, others trying to calm them. Adams put his hands down beside him, bracing himself, prepared for the next jolt, heard the lieutenant, up front, close to the cockpit.

"At ease! It's flack, antiaircraft fire! Nothing out of the ordinary! Stay calm! We'll be over the zone pretty quick!"

Adams felt a strange sense of confidence from Pullman's words, kept the thought away that this was Pullman's first combat jump. The plane dipped again, and Adams saw the flashes through the crack in the door and cursed himself now. What the hell were you thinking? Close the damned—

The plane rolled over hard again, tossing him to one side, his gear punching him in the side, awakening the sore ribs. The plane straightened again, rolling him back into his seat, and he reacted to the brief calm, reached for the door, gripped the edge to steady himself. The plane was a chorus of sounds, cursing, raw fear, and Adams knew there was nothing he could say to shut them up. There was more of the chattering of shrapnel against the plane, a blast on the far side, and he thought, At least close the damned door! Through the sliver of light, he saw a bright flash, different, gold fire, and heard the hard shock of thunder, the plane shuddering from the blast so close by. He stared, saw the fireball falling away, and knew now: A plane . . . one of us. He was pulled backward, the pilot banking hard again, and Adams held tightly to the door, steadied himself, and heard Pullman, shouting above the chorus of sound,

"Sergeant, open the door!"

Adams held his grip on the edge of the door and absorbed the words. Well, yeah, of course. If we're hit, if we go down, it's the only way out. He pulled it to one side, held himself steady, the gaping doorway now blasting him with cold air. Around him, the other planes were scattering, no order, diving and rolling, some climbing higher, pilots desperate to avoid the clouds of flack, some panicking as badly as the men they carried. Streaks of antiaircraft fire ripped through them, another flash close by; a chattering of metal bits sprayed up from below, rattling the floor beneath his feet, a hard shattering of glass.

A man screamed, and Adams saw him fall forward, holding his face, others pressing closer, helping hands. The man was still screaming, a high-pitched horror, and Pullman was up close, kneeling. Adams started to move forward—who is it?—but held himself back. Stay put. It's almost time. Nothing you can do. He wanted to shout at Pullman, Get up front! Do your job! Pullman was ripping open a med kit, bandages flying apart, the lieutenant now focused, careful. Adams could see his hands, the syrette, thought, Morphine, good. He turned away, wouldn't watch, thought, No time for this, for treating wounded. We have to get out of here. The plane bucked again. The man's screaming had stopped. There were more rattles against the plane, a sharp crack of broken metal, and Adams eased closer to the opening, thought, There's no protection. We need to get the hell out of here. He looked toward Pullman again, saw the man standing, holding himself upright with his hands against the roof of the plane, backing toward the cockpit.

"Stand up! Everyone up! Hook up!" Pullman shouted.

Men obeyed, and Adams suddenly understood something he had heard long ago from Gavin. When it's hot, put everyone on their feet. If something happens to the bird, you need to go now. He reached down to his side and felt for the static line—more instinct, his hand wrapping around the hook. He turned again to the doorway—nothing to see, only smoke, thick and heavy—and reached back and hooked his static line to the cable over his head, the precious lifeline that would pull open his chute. Pullman repeated the order, prodding the men, some of them frozen in place. Adams stared blindly outside, searching for glimpses of the other planes. Damn! he thought. Too much smoke, must be the engine! But the engine was fine, a scattering of sparks but no fire. The red streaks of antiaircraft fire were rising up again, partially hidden by the smoke, the plane dipping hard to one side. He looked down at faint specks of fire on the ground, a new burst, a fat sickening fireball. That's our guys, he thought, poor bastards. Hope they got the hell out before they hit. Don't think about that now. He glanced at the signal panel close by: Nothing yet; no, it's too soon. We've only been over the coast . . . what, five minutes? The orders said eight. Where's this damned smoke coming from?

He couldn't see the ground at all—the flashes of light were muted—but the rumbles came still, sharp pops, and he stared out, searching for some sign of . . . anything. A plane emerged from the blackness, stripes, one wing mostly gone, the plane diving close beside them, losing altitude, rolling over as it passed below. The words burst inside of him, and he wanted to shout out, yell to the men in the stricken plane: Jump! Get the hell out of there! He closed his eyes. Good God. We're sitting ducks. Thank God for the smoke. The thought flashed in his brain now, and he stared out into the thick blindness, looked up, no stars. You jerk. It's not smoke. It's fog. Clouds!

The red light was in his eyes now, surprising him, the men responding with instinct, training, pressing toward him.

Pullman shouted out, "Check your equipment!"

Adams kept his back toward the men, felt for the precious line that would open the chute. He reached up again, gave the static line a sharp tug, testing the cable. The routine came back, and he checked each of his buckles, the pockets, the reserve chute, all the gear hanging from the pistol belt. He felt hands on his back, more of the training, the next man checking all those places Adams couldn't reach, a hard tap on his helmet: *Okay.* Adams kept his eye on the red light, wouldn't blink, edged closer to the door. The plane banked again, a fountain of red ripping the air in front of him, another, shattering taps on the wing. The streaking fire was coming up thick again, and he felt the plane lurch, the speed increasing, the pilot gaining altitude. The engines were revving up, more airspeed, and Adams began to scream in his brain, *No!* What the hell are you doing! That's too fast! The plane was still gaining altitude. He heard Pullman shouting something to the pilots, and Adams stared that way, yelled out, "Slow this damned thing down! We can't jump this fast!"

The red light turned green.

One word from Pullman: *"Go!"*

Adams leaped into the crushing current of air, felt himself jammed backward, twisting, then the hard jerk from above, straps digging into his groin, punching him in the belly as the parachute ripped open above him. He tried to breathe, held his arms in tight—*Too fast, you bastard, you cowboy son of a bitch.* The parachute was fully open now and he grabbed the risers, tried to steady himself, to gain more control. He stared downward, nothing, still in the clouds, and cursed again. How high were we? That stupid idiot panicked. Too fast and too high.

Adams was in control now, kept his gaze down, his knees together, legs slightly bent, thought, It's blind all the way down. Get ready! But the fog was suddenly gone, and he saw specks of light, fire, could hear the steady chatter of machine guns. The ground was rising up quickly, blessedly flat, and he braced himself for the roll, another second. . . .

He impacted into water, a hard splash, made a muffled shout, was under the surface. He clamped his eyes shut, put out his arms, flailed madly, tried to hold his breath, water in his throat. His feet touched something thick, soft, and he fought not to choke, bent his knees, launched himself upward. His face was in the air, and he gasped, choking, kicked hard, kicked again, his arms driving downward, loud splashes, trying to keep himself on the surface. He coughed hard, filled his lungs with air, was underwater again, his brain racing. *Dammit, I'm not going to die in a lake!* The water seemed to suck him down, the straps from the chute strangling him, and he kicked to the surface again, his chest heaving, took one long breath, coughed again, tried to clear his lungs, screaming in his head, *Get out of the water! The knife!* His arms were wrapped in grass, his legs kicking through a thick tangle, and he held his face out of the water, precious seconds, took a long breath, released it, took another—okay, ready—*Do this, do it fast!* He dropped down, kept his eyes closed, reached down to his leg, found the knife—quick motion—sliced the straps around his arms and chest. He launched himself up with a hard kick, his face in the air again, another breath, dropped down, and cut the last strap, the knife slipping out of his hand, gone, lead in his legs, his energy draining fast. But the parachute had released him and he could keep himself upright more easily, his head above water. He searched frantically, specks of light, a thick mass to one side, a tree line. *All right, swim!*

He pushed his arms out heavily, dropped down again, probed the bottom with his feet, pulled away from the thick grass, came up, thought,

Don't get tangled up, for God's sake. He kept his eyes on the tree line, painful progress, breathing in short hard gasps, a burning in his lungs. He could feel grass with his hands, pulled himself along, probed downward, the bottom coming up, shallower. He tested, the water was shoulder-deep, and he stopped, took painful breaths; You didn't drown, lucky bastard! He heard a new sound, hard splashes, shouting, more men landing in the water, and he turned. Dammit, at least I cut free. How many can't? I have to help—

Machine-gun fire sprayed past him, streaks of light, parachutes above him, more splashing. One man came down a few yards away, raucous splashing, a hard cry. Adams pushed downward with his boots, fought with his legs, moved toward the man, saw him, moving away, the water more shallow. Adams followed the man—wanted to shout, *Go to the trees!*—but the splashing was noise enough. The machine-gun fire swept across again, higher, the gunners seeking targets still in the air, and Adams pushed himself in steady rhythm, the bottom coming up, knee-deep. The man in front of him was clear of the water, stayed low, and Adams followed, the man disappearing into the brush. Adams moved quickly, thick mud pulling at his boots, crawling, a row of small trees. He tried to see where the man had gone, but the machine guns came again, streaking fire. More shouting from behind him, and he turned, tried to see, glimpses of movement, churning water. To one side, another man emerged splashing, waist-deep, then out, scampering into the brush.

Adams waited, saw more chutes far to the side, soft reflections, lit by streaks of fire, the dull glare of flack blasts in the clouds above. More men were landing in the water, others up in the brush beyond, some voices, wounded and terrified men, some silenced quickly, dragged down by the weight of their gear. He was breathing heavily, coughed again, pressed his hand hard over his mouth, spread out flat on the muddy ground. *Get to the brush. Now!* He peered up, clumps of grass in the mud, the machine-gun fire silenced, no targets in the air. There were planes still above him, more of the vast armada rolling past, and he thought, No, God, somebody has to tell them. Don't jump here, not over water. He tried to find the chutes, nothing, black blindness. There was mud in his eyes, and he wiped frantically with his sleeve but still saw no chutes. Maybe they're empty already, jumped somewhere else. Thank God. How the hell did we jump over water? Far in the distance, firing began again, more machine guns, pops of rifle fire, every direction.

He pulled himself to his knees, slow and silent, searched the blackness, caught a glimpse of parachutes farther away, now one plane right above him, black shapes, chutes coming out of the clouds, and he wanted to scream, No! But there were no words, no warning. The men came down far out onto what seemed to be a wide grassy plain, preparing themselves to roll on flat ground that was not ground at all. They were too far away for him to reach, and his brain pulled him back, You'll drown. Or maybe it's shallow out that far, maybe they'll reach . . . what? The other side? What the hell is this place? It's not a river. If this is the Merderet River, it's supposed to be fifty feet across. Some mapmaking genius, killing our people with his stupidity.

Adams crawled slowly up a gentle rise, the mud giving way to dry land, into a thick row of brush. He rolled over on his back, listened to soft sounds farther along the brush, thought, Our guys. Have to be. Maybe not. He reached back behind him, the submachine gun still strapped to his back, and thought of the knife, the precious blade that had saved him in the water. Well, you're alive for now, but be damned grateful you didn't cut away the Thompson. He put his hand on his waist, felt for the pistol, but the belt was stripped bare. He felt a jolt of panic, realized the canteen and shovel were gone, the cloth bag, the grenades. He reached lower. One pants leg was ripped, no pockets at all, but the other was intact, a heavy bulge, precious ammunition. His mind was racing, and he glanced toward the black water, thought, I lost it out there?

He thought of the jump now: Damn! Son of a bitch! That Texas moron! He tossed us out too damned fast. What? A hundred fifty? My gear is scattered all over France. Everybody in the stick is probably in the same boat. We're lucky we didn't smack into the tail. Or, hell, maybe somebody did. He held tightly to the face of the Texan, the pilot who had succumbed to panic, who had dropped his men over water, who had put them out at far too much speed. I hope you made it home, pal. Because one of these days I will find you.

The gunfire was scattered, distant, then suddenly, one spray of fire, men calling out: German words. Adams stayed flat in the brush, furiously helpless, and readied the Thompson, preparing to wage his own war. They're moving up, he thought, trying to find us. He heard a truck, more sounds, knew that more were gathering, more guns. Streaks of tracer fire were coming from the far side of the water as well, and he tried to gauge the distance. The town, Sainte-Mère-Église—that's where we're supposed to end up. But where the hell am I? If this is the Merderet, it's a hell of a lot more than some narrow river. He searched his pockets for the compass, the small disk, but it was a useless exercise. Nothing to see until dawn anyway. No matches; they were in the damned bag.

The machine guns seemed to quiet, fewer bursts, and he thought, Yep, I know what you're doing. Any idiot can shoot up the night. You're going to start looking for us, and maybe just wait until daylight anyway. Time for me to find somebody. Gather up. He sat upright, listening for other sounds, felt the chill from the water soaking his jumpsuit, his socks, flexed his wet toes, thought, Wonderful. Don't need blisters too. As the gunfire grew more scattered, he began to hear movement around him, small cracks in the brush, footsteps and, now, breathing. He eased the muzzle of the Thompson that way, tried to keep silent, his own breaths betraying him, the annoying shiver, his mind racing. *The call signs* . . . lightning and thunder? No, dammit! That's not right! What is it? Lightning . . . something. He heard the whisper now, a low croak.

"Flash!"

One word flooded his brain, the perfect logical response: Gordon. He cursed himself. No, that's not right! The low croak came again. "Flash, damn you!"

"Thunder!"

The reply came from one side of him, movement in the brush, and now Adams felt his mind opening up, breathless relief. He said it as well. "Thunder."

The men moved in closer. Adams rose to his knees, saw four men, said, "Sergeant Adams. Who are you?"

"Sarge! Thank God! It's Nusbaum!"

There were more men moving through the brush now, a hard whisper. "Quiet! Celebrate later!"

Even in a whisper, Adams knew the voice. "Lieutenant. Glad you made it."

"I'm glad too. How many do we have here?"

Adams made a quick count. "Ten, looks like. We can gather up more, we just have to make ourselves easy to find. This is a good place."

"I'm not going to sit in one spot, Sergeant. We were supposed to come down between the river and Sainte-Mère-Église. I have to assume that's where we are. We need to find that town."

Adams said nothing. And where would that be? he thought.

Beside him, one man moved closer, a harsh whisper. "I don't have a rifle, sir. Lost it."

Adams knew that high squeak. It was Unger. "Take it easy, kid. We'll find you one."

Another man said, "I lost mine too. What are we gonna do?" There was too much volume to the panic in the voice—Hovey.

Adams moved close, gripped his arm. "Shut up! We'll find weapons. Stay close together."

Pullman moved into the center of the group and dropped to one knee, the others all down as well. "I think there's a road, just past those trees. I thought I saw a truck when I came down." He reached into his pocket, and Adams knew what was coming, the sharp click of a lighter. Of course, an officer would have a damned Zippo. The light flickered briefly, then another jarringly loud click, the flame extinguished. Adams had caught a glimpse of the compass.

"North is that way," Pullman said. "That's where we're headed. Unless we were dropped in some cockeyed place, the town should be that way."

There was a sudden rising chorus of gunfire, chattering bursts, the sounds expanding all around them. Streaks of tracer fire erupted from the trees, and the men all dropped flat. Adams slid on his belly, pulled himself farther into the brush, thought of Pullman's words. Some cockeyed place. Yep, this would qualify.

They stayed flat for long seconds, the fire increasing but farther away, no one aiming at them. They don't know where we are, he thought. Not yet. We should stay here long enough to gather up whoever made it, whoever got out of that damned water. But once it's light enough to see something, we need to go to work. He raised his head, eased himself through the grass, tapped Pullman on the leg.

"We should spread out here, form a perimeter, watch our flanks. Looks like this brush runs in a straight line. Good cover. I lost my shovel, but we can use what we've got to dig in. You said there was a road."

A burst of fire rolled over them, a machine gunner spraying wildly, and Pullman turned his head toward him, reached down, grabbed Adams's hand.

"We . . . have to go! You lead the way!"

"Easy, Lieutenant. We need to find more of our guys. They gotta be all over the place out here. We move now, we're stumbling blind. Best we dig some holes right here, close to this brush."

"Okay. Okay. North is that way. How long should we wait?"

Adams didn't like the question. Dammit, what a time for the looey to fall apart. The firing was increasing again, most of it in the distance, flashes beyond the trees, and Adams dropped low again, leaned closer to Pullman's ear.

"Sir, we need more rifles, and we need to find someone in command, someone with a radio, someone who knows what's going on."

There was a sharp *click,* farther down the brush line, then another. The men listened in silence, and Adams realized what it was: a toy cricket. He glanced at Marley, the man lying flat, No, it's not you. Pullman said in a faint whisper, "Thunder!"

"He's too far away, sir. I'll go get him. If he doesn't shoot me."

The cricket sounded again, sharp double *clicks,* and Adams pulled himself around in the grass, eased that way, crawled past Unger, another man. He stayed on his knees, moved close to a twisted tree, the brush covering a mound of dirt, rising up in a steep embankment, tangled with tree limbs. He pulled himself along, tested the ground with his knees, avoided the tangles of sticks and roots. He fought the chill in his clothes and thought of the missing knife, the pistol gone as well. This idiot better be one of us. His knee punched a rock, and he grunted, clenching his jaw. Dammit! He looked behind him, no landmarks, black shadows, the brush extending back in a straight line. He crawled again, ignoring the throb in his knee, long seconds, chattering machine guns far across the field, the distant blast of a grenade. He stopped and looked that way, thought, That was one of ours . . . maybe. Hope to God it was. He glanced back again, tried to guess the distance he had come: a hundred yards, maybe. Pay attention to that. Sound carries in the dark.

Click-crick.

The cricket was close, just on the other side of the brush line, and Adams ducked low, said in a sharp whisper, "American, you jackass. Stop playing with that damned toy."

There was a rustle in the brush, and he heard the man crawling, a whisper. "My rifle's aimed at your head. If you're a Kraut—"

"If I'm a Kraut, you're already dead."

"Where's your damned cricket?"

"Orders, you moron. Only the One-oh-one carries crickets."

"I *am* One-oh-one. Who are you?"

Adams understood now, felt a strange relief, realized he was breathing heavily. "I'm Eighty-second. The Five-oh-five."

There was silence for a brief moment, and the man began to move, punching through the tangle, and Adams waited, the man easing quietly up the far side of the embankment. He emerged through the brush, grunted, rolled over, tumbled down next to Adams.

"What the hell is the Five-oh-five doing here? I'm with Five-oh-one, Corporal Burkett. Captain Hadley's radioman. Lost my radio, though."

The man's speech had too much volume, stabbed the silence.

Adams grabbed his shoulder. "Shut up," he whispered. "Krauts everywhere! You hear those machine guns? Come on. There's a bunch of us over this way, a hundred yards or so. I'm Sergeant Adams. My lieutenant is in command there. More or less."

"You lost?"

"We're all lost. Any of your buddies around here?"

"Don't know. Nobody answered my cricket."

Adams didn't respond, thought of Gavin. Yeah, I'm sure you loved this cricket idea.

"Let's go. Until you find your captain, you're with us."

He began to move, crawling back toward the others, realized this part of the embankment was nearly the height of a man. To one side the field was open and flat, the embankment a stout wall of cover. He stood, kept himself low, and continued to move, Burkett silent behind him. Good. At least the One-oh-one teaches you how to be quiet. Adams stepped slowly, the ground soft, thick grass, and Burkett suddenly grabbed his arm. Adams froze, the man's fingers digging into him, a soft whisper, close to his ear.

"There! In the field!"

Adams turned slowly, Burkett crouching behind him, and lowered himself as well, the Thompson coming up. He saw movement, blind shadows, sounds of footsteps in the grass.

Burkett said in his ear, "Should I use the cricket?"

Adams put a hand on the man's chest, a silent *no,* stared at the dark motion, the shapes coming closer, no more than thirty yards away. He wrapped his fingers around the trigger of the Thompson, the shapes still moving, silent, more soft steps, closer still. Burkett raised his rifle, and Adams yelled in his brain, No, not yet! He wanted to grab Burkett's arm, but he kept his grip on the Thompson, pointed it at the closest shadow, easing it up to his shoulder, aiming. The shapes began to take form now, closing the space between them, the shadows larger, heavy steps, ten yards, closer, and now a single loud echoing sound, shattering the dark.

"*Moooooooo!*"

Adams jumped, fought the need to laugh, the other shapes now clear in the darkness, gathering closer, a small herd. He felt his hands shaking. Burkett was down now, sitting, breathing hard.

"I almost peed myself," Burkett said.

Adams grabbed the man's shoulder, fought to keep the whisper, ignored the man's embarrassment, said, "Let's go."

They were up and moving again, the embankment dropping away into the thick brush, the direction Adams had come. He slowed, listened, Burkett mimicking his movements, and the word drifted toward them in a whisper.

"Flash."

Adams didn't hesitate. "Thunder."

He saw them now, in a low line, more than he expected. One man crawled toward him, Pullman, and Adams said, "He's from the One-oh-one. Only one I found."

"A few others from the One-oh-one are here. Came in from that way. Looks like we're scattered all to hell." Pullman put a hand on his shoulder, leaned close. "You were right about staying put, Sergeant. As soon as it's light enough to see, we might have enough people do something. Sergeant Davies is over there, a few of his platoon. He thinks there's a bunch more of us past that far tree line. Krauts too."

Adams knew Davies well, another veteran of Sicily. Good.

Behind him, a low whisper. "Hey, Sarge, you capture us some steak?"

Adams was in no mood for Marley, ignored him, could see that Pullman was shivering, and Adams felt it himself. Have to take off these boots, he thought. He looked toward the men closest to him.

"I need a pair of socks. You spare any?"

One man rolled forward, silent, working the small cloth bag, held out a dark hand. Adams couldn't see the man's face, no sounds.

"Thanks."

He sat, untied the wet boots, heard a low voice at the far end of the line.

"Flash!"

"Thunder."

Three more men emerged from the brush, low whispers, chattering excitement. Thank God. More of us. Pullman's right. By dawn, we can get something done. Be damned nice if we could find someone with a BAR, or a heavy machine gun. Or a radio.

He stripped away the waterlogged socks, hooked them on his belt, slid the dry socks onto his grateful feet. The boots were miserably wet; nothing he could do about that. He pulled hard on the soaked leather, the boots sliding on reluctantly, and laced them up quickly. Around him, the men were spreading out, digging in, more strength, shielded by the brush to one side, an open field of fire in front of them. Adams thought of the water, someone's amazingly stupid mistake. Don't we have observers? They take pictures, for God's sake. How many did we lose? No, can't think about that. There's a flock of us all over these damned fields, and with a little day-light we can raise some hell. He stared out into darkness: nothing to see, the sounds of a truck in the distance, the rumble of artillery. Now the rum-bles grew louder, low steady punches, and he stared that way, searching for flashes of light, but saw nothing; too far away. The sounds continued to grow, like a distant storm.

Pullman moved close to him, pointed. "Northeast. You think . . . you think it might be—"

Adams already knew. He had heard this before, on Sicily, incoming fire from guns far larger than anything the army took to the field. The heaviest shells came from the big ships, the massive naval artillery that would batter the enemy positions along the beaches. He glanced skyward, could see more of the thick gray above him, the first hint of precious day-light. My God, he thought. That's coming from the beach. That's how it happens. The bombers start it, and then the battleships, and when it's light enough to see the men will follow.

He stared out toward the open ground, toward hidden tree lines, where the clusters of German machine guns were rolling into place, men who had been scrambled out of their outposts to meet this assault from the paratroopers, an assault that had not yet truly begun. He felt nervous, anx-ious, his hands holding tightly to the Thompson. Come on, dammit. Just a little more daylight. We need to find more of us, somebody in charge. He moved up to one knee, glanced at the men along the hedgerow, his own men, his lieutenant, the others, movement in the darkness, the soft work of the shovels. Some were stopping now, staring out as he was, the distant sound growing louder still, the rumble rolling all through him, low punches in his gut.

I wish I could see that, he thought, see it up close, right there, on the sand. Who's going to stand up to that? Come on, boys. Come *on,* boys! He raised the Thompson slowly and held it high over his head, one man's silent salute to so many others, those men who still had to cross the beach.

PART THREE

The spirits have been poured. It's time to take a drink.

WINSTON CHURCHILL

18. THORNE

By June 1944, the Twenty-ninth Infantry Division had been in south-western England for more than eighteen months, longer than any other combat division in the American army. Their training had been both brutal and fun, depending of course on the weather and what they were ordered to do. Through the rugged countryside, they had practiced every kind of infantry operation: storming rocky beaches, launching full-scale assaults on unsuspecting farms, surprising farmers who stayed at their plows, cheering the troops as they flowed past. More than once, the troops had slipped quietly through gullies and streambeds, surprising hikers or young lovers who had thought the isolated countryside would offer a bit of privacy. For most of their training, they had no idea what they were being called upon to do; not even the officers were completely aware until a few days before the operation would begin. But long before that, they had won a hard-fought victory of another kind, capturing the affections of a large percentage of the English civilians. Beyond the rugged beaches and mock battlefields, many of the young soldiers embarked on a different sort of operation. It took place in the dance halls and pubs of so many villages and towns, where the girls looked with smiling eagerness toward these Americans. The soldiers learned quickly that the enemy here was formidable and often as threatening as the Germans: the mothers who stood guard over the virtue of their daughters, vigilance that was often hopeless. Frequently, seduced by the uninhibited charms and deep pockets of the brash GIs, many of the mothers succumbed as well. But no matter their relentless assaults on the virtue of the Englishwomen, the soldiers had found a graciousness in the hospitality of most civilians, who seemed to recognize that these Americans brought something desperately necessary to this fight, that the loud voices and rude, boisterous habits of the GIs did not diminish the urgency of the job they had to do, a job the British could not accomplish by themselves.

Throughout the infantry's training, the high brass had come to the fields, Montgomery and Bradley and Eisenhower, with speeches and pep talks. The men were always grateful for the attention, if not for the speeches themselves. No matter what kind of encouragement the generals brought, it was a sign to the GIs that they were not forgotten, that the months of training had some meaning, that eventually they would be called upon to do something *big*.

The 29th was called the Blue and Gray Division, their shoulder patches a simple yin-yang design of the two subtle colors, a reflection of the geography of their makeup. Most were from the eastern seaboard, Virginia and Maryland, Delaware, Pennsylvania, and New York. The division did not come into existence until World War One, but the individual infantry regiments had an extraordinary history of their own. All four, the 115th, 116th, 175th, and 176th, could trace their origins to colonial times, and even before. One in particular, the 116th, had been assembled from men who spent their youth in and around famous battlefields of another war, descendants of many who marched through fights that ripped across Virginia in the 1860s. Those men had been raised with the glorious stories of the famous men that their grandparents stood beside and even worshiped. The 116th Regiment had evolved directly from the old 2nd Virginia, a Confederate unit whose extraordinary reputation had come under the leadership of a man whose legacy was a part of every Virginian, who had earned much of his legendary reputation in the Shenandoah Valley. It was natural that the 116th would name themselves after this most vivid hero of their homeland. They began to call themselves the Stonewall Brigade.

The 116th had filed aboard ship nearly a week before, a lumbering transport named the U.S.S. *Thomas Jefferson*. Before the men could even settle into the crowded bunk rooms, the ship had steamed away from port, and despite assurances from their officers, some of the men believed the great assault had already begun. But the ship only took them as far as a sheltered anchorage, a rendezvous point in peaceful waters off the Isle of Wight. For the first time, the men could see more of the great fleet, transports, larger landing craft, and the destroyers that gave them protection from any probing by German U-boats. Here the days crept by snail-like, and in the cramped and crowded confines of the ship, the men fought the boredom and anxiety of what was still to come. The tedium of their days was broken by the only kinds of recreation they could muster, card playing and crap games mostly, which the officers obliged by looking the other way. There was no privacy, no place for any man to sit alone with his thoughts. Even the men who made use of the time to send letters home wrote in crowded quarters, alongside men who would not stay silent, who deflected the sentiment in their own letters by teasing the others about the proper way to say *I might not see you again*. The letters wouldn't actually be mailed, not yet, security keeping everything on board ship, and even if the letters were to go out at all, they would pass first through the censors, those hated bureaucrats armed with scissors and thick black pens, who would remove any mention of place or time or conditions. But the men wrote anyway, the words on paper their only outlet for the fear they could not dare reveal to their buddies around them.

On the night of June 4, the routine of the sailors changed. The ship's crew scampered through the crowded decks with a contagious urgency that spread to the soldiers. The clatter of the anchor chain and the deep rumble of the engines jolted them, nervous voices rising, then squeezed away by waves of fear, so many grasping the hands of friends and companions, brutally aware that every rumor, every fantasy, every nightmare was about to be replaced by reality. As the ship moved out into open water, the violence of the wind and rain drove even the curious belowdecks, huddled in the smells of their crowded bunk rooms, the anxiousness giving way to seasickness. When the anchor chain released again, they were ecstatic to find they had returned to port, and their relief fueled energetic rumors that the operation had been called off; quite likely the Germans had surrendered to the threat alone. But that had passed quickly. Sanity was restored by the officers in orders relayed to the men that there was only a postponement. All day on June 5, the soldiers no longer cursed their boredom, the sickest men enjoyed a full day of recovery, the sailors sympathetic, the medics passing out more seasickness pills, eagerly accepted by men who had learned something unexpected about the sea and themselves. The brief journey was not their first ocean voyage, of course. The Twenty-ninth Division had come across the Atlantic on the enormous *Queen Mary*, a city at sea. Some had suffered then as well, but that was more than eighteen months ago, and the talk and anticipation then had been more about enemy submarines and what they would find in England. It was, after all, an adventure, the fear not yet real, so much attention on training and readiness, mock battles and easy talk. Now, with the clock ticking in every bunk room, all talk of a quick end to the war was set aside. These men now understood that the time had finally come to fight the enemy.

After a twenty-four-hour reprieve, the ship began to move again, churning past the darkened coast of southern England. This time, when they reached the final rendezvous point in the English Channel, the men could see that the small fleet that had given them such pride was no fleet at all. It was just one small part of a vast armada, thousands of ships that spread out beyond the horizon, protected by swarms of fighter planes and barrage balloons. As darkness came, the *Thomas Jefferson* surged seaward once more, the anxious misery of the rolling seas equaled by the tight anxiety in every man that this time the mission was a go. D-Day had arrived.

T ommy Thorne was one of a twelve-man rifle squad of Company A, 116th Regiment, most of the squad from his part of Virginia, their homes spread out in the green farm country around Fredericksburg. He was old for twenty-two, had married right out of high school, a common custom around his home. His wife, Ann, had given birth a year later, a fragile little girl they had named Ella. The baby was not yet a year old when he signed up, and now, more than a year later, he could only know her through his wife's achingly detailed letters. But with the letters came photographs, so Thorne had fastened the most recent photo in a place that was protected, the safest place he could find: inside his helmet liner.

When the call came to volunteer, Thorne did not have to be prodded. He had convinced himself that hesitation might mean the draft, and he might not have any choice about where he served. The recruiting sergeant had been a gruff, likable man who filled the young men with fiery stories of glorious adventure, how they would punish the Japanese for their obscene violence against Pearl Harbor. The attention was on the Pacific, the recruiting office papered with colorful posters about bloodying the cartoonish Japs. But the recruiter's enthusiasm for a quick victory was dampened by what Thorne had seen in the newspapers: horrifying reports of disaster, odd names like Corregidor and Bataan. He was assigned to the Twenty-ninth Division at Camp Blanding, near Jacksonville, Florida, and welcomed the rumors that very soon the division would go west, boarding the great transport ships that would carry them across the Pacific. The men soon learned what the senior officers already knew, and as the division continued to grow and find its identity, the truth of their assignment was passed down to the men who would carry the rifles. Long before anyone knew the specifics of Operation Overlord, the 29th was on its way to England.

ENGLISH CHANNEL
JUNE 6, 1944, 4 A.M.

As the ship rumbled and tossed through the windy darkness, Thorne had wanted to go topside, to escape the smells of seasickness but, more, to try to see the amazing variety of ships. He had never seen a battleship, but the lieutenant had told them that the great juggernauts would be there, providing thunderous cover for them, very likely obliterating enemy positions onshore, if there was an enemy to be found. When the naval barrage began, the Allied bombers would already have made their runs, thousands of tons of high explosives dropped along all five landing beaches, blasting the enemy fortifications and the artillery emplacements anchored behind them. Thorne had felt his lieutenant's confidence, shared by most of the men, nervous hope that the landings might be completely unopposed, that it would be an engineers' battle, their only task to clear away the debris so the infantry could have a clear path inland.

At 2:30 A.M., the regimental commander, Colonel Canham, had come through, carrying the word to any men who might be sleeping that the time had come to strap on their gear. Thorne had grabbed a nap propped up in a corner, a poker game unfolding right in front of him, his attempts to sleep a waste of time. But some had slept, those men who had that luxurious ability to nod off anywhere, and when the colonel gave the orders, they had emerged from cubbyholes and peered up from bunks where other men talked in low voices. At 3 A.M., food had been served, passed out by the sailors, a breakfast of franks and beans and doughnuts. The advice came from the officers: No matter how miserable your gut might be, no matter how scared you were, you had better eat. Talk of food always seemed to grab the attention of the troops far more than the usual briefings. Thorne had taken his lieutenant's advice seriously and thought of his words now.

"This is all you're going to have for the next couple of days, at least. I'd eat as much of this chow as you can hold."

Most of the men had obeyed, and Thorne had stuffed himself, a few extra doughnuts for good measure. Now, as the ship tossed and rolled through the windy darkness, he tried not to feel the uneasiness under his belt and what a full stomach might suddenly mean.

He was still in his corner, the poker players silent now, the game dissolving. He scanned the room: steel bulkheads, a network of iron pipes overhead, the smell of oil and cigarettes, some of the men still fumbling with bits of paper, an effort at one last letter. They were mostly quiet, sitting on the hard deck, leaning against their overstuffed packs, rifles upright beside them. Occasionally Thorne saw a smile, one man slapping a friend on the back.

"You know that every damned one of us is going to get a bronze star. All we gotta do is hike over that beach and get our picture taken. I hear the colonel's got his own flag, and his staff is having a race to see who sticks it in the ground first. Ernie Pyle's here too, on one of these tugs somewhere. I wanna meet him, get my picture taken. I hear he puts your name in the paper if he talks to you."

The man seemed to run out of energy. Thorne looked at the others, Sergeant Woodruff leaning back, his helmet pulled low, more men from his squad sitting together, one man rubbing his M-1 with an oily cloth. The lieutenant appeared at the door, his bass voice booming.

"Listen up. Make sure you've got your gear, your *own* gear. No screwups. We're close to it, boys. When the order comes to go topside, fall in and keep it orderly. Nobody gets points for being the first in line. You've done this before, so do it right. This tub's hauling thirty of those damned landing craft, and there's room for everybody. Any questions?"

"The tanks really gonna beat us in, sir?"

"That's what I've been told. There's supposed to be a couple dozen tanks in our sector, and if everything goes right, you'll be landing right behind them. I saw one of those amphibious ducks. Damnedest thing I've ever seen. The tanks are wrapped in a canvas balloon, like some big-assed

Christmas present, and they actually float. Some kind of outboard motor shoves them through the water."

Thorne tried to imagine a floating tank. To one side of him a man spoke.

"Just so long as their damned cannons work."

The lieutenant adjusted his belt. "The tank boys will do their job. You've got enough to think about." He paused. "One more thing. Those of you who bothered to listen to the speech from that major . . . what's his name, the division staff officer. I've been hearing those rules since I got my commission, and by damn you're going to listen to them too. One in particular: Shoot only at known targets. I don't want any of my people picked off by friendly fire. Shooting like hell at a concrete wall is more likely to kill you than hurt anybody on the other side. Pick your targets. You got that?" He seemed satisfied by the lack of response and adjusted his backpack, looked at his wristwatch. "Check your rifle. Then check it again. It can't be long now. I'm going to talk to Captain Bridger, see if he's heard anything. Meanwhile, check those M-1s."

There was authority in the man's rough voice, and as he moved out of the room the men obeyed, with a rustle of plastic sheathing, the water-proofing material that they had already used to wrap their rifles. It was the only protection the weapons would have against sand and salt water. Thorne felt the oily film on the steel barrel and pulled back the small bolt. Others were doing the same; there was a chorus of *clicks*. As he rolled the plastic back around the length of the gun again, he saw one man removing his watch and stuffing it carefully into a condom. Thorne laughed. "What the hell is that?"

The man looked at him without smiling. "Waterproofing my watch. My wallet too. Works really well."

"But . . . that's a rubber."

"It's not just *a* rubber, it *is* rubber. That's what counts. Tried to fit one over my boots, but it wouldn't stretch that far." The man held the watch toward him, said, "See? Works like a charm. My grandpa gave me this, and I don't want it screwed up."

Close in front of him, Sergeant Woodruff peered out from beneath his helmet. "The only thing screwed up is you. You meet some mademoiselle, you'll wish you had that damned thing in your wallet and not around it. Anybody in this outfit catches the clap, I'll kick his ass."

Thorne thought of the lone condom, had been embarrassed to take it, had thought of handing it off to the man who stood in line behind him. He had never succumbed to the temptations of the English girls and had taken a fair amount of ribbing. Don't need it, he thought. What would I tell my wife if I got the clap? Well, I wouldn't tell her, I guess. Better yet, don't catch it in the first place. He slipped the strap from under his chin, pulled the helmet off, and looked into the liner at the photo.

Beside him, the BAR man, Rollings, said, "Hey, Tommy, you forget what your wife looks like?"

"You're too young to have a wife. Stupid as hell."

The words came from Woodruff. The sergeant was as old as the lieutenant, Thorne guessing thirty, a stubble of beard on his creased face. Thorne had heard this before, ignored the comments. He glanced at the photo again, beautiful Ann, a smiling dark-haired woman, holding the baby in her arms. He left it untouched, knew the words she had written on the back: ELLA SAYS, COME HOME SOON!

Yep.

The lieutenant was there again, red-faced, breathing heavily.

"Up and at 'em, boys. It'll come over the loudspeaker in a minute or so. You know what I want now. Let me hear it."

The men knew the drill, the cheer that identified the entire division, the motto that had become their particular battle cry.

"Twenty-nine . . . let's go!"

Thorne said the words, but the enthusiasm wasn't in any of the men, the cheerleading suddenly empty, unimportant.

The lieutenant seemed resigned. "I'd hate like hell for the general to hear that sorry-assed yell. All right, check your gear! Right now!"

Thorne used his rifle as a crutch, was up on his feet, pulled to one side by the weight of his pack. The others were up as well, groans and grunts, the dull clanks of canteens. Thorne steadied himself and leaned forward to offset the awkwardness of the backpack. They were used to the normal infantryman's gear: the M-1, at least sixty rounds of ammunition, bayonet, grenades, and canteen. But word had come down from high above that on this operation they would haul nearly sixty pounds more than the usual load the infantryman carried. It was one of those so-called good ideas, passed down from generals who would not have to cross a beach under fire. Despite urgent complaints from the lieutenants, protests that a man did not require so much *stuff,* most of the men were issued a back-straining variety of equipment. Besides the normal supply of ammunition, each man was to carry bandoliers as well, three heavy belts of cartridges they would hang across their chests. Along with the bayonet and fragmentation grenades, they would receive phosphorus and smoke grenades as well. Their uniforms reeked of some stinking chemical, said to protect a man from poison gas, which made the uniform stiff and uncomfortable. They were issued gas masks and first-aid kits, three meals of K rations, and a handful of chocolate bars, known as D rations. Many of the men carried bricks of high explosive and satchel charges, what some officers said were to be used as an aid to digging foxholes, a level of instructional stupidity that no one believed. Some also carried bundles of pipelike tubing, which could be fastened end to end, what were called Bangalore torpedoes, designed to slide an explosive charge beneath barbed wire. Thorne had wondered if the command was congratulating themselves on what someone must have thought was a marvelous idea, that every man would be his own engineer, each one capable of blowing a hole through the enemy's fortifications. The questions had filtered back up the chain of command: If every man is supposed to be a demolition expert, why do we need engineers? And if we have engineers, why are we weighed down with so much explosive?

To accommodate the extra gear, the men had been issued an additional piece of clothing, a jacket with spacious pockets, since what they were carrying far exceeded what anyone could stuff into his backpack. And, since it was anticipated that some would have to deal with a watery landing, each man received a life preserver, a beltlike band wrapped high around the chest, which could be inflated by compressed air cartridges. More than one man had already discovered during the water drills that if the belt was too low, closer to a man's waist, the center of gravity would flip him upside down. Even men who were capable swimmers took little comfort in that. In deeper water, unless a man could shed most of the ninety pounds of equipment he carried, no one believed the inflatable vest would keep anyone afloat for long.

ELEVEN MILES OFF OMAHA BEACH
JUNE 6, 1944, 4 A.M.

Thorne's face was wet, salty spray from the wind, and he blinked through it, fighting to see anything at all. Before the sun had set the night before, he had ached for binoculars, hoping for some glimpse of the enormous warships, the amazing guns. There were so many of the transports too, so much activity. He had wondered what generals might be staring back at *him.* It was more than curiosity, more like pride, the same pride that had affected the others, encouraged by the sight of so much power, the sheer enormity of the invasion force. The briefings they had received had been surprisingly specific, much more information than an infantryman would normally hear. But once they had boarded the ships, there was no danger of loose lips, and the officers had seemed almost relieved to tell their men what was expected of them. It had inspired them all, knowing that in the darkness around them, the Twenty-ninth Division was only one small part of the whole, and Thorne knew that *right out there* was the First Infantry Division, the Big Red One, veterans of North Africa, who would land on Omaha Beach alongside the Twenty-ninth. Somewhere to the west was the American Fourth Division, headed to what the maps called Utah Beach.

He felt the line of men moving and moved with it, more salt spray, chilling, chattering conversations he tried to ignore, the fear rising inside him, inside all of them. He looked into the darkness, the deck sheathed in double layers of blackout cloth, hiding any hint of light. He wanted desperately to see, wished now he had gone up on deck earlier. They're all out there, he thought, the whole damned army. I hope they are. He tried to picture the British and Canadians, more transports hauling troops he had never seen, led by men who had faced the Germans before, veterans, heroes. Are we as good as that? What are they doing right now? This, I guess. Same damned thing we're doing. Are they scared?

He tried to push the thoughts away, moved forward again, heard shouting from officers, voices scattered in the sharp breeze. He glanced down at his boots on the wet deck, the ship rocking gently, side to side, uneasiness in his stomach. What happens now? What time is it? Are the boats ready? His hands were shaking and he pulled his arms in tight, crossed them against the life belt, realized it was sagging below his ribs. No, dammit! He had a moment of panic, pulled at the belt, slid it higher, tucked it under his arms. Remember that! But the lieutenant said we wouldn't need it. He told us . . . he couldn't remember what the lieutenant had said, thought of the plastic wrapping around his rifle. Will it work? No, you can't worry about that. They've been training us for too long for us to worry whether or not we're ready. He put a hand on his watch, useless to see it, knew it had to be close to four. The ship rocked again, the men tilting to the side, one man falling, helped to his feet by others. Thorne thought of the steel beneath him; he had always marveled at that. Floating steel. Like the tanks. It was something he had never grasped, how so many tons of steel could bob safely on top of the water. His brain was wandering aimlessly, and his hands were shivering. What keeps us from sinking right to the bottom? How deep is it anyway? How the hell do airplanes stay in the air? Amazing. Somebody figured out it would work. The Wright brothers, I guess.

The line moved again, and he heard the groan of metal, cables and cranes, saw something moving above his head. He stared up into thick blackness, heard more sounds: machinery, electric motors. His mind cleared, the terrified chatter quieting, men in front of him moving forward again, and he was at the blackout cloth now, a gap, the man in front of him, Woodruff, holding it open. Thorne stepped through, a hard blast of wind, the smell of the spray, his face wet again, sweat and salt water. He knew what the motors meant, the davits, hoisting the smaller landing craft, swinging them out away from the ship. They would be lowered to the level of the deck the men were on, the routine for loading. The troops had practiced this many times at Slapton Sands: thirty-two men in each boat, with a crew of three perched in back. The boat was called an LCVP, Landing Craft, Vehicle and Personnel. Thorne had always wondered about the *vehicle* part, the same question rising inside of him now. What the hell could they fit into the damned thing? A jeep, I suppose. Stupid damned way to haul one lousy jeep. It's a big steel bathtub. It floats, though. Steel. What happens if it fills up with water?

"Load up!"

He flinched at the loudspeaker, realized the man was right in front of him. There were officers now, identified only by their words, faces invisible in the salty darkness, voices crisp and nervous.

"Get moving! Let's go!"

He knew that one, his own lieutenant, gravel in his throat, older, a man Thorne wanted to believe had done this before. But the Twenty-ninth had never done anything like this before, and despite the long months of training, he wondered about the fear, did not expect this, the unstoppable shaking, no loud arrogance, none of the cockiness. He could see the closest LCVP, rocking precariously, bouncing slightly against the rails of the ship, sailors working ropes, holding it in place. The small craft were lined up all along the side of the ship, soldiers gathered at each one. There was another gust of wind, sailors still working, the boat secure, men in front of him climbing aboard, the lieutenant again.

"In you go! Let's move!"

Thorne grabbed the wet railing and tried to swing a leg up, the weight of his gear pulling him backward. He felt a hand under his arm, steady, wanted to thank the man, but he was pushed forward, up and over, more hands on his chest, tight grip on his arm. His feet were on hard steel again, the small craft rocking slightly, men cursing, another hand, pushing him from behind, the voice of the lieutenant.

"Step aside! Move to the front! Pack in tight!"

He tried to obey, felt for the butt of the M-1, the strap still on his shoulder, the crinkle of plastic, but there was no balance, and he fell forward, into the back of another man, the landing craft rolling side to side, more men coming in behind him. He had done this before and pressed forward, the number in his head, thirty-two, knew the riflemen would be up front and, with them, those men in each squad who carried a precious BAR. The bazooka carriers and flamethrower crews would settle in toward the rear, close to the boat crew. He pressed forward, pushed again from behind, no more spaces now, men huddled low, escaping the wind. He still wanted to see, tried to look upward, but there were no lights, just the ship, a massive shadow in the darkness, and around him the sounds of the waves and the wind, the men and their equipment, and the urgent shouts from the officers.

"Sit down!"

He put one hand down to soften the fall, but nothing was soft, the backpack jolting him from behind, wet steel, pain in his wrist. More men came in close to him, pressing against him, a hard slap on his back, the man slapping the others, shouting into his face, the lieutenant.

"Let's do this! Twenty-nine . . . let's go!"

The cables began to groan, and Thorne felt his stomach come up, the LCVP dropping unevenly, straightening, uneven again, rocking slowly in the wind. There was silence from the men, every man gripping something inside, waiting for the impact on the water. It came now, one hard roll to the side, shouts, raw fear exploding in the darkness. Thorne strained his eyes, saw only the shadows of the men around him. He heard a groan, a loud cough, the smell of putrid smoke: the engine of the small craft coming to life. They rocked again, men crushing into him, one man stepping above him, a sailor, cables unhooked, more shouts, and the boat surged forward. He held himself straight, tried to anticipate the movement of the boat, the waves rising up, then falling away, the engine coughing again, more smoke, the boat seeming to circle, turning in a tight arc, and he remembered the briefing now: The boats would wait and gather, all of us moving together. The boat continued to turn, leaning with the wind, rising up again, and Thorne couldn't avoid it now, all those doughnuts and baked beans. He tried to stand, impossible, felt the panic, the awful cold twist in his throat. He leaned down, curled his face over his boots, and threw up.

19. THE GRENADIER

VIERVILLE-SUR-MER (OMAHA BEACH)
JUNE 6, 1944, 4:30 A.M.

The colonel had breath like sour cabbage, his face inches away, and Reimer could only endure it.

"Is your weapon *clean,* Corporal?"

"Yes, Colonel!"

"Hmm. I wonder. Have you become so soft you have forgotten how to shoot the enemy?"

"No, sir! Absolutely not, sir!"

The colonel stepped back and looked at the next man, standing stiffly beside Reimer and bracing himself for the same questions. But the colonel seemed to lose fire for the inspection; he turned and looked toward the lieutenant, standing to one side.

"Your men are a disgrace to the Reich. I have been placed in command of a hopeless band of misfits. This regiment has a heroic past, has performed on the field of battle, has demonstrated to the enemy that Germany's soldiers are to be *feared.* Now you will inspire laughter. Worse, the enemy will ignore you and pass right through your lines without knowing you are there. How dare you call yourselves grenadiers!"

The colonel spun around and marched toward his car, the driver waiting stiffly. Reimer kept his head straight, his eyes watching the man. He had been through this many times before; Thank God he is leaving, he thought. The colonel was inside the car now, two staff officers waiting dutifully, then sliding into the car as well, a precision they had perfected. The car fired up, rolled away, was quickly gone, the night quiet again.

Reimer looked toward the lieutenant, a sad young man named Hochman, who said, "Colonel Goth does not mean what he says. You are the finest unit in this army. The colonel must say those things to keep you sharp. He will certainly say the same things to every platoon at every inspection. I am confident in you. You are dismissed. Return to your stations."

Reimer waited for the others to leave, spreading out in the darkness, low mumbles. He glanced up: a thick wet night, a hard chilling breeze rolling up off the beach. He tugged at his coat and moved closer to the lieutenant.

"What do you want, Corporal?" There was no energy in the question.

"Sir, Private Dieter says we have received additional ammunition. I have not yet seen any. My weapon has only six boxes, and should we drill again today I will use much of that."

"I have never seen a man so concerned with his ammunition supply. Every machine gunner in this regiment has sufficient supply. Are you so poor a shot that you would waste it?"

"Certainly not, sir."

"No, I know that." He paused. Reimer tried to see his face in the darkness. He liked the lieutenant, had never heard the man indulging in the mindless berating of his men so common to some of the other young officers. "Corporal, I have heard no orders about firing practice today, so I would suggest you concern yourself with keeping your weapon clean. But Private Dieter is right. A wagon came forward earlier, with ammunition for the machine guns and several boxes of grenades. I will be sure they are distributed. Your loader is . . . Schmidt?"

"Yes, sir."

"Your duty will end at eight this morning, so before you retire to the bunks, send him back to the depot, the one beyond the minefield. Two boxes more should be sufficient for you." He paused. "Wait for daylight, and tell him to stay in the road. There is a reason we put warning signs in place. I will not have any of you become casualties of our own mines."

"Yes, sir."

The lieutenant looked upward. "Daylight soon. At least it's stopped raining. I must write a letter to my wife. She is complaining again. What am I supposed to—?" He seemed to catch himself, and Reimer turned away, would not invade the lieutenant's privacy. "Never mind that. Man your post, Corporal."

Hochman moved away. Reimer hunched his shoulders against the cold, stepped carefully, and tried to avoid the mud, a futile effort. A stout wall loomed up in front of him, concrete, and he ducked, leaned into the narrow opening, stepped down onto concrete steps. The air was ripe with the smell of tobacco, delicious and intoxicating: Schmidt and his ever-present pipe; the man had an amazing ability to find something to smoke besides dried cow manure. The concrete walls were nearly a full meter thick, the floor of the bunker set down below ground level, and he welcomed the shelter from the wet chill, moved through a maze of pathways. The bunker had been completed for only a short time, a month perhaps, but Reimer had not been a part of that effort. He had arrived only two weeks before.

When the orders had come to move the grenadiers to the coast, most of the men accepted the new assignment without complaint. But there were always those who believed it was just more stupidity, generals shifting their units around the French countryside just because they could. Reimer hated that kind of talk, but it had become inevitable, so many of the men having already survived life on the Eastern Front, fighting not only the Russians but their own commanders, men who seemed unable to lead them to a victory.

Reimer knew a great deal about that. He had been summoned to the army the autumn before, as surprised as his officers were to learn he had an eye for marksmanship. The Germans were desperate for skills of any kind, and Reimer was gratified to be promoted to corporal in a grenadier regiment after only a few short weeks of training. But no training prepared him for the post he was first assigned to, a march eastward into the desolation of the front lines that were barely holding back the savage onslaught of the Russians.

He had an eager smile that brought him friendships, but when he arrived at the front he found men who had no use for smiles, who spoke in subdued curses. Despite his persistence, few would speak of their experiences. Very soon, the experiences found him, and his childlike eagerness to become a part of something glorious was replaced by utter misery. Deep into the numbing Russian winter, the two armies seemed content to pick at each other with halfhearted efforts. But the orders still came, plans hatched by generals whose feet were warm, and when word came to push forward, to launch some offensive effort in the deadly cold, Reimer soon learned why the men cursed their commanders. If the Russians were willing to wait out the worst of the winter, Reimer learned what many of the veterans already knew: The real enemy came with the first days of warming weather, and it was not the Russians. Like the German soldiers who came before him, Reimer had not been trained or equipped to suffer a march in sucking rivers of mud, knee-deep in fields of melting snow that dragged the army into paralysis. In early spring, neither army had attempted any kind of serious campaign. In the lull, the German High Command seemed to awaken to the notion that some of these men had seen enough of this particular horror and there might be a reason to add their waning strength to another part of the war. Reimer had never been wounded, but in one of those confounding mysteries of the army his name was placed on the list of those to be transferred out.

The orders that brought those fortunate few out of Russia were met with dreamlike disbelief. Railcars carried them westward, through soft hills and sunshine, a long glimpse of Germany itself, and then through the paradise of France. Reimer found himself reassigned to the 916th Grenadier Regiment, the High Command's efforts to strengthen Rommel's defensive forces along the Atlantic Wall. To the men who made the long train ride with him, the move had been a desperate relief, many carrying wounds, others broken down in so many other ways. As the spring warmed them, they grew more fit, but their spirit had been shaken, and despite the encouraging words from his new lieutenant, Reimer wondered if the men who were supposed to add power to the 916th had any strength left for another fight.

Throughout April and into May, the 916th Grenadier Regiment enjoyed the mundane duties of an army of occupation, mostly overlooked by the Allied bombing raids and overlooked even more by their own commanders. Despite the lack of adequate supplies, the men were doing well, the wounds of the veterans healing, and they continued to train, some contributing long weeks to Rommel's construction efforts. The 916th was one part of the 352nd Division, which had been formed the previous November. The 352nd had been brought up to what the army labeled full strength, and with the months of peaceful training, the German High Command had confidence that the 352nd was one of Germany's most efficient fighting units. Though Reimer heard grousing about their blister-inducing efforts as construction workers, he appreciated that digging into fortified positions along a stretch of peaceful coastline was far more enjoyable than what he had endured in Russia.

He had been assigned to a position in a massive concrete bunker that gave him a wide view of the rugged coastline. The bunker was sunk into the rocky cliffs, high on a bluff, protected by steep sandy walls, swept clear of brush and debris by the engineers. For long hours he would stare out to sea. Most of the men around him found the hypnotic peacefulness utterly boring, but Reimer's routine was pure joy: almost daily practice with his machine gun, an amazingly efficient MG-42, weapon of choice for so many of the grenadiers. The gun was lightweight and portable, belt-fed by his loader, the pipe-smoking Hans Schmidt. The MG-42 usually sat on a tripod, essential to protect the gunner from its amazing kick. The light weight meant recoil, and the rate of fire—fifteen hundred rounds per minute—meant that no man was strong enough to fire the gun from his shoulder. He had practiced firing a single round, nearly impossible; most of the gunners were able to fire only as few as three rounds with a quick flick of the finger. The speed of fire made the MG-42 a magnificent weapon, but it was the sound that inspired Reimer to volunteer as a gunner. The rate of fire was so rapid it didn't sound like a machine gun at all, no popping of individual shells. It was more like a loud ripping of cloth, a sound that gave the gunner a power on the battlefield that the riflemen envied. Reimer loved his MG-42.

There were a half dozen machine guns spread through the bunker, the gunners mostly lying flat, their loaders taking turns with them staring into darkness. In one corner was a stack of gun barrels, replacements for the MG-42s, several of the men having been designated as mechanics for the job, should the need arise. In the darkness, there were low comments, small conversations. Reimer moved toward his gun and checked the tripod, the legs anchoring the gun flat on the concrete floor. Schmidt was in the corner to one side, his back against the wall, sitting on the stack of ammunition boxes, his usual perch.

"The lieutenant offer to tuck you in this morning? Almost bedtime, you know."

Reimer had heard this before. "I asked him about ammunition. He told me to send you back to the depot, the larger one close to the village. Dieter is right. A wagon brought some more boxes up."

Schmidt held the pipe in his mouth, a soft glow coming from the bowl, brighter now, more smoke. "Now? You're going to make me leave this comfortable seat, just so you can stuff this place with your damned cartridges? How many do you need?"

Reimer pressed his hands on the concrete and peered out, the breeze chilling his face. "I want all they'll give me. And, yes, you can go right now, if you don't mind having to stand on your feet. But be careful. The lieutenant was concerned that you might wander off into a minefield. Stay on the road."

Schmidt laughed. "The Calvados is gone, I promise."

There was laughter to one side, the mention of the liquor stirring a response.

"Damn you, Dieter," Schmidt said, "I never should have told you I found it. Three bottles, and not a drop left."

Reimer stared at the sea. "You're both fortunate the lieutenant didn't find out. It was bad enough you got drunk. You could have cost me my rank."

"Oh, so I should worry they might break you down to my lowly level, Corporal? It was one night, one party. There was no harm, and no one wandered into a minefield. We earned a little celebration after that train ride. I'm beginning to love the French. Those little farmhouses have all sorts of treasures inside."

A voice in the dark—Dieter—added, "And they don't try to stick a knife in your throat, like the Russians."

Schmidt groaned and pulled himself to his feet, the pipe still in his mouth. "I wonder if Rommel will come out here. They say his inspections are worse than the colonel's by far. If he blisters you, you stay blistered."

Reimer shrugged; he had never seen Rommel. But every man had heard the stories, some more ridiculous than others. Reimer turned away from the breeze and looked toward the glow of Schmidt's pipe.

"Just go get the ammunition. And carry more than one box this time."

Schmidt tapped the pipe softly against the concrete wall, then stopped, silent for a moment. "You hear that?"

The conversations quieted, and Reimer turned toward the opening again. The ocean was a soft black blanket. In front of them, below the cliffs, he could see a faint reflection of wide sandy shore. It was low tide. He heard the hum now, and another voice came out of the dark.

"Bombers. Some lucky factory's going to get it."

"Or a railroad somewhere."

Reimer had heard the same sounds for two weeks, the planes coming in high over the beach, usually to the east. The planes seemed to subdue the men, the conversations over, silence in the bunker. Nothing we can do about that, he thought. They fly too high for even the eighty-eights to hit them.

Behind him, Schmidt said, "I thought we'd hear more from the fighters up here. I expect the Luftwaffe is hanging back a little, letting those boys get too far from home. I'd hate to be up there. Give me some concrete and my feet on the ground."

There was low laughter, more of the talk beginning, and Reimer focused on the wide stretch of sand. He could see flecks of black, the closest shore obstacles just visible, the first hint of daylight. The hum of the planes was louder. He looked up into concrete, thinking, That's strange.

Schmidt was beside him now. "What the hell? They've turned. Sounds like they're coming this way."

The men were all up, faces at the openings in the concrete, the sound of the planes droning overhead ever louder. Reimer heard a whistle, cutting through the hum, and backed away fast. "Down! Get down!"

The blast shook the ground beneath him, and he flattened out, men scrambling over one another, tumbling down: more blasts, hard rocking quakes. The explosions shook the concrete, dust raining down; for long seconds, there was no other sound but the hard roar of bomb blasts. Reimer closed his eyes, his face in his helmet, his arms in tight, holding the terror inside. But then, just as quickly, the blasts moved away, back behind the bunker, a thousand giant hammers, punching the ground farther away from the beach. He raised his head, one hand pulling his helmet on straight; he could still feel the shaking in the concrete beneath him, but the deafening blasts were distant, hollow. He blew dust out of his mouth. Men were coughing around him, and now a voice—the lieutenant—said, "Stay down! We're safe in here!"

No one answered. Reimer focused on the sounds, the bombs raining down far behind them, and then a different chatter of sounds, small bursts in a long chorus. "The minefield," the lieutenant said. "That sound . . . they're bombing the minefield!"

In short minutes the bombing had stopped, no sounds at all. The men were rising slowly, wiping concrete dust from the guns. Reimer's ears were ringing.

"They missed us!" Schmidt said. "They damned well missed us!"

The lieutenant was up now. "Anyone hurt?"

No one responded. Reimer saw him moving away, checking the others. No one responded, every man searching himself for injury, clearing his brain of the noise and the dust. Reimer pulled a handkerchief from his pocket, leaned close to the gun, and wiped the mechanism.

Schmidt punched him on the back. "Good thing I didn't get up like you wanted and rush back to the depot. I told you, give me concrete every time."

Reimer, still gaining his hearing, shook his head and thought of the depot, the new boxes of ammunition. Damn! "Lieutenant, you think they hit the depot?"

"I don't know, Corporal. We'll find out soon enough. For now, we should remain here. There could be more bombers, and these bunkers have saved us."

"My God. My God!"

Reimer turned. One of the others was staring out, his face pressed close to an opening in the concrete. He moved that way, saw the gray softness of daylight spreading out over the beach to the open water. For two weeks he had watched the horizon, the first glimpse of dawn revealing the water, either smooth and glassy or broken by waves and whitecaps. But now there was something else. The lieutenant was close beside him.

"Those are ships," he said in a low voice. "It's a whole fleet."

Reimer felt a jolt of ice in his legs. His eyes fixed on the sight: dark shadows, small ships and large. No words, no talk from anyone. His mind was racing: questions, a rising surge of fear.

Schmidt, close to him, said, "They're ours, right? That's the German navy. Somebody's going to catch some hell today."

"I don't know," the lieutenant said. "I need to get to the radio, see what's happening. Stay alert here!"

Reimer kept his eyes on the ships, the farthest ones, enormous, larger than any he had ever seen. He heard the low hum again, but faint, a single plane, rattles of gunfire, farther down the beach. There was a shout, some-

where outside, more machine-gun fire, the sound of the plane's engine
drifting away. He kept his eyes on the ships, his mind swirling with questions, one man in the bunker said, "Spotter plane. I bet that was a spotter
plane."

"Spotting what?"

There were flashes now, flickers and specks of light all across the horizon, and Reimer pulled back from the concrete. *Those aren't our ships at all.*

He glanced to the side, the lieutenant still there, frozen, staring out,
and the lieutenant said, "Spotting *us*."

The awful noises returned: screaming wails, the air above them ripped
and shattered. The shells began to thunder above them, jolting him, the
men tumbling again, more dust, the concrete shaking, deafening blasts.
He lay flat, held his helmet to his head, curled his legs in tight, felt himself
bouncing on the concrete, his hands hard on his ears, his brain screaming
into the roar of fire, the terror grabbing him, pulling him into a complete
and perfect hell.

A fter forty minutes it stopped.

Silence hung over them in the thick dusty air. Reimer felt it first
in his chest, the hard quaking inside him suddenly quiet. His hands were
still against his head but he opened his eyes, saw whiteness, the breeze
pushing through slits in the concrete, daylight and dust, the air slowly
clearing. Men were moving, crawling, some with hands still locked over
their ears. Reimer saw faces, wide-eyed shock, eyes fighting to see, and he
pulled his own hands away, hesitant, expecting more of the shocking
blows, but there was silence, no sound at all. The lieutenant was there,
close to him, a hand on his shoulder, and Reimer nodded, couldn't hear
the man at all, struggled to his knees, then up to his feet. He saw Schmidt,
on his feet as well, adjusting his helmet, blood on the man's face, a cut on
his nose. Schmidt looked at him, gray dirt accenting the whites of his eyes,
the sounds starting to come back, soft murmurs, and said, "You all right?"

The words were hollow and soft against the numbness in his ears, and
Reimer nodded. He looked past Schmidt, saw the machine gun lying on
its side, the tripod pointing in the air, and moved quickly, instinctively,
righting the gun. Schmidt was there as well, and then a hard hand on his
back and the voice of the lieutenant.

"Man the guns! All of you! Loaders, up and ready!"

The men responded, the machine guns put back in place, boxes of ammunition opened, belts coming out. Reimer looked toward the water again, could see the ships more clearly now, the sea alive with motion. My God, he thought. They're coming in. The lieutenant was moving among them, quick and efficient.

"Everyone ready!" He shouted, "No firing! If they put men on the beach, wait for that! Wait for the order!" There was panic in his voice.

Reimer glanced down at the gun. Schmidt was holding the belt of shells, looking at him, waiting. Reimer reached down, pulled hard on the bolt, clamped the first shell in place. He looked out again, saw a narrow crack in the concrete, but the thick walls were still in place, solid, the strength that had saved them from the shelling. The ships were everywhere, larger ones on the horizon, smaller ones, much smaller, moving toward the shore. He felt his stomach turning, rubber in his legs, sat down behind the gun, stared down the barrel, swung the gun from side to side, sweeping motion, wide field of fire. Alongside him, the others did the same, no one speaking, no words, every man focused on the job, the training. Most had done this before, but training was not like this, memories of target practice were swept away by what they faced now. He focused on one boat, strange, flat-faced, pushing awkwardly through the water, and aimed the gun, his hand gripping the mechanism. Around him, the men waited, no sound at all, no planes, no artillery fire.

"They're coming in right under our guns," the lieutenant said. "At low tide. This is too easy."

20. THORNE

They had rolled and tossed for nearly two hours, the men who were able staying on their feet, a pool of salt water and vomit washing around their boots. Despite the seasickness pills, nearly every man had succumbed, and adding to their misery, every man was soaked with the salt spray and the stink of the gas-fighting chemical in their clothing. Thorne had suffered as badly as any around him, but the lieutenant had screamed himself hoarse over a new problem, the rising level of water in the bottom of the boat. The men who could muster the energy began to bail with their helmets, tossing the stinking brew up and over the sides, much of it caught by the stiff breeze and blown back in. Thorne wanted to help, but the aching sickness kept his hands frozen at his chest, one crossed over to grip the rifle, the other hard on the cramp in his stomach. His backpack was pressed against a man behind him, who held them both up by leaning against the side of the boat.

They rolled forward toward the shore beneath a shroud of heavy clouds, faint daylight most of them had not yet noticed. Around him, men were talking, some of them loosening their hold on their fears, trying to fight off the misery by focusing more on what they were about to do. He felt a hand on his shoulder, one of the men standing high above him, and Thorne looked up, saw the man staring out over the side of the boat, a loud shout.

"Wowee! Look at that! It's a battleship. The *Texas,* I bet!"

The man was answered by a thunderous roar, the small boat quivering from the shock. The man fell backward, came down hard. Thorne was knocked back, men falling like dominoes, splashes in the boat. The thunder grew, the big guns on the warships opening up in a chorus of hard thumps and roars, and Thorne felt it in his ears and gut. The barrage of fire brought more men out of their sickness, more of them rising up to see, and there were shouts, cheers.

One of the sailors called out, a warning. "Hold on! Brace yourselves!"

A single wave came now, different, a wide swell that rolled the boat sideways, men tumbling back, falling, sloppy splashes. Almost immediately, Thorne felt the boat rolling again, back the other way, and tried to balance himself, move with it, his outstretched hands slamming hard against the bulkhead, men falling against his back, pushing his face into the steel. But the roaring thunder continued, and he fought against the sickness, struggled to see, pulled himself up, looked out, spray in his face again. He could see the battleships, long streaks of fire from the massive guns, more ships firing in the distance, on all sides, another battleship behind them. The lieutenant was close beside him, one fist in the air.

"Yes! Kill the bastards! Blow them to hell!"

Thorne held tightly to the top of the bulkhead and steadied himself, the pressure from behind lightening, the men finding their balance. The sailor called out again. "Brace yourselves! Another wake from the battleship! Hold on!"

With every salvo from their fourteen-inch guns, the great ships recoiled, and the wake they created spread through the tiny landing craft, adding to the roughness of the surf. But the men knew what to expect now, and when the boat rolled to the side again, they were ready, most huddling low, no one falling. Thorne stayed up, holding tight to the top of the steel bulkhead, straining to see, streaks of fire from every warship, the arc of the massive shells pointing the way, smoky blasts along the shoreline. The other landing craft were close, their own fleet of six boats, packed with helmets, men peering up as he was. To one side were the larger craft, the

LSTs, which carried tanks and artillery, and far in the distance, many more, large and small, every one pounding its way forward through the rolling swells.

The shock waves continued to roll the deep water beneath them, and Thorne looked ahead, the shoreline buried under smoke and fire, the sight energizing him, energizing all of them. But then the fire began to slow, the big ships growing silent, others, in the distance, quieting as well. And then, it stopped. The men were still straining to see, the crowded boat still plunging forward, rolling and pitching, some men still bailing water. Thorne stared forward, saw low clouds of smoke, the last remains of the naval bombardment. But it was clearing now, and he could see the shoreline, a chalky wall, cut by a deep V, hints of houses and buildings. The only sound was the smoky churning of the boat's engine. He scanned the horizon out to both sides of the boat and could still see the battleships and other warships, silent sentinels.

The lieutenant spoke beside him. "That's it. We're too close in. They can't shoot over us. Whatever is left out there . . . is ours."

Suddenly there were new sounds, high shrieking wails, the men flinching, heads turning toward the closest landing ships, sheets of flame pouring toward the shore. Thorne felt his heart leap in his chest.

"Rockets!" the lieutenant said. "Give 'em hell!"

Thorne had seen this before in the rehearsals at Slapton Sands, but only from a great distance. He had never heard the frightening screams before, the ships that carried the rocket launchers very close to them. Some were behind them, the rockets streaking right over their heads, every man flinching, holding their helmets, some kneeling down. Thorne wanted to see, fought the fear, the lieutenant again, "Damn! They're too close! Keep your heads down!"

Thorne obeyed, leaned his helmet against the moving bulkhead, the piercing screams whining in his ears. And just that quickly, it was over. Men responded as he did, standing tall again, staring forward, more smoke on the shoreline.

"That's our cover!" the lieutenant shouted. "Doesn't matter if they hit anything. Sure as hell they put holes on the beach!"

Cover. Thorne hadn't thought of that; there was nothing in the drills about making cover. *Do we need it? Who could survive all that shelling? There's nobody left out there.* He focused on that; surely, surely no one's left alive. Or they ran away. He was breathing hard, could see a wide flat stretch of sand; his heart thundered in his chest.

The men were talking again, a clatter of voices rising, all of them standing up now, and the sailor shouted, "Get ready!"

The words sliced through him, an icy bayonet. *Ready.* Get ready. I'm ready. He thought of the battle cry, all that pride drilled into them. *Twenty-nine . . . let's go!* All right, then, let's go. Let's go get our bronze stars. He thought of the man who had said that; maybe he was right. Bronze star. Words rolled through his brain. The colonel's last briefing: Get off the beach . . . get your ass off the beach . . . too many men coming in behind you . . . clear the way. That's the job, he thought. Clear the way. Blow the wire, find the draws, look for the church steeple. The church steeple. He stared out toward the V-shaped dip in the cliff, just like the drawings, and beyond, through the drifting smoke, a steeple.

The sight punched him, and he shouted, "There it is! The church!"

It was the first thing he had said since he boarded the small craft, but other men were calling out as well, and Thorne saw a sign, posted beside the ramp at the front of the boat, had not noticed it before: NO SMOKING.

His eyes froze on the sign, and for one moment his brain grabbed on to its pure nonsense. What the hell difference would it make anyway? He looked at the others, most of them staring to the front, smoother water, and his eyes caught motion, low along the beach, the sounds reaching him now, fighter planes, screaming past.

At the rear of the boat, the sailor called out again. "Another minute!"

The men were silent now, all eyes to the front, wispy smoke on the beach, small fires, the larger LCTs moving in closer; *the tanks will go in first.* Thorne was shivering again, tight pain in his stomach, the sailor's words: *another minute.* His eyes stayed fixed on the beach: no movement, nothing alive, no one there. There was silence from the men around him, and now a whistle, coming toward them, a soft punch in the water, a plume suddenly rising high. He looked that way, saw another rising farther out, close to another boat. Now the whistles rolled overhead, the air split by the sounds. The lieutenant shouted, "Artillery! Keep your head down!"

Thorne ducked, his helmet pressed against the bulkhead, one hand against the steel. *Steel.* Good. We're okay in here. He felt a hard jerk, the boat lurching to a stop, suddenly pulling backward, the engine reversing, and the sailor called out, "This is it! As far as I go! Lower the ramp!"

Beside Thorne, the lieutenant yelled out, "Not yet! Get closer!"

"No! This is it! We've got to do it now!"

"You son of a bitch! Get us closer!"

"I said, lower the ramp! *Now!*"

The sailor's crewmen obeyed, the ramp yawning outward, falling downward to the surface of the water. The lieutenant was still shouting and Thorne saw his face, raw fury. But the boat had stopped, and the training was in all of them. The lieutenant turned, moved toward the opening, yelled out one more time. "We might have to swim. Inflate your belts!"

Thorne saw the edge of the ramp dipping below the water in front of them, the wide expanse of beach still a hundred yards away, and the lieutenant stepped out onto the ramp, one glance back.

"Life belts! Let's go!"

And now there were new sounds, sharp cracks and pings, lead on steel, and Thorne saw the lieutenant's face, sudden shock in his eyes, the man dropping to his knees, falling to one side, tumbling off the ramp into the water.

Behind Thorne, the sailor shouted, "Go! Go!"

The men seemed frozen, most staring at the place where the lieutenant had been, but his body was gone completely. The bullets were coming into the boat now, another man falling forward, a hard grunt. Some of the men began pulling back, trying to escape from the inescapable, but one man moved out onto the ramp, jumped quickly into the water, and Thorne saw him standing upright, the water waist-deep, the man waving his arm.

"Let's go!"

Thorne slid the rifle off his shoulder, pressed forward, and waited while the men in front of him filed out. He was there now, the sloping ramp under his feet, chattering rips in the air, a hard crack, the man falling away, then another beside Thorne dropping to his knees, falling facedown on the ramp. A bullet smacked into the steel beside him, a whistle of artillery, a tall plume punched up to one side. Men were pushing at him from behind, hard cursing shouts, and Thorne jumped down, water in his face, his boots hitting bottom, heard a man crying out behind him, more splashes. He pushed hard through the water, ducking low, down to his shoulders, held his rifle in front of his face. Men were moving beside him now, as he was, pushing forward. There were more spits in the water around him, zips above his head, a sharp crack rattling past his helmet, a hard watery blast to one side, but he did not stop; he pushed forward, furious at the water that grabbed him, slowed him. The artillery shells ripped overhead, and he was swarmed by the hard stink of smoke, saw a thick black swirl, fire, wreckage in the shallow water. His legs kept moving ahead, water and smoke in his face and now a hard blast, a ball of fire, more black smoke. He looked that way, saw another boat, direct hit, men on fire, bodies in the water. He wanted to stop, thought of helping, but it was too far, the bullets were still cutting the water around him, and his legs did not stop but pushed him forward, his brain screaming, *Keep going!* It was easier now, shallow water, then he was out, hard sand, black steel in the sand, crosses and poles in front of him, men moving past, his lungs burning, his legs heavy, the weight on his back dragging him down. He fought that, looked straight ahead, smoke rolling past, screaming men, more blasts, more fighter planes overhead, wide flat sand, the cliffs so far away. He lowered his head again, heard another sharp cry, more thunder, a burst of sand beside him, whistling steel. There was no thought, just the motion of his legs, driven by the training and the terror. He could hear the steady rattle and rip of machine guns far out in front of him, thumping bursts of mortar fire in the wet sand. He was gasping, his legs cold lead, and he moved to one of the steel crosses, his hand out, holding himself, his knees giving way, his chest heaving. Men were around him, no words, desperate and exhausted, stopping, as he was, finding cover behind the steel, more men tumbling into the sand.

"Help! Medic! Oh, God!"

Thorne searched for the man but there were too many, stumbling and falling, helmets off, backpacks scattered, another blast, a chorus of *pings* on the hard steel beam above his head. He knelt low, kept his face down, both knees in the wet sand, another man down beside him, seeking cover, a hand grabbing his shoulder, panic in the man's voice.

"We can't do this! We have to go back!"

More men were down behind him, one man crying, uncontrollable wailing, but most of them were silent, heads down, some of them flattening out behind the protection of the steel, the shower of machine-gun fire relentless. Thorne heard more of the thumps, grunts and cries, sparks in front of him, bullets striking the steel. He tried to roll himself up tight, a smaller target, but a hand was grabbing his collar, a deafening voice in his ear.

"Let's go! Get to the beach!"

The man moved out in front of him, beyond the protection of the steel, and Thorne saw more men doing the same, running across the flat sands, some tumbling forward, one man tossed to the side, broken by a mortar blast. Pieces.

Behind him another man came forward, screamed, "Go! We gotta go!"

Thorne knew the voice, the old sergeant; Woodruff went past him, running low, holding his M-1. Thorne saw the plastic wrapping, thought of his own, the rifle clamped in his hands, his brain yelling instructions, Load it! Shoot back! He glanced up toward the beach again, nothing to see, in his head the idiotic instructions: *Know your targets.* He saw Woodruff, still moving, going up a rise, a low wall of rocks, Woodruff down now, waving his arm, calling them forward; more men moving up to him, more cover.

Thorne tried to move his legs, cramped, paralyzed, another hard blast, black smoke rolling over him, machine-gun fire striking the steel in front of him. He felt himself shaking, wanted to cry, terror holding him, but another wave of men was moving past him, some of them stopping close to him, behind the obstacles, seeking cover, but the mortar fire was finding them too. The thumping explosions came in a steady rhythm around them, throwing sand in the air, a direct hit on one of the steel obstacles a few yards away. He stared that way: pieces of men, an arm hanging on a steel beam, rocking slowly, fingers curling up.

You can't stay here! He realized now, there was water beneath him, a shallow wave coming slowly from behind. The briefing came back, one fact no one had paid attention to, something about the tide coming in, faster than anything they had seen. A helmet rolled past him now, carried by the flow, more clothing, and men were splashing past him, panicked cries, wounded men calling out. *You can't stay here!* He looked for Woodruff and saw dark shapes, men huddled low behind a rocky wall. *Cover.* Go!

He pulled himself up, fought through the stiffness in his legs, the burning weakness in his lungs. He held the rifle close in front of him and tried to run, slow plodding steps, splashing water. The machine-gun fire was steady, cutting the air over and around him, hard splashes, more heavy blasts behind him, a sharp explosion, more smoke. He focused on the wall, now closer—no more water, no more obstacles, just soft sand, the beach rising up—hard pain in his legs, fire in his chest. He was close to the wall, saw it wasn't a wall at all, just a mound of small rocks, spread out all along the beach, but it was all the cover they had. He dropped to his knees, crawled forward, moved through a cluster of men, lifeless, dark stains in the sand, a broken rifle, shredded backpack. He pushed past, saw faces watching him, one face, Woodruff, the sergeant staring back at him with black eyes, dull shock.

Thorne crawled up beside him, collapsed, gasping, spitting through the sand in his mouth. No one was talking, machine-gun fire chattering across the rocks above him. More men were coming up the sloping sand, dropping down along the rocks, soft cries; one man, blood on his face, helmet gone, running; men shouting at him, *Get down;* and Thorne saw the impact punching the man's chest, the man curling up, rolling forward. The cries rose across the beach in a horrible chorus, wounded men calling for stretchers, some still out on the open beach. Thorne looked back and saw a hand in the air, the man screaming, meaningless noises, one man running low, moving toward him, a dull red cross on the man's helmet. But the storm of fire blew over them and the medic collapsed, falling onto the man he was trying to help.

Thorne felt himself shaking, sick, the rifle still in his hands, still wrapped in plastic, watched as more of the men splashed through the shallow water, so many of the landing crafts in the distance. Some of the boats were close, had come in with the tide, pieces, broken and battered, no one at the controls, black smoke. He looked along the rocky embankment, out past the gathering men, and saw a tank on fire, still in the water; another, sideways, farther out in the surf. The larger landing craft were still coming in, spread out all across the rising water. His eyes fixed on one of the larger ones, close; he saw the big ramp come down and heard Woodruff's angry outburst.

"Tanks! They're coming in behind us! *Behind us!* They're supposed to be here first! This isn't going to work!"

Thorne didn't respond, his brain arguing, They did come in first! They just didn't make it! There weren't enough of them! He kept his stare on the wrecked tanks, those few that had led the assault, but they were gone, useless, no sign of their crews. More men were coming in through the surf, gathering in a cluster, kneeling behind a burning tank, using the wreckage for cover. But there was no cover; just machine-gun fire sweeping them from too many directions, the men suddenly collapsing into the surf. Farther out, more artillery fire erupted near an LST, the wide maw of its ramp hidden by smoke and tall plumes of water.

Now a tank rolled out onto the ramp, its gun firing with a hard thump, the tank spilling forward into the water, then upright, pushing toward shore, the gun firing again. Another tank emerged onto the ramp, more firing from both tanks, the second tank close behind the first, rolling through the shallow surf. Woodruff was still cursing, but Thorne ignored him, thought, Thank God. Thank God. They'll save us. He stared at the open bow of the ship, another tank appearing, magnificent power, another one emerging from behind. Yes! Keep coming! The first two reached the flat open sand, turrets in motion, guns firing upward toward the cliffs, and the sand in front of the first tank erupted, the artillery shell just short. The tank kept moving forward, up the incline of the soft beach, and now Thorne heard the sounds, shell after shell in the air close overhead. The sand erupted again, the first tank impacted by the blast, more sand and smoke, the second tank moving past the wreckage, another blast, direct hit, more shells falling farther out, on the landing craft itself. The surviving tanks continued to fire, but the enemy had the range now, and the water around the tanks flew into a fiery spray, more direct hits, an open hatch, men suddenly appearing, scrambling out of the burning wreck, tumbling away, sprayed by machine-gun fire.

Thorne felt sick again, heard low groans around him, and Woodruff, high panic in the man's voice. "This isn't working! It isn't working!"

The machine guns continued to fire, seeking targets, splintering the rocks over his head. Thorne looked to the side, saw a dozen men, most curled up tightly, one man frantically scooping the sand with his hands, others now copying him. Thorne looked at Woodruff, saw none of the older man's steel but only panic in his eyes.

"Sarge! What do we do? We're supposed to be going through the draw . . . toward the church."

"I'm not going anywhere. The lieutenant is dead. Hell, as far as I know, every lieutenant is dead. We have to get out of here . . . back to the boats!"

Beside the sergeant, a man began to dig frantically. "They're all dead! Captain Fellers is dead! I saw him!"

Thorne absorbed that: Fellers, the company's commanding officer.

"There are no boats!" Thorne shouted. "We can't stay here! We have to keep going!"

Woodruff said nothing, just rolled to one side, digging his own fox-hole, frantic hands working the sand.

Thorne was furious now, grabbed Woodruff by the shoulder and shouted, "Dammit, we can't stay here!"

Woodruff took his arm, hard grip, terrified anger in the man's eyes.

"Let go of me. You want to keep going, go ahead. Maybe we'll catch up to you."

Thorne was shaking again, realized the M-1 was still in plastic. He unwrapped it, saw wet sand in the breech, blew on it, then again, jerked the small bolt, the rifle loaded. He was panting heavily. Other men watching him with wild-eyed fear, some settling into shallow foxholes, tossing sand out in small scoops. Thorne felt helpless, weak. He glanced up at the rocks cresting a foot above his head. He looked back out toward the water, the vast fleet in the distance, useless now, more of the larger landing craft pushing in under their barrage balloons. Smaller craft came in as well, the next wave, some moving close to the steel obstacles, another explosion, the craft tossed backward, rolling over, men falling away, survivors jumping into the rising tide. Thorne watched the men pushing through the water, some stopping, dropping in shallow water, flattening out, seeking shelter from wreckage and pieces of debris.

All along the edge of the water, the tide had brought in a mass of horror, the slow ebb and flow of shattered men and equipment. But the machine guns did not stop, and the wreckage at the water's edge was no cover at all. On the beach itself, bodies were scattered in chaotic heaps, rifles and helmets, much of the gear they carried blasted into rubble. Thorne could see now that the sand was nearly smooth, no holes, none of the cover from the navy's shelling. He tried to shake the thoughts from his head, the lieutenant, the rockets. What happened? Did they miss . . . everything?

The fighter planes came over them again, one man shouting, "Krauts!"

But Thorne could see the distinct shapes of the P-38s. "No! They're ours!"

The planes began to circle, rips of fire into targets on the cliffs, the planes rolling over, moving away. But still the machine guns sprayed out all across the beach, unstoppable.

The flow of men continued, men fighting their way past the carnage in the surf, and Thorne could only watch them, coming up out of the water, running to reach the rocks.

"Get up!" one man shouted at the huddled men. "Get the hell off this beach! Get to the cliffs! Move it!"

Thorne knew that sound, the authority of an officer, saw captain's bars on the man's helmet and felt breathless relief—someone in command—but saw that the captain's arm was hanging loose, a flow of blood; the man fell to his knees and forward onto the sand. More men came up, a medic, not stopping, all of them seeking the cover of the rocks, but there was no space now, men pushing up hard against the others or scrambling to dig holes. There was a thumping explosion—no warning, a mortar shell—and sand sprayed over Thorne, screams, bodies tossed aside.

He turned toward Woodruff again, his anger boiling. "We're dead if we stay here!"

"We're dead anyway! There's nowhere to go!"

Thorne's hands ached from the grip on the rifle. He wanted to stick the barrel into the man's face. "You son of a bitch. You're supposed to be in charge! The officers are dead! Damn you, you're just a coward."

Woodruff turned away. Thorne saw faces, a dozen men watching him. He felt icy desperation, more mortar shells blowing sand in the air, some impacting the shallow water. One man pointed up at the top of the rocks.

"If we go up, there could be cover. If we're quick."

Another shell impacted the sand, close, showering them all. Thorne felt the energy, more men coming out of their shock, some watching him, hopeful, men who knew the job they were supposed to do.

"Yes! We can't stay here!" He pointed out toward the surf, more landing craft dropping their ramps. "They're sitting ducks if we don't get those machine guns! That's what we're here for!"

Another man called out, "Who's in command? Are there any officers here?"

Thorne looked out to both sides, no one responding. He thought of the lieutenant, Woodruff's words: *Every lieutenant is dead.* Out in the surf, a fresh wave of men was coming in, and he looked along the shoreline, no place for them, no cover at all.

He rolled over, checked the breech on his rifle, took a long quivering breath, and said, "We have to go! We have to get those machine guns!"

Others responded, nods, quick shouts.

"Let's go!"

He looked down, a brief moment, stared into sand, another breath, checked the rifle again, pulled himself up, jumped up on the loose rocks, his feet stumbling, the rocks giving way. He was in the open now, his eyes searching, frantic, a narrow stretch of road, the cliff beyond, no holes, no

cover at all. He ran, crossed the roadway, saw a deep cut in the hill, a valley, moved that way, the air coming apart around him, shrieks and pops
and cracks. He moved toward the base of a hill, a low mound of dirt, saw
barbed wire. Another spray of machine-gun fire cut the ground beside
him. He dropped flat, his chest heaving, and more men came up around
him, some of them firing blindly, curses and shouts.

One man rolled over toward him and said, "Torpedo . . . in my backpack!"

Thorne saw blood on the man's chest, the stain spreading, the man
staring blankly, then a soft gasp, empty eyes. Beside him, a man fell flat,
crawled close, said, "He's got a torpedo! I'll get it!"

The man grabbed the dead man's trio of metal pipes and cut through
the straps with his bayonet. Another man was there now and fastened
them together, a lengthening pole, the first man attaching the explosive
charge. Thorne pointed the rifle up the hill, pulled the trigger, pulled it
again, but there were no targets, nothing to shoot at.

The man beside him rolled to one side, the long pipe in his hands.
"Ready! Heads down!"

They all flattened out, the man shoving the pipe out beneath the
barbed wire, then a sharp blast, dirt falling on them, pieces of wire. Thorne
raised up and saw the gap, shreds of wire on both sides of him. The machine guns fired again, and now rifle fire, lower in the rocks, hard pops, a
sharp grunt from the man beside him, rolling backward. Thorne reached
for him, froze, the rifle fire cracking around him, blood on the man's face,
too much blood, and Thorne ducked low, gripped the rifle again, turned
to the side—more men had gathered, a dozen more—and he shouted out,
"Go!"

They rose together, but not everyone, the machine guns still finding
their targets. Thorne ran forward, searched the ground frantically, the
enemy firing from the rocks above them. He stopped again, lay flat, flickers of fire from a stout wall of concrete. He crawled forward, rolled into
a low dip in the ground, the guns firing over his head, German words
shouted above him. Thorne rolled over, faced the water, leaned his back
against the embankment, saw men hunkered down along the splintering
rocks, some moving closer, some firing their rifles. Thorne looked up,
straight above him; he could see slits in the heavy concrete, but too far. He
put a hand on his chest, felt for a grenade, and said, "We have to get up
higher!"

Men were watching him, others pulling at the grenades on their chests, understanding, one man starting to climb, keeping flat against the rock. Thorne watched him: Yes, good, go! Others were firing their rifles, covering fire, and the man worked his way up slowly, the rip of the machine guns still above them. Thorne wanted to help, to climb as well, but the rock above him was smooth, no steps, nothing to grab. He leaned back, aimed the rifle at the slits, but there was nothing, and he thought of the rocks on the beach, shattered into splinters. Maybe . . . just shoot at something!

There was a rattling in the rocks beside him and he heard a shout, looked that way, saw the distinct shape of a German grenade rolling, tumbling down the rocks, coming to a stop below his feet.

He felt himself bouncing, opened his eyes, saw a man standing below his feet, and realized he was on a stretcher. The bouncing stopped now, the stretcher down, his back resting on hard ground, more men around him, soft cries, gray light in his eyes. He wanted to talk, questions forming, but the fog was thick in his brain, dull aching in his arm, his eyes trying to close again. He felt a burst of panic, forced his eyes open, and the energy came now, his voice hollow, distant.

"What happened? Where are we?"

One man leaned low, dirty red cross on his helmet, low thin voice, very far away. "You're wounded. But we got you. I gave you morphine. You'll be okay."

Thorne felt his eyes close, forced them to open again, the word rolling into his brain: *wounded.* Where? How bad? The medic was gone, just gray sky above him, rock walls, shadows. There were thumps in the distance, and he felt the panic returning—artillery, mortar fire—tried to sit up, useless, no energy, realized now there was a bandage on his right arm. *Wounded* . . . where? I'm okay? Is he lying? Maybe I'm dead. Angels. He fought the fog, raised his head, all the strength he had, a blanket across his body, had to see, flexed his fingers, the left arm free, no bandage. He raised it slowly, looked at his fingers, saw them moving, heard more voices, one man calling out, flickers of movement to one side, men carrying another stretcher. He tried to see, blinked through the fog, thought, Where am I? The fog spilled through his brain, and he forced his eyes open, saw rocky walls straight up on two sides of him, Yes, that's good. Cover . . . protection. His hand dropped down to the side, his fingers curling up in soft sand. The beach? He tried to move his right arm: a bolt of pain, *wounded*. How bad? Dammit, where's the medic? His fingers flexed again, and he put the hand over his chest, reached for the other arm, felt the stiff gauze, the ache in his shoulder. He pulled the blanket away, slid his hand down, the uniform crusted, stiff and stinking, his hand moving to his genitals; nothing missing, thank God. His hand stopped at his thigh, no strength to sit up, no way to reach farther down. He flexed his toes, both feet, felt them wrapped in soft socks, no boots. *No boots.* Somebody took my boots!

"Hey! Hey! Somebody!"

The medic was there again, featureless face. "You hurting? Need more morphine?"

"My boots! They stole my boots!"

"What's he want?"

Thorne saw a second medic, a bag in his hand.

"I'll give him some more," the first man said. "He's asking for his boots."

"Oh, God. Yeah, it happens like that. He thinks he's feeling his toes. Okay, give him another shot. No time for this now."

Thorne felt his head swirling, the medic leaning low, close to his face. "Here. This'll help."

The fog rolled thick again, and he saw the barracks, men scrambling for inspection. "I don't have my boots! The lieutenant won't have that!"

The medic was there again, the man's face a soft blur, a voice, far away, meaningless words. "Get this one to the boat. The tourniquets won't hold much longer. He's lucky he lived. But he's lost both legs."

The men of the Twenty-ninth Division continued to pour onto Omaha Beach, alongside the continuous wave from the First Division, the Big Red One. On the other beaches—Utah, Gold, Juno, and Sword—American, British, and Canadian troops had a far easier time of it, confronting German forces who were caught utterly unprepared for the enormous onslaught of men and machines. In those landing zones, beachheads were quickly established and the enormous fleet of landing craft and transport ships continued to off-load an entire army onto miles of French coastline. As those successes mounted, Omar Bradley, offshore on his command ship, the U.S.S. *Augusta,* watched in horror as the Americans on

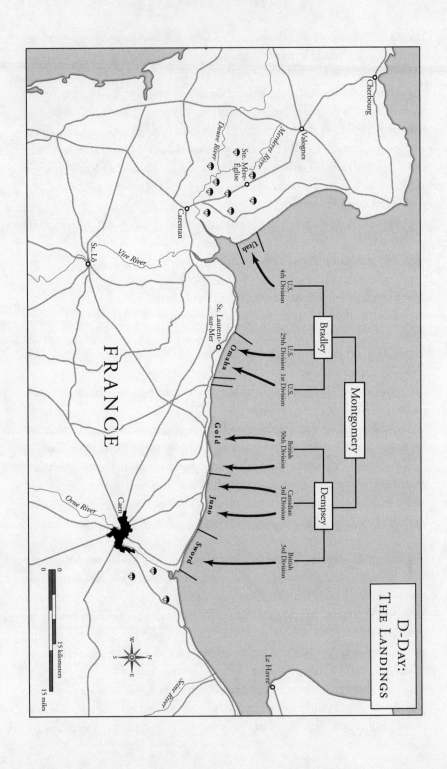

D-DAY:
THE LANDINGS

Omaha Beach confronted German resistance that no one believed was there. Instead of ill-equipped and worn-out German defenders, the Americans had stumbled into the crack 352nd Division. As the infantry, Rangers, and engineers struggled to find a foothold on Omaha Beach, the flow of reports that reached Bradley provided little optimism. What was supposed to have been a show of magnificent new technology, the floating tank, had instead been a disaster all its own. Of the thirty-two amphibious tanks destined for Omaha, twenty-seven had sunk of their own accord long before they could reach shallow water. Those tanks that were to be off-loaded from LCTs fared almost as badly. Most of the armor that was to have provided the opening fist for the American surge off Omaha Beach was instead reduced to burning wreckage along the water's edge. It was worse for the American artillery, in particular the 111th Field Artillery Battalion. Their mission was to support the infantry by landing a dozen 105mm howitzers. Those cannon would be hauled to the beach by another new technology, amphibious trucks. But the trucks had been launched too far offshore, and they were not equipped to ride through so many miles of rough surf. All twelve howitzers were lost, most of them disappearing with their crews beneath the rough seas before they ever fired a shot.

As the men and their equipment rolled into the firestorm on Omaha Beach, it was immediately obvious that the air attacks and the massive naval bombardment had accomplished very little.

Though the fight on Utah Beach had been far less devastating to the Americans than the ongoing disasters at Omaha, a struggle of a different sort took place inland. The mission of the 82nd and 101st Airborne divisions had been to secure the bridges, towns, and crossroads that would prevent German reinforcements from organizing a counterattack against the vulnerable American beachheads, exactly the sort of tactic Erwin Rommel had perfected. For the paratroopers, that fight had only just begun.

21. ADAMS

He had tried to sleep, if only for a few minutes, to ease the aching weariness in his joints. His foxhole was narrow and shallow, just enough to protect him from the machine-gun fire that might suddenly erupt around them. But the fire close by had stopped, and it was the silence that kept him awake. There was still sporadic firing in the distance, but none of the heavy naval guns and no bombers. The bombardments he could hear came mostly from the north, where the lieutenant believed the town had to be. He's probably wrong, he thought. That damned Texan could have dropped us anywhere. This is just like Sicily: blind pilots. Somebody's gotta figure out a better way to do this.

He eased himself up, his head above the grass, just enough daylight to see out across the field, the tree line on the far side less than two hundred yards away. He glanced along the brush line close to him and saw others stirring, anxious, as he was, to get moving.

One man crawled up out of his protection, a whisper. "Let's go!"

Adams responded quickly, was up out of the foxhole, the grass wet and cold, the men emerging from their shallow hiding places. He could see faces now, most still blackened.

Another whisper: Pullman. "This way!"

The men followed. Adams made a quick count: twenty-five, at least. He stepped into the brush, men behind him, thinking, It's a start. He thought of Scofield. We need to find him or someone else up the ladder. Sure wish we had someone in charge who's done this before.

They emerged out of the brush line to a flat hard road, a shallow ditch on both sides. Adams moved up close to Pullman, saw another man coming close, familiar, Sergeant Davies.

"We should split up, stay in the ditches, single file," Pullman said. There was a burst of fire in the distance, familiar thumps, and Pullman said, "We should keep moving in that direction."

Davies moved away, and Adams thought, Could, should. Dammit! Just give the order! Pullman was looking at him now, seemed to expect something.

"Anybody have a BAR?" Adams said.

Pullman looked around at the men. "I don't know."

Adams moved quickly, bent low, focused on each man, saw Unger, the high voice again. "I don't have a rifle!"

"Shut up! We'll find one! You've got your forty-five, right? Use that." He passed through the rest of them, saying, "BAR?"

No one responded. Adams reached the end of the line, looked back toward Pullman, and shook his head. Just dandy, he thought. Riflemen and a handful of Thompsons. Hope like hell we don't run into a tank.

Pullman moved up close to him. "You want to take the point here? I'll go across the road and take Davies with me."

Adams nodded, moved away. Just *tell* me to take the point, he thought. He kept low in the ditch, watched Pullman cross the road in a quick scamper, a dozen men following him, Davies bringing up the rear. Good. Davies knows what he's doing. He'll cover the lieutenant's ass. He looked at the men still with him, saw Corporal Nusbaum, and motioned him over. Nusbaum was there quickly.

"Bring up the rear on this side of the road," Adams said. "Keep them in the ditch. I don't like being in this road. Watch our backs."

"No problem, Sarge."

Nusbaum slipped past the others, whispered instructions, and Adams looked across the road. Pullman seemed to be waiting for him. Adams pointed, thinking, That's the way you want to go, isn't it? Pullman began to move, Adams as well, the men following. They crossed another road, a narrow farm lane, more of the hedgerows close on both sides. Hell of a place to wander through, he thought. Krauts could be anywhere. He glanced behind him, the men moving slowly, deliberate silence. Good.

They pushed straight ahead, another intersection in the distance, but the brush along both sides was tall and thick, small trees and tangles of limbs. He tried to see through to the other side, but the thickets were dense, impenetrable. He listened to his boots in the soft muck, the footsteps of the men behind him. Keep it quiet. If there's somebody on the other side of this mess, we need to find them before they find us.

It was close to full daylight, the sky still heavy and gray, thick mud in the ditch. Behind him, a man stumbled, a soft splash, and Adams looked back, furious at the sound, the man up again, Marley, a thumbs-up, nodding, and Adams turned to the front again, glanced to the right, across the road, Pullman watching him. Adams looked again to the front, the hedgerows tall on both sides of them.

The road ahead made a sweeping curve to the right, and Adams heard new sounds, the rhythm of boots, a man laughing. He froze, saw movement beyond the curve, dropped to one knee, men behind him doing the same. The sounds were closer, and he saw them now, a column of troops, two abreast, dark uniforms, helmets. He eased his eyes to the side, saw Pullman, frozen as well, watching him, aware. *Good.* Adams made no movement, no sign, thought, A hundred yards and closing. Just be still. Don't do anything, not yet. Let them get closer. How many? The men at the front of the column were marching toward him in a casual stride, oblivious, low chatter, the steady tramp of boots. His heart was racing, his breathing came in bursts, the Germans, still unaware, closer, fifty yards. He heard breathing behind him, the sound punching his brain, but it was time, the Germans too close. He glanced at Pullman, saw the man staring forward, motionless, so Adams fell forward and dropped flat, the muzzle of the Thompson level with the road, wouldn't wait for Pullman's order.

"*Fire!*"

The roadway erupted in pops of rifle fire, smoke and flashes, the Germans tumbling forward, men scattering into the ditches. Adams stayed low, the Thompson at his shoulder, short bursts, one man coming toward him in the ditch, facing him, wide-eyed and frantic, holding a machine pistol, the *rrrrip* of the gun wild, no aim. Adams squeezed the trigger, the man falling backward, another man behind him, down as well.

The Germans were returning fire now, the roadway too narrow, men on both sides trying to push into the hedges, the cover too dense, scattered fire finding them. Some were still in the road, lying flat, using the fallen for cover, taking aim now, cracks in the air above his head. He heard a hard grunt behind him—wouldn't look, not now, no time—he rolled to one side in the mud and grass and slid behind a small tree, but not far enough, his right side exposed. The Thompson was empty, and he curled tightly behind his narrow cover, ripped at the pocket on his leg, grabbed another magazine, slammed it into the gun, and jerked the bolt, ready again. The men behind him were still firing, and he stayed low, looked back, the muzzle of an M-1 above his face, deafening, smoky blasts. There was shouting all across the road, and Adams fired the Thompson over his shoulder, blind, sprayed the ditch, the road. Above him, bullets shattered the small tree, more of the *rrrrip* from the German guns.

He saw his men pushing into the hedge, a gap, escaping, frantic calls, "Go! This way!"

He watched the man above him back away, firing the rifle, empty now, the man fumbling for another clip, a crack of bone, the man tumbling backward, twisting, blood flowing on his blackened face, silent, motionless. Adams stared for a long second, didn't know the man, saw the others, jumping up, one at a time, pushing into the opening in the brush. Others were firing, muzzles pointed past him; he ignored the fallen man and yelled out, "Go! Through the gap! Pull back!"

The closest man was up and through the gap now, and Adams saw more men down, one man rolling over in the ditch, soft cries, blood. Dammit! Dammit! Adams rolled out from behind the tree, fired the Thompson, saw German helmets low in the ditch in front of him. But the firing had slowed, the Germans backing away, seeking their own cover, beyond the curve in the road. He reached down, grabbed the fallen man's jacket, saw the hole in the man's forehead, wouldn't see it, released him, looked to the next man, movement, the man only wounded. It was Buford, calling out, blood on his arm, and Adams grabbed his shirt, looked into the gap, and started up the embankment, dragging Buford behind him. There was another *rrrrip* from down the road, the mud splattering, a hard grunt from Buford, thumps in his chest, and the man fell out of Adams's grip. Adams turned, saw the German crouched low in the ditch, saw his face and his machine pistol, the man reloading, and fired the

Thompson again, wild, missed, the German turning, running, more men behind him, some still firing. Adams launched himself up through the gap, the brush shattering, splinters in his face, and pushed hard through the tangle, the hedge falling away, open on the other side. He slid down, put another magazine in the Thompson, and aimed it at the gap, his hands shaking. Come on! Try it! But the fire had slowed, a single pop and then nothing, voices in the distance.

He looked along the embankment—six men—and fought his breathing, looked at the faces, wild, terrified, one man without a helmet: Marley, no rifle, panic in his eyes. Unger was there as well—thank God—the young man flat against the dirt, his eyes closed, soft words. Hell of a time to pray, kid. Coulda used it ten minutes ago.

Adams looked up into the gap again, no movement, thought, They're pulling back. But there's not enough of us, and they know it. They'll be back, or they'll move around us. He thought of Pullman, the other ditch. He eased up slowly, the Thompson pointing the way, peered into the gap, could see across the road, no sign of anyone else. But the cries were there, hard sharp sounds, wounded men on both sides. Adams looked back at the six men along the embankment and said in a low voice, "Anybody hit?"

The men glanced at one another, heads shaking. Unger stared intently across the open field, Adams following his lead, stared out as well. The field was at least two hundred yards across, easy rifle range, another thick hedgerow on the far side.

"Krauts could be right over there," Adams said. "We have to get the hell out of here."

"What about the others?"

The words came from the last man, a corporal's stripes, Nusbaum.

"You wanna run back out there and see what they're doing?"

"We can't just pull back, Sarge. Guys got hit. We have to get the wounded."

Adams looked up into the gap, the awful cries, lowered his head. Dammit! There was a new sound now, the dull roar of an engine, shouts in German. Adams moved into the gap, pushed at the small limbs with the submachine gun, stared across toward the far ditch: no movement, one man lying flat in the road, the eagle on his shoulder, the man from the 101st. Adams pushed himself on his elbows, heard another truck, the squeal of brakes, and slid forward, his head turned sideways, peered out past the edge of the brush, saw them at the far end of the curve in the road. There were two fat trucks, twin machine guns mounted on top. German troops were gathering behind, officers spitting out orders, one man in the truck staring at . . . *him*. The brush above his head flew into pieces, and Adams shoved backward and slid down the embankment, the others flat against the dirt, eyes watching him.

"Two armored trucks," Adams said. "Looks like mounted fifties. A whole company of Krauts."

"Sarge!"

Unger was pointing, straight down the hedgerow, men emerging, spreading out into the field, the machine pistols erupting again, the pop of rifles.

Adams fired the Thompson, a wild spray, the Germans too far away, lying low. They returned fire, and Adams lay flat, heard the trucks moving in the road, closer, heavy-machine-gun fire splattering the brush in the hedgerow.

"Go! Back that way! Save your ammo! Just go! Head for that brush!"

He crawled backward, still firing the Thompson, but the Germans were too far away, one man standing, defiant. Adams cursed to himself, thought, If only I had an M-1, you bastard!

The Germans began to push forward, crawling, helmets bobbing in the grass, and Adams thought of the magazines in his pant legs. What, five more? It's time to go. His own men were far behind him now, and Adams turned and ran, a frantic sprint, following the others. The field ended at another hedgerow, right angles to the one beside them, and Nusbaum led the way, another narrow gap, the men plunging into the tangle, cracks and hums in the air. Adams stopped, waited for the last man to slide through, and fired the Thompson again. The roar of engines came from beyond the hedgerow beside him, the trucks closer still. As he stared into the blind thicket, he heard Unger.

"Sarge! Come on!"

Unger aimed a rifle, fired above Adams's head.

"Now, Sarge!"

Unger backed away, and Adams leaped into the gap, pushing Unger with him. They tumbled into another open field. The trucks were still there, moving past them, invisible, the thick hedge along the road hiding them. Adams worked his way back up to the narrow split in the brush, saw the Germans in the field moving back into the hedgerow, back toward the road. He was breathing heavily, his words in a grunt.

"They're not following us. Smart. We need to keep going. Too damned many of them. We can't fight that armor." He looked at Unger, saw the M-1, and said, "I thought you lost your rifle."

Unger motioned toward Marley. "It's his. He dropped it in the ditch. I borrowed it."

Marley was flat on the ground, his hands on his face, soft sobs, and Adams felt the rage, one more screwup.

"Leave him be, Sarge," Unger said. "He'll be all right."

Adams scanned the others, Nusbaum staring down, flexing his fingers around his M-1, the other three looking at Adams, unfamiliar faces. Unger said, "I said I got him, Sarge."

"Fine. He's yours." He stared out along the hedgerow, away from the road. "Let's go this way. We can't use that road at all. The lieutenant's probably doing the same thing, out the other way. Stay close to the brush. Corporal, bring up the rear. You see anybody chasing us, raise hell."

Nusbaum seemed to come awake, nodded. "What about the wounded, Sarge?"

Adams felt a fresh burst of fury, his words erupting in a soft hiss. "What the hell are we supposed to do? If they're alive, the Krauts have them. There's seven of us, Corporal, maybe a hundred of them. Now let's head out this way, follow this hedge. You got that?"

"Sure thing, Sarge."

Adams felt a burst of guilt, thought of Buford. I got him killed. Should have just left him. No, dammit. Don't do this. Nothing else we can do, not now. He saw Unger down beside Marley, grabbing his shoulder. The big man looked at him with red empty eyes.

"Let's go, Dex," Unger said. "We need to find you a couple rifles. I'll use one of them to give you some backbone."

They had walked through two more of the boxed-in fields, and each one could be its own battlefield, sealed from the outside by the thick hedgerows, most surrounded by narrow farm lanes. Adams had a routine now. As they reached the end of the row of brush, one man would slip through to the side, just a glance at the field beside them, searching for any sign of an ambush. In front of them, it would be Adams, crawling low, threading his way into the hedge, probing silently, as quiet as the brush would allow. They wouldn't stay in the lanes, the space too tight, so he would lead them up and over the next row into the new field. Then, they would move close to the hedge to one side and do it again.

They reached the end of another field. Adams glanced back, pointed, and Nusbaum slipped out on his knees through the hedge beside them. Adams waited, sat low with the others, and Nusbaum was back in only a few seconds, a thumbs-up sign, moved close to Adams, a soft whisper:

"No problem that way, Sarge. There are signs all across the field: ACHTUNG MINEN. I think that means—"

"Yeah. It means we're not going in that direction." He motioned to the others: *Stay low,* wait. The hedge was thicker than most, taller trees, a higher ridge of dirt, and Adams crawled up, felt the pain in his knees, the exhaustion. He stopped near the top, knew the men were watching him, winced at the pain in his knee, thought, Keep going, tough guy. He began to move forward, the Thompson in front, froze, a voice, just beyond the brush. He flattened out, heard it again, but different, hard whispers. His heart was racing again, and he glanced at the Thompson. Half a magazine, maybe. Reload before you do this, you jackass. He waited, silence now, and then pushed forward, thick leaves in front of him, vines, felt a sharp jab in his shoulder. The pain was searing, surprising, and he slipped his hand that way, felt the long thorn stabbing him, broke it with a small snap. There were more of the whispers and then silence again. He could see the hedgerow opening up in front of him, the ground falling away. What the hell do I do now, crawl down right into them? He listened for a long silent moment, thought of backing away, but the thorns had him again, stabbing his hip, and he twisted one leg slowly, trying to escape the agony.

"You give us a call sign or we're gonna feed you a grenade."

The word flooded his brain. "Flash!"

"Thunder, you lucky son of a bitch."

Adams still couldn't see past the brush. "There's a half dozen of us. We're coming out."

He didn't have to look behind him. His men were responding to the talk, already climbing up the embankment. Adams fought against the vines now, pushed through, the field in front of him open, as they had all been, hedgerows beyond, another perfect rectangle. In the grass, he saw them, helmets, rifle muzzles, the distinctive barrel of a magnificent BAR. And, rising up from a foxhole, Ed Scofield.

"You forget the damned call sign, Sergeant?" There was no humor in the captain's question.

"No, sir. Sorry. We've been used to keeping mum."

"You're smarter than that, Jesse. But never mind. Krauts are all over the place. We fought our way into this field, and they seem to have let us have it, at least for now. We surprised them pretty bad: some field head-quarters, eating their breakfast."

The others crawled down from the hedgerow. Scofield watched them.

"Five-oh-fivers. Good. There's about fifty of us here. I've got people on the perimeter, watching all four corners of this field. We saw you coming when you crossed the lane out there. First thing I wanted to know is if you had a radio. Apparently not. None here either. Most of the damned things dropped into the water or got busted all to hell. But we've got five BARs, a handful of medics, and one bazooka. A dozen of us are from the One-oh-one, including two lieutenants. I'm ranking officer."

Adams saw men peering up, curious, exhausted, blackened faces, some dropping back into their holes. There was a thunder of artillery in the distance.

Glancing that way, Scofield said, "Hell of a fight going on over that way. Probably the town. I was just getting ready to push out of here. I had the men dig foxholes in case we had to haul it back here again. You fit to travel?"

Adams looked toward the one bare head, Marley. "We need a weapon for this man."

Scofield pulled a rifle off his shoulder. "Here. Take this one. Lost my carbine in the jump, picked this one up from . . . well, it won't be missed. Hell of a mess this morning. Men in the water, men in trees. Krauts had target practice, picking us off—" He stopped, and Adams saw the familiar grim stare. Scofield handed the rifle to Marley, who nodded weakly. "Thank you, sir."

"You got ammo?"

Marley put his hands against the pockets of his jumpsuit, said, "Yes, sir. Sixty rounds. Lost my bandoliers in the jump."

Scofield didn't react. Sixty, Adams thought. Just what he jumped with. Never fired his rifle. He looked at Marley, no sign of the smart-assed grin.

Adams moved close, said in a low voice, "I've got your back, Private. You damn well better have mine."

Unger was there now, grabbed Marley by the arm, said, "We're ready to move out, Sarge."

Adams turned toward Scofield, saw a subtle flicker of understanding.

"Your *men* fit to travel, Sergeant?" Scofield said.

"They're fit, sir."

Adams heard a voice far down the field, saw a man standing, waving his arms. There was another man moving with him, head low, scampering frantically through the grass.

"What in hell is that about?" Scofield said. "That guy's not one of mine. He runs like a staff officer."

The two men joined them, the second man older, breathing heavily. Adams saw the smudged oak leaf on the man's helmet.

"Hello, Major," Scofield said. "Welcome to our fortress. You just happen by?"

The man was catching his breath.

"Captain! Thank God!" he said in quick gasps. "I've been searching all over for anyone who could lend a hand. We're scattered all over hell out here. And the enemy was just as likely to be in this field as you were."

Scofield glanced at Adams. "We specialize in lending a hand. Do you know where we are?"

The major seemed surprised at the question.

"I haven't the first inkling, Captain. But I do know where General Gavin is. He ordered the few staff officers he could find to come out here and bring in whatever strength we could locate. There's a road back that way, out past the far side of this field. The general has established a command post of sorts about a mile to the west."

The men close by were rising up from their foxholes, expectant faces. Adams saw a sergeant, unfamiliar, the insignia of the 101st, and Scofield motioned to him.

"Gather up the men. I'm pretty sure General Gavin has something useful for us to do. At least we might get a chance to kill some more Krauts."

The major seemed surprised at the number of troops who were suddenly appearing from their cover. "Yes. Most excellent. Um . . . Captain, tell me. General Gavin was most specific about my asking this. It seems the general has been unable to contact anyone, to find out—well, anything. We lost our radios in the jump, and nobody we've found has one. Do you?"

Scofield pulled his forty-five from his holster and checked it. "Of course not, Major. Why would anything out here go according to plan?"

22. ADAMS

They marched alongside the narrow road, hemmed in by the endless confinement of the hedgerows. But now there were men in foxholes, Americans, spread out through every glimpse of open space, some along the ditches that bordered the road.

Gavin's staff officer had assured Scofield that there was no danger. In his energetic efforts to gather up more troops, he had seen no sign of German patrols and nothing to prevent Scofield's men from reaching Gavin's position. But Adams understood Scofield's caution. In this strange hedgerow country, every field was a hiding place, every intersection a perfect place for an ambush. Scofield kept the men ready, two columns walking close beside the shallow ditches on either side of the road. Adams led one column again, avoiding the wide potholes in the road, blasted dirt and brush, the remnants of an artillery barrage. In the open fields, he could see men still digging, either narrow trenches or their own foxholes. Around them, the ground was ripped and smoking still; he caught the hard smell of explosives and saw equipment turned into rubble. Across the road, Scofield walked with the major, no conversation between them. Gavin's staff officer was clearly nervous, flinching at the sound of clanking metal, taking quick steps and pulling ahead of the column, eager to return to some kind of sanctuary. As they moved into the open ground, Adams could see more men, clusters of foxholes, gear and guns, a bazooka crew assembling to check a box of their rockets, the only antitank weapon these men could carry on their backs. Despite the numbers, Adams kept a wary eye on the distant hedgerows. The edges of each field had the same kinds of boundaries, thick rows of brush, tangles of vines and low bushes, rows of taller trees. But now there were rows of men, some up, lining the embankments, machine guns pointed out, well protected by the cover. There were more bazookas, and Adams saw more boxes of the small rockets beside each man. He had vivid memories of the clumsy weapon, Sicily, one lucky shot into a German tank by a man who did not live to brag about it. But the worst memory was of a duel, one man against a German Tiger tank, Lieutenant Colonel Art Gorham, responding to the chaotic nightmare of a fight by standing his ground against the massive machine. Gorham lost the fight, but Adams still kept the image in his mind, one man's extraordinary courage. It was the bravest act Adams had ever seen.

The exhaustion was still inside him, slow ponderous steps, wetness in his boots—mostly sweat this time—his uniform stiff and stinking. Adams had given up cursing the supply officers or engineers or whoever had come up with the idea that these jumpsuits could become shields against poison gas if they were soaked in some kind of chemical. Adams had heard no reports of gas from anyone. Idiots, he thought. One more case of the cure being worse than the disease.

They reached a wide opening in a hedgerow, the major pointing the way, and Adams saw the machine gunners, the lookouts, short nods, tired relief on their faces, as they watched Scofield's fifty men march past. Adams, behind Scofield, heard Gavin's staff officer chattering, his own kind of relief at surviving his particular mission. Adams ignored the talk, looked across the field, focused more on the machine guns, tripods, the heavier guns that had been bundled beneath the wings of the C-47s, guns that had survived the drop. Thank God, he thought. Not everything landed in the water. He began to scan for familiar faces, some sign of anyone from his own platoon—Hovey, Simpson, Moretti, Whidden—men he had not seen since they left their plane. But the faces who watched him pass were dark and dirty, the eyes sheltered by helmets pulled low. He thought of the lieutenant. Did he make it? If Pullman is here, someone oughta know that. Officers are supposed to make sure we know where the hell they are.

As they moved through the field, Adams saw more gear spread out on the ground, the far hedgerow more like a small wood, taller, parachutes draped through trees and tangled in the brush. There was a road there too, another narrow lane, ripped backpacks in the ditch, a broken rifle, and, now, a row of bodies. The major stopped. "Over there. General Gavin is the tall one."

Scofield glanced at Adams. "We know General Gavin, Major. Thanks for being our guide."

"Oh, certainly. Have you had any rations? We found a large drop bundle, food and water. Damned fortunate, that one. Your men can take what they need, if there's any left."

Scofield turned toward the men, a straggling line gathering, and Adams saw the lieutenants moving close, questioning.

"Unless General Gavin says different, spread them out right here," Scofield said. "Looks like everybody's digging in, so let's get to work. Send half a dozen men with the major here, get some grub, fill some canteens."

"Yes, sir."

Scofield motioned to Adams to follow, stepped around a muddy hole, the dirt churned and burnt, scraps of metal from . . . something. Good time for a shovel, Adams thought. The Krauts sure as hell know we're out here.

He heard the clanking of metal, more shovels, and a canteen, and was suddenly enormously thirsty. He hadn't thought of that until now, the hunger churning inside of him as well, the tension that gripped him so hard finally letting go. He saw men eating, small piles of tin cans tossed aside, more clanking canteens, and beyond, among a group of men in dirty jumpsuits, the lanky frame, one foot up on the dirt embankment, staring at a map: Gavin. The men around him leaned in close, Gavin speaking in low tones, a quiet briefing. Adams knew what it meant. They put them in the same uniforms we have, but it can't hide them. Officers stand out.

Gavin looked up, studied the new men spreading out in the field, and recognized Scofield. "Captain. Good to see you. Those men belong to you?"

"Not exactly, sir. I picked up some men from the One-oh-one, and there's a few from the Five-oh-seven."

"Yeah, I know. I've got about six hundred here, altogether. A lot of Five-oh-seven guys, plus strays from every damned unit that jumped. I guess than includes you." He looked at Adams now, put his hands on his hips. "Well, I'll be damned. I've gotta say, Sergeant, you look like hell. Makes you kinda miss London, wouldn't you say?"

"Yes, sir. It's good to see you too, sir."

Gavin rolled up the map and handed it to one of the officers.

"Anybody have any questions? Give it about fifteen minutes, time for these new men to grab a breath. Then we'll move out."

The officers moved away, each heading toward his own place in the field, and Gavin sat slowly on the embankment with a low groan.

"Sir, I'm sorry to report that we don't have any radios."

Gavin rolled his head to one side, blinked, and looked at Scofield through tired eyes. "Of course not. That would be too helpful. You lose them in the water?"

"Or busted 'em to hell on the drop."

Gavin punched a fist into his hand. "Damn! This is a royal bitch, Captain. I heard a report that the landing on Utah Beach was called off. Could be a rumor, but it's one hell of a rumor, and I have to take it seriously. If we're not supported pretty quickly from the coast, the enemy's going to chew us up piecemeal. Except for Colonel Kellam, I haven't heard from the regimental or battalion commanders at all, except that Krause and Vandervoort are both out of action. General Ridgway is . . . back that way somewhere. That's all I know for certain. We've got men on the far side of the river too, but I have no idea if anyone's still in charge over there, or if the whole lot has been snapped up by the enemy."

There was a sharp whistle, a tumbling *rip* in the air, men shouting, a blast erupting in the middle of the open ground. Men scrambled for cover, dropping down. Gavin rolled over, on his knees, and shouted, "Cover! Now!"

He crawled rapidly to a narrow slit trench and disappeared, and Adams flattened out in the short grass, Scofield beside him. The blasts came in a rhythm now, punching the ground around them, one blast shattering the brush behind them, Gavin's voice came again. "Get in here!"

Adams didn't hesitate, followed Scofield to the trench, both men rolling across the ground and dropping down, Adams landing on Scofield with a hard grunt. They lay still, the ground pulsing beneath them with each impact. There was no other sound, just the hard claps of thunder, and

Adams put his hands over his ears, felt one hard jolt, close, dirt falling on his back. He could smell the thick stink of explosives, sulfur smoke rolling over them, his lungs burning. The blasts slowed now, separate punches, and then silence. Adams eased his hands away from his ears, tested his hearing, blew a sharp breath, tried to clear the smoke from his chest. Close beside him, the voice of Gavin.

"You two can get the hell off of me now. This trench was made for one. Wish you'd been here ten minutes sooner, you'd have dug your own."

Scofield said, "Sorry, sir. It was . . . convenient."

Adams crawled out and rolled into the short grass, Scofield up as well. Gavin stood in the trench, thigh-deep, searched the field, and called out, "Anybody hit?"

Adams saw hands waving, medics gathering, shouting responses.

Gavin cursed. "Been like this all damned day. Ten-minute artillery attacks. They've been hitting every field around here, trying to soften us up. I don't think they know exactly where we are or how many. You can't see a damned thing from one field to the next." He squinted at Adams. "You remember all those observer reports, all that aerial photography? Everybody thought these hedges were three feet high. Some French farmer told me this morning, they've been here since the damned Romans. It would take a Kraut eighty-eight to blow a hole in this stuff." He scanned the field again.

Adams saw the wounded, medics working over them. Only three men hit, he thought. I guess that's good.

"We don't know where the Kraut guns are, but I'm ready to do something about that," Gavin said. "Our first objective was La Fière Bridge, but we have that in our pocket. The enemy put up a fight there, but it wasn't too hot. They had some machine guns in the farmhouses, maybe fifty Krauts, and we bagged most of them. Colonel Lindquist is the senior man there, and so far he's done the job. I'm a hell of a lot more concerned with the second bridge, about two miles south of here, Chef-du-Pont. Your CO, Ekman, is supposed to be there, but I haven't confirmed that. It's been quiet down that way, and that could mean trouble. Either we have nobody there, or the Krauts are dug in so heavily our boys have backed away. But those bridges are why we're out here in the first place, and sure as hell the Krauts know we're coming after them. We're not sure how many of our boys are cut off on the other side of the river, but if we raise enough of a ruckus down there, it'll give 'em a place to head to, and we might hit the bridge from both sides." Gavin paused, looked at Scofield. "Any chance you salvaged any of the field artillery?"

Scofield shook his head. "I know one of them came down in the water, sir. It landed right next to me. It's buried deep."

Gavin shook his head again, climbed up out of the trench, moved back to the embankment, sat. "We lost two of them right out here. One fell into the swamp about a mile to the north, and the Krauts have so many machine guns covering that ground, nobody could retrieve it. Another came down on dry ground in too many pieces. We reassembled the damned thing, only to find out the breechblock was missing. It'll make some French farmer a nice yard ornament. So, no artillery support, and no radios to let anyone know what the hell we're doing out here. And if that damned rumor about Utah Beach is accurate, we're doing all this alone. Captain, see to your men. We're going to move out toward Chef-du-Pont in a few minutes. I'll give the word. Anybody bitches, tell them they might be glad they have those holes waiting for them if this little party goes to hell. Leave your sergeant with me for now."

"Yes, sir."

Scofield moved away, and Adams watched him through a fog, the hunger returning, dust in his mouth. He brushed dirt from the stinking stiffness of his uniform. "Sir, is there a canteen around here I could use? I lost my gear in the drop."

Gavin pulled his own from his belt, handed it up to Adams. It was half full, and Adams took a brief swig, the water warm and perfect. He handed it back.

"What happened to your gear?" Gavin said.

Adams moved the last remnants of water around his mouth, the last swallow. "I came down in deep water. Had to cut myself free. But most of it left me in the air." He wanted to say something about the pilot, the idiot Texan, but thought, No, let it go. There'll be time for that jackass later.

Gavin searched the field. "Major! Get the sergeant here some rations. Whatever we have in that crate over there."

"Sir, I can get it myself. No need to—"

"Sit down, Sergeant. I know you too well. You're beat to hell, and you haven't had a damned thing to eat. We did find a crate of C rations. Only good luck we had today. That's a hell of a lot better than those damned K rations. Never figured out what deviled ham is anyway. But in the Cs, you can actually eat the beef stew. And the fruit cocktail's not bad."

The major hurried close, carrying a handful of small cans. He seemed nervous.

"Here you go, Sergeant. General, I wish you would stay down in the trench. The enemy artillery has been pretty consistent. They could begin again any time."

"Worry about yourself, Major. Use my trench if you want. The sergeant here seemed to like it. But don't get comfortable. We take that second bridge, I'll need you to send word to General Ridgway. I expect somebody from his staff will be nosing out here pretty quick, once the shooting starts again. First, go find Captain Grayson. Tell him to pass word to the officers. We move out in ten minutes."

Adams watched the major hurry away, dug into the beef stew with two fingers, then turned the can up and slurped the contents down his throat. He picked up a second can, hesitated, stuffed it into a pocket in his jacket. Yep, save that one for later. Gavin's right about that deviled ham stuff. But right now it wouldn't matter. Spam would work too. He noticed Gavin watching him, no smile, could see that Gavin was thinking, planning, his brain always working.

"This has been one hell of a mess, Sergeant. I'm not happy that all we've done is stir up the countryside and put our people on one bridge. Rommel's too smart not to sort things out, and when he does, those bastards will be coming. If they had any idea how much confusion there is in these swamps and hedgerows, they'd have hit us already. I'm surprised as hell we haven't had any Messerschmitts buzzing us. And I haven't heard anything about Kraut armor yet, but it's out there, and sooner or later it's coming too. If we don't get our people into a strong position by nightfall, we could get chewed up pretty badly."

"Yes, sir."

Gavin reached for a can of the rations and stared at it for a moment, rolling it in his hands. Adams felt a question brewing: If the bridges are close, we're not that far from the designated drop zones.

"Sir, where did all that water come from? I saw the maps. The Merderet—"

"The Merderet is now spread out all over hell. Rommel opened the dikes, or the dam, or whatever the hell else he could do. I know those maps, Sergeant. Got one right here in my pocket. At La Fière Bridge, the river is supposed to be ten yards across. When we hit them this morning, we found out it was five hundred yards to the other side. The Krauts, or

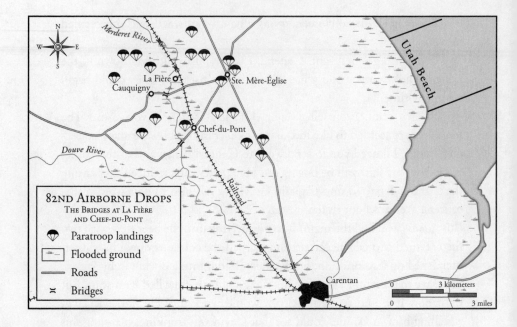

82ND AIRBORNE DROPS
THE BRIDGES AT LA FIÈRE
AND CHEF-DU-PONT

🪂 Paratroop landings

Flooded ground

Roads

⋈ Bridges

somebody, built a causeway on the far side of the bridge, to keep the road above water. The only thing I can figure is those idiots in the observation planes didn't notice. They probably saw all that grassy swamp and assumed it was dry ground. They expected to see a narrow river, so that's what they saw." He looked at Adams with the hard stare Adams had seen before. "You lose some people?"

"Yes, sir. I tried like hell to figure a way to get to them. Where I came down, it was over my head. Lucky to have made it. Some weren't. I think a few just . . . disappeared."

Gavin looked down between his feet. "Sicily all over again, Sergeant. The pathfinders helped some, but you know how that goes. Some of them jumped into God-knows-where. At least, this time, there's enough of us in one place. I've heard from other commands, officers gathering up scattered bunches, some organization here and there. There's been a hell of fight around Sainte-Mère-Église, and that's been going pretty well. Krause got himself wounded, and I think Vandervoort broke his leg on the jump, but General Ridgway's close by, and I think he can handle things there for now. Our job right here is to take those two bridges and occupy the villages beyond. We've got half a day of daylight in front of us, and we're going to do the best we can. There's a pot load of glider troops coming in at dusk, which should help us out in a big way. They'll be bringing in some artillery, for sure, jeeps, supplies, and ammo. Somebody sure as hell better have a radio."

NEAR CHEF-DU-PONT BRIDGE
JUNE 6, 1944, 11 A.M.

Gavin led two hundred men toward the objective, and along the way they found others, more senior officers, battalion and company commanders, engineers, and bazooka carriers. They advanced in two columns, parallel to the river, the checkerboard of the hedgerow country providing protection from any distant observers. Adams stayed close to Scofield and was trailed closely by the men of his squad, those few familiar faces. It was the same throughout the advance, sergeants and field officers assembling their own men whenever possible, adding in those men who had been separated by the chaotic jump. Up front, Adams's column was led by Lieutenant Colonel Edwin Ostberg, First Battalion commander of the 507th, another addition to Gavin's growing army. Adams didn't know Ostberg at all, but he had the same look as Gavin: no frills, no puffery, what every soldier needed a senior officer to be.

There had been shots from the direction of the other column, the sounds dispersed and muddled by the hedgerows, but it was all the reminder Adams needed that, in this blind maze, the enemy could be anywhere at all. He moved heavily, automatic steps, glancing continually into the hedgerow beside him. It was an uncomfortable habit, the thick brush too close, the fields beyond too obscured.

The men were moving off the roads, directed by Gavin toward a single railroad track, but the land around them had not changed; hedgerows still flanked the track. Adams glanced behind him, the men staying close, eyes nervous, silent, wary, everyone holding on to something inside, his own caution, fear, uneasiness. Adams looked to the front again, thought, At least we can't get lost. Sure as hell, this track will lead to a town. Or a bridge. I guess the officers have that one figured out.

Adams saw Ostberg raise his arm, the order to halt. There were men emerging from the brush, coming out onto the track, one man cradling a BAR on his shoulder, another man with a sergeant's stripes. Adams saw machine guns, more troopers dug in close to a thick row of brush, a long narrow trench.

Beside him, Scofield said, "I better see what's up. We must be close."

The captain moved up, joining the conversation, low voices Adams couldn't hear. But the talk was brief, arms pointed forward, and Ostberg looked back toward the column, a quiet stare, seeming to measure the men behind him. Adams heard quick footsteps, boots on gravel, Gavin jogging past him, moving to the front, more talk, and then Scofield came back toward him, his face red, alive.

"The village is up ahead, a half mile. The Krauts are there for sure, machine-gun nests at least. There are a few houses, so snipers could be anywhere. We're going to spread out, push in, and blast the bastards." Scofield was breathing heavily, put a hand on Adams's arm.

"You ready to go to work?"

Adams felt a strange quiver in his legs, ignored it, focused on the icy burn in his stomach. "Sure."

There was nothing else to say, numb acceptance. He looked behind him, saw Marley, a helmet now, someone else's M-1 held tightly across his chest. Marley made a sharp nod toward him, wide-eyed, anxious. Beside him was Unger, a dirty-faced boy, and Adams stared past, wouldn't see the boy's eyes, didn't want to know if Unger was scared. Of course he's scared. We're all scared. Even . . . me. Dammit, knock that off.

The others were spread out all around the track, officers moving quietly through them, passing the word, and Adams tried to feel the excitement, fought the strange numbness in his brain, the quiver still there. He looked at the Thompson, the short barrel a dull sheen of oil and dirt, his hands dirtier still. The large pocket on his pants leg was still heavy, four magazines for the submachine gun, four grenades still clipped to his jacket. He pushed at the gloom in his head, angry now. Dammit, you've got a job to do! He tried to pull energy—confidence—from the faces of the others, even from men who had never done this before. But there was just as much fear there, men pulling their rifles close, silent, some staring out past him, toward Ostberg and beyond, trying to see what was not yet there: the enemy, waiting.

Adams hoisted the Thompson in close, tucked the butt under one arm, and turned to Scofield again, the captain still looking at him, and Scofield said, "Let's get those sons of bitches."

They crept low, using the brush for cover, but the trees ended, the ditches alongside the railroad tracks more shallow. Down the road,

Adams saw the first house, small and fat, one window. Across the road, the men had more cover, and he glanced that way, saw Scofield, Unger, another twenty men in line, all crawling, silent, the slow stalk of a dangerous beast. Adams stayed close beside the mound of the railroad track, the ribbon of steel just enough to shield his helmet. He stopped, lying flat now, nursed the pains in his knees, raised his head slightly, and stared at the single window, a small black square, searching for any movement. The house was more than two hundred yards away, but the troopers were mostly in the open, in plain view of any machine gunner who might be inside. Adams heard puffs of breathing behind him, from others spread along the track, and thought, We're sitting ducks. But nobody's shooting at us. Where the hell are they? We need to get up and move, or . . . what? Artillery? Yeah, that would be nice. Blow that house to hell.

The noise was sudden, a hard blowing cough, and Adams dropped his head, his face in the rocks of the track bed. But the sound grew, more quick coughs. He looked ahead to a column of black smoke rising from the village, heard the roar of an engine. He felt the vibration in the rocks beneath him, and saw the train now, coming out from the village, the engine moving slowly. He felt himself pulling backward, oh, hell, and behind him, men were spreading out away from the tracks, the train coming toward them. He glanced that way, but his legs wouldn't move, the low rumble in the ground holding him. The rifle fire came now, shouts on the far side of the track, a burst from a Thompson. Adams slid his submachine gun forward, aimed, nothing but the green steel of the train engine, heard new sounds, shots from the train, splatters on the rocks, the pops of rifles. He held his fire, nothing to shoot, but the men around him had spread out, some flat in short grass, firing, the train a hundred yards away, still moving slowly toward them, and now, with a great groan of squealing brakes, it stopped. The firing continued, and Adams saw German uniforms, a flood of men leaping from the train, one man falling, the others running. He pulled the Thompson against his shoulder, but the uniforms were out of sight, his brain yelling, Don't waste ammo! From both sides of the tracks, the firing continued, by men who could see past the train, who had targets.

Adams felt the fury and frustration, nothing to shoot at. Men were up and moving, one voice, Gavin: "They're retreating! Get to the train!"

The train belched a great plume of smoke and, with a high groan of steel on steel, began to move backward, its own lumbering retreat. Adams pulled himself up, was running with the others, more Germans leaping down from the train, frantic, scampering away, some shot down, pops of fire out to one side. The Americans were at the train now, some climbing up, sprays of fire, the train stopping again. Adams was beside the engine, the Thompson pointed forward, still no targets, just flickers of gray, the Germans pulling back farther, disappearing deep into the village. The shooting stopped. Adams heard a cheer, loud curses, and kept his stare on the village, the small windows, his hands shaking, the tracks now swarming with Americans. And close beside him, the voice of Gavin.

"I'll be damned. We captured a train. Never thought they'd give it up without a fight. A half dozen cars. Let's see what they were hauling."

Gavin climbed up into the engine. Adams saw men moving between the cars, some climbing up on top, men gathering around one open car, antiaircraft guns, the train's protection.

"Hey, General! There's nothing but empty bottles!"

Adams looked toward the voice, the man tossing a glass bottle out onto the tracks, shattering it. Adams flinched at the sound, felt his legs weakening again, ignored the cheers. He moved to the steps at one end of a railcar and sat, looked at his shaking hands, his chest heavy, cold, his anger rising. He leaned out, looked into the village, no movement, saw two German bodies, gray uniforms, thought, Your unlucky day. Maybe you should have learned to run faster. He stared at them. Maybe you're faking it, he thought. Playing dead. Why don't one of you move . . . just a little? Then he saw the blood, a dark stain on a bed of small rocks. No, you're not going anywhere.

He slapped one hand against the breech of the Thompson, slapped again, pulsing frustration, and said aloud, "Dammit!"

"What? What is it?" He was surprised to see Scofield, smiling, the smile slowly disappearing. "You okay, Sergeant?"

"Yeah, Captain, I'm fine. I guess they got away. Pisses me off."

"They didn't all get away, and the rest of 'em might not go too far. The bridge is up ahead, down a hill to the right. There's nothing on the train to get excited about, one car full of some kind of ass-stink cheese. Not sure where the Krauts were going with that. A bunch of empty glass bottles too. General Gavin thinks maybe they were just hitching a ride, a couple platoons going to hit us at La Fière. We've got to keep moving forward. Let's fall in."

Scofield moved away, and the orders came now, the men lining up on either side of the train. Adams moved to the end of the row of cars, the tail of the train, saw Gavin and Ostberg, both men pointing toward the village, the men moving out quickly, staying low, close to the fat stone buildings. Adams kept his stare on the first building, but there was silence, the windows just windows, and Adams stepped into line, moved past the bodies of the Germans, hesitated, forced his finger off the trigger of the submachine gun, and thought of the train, the desperate scramble of the Germans. No targets. I didn't get my chance. Scofield was beside him now, and Adams kept moving, stared at his boots, then up at the scattered houses, the still silent windows.

He could feel Scofield's eyes on him, heard the captain's words. "I missed my chance back there. Never got off a good shot. You?"

Adams shook his head. "Nope."

"Pissed off about it, right?"

"Yep."

"Thank God. I thought it was just me. An officer's supposed to show some decorum, not lead the way by blasting everything in sight. But that's sure what I wanted to do. Kill everything that moved."

The words were strange, nothing like Scofield had ever said before, and Adams looked at him. "I think you're full of crap, sir."

"You're right. Maybe it was *you* who wants to kill everything in sight. Take it easy, Sergeant. I hate the enemy just as much as you do. We'll get our chance."

Adams chewed on the words. "First time I've thought of it that way. Never felt like I hated the Krauts. It was about survival. I knew damn well that if I didn't shoot him first, he'd shoot me. I've heard all that garbage about, Oh yeah, he's just like me, or Maybe he's got a wife and kids, all of that. You start thinking like that, you'll hesitate, and then you'll end up getting your own people killed."

"You never had that problem."

"No, sir. But it's different here. I don't know why. I didn't feel this way in Sicily. I don't like the shaking in my gut. I don't like worrying about that damned kid back there. I'm sick of crawling on my belly and I'm sick of watching my guys get picked off. I'm tired and I'm pissed off. It doesn't matter now if those Krauts are shooting at me or taking a crap in the bushes. Those bastards started this, and if it'll get this over with quicker, I'll kill every damned one of them."

23. ROMMEL

The trip back to France from Württenburg had been miserable, made worse by his infuriating ignorance of what was actually happening along the coast. The first call had come to his home at six that morning: Speidel, his chief of staff, more agitated than urgent. Speidel relayed the reports that had begun just after midnight, enemy paratroopers suddenly appearing in scattered sectors behind the Normandy beaches. Speidel was dismissive. Most of the German commanders had seen this kind of activity before, airdrops aimed at linkups with the French underground, spies coming and going, annoying pinpricks around the edges of German control. But Speidel had heard too many reports by dawn and there had been too much furious shouting by German field commanders. Orders from von Rundstedt had finally begun to flow outward: the panzer units placed on highest alert, the infantry mobilized for a move to the threatened sectors. And then the reports began to come in from the beaches. Despite his skepticism that the commanders were overreacting, and despite the insistence from von Rundstedt himself that the need for concern was greatly overblown, Speidel realized it was time to phone Rommel.

Rommel had not begun the drive back to his headquarters until after

ten in the morning, had spent precious hours gathering as much information as he could. The journey from his home to his headquarters took
Rommel eleven hours to complete, and along the way he continued his efforts to find out exactly what was happening, seeking answers no one
seemed able to provide. There was rampant skepticism, so many of the senior commanders holding tight to the theory that this so-called invasion
was in fact a ruse, that the Allies were staging a powerful demonstration
designed to draw German attention toward Normandy. In Germany, the
High Command remained entrenched in their belief that the full-scale assault was still to come at Calais. But throughout the morning, the seas off
Calais remained empty, and despite increasing speculation that the genuine thrust had not yet begun, the observers along that coastline had said
nothing about enemy activity.

"Where is the navy?"
        Speidel shook his head, and Rommel turned toward Admiral
Ruge. "Do *you* know? Do we even *have* a navy these days? A thousand
ships land on our doorstep and no one knows they are coming. Is no one
patrolling the tiny ocean that sits between us and the enemy?"

Ruge leaned forward in the chair, his hands folded under his chin. "All
I have heard is that the weather kept our normal patrols in port. Conditions at sea have been treacherous, at least as far as the meteorologists could
tell. Most of our weather observation posts have been bombed in recent
days, so we have had something of a gap in our forecasts."

"The enemy bombed weather stations. Why would they waste their
resources on such mundane targets? Is it possible they did not wish us to
know what the weather was likely to be? Is it possible they wished to keep
us in the dark about conditions at sea?"

Ruge stroked his chin. "I had not thought of that. Someone should
have seen the significance of those bombings, yes."

Rommel paced, dug his boots into the soft rug, spun around, crossed
the room in long hard strides. "*Someone.* Paratroopers landed hours before
dawn, and *someone* decided it was not necessary to mobilize the armor."

Speidel said, "That is not quite correct, sir. The Twenty-first Panzer
was put on alert, and orders were issued for them to prepare to advance to
the affected area near Caen."

"They *prepared* to advance? Did they actually advance?"

"Um . . . no, sir. General Feuchtinger could not be located for some time. His chief of staff told me what we already knew, that the general occasionally seeks . . . warmer company. No one at his headquarters would issue any commands to the armored units until he was found. And as you know, sir, General Dollmann was on his way to war games at Rennes when word came. It took several hours for his staff to return to Seventh Army headquarters."

"War games." Rommel stopped pacing and looked up at the high ceiling, intense pain now throbbing through his skull. "We were playing war games."

"Yes, sir, the maneuvers had been scheduled for some time. There were expectations that the enemy would remain idle while the weather was so uncertain. You must recall that, sir."

Rommel closed his eyes, put a hand on the back of his neck, rubbed hard at the twisting tightness in his neck. "Do not tell me what I should recall. I also recall our weather experts telling us there could be no attack. I also recall how so many agreed with me about the impossibility of the enemy coming ashore at low tide. I also recall my own flagrant stupidity at believing those beach obstacles would hold the enemy offshore, that our magnificent artillery would pulverize their ships, that our fine fighting forces would annihilate them from behind the perfect strength of our concrete wall!" He spun toward Speidel, pointing a shaking finger toward the man's widening eyes. "And when the reports arrived here, when the enemy made his landings, you did nothing! Did you require extra sleep? A little too much wine last evening?" Speidel stiffened, and Rommel was surprised to see defiance. "You have something to say, General. Have I slighted you? Insulted your integrity?"

"Sir, until dawn, every indication was that the enemy activity was . . . insignificant."

Rommel put his hands on his hips. He could not stay angry at Speidel. There are fools galore in this army, he thought, but Speidel is not one of them. He moved to his chair, lowered himself heavily, sat back, closed his eyes.

"I would suggest, General, that your indications were incorrect."

"Yes, sir."

He opened his eyes again and looked at Ruge. "Now the enemy is on our soil and he is strengthening, and he will continue to strengthen unless we can drive him away. We had a difficult task before. Now, we may have an impossible one." He looked at Speidel again. "What happened to von Rundstedt? Is the old man so oblivious that he also ignored the reports? Why were orders not issued for an immediate response? He is supposed to be in command out here, is he not?"

"Sir, Marshal von Rundstedt has been in contact with the High Command since early this morning. He could not authorize the advance of the panzers . . . you must recall that, sir."

Rommel glared.

"I apologize, sir," Speidel said. "But the panzer commanders would not accept Marshal von Rundstedt's orders without confirmation from the Führer's headquarters."

Rommel knew what was coming, thought of Keitel, Jodl, the others, so many nervous birds dancing around Hitler.

"Marshal von Rundstedt was told that the Führer was sleeping and could not be disturbed. No one else at the High Command would order the advance of the armor without the Führer's approval."

"So no counterattack has been made. We respond to the enemy's invasion by not responding. Does there seem to be a flaw in this system, General?"

"Yes, sir. It has been emphasized repeatedly that you—we do not have authority over the panzers."

"Yes, yes, one more thing I should *recall*. We cannot move unless the Führer gives us his blessing. Perhaps had the enemy landed their paratroopers on the rooftops at Berchtesgaden, Herr Hitler might have been sufficiently troubled to address the matter."

"Sir, despite our best efforts to convince the High Command that the enemy's actions should be addressed in the strongest terms, General Jodl did not believe the reports. He insists that the enemy has yet to show his hand. We are to remain on highest alert for the landings that must still come at Calais."

Rommel leaned forward, his arms resting on the desk, and stared down into dark wood. "I learned long ago that if General Jodl prescribes a plan, we must do the opposite. That is certainly the case now." He looked up at Ruge, saw a hard frown. Yes, you know all this, he thought. "So, Friedrich, what are we to do? Our most powerful forces are scattered, and no matter how hard we push them forward, the enemy has gained a foothold."

"It is not lost, Erwin. Surely, the enemy is in a confused state. You have always been the master of the counterattack. What worked in North Africa will work here, surely. Strike them hard, on a narrow front. Do not allow them time to organize and reinforce."

Rommel tried to laugh but leaned back in the chair again, the headache boiling inside him. "So, Admiral, you read my book."

"Well, yes, but I studied your campaigns as well."

"My campaigns did not result in victory, Friedrich. I had to wage war on two fronts, against two different kinds of enemy. It is no different now. The enemies of our country sit not only on their beachheads in Normandy but high on their thrones in the Bavarian Alps. No, we are not yet lost, and the situation is not yet hopeless. I agree that the enemy is most certainly in disarray, and we must take full advantage of that."

He tried to feel the old energy, all those things Ruge was describing. It had been glorious in Africa, crushing the enemy with devastating surprise. Before that, in France, at the beginning, Rommel had struck with lightning speed and ruthless efficiency, slicing through the French and English like a sword through butter. The result had been Dunkirk, three hundred thousand of the enemy pinned with their backs against the sea, a fat goose waiting for the slaughter. And then Hitler had ordered a halt, would not believe his own generals that complete victory was so easily in his grasp. So the moment slipped away, an entire British army rescued—carried off the beaches—to return another day. *This* day.

Rommel pulled himself out of the chair, moved to the window, stared out into fading daylight. Dark shadows filled the gardens. He struggled to clear his head, thought of Lucie and her birthday, the utter foolishness of his personal indulgence. If I had been *here,* if I had given the order, if that idiot Jodl had heard my voice on the phone instead of that feeble old man, perhaps we could have moved more quickly, hit the enemy hard before he could push us back from the beaches. But I never thought they would come at low tide. It was suicide, and yet . . . they have survived.

He turned slowly, Speidel still standing straight, staring ahead. Yes, Rommel thought, he has a guilty conscience. But what else could you have done, Hans? No general will risk being the man who cries loudest, no one will risk being made a fool over a false alarm. The quote came to him now, old lessons, Frederick the Great: *It is pardonable to be defeated but never surprised.* So, who is responsible for the surprise, after all? Was it the enemy's genius or our own ineptness? If I had been here, would I truly have made a difference? I also expected them at Calais. At high tide. Is there any pardon in that for me?

"I want Geyr here in the morning." He spoke slowly. "I want full reports on the enemy's activities. I want to know what those damned paratroopers are doing. I want to know why we have no air support for our defenses. I will demand that von Rundstedt—or whoever else thinks he is in charge here—cede me full authority to strike the enemy in the most advantageous manner. I want full mobilization of all reserve units, as far back as Paris. Once I have determined the enemy's strength in the various sectors, I want the Fifteenth Army mobilized to move south on my command. If I have to talk to Hitler myself, I will, and if I have to take a pistol into General Jodl's office to get some attention, perhaps I will do that as well."

He looked at Ruge.

"You are quite correct, Friedrich. The enemy has taken an enormous step, and he may very well have the advantage. But it is not yet over."

24. ADAMS

They had worked to clear the town of snipers, but the troopers at Chef-du-Pont had been unable to advance completely across the swollen river. As at La Fière, the raised causeway extended out past the stone bridge for several hundred yards; halfway to the other side, the causeway spread out in a wide bubble of land, occupied by several stone buildings. As the paratroopers fought their way through the village, the retreating Germans who did not escape across the marsh manned that fortified position. Throughout the afternoon, artillery and machine-gun fire poured over the town itself, keeping the paratroopers huddled down in whatever cover they could find. An assault would require artillery, which the Americans still did not have. To try to swarm the German machine guns on foot, across so much flat open ground, would be suicide.

As daylight began to fade, Gavin received word that his hold on La Fière Bridge was enduring a crisis of its own. Though the men left there had done good work, establishing a bridgehead on the far side of that causeway, there had not been enough strength to hold the position, and German armor and artillery had responded by overwhelming the meager force that tried to hold the village of Cauquigny, on the west side of the river. The paratroopers there had been forced to flee back eastward across the causeway, to the village of La Fière. But even with their armor, the Germans could not make an effective strike across the open causeway, the few bazookas in operation performing exceptionally well, destroying two German tanks on the causeway itself. By late afternoon, both sides held a tentative grip on their own side of the causeway, a situation far more dangerous for the outnumbered and outgunned Americans.

The worst news Gavin received was the casualty report. While Gavin was still at Chef-du-Pont, Colonel Ostberg had been badly wounded by machine-gun fire, and Gavin had placed that force under the command of a company commander, Captain Roy Creek. But the situation at La Fière was much worse. German artillery had taken an enormous toll on the men there: Along with the loss of dozens of troopers, the battalion commander, Fred Kellam, was dead, along with his executive officer, Colonel James McGinity. Command at the bridgehead had fallen on Colonel Mark Alexander, the executive officer of Adams's own 505th, until Colonel Ekman himself finally found his way to the bridge.

With nightfall spreading over both causeways, Gavin's frustration mounted. Despite the chaos of command changes, Gavin believed, with the more dangerous fight facing them at La Fière, the village was where he needed to be. Late in the afternoon he left Chef-du-Pont in the hands of Captain Creek and thirty-four troopers of the 507th, and pulled the rest back to La Fière.

LA FIÈRE BRIDGE
JUNE 6, 1944, 9:30 P.M.

"Cease fire!"

The shooting gradually stopped, and Adams tried to calm himself, the heat from the Thompson searing his face. He rolled over to one side, jerked the magazine away, tossed it behind him, reached into his pants leg. Two more. That's not good.

"Hold your damned fire! The Krauts are using your muzzle blasts for target practice!"

The voice was Scofield's, the man sliding through the taller grass, reaching the row of foxholes.

"Here, Captain. Good cover," Adams said.

Scofield crawled quickly, spun around, slid down into the narrow cut in the dirt.

"We're not going anywhere tonight. Too many Krauts on the far side, too few of us, and they've got all the advantages." Scofield peered up, the far side of the causeway lost in the darkness, brief flashes of fire, streaks of tracers. He scanned the ground close by—more foxholes, the best cover the men had—and called out, "Keep an eye on that causeway. The Krauts have moved machine guns up on both sides, and they know we're sealed up here. All hell might break loose in the morning, so no wasted ammo."

Adams felt the magazines again, through the filthy cloth of his pants, and said in a low voice, "Not much left to waste. I'm down to sixty rounds. Still have the grenades. Haven't been close enough to anything to toss 'em."

"That might change. Right now, we're looking at a stalemate here, which is a damned good thing. I'm not really interested in making a long-distance run across that open causeway. The Krauts have a dozen machine guns, and if so much as a frog moves out there—"

"I heard engines, trucks maybe."

"Yep. They're pouring people into line over there, but they don't want to cross that open ground any more than we do. I think our reputation for marksmanship is spreading. They'll probably try to soften us up with artillery and send some tanks across. Gavin is pulling back some of the five-oh-seven and five-oh-eight boys, forming a reserve to cover both bridges and maybe give some help to Sainte-Mère-Église."

Adams knew by now that the larger town, one of the jump's main targets, was five miles east of La Fière Bridge, a straight shot behind them on the same road that led out over the causeway. There had been sporadic firing from the town all afternoon, unnerving the men, who stared at German guns across the flooded river. Should the Germans recapture Sainte-Mère-Église, the men at the causeways would be cut off.

There was a lull in the firing. Adams peered up through the grass, the darkness almost complete. He thought of the men whose jump landed them on the far side of the river, the men Gavin had hoped would come to their aid. Those paratroopers had established their meager bridgehead in the village of Cauquigny and brief contact had been made with a number of those men, a small force mostly from the 508th. But with German armor overrunning that position, pushing the troopers back across the causeway, the men still on the west side were presumed to be either scattered again or captured.

"Any idea how many of our guys got stuck over there?"

"Gavin didn't say much about it. Best guess is that we only had fifty or sixty guys holding on to Cauquigny. Big mistake probably, but he hasn't said much about that either. Hell of a mess. If we'd had the whole bunch of us over there, we might have held the Krauts away, but then they might have broken into our rear on this side of the river and cut us off. We need to hold our position at this causeway, and at Chef-du-Pont, to give our boys at Sainte-Mère-Église time to organize and fortify the town."

There was a spray of tracer fire, men shouting, streaks of white light punching the air over Adams's head. He lay flat, Scofield doing the same. Out front, voices: "Pull back! Get off the open ground!"

Scofield cursed, looked up briefly, and said, "Who said that?"

"Colonel Lindquist. Orders!"

Scofield cursed again and said to Adams, "Lindquist has 'em pulling back! What the hell for? Damn!"

Scofield crawled up and out, moving forward, more voices, the officers arguing, the words finding Adams.

"Gavin's orders."

Well, okay.

Men began to crawl past, moving off the more open ground along the edges of the causeway.

"Foxholes! Watch it!" Adams said.

He heard tumbling boots: more men up, crawling to the thicker brush along the edge of the village of La Fière.

Scofield was there again. "Let's go! Find some cover, keep down."

"What the hell, we pulling out?"

Scofield was moving away; he glanced back. "No questions, Sergeant. We're consolidating, that's all. Pulling in the fingers. Let's go."

Adams crawled up out of the hole, the ground alive with men in motion, tracers coming again, pops and thumps, brief flashes that lit the ground. He knew the heavier brush line was up a short rise, rocks and low rocky walls; in the village itself were stone buildings that would endure only the lightest artillery fire. He tried to see Scofield, heard officers calling out, could see a vast sea of foxholes now, larger machine guns perched in their nests, bazooka crews, the best defense they had against what was still to come. Men were still digging, dirt tossed into short piles, adding to the cover, making room for the others, quickly filling up the holes. Adams saw one man standing in the brush, tall and thin: Gavin.

"Line up here! If you have a shovel, use it!"

There was a sharp crack above Adams, a streak of light, and he flinched, blinded. No! He blinked hard, fought to see, and called out, others as well.

"Sir?"

"General?"

Gavin's voice found them, high-pitched and angry. "Son of a bitch! They were aiming at me! To hell with this. We've lost enough officers today. Who's close by, Captain Scofield? Colonel Ekman?"

"Here, sir!"

"Scofield here, sir!"

Adams saw Scofield now, as the officers gathered, Gavin crouched low in the brush, and Adams caught pieces of the low talk.

"I've set up a command post where the road meets the railroad tracks. We finally found some radios, so I'm in contact with General Ridgway. He's holding position in Sainte-Mère-Église. We've got glider support scheduled to come in any time now, two huge flocks of those birds, set to land about now and again around eleven. If we're lucky this time, they'll bring us some artillery pieces we can actually put to use. Colonel, follow me. Captain, see to your men. Make sure everybody has some rations and some ammo. The gliders should help there too. Keep an eye out for anything moving on that causeway. I don't think the Krauts will come in the dark, but—well, hell, I didn't think I'd have this many guys in such a mess in the first place. Stay alert and get some rest."

Gavin slipped away through the brush. Adams saw Scofield moving out through the network of foxholes, heard low talk, orders to the lieutenants. Adams sat back against the dirt wall, his knees touching the dirt in front of him, in a hole he had not dug. He reached into his pocket for the D ration, a lone candy bar, all he had left. The paper came off easily and he bit off a piece, felt his thirst. Still no canteen. Take your time, he thought. I haven't seen any gliders, and I'm not so sure it'll matter anyway. He recalled Gavin's own words, weeks before: *Gliders don't land, they crash successfully.* Not me. I'm coming down on my own feet, not in some ready-made coffin. There's some serious guts in those glider pilots.

Around him, men were eating rations. Some were still digging, making their holes deeper than they needed to be. Some were talking, low mumbles, some sitting alone, as he was; some smoking cigarettes, absorbed by what they had seen and done. This has been one long-ass day, he thought. About this time last night, we were boarding up. Marley crying,

Unger full of conversation. Corporal Nusbaum . . . jerk. Well, maybe not. He did okay today. Takes a little machine-gun fire to find out what a guy's got in his pants. Lieutenant Pullman . . . God knows where he is now. Not here, that's for sure. Hope the Krauts didn't grab him. Buford . . . Dammit! He bit off another piece of the chocolate, could not shake the sound of the bullets hitting Buford's wounded body. I had to be a damned hero and pull him up out of that ditch. He'd be alive if I'd just left him there. He cursed himself, closed his eyes, his head against the dirt. Or maybe not. The Krauts would have found him, maybe nailed him right there in the ditch. They shoot the wounded? Who the hell knows? Let's not find out. Bastards.

He knew Unger was close by, had stayed true to his word to stick close to Marley. They made it through so far, he thought. Marley's a veteran now. Hell, after today, everybody out here is a veteran. But we lost a bunch of people. So much stupidity and bad luck. Or just plain old combat. Kill or be killed, and a bunch of us lost that argument. And tomorrow we've gotta do it again.

He heard a soft hum and the men quieted, listening. They all knew the sound, the drone of a vast flock of C-47s, hauling their precious cargo behind them. It was almost completely dark. The machine-gun fire started again, the Germans aiming skyward, red streaks arcing overhead. Adams stared into the night sky, but there was nothing to see, only the sounds of the engines. Even now, Adams knew, towlines were being released and men and equipment were drifting silently down through the darkness. The gliders were coming.

25. EISENHOWER

He walked beyond the tents and felt for the note in his pocket, the message he had prepared to read to the press, to the president, and to those families who waited for any word of their men, the soldiers Eisenhower had ordered into France.

> Our landings . . . have failed to gain a satisfactory foothold and I have withdrawn the troops. My decision to attack at this time and place was based on the best information available. The troops, the air and navy did all that bravery and devotion to duty could do. If there is any blame or fault attached to the attempt, it is mine alone.

It had stayed in his pocket all day, memorized, recited to himself a half dozen times. But it hadn't been read aloud. So far, it wasn't necessary.

The air was cold, and he looked up, a glimpse of moonlight through thick clouds, the weather still holding, a stiff breeze drifting past. It was the only error the weathermen had made, the prediction that the wind would die down. But the rest? He thought of Captain Stagg, the man's edgy confidence. *Guesswork.* All right, Captain, good job. All of you. He was blinking through wetness now, but it was not emotion, just pure rugged exhaustion, his eyes battered by the breeze, losing focus. He turned toward the tents. Better try to get some damned sleep, he thought. *Try.* It can't be as bad as last night.

The night before, with the paratroopers in their planes and the landing craft in motion toward the beaches, Eisenhower had tried to take advantage of those agonizing hours before any news could come in, before reports could be made by anyone whose feet were actually on French soil. But there had been no real sleep for him, just exhausted fitfulness, thunderous doubts rolling through him, horrible scenarios, every possible failure, questioning the wisdom and the certain cost of sending so many men into such an uncertain place. The doubts had rolled through his head in the voices of Churchill and Brooke and of the myriad staff officers whose torturous griping and petty jockeying for position had so often undermined this gargantuan undertaking.

Eisenhower had rolled in his cot, sweating and furious, fantasizing what he should have said to them, hard curses in the faces of those men he would never dare to blister outside his imagination. Through all the angry sleeplessness, he worked to turn his mind toward the positive, seeing the faces of the well-wishers and optimists, the men whose planning had been so meticulous. It can't *all* go wrong, he thought. And God knows it can't all go according to plan. No one expects every detail to unfold exactly as the maps predict. Except Montgomery, of course.

Eisenhower had kept the man's image in his mind, cheery with confidence, stern and condescending. With the interminable darkness still engulfing his tent, Eisenhower continued to ask himself the same question, silently repeating the words: Is all that confidence justified? Is Monty right and all of this will work? Is *he* sleeping right now?

And then, while it was still dark, the first call had come in, intercepted by Harry Butcher, who would generously believe his boss was fast asleep. Butcher had written down the details with breathless relief and could not wait for the waking hour to deliver the message, so it came to Eisenhower in soft morning darkness, Butcher creeping stealthily toward the tent, expecting snoring. But Eisenhower was up, sitting on his cot smoking a cigarette when Butcher came. Every possible disaster had boiled up inside of him when he saw Butcher's shadow, but then he had seen the man's smile. The caller had been Leigh-Mallory, and Eisenhower immediately understood why. Leigh-Mallory had been the greatest naysayer of them all, but as air commander he had received the first reports from the paratroopers in both armies, reports that might have confirmed his deadly pessimism. But the losses were not nearly as awful as he had predicted, barely thirty C-47s missing out of the thirteen hundred that had gone across. It was a staggering piece of good news, offered by a man who showed genuine graciousness in admitting he had been wrong. The word from the paratroopers and glider crews themselves had been slow in coming, but word did come, and despite the predictable chaos of a large-scale night jump, the British in particular were actively engaged around their designated drop zones. Word had been more sporadic from the American zones, nothing yet from Ridgway, brief reports from Maxwell Taylor. Leigh-Mallory had relayed more news as well, better news. There had been virtually no sign of German fighter planes, except in the one area with the name Eisenhower had desperately wanted to hear: Calais.

When word came from the beaches as well, Eisenhower knew by daylight that the landings had succeeded. The winds had been vicious, many landing craft lost, the technological wonders of amphibious tanks and trucks faring poorly as a result of the high surf. But the men had pushed ashore to minimal opposition, the beachheads spreading even now. Except for Omaha. There had been very little word from Bradley for agonizing hours, Bradley himself staring through binoculars at the horrific carnage that had engulfed the men of the Twenty-ninth and First divisions. Throughout the day, as successive waves of landing craft brought added troop strength to reinforce all the beaches, Omaha had suffered a catastrophic traffic jam. Because the first men ashore had been unable to push inland, they had blocked the way for the others coming in behind them. By midmorning, thirty-four thousand men had fought their way ashore on Omaha Beach, only to huddle in whatever cover the beach could offer them, many protected only by the disastrous waves of human and steel debris that clogged the shoreline.

Eisenhower shivered in the cold, started to move, then stopped and looked east, into the blackness. I will find out about that, he thought. That's the first place I will go. First thing in the morning. Bradley will know what the hell happened there, and Bradley will straighten it out. But I have to see for myself.

He didn't know numbers yet; it was too soon to tally the casualties. But it's bad, he thought. And it could have been just as bad at every beach. But it wasn't. They didn't know we were coming . . . that's the only answer. But why not? Was it as simple as our bombing their weather stations? Would they even be looking at their weather reports? He shook his head and rubbed a hand across his forehead. It would seem not. We prepared to meet their warships, and there were none to meet. We sent fighters to hold off the Luftwaffe, and the Luftwaffe didn't come. There was no sign that they were expecting us at all, except maybe at Calais. The intelligence worked. The deception . . . my God, it might still be working. What other explanation is there? They are not fools over there. That's Rommel, after all. But their planes were patrolling *Calais.* Even if Rommel knew we were coming, he most definitely did not know where. I'll be damned.

He turned toward the tents again, dim shapes moving in the darkness, the staff hard at work, gathering information, monitoring radios and wireless sets, passing messages through, some to London and Washington, others to ships that stayed close to the beaches. Eisenhower had sent his own message to Marshall that morning, as much information as he could offer.

Then the public broadcast had come, carefully worded, relayed through the BBC.

A landing was made this morning on the coast of France by troops of the Allied Expeditionary Force. . . . The hour of your liberation is approaching.

Broadcast messages had followed from various European heads of state, the king of Norway, the premiers of the Netherlands and Belgium. The one missing voice had been French. Charles de Gaulle had refused to have the timing of his own message dictated by Eisenhower or anyone else, so he had waited until six that evening before making his own pronouncement. Despite every effort to discourage him from inciting a nationwide riot in the ranks of the Resistance, de Gaulle had done exactly that, issuing an all-out call to arms that burned through Eisenhower. SHAEF still had hopes that, through its many contacts across France, the Maquis could be encouraged to lay low until the invasion had secured a viable foothold. Voices of reason might still prevent underground fighters from revealing themselves so that the enraged Germans would not begin a campaign to massacre Frenchmen. But de Gaulle seemed intent on defying all reason, ordering his people to obey only those commands of what he called the French government, virtually ignoring the fact that the invasion was an Allied affair. As a final straw, de Gaulle intimated that the Normandy inva-

sion was the genuine article, the single thrust. Despite agonizing efforts by
Eisenhower's staff and British government ministers to convince de Gaulle
to go along with the Calais deception, de Gaulle's message made no mention of Calais at all. To any German intelligence agents who were charged
with monitoring de Gaulle's statements, the conclusion had to be that
Normandy was in fact the sole operation, what de Gaulle described as "the
supreme battle."

Eisenhower reacted to de Gaulle's statement with as much self-control
as he could muster, but he pulsed with anger at the thought of the man's
moronic bluster. How many Frenchmen will die, he thought, because of
that puffed-up idiot? How many of *us*? But we can say nothing at all, cannot contradict him. There can be no public comment to the French people implying that the Allies and SHAEF don't support French national
interests. But de Gaulle's interests aren't French, they're de Gaulle himself.
He has put himself squarely at the top of the French government, when no
one has either elected or appointed him to the role. He's wrapped himself
in the tricolor, a one-man French flag. No, we missed our chance, he
thought. I should have included him in the operation in a far more meaningful way. We could have launched him out of a landing craft, a one-man
army. Who needs fighting divisions when we have de Gaulle?

As the day had worn on, encouraging details continued to roll in, and
one surprise visitor provided a remarkable contrast to the annoyance of
Charles de Gaulle. This visitor was General Frederick Morgan. Morgan
had been the engineer and architect behind the original planning for
Overlord, and now he was simply a bystander, the plan growing like a
child from Morgan's cradle to full adulthood. But there was no bluster in
this man, just a humble need to know anything Eisenhower was willing to
tell him, and Eisenhower understood the magnitude of the man's humility.
If the plan had not worked, Morgan could easily have been the goat, the
accomplishments of his long career crushed by the weight of the failure.
But with encouraging reports from the beaches, Morgan had gone away
with only a display of quiet satisfaction, leaving Eisenhower with a few encouraging words.

While it had once been Morgan's plan, it had been Eisenhower's to
carry out. More Morgans, fewer de Gaulles, he thought. But it would
never be that way. And these men will not become easier to command now
that this operation is in full gear. Montgomery, Bradley . . . just do your
job. It's all still on paper, and so far what was drawn on paper seems to be

working. But paper is never enough. Men died today, taking those beaches, and men are dying tonight trying to hold them. Never forget that. There is no victory here, not yet. I will see them both in the morning, and you can damned well bet Monty will be strutting like a bantam rooster. But dammit, this is just the beginning. We're ashore for now. He couldn't shake the name: Rommel. What are *you* doing right now? You have too much power and too many good people not to respond. It could still be a bloody awful mess, more than Omaha Beach. What about the paratroopers? We need to hear from Ridgway, anything, some word. Is he alive? Have they accomplished any of their objectives?

Eisenhower moved closer to his tent, his boots muffled by the cinders spread thickly on the path. The note was stiff in his shirt pocket, and he fingered it again: *I have withdrawn the troops. . . .* God help me. If I have to tell that to our people back home . . . well, I might as well not go home at all.

He was at the tent now, leaned inside, the speck of light from a small gas lamp, mostly covered, no light reaching the roof of the tent. The blanket was flattened neatly on the cot, his extra boots standing straight in one corner. He moved toward the small dressing table and reached for the porcelain pitcher, heavy with water. Thank you, whichever one of you did this. You coddle me too much. He drank from a tin cup, heard muffled voices outside, the work ongoing, men who would be working all night long. I have to know, he thought. I have to get out there and talk to people and see for myself. But there's nothing I can do now, and, dammit, I need some sleep.

He took off his jacket, always aware of the note in his shirt pocket, the awful message. He felt for it, pulled it out, and, held it up in the faint glow, folded neatly. So much at stake, he thought. This has been the first day of something that will possibly win us this war. Or lose it. So . . . what do I do with this? He looked toward the small wastebasket. No, not yet.

He put the note back in his pocket, moved to the cot, and sat and unlaced his boots. The tent shook above him, the wind picking up, the tent flaps snapping, canvas rustling, the darkness around him alive with hard whispers.

26. ADAMS

The glider landings had been a nightmarish blend of relief and catastrophe. The tight checkerboard pattern of the hedgerow country created fields that were mostly too small for landing even the smaller Waco gliders. Many of them avoided enemy fire only to plunge nose-first into the hedgerows themselves, shattering crashes that destroyed the aircraft and, often, everything and everyone inside. Throughout the night, many of the paratroopers had served as rescue squads for gliders impacting in fields close by, the night ripped by the awful cries of the injured. The enemy contributed their own nightmare, more than just Rommel's asparagus. Scattered German machine gunners were drawn to the sounds of the crashes, setting impromptu ambushes for paratroopers who did what they could to help. Even those gliders that were able to come down without killing their crews often spilled their cargo across wide-open ground, men and equipment set upon by both sides, small firefights that shattered the darkness with deadly confusion. No one knew how many of the 175 gliders had survived complete destruction from their landings, but some men did emerge unscathed, magnificent reinforcements, and with them came crates of ammunition, rations, and radios. Even Gavin received an unexpected bonus, a glider coming down close to his command post that brought an intact jeep. Better still, the heavier gliders brought a handful of 57mm antitank guns and, near Sainte-Mère-Église, at least three snub-nosed 105mm howitzers. As the antitank guns were brought forward at La Fière Bridge, the paratroopers understood, if the Germans came again, that this time it might be a fair fight.

Adams had slept for most of an hour, awakened more by the rumbling in his stomach than anything happening across the causeway. It had not been long after midnight when the artillery began again, most of it closer to Sainte-Mère-Église, a struggle for the essential crossroads, for the defensive value of the town itself, the houses and block buildings offering both sides cover for machine guns and heavier weapons. At La Fière, there had been sporadic firing, mostly snipers and sharpshooters, seeking targets in the dark. Adams had stayed low in his foxhole, grateful there had been no glider crash close by, nothing to draw his men up from their safe havens. But the supplies had come forward, Adams gratefully stuffing his pockets with magazines for the Thompson, all the while watching the movement of the new men and their magnificent weapon, an antitank gun positioned behind a fat mound of dirt a few yards away. With the addition of the glider troops he had expected orders, some kind of word from Scofield, another shift in the line, something officers seemed to enjoy. But Scofield wasn't like so many of the parade-ground officers, and the men near Adams had stayed in place. Adams knew only that the captain was close by, in a foxhole of his own, probably doing what Adams was doing now: eating his rations.

The fruit was sweet and syrupy, and he finished the small can with one gulp. He probed the rest, some kind of crackers, a packet of dried coffee. Forget that, he thought. They need to put more stew in these kits instead of junk that makes you thirsty. He took a quick drink from his new canteen, the water tasting like dirt. The canteen had belonged to another trooper, the only identifiable piece of equipment remaining beside the man's blasted remains. Adams had tried to ignore that, forced it away now. It's like Marley's M-1, he thought. Lose one, pick up another. You make do. Rifles and canteens are just like soldiers. One replaces another.

With the added rations had come a marvelous surprise, far more meaningful to the men than Gavin's jeep. As the men from the gliders made their way into the field, word had been passed—and Adams heard it directly from his captain—that the gliders had brought more than just troops and equipment. Throughout the day on June 6, the rumors of some awful disaster at Utah Beach had permeated the men in the field, angry officers doing what they could to silence the talk that the paratroopers were completely alone. Until the gliders had come in, not even Gavin or Ridgway had known if the rumors were true or if the landings had actually been made. It was the officers who came in on the gliders who brought Gavin the first word that, in fact, Utah had been a rousing success. Even in the darkness, American infantry was pushing inland. Adams welcomed the news as heartily as the men around him, but darkness had snuffed out the optimism. No one had actually seen any infantry yet, and to the east there was the ongoing fight around Sainte-Mère-Église, a major roadblock between Utah Beach and the paratroopers hunkered down along the Merderet River.

Adams looked up, a glimpse of stars in the clouds, and thought of asking somebody the time. No, he thought, keep your mouth shut. Doesn't much matter what the hell time it is. It'll be daylight pretty soon, and the only time that matters is when it's time to shoot at somebody. There were low voices around him, those men who had dug larger holes, accommodating several men. Not my guys, he thought. That's just dumb as hell. One lucky shell takes out half a squad. Why do some of these guys need a buddy next to them, somebody to chat with? I'd rather have dirt around me than somebody's guts.

The sharp whistle came now, and he saw the flash, the shell coming down behind him. He stuffed the last of the rations in his pocket, rolled over to his knees, stayed low, waited for more. It came now, whistles and shrieks, a hard *crack,* men calling out, the *pop* of rifles, and a voice close by: Scofield.

"Man your guns! They're coming out! Wait for something to shoot at!"

Adams straightened, his helmet easing up just above the dirt mound in front of his hole. The causeway was barely visible, lit by streaks of fire, muzzle blasts from the men farthest out, men who could see what was in front of them. The sounds were scattered—some men firing at nothing— and Adams looked to the side: more mounds of dirt, rifles resting on top, a glimpse of helmets.

"No shooting until you see the bastards! You hear me?"

"Yeah, Sarge."

It was Unger. Yep, he knows, Adams thought. Not as stupid as he looks. He knew Marley was there as well, and Nusbaum, and others in a line along the brush. No one spoke. Adams focused on the causeway again, heard a new sound, the dull rumble of engines, the creaking of steel. Tanks.

He strained to see, the darkness fading, the marsh around the causeway covered in a low blanket of fog. But the sounds were growing louder, at least three tanks, more, coming out of the thickets across the way. He heard Scofield now.

"Hold your fire! Let them get clear!"

Adams glanced at the Thompson, thought, Clear of what? He's not talking to me. Then he realized: the antitank gun! Yes! Hell of a lot better than a stinking bazooka. He thought of the gun crew, the men who survived their glider, who had crashed successfully. Guts. Luck too. He knew the knock against some of the glider troops, that the units were green, untested by combat. But good God, he thought, they rode those damned coffins to get here, and sure as hell they don't need to prove anything else to me. I just hope they can shoot straight.

Men were firing close by, rifles mostly, and Scofield was shouting again. "Cease fire! Let them get closer!"

But the firing continued, all along the edge of the causeway, more officers trying to control their men, the shouts useless. Adams had seen it before, men getting their first look at the enemy, and emptying their clips into the air, nervous hands squeezing the triggers in pure reflex, firing empty guns—an infuriating loss of control. He felt helpless. He could only command a small piece of the fight, but shouted out, "You hear me?"

"Yeah, Sarge."

"Yeah!"

"You see infantry around those tanks, take 'em out. You don't, sit tight. Let the big guns do the job! You hear me?"

"Yeah, Sarge!"

He knew the high pitch in Unger's voice, shared the boy's excitement. The rumble of the tanks was growing louder, and Adams leaned his helmet against the dirt wall in front of him, felt the ground rise beneath him, a shell landing close, ripples of machine-gun fire arcing overhead. His heart raced, sweat dampened his filthy clothes, voices blended in with the impact of the shells, *thumps* and *pops* again. And now, a loud *thump,* deafening, curling him up tight, the dirt crumbling around him with the shock. He shook his head, thought of putting his hands on his ears, but then it came again. And then there were cheers.

He forced himself to look up, his eyes just above the mound of dirt, and saw fire on the causeway, splashes in the marsh. The air was alive with streaks of fire, but his eyes stayed glued to the one spot, dead center on the wide-open stretch of raised ground. It was a tank, and it was on fire.

The men at the big gun continued their work, but Adams stayed up, stared hard at the foggy marsh, saw flickers of movement. All across the near side of the causeway, the Americans were firing, the German infantry tumbling down, another bright flash, and a second tank was engulfed in fire. But the Germans were swarming across the narrow stretch of dry ground, some wading in the taller grass, spreading out in the shallow water, returning fire. They were past their own tanks now, still coming, a steady wave. Adams leaned down and stared through the sight of the Thompson. Too far! Dammit, I need a rifle! But his own men were answering, the M-1s close beside him opening up.

"I got one! I got one!" Marley's voice.

"Shut the hell up! Keep shooting!" The second voice was Unger's.

The Germans were still coming, a dark stain spreading out on the causeway, fallen men, some crawling, many more still advancing through their own dead. They reached the first foxholes, fire on both sides, and Adams saw terror in faces and eyes, and he aimed again and pulled the trigger. The Thompson jumped in his hands to no effect, the Germans still flowing toward him, five more, ten behind them. Adams felt his own panic now, thought, Too many of them! He raised his head, ignored the gun sight, held his finger on the trigger, and sprayed the open ground in front of him, until the submachine gun emptied. He ducked down, snatched a magazine from his pants leg, stuffed it hard into the gun, jerked the bolt, raised up, saw boots, a rifle, the man stumbling, falling to one side. There was another man, a bayonet, and Adams fired again, the man's chest coming apart, helmet coming off, bullets thumping the ground beside him. He held the trigger until the gun emptied and slumped down again, two magazines in his hand, one in the gun. A man jumped over him, and Adams fired up, ripped the man's back, a shout rising up inside him. He sprayed the submachine gun blindly, saw the ground around him now, a carpet of fallen men.

The Thompson was empty again, and he rammed in the fresh magazine, but the targets were distant, running. The causeway was a surge of motion, most of it the other way, the Germans who had survived the assault pulling back. Behind them, the tanks still burned. He saw now that the wreckage had blocked the roadway, the rest of the German armor unable to move past. Those tanks were backing away as well, the antitank guns still firing, more fire from rifles close by. Men were screaming around him, wounded Germans mostly, and Adams felt his breathing, cold pain in his chest, his hands wrapped in a hard grip on the Thompson, and his eyes searched the fallen, weapons, hands, grenades. There was still firing, his ears ringing, the antitank gun again, and he looked that way, saw only the barrel, red hot, smoking, more smoke from the muzzles of the rifles. There was a silhouette beside him, a rifle whipping around, the muzzle past Adams's face, and he jerked the Thompson that way, but the rifle was one of his. There was a flash of fire, the sharp punch of the M-1, and Adams was frozen, the rifle aimed just past his face. The man yelled now, manic, screaming insanity, and Adams saw the eyes: Unger, the kid, red-faced, aiming the M-1 again, another flash of fire. Unger lowered the rifle and stared past Adams. Marley was up beside him, shouting. "You got him! Sarge, he got him!"

Adams followed Unger's stare, turned, and saw the German a few feet away, a pool of blood on the man's chest, bubbles and foam, and in his hand a grenade. Adams felt a hard quiver in his legs, leaned against the dirt, and looked at Unger again, still wild-eyed, furious.

"It's okay, kid! You got him!"

Unger lowered the rifle, seemed to get control, and looked out toward the causeway, Adams doing the same.

"He was crawling up behind you, Sarge," Unger said.

"I know, kid. You got him. Thanks."

Unger nodded slowly.

Marley said, "I got a bunch of 'em, Sarge! That was nuts! They just kept coming!"

Adams looked again at the dead German. The grenade, he thought. Better get rid of that damned thing. He pulled himself out of the foxhole, rolled across the ground—could smell the man now, sickening, blood and stink—and slid close to the man's arm, black dirty fingers wrapped around the grenade. Adams grabbed the hand, the grip loosening. He pried the grenade away, kept it tight in his own hand.

Scofield was there now, on his knees, said, "What the hell you going to do with that?"

Adams stared at the grenade, his fingers tight around it, and held it out. "Souvenir?"

"Funny man. Get rid of that damned thing!" Scofield began to move away, pointed. "There's an empty foxhole. Drop it here!" He called out, "Heads up! Fire in the hole!"

Adams crawled that way, Scofield flattening out, and Adams dropped the grenade into the hole, rolled away quickly. It's probably not armed, he thought, the words jarred away by the blast, the ground punching him, a spray of dirt billowing up, falling around him, on him, dirt in his ears, nose. He coughed.

"You satisfied now, Sergeant?" Scofield said. "Get your stupid ass back in your foxhole."

You too, he thought. He crawled quickly, felt the shivering again, slid back down into his hole. He looked up at Unger. The boy was still staring at him, strange, eerie, hollow-eyed, and Marley was talking again, meaningless jabber. Adams ignored him, keeping his eyes on Unger; he'd never seen the look, the pure frozen stare.

"Thanks, kid. Looks like you saved my ass."

Unger didn't respond. Adams heard more of the sounds now, soft cries, one moaning scream, medics scampering past, medical bags. Then he heard a new sound, soft and low, looked at Unger again and saw his face cradled in one dirty hand. The boy was sobbing.

The Germans continued to shell the American paratroopers at La Fière, but they would not repeat their costly mistake. There would be no more frontal assaults across the wide-open ground of the causeway. By late afternoon on June 7, the fight had settled into a lull, and the Germans offered a hearty surprise. They brought out a red cross, asking the Americans for a brief truce, to allow the Germans to collect their dead and wounded.

For one brief moment, the war seemed to pause, while men on both sides tended to those who did not escape the slaughter, the Germans hauling away nearly two hundred of their fallen. With the gruesome mission complete, the Germans again began their artillery and mortar assault. Adams could only stay low in his foxhole. All along the Merderet River,

Gavin's men endured the barrage until nightfall, when, again, their com-manders would plan their next move. But this time, there was added strength. At Sainte-Mère-Église, General Ridgway finally met the first in-fantry officers of the American Fourth Division. The bridgehead at Utah Beach had been secured.

27. EISENHOWER

By midmorning on June 7, Montgomery's British and Canadian forces, under Lieutenant General Miles Dempsey, had established strong footholds on all three of the easternmost beaches. Throughout the day on June 6, those troops had encountered considerable opposition, though not the stinging disaster that had met the Americans at Omaha Beach. But with so much confusion in their hierarchy, the Germans could not mount any coordinated effort to strike back when the Allies were most vulnerable.

At Juno Beach, the Canadians under Major General Rod Keller made their landings hemmed in by formations of rocks, which forced them to drive forward in wedges that were more narrow than the planners had anticipated. The result was two separate assaults onshore, which bypassed a German stronghold between them, the town of Courseulles-sur-Mer. But the Germans who held their ground were soon cut off, and by nightfall the tenacity of the Canadians had overcome the resistance they faced on Juno Beach. With much of the opposition eliminated, the Canadians had been able to drive inland nearly five miles.

On either flank of the Canadian landings, the British landings at Gold and Sword saw equal success. As at Juno, the British troops pushing ashore at Gold found a large escarpment of rocks, which limited their landing to a narrower slice of beach. Here, the British, under the overall command of Lieutenant General Neil Ritchie, drove inland across a more narrow front than expected, which gave the British the same advantage as the Canadians, allowing them to punch a hole through the German resistance. Though the Germans maintained several strongpoints, the British, like the Canadians, were several miles inland by dark. Farthest to the east, Sword Beach straddled the mouth of the Orne River, the vital waterway that led straight into the city of Caen.

Inland, the British Sixth Airborne had made their jump on the far eastern flank of the entire operation. At the very least, the British paratroopers would serve as a first wall of protection on that flank, should the Germans launch a counterattack from the direction of Calais. Unlike the Americans, a large percentage of the British troopers came down relatively close to their designated drop zones east of the Orne, and had fought effectively to capture vital bridges that crossed the river. At the key river crossings, British paratroopers and especially glider troops accomplished most of their missions with stunning success, and Montgomery's plan to capture the city of Caen on D-Day seemed within his grasp. Though the British on Sword Beach struggled with stout German strongholds, they too were able to drive a spear several miles in from the beach, pushing southward along the river with expectations that Montgomery's boast of grabbing Caen was about to come to pass. But British expectations met reality. The Twenty-first Panzer Division was the only serious armored force that Rommel's command had at their immediate disposal, and despite so much confusion and doubt among German generals, the Twenty-first was moved into position exactly where it needed to be to keep the British out of Caen. Late in the day on June 6, the panzers managed a counterattack of sorts, resulting in one column of German tanks actually reaching the western fringes of Sword Beach. But the attack lost steam, the panzers still reeling from confused orders and the dispersal of so much of their armor in small-scale battles scattered across the countryside. The panzer division had suffered from the unexpected dilemma of dealing not only with British infantry at the beaches but with the paratroopers engaging so many vital strategic targets along the river. By dark, the panzers had withdrawn to a formidable defensive position closer to Caen, and both sides understood that any significant contact would wait for morning. Though Eisen-

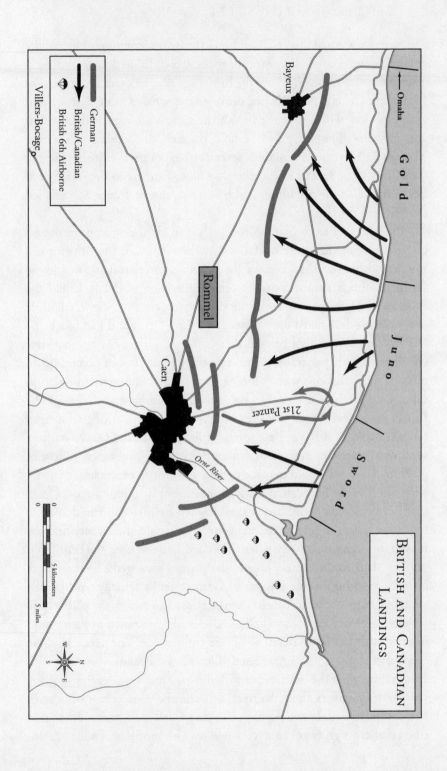

BRITISH AND CANADIAN LANDINGS

Omaha

Gold

Juno

Sword

Bayeux

Caen

Rommel

21st Panzer

Orne River

Villers-Bocage

German
British/Canadian
British 6th Airborne

0
5 kilometers
0
5 miles

N
W   E
S

hower had heard Montgomery's grand pronouncements that Caen would be in the bag by dark, that boast was just one part of the vast paper plan that had been tossed away by the stark reality of the assault. Operation Overlord had succeeded in landing 150,000 Allied troops on French soil. Their first priority was to drive the enemy away from the beaches and then keep him away. Once the beachheads were secured, an enormous number of troops were poised to flow in behind them, along with mountains of supplies and matériel. Despite the horror the Americans had confronted on Omaha Beach, Eisenhower knew D-Day had opened the door that might finally drive Hitler out of France and possibly end the war. The question now was, What were the Germans going to do about it?

OFF OMAHA BEACH
JUNE 7, 1944

They started early in the morning, transported on the minelayer *Apollo,* Eisenhower's temporary headquarters at sea. At Eisenhower's instructions, the small ship first cruised the waters past Utah Beach, which had become a virtual city of activity, large landing craft clustered in what seemed to be an enormous traffic jam, each ship waiting in turn to disgorge more men and equipment, supporting and adding more troop strength that would follow the American Fourth Division inland. But Eisenhower was far more anxious to see Omaha, knowing that, off that beach, Omar Bradley waited aboard his own command ship, the cruiser U.S.S. *Augusta.* The *Augusta* had supported the landings at Omaha Beach, its eight-inch guns contributing to the naval bombardment thought to have neutralized German opposition, a grotesque miscalculation.

As the *Apollo* maneuvered close to the *Augusta,* Bradley had already received word that Eisenhower was coming, and with a neatly executed transfer, Bradley moved from his own ship to the much smaller *Apollo* by crane, aboard a thirty-man landing craft, an LCVP, that never actually touched the water.

"Monty was here this morning, full of piss and vinegar," Bradley said. "Happy vinegar, I guess. Well, hell, Ike, you know Monty."

Eisenhower had not taken his eyes off the beach. "Yep, I'm sure of that. I talked to him earlier, and I should see him in about an hour. They had something of a rough go, particularly at Sword. The enemy was pretty heavily fortified, and it took the Canadians a little longer than they expected to get off the beach. But they're on the move now. Damned fine work, I hear. Monty says he has them in gear this morning, to keep up the push."

"He pushed me pretty hard to get the beachheads connected. His usual speech about speed and boldness. He thinks we have the initiative and must take advantage of it."

Eisenhower looked at him. "You disagree with that?"

"The plan called for us to drive south and cut off the peninsula. Now, he wants me to spread out the beachheads, so we link hands first. It's going to cost us time, Ike. All his chatter about phase lines just went out the window."

"Drop it, Brad. Not the time. Monty's right. We had better take every advantage we have, but we're too vulnerable right here. Until Omaha is in stronger hands, your part of this operation can wait. You can damn well bet that Rommel is over there making some plan to bust us in the chops. I'm surprised as hell it hasn't happened yet. I half expected to hear of a full-out counterattack hitting us across the whole landing zone, but there's almost no incoming fire at all around Utah. It's a big damned parking lot, which scares me a little.

"No matter what Monty says, I can't accept that Rommel is just going to let us waltz in without one hell of a fight. It's like waiting for the second shoe to drop. We had every reason to believe that all five beaches were going to be hot as Omaha. I was more afraid of that than anything, that we were going to catch holy hell every step of the way. It's almost like they sat back and let us land, and the only thing I can figure is that Rommel's about to give us one hell of a counterpunch."

"Could be, Ike. But every indication is that we caught them completely by surprise."

"Except right out there. What happened?"

Bradley leaned on the ship's rail and stared at the distant beach, low clouds of smoke drifting across. There were thumps, the ongoing fight that had spread inland, but on the beach itself the landing craft continued to pour out men and equipment.

"We stumbled into a mess. We were too blind to what was waiting for us." He looked at Eisenhower, a hard scowl. "I'm not casting blame anywhere. Be clear about that. This was my ballpark, and I got my people whacked hard. Most of the prisoners we picked up are from the Three-fifty-second Division, and we hadn't heard they were there at all until early yesterday. By then, it was too late to change anything, too late to prepare anything different. The whole operation was in full motion. The opposition at Utah was pretty much what we had hoped for, enemy units we knew weren't up to snuff. But here? The Three-fifty-second is one of the best German outfits in the theater, and they were sitting up there on those bluffs.

"I sweated blood out here, Ike. Saw most of it myself. Had to push Gerow a little bit, but I can't really blame him. The First Division had experience under their belts and we sure as hell needed that. And the Twenty-ninth fought like madmen. They lost most of their field officers and still kept fighting. I heard that General Cota took charge and did one hell of a job getting his people off the beach. Nothing like this at Utah. Over there, Collins was ready for anything. Anybody who's spent time in the Pacific knows what kind of hell these beaches can be, and Collins had his men in tip-top condition. But here . . . none of the senior people had been through anything like this before."

"We're all supposed to be in tip-top condition, Brad. Gerow is a good man, and his division commanders are first-class. That doesn't explain what happened here."

"You're right. The other fellow was up there waiting for us. I'm not saying he knew we were coming, but they had their best people in the right place at the right time."

"Bad luck?"

Bradley stared at the beach again, fingered his binoculars, kept them at his chest. "It's supposed to be my job to eliminate *luck*. We had a tough fight here, but dammit, we're getting the job done. The First and the Twenty-ninth took heavy casualties all day yesterday, and they're still taking them now. But we've pushed up past the bluffs, and the villages are fairly secure. We're in about a mile and a half. The Rangers took Pointe-du-Hoc, and it looks like they knocked out the big guns that were up there. At least, it seems so; enemy artillery hasn't been a factor at all. We don't know how many Rangers are left up there, because no one can get through to them. The enemy is still close, heavy-machine-gun emplacements and some deeply entrenched strongpoints. That's awfully high ground, and the infantry moving off the beaches hasn't been able to reach it. Those are Rudder's people, toughest sons of bitches in the army. We're pushing like hell to support them, but it's a slow go. The other fellow is giving us all we need, Ike."

The other fellow. Eisenhower knew Bradley's term, no insulting slang for the enemy. The Germans were simply . . . the other fellow.

"You been to the beach?"

"This morning. My own staff raised hell with me, but I had to see it." Bradley paused. "Keep the damned reporters away, Ike. We don't need pictures of that place on the newsreels, not yet. I saw Ernie Pyle out there, and I told him he better keep his damned dispatches to himself until we clear it. Not even sure how he got onshore so quickly, but he was as sick to his stomach as I was." Bradley paused again, seemed to search for words. "I've never seen anything like it. The dead . . . they were rolling up on the beach like seaweed. Our boys were still taking heavy fire, so for half the day we couldn't even pull the casualties out of the water. The troops in the later landings were stepping through . . . pieces. It's a little better now, but a lot of the seriously wounded are still on the beach, pulled into cover as much as possible. And the wrecked equipment is still playing hell with the landings. We kept the *Augusta* about two miles out from the beach, and we were bumping through debris even there. I asked the captain to put a bunch of men up in the bow to search for survivors, but it was mostly busted-up landing craft, pieces of God knows what. The engineers are telling me that right now we need bulldozers on that beach more than anything else. We were supposed to land sixteen of the damned things here; three survived. The rest either sank or got blown to hell before they could do the job. Not sure what the engineers were expecting. Too many rehearsals probably. They learned it's a lot harder to build your damned road when somebody's dropping mortar shells on your head. This morning, they were working up on the bluffs trying to flatten out a landing strip. We're getting there, Ike, but any idea of a timetable's been tossed out the window."

Eisenhower heard no complaint, no excuses in Bradley's voice. And Bradley would not exaggerate.

"Monty give you any orders?"

"Well, yes. He didn't want to hear much about what these boys ran into here. Called it a *bloody tiff,* said his boys had one at Sword. Like I said, he pushed me to link our left flank to his right, to seal the landing zones into one secure sector. He's afraid Rommel will punch through and keep us separated. Collins is doing what he can at Utah to drive some people this way, help us break through to the Rangers from the other direction." He paused. "That wasn't the plan, Ike."

Eisenhower nodded, thinking of the maps. The primary goal of the troops at Utah Beach was to drive hard to cut off the entire Cotentin Peninsula, isolating the crucial port of Cherbourg. Once the peninsula was cut, new troops would land at Utah to drive toward the city itself. One of the essential objectives of the entire operation was to grab a major port city, which would serve as the conduit to feed and equip the ever-growing army.

"Plans change, Brad. That's what Monty does best. He makes damned sure he's ready before he orders a move. We're not ready until these beaches are secure, and a mile and a half of bridgehead is not secure. Cherbourg will wait. It'll still be there. The floating piers should be coming in pretty soon, and that'll help a hell of a lot."

"Floating concrete boxes. Yeah, I saw those things. Pretty impressive, if it works. Mulberries. Who thought of that name?"

"Morgan's people. Pure genius, if you ask me. Until we grab Cherbourg or Antwerp, these beaches will be the best ports we have. No way the enemy could suspect we're bringing our own docks with us. I don't think I could have made it as an engineer. I'm like you. Never thought so damned much concrete could float. But it's floating right now, out there somewhere, big damned blocks of it, and as quick as they get it hauled in here, they'll sink those things right offshore, and—*bang!* A port. Mulberries."

Bradley seemed distracted, so Eisenhower stopped talking; it was just nervous energy. Bradley raised his binoculars, then lowered them quickly; there was nothing to see in the smoke.

"I hate to say this," Bradley said, "but somebody did a half-assed job with intelligence. Every report tells me how difficult the countryside is, and this is the first I knew anything like that. I saw a little of it myself this morning, beyond one of those villages: hedgerows tall as a house and just as thick. Every damned farmhouse and cow pasture is guarded by a wall of dirt and brush, and the enemy knows exactly how to use shelter there. Why the hell didn't we know about it?"

"We know about it now, and we'll do what we have to."

"Ike, the paratroopers are out there in the middle of miles of that stuff. It's probably why we didn't hear from Taylor until noon. Ridgway—well, we haven't heard much of anything from the Eighty-second. They're holding on to Sainte-Mère-Église, best as we can tell. Collins is pushing his people that way as fast as they can bust through the countryside, but there's plenty of the other fellow scattered all over hell. Monty was all puffed up about the British paratroopers and what a fine job they did. Can't fault him for that. He also says Dempsey's been able to push his infantry seven miles inland near Bayeux. Then he looks at me like he's asking, What the hell is *your* problem? I wanted to ask him if he knew what the hell a hedgerow was, maybe take him out there myself and show him the damned things."

Eisenhower kept his eyes on the beach. "Just do your job, Brad. I'll hear all that from Monty. I agree we've got to link up these beachheads. But he had big plans, all those damned maps. I'm wondering how much more he's been able to accomplish this morning."

"He won't tell me any of that, Ike. Unless it's good."

"He'll tell me."

"Oh, by the way. I did ask him about Caen. He didn't like the question."

ON BOARD *APOLLO*, OFF GOLD BEACH
JUNE 7, 1944

"Bloody magnificent day, Ike! I'll be setting up the command post on shore straightaway! Let the boys know we're right there with them."

"You been ashore?"

"Oh, no, not yet. Soon enough, though. Don't want to distract the boys from the job at hand. Keep them pointed toward Berlin, as it were."

Eisenhower couldn't fault Montgomery for his high spirits. The ship rolled slightly, in reaction to a larger cruiser passing by a half mile to one side. Eisenhower grabbed the rail and looked toward Montgomery's transportation, a British destroyer. Sailors were lining the deck, some with cameras. They're photographing *me*! Eisenhower realized. Well, no, not just me. Maybe not me at all. They might not even know who I am. He glanced at Montgomery, the ever-present sweater, the black beret. They love this man. All right, good. We need that. Eisenhower thought of Bradley, his barely hidden dislike for Montgomery. Patton feels the same way, doesn't hide it at all. That's one reason why Bradley has the job.

Montgomery seemed to notice the cameras now, stood straight, tugged at the sweater, a slight pose. Eisenhower said, "What's your plan to get through to Caen?"

"Ah? Yes, bloody nose on that one. Jerry surprised us. Didn't expect to run into the panzers so quickly. We're bringing up our own armor, and I expect we'll return the favor. Jerry did *us* a favor, though. Threw his tanks in piecemeal, gave us some fun." Montgomery looked at Eisenhower now, seemed to test his mood. "Jerry did us another favor as well. By having his available armor positioned on *this* flank, it means that for now he has very little on the *other* flank. That should be of help to your boys, eh? I tried to explain that to General Bradley—well, not in so many words."

Eisenhower thought of a response but let it pass. Monty was a lot of things, but he was usually right. He saw another ship moving past, a large landing craft—tanks, likely, or heavy armored trucks. He thought of Montgomery's words. Yep, bring up our own armor.

Montgomery seemed to read him, said, "Soon enough, Ike. We'll hit him in the soft spot, and keep hitting him until he calls it off. That's the idea, eh?"

"Any estimate how long it will take you to grab Caen?"

"You know I can't tell you a date. Bradley doesn't know when Cherbourg will be in our hands, does he? Not meaning to lecture you, of course, but these things have to be done in their own time. Soon enough. Remember, I've handled this chap Rommel before."

28. ADAMS

With significant manpower and more heavy armament pouring across Utah Beach, the American beachheads were becoming more secure by the hour. Most of the heaviest German resistance was anchored in the east, the British sector, Rommel's desperate attempt to prevent the city of Caen from falling into Allied hands. Though the fate of the port of Cherbourg was equally important to the Germans, Rommel didn't have enough power at his command to launch a counterattack that would be effective against the infantry and armor that continued to land at Utah. The hedgerow country was in fact a detriment to both sides, preventing anyone from assembling a massive strike force, and most of the hedgerows were in the American sector, a difficult barrier to Bradley's goal of cutting across the Cotentin Peninsula. Worse for the Germans, the pockets of American paratroopers tied down much of Rommel's available strength in scattered fighting, keeping the Germans from amassing the kind of punch they would need to strike back in any meaningful way toward Utah Beach.

As Montgomery had insisted, the two American beaches were finally linked up, and increasing numbers of troops began to come in at Omaha Beach as well. In time the artificial harbors, those strangely named Mulberries, would be in place. Other artificial breakwaters were being created by using scrapped and damaged transport ships, which were sunk offshore in a carefully designed pattern. From these artificial piers, the off-loading of even more men and equipment would proceed at a much faster rate.

Bradley was forced to acquiesce to Montgomery's more plodding approach. Despite his impatience to get on with the original goals of the Overlord plan, Bradley had to concede that those objectives could only be reached when sufficient power could be brought toward the front lines. Local fighting by the paratroopers around Sainte-Mère-Église had mostly cleared that area of significant German opposition, and American infantry from Utah Beach continued to move toward the flooded Merderet River. Both sides recognized that the river was a formidable obstacle. The various attempts by one side or the other to drive the enemy away had resulted in unacceptable casualties for anyone attacking across the flat open ground. But the paratroopers who hunkered down on the eastern side of both causeways could hear ongoing firefights across the river, evidence that a sizable number of beleaguered paratroopers were still holding out in isolated pockets on the western side of the river. For Adams, and for the officers above him, the sounds of that fighting tore at their frustration, no one certain how many of those troopers had survived.

With Sainte-Mère-Église in American hands and the infantry moving forward from Utah Beach, Ridgway and Gavin were suddenly faced with an annoying reminder of what their original mission had been. The Fourth Infantry Division had made the first landings on Utah and had been assigned the task of driving up the east coast of the Cotentin Peninsula, pushing toward Cherbourg from the right. They had been followed ashore by the Ninetieth Division, whose job it was to press westward, across the Merderet. The Ninetieth would be followed closely by the American Seventy-ninth and Ninth divisions, a force sufficiently powerful to cut across the peninsula at its base and then drive northward to engulf Cherbourg.

The Fourth and the Ninetieth were part of the Seventh Corps, commanded by Lightning Joe Collins, a rugged veteran of campaigns in the Pacific, where he had earned a reputation for pushing his forces into battle with a little more tenacity than some of his subordinates found comfortable. But Collins had the absolute support and confidence of Omar Bradley, and with Utah secured so quickly, Collins had done nothing to harm his own reputation. It was natural for Collins to take the next step, to drive his infantry across the flooded Merderet River as quickly as possible.

At Sainte-Mère-Église, Matthew Ridgway began to feel pressure from behind. Collins was pushing hard, implying that his forces could do what the paratroopers could not. For men who had repeatedly traded hard blows with the Germans across the river, that sort of boast didn't go down smoothly. Worse, the Ninetieth Division was completely untested in battle, and both Ridgway and Gavin realized that their inexperience could lead to disaster in the field. Though Collins was following the original Overlord plan, to Gavin and Ridgway he was showing a bit too much bluster by assuming his fresh infantry was certain to sweep across the Merderet, and he unwisely gave the paratroopers the impression that they should now stand aside while his infantry cleaned up their mess.

Though pride was a dangerous motivation for launching an attack, there was another problem for Jim Gavin at La Fière. The troops most fit to launch the necessary frontal assault were the newly arrived 325th Glider Infantry, one more part of the Eighty-second Airborne. Though Gavin agreed with Ridgway that there was too much risk in allowing the green Ninetieth Infantry Division to make the assault, Gavin knew that the glider troops had no more experience than Collins's infantry. With so much pressure coming from behind to resume the drive across the Merderet, Gavin positioned as many of his veteran paratroopers behind the glider men as he could muster. If the glider troops faltered, at least he would have veterans to back them up.

To the south of La Fière, a growing number of mixed forces continued to trickle into the positions at Chef-du-Pont, including more scattered elements of the 101st. The added manpower gave Gavin confidence that the stalemate could be broken, that he finally had the strength to drive across and link up with the troopers on the west side of the river. At the same time, a shallow sunken road was discovered to the north of La Fière, giving the Americans a third avenue across the marshes. To gain as much advantage as possible, Gavin ordered the assaults to begin at dark, but the attacks were uncoordinated and ineffective. Though the paratroopers did push across the river at both places, the Germans were too strongly entrenched and still outnumbered them. By early morning on June 9, the attacks were called off, many of the troopers returning to the east side of the river. Gavin had no choice but to admit failure, and his assessment of several of his inexperienced field commanders had changed for the worse. If the paratroopers were to make a successful push across the Merderet, it would have to be more than just some artful maneuver. Ridgway agreed. The Americans would have to drive hard across the causeways, straight into the German positions. The center of that push would be La Fière.

La Fière Bridge
June 9, 1944, 10 a.m.

The assault the night before had lit up the sky with streaks of light, flashes of fire that inspired Adams and then frustrated him. Around him, the men had cheered, but then, with the fight continuing past midnight, the enthusiasm turned to frustration. If there had been success, Adams knew they would have been ordered to advance across the causeway, adding power to those men who had driven the Germans back. But the order never came. Then, as the sleepless troopers continued to wait in their foxholes, frantic officers had come and radios had crackled around Gavin's command post, reports of horrific cost and no substantial gains. There had been one positive word, however, passed along to Adams from Scofield. The location of at least two groups of Americans had been confirmed, those men mostly from the 508th, who had come down on the west side of the river. It was valuable strength that Gavin hoped to call upon to lend a much-needed hand. Any enthusiasm for that report was dampened by the knowledge that the Germans were just as eager to gather up those stranded paratroopers as Gavin was. Though the stranded men had done what they could to aid the new attack, in the darkness, and with such a staunch defense by the Germans, there could be no rescue. Those men were still out there.

With so little communication, and the rampant energy of rumor, Adams had no idea who might be on the far side of the river. The river itself still held the visible bodies of men and their parachutes, dark smears in the grassy water, tangled parachutes in the brush. It was a constant reminder that a great many men had come down in water as Adams had come down, many of them not lucky enough to survive. But across, beyond the swampy marshes, there were only the sounds of scattered fighting, mortars and machine guns and hints of rifle fire. With each firefight, the Germans were consolidating, bringing more people to the front, still seeking one more way to eliminate those paratroopers cut off on the west side of the river.

Adams stared out that way, across flat grassy marsh. I never thought the five-oh-eight would be worth a damn, he thought. Too fresh, too much talk, and no experience. But there're some tough bastards over there. I'd like to shake somebody's hand, if they survive.

To one side, a mortar shell impacted, with no warning. He had grown nearly immune to the shock of the constant surprise, so many shells, the strange security of his one small hole. The officers continued to move about, Gavin as well, and Adams had cringed, thinking, All it takes is one lucky jackass over there, and we lose the best man we've got. But Gavin still came forward, holding the binoculars, giving fresh orders, officers scampering close, then back to their men. Adams would watch him, Gavin never flinching. It was too strange. Adams's thoughts went back to the offices in London: clean uniforms, all those weeks of planning and meetings, maps and arguments, with men who would never do *this,* who would never know what it was like to go about your business with the enemy trying to kill you. Then Gavin would be gone again, and Adams tried to visualize that as well: Gavin somewhere back by the railroad tracks, with staff officers, radios, even General Ridgway. I'll never be an officer, he thought. I have one job, and it's the best job in the army. Kill the enemy. To hell with arguments and generals. But not Gavin. God help him. If I don't survive this, I hope like hell he does.

Throughout the morning, more of the precious artillery had come forward, a total of seven of the snub-nosed howitzers now dug in, facing the causeway. There had been the sound of tanks as well, a glorious racket that pulled the men up from their holes. All through the village and beyond, a dozen Sherman tanks had appeared, sent forward by commanders who had brought their armor across Utah Beach. The tanks had spread out in whatever cover they could find, some of the crews digging shallow pits, the hulls of the tanks set low, only the turrets visible to the enemy across the way.

The arrival of the armor and artillery gave every man at the causeway a reason to breathe easier, talk drifting through the foxholes that with so many new teeth in the American position the Germans were not about to try another assault. But Adams heard other talk as well, talk that made more sense, coming from men who knew what was about to happen. He watched them now, Gavin coming again, standing low over a narrow slit trench, two infantry officers in clean uniforms beside him, dropping down, keeping low, a telltale radio aerial, the tool of the artillery observer. Gavin was pointing across the open ground, and Adams heard the words.

"Right there. The road on the causeway leads into Cauquigny, which is eight hundred yards or so beyond those trees. The enemy has it, and we're going to take it. I want you to blow hell out of the place, and anything else you see that looks like a target. How many 155s?"

"By now, sir, we should have all twelve in position."

"Good. Pick a target out there, and start zeroing them in. Let me see what they can do."

Adams heard low talk, one man using his radio, and in a few seconds, Adams heard a ripping shriek, the shell coming from behind, passing overhead, and then, a hard thump across the causeway. Now another shell came, another punch of thunder, smoke rising, men around him quieting, watching the spectacle.

Adams looked at Gavin again, saw him standing upright, binoculars, shouting, "One more time!"

The shelling continued, guns far behind the causeway seeking the range, zeroing in on the woods across the way. Gavin turned and scanned the men around him, helmets popping up across the sloping ground, more men gathering in the narrow streets of the village. Gavin motioned to an aide, a radio coming forward, the men ducking low, Gavin still upright. He spoke into the radio; Adams couldn't hear the words, but now the guns close by began to fire, then a sudden burst from a tank, then more, the entire village erupting with cannon fire. Adams held his ears, couldn't help a smile, watched Gavin again, the tall man seeming to wait, enjoying the moment, the power in his hands, one arm waving, a signal to the officers. Scofield was up now, motioning to Adams and the others, pointing, the order to fire drowned out by the roar of the big guns.

Around Adams, the heavier machine guns opened up, the beautiful rattle of the BARs, the men caught up in the enormous turmoil, firing their rifles. Adams raised the Thompson, aimed high at the dull tree line across the way, fired a short burst, then emptied the magazine. He stared out toward the causeway, streaks of white, impacts on the far side, trees across the way tumbling into fire, thick plumes of smoke rising. Save your ammo, he told himself. This thing isn't any good at long range. Let the big boys do the job. But damn. I do need to fire this thing once in a while. I need to smell the powder.

He searched for Gavin again, but the general was gone, back to his command post, where more of the radios connected him to Ridgway and to the men farther behind, the vast wave of infantry waiting to roll over this miserable stretch of open ground. Out front, closer to the causeway itself, the glider men had slipped into place, the men who would lead the assault. One man rose up from a foxhole, an officer Adams didn't know, a quick wave of his arm, a voice lost in the cascade of fire. The men rose up with him, several hundred from the cover of the stone bridge itself, a surge of green pressing across, moving onto the narrow mouth of the causeway.

Adams watched them, no sound except for the solid wall of firing from the tanks and artillery, the chatter of rifles and machine guns close by. They were on the causeway now, slow jogs, some staying close to the rows of brush on either side of the open lane, a futile grab for cover even as they made their advance. More men filed in behind, a single tight wave, helmets bobbing, rifles across their chests. They reached the slight curve in the causeway, still moving forward, nothing slowing them but their own tired legs, and Adams felt a knot in his chest. My God, keep going! Go! Faster! They were halfway across now, the shouts of the officers pulling them forward. Adams stared into the smoke, the artillery fire still blasting the far side of the flooded plain, but the smoke was drifting to one side, trees were visible, a spire from the village in the distance, and now from the smoke came streaks of fire, flickers and bursts from all across the far bank.

He flinched, pulled his shoulders in tight, hands hard on the Thompson, could see men falling on the causeway, the wave of green staggering, some men stumbling into the water, no cover, no protection. But the men in front pushed on and Adams couldn't turn away; he held the Thompson up in frustration, useless at this range, others around him aiming their M-1s to the side, to the enemy who fired back from cover so far away. He tried to see, but smoke was pouring over the causeway, mortar rounds coming down among the glider troops, flashes of fire, dirt in the air, men falling, staggering, some seeking cover in the water. The surge had slowed, so many of the men were down on flat ground or packing into the shallow ditches along the causeway. But others still moved forward and reached the far side, disappearing into smoke, hidden by the stream of men that came back, some wounded, some just running.

Adams stared in cold horror, felt his legs strengthening, tight springs, thought, Get out there, help them! What the hell are we doing back here?

The fight seemed to taper away, scattered shooting on the far side of the river, but the artillery had stopped its fire, the targets just as likely to be friendly. Officers were moving around the bridge, back up the rise toward Adams, toward the men who stared out as he did, the horrific sight, bodies on the causeway, blasts of mortar fire still falling, tossing the dead in the air, men flung into dark water.

There was a new sound behind him, the rattling roar of a tank, and Adams turned and saw the Sherman rolling toward the bridge and crossing quickly, men scrambling to clear the way, dragging the wounded and dead to the side of the road. More tanks began to fire up, moving into line, and the first tank was on the causeway now, the gun firing. Adams was suddenly furious. What the hell? You'll run people over! Where the hell were you when this started? Why weren't you in front? The tank bounced and rolled forward, a mortar shell coming down behind it, another to one side, a plume of water rising. The other tanks were moving toward the bridge, and Adams saw a flash of fire far out on the causeway, and the first tank spun sideways and tilted down, its gun pointed uselessly to the side, boiling black smoke. The other tanks halted now, the first tank a perfect roadblock, and Adams wanted to scream, jam his fist into someone's face. What stupid son of a bitch did that? He thought of the German tanks, wrecked on the causeway two days before, gone now, pulled into the water by the good work of demolition teams. Now we return the favor?

"Sergeant! Get ready to move! We're going in!"

Adams saw Scofield pulling himself out of a foxhole, others rising up all along the near side of the water. He saw Gavin as well, the thin silhouette, leaning against a small stone wall. Gavin was staring across the causeway, a man behind him shouting furiously into a radio. Gavin pointed to Scofield and said, "We're going across! The glider boys need some help!"

Scofield didn't look at him. Adams saw streams of sweat on the man's face, the hard stare in the eyes, and around them his own men were rising up, wide-eyed with fear.

Adams climbed up quickly and moved toward them.

"Those boys need us!" he shouted. "You got that? It's time to go to work!"

More men were gathering, most ignoring the cracks and whistles from guns across the river, other sergeants calling their men out from their cover, officers on the stone bridge. Adams tapped his heavy pants leg, a bundle of magazines for the Thompson, felt the grenades hooked to his chest. Unger was beside him now, talking, high-pitched words; *Be careful.* Adams tried to ignore him; I don't need that kind of stupidity, he thought. "Shut the hell up! Save it for the enemy!"

He looked past Unger, glanced at Marley, Nusbaum, and the others; he didn't want talk from any of them. They were strangers now, all of them, helmets and rifles and dirty uniforms.

Scofield shouted out, "Follow Captain Rae! Double-time! Let's go!"

Adams waited for the others to start moving and slipped in behind Marley. No one stops, he thought. No one turns around. A new flow of men was already on the causeway, pushing past others who were coming back. Around them, the enemy fire was increasing, mortar shells dropping again, some in the water, the smoke from the burning tank rising to one side, no cover at all. Men were down all around him, the glider troops, dead and wounded, green men who had not survived their first fight. Others were crawling, some in the water, hard cries, drowned out by the sheets of fire over their heads. Adams was close to the tank, a cluster of men seeking cover, an officer grabbing a man by the shirt, screaming profanity, the man up, moving forward again. The ditches were thick with men, some of them weaponless, no wounds, and there was another officer, pistol in hand, firing in the air.

"Get up! Move or I'll kill you!"

Adams didn't pause, stepped through the fallen men, one of them curled up, his hands over his head, and Adams felt rage, kicked the man. "Get up! Let's go!"

The man ignored him, paralyzed, and Adams could not wait, saw others rising up from the ditches, moving into the road again. In front of him, a man slowed, and Adams pushed him with his hand: Marley, the big man hesitating. A sharp crack went past Adams's ear, and he shouted, "Keep moving! No cover here! Get to the other side!"

Marley seemed to respond, jogging forward, more men on the causeway beside them. The trees ahead were filled with smoke; rifle and machine-gun fire rolled over them. Adams saw the ground rising, the causeway ending, the road narrowing, disappearing into a hedgerow. He tried to breathe, searing pain in his chest, saw men scattered in the grass, some firing into the trees. To one side, a cluster of gray, Germans, on their knees, hands in the air, one man's rifle pointed at their faces. Adams pushed past, saw Scofield, waving them forward, saw trenches now, German trenches, men dropping down into cover, firing into the trees. He scanned the ground on both sides of the road, searched frantically, men still going down, saw a thin trench, moved that way. Men were already there, one man firing, the others just curled up, weaponless, terrified, a dead German in the grass. He moved past, felt a hard blast behind him, a mortar shell, screams, and ducked low, looked back, and saw more men coming, spreading out away from the causeway, officers shouting, pointing, cover in the trees, bodies, bloody black shapes, a German helmet, the hard stink of explosives.

The fight was all around him, and he searched again for cover, saw a low rise, fresh dirt, and climbed up, his legs weak, stumbled, rolled forward, the ground falling away sharply. He was on his side now, hard jarring impact, the Thompson jammed into his face, but he kept his grip, fought to see, was down in a trench, soft dirt, more stink, a uniform, gray, the helmet, *Kraut*. He spun himself hard, jerked the Thompson forward, fired a burst, his own voice screaming as loud as the submachine gun. He fired again, the man's chest ripped apart, saw the face now, black tar, lifeless, realized—a corpse. He stared for a long moment, the sounds of the fight above him, a blur of noise, machine-gun fire and screams, and he held tightly to the Thompson, smelled the smoke from the barrel, the stink in the trench, felt the blind fury, his own terror, the animal taking over, and he stared at the dead man's empty eyes and pulled the trigger again.

They had driven forward to the village of Cauquigny, the Germans giving ground slowly, a brutal hand-to-hand fight, bayonets and hand grenades. By late afternoon the Germans had mostly pulled away, leaving Cauquigny a shamble of shattered buildings, smoke and dust and debris, the paratroopers digging into whatever cover they could find. Behind them, on the causeway, the wreckage of the Sherman tank had been cleared, the men astounded that the one officer who rushed forward to oversee the job had been General Ridgway himself.

With the causeway cleared, three more tanks rolled across, led by Gavin. The sight of their commanders was enough to rouse many of the cowering men from their terror, and all along the causeway, men found the strength to rise up and push forward to the village. With officers gathering, a command post was established at a small blockhouse, the command falling upon the senior officer in the town, Colonel Herb Sitler, executive officer of the glider regiment.

Gavin continued to traverse the causeway, adding strength to the men who held a fragile grip on Cauquigny, men too tired to make much of a defense. At dusk, the Germans came again, but Gavin's orders were explicit. The cost had been far too great simply to give ground again, and there would be no retreat back to the east side of the river. With the fight ongoing around the town, pockets of men on both sides stumbled blindly, the Germans relying on their artillery to pound places already pounded by the Americans that morning.

As darkness settled over the swamps and villages west of the river, the fight grew more scattered, any panic in the men replaced by utter fatigue. With the lull came new orders, Gavin still at work, other officers doing what they could to organize and prepare their men for anything the Germans might do. Adams had been sent north, along the river, a squad of men led by Captain Scofield. They had one simple mission: Do what they could to locate any pockets of stranded paratroopers.

WEST OF THE MERDERET RIVER
JUNE 10, 1944, 10 P.M.

The ground was wet and soft, one more narrow farm lane, set deep between tall hedgerows. To one side, the steep mounds served more as a dam, holding back the flooded Merderet. But there were gaps, low places, and Adams had stepped through water on the road, shuffling his feet, harsh words for the men who were clumsy, careless, whose boots made any kind of splash. During the fighting around Cauquigny, there had been signs that a fight had broken out to the north, a half mile or more above the town, the telltale rumble of American grenades, the pop of the M-1s, something Adams had heard himself.

Scofield kept to one side of the road, Adams across from him. They were fifteen men. Bringing up the rear was a lieutenant Adams didn't know, a name he had already forgotten. He moved with slow automatic steps, testing, the ground hard again: small rocks, tedious steps, urgent carefulness, nothing to break the silence. He stared ahead, fought to see any movement, the darkness alive with small sounds, insects mostly, some strange screeching bird. Birds, he thought. Wonder what they think about all this? Cussing us out probably. Men ripping their little piece of heaven all to hell. At least they can get out of the way. Not like us. He thought of the causeway, so many men, stepping through the dead. Someone's back there working on that right now. Gotta be. The graves people. Miserable damned job. More miserable than this? He looked to the side, the shadow of Scofield, and heard a stumble behind him, one man's boots skidding to a halt. He froze, and the others reacted, all of them still. The closest man moved up, a faint whisper.

"Sarge. There's somebody in the brush. Right here."

The whisper was Unger's. Adams focused, frozen, listening, heard a single low click.

"Down!"

The men dropped down, grunts and thuds on the road, and now there was a shout from the brush, a single word.

"Flash!"

Scofield responded. *"Thunder!"*

The brush came alive now, cracking limbs and heavy footsteps, shadows emerging through the hedge. The men around Adams began to rise. From the brush one man said, "If you're Krauts, you're all dead. We've got a thirty up ahead covering this road."

"If we're Krauts," Scofield said, "we took your damned password, and we picked up some pretty good English along the way."

One man stepped close in front of him, and Adams stood up, nervous finger on the Thompson.

"I'm Lieutenant Colonel Charles Timmes, Second Battalion, Five-oh-seven," the man said. "We were wondering if anybody was ever going to find us. Who might you be?"

"Captain Ed Scofield, Five-oh-five. We found you. How about we get the hell out of here, Colonel?"

"Sounds fine to me."

Timmes turned away, a quiet order, word spreading, more men emerging on the road ahead. Adams felt his hands shaking, unexpected. They've been out here for *four days,* he thought.

"Sir," Adams said. Timmes turned toward him. "How many have you got, sir? If you don't mind me asking."

"Fifty, more or less. There were a hell of a lot more, but they're still out there somewhere."

The men were gathering, no one speaking, and Timmes moved toward Scofield. "Captain, I assume you know the way out of here?"

"This way, sir."

Timmes's troops were in the road, some around Adams now, his own men moving close, a strange silent moment. Greetings and questions would come later, passing cigarettes and full canteens. Right now they shared a breathless flicker of relief, but no one among them knew what they would still have to do, how much more of this they would have to endure. Adams tried to see faces, but they were only shadows, dark shapes. So far, like the men who had found them, they had merely survived.

29. ROMMEL

The truck in front led the way, the car following closely, bouncing heavily on a narrow rocky trail. Rommel grabbed the back of the driver's seat and braced himself as the truck stopped abruptly and Sergeant Daniel jerked the wheel to avoid a collision. The rattle of antiaircraft fire came now, the twin guns on the truck pointed skyward, the gunner spinning furiously in his small turret. Rommel heard the planes, but there was nothing to see, the tall hedgerows sheltered them.

"Sir! Abandon the car! We must seek cover!"

He ignored the urgency of his aide and peered out, trying to see some sign of the planes, then caught a glimpse, more of them now, the roar of their engines flowing past. The antiaircraft guns continued to fire, aimed low toward the horizon, but then silence. Rommel saw an officer jumping from the truck, coming back toward the car, furious, shouting,

"Damn them! Damn them all!" The man seemed to gather himself and said to Rommel, "Sir! Corporal Weiss may have hit one of them. They were British, I believe. Single-engine, fighters perhaps."

"Or dive-bombers. We were not their target, clearly." He glanced at Captain Lang in the front seat of the car. "There is no need for panic. Return to the truck, Lieutenant, we should not delay. Captain, where are we exactly?"

Lang scanned a small map. "The Morain Bridge is three kilometers to the west. That is where we are to meet with General Bayerlein, sir."

There were more planes now, the roar of engines farther away, and Rommel saw the anger still on the lieutenant's face, the man who commanded his lone escort.

"Lieutenant, you may tell your gunner to be more precise with his shooting. If the enemy is going to come so close to us, that is an opportunity, not a reason to panic or waste ammunition. Am I clear, Lieutenant?"

The man stiffened. "Very clear, Field Marshal!"

"Then let's proceed. Lead us back to the main road. I would prefer not to keep General Bayerlein waiting." He leaned closer to his driver. "Sergeant Daniel, that was a fine piece of maneuvering. When this war ends, perhaps we should find you a racing car to drive. I have no doubt you would leave your competition behind."

"Thank you, sir."

Rommel sat back in the seat and waited for the armored truck to move away in front of them. Daniel is a good man, he thought. Remember that. It is not always best to scream at your aides. I should save that for the generals.

They began to move, the narrow lane curving, wrapping around a small field, the hedgerows leading them back to hard road. In the front seat, Lang turned to him.

"Forgive me, sir, but I must remind you of my concerns. General Speidel is most insistent that we not do this in the daylight. The enemy seems to be seeking out any target they can find, and I am concerned that they might find . . . you, sir."

"Thank you, Captain. But there is nothing to be gained by the constant delay, waiting for darkness so that I may conduct this command. I require General Bayerlein to advance the Panzer Lehr Division as rapidly as possible toward Villers-Bocage. Every report I am receiving indicates that the British are massing north of there. It is one avenue to circumvent our strength at Caen, and they will use that to try to come at the city from two sides. I would do the same."

"Of course, sir."

The truck led them onto the road, and he looked forward. The gunner was scanning the skies, three more men on the truck doing the same. Yes, you are awake now. If we are fortunate, you will not have any more targets this day.

The hedgerows were gone now, the road rolling slightly, low brush and thickets, a wide field, cows grazing. Rommel shook his head. Amazing people, the French. Why do they not leave here? How many of them will die because they insist on plowing their land and milking their cows where we fight this war? Well, at least there will be beef for the men.

He saw the bridge, half a kilometer away, rusty steel girders, could see trucks on both sides, an outpost, machine guns and antiaircraft guns, one large field cannon, hooked to a larger truck. He glanced skyward, a sheet of blue, broken by thick white clouds. Why did Bayerlein think this was a good idea? We should do this in the open?

He heard them now, more airplane engines, the truck halting in front of them, Daniel stepping hard on the brakes of the car. Rommel braced himself against the front seat, looked to the side, and saw the planes, a formation of four, very low, topping distant trees. The gunners at the bridge were already firing, the planes coming fast, four more now behind them. He slid low in the seat, nowhere else to go, wanted to shout at Daniel, Back away! But the planes were quickly past, climbing away, and now, in front of him, the bridge erupted in flame, a shock of explosion. He stared, frozen, the girders tossed skyward, falling away, tall splashes in the water, the antiaircraft guns still firing. Daniel jerked the car into reverse, backed away on the road, and spun the car in a tight loop.

Rommel grabbed his shoulder. "No! It is over! Move to the bridge! There will be wounded!"

Daniel obeyed, the car back on the road, moving past his own truck, which followed him, guns silent. They reached the bridge, black smoke, but the fires had extinguished themselves quickly, pieces of the bridge down in the narrow river, men still at their guns, staring up, no targets. Rommel pushed open the door of the car and stepped out, his aides doing the same. Men were gathering, some simply staring at the wreckage.

Lang shouted out, "Who is injured? Anyone hurt?"

Rommel saw an officer, a major—the man kneeling, terrified, holding to the side of a staff car—and moved toward him.

"See to your men!"

The major turned, seemed unable to speak, and Rommel recognized

him, one of Bayerlein's aides. Men were emerging from the smoke, the
breeze clearing the air, the hard smell of explosives drifting away.

"No one is hurt! No casualties!" one man called out.

Rommel had no patience for paralysis. He moved close to the major,
grabbed the man's shoulder, pulled him up. "Where is General Bayerlein?"

"They bombed the bridge, sir!"

"Yes, Major, I know they bombed the bridge. Where is General Bayerlein?"

"He is with the division, sir. He has established a command post near
Aunay! This is terrible, sir! A catastrophe!"

"It's a bridge, Major. The enemy has been bombing every damned
bridge in France."

"No, sir, I mean—the division!"

Rommel realized now. This is not right; Bayerlein should be here. If he
is not . . . ?

"Get control of yourself, Major! What has happened?"

The man released his grip on the car, closed his eyes for a brief second,
then said, "General Bayerlein sent me to find you, sir. The general offers
his deepest apologies for not meeting with you at the appointed time. I
have been instructed to tell you that the Panzer Lehr Division has taken
very heavy casualties and very serious losses in tanks and vehicles. The
enemy has located our advance, and their aircraft are striking us at every
opportunity. I have not witnessed this myself, sir; I was in the rear of
the column. I have not seen anything like this. The bridge just . . .
exploded . . . right in front of me."

Rommel felt a burn rising in his brain. The man is a child, and Bayerlein makes him a staff officer.

"Shut up, Major. So, now you have seen bombs drop. You will see a
great many more, I assure you. Is the Panzer Lehr Division advancing in
daylight?"

"General Bayerlein was most angry about that, sir. General Dollmann
ordered the division to advance as quickly as possible, and when General
Bayerlein objected, General Dollmann repeated the order and said that the
instructions had come directly from Marshal von Rundstedt. The division
was to move forward with all speed, no matter day or night. General Bayerlein was quite upset, sir, but he obeyed the order."

"Yes, and the enemy has bombed him to hell!"

Rommel made a fist, pounded hard on the major's staff car, felt the wave of anger rolling through him. Von Rundstedt. That stupid old man.

"Do you see this bridge, Major?"

"Yes, sir. It is a tragedy, sir."

"No, Major, it is war. It is the good tactics of our enemy. We cannot protect the bridges, and so they are targets, easy targets. But our tanks are the power of this army, and they are *not* to be easy targets! Do you understand that?"

"Yes, sir. General Bayerlein was most upset. We have taken heavy losses, sir."

"I will hear about losses later. Right now, you are to return to General Bayerlein and instruct him that if he moves his division during daylight hours, I shall put him in front of my personal firing squad. You tell him that if General Dollmann or Field Marshal von Rundstedt has a problem with my order, they may telephone me or summon me themselves. I shall happily explain to them why the enemy enjoys having the sun shine on a column of our tanks!"

He did not wait for a response, spun away, the door to his car held open by Sergeant Daniel.

Behind him, the major called out, "Um . . . sir? How do I get back across the river?"

HEADQUARTERS, PANZER GROUP WEST, LE CAINE
JUNE 10, 1944

"You are quite right, of course, Erwin. We must confine our movements to the nighttime. The loss of travel time will, however, cause us considerable disadvantage in moving our people into their necessary position. I hope you realize the cost of that."

Rommel held the phone away from his ear, stared at it. He put a hard clamp on his anger, formed the words.

"Sir, there is a far greater *cost* if our tanks are obliterated before they can reach their necessary positions. Or is that not a concern?"

Sarcasm never seemed to reach von Rundstedt, and he seemed not to hear it now. The old man's voice came through the receiver again.

"You should leave the matter of transportation to the division commanders. I must implore you to keep your focus on the larger picture. Despite the enemy's continuing bombing campaign in the Calais sector, the

Führer has concluded that the enemy invasion is confined to Normandy alone, that region occupied by your Seventh Army. General Jodl was most explicit on this point. Regardless of our *beloved* Führer's instincts, however, he does not wish you to withdraw the Fifteenth Army from their present position at Calais. Do you understand, Erwin? According to Herr Jodl, your duty is to destroy the enemy by driving him back to his beaches, and you will do so with the forces now available to you. General Witt is advancing the Twelfth SS Panzer closer to Caen, and despite their losses, Panzer Lehr is at your disposal as well. My reports tell me that the front is holding and the enemy is weakening. There is no need for any of your . . . how do I say this?" Von Rundstedt paused. "On this I must agree with the High Command. There is concern that you will claim defeat when none is to be found. I have advised General Jodl that we should withdraw our forces away from the coast, in order to establish a powerful defense behind the Orne River. Of course, the Little Corporal did not agree. According to Jodl, his exact words were, *Every man shall fight or die where he stands.* I believe there is little room for interpretation in those instructions, wouldn't you say?"

Rommel's hand was tight around the receiver, sweat in his clothes, and he fought through the empty helplessness, searched his brain for a response. Von Rundstedt's voice rattled again in his ear.

"Are you there, Field Marshal?"

Rommel pushed out the words. "Yes. I heard you. General Jodl believes that the Normandy landing is the enemy's sole plan of attack, and yet I am to leave the entire Fifteenth Army at Calais in the event that he is wrong? The enemy is only coming on one front, but I am to prepare for another front, a front on which we do not believe he will attack?"

"I am following orders here, Erwin. You shall do the same. I will hang up now. There are duties here that require my attention." Von Rundstedt paused again, and Rommel heard the sarcasm in his words. "Heil Hitler."

The phone line went dead. Rommel dropped the receiver on the table in front of him, a sharp tumble that startled Geyr's aides. Across from him, Geyr was watching him from behind a desk, cautious, curious. Rommel sat down on a small wood chair, feeling the usual weariness. He had endured too many explosions inside, the utter frustration of fighting a war with half his weapons.

"I assume that we are to continue with our current strategy, the armor advancing northward and then maintaining our position," Geyr said.

"Of course we are. Even von Rundstedt knows that's a bad idea. But never mind. He's busy pruning his rose garden."

Geyr turned toward the large map, and Rommel thought, Yes, look at your map. Make a good show of it. Pretend to plan something new. There is nothing new, General. We are fighting the inevitable.

Rommel stood slowly, and Geyr turned to him, "I had hoped our petroleum situation would have improved. It is difficult to resupply and refuel my tanks. We are rationing our ammunition, as well. The railroads—"

"The railroads are useless, and the roads are impossible except at night—yes, yes, I know all of that. It seems that finally that old man in Paris has learned this as well. So tell me, General, even if I could move a convoy of trucks, how do I send you gasoline when the supply officers in Paris won't even acknowledge my requests? Von Rundstedt tells me we have plenty of supplies, because he studies great rows of numbers scribbled on sheets of paper. It is those same pieces of paper that tell the High Command how powerful our fighting divisions are. It is so much fiction, General. But I will tell you what is *not* fiction. Right now, the enemy is continuing to strengthen, reinforcing on *his* beaches. He possesses an infinite ability to strengthen himself, and we cannot even summon our valiant Luftwaffe to protect a gasoline truck!"

Rommel paused, then said, "Reichsmarschall Göring cannot be bothered to respond to my requests himself, so he sends his minions to assure us that all will be well and our vaunted air force will soon sweep the enemy from the skies. In the meantime, he insists that we conserve our ground forces. Conserve! And you—I have seen the same tendency in this command, Herr Geyr. Too much conserving, and not enough attacking! If the armor had been at my disposal, I would have destroyed the enemy on the beaches. Now, when the tanks are finally brought forward, we are cautious; we do not wish to commit our greatest strength to the fight!"

He was breathing heavily, the fury tearing through him; he put his hand on the table and steadied himself. Geyr did not argue—surprising—and turned again toward the map. Good, he thought. Geyr is afraid of me. I should just kill him and make this simpler.

After a moment, Geyr said, "Sir, I have done all I can to prevent the enemy from damaging our armored strength with his naval guns. We never could have hoped to hold on to the beaches. They should never have been regarded as anything more that outposts, observation points! The armor requires fields of maneuver and cannot be used to prick the enemy like a handful of sewing needles. I have tried to explain this to von Rundstedt, and I have tried to explain this to you. We cannot fight a decisive battle on *this* ground. The conditions here are absurd: We are either in this obscene bocage country or hemmed in by small villages at every turn. We must choose the terrain that is best suited for our tanks! When the enemy comes, we will respond to him the way our armor has responded before, a hard strike in force on a narrow front. Yes, I am conserving our armor, because if we do not, if we continue to strike the enemy in small-scale assaults, we will accomplish nothing at all."

"General Geyr, what we *accomplish* is not our concern. I learned long ago that the High Command is concerned with methods and planning and lines on maps. Our orders have been made clear to me. We are directed to meet the enemy's thrusts where and when he makes them. We are to advance the panzer divisions where the enemy is pressing forward, to blunt his advances. Thus far, the enemy is making needle pricks of his own, probing, testing, trying to find our weak points. He is having just as much difficulty in the bocage country as we are, but since that is where he is, that is where we are ordered to strike him. Disagree with me all you wish, General, but had Hitler approved my tactics six months ago, the enemy would not be in this country at all. He would be fishing his corpses out of the sea."

"Sir, how else can I explain this? If not to you, to the High Command! We must have room for the tanks to maneuver! There is ample open ground to the south and east! Do they not understand?"

"What the High Command understands is that we are to obey the instructions they give us. I know something of armor tactics, General. I know what kind of *ground* is best." Rommel stopped, stared blankly at the map. He thought of North Africa, the maps so much simpler. Open and flat, no obstructions, speed and power and mobility. Paradise for the armor. And now, we run and hide behind rows of bushes.

Geyr was angry now, red-faced, pacing. "I cannot make my argument with the High Command, but I must protest once again to you! You hold on to this idea that the enemy could have been destroyed on the beaches! Even if the panzers had been positioned perfectly, if I had sent in my tanks directly to the beaches, the naval artillery would have crushed us. But none of that matters now! We must convince von Rundstedt, or even the Führer, that the most effective way to defeat the enemy is to pull back into open country where we can meet him on *our* terms."

"When?"

Geyr seemed surprised by the question. "When the enemy, um . . ."

"No, General, the time has passed. We have allowed the enemy to land his army, and now he is fortifying it. No matter what kind of fight we make, nothing will be on *our* terms. He will come only when he is ready to come. That is Montgomery over there! He will only move when he is comfortable, when he can stroll placidly through the lines with his cup of tea and feel no threat from us. Every day that passes he is stronger, one step closer to striking us in a way to which we cannot respond. Our only hope is to strike him right now, all across the front, to shock him and send his troops back in confusion."

Geyr shook his head. "I fear, sir, you are still fighting the African war."

Rommel saw nervousness on Geyr's face, a line crossed. But the energy for the argument was draining away, and Rommel stepped slowly to the map. "You mean, General, the war we should have *won*."

"I meant no insult."

"Insult me all you wish. I am accustomed to it." Rommel studied the map. "The enemy has linked his beachheads. It is obvious to me that Montgomery's intentions are to capture Caen and then drive us away from the favorable ground you so cherish so he might use it himself, to stage his grand assault toward Paris. The Americans will most certainly drive northward to capture Cherbourg. The enemy possesses complete air superiority over this front, and thus he can resupply himself at will, while we must struggle to shift our tactical positions in difficult ground at night. I would much prefer that we withdraw the armor to more suitable ground, where we can form up a massive strike. Those forward positions can be manned by infantry, but the infantry is slow to arrive because, like your tanks, they can move only at night. And because we cannot get sufficient gasoline and vehicles, and because the railroads are virtually worthless, we must advance our troops on foot. All the while, the enemy is expending lavish amounts of ammunition from infinite sources, and we must ration ours. Despite what von Rundstedt believes, none of our divisions are at full fighting strength, while the Americans are crossing the ocean in great waves of steel that we cannot hold back. We have lost the U-boat war and the battleship war; despite Göring's ridiculous boasts, we have lost the air war. The infantry and your tanks are still capable of delivering an effective blow, but every day those forces grow weaker." He turned, saw no expression on Geyr's face. "Is that too much *defeatism* for you, General? Should we all remain optimistic and content ourselves with gardening, like that foolish old man in Paris? Or should we all do what Reichsmarschall Göring does? When things become difficult, let us consume a draft of morphine, and all our ills will become perfectly pleasant."

Geyr glanced at his aides, who seemed to flinch. "Sir! I will not permit such disrespect."

"Be silent, General. I am not concerned what others think of me. I do not fear the Gestapo. I am too far removed—*erased*—from any kind of future, no matter how this war ends. Might we still prevail? I have heard the same talk you have, all that blather about our new secret weapons. The High Command whispers of great secrets: We will soon have doomsday machines, great powerful weapons no one has yet seen. Is that fiction as well? I don't know. Do you? Does von Rundstedt? But what do I care about that? If we have such weapons, and we turn the tide of this war—or even prevail—I will be tossed out the window by the sycophantic monkeys that surround Hitler. If the enemy defeats us, I will be held as a war criminal. I am a soldier first, General, and my duty is to attack the enemy. But I will say what I think. You may disagree with me, but you will not silence me with your outrage. You should be far more outraged by what is happening to your tanks."

T he car drove rapidly, the armored truck in front, and Rommel studied the map, ignoring the bouncing of the rough road.

"Sir, we should seek shelter until nightfall."

Rommel did not look up. "Yes, Captain, I know. But there is much to do, and La Roche Guyon will give us shelter enough. For reasons I do not understand, the enemy respects our antiaircraft batteries there. We must be grateful for small favors. I am quite certain the enemy spotter planes are searching for more meaningful targets than this one car and that single truck."

He set the map aside as the car moved up a rise and down again: rolling country, free of the annoying confinement of the hedgerows, the bocage. Geyr is right of course. In those conditions, one man with an antitank weapon can block a road by himself, hold up an entire battalion of armor. Why did the enemy choose to invade *this* place? The key to an invasion is to move rapidly, establish your strong base, yet they chose beaches that would lead them into that infernal bocage. I would not have done so. And because it is not what I would have done, I was surprised. We were all surprised. If the enemy comes at Calais, another invasion, then I shall be surprised again.

The car climbed familiar ground, green fields and tall trees, the stark beauty of the castle that was his headquarters. The road ran along the river, and he looked up at the pockets of antiaircraft guns, the batteries of machine guns and eighty-eights that kept him safe. The car rolled to a stop, the guards coming to attention, one man pulling open the door. Rommel stepped out into the usual respectful silence, but there was commotion at the grand entranceway, and he saw Speidel, more aides behind him, all coming forward.

"Sir! We have just received this! I have not yet confirmed its authenticity, but it appears genuine!"

Rommel felt the usual dread. What has happened now? "What is it, General?"

"We should go inside, sir."

"It's a little late for discretion, Hans. You have just alerted the entire compound."

Speidel leaned close, held a paper in his hand. "Sir, this came from Captain Merling, an observation outpost near Le Caine. The enemy has struck with their bombers. It is most tragic, sir."

Le Caine, Rommel thought. Geyr's headquarters. "Silence. Let us go inside."

They moved quickly with heavy steps, and Rommel felt the familiar cold in his gut, walked into his office, Speidel shouting orders to the staff: no disturbance. Speidel closed the door behind them.

"What has happened to General Geyr?"

"Apparently he is only injured, sir. But the enemy struck his headquarters with an air attack that seemed directed to the place. They must have discovered—"

"What is the tragedy?"

Speidel stopped and handed Rommel the paper. "From first reports, sir, it seems that the enemy has destroyed the entire headquarters of Panzer Group West. Most all of General Geyr's staff was likely killed. I have not yet spoken to General Geyr, and I do not know his whereabouts. But the observation post did say he had been seen by doctors and was probably not seriously hurt."

Rommel moved to the chair, sat, faced the tall window. "When did this happen?"

"The observer said they saw your car pass by . . . about thirty minutes before the raid."

"Thirty minutes. Well, Hans, those are the fortunes of war. I could have remained there arguing with him until—well, it is unlikely they were targeting me. But you're right. They somehow learned of the position of his headquarters. His entire staff?"

"Most everyone. There is no specific confirmation. Apparently everything was destroyed."

Rommel tried to see the faces. Geyr had good officers in his command, some of them tank commanders who had served with Rommel in North Africa. And somehow Geyr escaped. The fortunate placement of his latrine, perhaps. He turned in the chair, saw Speidel looking down.

"What do we do now, sir?"

Rommel sat back, rubbed the rough beard on his chin. "If you want to kill a snake, you first cut off its head. By this *success,* the enemy has caused us to delay any advance. There can be no coordination among the panzers now. I will meet with von Rundstedt at the earliest moment. Perhaps he can be persuaded to see this fight for what it is becoming."

"Sir?"

"Never mind. Do what you can to find out the condition of General Geyr. I must speak to General Witt. The Twelfth SS Panzer should be engaging the enemy west of Caen. General Witt must be told what has happened, so he can remain in communication with me and not Geyr."

"Yes, sir."

Speidel hurried away, the door closing again, and Rommel stood and stepped to the window, darkness rolling over the river, hiding the gardens. Thirty minutes, he thought. Was it betrayal, some French farmer working for their underground? Or exceptional work by the enemy's observers. Excellent way to die, I suppose. You would hear the whistle, perhaps a second or two, and then . . . nothing. It ends. I always thought a tank would be best, engaging the enemy, a duel, the better man making the good shot. If you lost, the tank was your tomb. If you prevailed, you would climb out, walk over, and admire what you had done, the good kill. There was plenty of that in Africa. Well, no, not really. There were very few duels. There was confusion and chaos and smoke and fire. And the better man didn't always win.

Rommel looked up into the darkness, thought, It could happen here, just like that. One of those B-17s, making it through the flak in one piece, one pilot's lucky day. Yes. An excellent way to die.

30. ADAMS

June 14, 1944

As more force poured across the causeways that bridged the flooded Merderet River, the Germans who had fought so tenaciously began to pull away. Worn out and underequipped, the scattered regiments of the Eighty-second Airborne were withdrawn and organized once more. But there was no luxury to be found, little time to rest and refit. Within a few short days, the need for experience on the front lines became painfully apparent.

As part of the original plan, the Ninetieth Infantry Division had moved forward from their landing zone at Utah Beach and pushed right through the paratroopers' positions along the river. Adams and his weary squad had been pulled back to Sainte-Mère-Église, to watch with rising enthusiasm as the men of the Ninetieth, so many fresh legs and clean rifles, took their place. The Ninetieth would continue the push westward, Bradley's hard slice across the Cotentin Peninsula, isolating whatever enemy units remained north of that advance, the last resistance the Americans would face before they began their assault northward on the city of Cherbourg.

But almost immediately, the Ninetieth Division had problems. The fresh legs quickly bogged down, and when faced with their first test, their first confrontation with the German strongholds in the bocage country, the infantry seemed to succumb to paralysis. The corps commander, Joe Collins, began to understand what others across the Atlantic had once feared, that the Ninetieth had been woefully undertrained. Bradley realized that, for reasons no one at SHAEF could adequately explain, the leadership was lackluster at best. Almost immediately, Bradley ordered Collins to act, and Collins removed the division head, Major General Jay MacKelvie, as well as the regimental commanders most responsible for the lack of fire in their men. In their place, Collins inserted officers who had shown some combat initiative. But the error had been made, and what should have been a hard strike across the Cotentin had become instead a mishmash of insignificant battles against an enemy who had been given time to regroup. Not willing to wait for the Ninetieth to find its spirit, Bradley reacted to the unexpected stalemate by authorizing Collins to call upon the most reliable and experienced troops he had in that part of the American sector: the paratroopers of the Eighty-second Airborne. Though many of the exhausted battalion and regimental commanders protested, Matthew Ridgway accepted the need for his paratroopers to return once more to the front. While the 507th and 508th would engage farther to the south, the men of the 505th would try to accomplish the job the Ninetieth Division could not complete: capturing the French town of Saint-Sauveur-le-Vicomte, the next major intersection on the roads that led to the far western coast of the peninsula.

SAINTE-MÈRE-ÉGLISE
JUNE 14, 1944

Adams hated Sainte-Mère-Église. Though the bodies had been mostly removed, the signs of the struggle were everywhere: blasted ruins of homes and shops, shredded parachutes splayed out over rooftops or rolled into filthy bundles in every corner. The workers of the Graves Commission had been efficient with the bodies of the Americans, but the enemy's dead were still scattered about, German corpses lodged in attics or on rooftops, snipers who were only found when their bodies began to decay. The men who did the awful work were mostly Negroes, assigned to the gruesome task of identifying and arranging the bodies for transport back to the coast or burying them in makeshift cemeteries around the town itself.

Adams had never served with a black soldier but watched them with curiosity, as he had as a boy in the dusty streets of Silver City. Negroes were rare in New Mexico, but they came for the work, the copper mines always looking for men to fill the gaps in their ranks, the backbreaking work that wasted the bodies of men like Jesse's father. Adams was twelve when he saw a black man for the first time, a hulking mountain of a man toting a fat suitcase, walking along the street with his small round wife. The white men of the town seemed to recoil at the sight, urgent whispers that the boy could not understand, low talk in the café that black men would bring a scourge no one seemed able to explain. But the Depression and the Dust Bowl brought more men from the north and east, black and white, desperate to earn a wage, seeking whatever opportunity would feed their families. The mine was prosperous, a rarity, and as the different races and cultures blended, most of the laborers discovered a halting respect for the men who worked beside them, their mutual survival more important than the color of any man's skin.

In basic training, the soldiers had been only white, and talk of Negro regiments and Negro divisions inspired rude insults and obscenities Adams couldn't understand. Anyone who knew something of history knew that there had been black troops in the First World War who had proven themselves beyond anyone's doubts, the Buffalo Soldiers of the 92nd Division and their counterparts in the 93rd. Talk had drifted through the camps that the Buffalo Soldiers were coming again, newly formed, would probably join the fight in Italy. Many of the paratroopers dismissed Negro soldiers with the matter-of-fact assumption that a black man would never have the courage to jump out of an airplane. It was a question that Adams had asked himself, and there was no answer. As far as Adams knew, none of the Negro enlistees had been given the chance. Now, in the blasted streets of the ruined town, the Negroes worked on the one job someone had deemed them suitable for: handling the dead. Adams studied them in spite of himself, had spoken to several and been surprised by the quiet dignity and confidence of men whose hands and uniforms were covered in death. If the black men despised their work or despised the officers who had put them there, Adams saw little of that. Instead, there was respect in both directions, the soldiers pointing out the 82nd's *AA* insignia on Adams's shoulder, sharing that same respect with the rest of the infantry who passed through the town. To the infantry, the men of the 82nd and the 101st divisions had opened the door. Every man in the Graves Commission knew that if the corpses were American, they were paratroopers.

"Hey, Sarge, there's mail back there, in the square!"

Adams looked up from his mess kit, struggling with a hard knot of gristle. "Mail? Way the hell out here?"

Unger held out a small blue square of paper. "Yep! Got a letter from my mama. I don't believe it!"

Adams spit out the offending lump of meat. "I don't believe it either."

"Lookee right here, Sarge! See? It's dated last month, so she doesn't know a thing about what we're doing. All kinds of stuff about Sally Lewis—that's a girl I was kinda hoping . . . uh . . ." Unger stopped, seemed to think better of divulging any more details. "Anyway, there's a whole truckload of mailbags. Somebody said they came through Utah Beach. You oughta go check. Maybe there's something for you!"

Adams looked toward the large open square and could see soldiers gathering, one loud whoop, more men emerging from alleyways, the word spreading. He scooped out the last gooey lump from the small can of stew, swallowed it whole, and pieced the mess kit back together.

"You want me to clean that up for you, Sarge? You're not allowed to leave it dirty."

"I know the order. Fine. Here, clean the damned thing. Make it all shiny. I guess I'll go see what's going on. Maybe there's some mail for some of the other guys." The name punched him: Buford. No, please God. No family. Not now.

He pushed himself up to his feet, handed Unger the mess kit, and moved past a pile of twisted steel, the remains of a stone wall and a German eighty-eight, the barrel ripped apart. From the open square, men were coming past him, joyous surprise, anticipation, men with paper in their hands, one man crying. He saw the truck, officers holding the troopers back, keeping order, mailbags passing along a row of men, clerks and sergeants from each company, names calling out, eager hands. I'll be damned, he thought. The kid's right. They got us mail.

He saw Scofield, the captain with a wide smile, standing behind the mail handlers. Adams moved forward, more men flowing back past him, shouts and laughter, more tears, and Scofield saw him, waved him forward.

"Here, Sergeant! We've got some mail for the boys!"

Anything for me? The words stuck in Adams's throat, and he pushed his way through the throng, suddenly annoyed by the enthusiasm around him, even Scofield's smile digging into him. One man bumped him from the side, oblivious, his face buried in sheaves of paper, and Adams wanted to push back, forced himself to let it go, saw Scofield's aide, a corporal, fishing through one canvas bag, emptying it quickly, the names flowing out, one name now startling him.

"Lieutenant Pullman!"

"Here!"

Adams saw him now, the small thin man slipping forward, his hand out, taking the letter. Adams wanted to call out, felt a strange breathless relief. He pushed toward him. Pullman was reading the letter, somber, his face clouded.

"Lieutenant!"

Pullman looked up. Adams was surprised to see raw anger and then surprise on Pullman's face.

"Sergeant! You're alive! Thank God."

"Hell, yes, I'm alive. I've been within a grenade throw of General Gavin for a week. Where the hell have you been?"

"Right here, actually. I got hooked up with some of the boys from C Company, and General Ridgway had us working on snipers on the north side of town. I heard about the fighting at the river. Messy stuff. Glad to see you're all right."

Adams looked at the letter in Pullman's hands. "Everything okay, sir?"

Pullman folded the letter carefully, slipped into a pocket. "Not really. Don't worry about it. I'm damned glad to see you. I've caught up with a few of your squad. Had a little problem with Private Marley. A few of the boys found some Calvados or hard cider or something. Had to stick them all in a makeshift stockade. He'll be out by now. Probably have his tail between his legs and one hell of a headache."

"I wondered where he was. Don't worry, sir, I'll handle him. Stupid bastard."

"Easy, Sergeant. We need every man. Orders came this morning."

Scofield was there now. "That's all the mail for today. Sorry, Sergeant, looks like there wasn't anything here."

Adams turned, felt the urge to salute, old habit, held it down. The word had been made clear by Gavin himself: no saluting anyone this close to the enemy. An officer would be a perfect target for any sniper. Scofield was sliding his own letters into a pocket.

"It's okay, sir," Adams said. "Didn't expect anything. My mom's not much of a writer."

Scofield seemed to measure the statement, a silent moment; then he looked at Pullman. "Gather up your platoon, Lieutenant. What's your latest head count?"

"About thirty, best as I can tell. Sergeant Adams would make thirty-one."

"Not too bad, considering. Let's assemble in the street beyond that church. We're moving out at eleven hundred. The Five-oh-seven is already on the march, and we're protecting their tail. The enemy is all over the damned place, pockets of holdouts hunkered down in some pretty tight places. This hedgerow stuff is a damn nightmare, and the sooner we push out past it the better. Warn your men about snipers. Every man pays attention to the trees." He looked at Adams. "Well, hell, you know what to do."

"Yes, sir."

Scofield backed away. "I'll see you in twenty minutes. Need to check some details with Colonel Ekman."

Pullman saluted. Adams saw a quick frown on Scofield's face, wanted to grab the lieutenant's arm. Pullman was oblivious. "We'll be ready, sir. Let's go, Sergeant."

Scofield moved away quickly, and Adams knew why. He's cursing under his breath, he thought. No snipers today, though. Not here anyway. God help this idiot lieutenant. Ridgway sent him on sniper patrol and he didn't learn a damned thing.

Pullman began to move, and Adams followed close beside him, the square thinning out, men returning to their commands. There was laughter in every corner, men displaying their letters, loud talk, more of the whoops. Adams felt himself bristling, the sounds sharp and annoying.

"Sorry you didn't get any mail," Pullman said.

"Forget about it, sir. Not important."

"Well, that's your business. It could be worse. You could get a letter from your wife, telling you she's going to have a baby."

"Congratulations—"

Adams held the rest, and Pullman said, "Yeah, sure. I've been away for just a tad more than the required nine months. She's trying to convince me it's okay, that I'm still the father in *her* mind. I am, after all, the *husband*."

"Sorry, sir."

"So, your mother isn't big on letter writing? She big on being a mother?"

There was no humor in Pullman's question, and Adams thought, None of your business. Then he glanced at Pullman's pocket and thought of the letter, the man's anger. Hell, I owe him something. He spilled his guts to me, dammit.

"My brother's a Marine, sir. He's in the Pacific. I'm scared as hell for him. Pretty sure whatever's he going through is worse than here. Jungles and Japanese. Like fighting savages, from what I hear. Maniacs."

"Yeah, and over there, they're hearing about what kind of monsters the Germans are. Get hold of yourself, Sergeant. Nobody's having a damned picnic. What's that got to do with your mother?"

Adams matched his pace with Pullman's, hiked the Thompson up tight on his shoulder, thought a moment.

"I think maybe I let her down by joining the army. My brother was all full of piss about the Marines, the elite fighting machine, all that. He's her baby, and I don't think she wanted to hear it. So she expected me to sign up with him, to look out for him. His name's Clay. He's three years younger, joined up when he was just eighteen. I tried to explain it doesn't work like that, the Marines don't care for somebody's big brother being a babysitter. Well, no, I didn't explain. You can't explain much of anything to either of my parents."

"You have a father? Never heard you mention him."

Adams sniffed. "We don't get along. He'd never write a word to anyone. Not sure he can even read. We've never been close or anything. He's not a nice guy."

"Sorry."

"It's okay, sir. Since I'm not wet-nursing my brother, and I'm not even a damned Marine, my mom expects me to make that up to her, I guess. Like I said, I can't help being scared for him. He's just a kid. Tough damn kid, though. Maybe it's why I joined the paratroopers. Show her I'm as tough as he is. Or maybe show him. If he's still alive, he's up to his ass in jungle rot, or malaria, or maybe some Jap prison camp. He gets hurt, or whatever else, she's probably gonna blame me. Only way out of that— well, hell, I guess I better go home some kind of hero."

"What? Sergeant, that's nuts."

Adams stopped, took a long breath. "Yeah."

EAST OF SAINT-SAUVEUR-LE-VICOMTE
JUNE 14, 1944, NOON

The infantry was still in place, holding their ground while the paratroopers pushed past. Unlike so many times before, there were no catcalls, no ridiculous insults, questioning why these men in baggy pants and tall boots dared to think of themselves as elite. Adams saw the faces of the men of the Ninetieth, soldiers whom the paratroopers now called ground pounders. They were not so different from the men in his own squad, young mostly, some with scraggly beards and dirty faces, grenades hanging on their shirts, the ever-present M-ls. But there was no swagger, no bravado. Adams had no idea what the infantry was going to do now: if they would follow a path the paratroopers would try to blaze or if they were going to be replaced by more of the troops still pouring across the beaches along the coast. For now, the paratroopers could only move ahead, seeking the enemy with slow careful steps, while, along the way, the infantry huddled in hastily dug trenches and foxholes and kept mostly silent.

The companies of the 505th were mostly intact again. The brief stay at Sainte-Mère-Église had given most of the regiments time to find their own, officers back on top, the units reorganized. There were yawning gaps in command, of course, appalling casualty lists from the fights along the river and the days of vicious combat around the town itself. Farther to the south and east, the 101st had endured the same scattered jumps and the same chaos, many of them picked off piecemeal or captured in small clusters by alert German infantry.

In Adams's own squad there were four missing faces, only eight men now who answered to him. Except for Buford, his other three missing men had likely come down in the water. Adams still carried the guilt of Buford's death, but talk of the missing men bothered him as well. He could not remove the memories of cries and splashes of helplessness. The others might only be found when the Merderet River was once again drawn down to its narrow banks.

As they advanced westward, they stayed off the roads, avoiding mines and booby traps. They pushed instead through the open fields, past one hedgerow at a time, climbing up and through the thickets, scanning and probing the field beyond. The men stepped now through tall grass, an untended field, no cows, no sign of a farmer. Adams's steps were slow and deliberate, with constant glances downward for signs of disturbed ground.

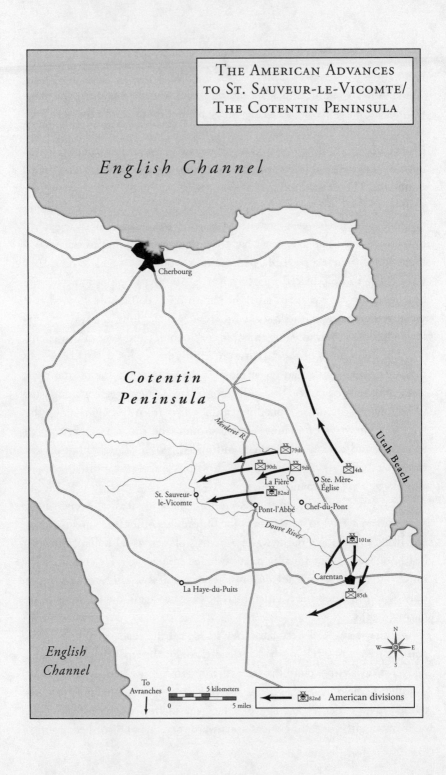

THE AMERICAN ADVANCES
TO ST. SAUVEUR-LE-VICOMTE/
THE COTENTIN PENINSULA

English Channel

Cherbourg

Cotentin
Peninsula

Merderet R.

Utah Beach

79th

90th

9th

4th

La Fière

Ste. Mère-
Église

St. Sauveur-
le-Vicomte

82nd

Pont-l'Abbé

Chef-du-Pont

Douve River

101st

Carentan

La Haye-du-Puits

85th

English
Channel

N
W   E
S

To
Avranches

0   5 kilometers

0   5 miles

82nd   American divisions

There had been word passed of scattered minefields, mostly close to the wider roads. But there were no telltale markers, and he had heard the terrible surprises, distant thumps, one man's catastrophic bad luck. The mines were gruesomely efficient, usually wounding a man rather than killing him outright, so the screams would come, limbs torn away, astonishing amounts of blood. The medics would be there quickly, so many of them ignoring the danger in the ground beneath them as they scampered across. If the medics were luckier than the men they tried to help, they would reach the wounded men, only to find that their help was no help at all.

He guessed the grassy field to be two hundred yards wide, typical, his own squad in the center, advancing in a ragged line. Adams was slightly in front of his men, Pullman and the other sergeants doing the same, the three squads moving closer to another hedgerow. He still searched the ground at his feet; then, farther out, he saw the thigh-high grass suddenly gone, replaced by a ditch of open earth. The earth was fresh, a trench, thirty yards wide, stretching along the front edge of the embankment, someone's unfinished task.

He froze, raising one hand. The men knew the signal: Everyone halted, silent, and Adams pointed the Thompson, eased forward again, then two quick steps, a one-man charge, the submachine gun sweeping the trench. Empty. Thank God. He motioned to the others without looking back, knowing the sergeants would wait for his signal—Let's go, advance—and eased himself down into the trench, searching for wires, any kind of booby trap, careful lessons from Scofield and others who had watched their men lose a hand or an arm in careless souvenir hunting.

The trench was mostly clean, no smells but soil, and he saw footprints, small dugouts to one side, one empty tin of someone's lunch, flies skipping around it. Someone changed his mind, he thought, and decided this wasn't the place. Make a stand somewhere else. He looked back across the open ground, the tall grass, the trench well hidden. Thank you, whoever you were. For the first time since the gruesome fight at the causeway, he felt the stab of fear, the cold shiver in his chest, and stood in the trench, thinking of machine guns, what could have been hidden here, the horrific *rrrrip*. He felt for the magazines pulling in the pockets on his pants legs and caught himself. Stay alert, you jackass.

The others moved up behind him, still spread out, began to climb down, then up, moving across the trench. They were silent still, the tall row of dense brush too close in front of them. No one's there, he thought. They wouldn't give us this nice little trench to use if they were on the other side of that hedge. He climbed up and saw Pullman down the line, watching him. Pullman pointed into the brush, made a short wave, and Adams took a breath. Yeah, I know. He nodded and moved forward.

The hedge was steep, the dirt embankment snarled in roots, all too familiar. Men were probing along the line as he was, seeking the opening, some kind of gap, and he heard a whisper, saw Marley, the big man wide-eyed, always afraid now, pointing into the brush. Adams eased that way, saw daylight through the hedge, and climbed up again, pushing the Thompson in front of him, crawling, slow and deliberate, the men in his own squad gathering behind him, a makeshift line. Adams crested the center of the hedge and scanned the open ground: another field, more grass, more silence. And then he saw the plane.

He slid down into the grass, kept his eye past the wreckage, any sign of movement. There was no smoke, the crash several days old, and he moved forward, closer. Keep low, he thought, good cover. The plane was only a few yards away, a burned hulk, small and, he knew now, a Piper Cub. It would have been an artillery spotter, flown by the insane daredevils who flitted and darted over enemy lines like so many pesky flies. But the Germans knew, when the Cubs appeared, that artillery would follow; the pilots were using their radios to call back to the artillery officers the location of enemy troop positions, camps, placements of tanks or big guns. Adams ignored the men behind him and kept moving forward, pushing back the grass with the Thompson: more fresh earth, plowed up by the impact of the plane. There was very little intact, one wing severed completely, the wreckage scattered farther into the field, the tail hanging from the body at a cockeyed angle. There had been fire, the grass out beyond the plane flat and blackened, crew-cut stubble. It must have been raining, he thought, or else this whole damned place would have burned, so it had to be a week ago. He saw the propeller, bent and curled, fought the urge to look into the cockpit, but men were moving up close; he saw Pullman, crawling up to the plane, standing now, a low voice. "Good God. He didn't make it."

Adams couldn't avoid it. He stood as well, saw a single mass of black cinder, no face, no limbs, the man still at his controls. He caught the first smell now, something new, backed away, fought it, and said to Pullman, "Let's get out of here."

The lieutenant said nothing but moved out past the plane and stepped into the open swath of burned ground. Adams looked that way, thought, No, bad idea—and there was a whistle, a sharp thump, Pullman staggering. The crack came now, the distant sound of the rifle, and Pullman fell forward, his body limp, crumbling, facedown in the charred stubble of grass.

Adams called out, *"No!"* and dropped to the ground: another whistle, *crack,* a single popping sound, voices behind him.

"They hit the looey!"

Adams rolled to one side, pointed the Thompson forward, shouted, "Shut up! No one moves!"

He tried to see to the right, Sergeant Tobin's squad, had not noticed if they were through the hedge. He glanced up, a quick motion—no one—and heard voices behind the hedge, damn them! Too damned slow!

"Corporal!"

"Yeah!" Nusbaum responded.

"Get back to the hedge! The medic's with Tobin's squad. Wait for our covering fire."

"Okay, Sarge!"

Adams was shivering now, the ice rolling through him. He pulled the submachine gun close to his chest and glanced up over the grass, measured the field, thought, A hundred fifty yards. Where the hell did it come from?

"Anybody hear a direction?" he yelled. "From the side, or straight in front?"

"I think it was straight ahead, Sarge!"

"Yeah. Pretty sure!"

He raised up again, a brief look, then dropped.

"Okay, aim at those trees on the far side! In five seconds, give them hell! One clip only! Don't use up all your ammo. Give Nusbaum time to get back into the brush! You ready, Corporal?"

"Yeah!"

"Five, four, three, two . . . one!"

They all began to fire, and Adams sprayed the tree line across the field, knowing that Nusbaum was moving quickly. Then the firing quieted, the men dropping again, low in the grass. Adams was breathing heavily, heard Unger.

"The corporal made it, Sarge! You see anybody out there?"

"Shut up! We're not going to see anybody. That was a sniper. Probably alone. Everybody stay down. We've got to get around this burned ground, stay in that deep grass. Wait for my signal!"

There was shouting behind him, from the hedge, and now a voice. "Stay down! BAR!"

The gun opened up, spraying rounds over their heads: more voices, men moving forward from the hedgerow. He saw the medic now, the red cross on the man's shoulder, dull red on his helmet, but it wasn't the man he expected. The man was older, gasping for air. It was Major Brubaker, the battalion surgeon.

"Doc! What the hell you doing out here?"

The doctor was flat in the grass beside him, seemed shaken, held a medical kit above his helmet, useless protection.

"Came up behind you a ways back. It's my day for fun, Sergeant. Captain Branning took a bullet in the shoulder, and your medic fell back to help. Colonel Ekman's back there, and he told me to get up close to the men. He gave me a look I couldn't argue with. Where's the lieutenant?"

"Out past the plane. He tried to cross the burned grass and went down hard, not moving. I don't think he made it, sir."

"I'll decide that. First I've got to get to him."

"We'll give you covering fire. Wait."

"No. Won't need it. That's why they put this big damned cross on the bag. They won't shoot at me."

The man began to crawl forward, the bag held high above him, and Adams said, "No! Don't be stupid!"

But the doctor was still moving away. He stood upright now, held the bag high, moved out into the short stubble. Adams cursed to himself, rose to his knees, aimed the Thompson, nothing to see, just trees, saw the lieutenant's body, motionless, the man's neck twisted, a pool of blood. The doctor was there quickly, kneeling, and the thump came, the *pop,* and the doctor fell back with a grunt. He was sitting upright, and his legs began to twist, quivering, his arms reaching for the medical bag; and now the second shot came, the helmet popping off, the man spinning around, eyes staring, mouth open, blood and surprise and death. Adams fired the submachine gun at the trees, more firing from the others, loud curses, stunned shock. He emptied the magazine, dropped down again, the BAR now filling the air above him. He stared down, blinded by fury; he was a *doctor,* you goddamned savage! Then he raised his head.

"Hold your fire! Cease fire! Anybody see the shot? Any smoke?"

No one responded. Adams jammed a magazine into the Thompson. "Stay in the tall grass, go around this damned plane! As long as the grass is deep, we can cross this field! Unger!"

"Yeah, Sarge!"

"Stay back here, keep behind the plane, use it for cover. Watch that far tree line. That bastard's still there, and I want you to watch for any flash or smoke! You see him, you kill him. You got that?"

"Yeah, Sarge!"

"Who's on the BAR?"

The voice came behind him, back in the hedge. "McGee, sir! Tobin's squad."

"Tell Tobin to move around to the right of us, stay behind that hedge on the right. There's gotta be more of these bastards out there! Keep an eye on us. We get close to those far trees, you push up quick past our flank, try to get behind that hedgerow in front of us and cut them off!"

"Yes, sir!"

Adams faced forward again, thought, *Sir.* I'm not an officer, you lame-brain. The only officers in this field are dead. Time to do something about that.

"Let's go!"

He slid to the right, crawled on his belly, kept the tall grass in front of him, heard the whistle of the bullet, the sniper trying again. But the men stayed low. He thought of Unger. The kid's got a good eye. Let's find him a target.

Adams pushed forward in a jerking rhythm, the Thompson cradled across his arms, pain in his knees and shoulders. The shots continued, but the cover was too good, and Adams looked up, a quick glimpse of the trees, thick and dark, thought of Unger again. Shoot something, damn you! His mind rolled over, something Gavin had said, at the causeway, and realized suddenly that there would be no smoke, the lesson they had only now learned in the field. The Germans used smokeless powder. He fought the image, his own submachine gun, spewing out smoke with every round. Finest weapons in the world. Good old U.S.A. That's what they tried to tell us. No army ever had better stuff. But it's *German* machine guns that shoot so damned fast—what, a million rounds a minute? Ours sound like sewing machines, shooting in slow motion.

He pushed forward again, the ground dropping, a low dip, a cluster of short bushes on the far side. He pulled his knees up, searing stiffness, wiped off the barrel of the Thompson, checked the muzzle, no dirt, took a breath, and thought, I'm gonna get that son of a bitch. He raised up again, a quick glance, the trees no more than fifty yards away. It was another hedgerow, fat and tall, too dense to see anything beyond. He dropped down, moved a few feet to one side, still in the depression, raised up again. Not giving you any chance to get your aim, you Kraut bastard. He glanced to the right, the hedge on that side of the field, and thought of Tobin: good man, tough as nails. Lousy jumpmaster, but he'll get his BAR up there quick if he doesn't want me kicking his ass. Yeah, that's what we need. Two idiot sergeants slugging it out. Even the snipers would laugh at that one. He could hear the men in the grass around him, no one talking, and now, a single voice, from the trees.

"*Kamerad!* No shoot! *Kamerad!*"

"Sarge!"

"Shut up!"

Adams raised up again, saw the German now, heavy camouflage, leafy branches in his helmet, his hands in the air, stepping down from the hedgerow.

"*Kamerad!* No shoot!"

Adams raised the Thompson, looked past the man, searched for any movement behind him, shouted, "Halt!"

The German obeyed, his hands still high, waving now, a voice behind Adams, Nusbaum.

"He's giving up, Sarge! He killed the looey and the doc, and now he's just . . . giving up!"

Adams stared at the German, felt the hatred, unquenchable, his hands holding tight to the Thompson, his brain screaming the words, just give me a reason, anything, run . . . *anything!* The German was smiling now, waving his arms in a wide arc.

"He's happy!" Nusbaum again. "He wants to be a damned POW. We should kill him, Sarge! He's probably out of ammo, so he gives up!"

Adams fought the pulsing urge to pull the trigger, heard more voices. "Kill him, Sarge!"

The man was still smiling, palms out wide, no weapon, and Adams curled his finger around the trigger, his hand shaking again.

The German was staring at him, said again, "*Kamerad!* Friend! America!"

Adams couldn't stop the quivering in his hand. He straightened his finger away from the trigger, thinking, It's the only English he knows. He thought of Scofield, Gavin, so many lessons, so much training. God help me. I have to do this. I have to kill this bastard. Stop smiling, you son of a bitch.

And now the crack came from behind him, the German staggering back, the smile still there, frozen, the man tumbling backward. Adams stared, the man twisting to one side, then nothing, red on the man's chest. Adams looked back toward the wreckage of the plane, saw the glimpse of a helmet, the barrel of an M-1, a faint gray wisp of smoke. Unger.

They continued to push forward throughout the day, small firefights far in front of them, but the worst had been absorbed by the 507th, most of the fields now peppered with dead and wounded, medics and stretcher bearers doing their work. As daylight faded, the order came from behind: Find cover, use the hedgerows as protection from enemy patrols, prepare to move again in the morning.

EAST OF SAINT-SAUVEUR-LE-VICOMTE
JUNE 14, 1944, 8 P.M.

He could see Unger in the darkness, the boy sitting on a fallen tree drinking coffee from a tin cup. Unger was silent, seemed unaffected by killing the sniper. Around him, the others were fishing through their K rations, faint reflections off tin plates, low talk, the glow of cigarettes. The coffeepot had been passed around, a happy benefit of the mess truck's having pulled up close by, covered now by a web of camouflage.

Adams knew Scofield was waiting for him at the command post set up just back of the nearest hedgerow, but he had no energy for new orders, no energy at all, ignored his own rations, his near-empty canteen. He kept his stare on Unger, thought of the German at the causeway, the man with the grenade, the first man Unger had shot at point-blank range. He saved my life. A fluke. Instinct. Good training. Kill or be killed. He reacted faster than the Kraut. And then bawled like a baby. He's a kid, for God's sake. That's what a kid is supposed to do. But now . . . he's not a kid anymore. He made a decision, the wrong decision. I hate those Kraut bastards, but I couldn't just kill a man who was giving himself up.

He wanted to ask Unger the question, but it wouldn't come, something holding Adams back, keeping him in his grassy seat, his back against a thin tree on the edge of the hedge. He watched the boy finish the coffee, wipe out his mess kit, and assemble it again, sliding it back now into the pouch in his backpack. Unger stood, stretched, rubbed his stomach, and Adams could see how thin he was. They had all lost weight, but Unger had little to spare, and the boy seemed to search for something, scanning the darkness.

Nearby, Marley said, "Hey, Wally. Latrine's over that way."

"No, thanks. Maybe later."

Unger searched again, then spotted Adams and moved toward him. "Hey, Sarge."

Adams watched him come closer, didn't respond.

"Sarge, can I talk to you?"

Adams pointed to the ground, an open spot in the hedge close by.

Unger moved that way, pulled his rifle off his shoulder, sat heavily. He reached in his pocket, pulled out something dark, said, "D ration? Got a couple extra from the mess."

Adams held out a hand and took the chocolate bar, a luxury he hadn't had in several days. "Thanks. What do you want? Make it quick, the captain wants to talk to me."

"Pretty awful today, huh? Killing the doc like that. And the lieutenant. I always liked him."

"So you made up for it?"

Unger didn't hesitate. "Guess I did. I guess that's how it works."

Adams felt a gnawing curiosity. He expected emotion, the same kind of sadness the boy had shown at the causeway. But Unger seemed at ease, calm.

Adams bit off a piece of the chocolate bar and sat back against the brush. "What the hell do you want, Private? You want me to tell you what a good job you did today? You looking for a medal?"

Unger tossed the candy wrapper out in front of him, pushed it with his boot. "You gonna report me to the captain?"

Adams was surprised. "Report you for killing a prisoner? What do you think?"

"I don't know, Sarge. I kept looking at the lieutenant, the doc, right there close to me. I kept thinking they would get up, move on back out of the way, that they were just hurt. Then I saw the German, and you, and I didn't know what to do. You told me to kill him."

"I told you to kill the sniper. Not the prisoner."

"That's bull, Sarge. The guys are saying he gave up when he ran out of ammo. You know this stuff. The Krauts will kill you as long as they can; then, when they're beat, they walk over and want to shake your hand like it's a baseball game." Unger paused. "Why didn't *you* shoot him, Sarge? I kept waiting for you to do it."

Adams felt a jolt, remembered the finger on the trigger, the shake in his hands. "You little son of a bitch. Don't you ever ask me a question like that. I've killed men in every fight we've had."

Unger seemed to recoil, held up a hand. "Sorry, Sarge. Didn't mean anything. I'm sorry."

"Shut up. Get away from me. I'm not going to report you to anybody. Not yet. But you better watch your ass. I know you're underage. You get in my way, I'll have you back in Iowa in a flash."

Unger stood, backed away, said in a low voice, "I'm eighteen, Sarge."

"You said you were eighteen a year ago. Get the hell away from me."

Unger was gone now, back toward the others, low voices, curious questions. Adams ignored them, stood, thought of the captain, the orders waiting for him. Damn that kid, he thought. Questioning my nerve . . . my *guts*?

He pulled the Thompson tight against his side, moved along the hedgerow, passed other men in small groups, some digging foxholes, idle talk, more rations and mess kits. He stared ahead into darkness, felt the weight of the magazines against his leg, the light thump of grenades against his chest. He was growing angrier, walked with hard precise steps, digging the heels of his boots into the soft ground. He saw the sniper now, the image unshakable, the Thompson pointed at the man's chest, the infuriating smile, the talk—*friend*—the surprise on the man's face as he died from Unger's perfect shot. His hand gripped the strap of the Thompson, and he saw Unger in his mind, stupidly childlike.

Damn him. I should have killed that Kraut son of a bitch and not even thought about it. And I didn't. I couldn't pull the trigger. God help me. Don't let that happen again.

"We found their bodies. The wreckage of the plane was an easy landmark. Pretty surprised we didn't run into anyone else, weren't you?"

Adams tried to keep himself at attention, had no energy for it. Scofield waited patiently for the answer, seemed to read Adams clearly.

"Yes, sir. We only found the one sniper."

"You were lucky. A half mile north, there were Krauts in every tree. Burdett ran into a storm there, pushed his men right through a minefield to get past it. Hell of a mess."

Adams had heard the commotion from that direction. "Yes, sir. I guess we were lucky."

"General Gavin says we'll get you a new lieutenant as quickly as we can. No time right now, and nobody available. You'll take command of the platoon for now. Pass the word to the other noncoms. Gavin . . . well, hell, you know what he said. He'd give you *my* job if he could get it past Ridgway. He thinks you'll command a corps one day."

"Thank you, sir."

"Coffee? The mess wagon sent a pot over here. Cold, but it'll do. Beats hell out of that powdered stuff."

"No, thank you, sir."

Scofield poured coffee into his canteen, sniffed it, made a slight frown. "Be ready to move at oh-five-hundred. We're pushing hard toward the coast. Gavin says Bradley's raising hell about how long this operation is taking. General Ridgway insists we're the men to get it done, so here we are. We clear the roads and get to those port towns, then the infantry can drive up here in their trucks and claim the bacon. Damned glad I don't have to deal with all that brass. Well, you know what that's like. But it's our own fault. We keep spouting this On-Time-on-Target business, and Bradley takes us at our word. Every damned division in this army has some kind of idiot motto. Those boys behind us? I think theirs is You Do the Dirty Work and We'll Show Up Later in Our Swim Trunks."

Adams tried to laugh, but his eyes were losing focus, his legs softening. He snapped himself upright.

"Dammit, Sergeant, get back to your men and order somebody to stand guard while you take a nap."

"I'm okay, sir."

"Like hell. I'm as pissed as you are about Major Brubaker. That was pretty damned stupid of him. But hell, surgeons aren't supposed to go wandering off into the field when we're supposed to have medics doing the job. I guess he didn't know that the Gentlemen's Code of War went out with Napoleon. Or maybe Robert E. Lee. I've heard of Krauts gunning down whole aid parties, stretcher bearers *and* their wounded. They hold up white flags, and when we ease up they hit us with machine guns. Our problem is we play by the damned rules. Those Krauts . . . " He stopped, drank from the canteen, spit to one side. "I'm tired of bitching. Get out of here. Get some sleep."

"Yes, sir." Adams started to move, stopped. "Sir, if you know where they took the lieutenant . . . he was carrying a letter from his wife. Pretty bad stuff. That ought not get out. It was in his pocket."

"I'll take care of it. What should I do with the letter? You think his wife might want it back?"

Adams shrugged. "Whatever you think, sir. Just wouldn't want some loose-lipped jackass spreading anything about him. Bad enough that he didn't make it."

"Sorry, Jesse. I guess you were pretty close to him."

Adams thought a moment, shook his head. "No, sir. Not really. It's just the decent thing to do."

"Whatever you say. Now, get some sleep."

Adams moved away, heard Scofield's words, *pretty close to him,* and thought of Pullman, tried to see the man, focused on that, and felt a strange anger, the same frustration he'd always had with Pullman's inexperience. *So he wanders out into wide-open ground and figures it's fine that we just follow him. Dumb bastard.*

Adams moved past men in foxholes—more sounds of shovels and mess kits—stepped past the end of a hedgerow, and saw movement around a heavy machine gun, the crew dug in, eating their supper. He saw his own squad now, moved that way, and thought again of the lieutenant. He had forgotten what the man looked like.

31. EISENHOWER

The first jet-propelled bomb had gone over the night before, coming down in a flash of high explosives that only warned the victims with a ragged sputter of the engine, an engine that would suddenly fall silent as its fuel ran out. Powerless, the bomb simply fell to earth, on whatever target happened to be beneath it, homes and shops of people who had seen too much of bombs. The self-propelled weapons had been launched from the Belgian coast, some possibly elsewhere, and if there was any aim toward any target at all, it seemed to be London and the chance destruction once again of England's civilian population.

It was a tactic Hitler had used before, in 1940, with the Luftwaffe's massive bombing campaign against British cities. It was called the Battle of Britain, and it was the extraordinary gallantry and skill of the Royal Air Force that had knocked the Luftwaffe from the skies and brought the horrific air assaults to an end. But now, German technology had changed, the bombs flying without pilots, no flying skill, no tactics at all except the random destruction of whatever unfortunate soul happened to be where the bomb fell. Ultra intelligence intercepts had given the Allies enough information to know that some new weapon was coming, but there had been no word of when or what exactly it might be. Ultra gave them Hitler's name for the jet-propelled bomb. It was the V-1, V for *Vergeltungswaffe:* vengeance weapon.

"Sir, the RAF has reported that they believe they can successfully engage the buzz bombs, if not by ground fire then by aerial attack. The estimate is that the things fly at about four hundred knots, and if more show up, the Spitfire pilots are confident they can shoot the damned things down. Rather impressive, I'd say."

Tedder was never one for hyperbole. Eisenhower absorbed the man's confidence, held his hands folded under his chin, and said, "Not *if* more show up. *When.* There's been too much noise from Berlin about this. It's not a one-night event. How many, so far?"

"Shot down? Oh, none yet, sir."

"No. How many bombs have there been? Total."

"Four thus far, perhaps more. They came down all over blazes, so it's sometimes hard to get the reports accurately. Only one did serious damage. Six dead, it appears."

"Civilians?"

"Quite so, I'm afraid."

"Keep me informed on this, Arthur. Hitler's been crowing about his secret weapons for too long. I can't really believe that this buzz bomb is the best he's come up with. We've zeroed in on their facility on an island in the Baltic Sea, a town called Peenemünde. The bombs are being tested there, so we assume they're building the damned things there as well."

"Right. Sir, we should most definitely ratchet up the air strikes along the Calais and Belgian coasts. Those ski jumps finally have some meaning."

"Pass that along to Spaatz, for certain. Leigh-Mallory should know as well. Well, hell, I don't have to tell you. Let's bust up as many of those damn launchers as we can before the enemy sends too many of those bombs this way. I know damned well Churchill is going to be on my ass about this. Your civilians don't need any more belly blows."

"Thank you, sir. We're on it." Tedder stood, one arm clamping his hat tightly to his side, turned, and went out and down the short steps of the truck.

Eisenhower sat back, heard the radio chatter, the unending flow of noise from the telegraph and code machines, manned by a staff crowded together shoulder to shoulder. He was suddenly anxious, could no longer sit in his small chair, staring at papers, statistics, and tallies. We've landed a third of a million men, he thought. Fifty-four thousand vehicles. All in a week's work. Now, if I could just get them to do the job we need them to do. No, keep that to yourself. You start bitching about it, and there'll be hell to pay, from Churchill on down. Best thing for me to do now is to put my face right up to Monty's and grab him by the ears.

Eisenhower flew in a B-17, specially equipped and delivered to him by the Americans' senior air commander in England, Tooey Spaatz. Eisenhower loved the B-17 and had often wanted to fire the machine guns himself, test out each battle station, crawl into the ball turret, maybe even test the tail gun. But he was too big. He marveled at the men who weren't, who volunteered for those jobs, no fear of claustrophobia and even less fear that as their number of missions increased, they were likely to be shot out of the sky.

There had been another B-17 put at Eisenhower's disposal, one provided by General Hap Arnold, the American air command's most senior officer, who held his post close to George Marshall in Washington. But that plane was delivered to Eisenhower without any machine guns at all, which Arnold must have thought was appropriate for the SHAEF commander, as though Eisenhower would never put himself at risk by flying the plane anywhere near a combat zone. Arnold's toothless B-17 remained parked in England. Whether or not Eisenhower would ever confront any danger in the air, he wanted machine guns.

MONTGOMERY'S HEADQUARTERS, CREULLY, NEAR BAYEUX
JUNE 14, 1944

"The landing strip was adequate, was it not? Really had to push those chaps to get it polished off. We'll have those strips in every village before this is over, I assure you."

Eisenhower was in no mood for Montgomery's exaggerations. "The strip was fine. What happened at Villers-Bocage?"

Eisenhower saw the man's chin tilt upward, the silent announcement that a well-rehearsed speech was about to begin.

"The Seventh Armored let us down, I'm afraid. Can't truly fault those chaps. They've done spectacular work since Libya, and for that I shall always champion their name. But we threw them into line against Rommel's finest. Any other time, it would have been a glorious victory. But there were difficulties, some errors that I would rather we avoided."

Eisenhower glanced at the others. General Dempsey was staring down with a deep frown. Miles Dempsey was Omar Bradley's equivalent, the senior ground commander in the British sector. He's got something to say, Eisenhower thought, but he won't do it here. This is Monty's show.

"How quickly can you resume the advance?"

Montgomery seemed to ponder the question, looked past Eisenhower toward a map on the wall.

"The seventeenth, no doubt. I'm still sorting through events here, a great deal of the administrative tail to gather up. But Jerry is showing his weakness, and in due time his entire front will collapse. For now I would suggest we focus on the positive. Our successes have been exceptional. The pressure is being released on General Bradley's forces, more every day. I count some five hundred Jerry tanks to our front, while no more than a hundred in the American sector. That should provide the energy for General Bradley to find his lost momentum. This entire strategy has worked as I planned it. I'm not seeking credit, of course. History will be the judge. There is a great deal of work still to do here, and this army will answer the call. Rommel knows he has met his match."

Eisenhower felt the air thickening around him. No one shared Montgomery's astounding level of cheer. Eisenhower stood, moved to the map, put a finger on Caen. He wanted to ask the question When the hell are you going to take that place? But there would be no answer, not with Montgomery in full bloom. Thank God there are no reporters here, he thought. Monty's so full of hot air he might explode.

Eisenhower scanned the others. Dempsey was still looking down. He looked at Tedder, but there was no real role for the air commander here. Tedder had come along on the trip across the channel at Eisenhower's request, both men welcoming the break from the offices at SHAEF. He knew Tedder had very little affection for Montgomery, could see it in his face. Yep, Eisenhower thought, all he wants to do is leave.

The meeting had lasted for two hours: reports of failure, senior commanders tossing their men into confused attacks. In the west, the

Americans were finally making progress, the overall strategy there still emphasizing the capture of Cherbourg, the port that they all believed would open a vital artery for Allied supplies into France. But in the east, the British and Canadians had not met any of Montgomery's goals. Eisenhower could not help thinking of Bradley's disgust at Montgomery's *phase lines,* so easy to draw on a map but now long forgotten even by Montgomery himself.

The Overlord strategy had called for envelopment and capture of the city of Caen as quickly as possible, and Montgomery's boast that he could accomplish that in one day had been loudly broadcast to his officers. Now, more than a week later, the Germans held tightly to the crucial crossroads, and every attempt to dislodge them had failed. The latest had come two days before, the British armor driving to the right of Caen, to grab the town of Villers-Bocage. Capture of that town would open up a route into Caen from the west, a pincer movement that might compel the Germans to pull away from the city. But the attack on Villers-Bocage had been poorly managed and poorly fought, and nothing had been gained at all, despite many casualties. The British Seventh Armored Division had already proven themselves to everyone's satisfaction. In North Africa, they were the fabled Desert Rats. Now, they were an overworked shell of what they had once been, and Montgomery's attempt to use them as a hammerhead into the German defenses had been a near disaster.

Eisenhower still looked at the map, weighed his words.

"We need Caen, Monty. That is still Rommel's major thoroughfare to Calais, and once he begins to bring those people into our front, we have a problem."

Montgomery seemed annoyed. "You shall have it. No great victory can be won without considerable effort, and we are making that effort. You of all people should know, Ike, that we cannot be swayed by the doubts of others."

OVER THE ENGLISH CHANNEL
JUNE 14, 1944

"What do you suppose he meant by *others*?"

Tedder sipped at his coffee, shrugged. "Monty sees ghosts in his closet, Ike. He knows he doesn't make friends, and he knows he has enemies."

"I'm not his enemy, dammit. I'm his commanding officer."

"We're all his enemy until this is over. He has *his* way of doing things, and the rest of us are just . . . interlopers."

Eisenhower stared out the window, complete darkness, no light but the soft glow from the massive engines of the B-17.

"To hell with that. He shot his damned mouth off about taking Caen in one day. We're no closer now than we were a week ago. Dammit, Rommel was fooled completely. I *know* that. He didn't prepare for us to punch him where we did. We put a couple hundred thousand men ashore and the Germans still thought we were coming in somewhere else. From everything I can see, they *still* think we're coming in at Calais too. Damnedest thing I've ever seen. A marvel. But we didn't take advantage, Arthur. Not like we should have. Despite what Monty says, we're bogging down. I've seen this before: in North Africa, in Italy. All those damned *plans*. We chose this ground and this enemy because they were not expecting us. And by damn, it worked! But we have failed to use that to our best advantage."

Tedder said nothing, continued to sip his coffee. He glanced back at the machine gunners at their stations a few feet behind them, the wide openings at the waist of the plane. The young men seemed relaxed, each with one arm up and over his gun, staring into black night. Eisenhower caught Tedder's look.

"Sergeant!"

One gunner jumped. "Sir!"

"Could you two give us a moment alone."

The gunners glanced at each other, the sergeant pointed forward. "We'll have a peek at the bombardier, sir. He's a funny one, always with a dirty joke."

Eisenhower waved them away, both men moving toward the front of the plane. Eisenhower looked down at the top of the ball turret, just beyond the bomb bay, and pointed. "I doubt he can hear anything."

Tedder shook his head. "If that was me, you wouldn't have to worry. I'd have fainted dead away, or they'd have had to pop me in the noggin to load me down there. He's probably asleep anyway."

The turret suddenly moved, a slight turn to the right, a silent response to Tedder's words. Eisenhower remembered the man's name, Brown, from somewhere in Georgia. He can't hear us, but to do that job, to climb down inside that damned bowling ball—he's the bravest man I ever saw. Doesn't really matter if he can hear us or not. I trust him.

Eisenhower sat back, felt the cold, and pulled his coat tighter. "Monty's tossing off some of this delay on Bradley. Glad Brad wasn't there today. He'd have blown sky-high."

"Suspect you're right. Your man Bradley's got some steel in his spine. Just a feeling I get. Monty doesn't care for him. Doesn't care for me either. Good perceptions all around."

Eisenhower didn't want this; he knew how Tedder felt, knew there were serious grumblings about Montgomery from almost everyone he commanded.

"This is still his command, Arthur. Overlord succeeded on those beaches in large part because of Monty's planning. He's entitled to see those plans through."

"Is he, Ike? No matter what? You don't hear the things I do, the things every British officer hears. There is real fear, fear that we're going back to 1914 again. The worst curse word you can use to an Englishman these days is *stalemate*. Monty gripes about the Seventh Armored, but it's the whole British army. I could never say this to him—or to anyone in my command. But what happens if we're forced to sit in one spot and dig trenches? What happens if Rommel brings his Fifteenth Army down from Calais and swallows up Monty's flank? I'm not talking about tactics and casualties. I'm talking about *defeat*. Churchill knows this. The British people can't bear this much longer. This damnable new weapon Hitler has, the buzz bomb. That's one more heavy blow, one more reason for people to say *enough*. Every family in England has lost someone, and they haven't stopped grieving from the last war. We put an army in the field, but it's not what we'd like it to be. All that blather about tradition, all that history: empire, kings, and great warriors. It's done, Ike. England is bled dry. Right now, Monty is still a hero, and he still looks damned good in the newspapers, the rooster strut, that ridiculous beret. But he's fallen on his face. Miles Dempsey knows it, de Guingand knows it. Monty's putting on a good show, and he'll keep strutting as long as you let him. But we should have knocked the enemy back on his arse, and we didn't."

Tedder paused, looked into the coffee cup.

"Monty can be as dismissive of Bradley as he likes, but I believe Bradley's the best hope we have. Monty keeps insisting that everything is going according to plan, that he's doing exactly what he planned to do, tying up the enemy's armor around Caen to take pressure off the American flank. That's pure bull, and you know it. But it doesn't matter what Monty says. The fact is, the enemy is more heavily concentrated on our left, and the greater threat from Calais is on our left. If we have any advantage, it's on the right, and Bradley has to act on that, whether he's insulted by Monty's attitude or not."

Eisenhower felt the plane slowing, on its approach to the base. "Brad knows what he has to do. It's my job to give him the means to do it. I can't judge Monty yet. As I said, it's still his command. One thing I've always believed, something I learned at command school: Rigidity defeats itself. Monty isn't rigid, he's just . . . methodical. He hasn't been defeated, he's been punched in the nose. I understand British fears, Arthur. I have no intention of digging into another Western Front. Monty should probably bypass Caen altogether and head inland. Better ground, room to maneuver. Bradley's making good progress in cutting the peninsula, and we'll have Cherbourg soon, even if the timetables are tossed out the window."

"Monty won't bypass Caen. It would be an admission he just can't make. He'd be telling the world that his plans were wrong, his tactics and strategy didn't work. Unless you tell him otherwise, he'll dog it out. He'll beat on the door to that place until the Germans do something to open it."

Eisenhower stared out through the window, felt the air in the plane warming, saw small flecks of blue light, the only lights on the ground. There were faces looking back at him, the crew readying for landing, the two gunners standing obediently away. Eisenhower motioned to them, pointed back toward their small seats, the men returning to their place at the machine guns. He looked at Tedder, the man's head back, eyes closed, stretching his neck. You're a good man, Arthur, he thought. And everything you say might be dead on. But right now . . . there's nothing else we can do. Monty has good people at the controls, and he has the strength, and he's keeping Rommel busy as hell. I have to keep him going in that direction. Bypassing Caen could open up a whole new set of problems. Monty couldn't handle that. It's not . . . methodical.

He wasn't sure about Tedder's pessimism, whether the British were as close to defeat as the air marshal seemed to think. But now, he thought, they have V-1s dropping on them. How would we react to that? What if bombs started falling on New York or Cleveland? Chicago? How much of that could we take? They've had a generation of young men swept away by one war, and now it's happening again. How much more can they give?

Tedder looked at him, pulled his hat firmly on his head, gave a sharp single nod, and faced forward. Eisenhower knew the look. Yep, he thought, he knows it's on my shoulders. Regardless of what Monty thinks.

The plane settled low, the engines almost silent, drifting, a final drop, hard rattling impact on the runway. Eisenhower let out a breath—he was always tense on landing—and watched the crew surge into motion, the last preparation before they disembarked. He looked again out the window, ground crews moving close, a single flashlight beam, the taxi signal for the pilot.

He leaned back, closed his eyes, thought of Rommel. We're fighting a legend, for God's sake. But dammit, you're not so perfect. We surprised you on the beaches, and then you brought your tanks in piecemeal. *Two* major mistakes. We just need a few more.

32. ROMMEL

JUNE 17, 1944

After weeks of urgent calls to the High Command, calls that forced Rommel to hold his anger to a discreet boil, it seemed that someone might finally be listening. The word had come both to Rommel and to von Rundstedt, a simply worded summons to meet with Hitler. But where the meeting would take place was a surprise. Instead of the usual lengthy journey required to accommodate Hitler in one of his hideaways, Hitler was coming to them.

For days now, Rommel had motored carefully to every crisis point in the front lines, had personally overseen the positioning of troops and armor, had dealt with the loss of two of his key generals, Wilhelm Falley and Erich Marcks, men whose deaths left a gap in leadership that he could not afford. Rommel continued to suffer problems of supply and logistics, and the Allied domination of the air continued to take a horrifying toll on any movement the Germans attempted during daylight hours. Rommel suffered as well from the lack of authority to move the different parts of his army where he needed them to be.

It was the ongoing chess game from afar, Hitler assuming more and more control over individual units in the field, mostly armor and artillery, preventing both Rommel and von Rundstedt from exercising the discretion so essential to confronting the rapid flow of change on various fields of battle. In some cases, Rommel's hands were completely tied, some of his key subordinates knowing they had to await orders that came from above Rommel's head. Even von Rundstedt could not override the order that called for every communication to pass from the front lines through Hitler's own headquarters, six hundred miles away. Rommel had continued to despair that his war was in fact being controlled by men who relied only on maps and exaggerated confidence in the strength of his various combat units, men who were trying to wage war from what Rommel referred to as their *green tables.*

But the fight had swayed back and forth, momentum shifting as more troops arrived to bolster Rommel's lines, some units moving up from southern France, others, amazingly, shifted westward from the Russian front. Despite Hitler's insistence that von Rundstedt oversee hard-nosed offensive strikes against the invaders, Rommel knew his best chances now lay in the bolstering of a stout defensive position, a position strengthened by the arrival of additional panzer divisions. He also understood that the British in particular were suffering from serious exhaustion in the field. As Rommel predicted, Montgomery was taking his time, regrouping and organizing; true to form, Montgomery's attacks began to bog down as the Allied troops on the eastern end of the front discovered not only a strengthening in German resistance but their own limitations as well. This had been no surprise to Rommel. His experience in North Africa had been a constant reminder that the terrain of Normandy was far more suited to a defensive fight and that exhaustion and the chaos of battle would affect both sides. The army with the heavier concentration of defense would be the army capable of inflicting greater damage. Though Montgomery would be cautious, he was still the aggressor.

With the British advances seeming to unravel, Rommel's defenses around Caen were holding steady, despite the additional strength the Allies were still bringing across their beaches. Rommel knew Montgomery would attempt various flank attacks and pincer movements at Caen, a pattern familiar to Rommel from his past confrontations with British forces in North Africa. As had happened in Libya, the British seemed unable to sustain a prolonged massed attack. Since much of their armor was coming forward in smaller packets, the Germans so far had been able to blunt their every thrust. But the British were giving as good as they received, and

Rommel knew he could not afford a war of attrition. Montgomery was adding to his strength daily from a seemingly bottomless well of resources. Despite the trickle of reinforcements that slowly made their way into Rommel's lines, the ongoing pounding from long-range naval artillery and the daily ravaging from Allied fighters and bombers had produced a crisis in the German lines that Rommel could not counter. His divisions were being eaten away.

To the west, the Americans had continued their push inland from their beaches, and Rommel knew he did not have the strength to bolster those lines as stoutly as the defenses anchored in front of the British. It was a decision he had made on his own, a risky move in the face of Hitler's intransigence. But then, Hitler had seemed to accept that the American intention to drive across the Cotentin Peninsula was an inevitability, one part of an obvious campaign to cut off and then capture the port of Cherbourg. Even Hitler seemed to accept that Rommel's army was not strong enough to stand tall in both sectors.

The priority for now had to be Caen. As long as the Germans held that city, it provided Rommel with an open door to move the enormous power of his Fifteenth Army down from the Calais sector, where they had remained since the invasion, idly guarding the beaches there against a second invasion, which even Rommel believed was still a possibility. Though the High Command seemed reasonably confident in their shaky conclusion that the Normandy invasion was in fact all the Allies intended, there were still doubts. An invasion at Calais had always made the most sense, the closest point where Allied troops could launch a direct strike into Germany's industrial heartland, the critical Ruhr Valley.

So, as Rommel's desperate fights continued in Normandy, two hundred thousand men of the Fifteenth Army posted at Calais watched over silent beaches. Rommel knew that as long as Montgomery was held in check in front of Caen, an opportunity existed. If Hitler could understand that, the order might still come to shift the Fifteenth Army for what could become a massive flank attack on the British left, which might swallow Montgomery up completely. But no one in Hitler's headquarters seemed willing to consider that as a reasonable strategy. Even von Rundstedt seemed to grasp the possibilities of turning the Fifteenth Army loose at Normandy, but the old man had shown no interest in aggressively challenging Hitler or his armchair generals.

Now, with Hitler agreeing to meet with both of them, Rommel realized this might be his best chance to convince the Führer that there might still be a way to salvage some kind of success. If Hitler would agree to a withdrawal to a stronger defensive line, a war of attrition might begin to favor the Germans. No matter how much strength the Allies could bring across their beaches, a fully entrenched stalemate might convince them to offer some kind of agreement for peace. Rommel knew it was most likely a fantasy, but with so much destruction rolling over both sides, it was a fantasy he had to embrace.

The meeting place was a fortified underground bunker an hour northeast of Paris, which had been constructed to serve as Hitler's forward command center for his invasion of England. But those plans had dissolved four years earlier, the results of jumbled uncertainty and maddening doubts among the High Command. Now the bunker sat unused, a hulking monument to indecisiveness. Rommel had repeatedly invited Hitler to come directly to his headquarters at La Roche-Guyon, but Rommel would offer no protest about the drive to Soissons. With so much now at stake, he would take whatever crumbs the High Command was offering.

MARGIVAL, NEAR SOISSONS
JUNE 17, 1944

Hitler sat in the center of the room peering over a map table, and Rommel was shocked by the man's appearance. His face was drawn, pale and sickly, his hands shaking, his shoulders slumped forward in frail weakness. In his hand, Hitler grasped a strange mix of colored pencils, as though prepared to make his marks on the map, but instead, he fingered them with noisy clicks and only stared at the map in front of him.

"You have allowed the enemy to whip you like so many little boys. I have been told that our troops were caught in their underwear, sleeping on the beaches, enjoying an idle holiday when the enemy arrived."

Rommel looked at von Rundstedt but saw no energy for protest against Hitler's absurdity. Rommel had heard that report from the BBC as well, nothing more than rabble-rousing propaganda for the benefit of British civilians.

"My Führer, that is not true. It is not true at all. We inflicted costly blows against the enemy landing forces. But we were not equipped to drive him away. Despite all my urgings, we had neither naval nor air support, and we did not have the time to complete the construction that was under way. Nor were sufficient materials provided to my command, the materials I had urgently requested."

Hitler did not look at him but stared at the map still, seemed to struggle to focus, his eyes blinking rapidly. "You always have excuses."

Rommel looked toward von Rundstedt and shook his head, a silent request for help.

"Herr Rommel is correct," the old man said. "The fighting spirit of our troops has never been higher, but we are facing an enemy who brings far more to the fight than we can offer him."

Rommel waited for more, but von Rundstedt seemed content to offer a small show of support for Rommel's report and little else. Rommel looked beyond Hitler, at Jodl, but the man's face showed perfect mimicry of Hitler's dissatisfaction. Rommel looked around the room: Speidel in one corner, no emotion on his face, others wary; no one offering anything at all. He moved a step closer to the map, trying to see where Hitler's focus might be, something specific he could address. But Hitler seemed to be staring at nothing at all. The only sound in the room was the pencils clicking together in his hand.

Rommel waded through the silence. He leaned closer to the map, could smell something in Hitler's breath, sour and medicinal.

"My Führer, the enemy has total dominance of the air and the sea. In those areas . . . here . . . where we are still within range of his battleships, our troops are absorbing hellish losses. The armor . . . The Twenty-first Panzer is down to half strength. Panzer Lehr and the Twelfth SS Panzer have lost a third of their manpower and armor. The Hundred-and-first Panzer have lost half their strength from air attacks alone! If we remain where we are now, the enemy will continue to engage us in a war of attrition. Mutual destruction damages us far more than it damages him. I propose—"

"You will not propose anything right now. We will have lunch and take a fresh look at the maps. I cannot concentrate. There is too much gloom in this place."

Hitler stood, the others stiffening, and Rommel could only watch as Hitler waved them toward the door.

"Go! My chef has prepared something, I am certain of it."

Rommel waited for more, some sign that Hitler intended to speak to him privately. But Hitler ignored him and stared at the map, rocking on his heels, his hands clasped behind his back, the pencils still clicking. He had not paid any attention to von Rundstedt at all.

"Come, lunch awaits," von Rundstedt said. "We shall resume this afterward."

Hitler turned abruptly and marched out of the room. Rommel waited still for some kind of instruction, some hint that this meeting might have actual meaning.

Von Rundstedt moved closer to him. "Lunch," he replied.

They moved through thick wet walls, stale air, and climbed a short flight of steps. The mess was brighter, a hint of warmth, but there was no sun, the room lit by a row of lightbulbs. On all sides they were held in by thick wet concrete; Rommel saw guards manning machine guns along a parapet high up on three sides of them. The table had been set, servants scurrying quickly, under the deadly gaze of a colonel, a particularly fierce-looking man Rommel knew as Stürtz.

Hitler sat himself quickly, the others tentative, the usual custom. No one would presume to sit at Hitler's right hand, the chair often left vacant. Several chairs away from Hitler, Rommel watched the routine he had seen before. Hitler's plate appeared, a mix of overcooked vegetables, surrounded by a dozen pills of various shapes and colors and, alongside the plate, four small sherry glasses, each one filled with various shades of dark liquid. Rommel thought of the pungent odor of Hitler's breath and rolled the word around in his mind: *medicine.* Alongside the plates of the others, wineglasses sat empty, ashtrays conspicuously absent. It was another custom. Hitler allowed no one to smoke in the presence of his food, and no officer would dare to risk any sign of alcohol impairment.

A man stepped forward, familiar to Rommel: Hitler's doctor. The man leaned low beside Hitler, a fork in his hand, scooped a piece of something yellow from Hitler's plate, and tasted it. He seemed to enjoy the ritual. He made a pronounced swallow and then stood back, keeping a mothering stare on Hitler's back. Hitler ignored him, but Jodl and the other members of Hitler's staff watched the man, as though expecting some horrible result. Rommel couldn't help glancing at Speidel, saw his own chief of staff looking purposefully at the empty plate in front of him, avoiding the doctor altogether. Rommel felt uneasy now, thought, What do you know, Hans? He looked again at the doctor, who kept his pose.

Hitler seemed to know how long to wait, then leaned over close to his plate and scooped up a handful of food with his right hand. He kept his face close to the plate, stuffed the food into his mouth in audible slurps, and then repeated the motion. Around the room, food appeared, plates of meat and more vegetables set on the table, Hitler's staff officers helping themselves with as much silence as they could muster. Rommel did the same, stabbed a piece of dark brown beef, dropped it on his plate, then studied a bowl of what seemed to be peas, a dull green mass of paste. Settle for the beef, he thought. Hitler sat upright, looked at the others, motioned with his left hand, said something in a full-mouthed mumble. He leaned low again, his right hand scooping more of the mushy food into his mouth. It was the signal the others seemed to wait for, and they began to eat as well. Rommel pushed the piece of meat around the plate and felt a wave of sickness at the hopelessness of the exercise. This is the man our army is dying for.

"My Führer," Rommel said, "if you will allow me to add to what I said earlier—"

Hitler glared at him, food on his chin, and shook his head. "Enjoy your meal, Field Marshal." Hitler sat up now, ignored the napkin, his spirits suddenly changing, a broad smile. "Have you heard about our new weapons? It is a glorious triumph for us. We shall destroy any will to fight that the English still possess."

"Yes, we have heard," von Rundstedt said. "The launchers are in our command sector."

"Ah, yes, of course. It is our greatest achievement of the war! Launch a bomb into the sky, and the enemy has no way to stop it, no way to know where it will come down. Total surprise! Devastating! It is truly a wonder. It is our scientists who will win this war. I have no doubt of that."

Rommel watched von Rundstedt eating his meal, the old man not commenting at all now. Fine. Someone has to say something.

"My Führer, would it not be of some benefit to direct such weapons onto the enemy troops? It could be a most effective way to damage their supply system, their support. The shock value could be very effective in turning his morale to our favor."

Hitler sat back from the table. "Are you familiar with General Heinemann of the Artillery Command? He has earned our respect for his study of the best use of the V-1. General Heinemann says that because the V-1 has a random target radius of fifteen kilometers, we cannot choose a precise target. Launching this weapon toward enemy troops would offer no guarantee that any targets would be hit, and there is a danger they could harm our own people. However, when launched against a large city, such randomness is the perfect advantage. There will most certainly be targets hit! That is the genius of it!"

"But why target civilians? We attempted to do that once before, and it did not drive the British out of the war."

Rommel stopped, saw an open mouth on Jodl, knew he had trodden dangerously. But Hitler seemed unaffected and strangely cheerful still.

"Do not concern me with such musings. Your responsibility is the battlefield. The V-1 is a masterful weapon that is perfect for destroying the will of a people to support their army. I should thoroughly enjoy observing Herr Churchill's face as the bombs fly over his head. The uncertainty, the fear. That is how wars are won!"

The doctor leaned close and said something in Hitler's ear, and Hitler reached for one of the small glasses and drank one of the concoctions, his face twisting in response.

"I am not certain we can prevent the enemy from cutting the Cotentin Peninsula," Rommel said. "Perhaps the V-1 could be used to hold back his push in that sector. Precision is not as critical in that kind of tactic."

Hitler shook his head. "The peninsula itself is not my concern. Our priority is Cherbourg. We shall pick the best man possible for the job and place him in that city with instructions for the garrison there to hold to the last. It is already a fortress, Field Marshal, a mighty wall against which the enemy shall bash out his brains. If we deny him Cherbourg, he will have no way to support his army in the field. We shall starve him. All we require is that Cherbourg remain in our hands for another month or two."

"My Führer, the enemy is resupplying himself now, on the very beaches where he made his landings. Perhaps I can convince you to come to the front with me, to make an inspection yourself. The morale of the men would be enormously bolstered by your presence. Marshal von Rundstedt and I assure your safety, and you can see for yourself the conditions our men must confront and what the enemy is bringing to this fight."

Hitler seemed amused by the suggestion and glanced at Jodl, who smiled in turn. Then he looked at Rommel again.

"I am well aware of conditions in your front. Be clear about this. I know your concerns about the enemy's air superiority. I promise you, Field

Marshal, we will soon have available many times more aircraft than we have had before. Our factories are concentrating precisely on those tools that you require. There has been increased production of Tiger tanks and long-range artillery pieces. In a few short weeks, these weapons will begin to arrive in your sector. The navy is now engaged in a plan to greatly expand our minefields off the French coastline, with special attention to the port at Cherbourg. We will soon begin a significant operation to drive away or destroy those battleships which concern you so. I assure you that such things will greatly bolster the army's morale. I also assure you that once the might of our scientists and our factories is put into line against the starving enemy, you and I will have no further need of these discussions."

MARGIVAL, NEAR SOISSONS
JUNE 18, 1944

It had come well before dawn, a thunderous blast that could only be a bomb. The impact had shaken the bunker itself, and Rommel had sat up in his bed, staring into darkness, waiting for more. But there had only been the single blast, and very soon guards had come, Hitler's staff officers spreading the word, no cause for alarm, no one injured. Then the explanation reached the bunker, furious apologies pouring in from launch sites to the west. It had been an accident, an errant V-1 whose gyroscope had likely been faulty. As Rommel dressed, a guard had come to him with an unsealed note from Hitler. The note had been brief, to the point, and entirely expected.

You will hold fast to every square meter of soil.

But for now there would be no more meetings about the matter, no more of the discussions that so annoyed the Führer. The guard relayed word that Hitler had gone, well before dawn, shortly after the bomb had exploded.

Rommel had waited for daylight, and after a brief farewell to von Rundstedt, had boarded his own car with Speidel, for the trip back to La Roche-Guyon. As his car bounced slowly past blasted bridges and pock-marked countryside, Rommel absorbed the obvious: The stray V-1 had done what his own generals would not dare to do, awakened Hitler from his drugged sleep. But Rommel knew as well that the timing of the Führer's departure was not coincidence. As his car finally rolled into the grounds of his palatial headquarters, Rommel understood with perfect clarity that the Führer had no stomach for the sounds of war. He would never choose to visit the front, would never *see* the condition of his withering army, would never bother to gaze upon the fantasy of his mighty Atlantic Wall.

33. ADAMS

As the American push across the base of the Cotentin Peninsula continued, many of the German forces who had so brutally confronted the paratroopers seemed to give up the fight, even hard-core regulars realizing that, with their backs against the wall of ocean behind them, their priority should be to preserve themselves. The German divisions that had faced the Eighty-second Airborne had for the most part been decimated, their commands dissolving under the increasing pressure of American infantry, artillery, and air assaults. With the inevitability of the American advance to the western seacoast, some of the Germans escaped southward, withdrawing deeper into France. Despite Hitler's absurd demand that his troops yield no ground, the generals under Rommel's command accepted the reality of their situation. Many of those units who had survived continuous combat with the Americans were ordered northward, to add their numbers to the garrison at Cherbourg.

The American advance toward the port city was inevitable to the men on both sides, and Adams had wondered about it: how strong the city was, how heavy the fortifications and the weaponry, how many men held the place. But the paratroopers were still facing a challenge in front of them, the last remnants of the German efforts to keep the Americans away from the crossroads at Saint-Sauveur-le-Vicomte. Before anyone could think about Cherbourg, they first had to complete the punch westward to the sea.

The 507th had driven close to the town, but now Matthew Ridgway had ordered the 505th to make the final assault. On their right flank, infantry, the American Ninth Division, would add to the punch. The Ninth, under Major General Manton Eddy, brought the experience of Sicily and the swagger they had earned. Though their advance was predictably more aggressive than that of the poorly trained Ninetieth, some units of the Ninth were populated by a great many replacements, new arrivals from the States, who had not yet seen combat. As had happened to the Ninetieth, units of the Ninth bogged down, reacting badly to German firepower. Despite the Ninth's swagger, the Eighty-second Airborne would continue to be the spearhead.

EAST OF SAINT-SAUVEUR-LE-VICOMTE
JUNE 17, 1944

They were moving slowly through hilly grasslands when Adams saw Scofield give a quick wave, the order to lie low. He looked back toward his own men, saw them obeying, and knelt, his head just above the grass, saw nothing in front, flattened out himself. He was breathing heavily, coughed, the dust from the grass in his lungs. Good hills. Like Sicily. Hard for us to be seen. He looked toward the place Scofield had dropped; Okay, we're gonna talk about this. Adams began to crawl, his own men staying put. Good, he thought, catch your breath. He pushed forward on his elbows, cradling the Thompson, saw boots, toes up, Scofield, lying on his back.

"Hey, Captain! You asleep?"

Scofield raised his head and peered at Adams from beneath the rim of his helmet. "Smart mouth, Sergeant. You're not running this show yet. Corporal Coleman has a radio, got a call from Company C that the Krauts have mortars all over the place beyond that next draw. Not sure what they're waiting for. Anybody in a tree could see us. Might be saving their ammo. I'd rather stay in this grass than go marching in a parade. Problem with that?"

Adams shook his head. "Not a one, sir."

That's why he's the captain, he thought. The veterans had learned to hate mortars, knew that the only hint of a mortar attack came from a distant *thump* that most of the men wouldn't hear. Then the shells would come in a high arc, no sound, none of the whistle or whine of the artillery, the shells suddenly dropping in your lap. The mortars could be anywhere, a hundred yards away or half a mile, a single bush hiding the crew.

"Hey, Captain, how about we keep moving?"

"Yep. We've had enough rest." Scofield was up on his elbows. "Lieutenant Feeney! Sergeant Tobin! Corporal Coleman!"

"Sir!"

"Here, sir!"

The men moved close, pushing through the grass; Adams saw Coleman, crawling with the radio on his back.

When they were within feet of Scofield, the captain said, "On my order, double-time to that draw in front of us, move down, find cover wherever we can. There could be Krauts anywhere, so hit the ground hard if anybody starts shooting."

Scofield pointed to Coleman's back and the corporal rolled over, handing him the radio. Scofield turned a knob and spoke into the receiver.

"Scofield to Harris. You there?"

Adams heard the crackled response, too loud, and Scofield cursed and turned a knob.

"We're moving forward. Watch those trees on the right."

"Grrrfffts."

The captain held the receiver away from his face and stared at it. "Piece of crap. The Krauts probably gave us these things as Christmas presents."

He handed the receiver back to the corporal.

"Looks like there's some brush along the edge of the drop-off. We need to get through that quickly, then push hard to get up the far side. No sign yet of Krauts on that next ridge, but they could be smarter than we are. I don't want to send us into an ambush. You ready to run?"

Adams said, "Ready."

The others responded as well, and Scofield nodded, pulled himself up to his feet, waved his arm. "Let's go!"

The men rose up from the grass, their own lieutenants driving them forward. Far to the left, more of the 505th was in motion, pops of scattered firing through thickets of trees. Adams looked back, checked his own men, saw Marley lagging behind, and slowed, waving them past.

"Damn you, Private! Let's move!" he said in a low voice.

Marley seemed to struggle on the uneven ground; he was past Adams now and said nothing, just small grunts as he ran. Adams fell in behind him, saw the limp, and thought, Yep, he's turned his damned ankle. Or got a rock in his boot. Adams slowed his pace, keeping Marley in front of him. They reached the falloff now; there was scattered brush below them, too thin for enemy cover. Adams scanned the hillside as the entire company poured down. The draw was steep and narrow, only a hundred yards across from crest to crest, the dip only thirty yards deep. Scofield, already in the thicker grass at the bottom, was climbing out, up the other side. The far face of the hill was mostly open, one cluster of trees to the right drawing Adams's eye. Other men were moving that way, pulled by a lieutenant. Adams kept Marley in front of him, heard the grunting as the big man stumbled down into the draw. Adams moved close behind him, kept his gaze to the right, watched the lieutenant, the trees, thought, Careful, there could be somebody in there. Marley reached the bottom of the draw and began moving up the other side. Adams lagged back, watching the lieutenant's squad moving into the trees: no other sounds, no hidden machine guns. Thank God.

Adams pushed through the bottom of the draw and climbed up on smoother ground, most of the men already hunkered down along the top of the ridge, keeping back from the crest. Scofield was there, watching him, watching the others. Adams saw movement from the cluster of trees, the lieutenant signaling, okay, nobody—and the trees erupted, a flash of fire, thick smoke, and the lieutenant was gone. More explosions came now, a steady rhythm across the face of the hill, some shells coming down behind them, in the bottom of the draw. Adams lay flat, the ground jumping beneath him, cries from men to one side, his own brain screaming the word: *Mortars!* Dammit!

Shouts came: Scofield, men along the ridgeline firing their rifles, the thumping rattle of a BAR, Scofield shouting again. The mortar blasts slowed, the rhythm broken, and Adams tried to count in his mind: a half dozen of them, maybe more. Find them!

He crawled up the hill—ripped earth in front of him, the stink of explosives, smoking metal—and pushed quickly past, the ridgeline only a few yards above him. Scofield was still there, pointing, giving orders, the men responding with their rifles. Adams pushed himself hard, heard more screams, close, ignored them, and drove himself up toward the captain, machine-gun fire in the distance, a distinct sound, streaking overhead.

There were new sounds now, the drone of a small engine. He rolled over and saw the glimmer, a Piper Cub, darting low, moving out past the ridge, banking hard, now another one, far to the left. The machine gun was still firing. Adams rolled over, staying face down in the grass, angry, hot, sweating, and gripped the Thompson, aching for a target. He could still hear the planes, the sound fading, more machine-gun fire, then a chorus of soft thumps.

"Incoming mortars! Keep low!" Scofield shouted.

The blasts peppered the hillside, one on the ridgeline close above Adams, jarring him, the whistle of steel splinters past his head, dirt falling on his back. He waited for the lull, the mortar shells punching down behind him, then quiet. He raised up: smoke and dust, Scofield, waving.

"Let's go! Hit those bastards!"

The men began to rise, Adams moving with them, saw wounded, one man crawling, dragging a shattered leg, a medic moving close to him, now another, scrambling low. Adams pushed to the top of the ridge, saw trees beyond, a hill, brush, specks of light, the sound of the machine gun. The air was streaked with fire, one man screaming in raw fear, the others pushing forward, silent rifles, closing the gap, men dropping, short cover in the brush. Adams ran hard, bent low, saw one small clump of brush, a smoking crater, threw himself down. The machine gun was close and he rolled over quickly, snatched a grenade from his shirt, and measured the range by the sound: thirty yards, less, more. Hell! He tried to see, the streaks of fire just over his head, one punch in the ground beside him, and searched, frantic, another punch in the dirt, coming from one side, fire from two directions. Men were shouting. He saw a flash of motion, heard a man running forward, one of *his* men, pushed the Thompson out, sprayed the brush in front: covering fire. The man was close to the machine gun, dropped to his knees, slinging one arm, tossing the grenade, then falling flat in the grass. Adams ducked, waited, the blast coming now, the machine gun silent, cries from the brush. There was rifle fire on both sides of him—targets, finally—the men around him responding. The BAR began again, ripping the brush to one side, the M-1s peppering the enemy. Adams pushed himself up, saw the man at the brush moving in, firing the rifle, empty clip, the man still jerking the trigger, silent, and Adams was there now, beside him, the ground littered with pieces of the machine gun, the bodies of its crew. Adams grabbed the man, pulled him low, stayed low himself. His own men were flowing through the brush, the BAR pumping fire into a thin line of trees in front of them. He saw the enemy now, dark uniforms, running away, and he planted the Thompson on his shoulder and fired, others alongside him firing as well. The enemy disappeared behind the trees, still running, some falling, shot down, no fight left, pulling away. Adams emptied the magazine, slammed in another, swept the ground close around him with the barrel of the Thompson, saw only dead men, and, beside him, Unger, the man who had thrown the grenade.

"Got 'em, Sarge! I got 'em! I got 'em!"

Adams grabbed Unger's arm, the man shaking, eyes wild, frantic, searching, and shouted into his face, "Private! Reload your weapon!"

The words seemed to reach the boy, and he looked at Adams, comprehending, then looked to his rifle, the barrel still smoking. He moved automatically now, the clip going in, the quick yank on the small bolt. Adams moved past him, close to the dead Germans, a crew of three, their machine gun in pieces, tripod broken, the work of Unger's grenade. Men were shouting, Scofield responding, and Adams looked that way, saw a German mortar, unmanned, and another, dug into a shallow pit. The paratroopers were swarming around their prizes, their lieutenants and sergeants pulling them back into line, Scofield moving among them. Adams looked behind him and saw Corporal Nusbaum, others from his own platoon, searching through the low brush.

"Sarge, we took some casualties," Nusbaum said. "Mortar round. Medics are working on it."

"How many?"

"Three, I think. Edwards is the worst. Shrapnel in the chest, but he's being tended to. I passed two more, bloody noses. You want me to stay with them?"

"No. We need to keep moving."

He looked for Scofield again, saw the antenna of a radio, the captain on one knee, speaking to someone.

"Dammit, let's do something," Adams said. "We're wide open here."

Scofield lowered the radio and scanned the field, his two lieutenants, the platoon commanders, moving close, Adams responding, doing the same. The captain waited for them, pointed to the right, back behind them, spoke in a low voice.

"Infantry's out that way, some of 'em having a rough time. Pinned down by mortars. I can't hear it from here, must be the hills. Some green regiment of the Ninth, stuck in their own tracks. Nothing we can do but push forward. But nobody's on our right flank. You got that? Keep an eye out. Those Krauts gave up pretty easy, so they're either pulling back to hit us again or they've skedaddled out of here."

Adams heard the sound, a rush of air, the ground erupting at the tree line. Now another, and all around them the men dropped down. Adams flattened on the ground, more shells rolling overhead. All through the brush the shells impacted, the ground ripped and tossed high, smoke and dirt choking him. He heard Scofield: "Radio!"

The shelling began to slow, one impacting in the distance, beyond the trees, and then silence, hard ringing in Adams's ears. The smoke was drifting slowly, a sulfur stink, and Adams blew dirt from his nose, rose up, and saw Scofield, the radioman beside him, shouting, "Stop! Tell the artillery to stop! You hear me? Cease fire!"

Adams realized the direction now; those shells had come from the rear. He felt a wave of cold, thought of the Piper Cubs. Scofield was yelling again, but the firing had stopped, and Adams looked out across the brush, the smoke drifting away, men pulling themselves up, calling out, the single word, "Medic!"

Adams moved that way, saw the craters, shattered brush, one shell impacting the German machine-gun nest, obliterating men who were already dead. More men were moving around the wounded, and Adams stared back, toward the draw they had crossed, beyond, where the artillerymen had relied on the instructions from the observers in the Piper Cubs who had brought the fire right onto their own men.

He moved quickly, saw the medic and his medical bag, the man rising up, leaving one man and running to another. Adams reached the first man and saw a huge gaping hole in the man's side, black blood and guts, the face pale white, the man already dead. Adams knew the name, one of Tobin's, pushed it away, and followed the medic again, saw him kneeling, the bag ripping open, white bandage unfurled. Adams heard the voice, had heard it too many times, but not like this. It was Marley.

One leg was completely gone at the knee, shreds of black cloth across his groin. The medic was wrapping the stump where the leg had been. Adams got down close, shouted into the medic's face.

"What can I do?"

"Morphine!"

Adams slapped his waist where his medical kit should be: nothing, swept away long ago by so much crawling. He searched Marley's clothing, the belt broken, canteen cracked, bloody water on the ground, but the medical kit was there. Adams fumbled frantically, found the syrette.

"Into his leg!" the medic said.

Adams was unsure, didn't know what to do.

"Forget his arm!" the medic said. "Into his leg!"

Adams obeyed, jerked at Marley's ripped pants, blood in his hand, the leg exposed, stabbed the needle. Marley was making low sounds, moans with each breath, the medic still working on the awful wound. Adams felt sickening helplessness.

"What else? What else can I do?"

"Nothing! Hold his hand! Hell, I don't know!"

Adams couldn't avoid Marley's face; the man was staring at him, blinking, more low sounds, and Adams pulled Marley's helmet off, saw frightened eyes, the mouth open, words—no, just sounds—choking terror. Adams felt his sickness coming, fought it, thought, Talk to him. His name.

"You'll be okay, Dex. We'll get you out of here."

Adams felt it coming, overwhelming, and spun away quickly, vomiting into the ripped earth. Dammit! He fought it but it came again, a hard twisting spasm, and he waited, the spasm passing, and swept his hand over the dirt, covering up.

"It's okay, Sarge. Nothing we can do for him now." Adams felt the hand on his back, turned, and saw Unger. "Come on. The captain's looking for you. He's mad as a hornet. Says our own boys did this. He called it friendly fire."

Adams nodded, spit, tried to clear his mouth. "Yeah, I know. Those damned spotter planes."

Unger knelt now, put a hand on Marley's forehead. "Hey, Dex. Like the sarge says, you'll be okay. They'll get you in an ambulance pretty quick, right?"

The question was for the medic, who had finished the bandaging, and the medic looked at Unger, tired eyes, shrugged. "Yeah, right, he'll be fine. We'll get him out of here as quick as we can."

The medic was up now, moving to the next man, and Adams watched him, saw one more wounded man, sitting up, no helmet, blood in his hair. But the man was talking, a cigarette in his mouth, the medic wiping the wound, nothing that seemed serious. Adams stood, Unger beside him.

Marley made a coughing sound. "Sarge! I can't be wounded! It's worse . . . I can't go home in pieces!" Adams forced himself to look at the man's face, the panic. "It hurts! What do I do? I'm hurting, Sarge!"

The medic was back now. "There's stretcher bearers coming up behind us. We'll be moving him to the aid station."

Adams said, "Give him some more morphine, dammit! Knock him out!"

The medic moved away, motioning for Adams to follow, Unger right with him.

"Look, Sergeant, we can only do so much. His leg's gone. I wrapped him up, but I think he lost too much blood. He won't survive the aid station."

"What the hell do you know? Give him some more morphine! He's a big guy. He needs more!"

Behind them, Marley was talking again, crying, garbled words. "Sarge . . . I can't go home like this . . . please. I'm not gonna make it. Please."

Adams said, "We'll get you some morphine! It'll feel better!"

The medic cursed, dropped down, jabbed another morphine syrette into Marley's leg, said something Adams couldn't hear, and moved away. Marley seemed to calm down, but the words still came.

"Please . . . I can't. . . ."

Adams leaned low. "We gotta go. You'll be okay."

Marley looked at him with clear eyes, low quiet words. "Sarge . . . please . . . shoot me."

Adams felt his gut turn over again, his own tears, backed away. "Damn you! Take this like a man!"

He felt idiotic, the words meaningless. He was furious now, felt a hand on his arm, Unger, felt an explosion growing inside, wanted to grab Unger's arm, snap it off.

"Sarge . . . we gotta go," Unger said. "The captain."

"The captain can wait! This is your buddy, kid!"

Unger leaned close, and Adams realized he was crying. "There's nothing I can do for him, Sarge. You either. We gotta go."

Adams felt black rage, turned away from the blood and horror. He knew Unger was right and was angry at himself. You can't do this . . . you could never do this. What the hell's the matter with you? He glanced up, thought of the Piper Cubs, felt the Thompson in his hand. You stupid bastard. You ever fly past me again, I'll blow you out of the air.

He looked out across the field, heard low voices, the soft cries of the wounded, medics in motion, the officers calling out, their men responding. Adams followed the flow and moved back into line with Unger, the only thing he could do.

SAINT-SAUVEUR-LE-VICOMTE
JUNE 18, 1944

The village was silent, utterly destroyed. The 505th had moved through, the Germans making little effort to stop them, the village now just a crossroads of blasted gravel roads, a point on a map. As the paratroopers advanced to the next objective, the French civilians began to emerge from hidden places in the countryside, finding their way back to their homes. Most of them discovered what the paratroopers had already seen, that nearly every structure in the small town had been obliterated.

For the most part, the enemy in front of them had nearly gone, the only danger coming now from pockets of Germans trapped by the rapid push of the Americans or smaller groups driven by the suicidal fanaticism of an officer they still obeyed. The snipers had mostly gone as well, but it had not been for lack of ammunition. As Adams led his platoon through the village, word had passed back through the column of stores of German artillery shells and mortar rounds, preparation for a fight the German soldiers had already lost. Adams had seen some of the captured arms and had marveled at the *Panzerfaust*, the German equivalent of the bazooka. It was far superior to the weapon the Americans had brought to the front, packing a much larger wallop and far greater accuracy than the clumsy tube-fired rocket. There were scattered souvenirs to be found as well, and many of the men began collecting machine pistols or the so-called potato-masher grenades. But the treasure hunt was short-lived; the officers ordered the weapons to be deposited in dumps, where they would be destroyed. Most men understood that no matter how superior the German small arms might be, the quickest way to draw fire from your own men would be to make use of a German weapon in combat. Their sounds were just too distinct. Too many of the paratroopers had heard all they needed to hear of the telltale *rrrrip* of the German machine guns.

They moved once more through low hills, but the ground was flatter now. Most of the hedgerow country was behind them. It was still farmland, but there was far more visibility, small houses perched among small orchards, or wider fields of some kind of grain. The men stayed mostly in the gravel road, and as he plodded along Adams stared at the machinery of war, the wreckage of German tanks and trucks, burned-out hulks of machines. The air above them was busy, a continuous roar of low-flying fighter planes, British and American, patrolling the countryside for any sign of a German stronghold or any foolish movement by the enemy in daytime. And then the Piper Cubs would come, on the same deadly mission as before, seeking targets for artillerymen who did not have to see what they destroyed.

Adams's feet were hurting, and his canteen had been empty for a while. The latest Piper Cub droned above him, and behind him men were calling out, empty boasts emerging from their anger. There would be a report of course, Scofield already sending word to Colonel Ekman, word that would flow through Gavin and Ridgway and beyond. Adams drove that from his mind, studied the gravel road, and looked toward a pile of black rubble, the remains of a truck, an artillery piece missing its wheels, the long barrel cracked. That's what's left of their army, he thought. Here, anyway. There were human signs as well, a German helmet, one hole drilled neatly through the top. He saw a coat, laid over a small bush, the insignia still attached, and thought of picking it up, but he had no energy for anything but the slow march, and the coat drifted past. Someone will grab that, he thought. Rear echelon, probably, an ambulance driver, something to take home and show his grandkids, tell them all about the day he took it off the back of a Kraut officer at knifepoint. Yeah, buddy, make it a good story. No one will want to hear mine.

They passed another village, more destruction, the few buildings mostly rubble, sharp jagged rocks and broken steel. He heard a voice in front of him, saw a hand pointing, and Adams looked that way and saw the wreckage of a British plane, one wing straight in the air, the rest in pieces, spread out across an open field. The voice in front said, "We should see if he's okay."

Then Adams heard the man's sergeant, Tobin. "Keep your ass on the damned road! If the Brits want their pilots, they can come get them!"

Adams wanted to smile, but there was nothing funny in Tobin's words, too many pilots were lying in too much wreckage all over this country.

And now came the smell.

It rippled along the line of men, staggering each one, Adams feeling it on his skin, all through his brain. He tried to pull away, flinched as the men in front and behind him flinched. But there was no escape, nothing to do but march past and hope the wind shifted. He had thought he would get used to it, every day now, but it was still a shock, a smell like nothing else. After the first few days in the hedgerows, the smells had emerged, a grisly surprise often waiting behind the dense rows of brush. The Germans had prepared their defenses well, trench works placed to allow the perfect ambush, machine guns protruding through hidden openings in the hedgerow that a man would never see. But the ambush did not always work, and when fights erupted, men on both sides would die. As the Germans conceded the hedgerows, they had often left their dead behind. The Americans cared first for their own, the graves registration officers more concerned for the men wearing the right uniform. So, often, the Germans remained where they fell, and as more troops moved past on the narrow lanes between the hedges, the hidden trenches spilled out the horrific odor, unmistakable and sickening, no one allowed to forget that every field had been a battleground.

Adams heard Scofield's words in front of him—"Take a break! Five minutes"—and repeated the order to the men behind him, word filtering back along the line.

The men responded gratefully, moving out along the roadside, some seeking shade in a farmyard, others gathering around a small well. Adams felt for his empty canteen, his thirst compounded by the sight of the well, and moved that way, standing in line behind a nameless uniform, the man's stench nearly overpowering. Beside the man stood Nusbaum, the corporal pushing the man away.

"Damn, Newley! We could all use a bath, but you've set a damned record for BO!"

"Hey! Not my fault, okay? I sweat a lot!"

Adams tried to ignore the smell, was surprised to see Scofield walking toward him. He stood back, held out his canteen, and said, "You're allowed to jump in front, sir. Nobody'll bitch."

"Thanks, Sergeant. Don't need any water right now. Come with me, will you?"

Adams handed his canteen to Nusbaum, who said, "I'll take care of it, Sarge."

The men in Adams's platoon were used to their sergeant talking to officers, and Adams ignored the stares, had endured too much of that because of his friendship with Gavin. He walked beside Scofield, who led him out into a field beside another house, stripped bare, the doorway yawning open, Scofield stopped, said, "We've got about a mile to go. Orders are to pull up and wait. But I think it's done."

Adams sorted through the words: *Done.* "What's done, sir?"

"We are. There are tanks moving up behind us and they'll push to the coast, begin the drive toward Cherbourg. We haven't received any specific orders yet, but I'm guessing General Bradley is about to cut us free. Maybe send us home."

Adams forced a smile. "We've gotten no orders, but you've figured this out yourself? I thought we weren't supposed to be spreading rumors."

Scofield didn't smile. "Maybe I just want it to end," he said, after a pause. "How about you? You need a rest?"

"That's what this is about, isn't it, sir? You're watching me, to see if I'm cracking up."

"We're all cracking up, Sergeant. This has been a hell of a lot more than anyone thought it would be. This . . . right here . . . this wasn't supposed to be our job. The enemy . . . most of 'em were from the German Ninety-first Division. Tough bunch. Word from the Five-oh-seven was that they found some nasty stuff, atrocities committed against our boys. The enemy cut some prisoners' throats. We're in a bad mood, Sergeant. If we pick up any Krauts, this could get a whole lot uglier than it is now. I'm not sure I can control what might happen. We're breaking down, losing our discipline. Look at you. I saw you puking your guts out yesterday over your man. That's not you, not one bit. Bad enough we get shelled by our own guns."

"I don't want to talk about that, sir. I let something slip. Won't happen again. Caught me off guard."

Scofield stared at him. "You really believe that? Fine by me. But what I saw—well, hell, never mind. I still think you're the best man in the company, and that's why it bothered me. We still depend on each other, and I have to know I can depend on you. What was that man's name?"

"Private Marley, sir."

"Marley? The troublemaker?"

"Yes, sir."

"Damn, that's a shame. Hell of an athlete, you know. Played ball somewhere, Oklahoma, I think."

"I don't pay much attention to where the men come from, sir."

"Oh, yeah, I know. You keep your distance. But you didn't keep your distance from Private Marley. You slipped badly. That's something I don't want to see, something Colonel Ekman is concerned about too. We're not combat-ready anymore. We need a rest."

"If you say so, sir. I'd just as soon go out shooting holes in some Kraut machine gunner."

Scofield tapped him on the shoulder. "Yeah, I know. Just make sure you outdraw him, Cowboy."

They marched until nearly sundown, the footsteps automatic, the full canteen prodding him on the side. They had moved to the side of the road one more time, as a column of tanks went past in choking dust, calls from the men sitting high in their steel fortresses that these grimy foot soldiers were now being rescued by the elite of America's army. The taunting words of the tankers had been a dangerous mistake, difficult for Adams to ignore. He knew Scofield had been right. Any one of the paratroopers could have been sufficiently offended by the tankers' arrogance to respond with a kind of violence that would have driven the tank commanders quickly down into their hatches. As the last of the tanks moved past, Adams had been quietly grateful that no explosions had occurred. We don't need a civil war, he thought. Besides, we'd be outgunned.

The road curved, a wide sweep to the right, downhill, the roadbed harder, less of the annoying gravel. Adams walked with his head down, realized now the sun was low, and looked up to see the orange ball just over the horizon. The column moved through the curve, the road dropping down, and he stopped. The road ended below in a T, a highway, tanks and trucks gathering in a long column. He stopped, moved out to the side, and let the others pass by, one man coming up close beside him. Adams wanted to tell the man, Get back in line, but saw it was Unger.

"I'll be, Sarge. What do you think of that?" Unger said.

"I think, kid, we've reached the end of the line. That's the ocean."

PART FOUR

Monty is a good man to serve under; a difficult man to serve with; and an impossible man to serve over.

DWIGHT D. EISENHOWER, 1947

To Hell with Compromises.

GEORGE PATTON

34. EISENHOWER

As the Americans gathered their strength for the surge northward into Cherbourg, the entire Normandy theater was set upon by the kind of contingency no general can adequately prepare for. On June 19, a storm of astonishing violence swept eastward through the North Atlantic, a storm more powerful than any weatherman in England had documented for forty years. The conditions were so hazardous that no plane could leave the ground. In the Cotentin Peninsula, Joe Collins's ground forces were kept immobile as well, the driving rain and winds turning every farm lane into a river of mud.

The worst impact of the storm came on the beaches, where haggard supply officers were straining to unload extraordinary mountains of ammunition and other supplies for the growing number of men the Allies were sending into the field. The only threat to the beaches now came from sporadic long-range artillery fire or the occasional night raid by small numbers of Luftwaffe bombers, and so the flow of supplies was increasing daily. Before the storm erupted, the Mulberries at Omaha and Gold beaches had provided man-made docking facilities that were more effective than even the engineers could have predicted, enormous tonnage flowing onshore from fleets of supply ships. But the storm rapidly took its toll, and the high winds and tumbling surf almost completely destroyed the wharf at Omaha Beach.

The worst of the storm took three days to pass, but the weather remained dismal, the rain and cloud cover still preventing the air support the Americans needed for the rapid full-fisted assault on Cherbourg. It was one more delay, one more enormous thorn in Eisenhower's side, one more blow to the ambitious designs of the planners.

BRADLEY'S MOBILE HQ, NEAR ISIGNY
JUNE 24, 1944

"We have a larger problem than air support, Ike."

"I'm listening."

Bradley rose from the narrow leather bench and paced across the small space. Eisenhower sat on a small sofa placed against one wall of the truck trailer. He had always marveled at Bradley's efficient use of the limited area inside the trailer, every wall papered with overlapping maps. There was one small writing table and a coffeepot in one corner. Eisenhower glanced into his cup—empty—but thought, Enough for now. To the front of the trailer, Bradley's sleeping area was cordoned off by a short wall, perched up on an elevated platform. Eisenhower couldn't help thinking of the tents in his own forward command post. Brad's got the right idea, he thought. He can move anywhere he wants to go and keep his feet dry doing it. There's a lesson here.

Bradley continued to pace. He kept his hands on his hips and seemed reluctant to speak, so Eisenhower knew that what was coming wouldn't make either of them happy. After a long moment, Bradley stopped and looked at him.

"I wish I could lather you up with good news. Nothing good about this storm. I know damn well the enemy has taken full advantage of our inability to hit them from the air. Well, hell, you know that." He paused. "Dammit, Ike, this is tough. Lee's your man, and I know he has your respect. But the supply situation has gone from awful to—well, more than awful. I've been bitching like hell at the SOS for weeks and haven't gotten anywhere. I haven't been needling you about this because I assumed you had more important things to worry about. But it's so bad now it's causing a reassessment of the entire operation."

Eisenhower had heard complaints before and knew the Service of Supply was never as efficient as it should be. The logistics commander, General John Lee, was generally disliked by everyone but Eisenhower, which Eisenhower considered something of a mystery. Lee was a powerfully driven man and fought tirelessly to bolster the resources of his supply service. But as the realities of Overlord had grown more complex, the grumbling from the field commanders had grown louder. Eisenhower had begun to accept that Lee's biggest problem might be an ego that needed constant massage. Even though Lee was tackling the enormous logistical problems that Overlord presented, he was spending just as much energy building his own kingdom, noisily inflating his own importance. The result had been constant wrestling matches between Lee's supply offices and the frustrated commanders in the field, notably Bradley. It was one reason why the port of Cherbourg was considered so vital to American needs; presumably, it would offer a far more open conduit for the flow of supplies so desperately needed by Bradley's army. But now, with the thrust toward Cherbourg delayed by the storm, Bradley's supply problems were increasing.

"Reassessing the entire operation? What kind of reassessment are you talking about? I've heard nothing about that from Monty."

"Have you seen Omaha Beach?"

Eisenhower shook his head. "The destroyer brought me across Utah. I haven't been there since the storm hit."

"It's the biggest mess you ever saw. I'd say it looks worse now than the day we landed." Bradley moved to the small desk, searched through papers, picked up one, handed it to Eisenhower. "Do you realize that if we had delayed the June 6 landings, our alternate timetable would have put us on those beaches the same day the storm hit? Do you have any idea what kind of disaster *that* would have been? You're a charmed man, Ike."

"Knock it off. We landed when we did because it was the right thing to do. I'm just the guy who had to dot the *i*'s. Believe me, I've been giving considerable thanks to the war gods."

"If you say so. But we're still looking at a disaster. I had to push like hell to get the navy to tell me how bad the storm hurt us. Admiral King finally got me these figures, before he wanted to release them to anybody else, even you. Ike, we lost eight hundred ships! Everything from beach landers to LCTs to full-sized cargo ships. *Eight hundred ships,* busted to hell or sunk. It'll take the engineers a month to clear that damned beach of the wreckage. And the mulberries at Omaha are shot, useless."

"I know about the Mulberries. That's why we need Cherbourg."

"Fine, we need Cherbourg. But my orders are to send Collins up there and, at the same time, send Middleton's Eighth Corps south, to capture Saint-Lô and open the door out of the Cotentin. We sure as hell can't stay penned up the way we are for very long. The enemy is building up his defenses every day. Monty assumes that our next step is to hammer the Saint-Lô area, maybe bust through, but right now that's where Rommel is the strongest. I've been talking to Middleton about bypassing that to the west, keeping the Eighth Corps closer to the coastline. It's pretty clear to me that we'll make better progress if we strike toward Avranches. We could cut off a hell of a lot of Rommel's people by moving around that way, maybe surround them altogether. But not anymore. Middleton can't move until Collins finishes the job at Cherbourg."

"Why not? Dammit, Brad, this isn't like you. I'm already hearing too much about what we can't do from Monty. Is this about supplies?"

"More specific than that; it's about ammunition. We can't supply the artillery fire for both operations. We don't have enough damned shells! Admiral Kirk's a good man, Ike, a good friend. He's agreed to send the navy's big guns to bombard the port. Until the heavy bombers can help us out, it's the only real power we can bring to bear. The Germans have poured enough concrete at Cherbourg to cover Kansas a foot deep, and we can't just prance up to those walls with a big show of uniforms and expect them to surrender. It's a damned citadel. You know they'll fight for it." He stopped. "Part of this is my fault."

"Which part?"

"I haven't climbed on the backs of the artillery people the way I should have. Every time we launch a ground attack, we've started with the biggest damned artillery barrage you've ever seen."

"I would hope so."

"No, Ike. *The biggest damned barrage you've ever seen.* Some of the infantry commanders won't send their people forward until every living thing in front of them is wiped off the map. Every damned mortar company is crying about ammo, every tank commander, every artillery officer. So far, no one has shown me that it actually works. We've stepped off several times, thinking it'll be a walk in the park, and—son of a bitch—the enemy's still there, still putting up a hell of a fight. So when our boys get resupplied for the next attack, they do it again, more this time, fire every shell they have. Stupid mistake, but it stops here. It has to. With the problems we have getting ammo into France, I can't supply Middleton with enough firepower to drive south until Collins takes Cherbourg. Neither you nor I have any idea how long that will take."

"Give me an idea anyway. I know you, Brad. You've thought about this until you're blue in the face. Don't tell me you don't have an estimate."

Bradley sat on the narrow bench again and leaned forward, his elbows on his knees.

"Okay, Ike. This damned weather will decide a great deal. Collins is already moving north, and if we can send the bombers up to help him, Cherbourg might fall in a week, maybe sooner. If he can secure the city and turn south to link up with Middleton, we'll be strong enough to hit Rommel."

"You're talking July."

"Yep. July."

"What does Monty say?"

Bradley seemed surprised. "You haven't talked to him?"

Eisenhower felt the weight of the question. "Not today. De Guingand is supposed to meet me here this afternoon."

Bradley sat back, frowning, and Eisenhower knew what he was thinking. Freddie de Guingand, Montgomery's chief of staff, was an affable, efficient man, who had always worked well with his American counterparts. Eisenhower liked him immensely and had grown accustomed to meeting far more often with de Guingand than with Montgomery himself. De Guingand seemed to accept his role as Eisenhower's preferred go-between, but Eisenhower had to wonder if Montgomery's own chief of staff was aware how difficult it was for Eisenhower every time he had to face Montgomery. Eisenhower's patience for excuses and bluster was wearing thin. He looked at Bradley, saw the stern-faced frown, couldn't tell if Bradley was reading him.

"This isn't something we need to discuss, Brad. I should go to see Monty anyway. He's made it plain that when I show up I'm taking him away from the business at hand, interfering where I don't belong. Not sure how much longer that game can be played. He hasn't delivered what he said he would deliver, and I know damned well that Churchill is grousing at him, and a few British newspapers are raising hell."

"That's not justified, Ike, not at all. I know he's got his problems at Caen, and some of that's his own doing. And you know damn well I'm not smitten by the Legend of Monty or anything like that. Right now, Rommel's got seven panzer divisions in front of Monty, and we're facing no more than two. Monty has never stuck his nose any further into my command than it needed to be. His biggest problem is that he shoots his mouth off. When you tell the whole world what you're going to do, and then you do it, that makes you a hero. If you don't do it, you look like a jackass. I'm mad as hell about our delays and our problems, but I'm not blaming anything on Monty. I've got my hands full right here."

Though the foul weather continued, on June 26, the commander of the German garrison at Cherbourg, General Karl-Wilhelm von Schlieben, was captured, along with eight hundred defenders of the primary defensive position at the heart of the fortress city. Over the next few days, the remainder of the city, including the critical waterfront, fell completely into American hands. But Cherbourg was not the supply panacea that Eisenhower had assumed it to be. With the Allied attack coming from air and sea as well as by land, von Schlieben had known that Hitler's orders to hold the city "to the last cartridge" was a hopeless task. Bowing to the inevitable, the Germans had instead wrecked as much of the harbor facilities as they could, clogging the shipping channels with sunken ships and debris and in general making the port virtually useless. It was yet another difficult challenge for the Allied engineers, the men who were charged with repairing what the Germans destroyed. For Bradley's army, that destruction meant more delay and more shortages of the matériel they had to have before they could consider their next major attack.

While Bradley wrestled with the challenges of confronting Rommel's forces at the base of the Cotentin Peninsula, Montgomery struggled again to take the increasingly fortified city of Caen. On June 26, he launched what he referred to as the showdown stage of the campaign, but the Panzer Lehr Division rose to the challenge and blunted the British attack. With the weather preventing British air support, the Germans launched a counterattack of their own, resulting in a hard fight that cost both sides enormous casualties. But neither side could hold the momentum, and by July 1, the front along the Caen sector continued to show disturbing signs of becoming a muddy stalemate, too reminiscent of what these two armies had endured thirty years before. Despite Montgomery's insistence that the attack on June 26 had achieved a notable victory, Eisenhower saw the reality on the maps. Though the Germans had suffered a higher toll of casualties, losses Rommel could not afford, the British had gained very little ground and were no closer to occupying Caen than when the attack began. Despite all the planning, despite Montgomery's confident certainty in his own predictions, Eisenhower was becoming increasingly concerned that if there was to be a turning of the tide, if a great hole was ever to be punched through the German lines, that punch would have to come from the right, on Bradley's front. Whether Montgomery would ever admit that his failure to capture Caen was in fact a failure at all, he continued to insist that his efforts there had accomplished his goal of drawing German strength away from the Americans.

Montgomery's raw-nerved defensiveness was producing strains in England that Eisenhower could not avoid. The heavy hand of politics was being felt, a grumbling toward Montgomery that was growing louder. But Eisenhower had no reason to step into that fray, not as long as the battle-grounds were still so dangerous and the outcome still very much in doubt. Montgomery was right that Bradley was facing far fewer German tanks than were bloodying the British at Caen, and American troop strength was continuing to increase. Despite supply issues and weather, if there was to be a major success in the Overlord campaign, the Americans were in the best position to make it happen.

With Collins's Seventh Corps now able to turn south, Bradley was finally able to assemble the enormous strength required for a large-scale push against the Germans, whose best efforts were aimed at keeping the Americans bottled up in the Cotentin Peninsula. The Seventh Corps would push southward alongside the newly arrived Eighth. To their left, the Nineteenth Corps, also newly arrived, would fill the space closer to the British positions. Bradley's force totaled fourteen American divisions, who outnumbered their German opposition by nearly three to one. Their overall objective would be to drive south, from the western coast of the Cotentin, on a front that would extend east, past the valuable crossroads of Saint-Lô. It was the Americans' most ambitious attack of the entire Overlord campaign. With the British continuing to hold the majority of the German armor at Caen, Montgomery enthusiastically championed the plan, insisting it would throw open the door to a collapse that could consume Rommel's entire front. But the failure of the Ninetieth Division was still fresh in Bradley's mind and, like Eisenhower, he recognized that placing so much dependence on freshly arriving troops was a serious risk. Bradley decided to rely upon the most experienced troops in his command. No matter how worn out the paratroopers were, Bradley insisted the Eighty-second Airborne lead the next attack.

35. ADAMS

"General Gavin's as pissed off as I've ever seen him." Scofield took a drink from his canteen. "Probably as pissed off as *you've* ever seen him."

Adams, his back against a tree, stared at the mess tent in the distance, trucks in a line on the road, men milling around, most holding plates of food. He shook his head. "Again?"

Scofield didn't answer, chewed the corner off a thick cracker. Adams saw men gathering, talking, helmets in their hands, a larger crowd around one of the lieutenants. The captain's news was spreading throughout the company, the men reacting with curses and numb shock, the entire camp building into more of an angry rabble than a regiment of soldiers. Adams reached down beside him, grabbed a tuft of dry grass, and pulled it up by the roots, a feeble show of anger, the most energy he could muster.

"What the hell's wrong with the One-oh-one? They've been kicked as hard as we have. Aren't they involved in this war too?"

"Not this time. Not here anyway. According to General Gavin, the One-oh-one has already been moved off the line. They're up north, on the

coast, Cherbourg's new police department." Scofield let out a breath.
"Keep your mouth shut about that. You don't need to know about our
troop positions. I know better than to talk about that."

"Don't worry about it, Captain. I'm not drawing any maps, and no
one in my platoon will hear a damned thing. I'd love to tell 'em though.
Might fire 'em up."

"Not funny, Sergeant. I heard enough cracks about that. Gavin was
pretty steamed about Ridgway, something Ridgway told the higher-ups.
Doesn't matter how beat to hell we are, he said. *We might be weak in numbers, but our fighting spirit is unimpaired.*"

"Oh, for crying out loud. It's Ridgway who's impaired."

"Can that, Sergeant. There's already enough bitching about generals at
Gavin's CP. I don't want to hear it from you."

"I'm entitled, sir. How many men are in this damned army? We've
lost—what, half our strength? And we're all they have to make this attack?"

Scofield put a hand up. "Shut it! Now look, Sergeant, I hate this as
much as anyone in this outfit, but we've got a job to do. Gather your platoon, and make sure they know what we're doing. The Ninetieth will be on
our left and the Seventy-ninth on our right. The Eighth is coming up behind us, and Gavin says they'll replace us in line as soon as we reach our
objective. But they need people leading the way who won't stumble over
their own feet. Like I said, Gavin's madder than hell about this, and the division has made protests all the way to Bradley. But the orders come from
the very top, and it doesn't much matter what any of us think out here. We
jump off at Oh-six-thirty, and advance toward a town called La Haye-du-
Puits, about eight miles south of here. Colonel Ekman wants everybody
rested, so make sure your guys get some sleep. No cards, no dice."

"Who's leading the advance?"

Scofield looked down, another long breath.

"That was Colonel Ekman's decision. The Five-oh-seven is more beat
up than we are, and most of the Five-oh-eight is already off the line. The
Three-twenty-five hasn't exactly impressed Gavin, and so, they'll come in
on our flank and rear, along with the Five-oh-seven." He paused, and
Adams waited for the words. "The Five-oh-five is the point."

"Of course we are."

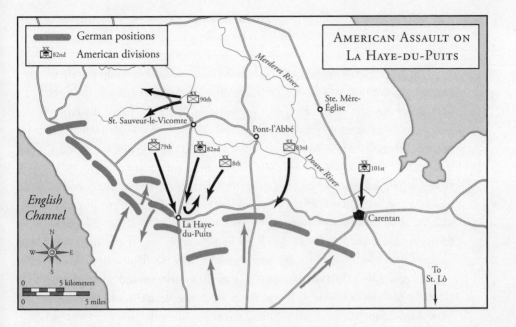

Merderet River

90th

Ste. Mère-
Église

St. Sauveur-le-Vicomte

Pont-l'Abbé

79th

82nd

83rd

8th

101st

Douve River

English
Channel

N
W   E
S

La Haye-
du-Puits

Carentan

0   5 kilometers
0   5 miles

To
St. Lô

SOUTH OF PONT-L'ABBÉ
JULY 3, 1944

The swamps and hedgerows were mostly behind them; the terrain now
was wooded, the ground rolling, only a few grassy fields and pleasant
farms. The roads were dismal, sloppy with mud, and the tired legs of the
paratroopers made slow progress. Adams could feel the wetness in one of
his socks, water seeping through a gash in the side of one boot, the same
boots he had worn since the operation began. There had been no supply
trucks for the personal needs of the men; most of the trucks they had seen
brought K rations and tanks of drinkable water.

The ammunition trucks had been scarce as well, and Adams knew
from the telltale tugging on his pants legs that he had only a half dozen
magazines for the Thompson. For reasons no one explained, there had
been ample supplies of grenades, the men scooping them up from habit
and attaching them to their shirts without comment. Whether or not it
was an accident, a chance delivery from the supply convoys, the inevitable
talk began. If the commanders were issuing more grenades, it meant they
expected a close-up fight. Adams felt it as well as his men. No one wanted
to charge yet another machine-gun nest. No matter how much Adams had
grown to hate Germans, the thought of hand-to-hand fighting opened up

that cold hole in his gut. If I have to kill them, he thought, I'd rather not look 'em in the eye. Not anymore. It'd be awfully nice if that Hitler bastard would just up and quit.

His own platoon stretched out behind him, no one talking, the men conserving their energy for the terrain. Scofield's briefing had offered few details beyond the description of their ultimate goal, La Haye-du-Puits. But before they reached the village, there would be a sizable hill, what the maps called Hill 131, where the enemy would certainly be dug in. Beyond that was La Poterie Ridge and then Hill 95, the final obstacle before the village itself. Adams had no idea of a timetable, if anyone above Scofield had even guessed how long the mission was supposed to take, or just how many enemy troops were waiting for them. It was obvious to the paratroopers that someone far above them had decided that if the fight was likely to be a tough one, the airborne should throw the first punch.

He marched in a daze, fighting to stay alert, an essential with woods close on both sides of them. It was more than sleeplessness, or the weariness of too many marches. Adams had felt the numbness growing for days now, even before the death of Marley. It angered him, quiet fury in his brain he couldn't sweep away. The men around him rarely talked about anything like this, seemed to go about their routine in the camps with matter-of-fact acceptance. Even Unger was still annoyingly chipper, the boy who had learned to become such an utterly efficient killer. Corporal Nusbaum still did his job with the same uninterested effort, always a hint that he would rather be doing anything else, probably outside the army. Adams assumed that before much longer Nusbaum would make sergeant, the regiment's need to fill the gaps left by the cost of so many hard-fought engagements.

There were hints, often from Scofield, that Adams himself would be promoted, a field commission to second lieutenant. There was nothing appealing to Adams about a lieutenant's bars, even with the raise in pay. I'm already the first one in line, he thought. They already do what I tell them to do, and as long as I'm a sergeant I can kick asses without getting court-martialed. It was a tired theme now: the training, jump school, curses, and screaming, what every instructor inflicted upon his men. He thought of Fort Benning, the jump towers, the first rides in the C-47s, terrified men, some who wouldn't jump at all, men who couldn't handle the training and would disappear without fanfare. How long ago, two years? His brain wouldn't do the math, so he tried to bring himself back to the march, the woods, the men in front of him stepping slowly through the mud. Didn't much matter how much ass I kicked at Benning, he thought. No matter what the army told me, I couldn't make paratroopers out of men who weren't designed for it. I sure as hell couldn't make heroes. You can never predict that, no one can, not even Gavin. Unger . . . I figured the first time he heard machine-gun fire, he'd crawl under some rock and cry his eyes out. Now I know damned well he's got my back, a kid! But he'll never make sergeant. He's too clean-cut, won't say a single cussword. Never even heard him raise his voice. His mama'd be proud. What would my mama say? The cussing wouldn't bother her. Wasn't a day gone by that my old man didn't spew out some kind of filth, most of it at her. Bastard. He still thinks soldiers are scum, the bottom of the ladder. What are you, old man? You dig holes in the ground. Try *this* for a couple days.

He fought it, the same anger that came to him at night, breaking his sleep. With the exhaustion of so many days in combat, his brain had no power to resist, so the sleep was never complete and never enough. I need to write her, he thought. I need to know if Clay's all right, what the hell he's doing in the Pacific. He won't tell her of course, even if he could. Hope like hell he's alive. That's the main thing. Probably ought to tell her I'm alive too.

He stepped in a hole, jarred, mud up to his knee, sharp pain in his ankle. "Dammit!"

In front of him, faces turned back, and one man was up beside him quickly, a hand under his arm: Unger.

"You okay, Sarge? Gotta watch those holes. You'll bust an ankle."

"Get your ass back in line, Private. I need a medic, I'll holler for one."

Unger said nothing, just backed away, and Adams felt a strange sensation: guilt. He wanted to say something, an apology, but he stared ahead, glanced into the trees, thought, You're getting too damned soft. Don't do that. We're not a damned social club. That idiot Marley did something to you. You better damn well forget about him. Buford too. Hell, I don't even remember what they looked like.

But one part of his brain opened up, exposing the lie, and he saw Marley now, the horrible image of the missing leg, the man's awful words: *Shoot me.* No! You son of a bitch. You had no right to say that to me. Show some guts! He stared down at his feet, slow footsteps in the mud, the pain in his ankle not as bad. I can't keep thinking about this stuff. This job oughta get easier: every day, every damned fight, every time I fire this damned submachine gun. I've never lost my nerve, never thought what it'd be like to get hammered, cut up by shrapnel. You dwell on that stuff, you'll end up hiding under a rock. Maybe I just need a few weeks' rest. Some of these morons talk about how they'd love a nice little wound, like that's all they'd need to get them home. Ask Marley about that.

He forced himself to watch the trees, pulled the Thompson off his shoulder, held it in his hands, flexed his back. He heard the rustles and clicks behind him, others doing the same, men who had learned to follow his lead. I guess if I did a bunny hop, they'd do that too. That's what happens when they get tired of hearing you cuss them out. They start paying attention.

There were sounds in front of him, the chatter of a machine gun, men moving into the woods on either side of the road. Adams was alert again, energized, motioned to his men, called out, "Cover!"

He stumbled into the brush, his foot stabbing a hole, cold water over his boots. He pushed farther into the cover, knelt, listened over the sound of the men behind him, the firing scattered, nothing in the air above their heads. There were voices on the road now: Scofield.

Adams looked at the dirty faces watching him and said, "Stay put. Let me see what the hell's going on."

He realized he had been the first one in his platoon to hit the cover of the woods and was annoyed with himself. Dammit, you command these guys. You shouldn't be the first one to take cover. Grab hold of it, Sergeant. He saw Scofield, talking into a radio, saw one of the lieutenants moving up the road quickly, a hand clamped down on his helmet.

Scofield waited for them both to move close, then said in a low voice, "We ran into an outpost of some kind. They didn't put up much of a fight. We grabbed a few prisoners. Colonel Ekman says, No slowing down. Drive hard, straight ahead. They don't seem to know we're coming. Hill 131 is right there."

Adams saw now: steeper ground to one side of the road. He looked at the lieutenant, who stared at the incline.

"I guess we climb," Adams said.

"Right now, Sergeant."

Adams moved to the edge of the woods, waved his men out, waited for them to gather. Unger moved up close.

"Where they at, Sarge?"

"Shut up. You see that hill? They're waiting for us on top. They're not coming down here, so we have to go up and get 'em." He looked around, saw Scofield on the radio again. The captain caught the look, nodded, pointed toward the woods across the road. It was time to climb.

They moved quickly, the fire from the German machine guns mostly ineffective, much of it passing over their heads. The rain had begun again, softening the sounds, and Adams led his men up through grass and rocks, natural cover, stopped behind a flat rock, his head down, raised up quickly, then down again. There was no response from above, no firing, and he thought, I'm not giving you a damned target, you Kraut sons of bitches. There was low brush scattered across the hill above him, dips and valleys, hiding places, and he heard voices, German, yards above him: urgent orders. The flat rock was a foot above his helmet, and he used the cover, looked back behind him, saw Unger behind another rock, watching him, the M-1 cradled close to Unger's chest. All along the hillside, his men seemed glued in place, motionless, some behind fallen trees, some in the rocks, no sounds above the hiss of the rain. Higher up the hill, the voices came again. Adams wanted to peer up, but the men were moving down the hill, closer, and he froze. The first voice was an officer, certainly. Okay, so the Kraut told his men to move down to a better position. Mistake, pal.

Adams could hear footsteps coming closer, dislodged rocks, the clack of metal, and he clenched his jaw, stared at the wetness on the Thompson. A small rock rolled past him, tumbling over his boots, and he heard a voice right above him, the man standing on his flat rock. Adams felt the burst in his brain. *Close enough.*

He pushed himself up with one hand, the Thompson in the other, already firing, the German was knocked backward, falling off the rock. Behind the man were four more, carrying a heavy machine gun, some hauling boxes of ammunition, all of them staring down the hill in stunned shock. Adams's men began to fire, the gun's crew was swept down, and above them more Germans were caught in the open, another gun crew, some returning fire, some of them ducking low, others running back up the hill. But the surprise was complete. Adams sprayed the hillside above him, saw the last man falling, more men wounded, crawling in the rocks, pops of fire from behind him, Unger, aiming at the wounded German.

Adams jerked another magazine from his pants leg, reloaded on his knees, the big rock still his cover, and scanned the hillside with the barrel of the Thompson, felt himself gasping for breath. There was scattered firing to one side, more of the 505th moving up the hill, some higher up, faster progress, and Adams wanted to move. We need to keep going, he thought. He looked at the boots of the man he had shot, the man lying on his back, just off the edge of the rock, his feet up in the air. Adams couldn't see the face. He leaned forward across the rock and pushed with the barrel of the Thompson, the man's legs falling to one side. Adams ducked low again, looked to his men, still in good cover, and listened through the hiss of the rain, more firing, both sides, muffled sounds. Then he stared up the hill, past the bodies of the enemy, and made a wave with his arm. *Let's go!*

They captured the hill before noon and pushed past, swarming up and over La Poterie Ridge. Throughout the day, German resistance had become fierce and far more effective, but the drive of the paratroopers overwhelmed their enemy's defenses. By dark on that first day, the 505th was perched high up on the ridge, facing Hill 95, the last obstacle before they reached the village itself. The following morning, they moved out early and, alongside several squads from the 508th, the 505th pushed up Hill 95, sweeping away the last resistance of an enemy who was unwilling to die for a hill they could not expect to hold.

HILL 95, NORTH OF LA HAYE-DU-PUITS
JULY 4, 1944, EARLY MORNING

"We pull back."

The others reacted, one lieutenant open-mouthed, slapping the top of his helmet with a dirty hand.

"What? Colonel, what the hell are you talking about?"

Ekman ignored the man's fury. "I'm as mad as a hornet about this," he said to Scofield, "but it's the order we've been given. The infantry on our flanks hasn't done the job. We're out here in a salient. If we continue to move forward and occupy the village, we'll be all alone, an easy target for a German counterattack."

Scofield pointed. "Sir, the village is right in front of us. We've observed the enemy retreating, dragging every gun he can carry. There might not even be any machine guns there. It's ours for the taking. The men have earned this, sir."

Adams could see the anger in Ekman's face, directed now at Scofield. "Dammit, Captain, don't you dare tell me what these men have earned! This comes directly from Corps HQ, and they didn't tell me to use my discretion. We're out here by ourselves, and we have been ordered to pull back and link up with the infantry on our flanks. You think I'm happy about that? We kicked the enemy in the ass and have nothing to show for it except casualties. You want to bitch some more? Save it for Ridgway. But I can tell you right now I'm not going anywhere near Division HQ until I have to. Ridgway's puking fire, and I've had to listen to enough of that already. Now, Captain, put some men out as a rear guard and withdraw back up those roads we used to get here!"

Ekman turned away and went quickly down into the trees. For a long moment, no one spoke. Adams pulled the Thompson tight against his side, the strap digging into a sore groove on his shoulder. He was too tired to feel anger, only the numbing fog coming back into his brain. Scofield took off his helmet and wiped a hand across his face.

"I'm going to make damned sure everyone hears about this. We were given a job to do, and we did it, and they pulled the rug out." He paused. "All right, assemble your men. Make sure they have something to eat, and then get them ready. Fifteen minutes. I'll give the order to move out."

The others moved away. Adams had no strength in his legs and blinked hard, trying to clear the fog. Scofield put his helmet back on.

"Retreat. I hate that word. Hate it more than—well, hell, maybe more than *surrender*. You surrender, it's because you're whipped, no choice except maybe to die. But *retreat*. That just means you screwed up, or some idiot in command did something stupid and put your ass in a sling."

Adams shrugged. "Sounds to me like we're pulling back because we did too good a job."

Scofield looked at him, said nothing. Adams felt a growling hunger, thought of the K rations, felt for the weight in his backpack. The radioman had stayed back from the gathering of officers and was moving up the hill now, a young corporal named Griffin, a fixture close to Scofield's side. Adams looked out across the side of the hill and saw a cluster of his own men, most lying in the rocks and grass, some eating from tin cans. He turned to Scofield again.

"Think I'll have some breakfast, Captain. Got an extra can of some-thing here, Spam maybe, if you need anything."

"Thanks, but I've got my own. I could use some coffee, even if it's the powdered stuff."

"You're a brave man, sir. I'll have the platoon ready to move in ten minutes."

He had the urge to salute Scofield but fought it, thinking, There could always be snipers, even up here. We get through this, there'll be time for salutes later. Maybe a hell of a lot of salutes. Put us in a parade ground somewhere, snapping salutes all day, make up for lost time.

Adams walked along the side of the hill. He could see the village below, silent, no movement. He was among his own men now, familiar faces, saw Corporal Nusbaum toss a small can toward a bush, benign tar-get practice. Nusbaum looked up at him.

"How long before we move out, time enough to make a hole in the ground? Haven't seen any sign of a full-blown latrine around here."

"A small hole. We pull out in ten minutes. You eat?"

"Yeah. Everybody has. I was really looking forward to that village down there. Figured we could find something better than this stuff. Maybe some good stinky cheese or more of that damned Calvados."

Adams thought of Marley, the drunken spree in Sainte-Mère-Église. "Time for that later. One thing this country's not short of is cheese and al-cohol. I'd settle for a peanut butter sandwich."

Nusbaum laughed. Adams saw Unger, another toss of an empty ration can. Unger stood, blew into the breech of his M-1, and hoisted it on his shoulder.

"Hey, Sarge. You know what day this is?"

"Your mama's birthday? What the hell difference does it make?"

"It's the Fourth of July, Sarge. We oughta celebrate."

"Not in the mood. Maybe somebody'll shoot a rocket or two in camp tonight." He felt the hunger again, a rumble in his gut, reached for the backpack, pulled out a can of Spam, and rolled it over in his hand, a ges-ture of resignation. "I bet George Washington never had to eat this stuff."

On July 2, the Allied command recognized a milestone that might have been the only part of the entire operation that had fallen close to its timetable. The one millionth soldier crossed the beaches into Normandy. That singular success provided a glimpse of inspiration to the commanders in the American sector, but there was another gesture that carried weight all through the ranks. The order for a July Fourth celebration came directly from Omar Bradley, what he knew to be a tradition for artillery units since the Civil War. The custom called for the firing of forty-eight artillery pieces, a salute by the army signifying every state in the union. But Bradley had a better idea, born of his frustration with the plodding progress of this fight. At precisely noon, every artillery piece in the sector, eleven hundred guns, each launched a single shell into the closest German position to their front, the largest salute of its kind since the tradition began.

As the men of the Eighty-second Airborne marched northward in their muddy withdrawal, the thunder of the guns was met with a weary mix of pride and apathy. Adams led his men back through their own footprints, and the sudden clap of distant thunder was no distraction at all. He moved again in a slow rhythm, the Thompson on his shoulder, his mind holding fast to his memories, so many of them bad. There were no thoughts of the next mission, or the next campaign, no concern for captains and colonels and generals. He tried to think of home, of the letter he should write, or his brother, somewhere in some hellhole in the Pacific. But his mind brought him back to the march, one foot in front of the other, rocks in the soft mud, the soft echo of footsteps of so many who were no longer there.

For another week, the paratroopers stayed in their camps, while the infantry massed and organized along the front lines, waiting for the orders that would send them forward once again. But on July 11, the men of the 82nd Airborne received an order of their own. Three days later, on July 14, they boarded transport trucks, a long snaking convoy that carried them through the awful bocage country, the country they had given so much to capture. The trucks moved north, toward Utah Beach, the 82nd sharing the same embarkation point as the 101st. Both airborne divisions were ordered aboard transport ships that would carry them back to England.

Whether he would ever see the enemy again was not a question Adams could yet ask himself, or anyone above him. His men had endured thirty-three continuous days of combat, and for now the questions were more about what they would find in England, whether they would enjoy the luxury of cots and roofs over their heads, hot food and quiet nights, and a dawn with breakfast instead of a bloody attack into enemy guns. Rumors began to fly, many of the men believing they were going home. But Adams had heard none of that from the officers. They were, after all, some of the most highly trained men in the army, with a specialized talent that might still be required. They were paratroopers. And the war was not yet over.

36. ROMMEL

There had been another meeting with Hitler on June 28, at Rommel's urgent request, but this time the Führer did not travel. The meeting was at Berchtesgaden, Hitler's fortified Eagle's Nest in southern Bavaria. Once again von Rundstedt accompanied Rommel, and once again, Rommel made a plea to Hitler, more details of losses and supply shortages, the position and strength of the enemy, estimates of just how long German lines could hold. But Hitler would hear none of it. He had every question answered in his own mind, and as always he furiously denounced Rommel's pessimism.

By now, Rommel had come to expect this reaction from Hitler, but there had been surprises at this meeting, an audience he did expect to have. This meeting was to be something of a show, as though scripted by the propaganda ministry, contradicting the gloom of both Rommel and von Rundstedt. It was more for the presenters themselves: Hitler's own staff, an audience trained not to question. Hermann Göring was there, the Luftwaffe chief, strutting as he always strutted, insisting that Germany's production of aircraft was at long last accelerating, that a thousand new planes were coming on line in a matter of days. Admiral Dönitz was there as well, the Kriegsmarine's senior commander, who did nothing to dispute Hitler's insistence that the vast waterways off the coast of France were soon to be made impenetrable by newly laid mines and patrolled by legions of newly minted submarines and gunships. There was boisterous talk of new secret weapons, the V-1 already wreaking havoc on British civilians, and another weapon, far more fierce, the V-2, soon to fill the skies over England, igniting its cities into flaming terror. The V-2 was a rocket, far larger than the V-1, which would fly with a high arching trajectory, coming down with none of the V-1's telltale noisemaking. Throughout the show, all the glorious optimism that was laid out before them, Hitler lectured both of his ground commanders on their defeatist attitudes, insisting with perfect certainty that the most effective strategy still was to drive the invaders back into the sea.

Von Rundstedt had listened to the extraordinary fantasies in stony silence, but Rommel could not let the opportunity pass, so he had repeated his darkest concerns, in one more attempt to shine reality into the Führer's eyes. Von Rundstedt had offered support for Rommel's plea yet again, echoing Rommel's insistence that German forces be withdrawn to a more defensible position. But Hitler was inside his own reality. No matter the facts, and Rommel's estimates on how the German infantry and armor might still salvage a breath of hope, the Führer was in no mood to have anyone tell him what he did not want to hear. Rommel's final argument had not been military but political, that the Führer should at the very least consider the future of Germany. It had been the final straw. Hitler ordered him to leave the room and not return.

LA ROCHE-GUYON
JULY 3, 1944

"Sir, Marshal von Rundstedt has arrived. He has told his staff to remain behind. I believe he wishes to meet with you in private."

"Certainly, Hans. I suspect he brings *good news*."

The room emptied of staff officers, but Admiral Ruge hesitated.

"Go on, Friedrich. The old man would not come out here if he didn't have a very good reason. I'm pretty sure I know what it is."

"Use caution, Erwin. These are dangerous times."

"For whom, me? Hardly. What will they do to me, send me home? The worst that can happen to me is that I am ordered *not* to go home until I win this war."

Ruge did not smile at Rommel's joke. He nodded and left the room.

Rommel heard noises in the corridor and waited, the old man appearing, moving in quickly, no formal greeting, no words at all. Rommel was surprised to see von Rundstedt's uniform so sloppy, the man's age too obvious: unkempt hair, dirt on his boots, tracks of mud behind him from the never-ending rain.

Von Rundstedt chose a chair close to Rommel's desk, sat heavily, looked up at him, and said, "It seems you've finally gotten your wish. It's your war now."

"What do you mean?"

"I've been relieved of my command. Surely you knew that."

"I thought we were both to be relieved."

"Oh, no, not you, not the Desert Fox; the Little Corporal must have his heroes. I would imagine Herr Goebbels put up an argument on your behalf. They still need your name in the newspaper." Von Rundstedt paused. "You owe a debt to Geyr, you know."

"Geyr? Why?"

"He sent Hitler a letter, outlining much the same conditions and the same strategy you had proposed. He was pretty detailed too. I always admired that in the man. Geyr insisted we pull back to a more defensible position behind the rivers. He asked me if I would allow him to send the letter directly to Hitler, and I agreed. It was an act of courage on his part. And so he was rewarded as I was rewarded. Geyr is gone too."

"What?"

"You heard me. The Little Corporal has pulled our boots off and sent us home. So far, we still have our lives. That could change."

Rommel moved close to his chair but did not sit, one hand rubbed his jaw.

"I did not expect—"

"Of course you did. Don't treat me like an old fool."

"No, truly. I knew Hitler was angry with us. He has been angry with me for longer than I can recall. He gets angry at everybody sooner or later. But he needs us. Even his idiot sycophants know we have no hope of winning this war."

He stopped, saw von Rundstedt looking at him, a tilt of the old man's head.

"You don't think this war can be won, eh?"

Rommel shook his head. "Of course not. The best we can hope for is a peace that does not destroy us."

"That's a curious way to put it."

Rommel sat down in his chair, no permission asked, no formality now, already accepting the old man's lack of authority.

"I overheard a staff officer this morning, Major Jürgen," Rommel said. "He said something I've heard before, in various ways: *Enjoy the war, because the peace will be terrible.* He didn't know I heard him, certainly he would have held his tongue. But they know, all of them. They know what the maps say, they know what the enemy is bringing to our front. They know we will never drive the enemy out of Italy. They also know of the reports from the east. That news is more frightening to me than anything happening here. The Russians cannot be stopped. They are driving us back across Poland, they will drive us into our own territory, and then they will follow. I had hoped that Hitler would hear what I had to say, my fears of what would happen to Germany if we allow the Russians to conquer us."

"He scolded you, did he not? *Do not talk to me of politics.* He does not believe anyone can save Germany but himself."

Rommel turned in his chair and stared out the window: thick gray skies. "He told me once, *Do not be concerned with peace. No one will treat with me.* I understood what he meant, and I understand it now. There can be no negotiation. All our enemies have one goal, to crush *him.* But we must fight for more than *him,* for more than his insane dreams."

"Careless words, Erwin."

"So, you are working now for the Gestapo? You know that what I am saying is true, you have always known it. The English and the Americans have no affection for the Russians. Surely, if we could approach them with some sort of entreaty, some discussion of how the fight *here* can be brought to an end, perhaps they will join with us to keep the barbarians from consuming Germany."

"Good God, Erwin. You are still an idealist. You may be the only one left. But your ideals are fairy tales. As long as Hitler is alive, no German will have authority to offer any kind of *entreaty.* The American leaders have made it plain that they will only accept unconditional surrender. I am very sure that those words came from Roosevelt himself." He paused. "Erwin, you still have your command here, you still have a job to do, one duty, to obey your damned Führer. You recall the oath? I do. I signed it ten years ago on a day much like this one, rain and misery. *I swear by God this holy*

oath, that I will render to Adolf Hitler . . . unconditional obedience, and I am
ready as a brave soldier to risk my life at any time for this oath. Now we risk
our lives just by speaking to him."

Rommel stared down at the desk. "Yes, I recall. We all signed it. No
one complained. I thought he would save Germany."

"What do you think now? No, it's all right. I already know, and you
should watch your words carefully. But you are still a soldier. You are still
pledged to unconditional obedience." The old man paused, a small laugh.
"You have never been terribly obedient to me. Now your orders will come
from someone else. Perhaps you will find them more to your liking." He
reached into his pocket, pulled out a small box. "They gave me this yesterday. My reward for being fired. The Oak Leaves for the Knight's Cross.
Very nice note signed by the Little Corporal too. Written by someone else,
no doubt. This morning, General Keitel called me. The Führer's staff has
apparently realized that there could be problems removing senior commanders while they are trying to fight a war. It's as though no one thought
of that before. I gave him one piece of advice. Make peace." Von Rundstedt stood slowly, a grimace of pain on his face. "I don't think he appreciated the irony of that."

Rommel suddenly realized how old von Rundstedt was, the stiff
joints, the haggard face. *He is saying good-bye. I may never see him again.*

Rommel stood as well. "What will you do now?"

Von Rundstedt steadied himself on the back of the chair. "I'm going
to a spa, the facility at Bad Töelz. I have various ailments that require some
attention. You should go there yourself." He moved toward the door, then
stopped and turned toward Rommel. "But not today."

Von Rundstedt's successor was sent to France immediately. Rommel
had served with the man before, had disliked him immensely, and
had no reason to believe that would change. His name was Hans von
Kluge, and Hitler seemed to love the man, had long ago spoken to Rommel of von Kluge's successes with a glowing pride, sure that this was the
man who could lead the German army into glorious victory. Von Kluge
had served first in Poland and France, as had Rommel, but then von Kluge
went east and, in Russia, he led the campaign that nearly put the German
army into Moscow. But glorious or not, von Kluge could not find the
means to complete the job, to destroy the Russians who confronted him.

Unlike the other German generals who paid a price for their defeats in the east, von Kluge was not condemned for the failures of his army. Hitler was still a champion of von Kluge's talents, so it was little surprise even to Rommel that von Kluge would be sent to France.

LA ROCHE-GUYON
JULY 4, 1944

"You are by nature disobedient, and you have ignored the Führer's wishes on occasions too numerous to count! I do not care that you are a field marshal, you will learn to obey orders!"

Rommel stood taller, von Kluge's words igniting a fire inside him, his head throbbing. Speidel stood to one side, ramrod straight, two other staff officers on the far side of the room. Von Kluge was red-faced. He took a step to one side, then turned and leaned close to Rommel.

"In Russia, we fought a *real* enemy. We fought an army that chose to die in a glorious charge rather than retreat. But they were too many, and we were unprepared. I have learned that lesson. And one more lesson as well. In war, men suffer and men die. But if they make mistakes, they will suffer more, and more will die! There have been too many mistakes here! For weeks I have been in conference with the Führer and his staff, and I have studied the situation. This army is a beast, kept in its cage by the unwillingness of its generals to release it! *Your* unwillingness! You cower in the face of the enemy's weapons, when ours are superior! It is a mystery, but it is one I shall solve!"

"Solve *how*?" Rommel dropped the guise of standing at attention, any hold on his temper loosened by von Kluge's insulting tone. "I have heard speech after speech about what we shall do to the enemy, made by men who tour stadiums and monuments but never by one who has walked in my boots! You believe that your new authority allows you the privilege of tossing aside my experience and my strategies, just because some armchair cowards in Berlin—"

Rommel stopped himself, seeing surprise on von Kluge's face. But von Kluge recovered quickly. Rommel could see the firm jut of his jaw; the man was not backing down.

Von Kluge said in a quiet hiss, "Field Marshal von Rundstedt was dismissed because the Führer had lost confidence in his ability to carry out his duty. You do not enjoy the Führer's complete confidence either, and you are still in command here only because of the Führer's generosity. I am giving you excellent advice, Herr Rommel. Obey the Führer's orders without hesitation, or you will suffer the consequences. I do not require explanations or excuses from you. I have already made arrangements to visit the front immediately, to speak directly to the infantry and armor commanders, and I will instruct them, as I will instruct you, on how we will succeed in destroying our enemy. And you shall not only obey the Führer, you shall obey me!"

"I obey orders, Field Marshal, when those orders are not suicidal to my army."

Von Kluge seemed to explode. He waved his arms and pointed a fist toward Rommel's face.

"You obey those orders you find to be convenient! This is not your war, Herr Rommel, to be fought in the way you see fit to engage it! You do not draw the maps, you do not position the troops, you do not plan the strategy! You have somehow survived in this command, but unless you eliminate your bad habits, I assure you, neither Berlin nor I will tolerate your lust for independence!"

Von Kluge spun on his toes and marched quickly toward the door, his aide pulling it open with perfect timing and following von Kluge out. Silence hung in the warm air, but after a long moment the room seemed to deflate. Rommel felt sweat on his forehead and in his clothes; his fists were clenched, his legs stiff.

He pointed to the aides. "Leave me."

They seemed grateful to escape. Speidel moved to the door, waited for the others to leave, and closed the door behind them.

"How dare he say that to you! Who does he think he is, to come in here and humiliate you?"

"Quiet, Hans."

"Sir!"

"*Quiet,* Hans. He thinks he's the commander of Army Group West, and he is correct. He has come here to *fix* things, and it is quite obvious the High Command has convinced him that I am one of the things that requires fixing." Rommel was still breathing heavily, and he flexed his fingers, trying to release the anger. "The most *notable* thing he said was that he has been in conference with the Führer's staff. The Führer's staff has no concept of what is happening out here, and so neither does Field Marshal von Kluge. I welcome his tour of the battle lines. He should hear of our situation as soon as possible from generals who face the enemy. I should like him to inspect our vast reserves of power and strength that those idiots in Berlin have shown him on all those fine pieces of paper."

"But sir, he should not have shown you such disrespect! Not in front of your own staff!"

"No, he should not. But he is a strutting martinet. It is his nature to infuriate people, to embarrass and humiliate them. It is how he gains *respect.* I will inform him that his tirade was inappropriate. In the meantime, I must deal with conditions that are more pressing. Have Sergeant Daniel prepare the car, and call General Dietrich. I must know what is happening on his front, if the British are moving their lines in front of Caen. I shall also see Colonel Lattmann. He has reported serious shortages of artillery shells, and I must prepare a report for my new commanding officer with numbers that are reliable."

Speidel seemed resigned to the job. "Yes, sir. Right away. But I must say, sir, if anyone were to speak to me in that manner, in front of my aides—"

"I have no doubt you would take it without comment."

Speidel seemed to chew on Rommel's words, still showing his anger.

"Yes," Rommel said, "you would take it, and you would do your duty."

LA ROCHE-GUYON
JULY 5, 1944

Rommel did not stand but watched as von Kluge paced the floor. He stared at the man's medals, which von Kluge seemed always to wear, something Rommel had rarely done himself. To one side, Speidel held his usual pose, stared ahead obediently, none of the fury from the day before in any of them. Rommel waited patiently, his hands folded on the desk. He had already heard from four of his generals as to what kind of reports they had given von Kluge.

Von Kluge stopped pacing, faced Rommel, seemed to attempt a smile. "Field Marshal, how long have you suspected that conditions here are not what we require to defeat the enemy?"

Rommel was not surprised by the question. "The enemy made his assault on June sixth. That is the day I knew we were not prepared."

Von Kluge nodded, paced again. "I do not believe we can hold the city of Caen. The British are very strong there, and their strength is increasing daily. Our greatest effort should be there because, if we give way, Mont-

gomery will have open roads to Paris and possibly into Germany itself."
He paused, looked at Rommel. "You know this, don't you?"

"Of course I know this. We cannot hold against the Americans either.
They are massing for a drive into our lines near Saint-Lô. Except for Cherbourg, we have done a reasonable job of holding the enemy away from his
objectives, and we have inflicted considerable loss to his forces. But we
have lost far more. Without air support . . . without *any* air support, we
have no chance of defeating him."

Von Kluge moved to a chair and seemed to debate whether to sit. "I
am not a friend of Reichsmarschall Göring. He can be . . . difficult."

"Choose whatever words you wish. In my opinion, Göring has betrayed our efforts with perfect precision. If we had struck the enemy on his
landing beaches with both armor and air power, our situation now would
be decidedly different."

Von Kluge frowned and rubbed his stomach.

"Are you ill? General Speidel can send for a doctor." He knew he had
done a poor job of hiding his sarcasm, but von Kluge seemed not to notice.

"No, not necessary."

"Supper, then? We have some truly fine French beef."

Von Kluge looked at him, puzzled, finally absorbed his words, and
said, "No, perhaps later." He took a deep breath. "You were correct, Herr
Rommel. I have seen your reports to the Führer, reports that he does not
believe. But those reports were accurate. The best course open to us is to
withdraw our forces back east and south of the Orne River and south of
the Vire. We cannot maintain a front as extensive as the one we are facing
now. That part of the Fifteenth Army which remains at Calais must be
brought southward, to protect from the enemy's ability to reach into the
Ruhr Valley."

Rommel said nothing. He was surprised at von Kluge's strange show
of acceptance and impressed by his quick grasp of the battlegrounds. He
might be a martinet, he thought, but he understands how to fight a war.

"So, will you advise the High Command of these things?"

Von Kluge seemed suddenly uncertain. "Of course. But you already
have. As did von Rundstedt."

"Don't forget Geyr. Never liked the man, but he occasionally understood how to use his tanks."

Von Kluge absorbed the sarcasm, nodding slowly. "Allow me, Herr

Rommel, to withdraw my complaints against you. My criticism was un-warranted." He seemed embarrassed, moved quickly to the door. "I am still establishing my staff and my headquarters. I shall not be as far from the situation as von Rundstedt. But there is much to do. Good evening."

Von Kluge's bootsteps faded away in the corridor. In the silence, Spei-del closed the door, looking at Rommel with open-mouthed surprise.

Rommel said, "I dislike him less today."

"He apologized to you."

"Yes, he did. That took courage. The question is, What does he tell Hitler? Our Führer has a short fuse these days, so von Kluge has a problem if he wants to keep his new command. Do we fight the war we are fighting now, or do we fight the war we must fight to preserve our country?"

"Sir, what do we do?"

Rommel felt the gloom returning, thought a moment. "Hitler was correct when he told me that no one would negotiate with him. More so now. There is no reason why our enemies here should listen to any kind of *talk*."

"Sir, may I sit?" Speidel asked.

Rommel pointed to a chair, and Speidel slid down slowly, seemingly consumed by thoughts.

"Sir . . ."

"I fear, Hans, that if this war does not end very soon, Germany will cease to exist. I would rather die right here and now than have my family live under the thumb of Russian savages. Our only hope is to cease the de-struction of this army, *my* army. I faulted Geyr for not using his armor, thought he was timid for preserving his forces. Now I see he was right. We must preserve what strength we still have. The most important fight we must wage has yet to come, the fight to prevent the Russians from con-quering our homeland. I still believe that if the British and the Americans understood that we hold no hatred for them, if we could communicate to them that we share a common enemy . . ."

"We cannot offer any kind of negotiation, sir. We cannot even sug-gest it."

"No, not while Hitler is alive. And so there will be no negotiation."

Speidel leaned back in the chair, his eyes in a narrow stare. "There could be a solution, sir. All Germans who love their country—"

"Quiet, Hans. I know your solution. No army officer can speak of . . . solutions, not in this office. Do you understand me? I will not hear of any . . . solutions. I have one duty, and that is to do what is best for my country and for the men who serve me. I cannot be involved. . . . I cannot be distracted by those things that do not concern me right here."

Speidel stood, stiffened, and said, "Sir, thank you. I should attend to my duties."

"You are dismissed, Hans."

Speidel spun around, left the room, and silence surrounded Rommel again. He sat for a long moment, then rose up from the chair, felt the old aches in his side, stiffening joints, and moved to the tall window. It was dark outside, a light rain falling, nothing to see, and he stared out, thinking of his son. What will the world hold for you, Manfred? What things will you endure and suffer because men like me did not have the courage to stand up and say *no*. Who has the courage now?

37. EISENHOWER

Late on the night of July 7, more than 450 British heavy bombers
launched a massive assault on the city of Caen. The following morning, July 8, Montgomery's beleaguered army stepped off to confront what
they believed would be an enemy who had been blasted into oblivion.

Though Montgomery had often feuded with the "air barons," he had
convinced most of them, particularly Leigh-Mallory, that bomber support
was essential to the operation. Eisenhower welcomed any sign of cooperation, had endured enough of the back-biting among the air commanders.
There was still a strong feeling among both American and British air commanders that heavy bombing of German cities was the easiest path to winning the war and that chewing up ground forces was a wasteful cost of
lives. Neither Eisenhower nor Montgomery agreed, and the rivalry and
clashes of personality had continued to be a serious nuisance to the har-
mony of Eisenhower's command.

The normally disagreeable Leigh-Mallory had surprised Eisenhower
by coming around to Montgomery's point of view, that the heavy bombers
should be readily available to assist any major ground offensive. But, as

usual, many of Leigh-Mallory's subordinates disagreed with him, voicing needling opinions that Montgomery was wasting their time, time that could be better spent dropping bombs on German factories. It helped matters very little that many of the air commanders continued to have so little regard for Leigh-Mallory that, if he supported a plan, they felt obliged to oppose it. But Montgomery had always been persuasive, and after considerable cajoling, the air barons agreed to cooperate. But the execution of any plan this large was never simple. Even Leigh-Mallory realized there could be problems caused by the close proximity of Montgomery's troops to the German positions. British pilots were deeply concerned that any inaccuracy by their bombardiers could have a catastrophic impact on their own troops. So during the crucial first hours of the operation, those air crews made the same mistake that had been made at Omaha Beach a month before. When the nervous bombardiers reached their designated targets, they chose to wait a few additional seconds to release their bombs. That delay caused the bomb loads to fall just beyond the German positions, and, instead of blistering the enemy's lines, they impacted the historic city itself. Fourteen thousand buildings were destroyed, nearly every recognizable landmark in Caen reduced to rubble.

Once the bomb runs were completed, the command was given for the British troops to begin their ground assault. Among the British tank crews and infantrymen, there was an air of celebration, the expectation that finally the enemy that had so doggedly stood his ground had now been obliterated and Montgomery's boasts of capturing the city would be realized without much cost. Instead, the British stepped straight into the mostly undamaged guns of the Twelfth SS Panzer Division, one of the most fanatically loyal units in the German army. The fight lasted three days, the Germans still holding their ground, backing away only as the war of attrition weakened their ranks. As Montgomery's troops finally began to capture strongholds in the city itself, they learned what effect the bombs had truly had. With the city so completely destroyed, the roadways were piled high with debris, so much so that British tanks and trucks could not pass through. That job fell to the British foot soldiers. By July 10, the Germans had backed away just enough for Montgomery to claim that the city had been captured, but even then, British troops only controlled a portion of the city itself. Fighting continued, the casualty lists on both sides lengthening by the hour.

With so much German effort being expended to hold Caen, Omar Bradley knew exactly the opportunity he had been given. The swamp and hedgerow country along the American front had done as much as the Germans had to frustrate every American effort to break out of the confinement in the Cotentin Peninsula. Eisenhower and his commanders understood that Rommel was using the natural defensive terrain to hold the Americans back with as few troops and as little armor as he could. It was frustrating to Bradley that he had not been able to take advantage, that the bocage country had proved to be far more difficult to break through than anyone had expected. Bradley continued to be strengthened by fresh American divisions coming ashore, adding to his numerical superiority. With Montgomery finally punching into Caen, the heavy concentration of German armor there would most likely stay put. Though Montgomery had boasted of a breakthrough at Caen, the reality was clear to both Eisenhower and Bradley. Once again the British had been stopped short of their goals. If the German lines were finally to be cracked open, both generals knew that the strike southward had to be an American operation.

Even as the fight raged around Caen, Montgomery made loud claims that his mission had been accomplished, a claim some of his own generals were quietly disputing. The air commanders in particular were livid, explaining away the errors among their own bombardiers by claiming that Montgomery's planning was, once again, faulty. Once more, Eisenhower had to hear the backbiting darts being tossed back and forth among his generals, a spitting match over territoriality, men guarding their turf and their reputations. Through all that annoyance, Eisenhower knew that the prolonged fights around Caen had cost both the British and the Germans far more resources and casualties than they could afford to lose. Secret Ultra intercepts had given Eisenhower the clear signal that Rommel's army was facing severe shortages across the entire front. But British losses were equally devastating. Though British and Canadian troops were massed on the beaches behind their front lines, awaiting a breakthrough Montgomery still insisted was imminent, the losses he had suffered were having a dangerous effect on morale, not only at the front but in the offices of the British government.

On July 10, as Eisenhower made one of his frequent trips from SHAEF headquarters near London to his forward command post at Portsmouth, he made a stop, at the request of the one man who was never afraid to voice his opinions about anything.

CHEQUERS, HOME OF WINSTON CHURCHILL
JULY 10, 1944

"For such a small man, Monty has an enormous mouth. Large enough to fit both boots. I admit, though, I was seduced by him." Churchill filled Eisenhower's glass, then his own. "I put too much vinegar on his claims for instant success at Caen. I should have known better."

Eisenhower sat in a soft chair across from Churchill's bed and set the glass of cognac on the small table beside him, the warmth of the room playing on his weariness. He had not expected the meeting to take place in Churchill's bedroom, but Churchill had insisted, and Eisenhower knew that the prime minister was far more interested in the conversation itself than where it took place. Churchill continued to talk, having said nothing yet that Eisenhower had been surprised to hear.

"The damned newspapers love him still. Saw a story in the *Times* by that buffoon Berkeley, something about Montgomery's magnificent talent for *economy of casualties*. The suggestion was that we should only fight those battles where no one would get hurt; lo and behold, Field Marshal Montgomery had performed admirably, to the benefit of our gallant boys or some such nonsense. I paraphrase, of course, but not by much. How's the cognac?"

Eisenhower picked up the glass, copied Churchill's obligatory swirl of the dark liquid, and took a taste. The warmth rose through his nose, the burn spreading down through his throat, and he responded with a forced smile, a slow approving nod. Churchill seemed not to notice but padded around the room, his slippers flopping noisily.

"Oh, be sure to tell your man Butcher I appreciate the cigars. Hard to believe Hitler understands tobacco. Fine smoke."

The cigars had come from Cherbourg, a souvenir Harry Butcher had brought back to SHAEF headquarters. Eisenhower had agreed with his staff officer's perfect logic that they were a most appropriate gift for Churchill.

"Thank you. I'll tell him. I would imagine they come from somewhere else though. Cuba, perhaps. I don't think the Germans grow tobacco."

"I didn't mean to change the subject, Ike. Monty's a problem. Patience is running out."

Eisenhower took another sip of the cognac, saw now that Churchill expected a reply. "Monty has his problems, certainly. But he's doing the job. I know that people are impatient with him, expect him to accomplish every objective."

"They expect it because he tells them that's what he's going to do! Dammit, Ike, no one's faulting Monty because of *you*, because you gave him some impossible job to do. He spews out his own bilge, and after a while, it washes back up around his own damned feet!"

Eisenhower thought, Be careful. He's testing me. This can't help us at all. After a long moment, he said, "Monty has accomplished a great deal. His engagements haven't always been successful, but results have come. No one can expect our plans to remain unchanged. We have done a great deal to adapt to what the enemy has given us. I had doubts that Monty could take Caen the first day, and I damn well wish he had pushed harder when he had the chance. But that's behind us. What's important right now is that the enemy has responded in a way that offers us another opportunity. The Germans have concentrated their greatest strength on Monty's front, and we believe that made it possible for Bradley to make a strong move. Because Monty tied up so much German armor, we were able to capture Cherbourg damn near on our timetable. Bradley's people are planning their next move right now, and it will be big, a major drive against the enemy's positions along the base of the Cotentin Peninsula. The only way we could expect to pull that off without getting our asses handed to us is by Monty's holding so much of the enemy around Caen."

Churchill lit a cigar and stared at Eisenhower through the smoke. "Monty paying your salary?"

Eisenhower knew the meaning, lowered his head, and stared at the dark wool of the rug beneath him. "It's working. It's just taking longer than we would have liked."

"Rubbish. What Monty said would happen in a single day has taken more than a month. That's the rub. You may call that adaptation if you wish, but there is more at stake here. I have pushed him myself, made it very clear that I will tolerate little of his absurd need to plan every move as though he's some kind of grand chess master. That's the image he wants us to have. It's pure rubbish. I've heard all about how he's the only man who could do that job. Brooke yells at me that I'm just gunning for Monty because I don't like his beret or something, that I should be giving him more credit. That's what you're saying too, isn't it?"

Eisenhower absorbed Churchill words, thought, Have you been in contact with Monty directly? He was growing angry now. No. I can't tell him he shouldn't be talking to my generals. They're not really *my* generals after all, never have been. But dammit, they're not his either.

He watched as Churchill continued to pad around the room, the round man's nervous energy infectious, cutting into the fog from Eisenhower's cognac.

"Regardless of what you may think of Monty," Eisenhower said, "he's the only alternative we have for this operation. It would be a serious mistake to think otherwise. This thing is far from decided, but I know damned well we're winning. The people who thought Monty ought to be making the big breakthrough simply didn't know the whole story. What he accomplished by holding so many German tanks at Caen—"

"You can give that a rest, Ike. I know you're spouting what you have to spout. I've never faulted you for staying on the fence. You've busted your blooming arse to keep politics out of your headquarters, and every damned one of your senior people love you for it. You won't come out and say what you really think about any of these generals, will you? You won't even say what you think about me. You think I'm a bloody pest, sticking my nose in where it doesn't belong. Yes, I'm a pest. I *like* to be a pest. I like people to shut the hell up when I walk into a room. I like raising the blood pressure of stodgy old farts, causing them to rise up off their soft cushions just a bit. No one should be *comfortable* in a war, Ike. No one. Not you, not me, and not Monty. I know you have a bit of a temper, heard about the dressing-downs you've given some of the misfits. Has to be done, of course, from time to time. But you're not prone to spout off just because someone's stuck a thorn in your arse. That's not you at all, is it? Can't say I've ever seen you really bitch out loud about Monty or anyone else."

"Opinions aren't what this job is about."

"Oh, very noble of you, Ike, but you're wrong. Every damned day starts with an *opinion* about what's going to happen and what your next move should be. You're right, this thing is far from decided, but in my *opinion,* we need more bite from the bulldog. We're getting too much out of the other end. I'm tired of cleaning it off my shoes." Churchill paused, seeming to enjoy his choice of words. "All I'll say to you is this. General Marshall sent you here with the absolute authority to transfer or remove from this theater any American who doesn't measure up. I'm telling you that if you feel there is any *British* soldier in your command who fails those standards, you report your dissatisfaction to me or to General Brooke, *no matter his rank.* You understand me?"

"I appreciate your confidence, but I don't see any sort of report forthcoming."

Churchill stuffed the cigar into the corner of his mouth, put his hands on his hips, and stared at him for a long moment. "You had any V-1s come down in your backyard?"

Eisenhower was surprised at the question. "Yes, a few. Broke a window at SHAEF, rattled us a few times."

"You're bombing hell out of the launching sites, right?"

"When we find them. It will cause more problems with the French, since the enemy has placed most of the launch sites in civilian zones. There are surely French casualties from our raids."

"I'm not concerned right now with French casualties. There have been more than two thousand civilian deaths around London. Did you know that?"

"Yes."

"*Time,* Ike. As much as anything else, the enemy here is *time.* Every day, more graves are filled. Every day, another family suffers a disaster. I don't know how many more disasters we can take. If you've got the right people in place to do the job, fine. Do the job. But do it soon. You get that?"

Eisenhower had heard those concerns before. *How do I tell him to have patience?* Every senior British general carried the burden that the British had given all they had to this fight. In Normandy, the Americans now outnumbered them by three to one, and every day, that disparity was growing. Eisenhower finished the cognac and let the burn drift downward.

"Very soon, General Bradley will launch a major assault against the enemy in his sector. I cannot give you any more details than that, because the plans are not finalized. Monty supports the idea, because he knows that we—that Bradley is in the best position to make that attack. What else can I say?"

Churchill moved to his bed, sat, refilled his glass from a fat black bottle. He put the cigar on the edge of the small table and downed the entire glass in one short gulp, the cigar quickly back in his mouth.

"You've said all you can. Except one thing. If Bradley breaks a hole in Rommel's lines, how will you exploit that?"

It was an odd question, and Eisenhower felt caution again. *Why would he ask?*

"We'll exploit it any way we can. Drive as much armor through the gap as we can, follow it with infantry, make every effort to widen the hole. The enemy will either retreat or we will work to cut him off."

Churchill rolled the cigar with one hand, looked at it, a shortening stub, jabbed it down into an ashtray, and said, "Bradley's a good man."

"One of the best, I think."

"See? That's one of those pesky *opinions,* Ike. All I'm telling you is, just get the job done."

All across the base of the Cotentin Peninsula, Bradley's army was continuing to grow, fresh troops landing on the beaches, a total of fourteen divisions coming into line. The plan, now labeled Operation Cobra, was aimed at punching around and through the French town of Saint-Lô, a key intersection that would allow American forces to drive out of the confines of the bocage. As Bradley's plan evolved, Montgomery offered a plan of his own, Operation Goodwood, that would send British troops around Caen on their own surge southward, pushing well past the city into precious open country that would allow British tanks to maneuver more freely. The plan Montgomery proposed was enthusiastically supported by Eisenhower and Bradley, both men realizing that a breakthrough on the British front could force the Germans to make a general withdrawal. If the Germans chose instead to obey Hitler's orders and hold their ground, it was possible that Rommel's entire Seventh Army could be swallowed up and destroyed.

As both plans came into focus, there was one more ingredient to the Allied effort that had yet to make its appearance on the battlefront. On July 6, George Patton made a noisy arrival into France at an airstrip near Omaha Beach, to begin preliminary work on organizing his command, the new Third Army. That command wouldn't become official until August 1, but Patton had suffered through his own inactivity long enough. He did not yet have an army in the field, but when the time finally came he would be ready from day one. While the Allies prepared their next best effort to break through the Germans who were holding them in place, Patton seethed at what he saw to be the woeful inefficiency of those men who were supposed to be his superiors. But, until Bradley could push open some sort of doorway through the enemy's stranglehold on the bocage country, there was nothing for Patton to do but wait.

In England, Patton's phantom command, the First Army Group, was still in place, and the extraordinary deception that had so baffled the Germans was still providing fodder for German intelligence. In the event that anyone noticed Patton's sudden absence from England, stories were planted throughout the spy networks, hints that Patton had been dismissed, that his clumsy indiscretions had finally overwhelmed Eisenhower's patience. Through every clandestine channel controlled by British intelligence, word was passed not so discreetly that Patton had been replaced by Lieutenant General Lesley McNair. McNair was one of the American army's most respected commanders and had run the entire system of training and organization of all army ground forces in the States. To the receptive ears of German intelligence, there was perfect logic for a man as capable as McNair to replace a loose cannon as seemingly unreliable as George Patton. To Eisenhower's astonishment, reports continued to filter through Ultra intercepts that the Germans had bought the ruse and still believed the fictitious First Army Group was a force to be feared. Even more gratifying were reports that the German High Command was vacillating again toward a belief that there could still be a second Allied invasion. Despite all visible signs to Rommel's front, despite the mammoth buildup of Allied divisions that poured across the Normandy beaches, von Kluge and Rommel had been ordered to maintain a sizable force of Rommel's Fifteenth Army at Calais, its sole purpose to confront another massive invasion.

SHAEF FORWARD COMMAND POST, PORTSMOUTH
JULY 11, 1944

Tedder read the report, one hand holding his pipe, the tent filling with the sweet fragrance of something Eisenhower thought to be cherries. Eisenhower lay back on the cot. "Patton's already driving me batty. He's scared to death the war will end before he gets his shot at sticking a knife in someone's belly."

Tedder chuckled. "Hitler's, I presume."

"George would say so. Did say so, actually, a while back. Algeria, I think. He's caused his share of headaches since then. Damn shame. But if he hadn't, he might be in Bradley's shoes, and I don't want to think about that. He would have probably knocked Monty's teeth out by now. I hate that cowboy crap."

"Let's assume, dear boy, they would have fought a duel instead. Far more civilized."

Tedder returned to his reading, the pipe rolling out more of the sweet smoke.

"Leigh-Mallory's mad as a hornet, you know," Eisenhower said. "Says the bomber problem at Caen was all Monty's fault."

"Oh, for God's sake, Ike. Leigh-Mallory has a problem with every sunrise. He bitches because no one will give his air chaps a job to do; then, when he's needed, he bitches because he wasn't given any time for preparation. The bombers aren't his responsibility anyway. That's Harris's problem. Those air boys are every bit as much nuisance as your man Patton."

Eisenhower smiled. "You should know. You're one of them."

Tedder ignored the joke. "I knew Monty was asking for trouble. We can't expect the heavy bomber people to rush into action every time a ground commander shouts out for air support. I've heard talk it was the prime minister who pressed Harris to give Monty the bombers he wanted. Now Harris's boys are catching bloody hell for their inaccuracy. Can't have that sort of thing, Ike. Can't have the civilian government trying to tell us what we should be doing out here."

"You have a plan to stop Churchill?"

Tedder sucked on the pipe. "Can't say one's occurred to me."

"The best way to keep Churchill's nose out of things is to win. He's just doing what the rest of the civilians and politicians wish they could do; he's putting in his two cents. The newspapers in the States are raising more hell than you can imagine. When word went out that we made it ashore on those beaches, the whole damned country thought, Well, that's it, we've won. I've seen a hundred columns written by dyspeptic know-it-alls who think we're dragging our feet on purpose. Someone suggested this is a conspiracy, that we're taking our time on purpose, so Hitler will have a chance to bleed the Russians first. Where the hell do these people come up with this stuff?"

Tedder held the pipe in his hand now. "At least FDR is on your side. His point of view carries a lot of punch in your papers."

Eisenhower thought a moment. "The president is in pretty bad shape, Arthur. It's being kept under wraps, but he's not doing well at all. Marshall won't say much about it, but you can bet everyone at the War Department is watching that one pretty closely." He sat up, slapping his hands on his thighs. "Damn it all, anyway! I don't want to talk about politics. I've got enough gum up my shorts just worrying about Monty. I had to dance a jig around Churchill, wouldn't dare let him know how pissed off I am."

"Churchill knows jigs when he sees them, Ike. You can bet he knows what's going on. Churchill feels just like I do, and that's not something I can say often enough. Monty doesn't attach enough importance to *time*. Summer isn't going to last forever, and when autumn hits, the weather's likely to be worse than it's already been. Every British commander remembers Flanders; no one wants to march through two feet of mud. It didn't work thirty years ago, and it won't work now. We have to get across the Seine, and if Monty can't be convinced of that, you need to find someone who can."

Eisenhower put a hand on his jaw, rubbed a day's growth of beard, looked at Tedder's pipe.

"That thing stinks, you know. Can't you come up with something a little more like tobacco?"

Tedder nodded, tapped the pipe into an ashtray. "Gift from Rosalinde. Carry it around even now, trying to use it up. Can't just toss it in the bin, you know."

Eisenhower was suddenly embarrassed, annoyed with himself. Tedder's wife had been killed in an air crash in Egypt a year before, a horrifying event Tedder had actually witnessed. It had been one more tragedy for a man who had already lost a son to the war.

"Very sorry, Arthur."

"Thank you, but no matter. It is pretty ghastly stuff. I'll leave the pouch behind next time."

Eisenhower still felt awkward.

Tedder seemed to sense it and said, "Bradley's operation could be the tonic everyone needs. Monty's cheering him on like he's America's last great hero. He knows that if Bradley breaks through, the enemy in front of Monty will probably dissolve away. Not sure I agree with that. Rommel's too smart to let himself get surrounded."

"I wish I knew what Rommel was thinking. We know Hitler keeps telling everyone to hold every inch of ground. If Rommel had his way, they'd already be back behind the Seine, with enough armor in place to keep us here for years. He probably wishes Hitler would drop those damned V-1s on our troops instead of London shopkeepers."

"I respect Rommel as much as you do, Ike. No matter what Ultra tells us, there's a lot more going on than we're hearing about. If Hitler has some new secret weapon, Rommel's job might be just to hold us in place as long as he can. He's done a pretty good job of that so far."

Eisenhower shook his head. "No, Rommel's job is to win. He hasn't been able to do that, and every day we're stronger. You're right, there has to be more going on than we'll ever know about. But I'm a lot more worried about our operations right here. I'm pushing Brad as hard as I'm pushing Monty, and Patton's bouncing off the walls of his HQ, wondering how hard he can push *me*. The newspapers think the war should have ended yesterday, and Churchill wants it to end tomorrow. What about you? What can I do to make *you* happy?"

Tedder slipped the pipe into his shirt pocket and smiled. "Right now, you can take a nap. Bradley and Monty have every wheel in motion. Churchill is home. And Rommel . . . I'm guessing Rommel has problems enough of his own."

38. ROMMEL

Rommel waited patiently while von Kluge read his letter. To one side, Speidel watched, seeming far more nervous than Rommel himself. Von Kluge stopped reading, glanced at Speidel, and said, "You approve of this, of course."

Speidel stiffened at the question. "Yes, Field Marshal. Most emphatically."

"Your loyalty to Marshal Rommel is a virtue. The Führer would agree with that, whether or not he agrees with . . . *this*."

Von Kluge continued to read, and the words echoed through Rommel's mind, words he had written in the frustrating urgency of trying yet again to convince Hitler that the war was not the Führer's private board game.

> The situation in Normandy is growing worse every day and is now approaching a grave crisis. . . . Our casualties are so high that the fighting power of our divisions is rapidly diminishing.

Von Kluge looked up from the paper, eyes wide. "Are these numbers truly accurate? We have suffered ninety-seven thousand casualties, and the replacements—"

"The replacements total ten thousand, as of today, and many of those have either not yet reached the front or are not fit for combat. We have lost at least two hundred twenty-five tanks, and for those I have seen seventeen replacements."

"My God."

Von Kluge returned to the paper, his frown deepening.

The newly arrived infantry . . . are in no state to make a lengthy stand against major enemy attacks. . . . Supply conditions are so bad that only the barest essentials can be brought to the front. These conditions are unlikely to improve, as enemy action is steadily reducing the transport capacity available. . . .

On the enemy's side, fresh forces and great quantities of war matériel are flowing into his front every day. His supplies are undisturbed by our air force. In these circumstances we must expect that in the foreseeable future the enemy will succeed in breaking through our thin front . . . and thrusting deep into France. The unequal struggle is approaching its end. It is urgently necessary for the proper conclusion to be drawn from this situation.

Von Kluge lowered the paper. "What would you have me do?"

"Endorse my signature and allow me to send this to Hitler. Jodl and Keitel will ignore anything that comes only from me, but they cannot ignore you."

Von Kluge began his routine; the slow pace, stared at the floor. "It could be the end for both of us."

Rommel felt himself rising in the chair. "The end is already here! There is no exaggeration in that letter, none of what those idiots refer to as my mindless defeatism! Those numbers are real, the description of conditions here is accurate! My predictions for the outcome of this absurd drama are entirely correct!"

Von Kluge stopped, looked at the letter again. "I know that. Calm yourself."

Rommel lowered himself into the chair again, sagged, and watched as von Kluge placed the letter on the desk. Von Kluge stepped back, seeming to weigh the obvious, and Speidel moved forward silently, already prepared with a pen.

Rommel nodded toward him, and Speidel said, "If you require a pen, sir."

Von Kluge did not look at him, took the pen, bent close to the letter, scratched quickly. Rommel felt a brief burst of energy, a small glimmer of gratefulness. The man has some spine, he thought. Von Kluge picked up the letter and said to Speidel, "You will courier this to the Führer today. He should see both signatures."

"Yes, sir."

Rommel nodded again to Speidel, who took the letter and made a quick silent exit. Von Kluge moved to a chair. He did not sit but leaned one arm down on the back, supporting himself.

"Thank you," Rommel said.

"It should not be like this. It should *never* have been like this. You should have been given the tools."

"Were we ever given the tools? Did you have everything you required at Moscow?"

Von Kluge shook his head. "I will not discuss the past. Our duty now is to preserve this army and strike the enemy where it will do him the most harm."

"He will strike us first. I am motoring out to see General Eberbach, and I will confer as well with General Dietrich. The armor is strong at Caen, and that must still be our priority."

Von Kluge looked toward one wall, draped with a map. "You still believe we should defend the city, try to regain what they have taken from us?"

"I am not concerned with buildings. The city is lost, but the infantry has been pulling back slowly, and we are hurting the British with every step. That is more valuable than how many street corners we control. We still hold the south bank of the river, and we must prevent Montgomery from cutting through our position there and driving farther inland. I must be certain that Eberbach knows that."

Von Kluge nodded, looked again at Rommel. "He should know what he has to do. I knew him well in Russia. Fine officer."

Rommel shrugged. "He was ordered to replace Geyr. I had nothing to say about that. The High Command still does not believe I am capable of exercising command over the panzer group. If you say he is a good man, I shall offer him the chance to prove it. He must keep Montgomery from breaking through."

"He will. If he has the tools."

"He has Dietrich and he has Meyer."

Von Kluge pulled his jacket tight, a signal he was preparing to leave.

Rommel saw age in the man's face: Sixty, I guess, he thought. Looks older today.

Von Kluge looked at Rommel with tired blue eyes. "He also has you."

Rommel was suddenly uncomfortable, avoided the compliment, heard weakness in von Kluge's words. He glanced at the papers on his desk. "Our best hope is that the Americans delay. If we are fortunate, they do not know our precise weaknesses there, the thinness of our lines. That entire front is difficult ground, and it is our best advantage. But they are coming as well. It is only a matter of time."

Von Kluge seemed preoccupied and nodded slowly. "I will travel up that way as quickly as I can, speak to Hausser. Perhaps you should do the same."

"My first priority is Eberbach, the armor at Caen."

Von Kluge moved absently toward the door, his mind somewhere else. He gathered himself and pulled again on the jacket, finding control, the good show for the staff outside. He looked back at Rommel, a silent stare, then said, "Go to Eberbach. Drive some steel into him. Into all of them. It is . . . all we can do."

NEAR LIVAROT, SOUTHEAST OF CAEN
JULY 17, 1944

The defenses near the river were strong, the panzer commanders digging in south and east of Caen for the inevitable push they knew Montgomery was preparing. The generals had been upbeat, confident; new reports gathered from the claims of captured soldiers suggested that the British and Canadians who faced them were rapidly losing their will to fight. Rommel paid little attention to that kind of optimism. He had heard too much talk from enemy prisoners before, men whose war had ended with their hands in the air. It was common for prisoners on both sides to speak of the collapse of morale in their army, as though it justified their own failure to fight to the death. But Rommel knew too much of Montgomery, knew the Allied commanders were pushing their men through the streets of Caen, massing them close on the north side of the Orne River. They had one intention, and it had nothing to do with surrender.

Rommel rode in a large open-topped Mercedes, the glass windscreens fully raised around him as protection from the dust of the primitive roads. Captain Lang was in his usual perch in the front seat, with Sergeant Daniel at the wheel. There were two other aides as well, one a fierce-looking corporal named Holke, whose sole duty was to keep watch on the skies behind them for any sign of enemy aircraft. The car bounced and tossed from the miserable necessity of keeping to the farm lanes and side roads. Rommel had a firm grip on the door beside him, glancing out through the glass at thick patches of trees and the occasional encampment, artillery supply depots mostly bare of anything but empty crates and guns in need of repair.

He had not yet received any response to his letter to the Führer. The question rolled through his mind. Had the letter produced a flurry of activity around a furious Hitler, his staff officers making the hurried effort to choose a successor for Rommel's command? They could remove von Kluge as well, he thought. But surely Hitler would see that as utter foolishness. The man was chosen to replace von Rundstedt because he was a good man for the job. Hitler knows von Kluge is capable and effective and loyal. If they replace him, it will be pure stupidity, the manic scampering of so many blind mice. And then what? Rommel knew how so many of these decisions were made. Each of Hitler's armchair generals would have his own favorite. Jodl will suggest someone, offer Hitler that same moronic seriousness, his oh-so-very-earnest advice that *this* new man will not only do the job, he will not complain, not like the misfit Rommel. Who would that be? Hausser, perhaps. Papa Hausser. He's older than von Kluge, but he might be the best man for the job. I wonder if Dollmann would have been considered, one more of Hitler's *good choices.*

Rommel had named the aging veteran Paul Hausser to replace Friedrich Dollmann at the head of Rommel's Seventh Army. Dollmann had been elderly as well, in his mid-sixties, a tall, elegant man who had done as much as anyone could to prevent the enemy's success on the Normandy beaches. As the Allies increased their pressure and drove inland, those failures had taken a toll on Dollmann that Rommel did not expect. Word had come that the old man had died after suffering a heart attack, but Dollmann's staff officers had finally revealed the truth: General Friedrich Dollmann had committed suicide. It was an unnerving piece of news and few would speak of it, even now. What good is loyalty if you don't have the stomach for a hard fight? Suicide is just another form of desertion.

Rommel pushed the thoughts away and focused on von Kluge, still grateful for von Kluge's endorsement of his letter to Hitler. He came here expecting glory, Rommel thought, the grand reward for his good service.

Now he has put his neck on the chopping block alongside mine. I should not forget that. Hitler certainly won't.

The car turned down a narrow lane, a white gravel road so common in the farm country. Rommel glanced at his watch: After four, he thought. We should reach La Roche-Guyon by dark. I need to speak to Speidel about the artillery—

"Aircraft! Behind us!" The voice was Holke's.

Lang did not hesitate, shouting to Sergeant Daniel, "Quickly! Those trees up ahead! Turn in behind them!"

The car surged forward. Rommel twisted in his seat, saw two planes coming toward them, fast and low over the distant trees. He felt cold in his chest, began to duck, but there was no time; his eyes were frozen on the nearer plane, the screaming roar of the engine, bursts of smoke from the wings. Streaks of fire hit the rear of the car with punching force: a fiery explosion. Rommel tried to lean over but the glass shattered beside him, a blast that blew hard into his face and neck. The car swerved, and Rommel tried to hold tight, grabbed at the man beside him, but the pain was ripping through his head, and he felt wetness in his eyes, blindness, heard the roar of the planes swirling above him, the echoing shouts of his men. The car swerved, a sudden jolt, rolling on its side, and Rommel was falling, landing hard on his face and arm. He gasped into dirt, tried to cough, but there was no air, no sight, and now the sounds were gone, darkness, his brain carrying him to some silent place very far away.

Captain Lang and Corporal Holke escaped from the wreckage and kept Rommel and Sergeant Daniel in hiding until another staff car rolled past. Still unconscious, the two men were carried to the village of Livarot, but there was no facility, no adequate place for the wounds to be treated. Desperate, German officers transported them to a larger town nearby, Bernay, where the Germans had a field hospital. The officers who carried them expected the worst, reacting with sickness and tears to the bloody wounds to Rommel's head, a cracked skull and shattered cheekbone, wounds every man thought to be mortal. Though Rommel remained unconscious, the doctors at the field hospital were able to stabilize him. But their other patient was in far worse condition. Within an hour, Sergeant Daniel was dead.

Word was quickly sent to the senior commanders and to La Roche-

Guyon, where Hans Speidel received the message with a soft cry of hopelessness.

*At the time we most needed him . . . we were deprived of our pillar of
strength.*

The German commanders in the field could only keep to their posts,
every man knowing that the Allies were coming again, their next attempt
to smash an opening in the German lines. Without adequate strength and
resources to launch an attack of their own, the Germans could only wait.
But closer to Hitler, one man would not wait.

H is name was Klaus Philip Schenk, Count von Stauffenberg. Like
Rommel, he came from the south of Germany and did not hold
the pedigree of those elite military officers from Prussia. But Colonel von
Stauffenberg had a different kind of prestige, a long family lineage of noble
service to Germany and an education far beyond that of most military officers. He carried knowledge and an air of culture and artistry that far out-
shone his own Führer, so much so that Hitler never completely trusted the
man and was always uncomfortable in his presence.

As German disillusionment with Hitler grew, it was mostly the intel-
lectuals, the men of breeding with a strong link to German aristocracy,
who had begun conspiring to remove him from power. But these men were
not always soldiers, were not schooled in the art of killing, and few of them
had direct access to Hitler. Von Stauffenberg, badly wounded in an air attack in North Africa, had lost an eye and had one arm badly crippled.
Hitler admired men who seemed willing to absorb such wounds in service
to their country, and so, despite his distrust of von Stauffenberg's position
in the German intelligentsia, he had made the count something of a confidant.

As Hitler's great dreams were replaced by catastrophic military failures,
the conspiracy against him grew and congealed, the plots unfolding. But
most were clumsy insipid attempts that usually went unnoticed by anyone,
including Hitler himself. These attempts usually involved bombs, but
there were bad fuses and mistakes of timing. The Führer seemed to be a
charmed man, with a sorcerer's knack for foiling his enemies.

Hitler was far from unaware of the potential for threats to his life. On
most occasions when crowds were present, he wore a bulletproof vest, and
his hand-picked bodyguards were ruthlessly efficient, highly trained elite

marksmen. No matter the passion of those who wanted Hitler dead, no one believed that any man could simply walk up to Hitler and shoot him.

Of all the men who plotted against him, none were able to stand beside Hitler with as much predictable regularity as von Stauffenberg. And so von Stauffenberg had accepted his role as the triggerman. But his luck had been no better than any other would-be assassin. On three prior occasions, careful planning had failed to produce results. All involved poorly constructed bombs and errors in timing, and all seemed to inflate Hitler's freakish aura of invincibility. But von Stauffenberg would not be swayed. On July 20, a meeting was scheduled at Hitler's field headquarters, the Wolf's Lair, one more discussion about maps and planning, where Hitler's generals would offer reports as inoffensive to the Führer's temper as possible. Von Stauffenberg was invited to attend. In his briefcase, he carried yet another bomb.

The meeting took place in a small building, aboveground, separate from the heavy stone bunkers that would usually protect Hitler. It was a miserable surprise for von Stauffenberg, who had expected the meeting to be belowground, inside concrete, where any blast contained in a tight space would certainly kill everyone in proximity. But the conspiracy was in place, the unstoppable commitment that this time there would be no failure. With the bomb by his side, von Stauffenberg entered the meeting.

There were twenty-five people in the airy space, gathered around a heavy wood table. Von Stauffenberg maintained as much composure as he could muster and set the briefcase down on the floor, a few feet from where Hitler stood. Then, feigning a sudden need to answer a call from nature, he left the room.

The blast destroyed the structure, shattering windows and walls and punching the roof skyward. The heavy wood table was tossed upright, collapsing to one side and falling on top of Hitler himself. Four men died in the explosion, and every other man in the room was wounded. After the explosion, von Stauffenberg left Wolf's Lair in a waiting car. His objective was the nearby airport, where a plane waited to ferry him to Berlin. There, the word would go out quickly to the other conspirators, expanding in a spiderweb of messages and setting in motion an elaborate plan to seize control of the German government and military in the certain chaos that would result from Hitler's violent death, before the Gestapo or anyone else could fill the vacuum. Across Germany and beyond, the calls were expected by anxious men who sat nervously in offices and homes from Berlin

to Paris to La Roche-Guyon. The conspirators hoped that Hitler's death
would begin an elaborate chain of events aimed at reaching out toward the
Allies, who were already battering the German defenses in Normandy.
There was a desperate hope that, with the death of Hitler, the war could be
brought to a rapid close.

But Hitler did not die.

The bomb had detonated beside a thick wooden table leg, which had
blocked Hitler from the major force of the blast. Though pinned beneath
the table, his worst injury had come from the sound of the blast itself. He
suffered a punctured eardrum.

Believing that the plan had succeeded, von Stauffenberg made his way
to Berlin, but within hours, word rang out from Wolf's Lair and the
Gestapo reacted immediately. Before anyone could make any real attempt
to seize power in Berlin, the entire conspiracy collapsed. Less than a day
later, von Stauffenberg and many others had been arrested and were
quickly executed.

Though Hans Speidel had known of the July 20 plot, he had never informed Rommel of its specific details. As it unraveled and the conspirators
were gathered up by relentless Gestapo investigators, Rommel remained
completely unaware. He had yet to regain consciousness from his wounds.

Over time, Hitler's revenge brought more than seven thousand people
into Gestapo custody, anyone who might have had the faintest link to the
conspiracy. More than two thousand were executed.

Speidel would not be arrested until September.

39. ADAMS

The beer was warm, but no one complained. Adams leaned back in his chair against a knotty wooden wall, focused on a woman on the far side of the room. She had tried to avoid his stare, but then he had caught a stare from her as well, brief, discreet, just a hint of warmth in her dark eyes.

The room was noisy, chatter flowing mostly from the Americans, their attention directed squarely at the women who were sprinkled among them. Adams had tried to stay out of that kind of combat, but the woman he watched now was not speaking to anyone. She seemed uncomfortable, out of place, and his mind went to work, a swirling fantasy fueled by the dark beer.

I bet she works in Leicester, he thought, in someone's office, stodgy and stinking of cigar smoke. Do the Brits smoke cigars? Well, sure. Churchill, you moron. She hates her boss, waits desperately for the weekends, when she can take the train down here, a getaway, maybe meet some of her friends. She doesn't come here by herself. She's no chippy, no bar girl, so she has to get talked into it by her friends. She's curious as hell, wondering what Americans are really like, all these veterans, paratroopers, different from the infantry. Hell, anybody can be infantry, but these men are different: tough bastards, floppy pants and tall boots. And me, over here against the wall, toughest in the bunch, but kind, smart. Yep, brains would matter. She wants brains. She's hoping for a quieter place than this, to have a conversation with a man who can explain this war, who can tell her stories without shocking her, who doesn't need to impress the hell out of her with all the glory.

The woman stood suddenly, her attention drawn toward the door, and his mental narrative jerked to a halt. She glanced at Adams, and then another man came in, American: broad shoulders, a loud voice. She waved with a smile, no coyness, nothing discreet about her reaction to this man, who now engulfed her with his arms. Adams felt his fantasy blasted away, raised up in his chair, fought to see them through the crowd. It was an officer, someone he didn't know. Someone else.

Well, hell.

"Hey, Sarge! I just saw Captain Scofield outside. Said he'd like to talk to you later. I wasn't sure you were still in here."

Adams glanced at the voice, Nusbaum, oblivious to the trauma that had unfolded in Adams's mind.

"He still outside?"

"I don't know, Sarge. I'm in here."

Beside the corporal, Unger stood smiling, seemed to sway, his eyes watery.

"How many beers you had, kid?"

"Beers . . . I hate beer. They told me about this malt stuff. Highland brew, Scotty something. Wow, Sarge, it kicks you in the head, burns every inch of you on the way down. . . . " He seemed to drift away for a second, then focused again, a broad smile. "I like it. It's good stuff."

"Scotch, you idiot. It's called Scotch. Watch yourself. You carrying any dough on you, it's liable to disappear."

"He'll be okay," Nusbaum said. "We're heading back to the camp." He was weaving slightly himself.

Adams swallowed the last gulp of his beer. "I'm leaving too. Had enough fun for one day. Guess I gotta find the captain."

He stood, a brief wave of dizziness, looked again for the girl, but there was only the crowd, noisier still, someone offering a drunken toast, drowned out by the men he was toasting. Adams felt the room spinning slowly, a hard belch rising up inside him.

"I want some more of that Scotch stuff," Unger said.

Adams pointed toward the door. "Let's get him the hell out of here. He'll pay for this tomorrow morning as it is."

They eased through the crowd, perfume and smoke washing over them, the door opening, more men coming in, smiles and anticipation. Adams pushed past unfamiliar faces, was outside now, the sun low, heard Nusbaum behind him.

"Damn, it's late. This day's already done for."

Unger stumbled, the two men now holding the boy upright between them.

"He cleans up his own damned puke," Nusbaum said.

"I promise you that. We oughta leave him in the alley over there."

"Can't do that, Sarge. Somebody'd roll him, for sure."

"I know. I wouldn't do that to the kid. Let's just go back to base." Adams adjusted his grip beneath Unger's arm.

"I guess this means he's a man now," Nusbaum said.

"No. It just means he's as stupid as the rest of us."

H e lay still, his brain working in the darkness, could not escape it. It had been this way every night, sleep broken by the sudden jolt of awareness. Adams knew to expect some kind of nightmares, something the doctors called shell shock, and he had waited for it. Some of the men were having problems during the night. The number of sick calls was increasing, no officer begrudging any man's need to see a doctor, seeking something to help him sleep. But there was nothing the doctors could do about nightmares. Adams had heard some of the others at night: a sudden shout, jarring the entire barracks awake, cursing and taunts, and then silence or a soft apology from the man who had suffered the dream. But Adams had gone through none of it, no nightmares at all, the memories of France, of hedgerows and drowning troopers, held away by a great gray wall. He forced himself to think of the dead, Marley and Buford and Pullman, the lieutenant who didn't have the brains to keep low in sniper country. But those details were clean and clinical now, no screams, no blood, none of the images that seemed to haunt the men around him. The sleeplessness would make him angry, mostly at himself, questions about his own sanity, all those things that psychiatrists were supposed to hear about. But no man would ask to see a shrink unless he was faking something. Adams stared up, thought, No, the crazy ones don't know they're crazy. Someone else has to figure it out for them. So what the hell is wrong with *you*?

He rolled over on one side, heard snoring, always snoring, a chorus of soft rhythms, the occasional snort and cough, curses. There would be cigarette smoke too, a soft glow down the way, someone else not sleeping, afraid of the nightmares or—like me, he thought. Maybe they're just . . . *bored.*

G avin was waiting for him, the tall thin man even thinner now. They were all thinner, but Adams was surprised to see how gaunt Gavin was, a reminder that in France even generals ate K rations. Gavin was shuffling through papers and glanced up, a brief smile.

"About time you showed up. You operating on civilian time now, Sergeant?"

"No, sir. Sorry. I didn't get the order until a half hour ago." Shut up, he thought. Gavin doesn't need excuses.

Gavin read from a paper, set it aside, picked up another, then reached behind him—one flow of motion—grabbed a coffeepot, and set it down on a flat piece of cork on the desk in front of him.

"If you root through that pile of reports over there, you'll find a cup. Probably dirty, but it'll be a general's germs."

Adams saw the cup, half hidden by a stack of blue paper, retrieved it. He filled it from Gavin's pot, and Gavin returned the pot to the hot plate behind him, still reading the papers. Adams smelled the coffee, his eyes instantly watering.

Gavin didn't look up. "I wouldn't drink too much of it. Some things never change."

"Yes, sir."

The general tossed a paper onto a growing pile to one side and sat back. "Your corporal, Nusbaum, got his third stripe today. He'll head a squad under the new lieutenant, Lewiston. You meet him?"

"No, sir."

"Brand-new, right out of officer school. Introduced himself to me like he was General MacArthur. Wish he'd done that to Ridgway, love to have seen that: *Lieutenant Lewiston, killed in action, burnt to a crisp by General Ridgway's wrath.* Well, he'd get a Purple Heart, anyway. Damn replacements. They're supposed to be training these guys before they get here, qualify them to jump. Someone up the ladder's falling down on that one. The damn repple depple is swarming with these guys, ready to be war heroes. Half of them are volunteering for the airborne. Pain in the ass, trying to sort through them all."

Adams had already met too many replacements, men who came through the Replacement Depot, or repple depple. They were the army's orphans, men who were drafted and had been assigned to no particular unit in the States. It was the necessity of war, a means of plugging gaps in the ranks of the frontline units. It made perfect sense to Adams. If a man had no idea where the army was going to put him, why not volunteer for the most elite unit there was? Let someone else worry about whether he could cut it or not.

Gavin drank his coffee, seeming immune to the taste; Adams glanced at his own cup, fighting the need to drink.

"Scofield's getting his oak leaves," Gavin said. "He'll be a major by this weekend. Still command the company, though. I tried to get him booted up to battalion commander, but Ridgway had his own people in mind. I've got the list right here, all the promotions. Your name's not on it."

"That's all right, sir. I wasn't expecting—"

"Your name's not on it because I wanted to talk to you first. I ran this by Scofield, but he thought it ought to come straight from me. One thing the army doesn't usually give anybody is options. But I have a couple for you."

Adams felt a stirring inside, saw Gavin reach for another piece of paper.

"I've written a letter about you to General Ridgway, and he has endorsed my recommendation. But nothing's final." He stopped, looked up at Adams. "You know how damned rare this is?"

"No, sir. I'm not sure what you mean, sir."

Gavin smiled again. "You have a *choice*. That's what's so damned rare. I've put in for you to receive a commission: second lieutenant, effective immediately. But there's a catch, and that's why you have a choice. If you accept your commission, you will return to the States: Fort Benning, actually. As I said, there are a wad of new men volunteering to jump, and we need a whole load of new instructors. Those instructors need the best training they can get, and in my mind you're the man to train them. In addition, you'll be designated as the Five-oh-five's senior jumpmaster. As such, you will determine who receives jumpmaster training and who makes the grade."

Adams digested the words. Fort Benning, one word rising up: Georgia.

"Well?"

Adams still didn't respond, felt a cold gloom flooding his brain. Gavin seemed unusually patient, and after a long moment Adams said, "Is that my . . . choice, sir?"

"I knew you'd ask that. That's *one* choice. The other is a bit less glamorous. The paperwork can be completed on this one pretty quickly. You will be promoted to first sergeant and return to your assigned company. You will remain under the command of Major Scofield and God knows which lieutenant. They're falling out of the sky around here every day. If you're lucky, you'll get a West Pointer." Gavin paused. "There's a catch to this one too. We're beginning a new training regimen for the entire division. No details yet, but there are expectations that the Eighty-second isn't ready for the dustbin just yet. In other words, you'll resume your place as the company's senior jumpmaster and qualify as many new men as you can."

"And I won't be going to Benning, sir."

Gavin shook his head. "No. You'll be staying here. You'll still be mine. And when we get our next assignment, you'll still be carrying that damned Thompson. That's what you're going to do, isn't it? You dumb son of a bitch."

"It's not a hard choice, sir."

"No, it's not. I'd do the same thing."

MARKET HARBOROUGH, NEAR LEICESTER
JUNE 24, 1944

The day had been long and muddy, and every new man in the company was learning to hate him. Even the veterans had begun the new round of physical training, and those who had slogged their way through the French bocage were discovering that they weren't in nearly as good shape as they thought they were. Already, Adams had heard the groans, a five-mile jaunt through the English countryside that had given them blisters and sore ankles, cramped legs, and gasping exhaustion. And it was only the first day.

He still had not met his new lieutenant, word filtering down that too many officers were not making the grade, that the qualification training had washed out a sizable percentage of the young lieutenants who had thought themselves capable of bringing down Hitler all by themselves. The replacements in the ranks were annoying enough, and Nusbaum had slipped easily into the role that Adams had once enjoyed, the sergeant with no tolerance. As Nusbaum pushed his men through their paces, the new men were hating him too, something Nusbaum actually seemed to enjoy. Adams had laughed at that, the first real laugh he had experienced in England, Nusbaum mimicking so many of the curses and blistering insults that Adams had long ago laid on *him*.

As daylight faded, the men stumbled back to the barracks, all of them anxious for the signal that the mess hall was open. It was as it had always been before, the men ordered to run everywhere they went, and it was no different now. Adams had already given word that they be allowed ten minutes to nurse sore feet and probe the various wounds from the long jog, a low chorus of misery Adams had heard too many times. He was suffering as well, a pain in his knee, remnants of something from France, flashes of memory he tried not to digest. He fought the need to limp and watched Nusbaum, chiding a new man unmercifully, following him into the barracks. Adams stopped, flexed his knee, and took a long breath: more pain, the stiffness in his ribs always there. He moved toward the barracks thinking of his cot, delicious, his private space at one end, a small piece of luxury for the new first sergeant. I need five minutes, that's all. Just five.

"Hey, Sarge!"

Unger was running toward him from across the parade ground. Adams was not in the mood for anyone's cheerfulness.

"Sarge! Look! Look here!"

Unger had reached him, breathing now in heavy gasps, pointing to his shoulder. He was wearing a corporal's stripes.

"How about that, huh, Sarge? I got a promotion! My mama's gonna be so proud!"

"I know, kid. I put you in for it."

"Wowee! Thanks, Sarge! Thank you!"

Adams couldn't help laughing. Unger made that five-mile run, and he's ready to go out and do it again. He began to move, slow steps, struggling not to limp, the barracks door achingly far away. Unger moved in beside him.

"I gotta ask you something, Sarge. I've been having a lot of trouble getting any sleep. Not sure what to do. I don't feel sick or nothing. I'm just wide awake, for hours, maybe."

Adams stopped, nursed the pain in his knee, saw a dark seriousness in Unger's eyes.

"Sorry I mentioned it, Sarge. You're hurting. We ought to head inside."

"Who says I'm hurting?"

He regretted the anger in his voice, but Unger didn't react to it. "It'll pass, I guess. Not sleeping, I mean. Whole lot better than what those boys in the hospital are going through. Heck of a thing, though. When I was a kid, I always wanted to stay up all night, see what it'd be like. Now, all I want to do is get some sleep. I guess we stayed up too many nights already. Maybe I'm used to it."

"Shut up. You think you're the only one who can't sleep?"

He voice was rising, and he felt helpless, couldn't control the anger now, saw Unger flinch, surprised.

"Sorry, Sarge. . . ."

Adams forced himself to look away. He was still angry, his brain shouting in meaningless fury. Unger seemed to watch him, and Adams looked at him again, saw the darkness, that small flicker in the eyes of this man who had learned to kill.

"How old are you really, kid?"

Unger looked down, seemed to debate the response, then looked up into Adams's eyes, cold and direct. "I'm eighteen, Sarge. Three weeks ago. The day Dexter died."

Adams fought the image: Marley's leg gone, the man's cries, the medic with too much work to do. He thought of Unger too, that same fight, running past Adams with the grenade and taking out the machine-gun nest, the sort of act that earns medals.

"Eighteen. It's a damned good thing."

"Sorry I lied to you, Sarge. I had to—"

"I don't care about that now. And I don't want to hear about Private Marley or any of the rest of it. You got that?"

"Okay, Sarge."

They stood silently, Adams ignoring the pains, a cold hand tightening a grip in his chest. He wanted Unger to go away, push all this from his mind. But the words came, unstoppable.

"I've been having a little trouble too. Sleeping."

Unger studied him, nodded. "Yeah, I know. Seen you a few times, could tell you were awake. What's it mean, Sarge? It's just . . . sleep. I'm tired as heck, feel like I could go to sleep in the chow line. But at night . . . I just lie there."

Adams thought for a moment. "All I know is that I'm so damned sick of lying in that cot and hearing . . . nothing."

Unger nodded again. "Awful darned quiet in that barracks." He paused. "You think they'll send us to France again? I really wanna go back, Sarge. I think I miss it."

Adams absorbed the words, saw the dark in Unger's eyes.

"That's it, kid. You miss it. So do I."

40. EISENHOWER

On July 18, Montgomery finally launched Operation Goodwood, designed to crush the final German lines of resistance around Caen and allow the British tanks to surge south into open ground. The advance had been preceded by another extraordinary effort from British heavy bombers, one more attempt at cooperation with Montgomery's plans. The goal, again, was to obliterate the enemy before the British ground forces would have to confront them. Seven thousand tons of bombs were dropped on German positions, and the bombardiers were far more accurate than before. Once the bombing had ceased, the British ground forces advanced into damage they could plainly tell had been horrific. But it was not horrific enough. Though frontline troops and their heavier weapons were shattered, the German tactic below Caen called for a stronger second line, to contain any immediate breakthrough. The British bombers damaged those positions as well, but large pockets of tanks and artillery were left unscathed. As the British armor advanced, expecting to find a disheartened and defeated enemy, they drove instead straight into batteries of eighty-eight-millimeter antitank guns, the most devastating ground weapon the Germans had.

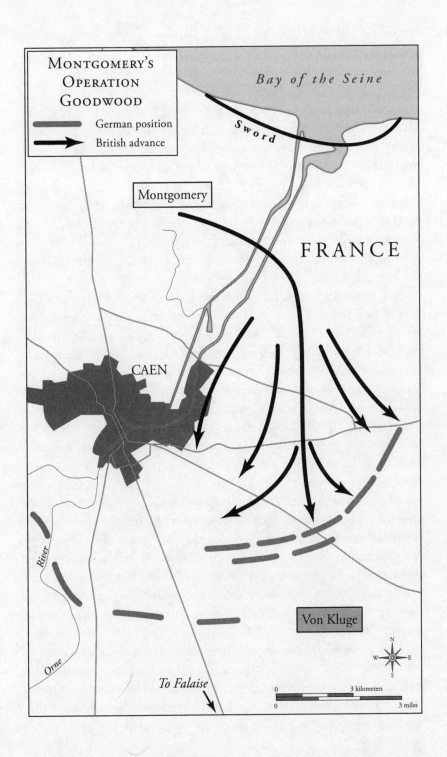

MONTGOMERY'S
OPERATION
GOODWOOD

German position
British advance

Bay of the Seine

Sword

Montgomery

FRANCE

CAEN

Von Kluge

River

Orne

To Falaise

N
W E
S

0   3 kilometers
0   3 miles

Montgomery had given Eisenhower and everyone else loud assurances that Operation Goodwood would create a significant rupture in the German lines and allow the British forces to drive as far south as the town of Falaise, a boast that invigorated everyone at SHAEF. But reality interrupted Montgomery's hopes. Sensing problems with his advance, Montgomery altered his own plans, tempering his ambitions considerably. Unfortunately for everyone concerned, Montgomery neglected to tell anyone at SHAEF that his plan had been drawn in. Worse for Montgomery, ongoing German resistance far exceeded his expectations. Montgomery recognized that pursuing Goodwood any further could lead to losses that the British could not absorb. On July 20, two days after it began, Montgomery called off the attack. Instead of the capture of Falaise, which would have required a breakthrough of some twenty-five miles, the British had a tentative gain of only seven miles of ground.

The original schedule for Goodwood had called for Montgomery's assault to begin two days before Bradley's Operation Cobra. Ideally, with Montgomery's attack in full swing, the Germans facing him would be held fast, and German commanders might even be persuaded to draw reinforcements from the troops who faced Bradley. Once again, what was drawn on paper did not happen in the field. Bradley's plans for Cobra required the same sort of heavy air support that had preceded Montgomery's attack, but by July 20 the weather had turned again, heavy rains and fog preventing the bombers from leaving the ground. Bradley was forced to delay his attack until July 24. The Germans would certainly determine that Montgomery had taken his best shot south of Caen and failed. The most logical plan for the Allied command would now be to launch the Americans against the German left flank, at the base of the Cotentin Peninsula. Eisenhower understood that the delay caused by the weather had negated any benefit to Bradley from Montgomery's operation. The Germans who faced the Americans in the bocage country would have ample time to prepare themselves for whatever Bradley was going to do, knowing they still held the defensive advantage in the hedgerows and swamps.

Montgomery's failure was one more straw on Eisenhower's back. The hostile grumbling, particularly among the British air commanders, was growing more fierce every day. Once again they had offered heavy bomber support to the ground forces and had virtually nothing to show for it. Whether or not they shared the blame, the "bomber barons" were openly outraged by Montgomery's apparent sluggishness. More and more, they just wanted him gone.

SHAEF FORWARD COMMAND POST, PORTSMOUTH
JULY 24, 1944

Eisenhower stood outside his tent, stared skyward. There had been reports of V-1s coming in much closer to Portsmouth, and he could not ignore them. Though the buzz bombs continued to take a horrific toll on the British citizenry, the Royal Air Force had been increasingly successful at targeting the flying bombs before they reached their targets, intercepting some of them far out over the English Channel. The V-1s were faster than even the fastest fighter plane, but the pilots were growing more skilled at interception. On the ground, the gunners were gaining skill as well, new technology emerging in the form of radar-sighted antiaircraft guns. But the quantity of V-1s had increased, hundreds in the past two weeks, and no matter the effectiveness of the efforts to intercept them, a number of them continued to get through.

He listened, heard the drone of aircraft engines, a squadron of fighters low on the horizon, nothing for him to see. Tedder emerged from the tent behind him, papers in his hand.

"Harris and Leigh-Mallory are in perfect agreement about this. Damned rare, that one. They're claiming Monty sold them a bill of goods, convinced them to toss all their eggs into his basket, then pulled the rug out."

Eisenhower looked at him. "How many metaphors can you put into one statement?"

"Sorry. Thought I'd toss a smile your way. Not appropriate, I suppose. But I've been chewing on this for a while now. I've not grumped as much about Monty as some of the others, you know that. It's not a simple task to come down hard on one of our own."

"Since when? Dammit, Arthur, one of the parts of this job I've grown used to is the bitching. I've heard it all, from your people and mine, and the French as well. Nobody's happy, ever. We win this thing, they'll be bitching about what happens next, who's in charge of what, all that political crap."

He paused.

"Monty has damned sure screwed up. We can't keep launching these attacks and sucking up these casualties when we accomplish so damned little. Seven thousand tons of bombs for seven miles gained. If that's how much this real estate is going to cost us, we're not going to make it to Germany. Churchill is raising hell every day, pushing me to *use my judgment,* his way of telling me to get off my ass and do something. The newspapers in the States are raising hell about Monty, as though he's losing us this war. Marshall's soaking up a lot of that, but it's still kicking me from behind, and I'm damned tired of it. I wish I could tell those jackasses that, by God, we *are* doing something to try to win this war, that Bradley's people are on the move. Damned know-nothings with all the answers."

"Ike, some of your own people are saying you have to sack Monty, and if you don't you're selling out to the British. I'm hearing more and more of that."

Eisenhower had rarely been angry at Tedder before but he felt the burn, the explosion building. "Don't you tell me what my people—" He grabbed the next words, pulled them back, spun around, and moved into the tent. Tedder came in behind him. Eisenhower sat on the cot, tried to hold his temper. "Dammit. I'm doing it too. Your people, my people. Sorry."

"Ike, I'm your second-in-command. I know how much bull is floating around. I know all about rivalries and patriotic spirit. I also know you're above all that, no matter how annoyed you get, with Monty or me or anyone else. I'm not suggesting you take any action with Monty one way or the other. But you have to know what the weather's like in your command."

"Look, I could fire Monty today. Churchill would raise a glass to me, every American general in this army would salute me—and then what? The British newspapers would spew out every invective that exists. Every damned story I get here refers to *Monty's troops.* From the very beginning the British papers were calling this Monty's invasion, Monty's paratroop drop, Monty's victories. I've had to take steam for that from the States and from right here. But, fine, I understand what the British papers are doing, how badly your people need him. If I sack Monty, your Parliament will erupt like a volcano. Churchill has enough problems as it is; he'd be facing a revolt."

He paused, shook his head.

"Brooke would never speak to me again. And he's my superior. And if Monty goes, who replaces him, Dempsey? He's a good man, but he hasn't set any records at Caen either. The best man might be Crerar, but he's

Canadian. There's a laundry list of good people in the British command and, I guarantee you, every one of them would think twice about stepping into Monty's shoes. And, what about *this* command? How effective would I be in dealing with anyone who thinks Monty got a raw deal? Damn it all, from the very beginning—in North Africa, in Italy—this command has always been about *cooperation.* It's the toughest thing I've ever tried to do. We are allies, but no matter how hard I try to change things we're two separate armies with two separate goals. Churchill says he admires me because I'm *on the fence.* He thinks that's a compliment, so I guess I should take it that way. I shouldn't have to explain this to you. I'm up here because I have to be. It's the most important part of my job."

"What the British are trying to preserve, Ike, is more than a victory. It's pride, survival of the empire, all that. It's a damned chain around the neck of every British general. We've lost so much already, and now the cupboards are bare. Every division we lose is . . . lost. Every pilot, every tank driver. Every mother's son."

"And every general. Monty's still a damned fine field commander, and despite what a jerk he can be, he knows how to win. Sometimes—hell, most of the time—his problem is that he's too damned careful, has to pull his tail up behind him, get everything organized before he makes his next move. Sometimes that's a mistake, and it's my job to keep him from doing it again. I've spoken to him a half dozen times, and I even put it in writing: some pretty strong stuff, pushing him hard. I went through the roof when I heard he changed the scope of Goodwood without telling me. I still had a big red circle around Falaise on the map in the truck out there. But, dammit, he's still holding a hell of a lot of Germans in place, which will help Bradley enormously. I promise you, the Germans aren't as dismissive of Monty as our own people. They won't just let him be and shift everybody out of position so they can confront Bradley."

"How many more mistakes will he be allowed to make?"

Eisenhower stood—needing to walk, to stretch out the frustrations—but stopped at the opening of the tent. "I'll know that when he makes them."

He stepped outside, still annoyed, a hot weight he was too tired of carrying around, and saw Butcher coming down the path, more papers and none of the usual smile.

"Chief! I have word from General Bradley."

"It's awfully quick for that. What's wrong?"

Tedder emerged from the tent behind him, and Butcher moved close, saying in a low voice, "We might want to step back inside, sir."

Eisenhower felt the weight increasing, slipped back into the tent. Butcher followed, Tedder staying just behind them, standing at the opening. Eisenhower turned to Butcher and saw hesitation, even dread, unusual.

"What the hell happened?"

"Sir, General Bradley reports that he has scrubbed his attack for one more day. The weather in his sector was just too lousy for the advance air assaults. But the bombers didn't get the word until they were airborne. The recall order was given, but some of the planes reached what they thought was their target zones and dropped their loads. It seems a good many of the bombs fell short and hit our people. The Thirtieth Division took some heavy casualties."

Behind Butcher, Tedder whispered, "Good God!"

Eisenhower felt a hard twist inside him. "How bad?"

"Not sure yet, sir."

"All right. Let's go. I've sat here long enough. Bradley's about to get some company. Find me a plane that can fly or a destroyer that's ready to go. If you can't, I'll swim the damned channel."

The B-17 swooped low, seeking a small opening in the heavy clouds. Eisenhower felt his stomach pulling up, fighting the dive of the plane. The trip across the channel was brief, made shorter by Eisenhower's own thoughts, his brain spilling over with rambling tirades to Montgomery, rebukes to Leigh-Mallory and Churchill and Bradley, furious words he knew he could never actually deliver. There is only so much a man can take, he thought. I never dreamed I would be more agitated by my own command than by the enemy. Dammit, I have no patience for this, not anymore.

He looked out the small window—a glimpse of water, the coastline, the plane still dropping—France. He searched through the overcast for the beaches, some sign of the enormous buildup of matériel, all that power creating an enormous traffic jam, held in place by the inability of his army to break open a hole. Eisenhower had seen the bocage from the air many times and short glimpses of it on the ground, in fast-moving staff cars and nervous guards. Not enough, he thought. I need to get out there and see more. Drive Butcher nuts, and Beetle Smith. My two nannies. Marshall won't be too happy either. But damn it all, I'm sick of sitting back in my own headquarters, listening to bellyaching from generals who should be above all that. God, I'd love to see the real war, one damned firefight. What would that be like? Hedgerows and machine-gun nests. Hell, do I even remember how to toss a grenade?

For weeks now he had felt a nagging emptiness, an aching hole inside, no matter his exalted position atop the command ladder of SHAEF, all the attention from politicians and generals, so many plans and maps and reports. With so much happening in the field, so many battles, and so many casualties, the feeling was growing that he had missed the most important part, the part that mattered.

I know why Patton's going nuts, he thought. He already knows what it's like to ride a damned tank into battle, and he's punching the walls because he wants to do it again. My job is to stay the hell out of the way of those people and stick with the papers and maps, the bitching and the egos. My job is to *administrate* the fight. Ridiculous. There's no such thing. This is a GIs' war. Those damned hedgerows, every man fighting his own battle against the guy on the other side of the bushes. Generals have damn little to do with that. And I'll never know what it feels like: death . . . a buddy going down. Well, no, I know what it feels like to lose someone close. Sometimes it doesn't take a bullet to do that job.

In all the shuffling of new commands, several names had risen to the top, men who were being moved along the chain of command, replacing those who weren't up to the task. Teddy Roosevelt, Jr., was one of the good ones, a close friend to both Eisenhower and George Marshall. During his first major command, Roosevelt had served as assistant division commander of the Big Red One. He had been popular with his troops, but he hadn't brought himself many accolades from the top. In North Africa, the First Division had seemed to fall apart after their successes in Algeria; there were violent lapses in discipline and, as always, the top brass had to accept the responsibility: Roosevelt had been relieved, along with the division's commander, Terry Allen.

But with so many new divisions coming across the Atlantic, the need for experience overshadowed the need for perfection, and, of course, Roosevelt had powerful friends. For Overlord, he was assigned the position of assistant commander of the Fourth Infantry Division, and Eisenhower was gratified to learn that the old shadows had been swept away. Roosevelt gained the respect of his men and every senior officer around him and had been the only general to go ashore with the first wave at Utah Beach. It was the sort of act that always endears a commander to his men, and ultimately his name climbed high on the list of those chosen to fill the gaps left by generals who had fallen flat. One of those gaps was at the top of the Ninetieth Division and so, in early July, Roosevelt was given that command. The day before he was to report to that duty, he suffered a fatal heart attack.

Eisenhower kept his stare out the window, mulled over Lincoln's words, *fitting and proper,* that one small piece of the Gettysburg Address. Yep, it's fitting and proper that Teddy be buried right here, alongside his men. That's what he deserves. Dammit, I'll miss him. Miss him now. We need every good man, every man who can get those damned reporters to tell a different story rather than constantly bellyaching about Monty.

The plane banked sharply and he pushed back in the seat, one hand on his stomach. Okay, I'm ready for this one to be over with. What the hell did I eat today? It's swimming around, that's for sure. His hand touched a piece of paper in his shirt pocket, the Ultra report that revealed the stunning details of the assassination attempt on Hitler. What the hell was that like? He had often thought of Hitler, his day-to-day routine, the strangeness of the man, wondered if Hitler even had a routine at all. Eisenhower felt the plane lurch, slowing. Do you fly much? he thought. They ever take you up in some big damned Heinkel, so you can watch the bombs drop? What kind of things keep you awake at night? Or do you sleep like a damned baby? You can't possibly have a conscience. But there's weight on you, no matter who you are or how nuts you might be. Even a damned dictator has to answer sooner or later, and you have to know your time is coming. Your own people tried to kill you, for God's sake. They've probably tried a dozen times. Don't think that's happened to me yet. Churchill, maybe. FDR, yep.

There had been raucous cheering at the news of the attempt on Hitler's life, Churchill echoing what many were saying: "They missed the old bastard. But there's time yet." But Eisenhower hadn't shared anyone's elation, had stiffened the mood of his own staff, a sharp reminder that on the front lines across from Montgomery were the SS panzer divisions, the most fanatical units in the western theater. How do you expect they will react? he had asked them. Their boss almost got assassinated. Don't you think that might just invigorate them to fight with a little more . . . gusto?

He looked out the window again, fog and open fields, trucks and supply depots. But the assassination attempt was still in his mind. That took some serious guts. Heaven help you folks who had something to do with the plot. Not only will the Gestapo hunt you down, there are whole divisions in your army who would do the same thing. The only plot I want to hear about is the one they bury him in, when someone actually kills the son of a bitch. We'll make sure we put his whole High Command in there with him, every damn one of them. Wish I could be a part of that, but that's not my job either. Damn shame. I'd volunteer for it, though. Hell, it might end up being the Russians. The way things are going, looks like they'll get there first. And, of course, I have to deal with stupidity like Monty and his big mouth. And bombardiers who can't hit the side of a damned barn, unless it belongs to their own people.

BRADLEY'S HEADQUARTERS, NEAR ISIGNY
JULY 25, 1944

Bradley was fuming, pacing, one fist pressed into his other hand.

"Dammit, I told them. I made it very, very clear. Bring the bombers in parallel to the road, and drop your bombs on the south side of it. Very damn simple. The road was the boundary, our boys on the north, the enemy on the south. Then I find out from my own people that, no, they flew in perpendicular to the road, came in right over our heads. Exactly wrong, exactly what I knew could cause problems. So, with the weather bad, they made blind drops, could only guess where the enemy was. And they guessed wrong! Leigh-Mallory says, Well, it would have been inconvenient to make the change in their flight path, would have taken a couple hours to rebrief the pilots. This has been on paper for *five days*. For *five days* the air command had their instructions! They made their own change and didn't say a word to me or anyone else. Leigh-Mallory tells me that the air commanders are scrambling around, telling each other, Well, of course General Bradley was informed of the change. We could never agree to fly in parallel to the road, that's just not how we would do it." Bradley pounded the fist into his hand.

"Five days ago they agreed to do it! I wanted to punch that smug self-righteous bastard right in the teeth. No one called me before the attack, Ike. No one called to tell me they had decided to ignore my instructions!

The Thirtieth took *a hundred fifty casualties!* They know they'll be some hell to pay and they're covering their own behinds."

Bradley was as angry as Eisenhower had ever seen him.

"Don't you think I'd have pulled our people back, if I thought there was even a *chance* we would get blasted to hell by our own planes? That's what I told Leigh-Mallory. Didn't faze him a bit. Arrogant sons of bitches!"

Eisenhower let Bradley finish without scolding him for his temper. It was one more problem, one more mistake, and he knew Bradley was right: There would be hell to pay. But not right now.

"I'll talk to Leigh-Mallory, find out what I can," Eisenhower said. "Get more details from the Thirtieth about their casualties. We'll have to figure out some good way to handle that, before the press blows it up."

Bradley seemed to calm, sat on a bench to one side, his hands propped on his knees. "Dammit, Ike. How much more has to go wrong?"

"Tell me about your ground attack. You've changed the plan for Cobra."

Bradley looked at him through tired eyes, and shook his head. "Not really. I've been hearing from Monty, indirectly, that he's not a fan of my tactics. I'm not aware that *his* tactics have put us any closer to Berlin, but that's not a comment for me to make. We have to do something different to work through the kind of geography we're in here; so far, our best progress has been too slow and too costly. I always thought that if you smacked the enemy across his whole body, you'd find his weak spot. But it hasn't worked here. The countryside is just too tough, too many places to hide. Hell, one eighty-eight can hold up an entire tank column, just by clogging up the road. One damned German soldier can stop a whole battalion, if he's got his machine gun in the right place. Monty thinks we should try to punch a tighter hole through the enemy lines. Okay, we'll try it his way."

Bradley stood, moved close to the map, and picked up a long pointer.

"We're hitting them on a more compact front this time. I'm pushing armor and infantry into a drive only four miles wide. Let's just say I'm going to try my own brand of blitzkrieg."

Bradley's fury had changed to enthusiasm. Eisenhower got up from the couch he had been sitting on and focused on the details of the map. He wasn't accustomed to seeing this kind of raw energy from his general. Bradley moved the pointer to the red circle drawn around the town of Saint-Lô and tapped the map.

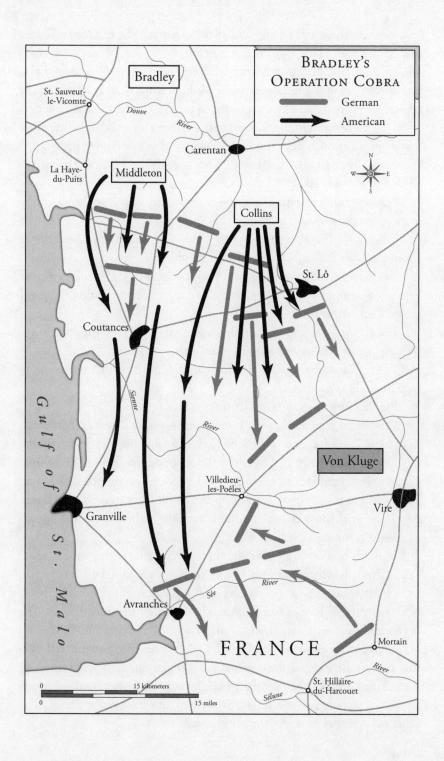

BRADLEY'S
OPERATION COBRA

German
American

Bradley

St. Sauveur-
le-Vicomte

Douve   *River*

Carentan

La Haye-
du-Puits

Middleton

Collins

St. Lô

Coutances

Sienne

River

Von Kluge

Villedieu-
les-Poêles

Vire

Granville

Avranches   *Sée*   *River*

FRANCE

Mortain

River

St. Hillaire-
du-Harcouet

Sélunee

Gulf of St. Malo

0   15 kilometers
0   15 miles

"We'll go at them right here, and if we can push them back we'll lean toward the coast. That way, we can pinch out any German divisions coming up from that direction or, better, drive some away. That should also pull some enemy strength away from Monty's front. Call it returning the favor. The more we lengthen the front to the west and stretch the enemy's lines, the more strength they'll need to move over this way. And if the other fellow moves enough people this way, Monty's front will open up."

Eisenhower studied the map. "That's assuming Monty can be persuaded to move at all."

Bradley didn't respond. Eisenhower watched him lean closer to the map, pretending to study some finer point.

"You have that map memorized, Brad. You want to speak up about Monty, you go ahead. Hell, everybody else does."

Bradley turned, shook his head. "Got nothing to say, Ike. He's mostly kept his nose out of this headquarters, let me run this operation the way I see fit. Can't complain."

Eisenhower had hoped for more, some kind of moral support for his own agonizing. He moved back to the couch.

"There's a strong current flowing through SHAEF that wants me to recommend his dismissal."

Bradley turned away from the map.

"I've heard a lot about that. I won't get involved. There's plenty to do right here. Oh, I forgot to mention. We had a GI come up with an idea to bust up the hedgerows. A sergeant in the Second Division, Culin, I think. Came up with the idea of fastening a big steel claw to the front of a tank, like a fork, to punch in and scoop up the brush from underneath. Damn if it didn't work like a charm. The tank rams the embankment and knocks a hole clean through the hedge."

"Sounds like something we should have come up with a month ago."

"Genius is where you find it. Listen, Ike, I thought I'd head over to Collins's command post, get reports on the progress of the ground assault from right there. Joe is expecting us. This is his moment in the sun. The Seventh Corps has seven divisions under its cap this time. If Collins can push his boys far enough, Middleton's Eighth is ready to come in right beside him to drive down the coast. If we can just open up some lanes, do something to make the Germans back away. . . . Dammit, Ike, I know about our screwups. But I still don't see why this has been so tough. The other fellow is better than I thought he was."

"The Germans?"

"Yep. Never thought they'd fight this hard. They had the good ground, and no matter how superior our numbers are, they've held the line. Didn't expect this."

"Neither did Monty."

Bradley seemed antsy, tossed the pointer on the narrow table beneath the map.

"We need to get going. The boys have stepped off by now. The bombers dropped their loads at nine-thirty. After the ass-chewing I gave Leigh-Mallory, I would guess the bombardiers were a little more careful this time. But I want to hear that from the ground commanders. I want some *good* news for a change." Bradley picked up his jacket, seemed to delay putting it on his shoulders. Eisenhower caught the hint. "You do what you have to do, Brad. I'm not trying to be in the way here."

"You're always in the way, Ike. That's your job."

When the B-17 put him on the ground near Portsmouth, Butcher was waiting for him. Eisenhower knew the look on his aide's face, the same look he had seen the day before. The staff car was waiting for them, Butcher obviously anxious.

Eisenhower stepped down from the bomber. "What is it, Harry?"

"They did it again, Chief. The bombers hit our own people . . . again."

"*What?* Who?"

"The Thirtieth took it the worst, sir, and some units of the Ninth. No word yet on the number of casualties . . . except for one."

Eisenhower saw Bradley in his mind, imagined his fury, the utter frustration, My God, I should have stayed there, he thought. I should have waited to hear the reports. Brad is going to rip someone apart.

Butcher seemed to be waiting, and Eisenhower realized what the man had said.

"One what?"

"Sir, General McNair had gone to the front, to observe the operation at first hand. He was . . . killed in the attack."

Eisenhower felt a punch of cold. "Lesley McNair? He's dead? We lost a lieutenant general to"—he paused, hating the term—"*friendly fire?*"

"Yes, sir. He was killed instantly, as far as we can tell."

Eisenhower looked past Butcher, at the aides waiting at the car, no one close enough to hear. "We have to keep this quiet, Harry. Not a word, you hear? Not a damned word."

"Yes, sir. I understand. It'll be tough, though."

"Everything's tough, Harry!"

Eisenhower's mind filled with details, the deception, McNair's new place at the top of Patton's fictitious First Army Group. We'll need some-one else. Just like that, someone else. Good God. He moved numbly to the car and sat down in the back, the door closing. Butcher came in on the other side, sat quietly.

"We have to wire General Marshall," Eisenhower said. "I'll recom-mend that McNair be buried right here, quietly, no ceremony. I know he'd have preferred that, to be closer to his men. We sure it was our own bombs? Could it possibly have been enemy shelling?"

"It's . . . unlikely, sir."

The car began to move, and he glanced at Butcher, who stared ahead, wrapped in his own gloom.

"What's it going to take, Harry?" Eisenhower said. "What else do we have to do?"

"Don't know, Chief."

Eisenhower sat back and tried to rest his head on the seat, but there was no rest. His brain was boiling over with details: the hopes; the plan-ning, problems, and controversies; and the death of men because of some-one's pure stupidity. He thought of Bradley: his map, his enthusiasm, his red circle around Saint-Lô. God help us, he thought. Can't *something* go right for a change?

For the first two days of Operation Cobra, the going was as slow and difficult as it had been since early June, a heavy-handed slugging match between two blind boxers. The reports flowed back to Bradley and Eisenhower, meager gains, minor breakthroughs, setbacks, losses, the bocage country still as formidable a foe as the Germans. Then the reports began to change. Even though there had been no great collapse, no surren-der, nothing that would tell Eisenhower there had been a victory at all, Bradley's optimism was ignited with each passing day by word of solid gains. The Americans had finally pushed southward far enough to draw clear of the hedgerows. In front of them, the haggard Germans seemed to realize that their best efforts were not enough, and their stout resistance had begun to give way.

Bradley's forces now totaled twenty-one divisions, and any war of attrition had shifted even more strongly in favor of the Americans. As Joe Collins's Seventh Corps fought their way through the rugged ground south of Saint-Lô, closer to the coast, Troy Middleton's Eighth Corps pushed hard to break the far left flank of the German defense. On July 30, Middleton captured the town of Avranches. The Americans had driven thirty-five miles from their starting point at Saint-Lô.

As the Americans paused to catch their breath, a call was made to Adolf Hitler from the headquarters of Army Group West. Field Marshal Hans von Kluge notified his Führer that the German left flank had completely collapsed. What von Kluge did not know was that behind the exhausted Americans, who were only beginning to realize the scope of what they had accomplished, another massive fist was ready, fully prepared to resume the push. On August 1, the American Third Army officially began its existence. After so many months of infuriating inactivity, George Patton was finally returning to the war.

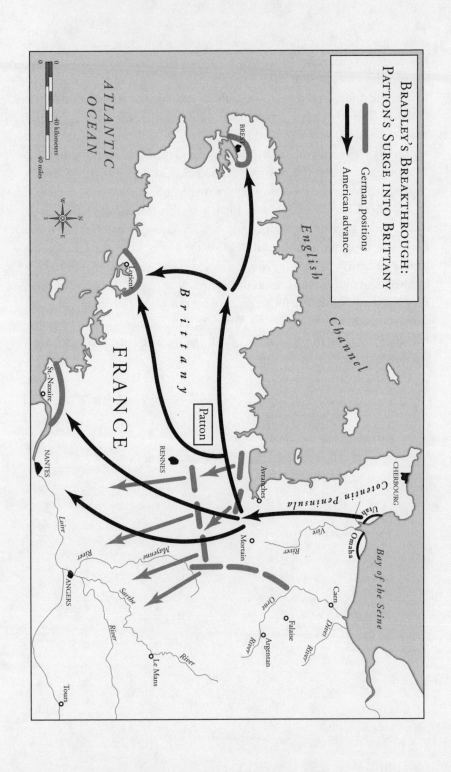

BRADLEY'S BREAKTHROUGH:
PATTON'S SURGE INTO BRITTANY

German positions
American advance

ATLANTIC
OCEAN

0
40 kilometers
0
40 miles

N
W   E
S

BREST

English

Channel

CHERBOURG

Cotentin Peninsula

Lorient

Brittany

Patton

FRANCE

St-Nazaire

RENNES

Avranches

Utah

Omaha

Bay of the Seine

NANTES

Mayenne

Mortain

Vire

River

Caen

Loire

Sarthe

River

ANGERS

River

River

Falaise

Argentan

Dives

Orne

River

Le Mans

River

Tours

41. PATTON

The image was still fresh in his mind, his deliberate tour of the enormous parking lots inland from Omaha Beach, wooden crates and canvas-covered mountains. The ships were unloading every day the weather would allow, so the mammoth stockpiles of supplies and hardware continued to increase. He had met the soldiers as well, his new army, men who greeted him with cameras and hearty cheers. Patton had obliged them with a brief speech, off the record, nothing of course for the reporters. He didn't need Eisenhower telling him to shut up. That was a lesson he had learned. But the soldiers would hear what he wanted them to hear, and so the words had come.

"I'm proud to be here to fight beside you. Now let's cut the guts out of those Krauts and get the hell on to Berlin. And when we get to Berlin, I am going to personally shoot that paper-hanging goddamned son of a bitch just like I would a snake."

The scattered cheering had burst into an eruption of pure affection, the soldiers seeming to realize that this man was one of their own. With all the talk of delay and indecision, the griping that filled the ranks, someone had finally come to France who knew how to win the war.

Patton did not share their joy or their unbridled optimism. As he left
Omaha Beach, the inspections began, his daily visits to the various division
commanders and the men who served them. There were the veteran units
and those newly arrived, and it was the veterans who concerned him most.
As he marched through their camps, he carried the reports on what they had
failed to do, the sluggishness and lackadaisical advances toward an enemy
that seemed far more prepared. Too often, the new men seem underprepared
and the veterans worn out. Patton understood why there had been so many
failures. No matter how much they cheered their generals, it was the soldiers
themselves who had to do the work, who had to show the enemy who the
better man was. It was the army's dirty little secret that too often the infantry
had bogged down or, worse, had been driven back when they confronted an
enemy they had been told they would simply sweep away.

Patton studied those men and began to realize that many of the same
soldiers who so raucously welcomed his words had not been sufficiently
trained and, worse, were not being led by the kind of officers Patton believed the army needed. He did not share his views openly, would not open
up a messy controversy when his command was only hours old. Though he
groused to his diary about Eisenhower's leadership, he appreciated that privately Eisenhower shared his views about the inadequacy of the training.
Both men were aware that propaganda was not confined to the Germans.
In the training centers throughout the United States, the American troops
had been surrounded by colorful posters, drenched in speeches from their
officers, drilled to believe they were unstoppable, the best equipped and
the most feared fighting men in the world. But the training itself had not
met that promise. Patton knew he faced a challenge. The sting of failure
had infected several of the infantry divisions, particularly the Ninetieth.
The army clearly needed something or someone to inspire them to become
better soldiers. In Patton's mind, no one was more suited for the job than
George Patton.

Patton's Third Army was now one of two such commands under the
overall leadership of Omar Bradley, who, in North Africa and Sicily, had
been Patton's subordinate. Bradley's original command during Overlord, the American First Army, was now commanded by Courtney H.
Hodges, a man Patton had known well, even before World War One. Like
Patton, Hodges had once fought under Black Jack Pershing in Mexico, in
futile pursuit of the bandit Pancho Villa. Patton's Third Army was the second half of Bradley's new command, which was designated the Twelfth

Army Group. The change in command structure put Bradley on equal footing with Bernard Montgomery, who still commanded his Twenty-first Army Group. Montgomery's command now consisted of Henry Crerar's First Canadian Army, and Miles Dempsey's Second British Army. The changes meant a significant promotion for Bradley and, in the eyes of many Brits, a demotion for Montgomery. Patton paid little attention to anyone's complaints about whether or not Montgomery had received justice.

Patton's new training regimens for the Third Army had become brutal, but there was more to the army's problems. The weapons weren't measuring up, the tanks in particular proving woefully inadequate to match the firepower and strength of the German machines. The antitank guns were inferior as well, particularly the clumsy bazookas that were more likely to draw deadly fire onto their own crews than to take out an enemy tank. Washington's weak reply to the complaints had echoed what Montgomery too had insisted, that force of numbers would overcome the inadequacies. But Montgomery had been unable to prove that theory. Patton realized, as did Eisenhower, that throwing greater numbers of weaker tanks at a well-equipped enemy only killed more tank crews.

As his army organized and grew, Patton grew as well, accepting that the increased responsibility he had so lusted for had finally come his way. His incessant griping was silenced by his new role, and his army had responded well to the man who would lead them. He knew there would be no miracles, that many of the same problems would still plague his men as they drove forward to face a fanatical enemy. Patton was delightfully aware that Montgomery's failures were due to his cautiousness and set-piece management on the battlefield, traits Montgomery had built his reputation on. Patton despised Montgomery's tactics as deeply as he despised the man himself. Whether or not his troops and their weapons were equal to what the Germans would put in front of him, Patton brought another factor that the Germans had not faced before. The inspiration came from another general and another time, the Shenandoah Valley of Virginia. Then it had been a Confederate, Thomas "Stonewall" Jackson, who crushed a far superior enemy by combining audacity and speed. Patton was supremely confident that, if it had worked for Jackson, it would work for him.

During the first week of August, he proved it.

Once his command became official, Patton's mobile forces pressed south and west from the breakthrough that the Americans had wedged open around Avranches. The overall plan called for a sweep west, to occupy the Brittany peninsula and capture the valuable port cities along that western coast: Brest, Lorient, and Saint-Nazaire. Patton would certainly comply, but shifting a major part of his army away from the main theater in Normandy caused a knot in his gut that he could not meekly accept. The open country of the Brittany peninsula was an easy mark, and Patton's troops had little trouble sweeping over miles of farms and villages that the Germans seemed unwilling to fight for. But the ports were a different story, and Patton found that what Bradley and Eisenhower assumed to be ripe picks were in fact well-entrenched and fortified German outposts, manned by inspired officers who were still enthusiastically obeying Hitler's orders to hold to the last man. There would be no easy prizes for Patton on the coast of Brittany. As Hodges's First Army faced off with the heavier lines of German resistance along the base of the Cotentin Peninsula, Patton chafed for a more meaningful role, some way to convince Bradley that the Third Army should drive east, not west. On August 7, the Germans opened that door.

BRADLEY'S HEADQUARTERS, NEAR ISIGNY
AUGUST 7, 1944

Bradley held the pointer and stabbed at the map.

"They hit us this morning, all along this area here. The Thirtieth took the brunt of it."

Patton felt the nervous excitement in the room, the staff officers behind him studying the maps, reports shuffling through their hands. Patton pointed to the "30" on the map. "How are they holding up?"

"All right for now. But the German has given himself an opportunity. If the Thirtieth gives way, the enemy might drive through to Avranches and anchor himself back on that damned coast. That'll cut you off. That's their plan, anyway. I'm sure Hitler looked at this same damned map and thought he could drive a knife into our front and split us apart. There's danger of a gap opening up south of the Thirtieth's right flank, so I'm pulling your Thirty-fifth Division up that way and putting them under Hodges for now. I don't want to hear any griping about it, George."

Patton had already noticed the weakness in the American position, said, "No griping. Plug the hole. If you don't, the Krauts will push right into Avranches. But that's as much gas as they'll have. Damn, this is one stupid attack. There's no chance in hell of this working. There's too many of us on his flanks."

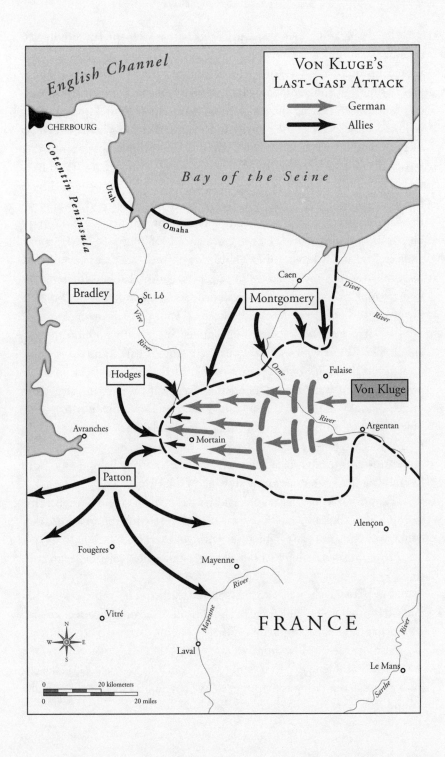

"It's desperation, George. And it gets better. I was pretty sure he was coming." Patton saw a hint of a smile on Bradley's face, unusual. "We picked up quite a few reports, the communications between von Kluge and Berlin. Von Kluge probably bitched like hell about this, any good soldier would. I'm betting the order came from Hitler himself, more of his hold-every-inch crap. Hitler looks at a map and sees his invincible army like you would see your queen on a chessboard, so von Kluge got the order to jam that army—specifically, his panzers—down our throats. It just happened to be bad luck for the Thirtieth Division that they were sitting in the dead center of the line. They took a heavy hit, but they're busting up the panzers too. The weather's been perfect for our air people, and they've taken a hell of a punch out of the German lines. Right now, we have two choices, and Ike is leaving the decision up to me. One, we can pull you back this way, seal the weakness in our lines, consolidate our forces into a tighter front. You've got twelve divisions, George, and four would probably be all we'd need. The rest would keep up your drive through Brittany."

"What drive? We've taken the damned place with nothing to brag about. The Krauts who were still out there wouldn't stand up to us. If we didn't grab them, it's only because they hauled their asses back into the port cities. You want me to spend the rest of this war laying siege to a bunch of rinky-dink ports? You want four of my divisions just to plug a hole? Why, so we leave it to the Krauts to decide what they want to do next?"

Patton realized his voice had risen and heard stirring behind him, both his and Bradley's aides nervously shifting in their chairs.

"Dammit, George, let it go. I said we had two choices. Ike expects me to think this through, not just bust out of here with the first idea that comes to mind. You can't fight a war with your temper."

Patton bristled, held it, let out a breath, and waited for Bradley to continue.

"The second choice is to go hell-for-leather. The other fellow has opened himself up to flank attacks on both sides, creating a perfect salient. Monty has three corps lining up . . . here . . . to move south pretty quickly."

Patton sniffed. "How quickly?"

"Can that, George. Monty's not your concern. You've been bellyaching for ages about doing something, so I've got an idea that ought to make you pretty happy."

Patton heard the seriousness in Bradley's voice, grew more serious himself and stared at the map.

Bradley continued. "I know damned well von Kluge sees what he's done to himself, but with Hitler chewing his ass he had no choice. He's given us a chance, and we should take it. We need to hit them as hard as we can. As hard as *you* can. Use the Loire River as your right flank, and drive those four divisions east. Try to reach Le Mans. If the enemy doesn't pull back to meet you, we might have an opportunity to hit him from behind, to pinch him between you and Hodges and Monty."

Patton studied the map, saw Bradley smiling at him.

"Well? You like choice number two better?"

"I think we should go farther east: Chartres, Dreux. That'll put us thirty miles from Paris. This thing could be over in ten days."

"Dammit, George, keep your head on straight! Paris? The enemy is right in front of us, and he's dangerous as hell. We have an opportunity to cut him off and maybe destroy the whole German Seventh Army in the process. I don't care a damn about Paris. You don't have to conquer all of Europe to do your job."

Patton absorbed the scolding, studied the map. "Le Mans, huh? I guess that'd work."

"No sulking, George."

Patton shook his head, kept his eyes on the map. "You want Le Mans, we'll get it. You want the Seventh Army, we'll get that too."

Bradley crossed his arms, still holding the pointer. "This is an opportunity, George. Let's see what we can make of it."

Patton turned, the silent order to his aides to head for the door. He felt his heart racing, so very rare now, the flash of excitement building. He glanced back at Bradley, forced a smile, saw seriousness, concern, doubt.

"I'll handle it, Brad."

He passed by Bradley's aide, ignored him, and followed his own people out the door, his mind filling with thoughts of Stonewall.

NEAR AVRANCHES
AUGUST 8, 1944

He shouted furiously, the truck drivers staring at him with open mouths, obeying his order.

"That way! Step on the damned gas!"

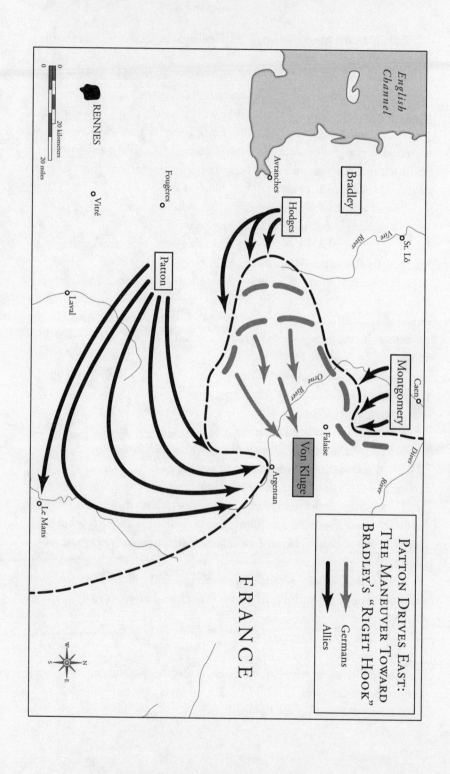

PATTON DRIVES EAST:
THE MANEUVER TOWARD
BRADLEY'S "RIGHT HOOK"

→ Germans
→ Allies

FRANCE

English Channel

RENNES

20 kilometers
20 miles

Vitré

Fougères

Avranches

Bradley

Hodges

St. Lô

Vire River

Laval

Patton

Montgomery

Caen

Orne River

Dives River

Falaise

Von Kluge

Argentan

Le Mans

N
W   E
S

The column surged through the intersection, a dozen two-and-a-half-ton trucks coughing black smoke as they rolled past him. He glared at the drivers as they passed him, one hand on the butt of the pistol in his belt, his chest out in a hard defiant stance. They know who I am, he thought. No one else out here has three stars on his damn helmet.

The column had spread out, a benefit of the faster speeds, and he waited for a gap, the end of one particular line, one regiment. The gap was nearly a hundred yards wide, and he stared at the distant truck, sniffed out loud.

"You're too damn slow. It's gonna cost you."

He turned and stared at the dumbstruck driver whose truck sat idly, crowding the side road, the low rumble of trucks behind, another column. All right, he thought, it's your turn. He held up a hand and waved the truck forward, the driver responding, the truck lurching into the intersection, more following closely behind. The column turned onto the single road, filling the gap in the advance. Patton tried to ignore the dust, fought the need to cough, the show of weakness he would not allow them to see. Damn this anyway.

"All right! Speed it up! Let's move!"

They continued to roar past him, a solid line of olive-green vehicles, every one filled to capacity with men who now saw their commander for the first time. The cheering came again, hands in the air, some scrambling to pull a camera from a backpack, futile, the trucks moving away too quickly. But they called to him still, word seeming to spread magically through the enormous column as to just who the traffic cop was at this clogged intersection. Good, he thought. Let them know who runs this outfit. Even if I have to bust up the damn traffic jams myself.

After long minutes, he repeated the maneuver, waiting for a gap in the column on the smaller road, bringing forward the waiting column from the larger road. He had predicted something like this, knew from the maps about this astounding annoyance, two main roads funneling into one. For more than an hour, Patton's jeep had crept along at a snail's pace, the shouts of the men around him more infuriating than pleasing. When he finally reached the intersection, he had seen the police box. It was standard procedure, the boxes put into place so an MP could direct traffic without being run over. But the box had been unmanned, someone's failure, and the converging columns had ground to a virtual halt, neither one able to figure out the mathematics of two roads merging into one. Patton had ex-

ploded, stepped furiously into the box, and for more than two hours he
had directed the traffic himself.

He saw a jeep now, and the helmets of two MPs, bouncing along the
side of the wider road and skidding to a halt. They emerged, scrambling
into the intersection, and saw him now, but he pretended to ignore them,
motioning crisply to the oncoming trucks, calling out, "That's right. Step
on the gas. There's a war up there, you know!"

"Sir! Good God, it's—"

He turned to the MPs with an evil smile, continued the steady waving
motion of his arm, and said, "Hello, boys. Someone sleep late this morning?"

"No, sir! No . . . sorry, sir. We'll take over . . . if you want us to!"

He spun toward them, both hands on his hips. "I'm doing just fine,
thank you! Get back in that vehicle and drive back along this column and
tell each driver to keep close to the man in front of him! These are soldiers,
boys! This is an army! I want them up where they can kill the enemy!"

They hesitated, one man still unsure. "Sir, we should be doing . . .
that."

"Yep, you should. But I'm doing it now." Patton turned back to the
line of trucks and waved them forward: more cheers, men standing up in
the beds, raucous calls, cameras, his name. "You heard me. Get going!"
The MPs scrambled back to their jeep, spun around in a cloud of dirt, and
disappeared behind the column.

Morons, he thought. There was artillery now, a long row of cannon,
pulled by smaller trucks, and he motioned them into the intersection. He
studied the guns as they passed, thinking, This is kind of fun, actually.
Can't do it too much longer, though. I'm already late to the war.

His aide was Lieutenant Colonel Charles Codman, whose clipped,
precise manners made him an odd contrast to the man he served.
Codman had joined Patton's staff in Sicily a year before, bringing with him
the culture and grace of a well-traveled businessman. He spoke several lan-
guages and seemed comfortable in any company, but he was a soldier as
well, having been decorated as a pilot in the First World War, that particular pedigree Patton would always value in any man he served with. Even
better, Codman took every dressing down Patton had given him and stood
tall in the process. Patton knew, as did everyone in his command, that

cursing and shouts went with the job, at least in Patton's headquarters. If you didn't take it personally, and did your job to Patton's satisfaction, you got along with him just fine.

They rode alongside marching columns, soldiers in motion, all forward. Patton nodded to them as they reacted to the jeep, more of the same enthusiasm he had grown used to. He leaned forward.

"This still the Ninetieth?"

"Yes, sir."

"Good. They don't look too bad. Make damned sure they keep moving. This isn't a vacation, for God's sake. I want these men to win something for a change."

"Yes, sir. They will, sir."

"Damn right."

Patton had attended Teddy Roosevelt's funeral, one of the select few invited to the low-key affair. But the business of war took precedence to sentiment, and immediately Patton had sought out Ray McLain, the man Eisenhower had selected to take the job left open by Roosevelt's death. McLain had commanded the Forty-fifth Division in Sicily, and Patton had been gratified and relieved that the Ninetieth, for all its difficulties, was finally in the hands of a man who would by all accounts whip it into shape. The Ninetieth was now assigned to Patton's command, a homecoming that McLain had seemed to appreciate as well. As the surge continued eastward, Patton had positioned the Ninetieth on the vanguard of this part of the infantry advance, testing whether or not McLain had truly turned their fortunes around. So far, they had yet to meet a real test. As had happened throughout most of Patton's extraordinary advance, German resistance had seemed mostly to collapse from the pure weight of Patton's audacity. No one in the Allied command had ever raced so many troops forward with so much raw speed. Before German resistance could jell into a cohesive defense, Patton's forces would be past them. Those units who did form some kind of wall were simply overrun by the stampede of the Americans. Patton had no interest in stopping anywhere along the way to wage a static battle. To Patton's staff, the greatest challenge was coming up with maps that Patton had not yet driven his army beyond. On August 8, the first units of Patton's Fifteenth Corps reached Le Mans, seventy-five miles from Avranches, rolling into the city with virtually no opposition. Almost immediately, the order was given, and the vanguard of Patton's forces turned north. To their west, von Kluge's Seventh Army was still prodding the

American front, but with Bradley's strengthening of the lines, and the incessant air assaults on the German positions, the steam had been drained from von Kluge's futile attack. With Patton now moving up behind them, the Germans were in danger of being surrounded. Bradley's plan was working.

42. PATTON

"Too slow, Ray! I want that damned town under our belt by three o'clock!"

McLain stood tall, didn't flinch. Patton had gone through this exercise before and knew McLain had a perfect handle on his men. The job would be done.

"Three o'clock it will be, sir."

Patton raised the binoculars and saw movement on the horizon: a column of tanks—his own.

"Look at them, Ray! Wide open ground! Your boys can make damned good time if they'll just stick close to the armor. Nobody in our way! You've got too many men on foot!"

"We're trying to close up to them. The trucks are pushing hard, but the traffic's pretty rough. There are too few trucks up this far, and some of my boys have no choice but to walk. Slows us down."

Patton lowered the field glasses. "Too few trucks?" He turned and saw Codman at the jeep. "Where's that supply convoy we passed?"

Codman responded immediately. "Five miles back, maybe closer. They should be up this way pretty quickly, if they keep pushing."

Patton stared back down the road, dust everywhere, cursed to himself. "I want them up here now. Right now! Get on the radio, find out who's in command of that column. They're hauling . . . what, blankets? Damned waste of gasoline."

He heard the roar of engines, the dust clouds billowing up on the road, and was surprised to see the lead truck. Good, he thought. Very damned good. We'll see about *walking*.

"Hold those people up, right here!"

Codman obeyed, aides scrambling into the road, arms waving, the lead truck skidding to a halt.

Patton moved that way, ignored the dust, shouted, "Who's in command here?"

The driver stepped down, saluted, wide-eyed, said, "Captain January, sir!"

"Who? What kind of stupid-ass name is that?"

"Uh . . . I don't know, sir!"

"Well, where the hell is Captain January?"

Men were emerging from the trucks farther back, some staring in frozen disbelief at Patton. One man moved quickly forward: clean uniform, a voice like a child.

"What's the meaning of this? I'm under orders from General Patton to get these supplies into Argentan!" The man stopped, stumbled, caught himself, his eyes on Patton. "Oh!"

Patton waited for the man to compose himself. He's twelve years old, for God's sake.

"You would be Captain January, then?"

January saluted, stood stiffly. "Yes, sir. My column has arrived on schedule, sir."

"Oh, stuff that noise, Captain, I want your trucks. Get your cargo unloaded immediately. We'll make a dump right out here in this field."

"Sir? Unload . . . here?"

"You deaf, January? Right here! Right now! I need these damned trucks."

The man seemed to quiver. "But, sir, these trucks are assigned to me. General Lee will want to know what happened to them—"

"General Lee is back in London sipping tea in his castle. I'm in charge out here, and as far as you or anyone else is concerned these are my trucks.

I have rifle-toting soldiers who are walking when they need to ride. You get that? Why in hell am I explaining this to you? Unload this junk right now!"

"Yes, sir!"

Patton turned and saw McLain watching him with a slight smile, which McLain tried to hide. Patton moved that way again and gripped the binoculars.

"Morons. An army of morons. If John Lee ever pries himself away from his caviar long enough to actually visit this war, I'll drive him right up to the Kraut lines and show him what this army is *supposed* to be doing."

McLain couldn't help the smile now. "The army needs supply people too, sir."

"Bull. The army needs *supplies*. The people I can do without. January! I should put a rifle in that kid's hands, see what kind of soldier he is."

Patton raised the glasses again, stared across a wide hilly plain, a column of trucks in view now, the tanks gone, over the horizon.

"Time to go, Ray. I need to look at a map. We should be in Monty's front yard about now."

NEAR LAVAL

AUGUST 12, 1944

"Where the hell is Monty? I thought the Brits were supposed to be here by now!"

Bradley didn't respond, the phone silent for a long moment. Patton raised his voice. "You hear me okay, Brad?"

"I hear you, George. Monty's had some trouble. The Canadians haven't pushed through Falaise yet."

"Trouble? Dammit, Brad, we're right where we're supposed to be! You ordered me to hold up at Argentan, and that's what we've done! Monty was supposed to be staring at us. Now, you're telling me he's still—what, twenty miles away?"

"He's doing what he can, George. It's been a tough go. I need you to hold at Argentan for now. The enemy is finally pulling back from Hodges's lines, and he's going to be heading your way."

Patton felt the explosion coming, shouted away from the phone. "Of *course* he's coming! That's why we're *here*!" He tried to calm himself, saw officers watching him: the corps commander, Haislip; McLain; others; none

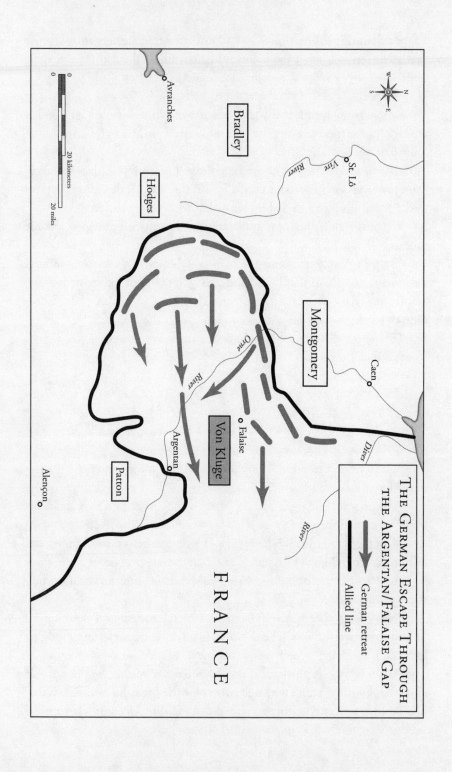

THE GERMAN ESCAPE THROUGH
THE ARGENTAN/FALAISE GAP

German retreat
Allied line

FRANCE

Avranches

Bradley

Hodges

St. Lô

Vire River

Montgomery

Caen

Orne River

Falaise

Argentan

Von Kluge

Patton

Alençon

Dives

River

20 kilometers

20 miles

of them happy. Patton gripped the phone, tried to hold his control, spoke slowly.

"Look, Brad. We can advance to Falaise ourselves, put some tanks up there in an hour. The Krauts are still to the west, and we've got a perfect shot at cutting them off completely! That was the plan, right?"

There was silence again.

After an agonizing pause, Bradley said, "Yes, that was the plan. But you have to hold at Argentan. I want no confusion on that point, George. None at all. Falaise is inside Monty's boundary. It won't do for you to cross over. It could cause problems."

Patton felt the hot burst in his brain, that word again: *problems.*

"Brad! Let me send my boys up there. Haislip already has tanks moving that way. What the hell difference does it make about Monty's boundary? We'll drive the British back into the damned sea. We'll make our own Dunkirk! But we have to close this gap!"

"Nothing doing! You button up at Argentan, and build up your shoulders. The enemy could hit you pretty quick."

"To hell with that! The enemy won't come anywhere near us! He's got a twenty-mile gap to slip through!"

"It's eighteen miles, and Monty knows what he has to do. If you extend to Falaise your lines will be thin. The German is bringing his whole force back your way."

"He's bringing his whole force because he's retreating! He's beaten! All we have to do is scoop him up! Dammit, Brad!"

"Enough, George. You have your orders. Hold your position at Argentan!"

The phone clicked: silence. Patton still held it to his ear, in desperate hopes that Bradley would change his mind. But Bradley was gone, and Patton knew what he had to do. He looked toward Haislip.

"General, order the recall of your armor. We are not to extend our position north of Argentan."

"What? Sir—"

Patton shook his head, silencing the man. He stepped away from the communications truck and walked up a low rise, Codman following.

Patton waved him away. "No. Everybody stay put."

He moved up to the top of the rise, saw the last glow of the sun. Patton stared that way and thought of von Kluge. The German attack against Hodges had been a desperate gamble: idiotic strategy, *Hitler's* strategy.

Now von Kluge has to get his people out of a hell of a jam, and we're going to sit here and let him do it. God help me. Won't anyone let me win this war?

For the next week, the Argentan–Falaise gap flowed thick with German soldiers, who endured an unending horror of air strikes and artillery barrages. But there was no armor and no infantry to bar their escape. The cost to von Kluge's army was catastrophic, but even in catastrophe, tens of thousands of German soldiers survived the desperate march. On August 19, Montgomery's army finally pushed southward to close the door, Crerar's Canadians and elements of a Polish division meeting the Americans face-to-face at the town of Chambois. For the Germans who did not escape the pocket, the statistics told the tale of the damage that had been inflicted on von Kluge's army: ten thousand dead, fifty thousand prisoners. Predictably, von Kluge bore the full brunt of Hitler's rage, yet another commander who could not fulfill his Führer's dreams. On August 17, von Kluge received the order to return to Berlin, to make way for yet another of Hitler's ambitious generals. It was von Kluge's final order and one he would not obey. The next day, as his car took him away from his army, he ordered his driver to stop along the side of the road, and there Hans von Kluge swallowed a capsule of cyanide. He was dead in seconds.

Within days, Patton's army continued their push eastward, far outstripping the ability of a seething Montgomery to match either Patton's speed or his achievements. Despite Montgomery's ongoing sluggishness, and brewing disagreements with Eisenhower and Bradley over the next phase in their operations, Patton's focus remained on the goal he had set for himself, the liberation of France and the obliteration of the German army.

On August 15, the Allied cause received a considerable boost, the launch of Operation Dragoon, a massive American-led invasion of southern France. Though the operation had been a hot topic of debate, supported by Eisenhower and dismissed vigorously by Churchill, the operation was as great a success as Eisenhower had long predicted. Within short weeks, Allied forces driving northward from the Mediterranean would liberate the crucial port city of Marseille and then sweep all German resistance completely out of southern France, driving them back toward Germany itself. At the same time, Patton's forces had reached the Seine and the Meuse rivers. On August 25, the Germans surrendered the city of Paris.

Though every thought turned toward the end of the war, the escape by so many German soldiers through the Argentan–Falaise gap would come to haunt the Allies. Far from being beaten, those same soldiers would regroup. Even with Germany's resources so drained, they would resupply, and they would fight again. In the words of General Jim Gavin:

> The battle of Normandy ended on a very bad note. What could have been a battle of annihilation had been a battle that allowed many Germans to escape and fight again. As they went reeling across France to their homeland, using horses, bicycles, broken-down vehicles, and any other form of transportation they could get their hands on, many French, Belgian, and Dutch people who saw them making their way through the occupied countries were convinced that the war was over.

Those people were mistaken.

43. ROMMEL

He had been carried home by car on August 8, but the wounds were still severe, the pains—headaches mostly—never leaving him completely comfortable. His skull had been cracked in four places, that fact driven into him by a frustrated doctor. Rommel was a miserable patient at best. After too many days of his angry impatience, gripes about hospital beds and snail-like nurses, the doctor presented Rommel with a human skull and, with one blow of a mallet, demonstrated just what Rommel's injuries involved. The skull had been shattered into bits across Rommel's bedsheets. Though Rommel continued to suffer through the aggravation of his recovery, after the doctor's graphic illustration he endured with a bit less complaining.

But now he was home. He was still impatient, the damage to his eye so severe that he wore an eye patch, and the farsightedness in his healthy eye meant that he could not read without incurring yet another headache. But there had been help, from Admiral Ruge to Lucie to Speidel, those close to him reacting with infinite tolerance, helping him pass time by doing the reading for him. In mid-August, his son, Manfred, had come home, a leave granted the boy by officers who did not question when he might return. Now it was Manfred who read to him, Rommel and his son sharing time together that had been very rare before. Rommel had always known that his duty would keep him from home, so the boy had grown into adolescence rarely spending time with his illustrious father. Now, for a time, the yawning gap between them could be remedied. Even now, the boy did not talk of their years apart, as aware as his father that a soldier's life did not inspire close-knit families. But Rommel took advantage of these precious days, delighted by the fifteen-year-old's bright mind. Throughout long conversations Rommel learned something new about his son that had far larger meaning than their own relationship. Manfred had grown up in a world where Adolf Hitler reigned supreme, and Rommel could not just dismiss his son's continuing loyalty to the Führer. Hitler had, after all, indoctrinated an entire nation and was still supported by the fanatical loyalty of much of his army. The Gestapo's wide sweeping net had brought prominent names into the public eye, those men who had dared to conspire to murder the Führer, and Rommel had not been surprised that the army and the public had responded with carefully orchestrated outrage toward those men now labeled enemies of the Fatherland. Even his son reacted with furious umbrage that anyone who called himself a German would participate in such a grievous act. It was a conversation Rommel would not pursue. In his own mind, Rommel was disgusted with the conspirators, but not out of any loyalty or affection for Hitler. He despised the notion that any army officers could toss aside his oath and accept the murder of a superior, no matter the circumstance. But his soldier's mind saw deeper into the tactic, appraised and weighed, and he was just as disgusted by their amateurish planning. The plot had been created by a network of aristocratic drawing-room strategists who had depended on a crippled man to arm and place a bomb. Those men were mostly dead now, executed in ways too brutal and too graphic for him to discuss with his son. And it was not yet over. The Gestapo was continuing a relentless purge of anyone who could be drawn into some connection with the plot itself or even with the conspirators.

Rommel's recovery relied partly on exercise, and for days now Manfred had accompanied him on frequent walks, winding paths near the house, through the woods that Rommel loved. But word had come, from friends and from visiting officers still loyal to him. The Gestapo was watching him and had established an unnerving presence in the small town, men in black uniforms who seemed to enjoy frightening the local prefect. Their presence had clear meaning to Rommel. As the walks with his son continued, Rommel armed them both with pistols. If the Gestapo or anyone else sought to eliminate him with a clumsy assassination attempt, there would at least be a fight.

"How are you, Hans?"

Speidel bowed slightly. "I have been removed as chief of staff of Army Group B."

Rommel sipped from the cup and held it close to his face, the steam from the tea dampening the eye patch, soothing the rough dryness. "I heard."

"They did it with some decorum, as though there will be some post for me in the future. I should be honored not to have been dragged away in chains. I don't know who they intend to replace me with a job that is, I suppose, impossible."

"The job is a fantasy. What remains of Army Group B? How much *staff* were you *chief* of?"

Speidel looked toward a chair, a request to sit, and Rommel pointed. "My apologies. Rest yourself. We need not have any formality between us. Not any longer."

"So you do not expect to return to service?"

Rommel glanced down at his clothes, no hint of a uniform. "Service to what? Sorry, that is an inappropriate question. If my Führer summoned me to command, I would go."

"I am certain, sir, that *my* service has concluded."

Speidel seemed nervous, his hands fidgeting in front of him, one hand now up on his wire-rimmed glasses, a needless adjustment. Rommel felt the man's fear and searched for reassuring words.

"They have not yet arrested you. Surely if they intended that, it would have happened."

"It is coming very soon. I have been informed, discreetly. My time is short."

"Nonsense. You have friends, loyal friends. Loyal to the Führer. Even if they do arrest you, I will do what I can to speak out for you. As far as I know, even I have some friends remaining."

It was a weak attempt at humor, and Speidel did not smile. After a brief silence, Speidel said, "I have been reading *Mein Kampf.* Rereading it, of course. I thought if I grew more familiar with the Führer's ideals, it would be useful."

"It has been a while since I read it. Any revelations?"

Speidel nodded slowly. "Yes, actually. Not what I expected, though. He talks about the rights of officers. He claims that if any professional soldier believes he has been given an outrageous order, he has the right to rebel, to speak out, to act against it. It is the duty of a soldier to fight for the good of his fatherland, not merely the wishes of his superiors. I hadn't recalled reading that before."

"It wasn't relevant before."

"But it is relevant now!"

Speidel's voice had grown louder, and he was self-conscious, seeming to shrink slightly.

"No, I'm afraid you are wrong, Hans. There is only one relevance, and it need not appeal to you or to me. This is not a world in which a soldier has any importance. We are merely the pieces of a broken machine, broken ourselves."

"Sir, will you try again? Can you talk to Hitler, offer him some reasoning, some clarity? The war in the west is all but lost. We are in full retreat, and only by the grace of God does our army still have the means to fight. But there can be no victory! You must try to convince the Führer that some kind of entreaty must be made to the Americans."

"No. There is no longer any point. The High Command has insulated itself from any reality because that is what Hitler requires of them."

Speidel rubbed his hands together again, stared at the floor. "How different things would be if they had killed him."

Rommel sat up, tried not to feel the throb of pain in his head. "Different? How? I can tell you, Hans. Hitler would now be a martyr to those who believed in him. Those who were the most loyal would fight to maintain power, and that would mean civil war. Hitler's power was given to him by a fanatical belief that he would preserve us, eliminate the enemies of Germany who tried mightily to destroy us after the last war. He convinced us that he spoke only for the good of Germany, that he would bring a unique peace to the entire world, a world ruled by German ideals. Too many of us believed him, believed that was a *good* thing. Many believe it now! If Hitler is killed by our hands, those who believe in him will draw strength from his message, and that alone would inspire enough fanaticism to continue this war. Worse, they will wage war on anyone inside Germany who does not agree.

Rommel paused. "That was always the mistake, always the stupidity of the plan! All of you seemed to think that Hitler's death would bring about some kind of peaceful breeze to Germany, as though all the hate and anger and brutality would simply vanish! I admit, for a time I believed that the British and the Americans would accept that *we* are not their enemy! I struggled with the idea that we should make direct contact with them, that I should commit treason by sending someone, *you,* perhaps, through our lines, to communicate to them that we were willing to end the war on their terms. For a while, I believed it would work, I truly did. But then I saw what was happening to our army. I saw what kind of effort they were making to kill us. And not just our Führer but all of us! The bombers do not target the Führer, they target German cities! I thought we could ask them to join with us, to save Germany by helping us stand up to the Russians. A fool's dream."

He paused again, rubbed a hand softly on the patch on his eye.

"There will be no peace without unconditional surrender. It is not merely Hitler who wages this war, it is the German army. We pledged an oath to him and we fought for him, and whether he dies tomorrow or lives for fifty years, we must accept that the defeat belongs to us. This is our responsibility, Hans! Ours!"

Rommel stopped, felt drained of energy, saw Manfred standing at the door.

"Come in here, son. Sit down."

The boy obeyed, a short respectful nod toward Speidel.

"Manfred, do you remember what I told you about obedience?"

"Yes, sir."

"What I told him, Hans, was that if he intends to be a soldier, he must learn not to question. I told him that one day he will receive an order he does not understand or does not agree with. He has no choice but to obey that order unconditionally." He looked at Manfred. "Now I am telling him that such obedience has destroyed us. He does not yet believe me, but he will."

Speidel looked toward the boy, who stayed silent. "Your father is correct. Each of us must pay a price for our obedience." He looked again at Rommel, stood slowly. "I will pay my own very soon, I fear." Speidel snapped his heels together, raised a salute. "I am honored to have been in your service, Field Marshal."

Rommel did not want Speidel to leave, but there was nothing else he could say, no words of comfort. He felt a knot rising in his throat and pushed himself up from the chair, Manfred surging forward to help, grabbing his arm, lifting. Rommel stepped closer to Speidel, ignored the salute, held out a hand. Speidel glanced down, seemed to fight for control, took the hand, and Rommel felt the firmness, the man's resolve.

"There is no justice, sir," Speidel said.

"Oh, yes, there is, Hans. In the end, there will be justice for all of us."

S peidel was arrested the next day. Rommel went to work immediately on his behalf, producing a lengthy letter to Hitler, imploring him to remember Speidel's efficient and loyal service, to the army and to the Führer himself. But no word came from Berlin, no response at all. Rommel had no idea where Speidel was or if anything had yet happened to him.

HERRLINGEN, SOUTHERN GERMANY
OCTOBER 14, 1944

Rommel sat alone in his study, glanced up at the clock—nearly noon—knew that Lucie would have some sort of lunch put out soon, to accommodate their guest. Captain Hermann Aldinger was one of Rommel's most long-standing aides, a friend as well as a subordinate, who had served with Rommel as far back as the First World War. Rommel welcomed Aldinger as he had welcomed the steady parade of well-wishers and former comrades-in-arms, but the visits from friends had grown less frequent, word continuing to spread that the house and Rommel himself were under the watchful eye of the Gestapo. Rommel felt restless. He picked up a paper on his desk, read it—his eyesight had improved—and thought, My friends have jumped this ship like so many rats. But do I blame them? What future is there for anyone who lingers around here? He focused on the paper, scanned the small sketch of a map, studied for a long moment. If this is accurate, he thought, it seems there is some hope. A delay in the inevitable, I suppose.

Rommel continued to receive reports from the battlefronts, passed

along by former staff officers and loyal subordinates. He had been surprised that despite the chaotic annihilation of so much of his army, some
organization was returning, the defenses that kept the enemy out of Germany still holding. It was logical to a soldier that no army, no matter their
success, could maintain the kind of aggressive push the Allies had thrown
against the Germans. Even victorious men must have rest, he thought, and
so there will be delays. They must rejuvenate and bring in replacements
and supplies. We must make good use of that small favor. It might be all
we have. He glanced again at the map, names of units and commanders,
good men, some of them, men who will still fight. And someone will step
forward to lead them. But it will not be me.

He tossed the map aside and glanced at a lone paper, sitting separately
on the corner of his desk. It had come on October 8, a note from General
Keitel, a summons for Rommel to travel to Berlin. The request had been
formal but not hostile; arrangements made for a private train to carry him,
as though protecting him from the crowds. The thought echoed through
him now, as it had on that day. How utterly stupid do they think I am? Is
this someone's idea of a well-conceived plot? He had already heard hints
from several friends closer to Hitler, word slipping out that Rommel was a
marked man. Hitler himself had lost faith that Rommel could ever be
trusted again. Rommel knew there was no direct connection tying him
to the plot to kill Hitler, because no such connection existed. But the
Gestapo relied less on facts than on their own paranoia, and he knew they
were continuing to gather up anyone who had demonstrated any vague an-
imosity toward Hitler. That would certainly include me, he thought. You
do not have to be an inept conspirator to understand why Hitler cannot
win this war, and I have been too honest about that. So now they will remove me. A train, no less. So what would they do? Would there be a bomb
on the tracks, something the High Command could trumpet loudly was
the outrageous act of some underground agent? Perhaps some itinerant
madman will jump aboard and shoot me in his deranged lunacy. He would
then shoot himself, of course, the neatest way to solve the problem of any
witness. It would be a terrible accident of fate, so the headlines would say,
inspiring sorrow from every corner of the Reich. The Führer could then
wring his hands publicly and declare that, all over Germany, the insane in
the hospitals must be executed as reprisal for the tragic death of the great
hero, the Desert Fox. Why should he exclude them, after all? Has he not
already executed anyone whose culture he found repulsive?

He sat back, blinked the injured eye inside the patch, and squeezed it shut for a long painful moment. *Perhaps the train would be safe, and they will wait until I reach Berlin. A trial perhaps, some general reading aloud carefully edited excerpts from my letters to Hitler, all my traitorous pessimism. No, they will risk none of that, no public show, no chance for me to speak out, to tell my own truth. It could prove embarrassing. Instead, they will do it . . . here.*

When the letter arrived, he had phoned Keitel, who had been far too busy to take the call, consumed of course by the business of the High Command. Rommel had been tossed off to Wilhelm Burgdorf, an old acquaintance from before the war, a man who knew very well why Rommel had called and why Keitel would not speak to him. Rommel had been careful but direct to Burgdorf. There would be no visit to Berlin, no need for some special train. He was, after all, still recovering from severe wounds and he was not yet fit to travel. Burgdorf had been compassionate and understanding, but then, five days later, word came to Rommel's home. Burgdorf would travel instead to see *him*.

He heard footsteps above him, thought of Lucie, padding around on the second floor, nervous, fiddling with laundry or bed linens. Manfred was there as well, home again after a brief return to his antiaircraft battery. Rommel heard a car outside, gravel and tires, and felt a rumble in his gut, the tight knot he had felt so many times before. *Burgdorf. Damn you.*

The conversation had a solemn air, nothing openly hostile, Burgdorf reading an order from Keitel, emphasizing Keitel's assurance that it came directly from Hitler. Rommel didn't need that assurance. He knew Keitel had never made an independent decision. If Rommel was to be eliminated, Keitel would merely be the messenger.

Burgdorf was accompanied by another general, Ernst Maisel, a skinny ferret of a man whom Rommel barely knew. As they spoke, Maisel stood silently to one side, and Rommel knew he was there more to witness the conversation, and perhaps to protect Burgdorf, the pistol on his belt conspicuous, the flap over the holster unfastened. Rommel could be dangerous, after all.

Burgdorf spoke to him in earnest tones, reminiscing about Rommel's more glorious days, a useless rehashing of exploits that Rommel himself had no interest in recalling. But then, after long minutes of pointless conversation, Burgdorf got to the point. The papers emerged from a narrow briefcase, excerpts of testimony from the many secret trials of the conspirators in the assassination plot, some of the accused mentioning Rommel by name, as though he were certainly aware of the plan. After a half hour of emotionless accusations, there had been a final order, Burgdorf allowing Rommel time to speak to his family. Then, the two officers stepped outside, to wait in Rommel's garden. He had been granted ten minutes.

He changed from the civilian clothes and buttoned up his jacket, the tan tunic that bore the insignia of the Afrika Korps. It was his favorite uniform. She sat on the bed and watched him, her hands wrapped together in her lap.

"How can they do this, Erwin?" The emotions were rising in her, redness in her eyes.

Rommel glanced at his uniform in the mirror. "They do this because they believe it is the right thing to do. They are doing their job. They have evidence that claims I am in conspiracy with people I have never met. They have volumes of ridiculous proof that I am a traitor to the Reich. It does not matter if it is false."

"Well, tell them it is false!"

"I have told them, my sweet. There is no argument here, no room for debate. This is all some sort of ceremony, and they are both good officers. I had thought perhaps they would want to extort something from me, that Hitler would still believe me useful. I had hoped perhaps he would force me to make some sort of public speech, some valiant call to arms supporting the fantasy that this war can be won. That was . . . optimistic of me. I know now that my fate was decided before they left Berlin. They first offered to have me stand trial, to accept public humiliation."

"Well, yes! Do that! What does it matter now?"

His own emotions were loosening, his voice rising. "It is a sham! I would never survive long enough to reach my own trial. If I accompany them away from here, I promise you, my assassination has already been planned. They don't dare give me a trial and will not risk having me speak out. And I would not risk it either. If I had dared to give them any kind of truth, anything they did not want to hear, it was very clear that there would be a price for *you* to pay. You and Manfred would become targets as well, enemies of the state. I will not have you suffer. There is nothing to be gained by *truth*. Not anymore."

She began to cry now. "I cannot understand this. You are accepting death. What am I to do? How do I respond to that?"

He tried to hold back his own tears, but there was no need now. "You are the wife of a soldier. You accepted my death when you married me."

"Father?"

Rommel turned, saw Manfred at the door, the boy staring at his mother with alarm. "What is it? Are they arresting you? I saw more cars outside . . . civilians."

Rommel motioned for the boy to enter. "Yes, I know. They are Gestapo. Manfred, I must be brief. In one quarter hour, I will be dead."

Lucie made a gasping sound, the tears flowing.

"No . . . that cannot be," Manfred said. "Why?"

"It is done, Manfred. Those men have evidence that I am complicit in the plot to assassinate the Führer. It is all lies, confessions drawn from tortured men, but they must have their prizes. I am . . . regrettably . . . a prize. I have been granted assurances, that by doing this now, my family will not be harmed or disgraced."

"Do *what* now?" Manfred moved closer to his mother, put a hand on her shoulder.

"I must go with those men." He saw the fear in his boy's eyes, the questions, the anger. Rommel moved closer to them both, said in a low voice, "I knew my life would end because of this war. I always knew. I have survived many times when I should have been killed. But there is nothing else that can be done now. To die by the hand of one's own people is . . . difficult. But you have seen it yourself. The house is surrounded, and those men are here for one reason."

"We can fight them, Father! I have the pistol—"

"It is of no use. We would be killed in seconds. I will not have you harmed, either of you. Obey me now."

The boy began to cry now, soft sobs, and Rommel put his hand on the back of the boy's neck, gripped him hard. He leaned low, Lucie looking up at him, and kissed her, tasted her tears. He stepped back, took a long breath, and fought for calm.

"I must go now."

The car rolled slowly, Burgdorf in the backseat beside him, Maisel in front beside the driver. Rommel had seen Burgdorf's pistol, knew that both men were prepared for him to resist, and that somewhere behind them the men in civilian clothes had their orders and would certainly obey them.

The car moved out through the garden gate, and Rommel stared out into darkening trees, hearing every sound: the crunch of gravel beneath the wheels, the breathing of the man beside him.

"May I inquire . . . where we are going?"

Burgdorf pointed ahead, spoke to the driver.

"Up the hill. Through those woods. There is an open field, enclosed by thick trees. It is very secluded there."

How do you know that? But then Rommel thought, Of course. Every detail has been planned.

The car rolled past the narrow stretch of woods, the trees giving way to open ground, the wide field Burgdorf had described. It was familiar, a place Rommel had taught Manfred to shoot.

Burgdorf said, "This is far enough. Halt the car."

The car stopped abruptly.

Burgdorf looked at Rommel. "This is the best way, you know. It will take only three seconds."

Rommel saw him glance downward, saw the small capsule in Burgdorf's hand. The hand opened wider, and Rommel took the capsule, rolled it over between his fingers. Burgdorf looked toward the front of the car.

"You may leave us now."

The front doors opened, and the driver and Maisel left the car, another well-rehearsed detail.

Rommel watched them moving away, no talking, their backs to the car. He felt a shiver, fought the fear, and said, "I am a loyal German, Wilhelm."

"So are we all, Field Marshal."

Rommel stared at the capsule in his hand. "You have given me your word that no harm will come to my family."

"I have. There is nothing to be gained by harming them. They will not be disgraced. You will always be a hero, Field Marshal."

Rommel felt his breathing in short bursts, cold thunder in his chest, thought of Lucie, her tears. There is nothing else I can do. His jaw clenched, his only protest, and he forced himself to relax, opened his mouth, slapped the capsule inside, a brief burst of bitterness, forced himself to swallow. He stared ahead, his throat tightening, no air in his lungs, a cold hard claw curling through his chest, the car swirling, his mind holding to a brief glow of sky, sand and tanks, and Africa.

AFTERWORD

The fact that your husband, Field Marshal Rommel, has died a hero's death as a result of his wounds . . . has deeply touched me. I send you, my dear Frau Rommel, the heartfelt sympathy of myself and the German Luftwaffe. In silent compassion, yours,

REICHSMARSCHALL HERMANN GÖRING
LETTER TO LUCIE ROMMEL, OCTOBER 1944

Of course Rommel, ultimately, was beaten. He lost. But, although what must matter in war is to win, that truism cannot provide the sole criterion for judgment of military talent. War may be considered as a business, open to audit, but its conduct is also an art. Napoleon was beaten. So was Montrose. So was Lee. Few could deny their genius. With all his imperfections, as a leader of men in battle, Erwin Rommel stands in their company.

BRITISH GENERAL AND HISTORIAN DAVID FRASER

God deliver us from our friends. We can handle the enemy.

GEORGE PATTON

THE GERMANS

HANS SPEIDEL

Rommel's most valued aide testifies before two separate courts of inquiry and confounds the Gestapo prosecutors with his carefully conceived explanations. Ultimately, he cannot be linked specifically to any of the conspirators. Unable to justify his execution, the Gestapo holds him in prison for seven months. Days before the war's end, he escapes captivity near Lake Constance, close to the German-Swiss border, and evades capture until Allied troops liberate the area. Speidel is the most closely involved participant in the plot to assassinate Adolf Hitler to survive the war.

Speidel is never implicated in war crimes and thus is not included in the Allied prosecution of Germany's elite generals. After the war, he returns to academia and enjoys several years as a professor of history at Tübingen University. He continues to be active in political affairs, works vigorously to have (West) Germany included in the unified front that becomes NATO, and believes—as did Rommel—that the Soviets will continue to be the greatest threat to a peaceful Europe.

He writes often of Rommel and his campaigns and in 1950 publishes *Invasion, 1944—Rommel and the Normandy Campaign,* considered by military historians to be a prime resource for insight on Rommel and his command. He takes temporary leave of academia and returns to the military, rising to the rank of full general in Germany's NATO command. In 1957, Speidel is named commander-in-chief of NATO ground forces in central Europe. He retires in 1964 and returns again to teaching at Tübingen. Speidel dies in Bad Honnef, Germany, in 1984, at age eighty-seven.

LEO GEYR VON SCHWEPPENBERG

The panzer commander who was so often Rommel's nemesis is best known for his stubborn unwillingness to agree with Rommel's tactics against the Allied invasion, at a time when cooperation might have turned the tide of the entire campaign. After the Allied bombing raid on June 10, which causes the near-total loss of his staff and headquarters, a wounded and demoralized Geyr begins to accept that the Allies cannot be turned back. He infuriates Hitler with what the German High Command labels the "mimicry" of Rommel's defeatist attitudes, so his July 2 dismissal is inevitable.

Geyr is captured by the Americans at the end of the war and is imprisoned for two years. Upon his release, he writes several articles on military tactics and strategy, repeatedly engaging in a one-sided argument against Rommel's tactics in Normandy, for which he receives little attention. Geyr dies near Munich in 1974, at age eighty-eight.

MANFRED ROMMEL

The field marshal's only child surrenders to the French in 1945, and with the war at an end he is allowed to return to his mother's home in Herrlingen. Within two years, he enrolls at the University of Tübingen, where he maintains a close acquaintance with Hans Speidel, but Manfred chooses a different field of study and earns a law degree. As his father's son and by his own abilities, Manfred quickly establishes prominence in the legal profession. He pursues a career as well in politics, serves in several municipal-level offices, including a term as mayor of Stuttgart. In 1995, he is appointed by German chancellor Helmut Kohl to the prestigious (and somewhat ironic) post of supervisor of Franco-German affairs. He retires from public life in 1996 and lives today in Stuttgart. His first-person account of Erwin Rommel's final days is arguably the most reliable and the most oft-quoted perspective on the extraordinary drama of his father's death.

FRIEDRICH RUGE

Erwin Rommel's closest friend during the Normandy campaign, the German admiral survives the war and writes of his experiences in a number of books and articles, most notably *Rommel and the Invasion*. He continues his service in the now-downsized German navy and serves as chief inspector of the Bundesmarine for six years, retiring in 1961. Like Hans Speidel, his reputation as an excellent officer and markedly intelligent man lands him a teaching post at the University of Tübingen. Admiral Ruge serves as president of the most prominent organization of German war veterans, the League of the Veterans of the Bundeswehr.

As a much-sought-after lecturer on naval strategies and applications, Ruge is a frequent visitor to the United States, lecturing often at the U.S. Naval War College at Newport, Rhode Island. He dies in 1985, at age ninety-one. A collection of his papers is housed today at the Citadel, in Charleston, South Carolina.

THE BRITISH

SIR ARTHUR TEDDER

Throughout his tenure as Eisenhower's second-in-command for Operation Overlord, the British air marshal continues to serve with admirable restraint through the tumultuous weeks of controversy between the ground commanders Montgomery, Bradley, and Patton. In October 1944, he returns to a more hands-on role over his beloved tactical air force, when he is named to replace the abrasive and universally disliked Trafford Leigh-Mallory. As senior air commander in Europe, Tedder continues to impress Eisenhower and is widely regarded as the finest British air force officer of the war. As Germany becomes pressed between the advances of the Allies and the Russians, tactical coordination with the Russian air force becomes essential, and Tedder assumes he will move into that role. But he is considered "too American" for some British tastes, notably including Alan Brooke and Bernard Montgomery, and in early 1945, pressure mounts to replace him with Harold Alexander. But Eisenhower lobbies against that change, for despite Eisenhower's affection and respect for Alexander, he knows Tedder is better qualified for the job. It is one more controversy of ego and personality that Eisenhower must wrestle with, and his loyalty to Tedder ensures a lasting friendship between the two men.

At the war's end, in May 1945, Tedder serves as senior Allied delegate to accept Germany's surrender in Berlin.

After the war, Tedder accepts the position of chief of staff of the Royal Air Force. He retires in 1950, to assume the post of chairman of the British Joint Services Commission in the United States, and steps down from that role in 1951 to become chancellor of Cambridge University. In 1966, he writes his memoirs and dies a year later in Surrey, England, at age seventy-six.

TRAFFORD LEIGH-MALLORY

For reasons that frustrate and perplex only him, Leigh-Mallory is never given credit for his positive accomplishments in command of the Allied tactical air forces throughout the invasion of Normandy. Seen as petty, vindictive, and generally ineffective, he is widely ignored by the men he allegedly commands. Eisenhower never warms to the man and, in October 1944, welcomes the opportunity to replace him with Arthur Tedder. But Leigh-Mallory has earned respect for his longevity of service to the air command and thus receives appointment as commander in chief of air services in southeast Asia, under the overall command of Lord Louis Mountbatten. In November 1944, Leigh-Mallory and his wife begin the arduous airplane journey to his new command in Burma. The plane crashes en route, and both are killed. He is fifty-two.

SIR FREDERICK MORGAN

The officer responsible for the plan that becomes Operation Overlord is for the most part a forgotten footnote to the history of that event. Morgan's extraordinary efforts produce the blueprint for the Normandy invasion, and though it is changed considerably by the addition of more troops and a wider invasion landscape, it is Morgan's concept to drive the assault into Normandy, rather than the more obvious point of attack at Calais. Perhaps Morgan's greatest accomplishment is assembling a team of British and American planners who manage to maintain a cohesive and productive working relationship, something Eisenhower struggles with throughout his entire command.

Morgan serves under Eisenhower at SHAEF for the remainder of the war and goes to Germany at the war's end to assist in coordinating the fledgling United Nations' support efforts for the devastated German economy. He retires from the British army in 1951 and is appointed controller of the British Atomic Energy agency. For three years in the mid-1950s, he is Britain's senior controller of atomic weapons.

He writes his memoirs and dies in 1967, at age seventy-three.

THE AMERICANS

JESSE ADAMS

In late August 1944, while the Eighty-second Airborne's newest first sergeant awaits his unit's next assignment, Adams is seriously injured during a training jump. He breaks an ankle and both arms when his parachute tangles with another trooper, who does not survive the fall. Thus, Adams misses the Eighty-second Airborne's involvement in Operation Market-Garden in Holland in September 1944. He never fully recovers from the injury, and is again offered an opportunity to return to Fort Benning, Georgia. Knowing his combat days are likely past, Adams considers the transfer, though, despite James Gavin's support, Adams's proposed commission as second lieutenant is never approved. Adams swallows the slight and returns to Fort Benning in January 1945, but his enthusiasm for training new recruits cannot match the passion he feels for the fight that he is missing in Europe. While on a brief leave in Columbus, Georgia, his injuries are aggravated by a serious jeep accident, and he will never jump again. In June 1945, Adams is discharged from the army and begins the journey home by train to New Mexico. The end of the war affects Adams as it does a great many who served in the most grueling fights, and he has no enthusiasm for the life he expects to find in peacetime. However, on the journey home, he meets Nancy Forbes, a former army nurse, who is returning to her home in Los Angeles. Over the course of the three-day journey, Adams finds a new direction for his passion. They marry in September 1945, after a two-month engagement, and he fathers four boys, two of whom will enlist to fight in the Vietnam War, both serving in the Eighty-second Airborne Division.

The family settles in Santa Barbara, California, and Adams pursues a career in real estate, surprising himself with his talent for deal-making in the fledging boom market of 1950s California. He is enormously successful and enjoys traveling with his family, including his mother, whom he brings into their home upon the death of his father. Though they sail the Pacific and vacation in Hawaii and Asia, he will not return to Europe.

He frequently attends the airborne's reunions and in 1954 is reunited for the first time with the one man who eventually becomes his closest friend, Wallace Unger. Because the men will rarely talk with others about their shared experiences, their time together is most often a closed-door affair, both men accepting that few can understand their need to release the memories. They also share a common bond, provided by the army and the efforts of Jim Gavin. Both men are awarded the Bronze Star, Adams for his gallantry in Sicily, Unger for his actions in the Cotentin Peninsula.

Adams retires in 1990, a wealthy landowner, and lives with his wife in Montecito, California.

Hell, I'm not a hero. I just liked to jump out of airplanes. It didn't much matter that along the way I had to kill Germans. They shot at me, and missed. I shot back. And didn't.

JESSE ADAMS

TOM THORNE

The young soldier who survives the 116th Regiment's disastrous landing at Omaha Beach returns to the states in August 1944, after a lengthy stay at a hospital in England. The loss of his legs confines him to a wheelchair for the rest of his life. Thorne will not accept repeated efforts from his family or various veterans' groups to furnish him with artificial legs. He is awarded a Bronze Star for his actions on Omaha Beach, will not display it, and never attends reunions of the 116th Regiment, the men who embellish their nickname as the Stonewall Brigade. Despite many invitations from local civic groups in and around his hometown of Fredericksburg, Virginia, Thorne will not speak publicly of his experiences during the war. Thorne's marriage fails after ten difficult years. His daughter, Ella, remains as close to her father as he will allow, and he never parts with the photograph of her as an infant, which he somehow managed to retrieve from his helmet liner on the day of his wounding. But he never accepts his fate and dies in 1958 of a self-inflicted gunshot wound at age thirty-six.

EDWIN SCOFIELD

Major Scofield jumps into combat yet again during Operation Market-Garden in Holland in September 1944 and, as in Sicily and Normandy, he leads his company with considerable gallantry. But like so many of the paratroopers who witnessed the birth of the Eighty-second Airborne, Scofield cannot survive so many tests of his own luck. On September 20, 1944, he is seriously wounded at Nijmegen, Holland. He spends four months in a British hospital and then returns to the States. An unwilling participant in the army's downsizing after the war, Scofield suffers lingering effects of his wounds and retires in 1947. He returns to college, graduates with an accounting degree from Penn State University, and lives a peaceful life as a bank examiner until his retirement in 1977. He regularly attends reunions of the Eighty-second Airborne, writes several articles about his experiences, and is always quick to mention his respect for the men in his command, notably his favorite noncom, Jesse Adams. He dies in Austin, Texas, in 2005, at age eighty.

JAMES GAVIN

"Slim Jim" succeeds Matthew Ridgway as commander of the Eighty-second Airborne Division in August 1944, and thus, at only thirty-seven years old and still a brigadier general, he becomes the youngest division commander in the American army since the Civil War. He receives his second star in October 1944, which also makes him the youngest major general in the army. Gavin not only earns the respect of his men but is singled out repeatedly for his actions on the battlefield and is awarded the Distinguished Service Cross, the Distinguished Service Medal, and the Silver Star, as well as a Purple Heart for having been wounded in combat. He is also awarded the British Distinguished Service Order, only rarely awarded to soldiers who serve outside the armed forces of the British Commonwealth.

Gavin remains in command of the Eighty-second Airborne until 1948, and throughout the 1950s becomes an outspoken advocate for a strong military, at a time when prevailing sentiment calls for downsizing. Frustrated that his is merely a voice in the wind, he nonetheless energizes various projects and the development of technology that advances a more mobile American army, including the utilization of helicopters, a practice that becomes the norm during the Vietnam War. But Gavin is not a man who flows with the tide, and despite earning his third star in 1958, he retires, believing the army has deteriorated because of infuriating interference from self-serving politicians, armchair strategists, and policy makers, all of whom Gavin despises.

He enters the world of private industry, serves eventually as chairman of Arthur D. Little & Company, a research and consulting firm, which he heads with great success until 1977. In 1961, he takes a brief leave of absence from the company, at the request of President Kennedy, and serves his country once more as ambassador to France, a post that thrusts him back into the world of political wrangling that he can tolerate for little more than a year.

Gavin writes several books that deal both with his personal experiences in the war and with his very opinionated take on the war in Vietnam, as well as various political and foreign-policy issues. Regardless of the controversy and the enemies that he creates by his outspokenness, he is beloved by the paratroopers who served under him.

He dies in 1990, at age eighty-two, and is buried at West Point.

WALLACE UNGER

Corporal Unger serves until the end of the war and makes his final combat jump into Holland during Operation Market-Garden. He is discharged in May 1945, and returns to his family home in Iowa. Like Jesse Adams, Unger finds civilian life unsettling, until he meets a woman who will unsettle him even more. He marries Rachel Todd in December 1946, and the couple has two children. Unger remains on his family farm and retires in 1996 at age seventy. Despite persistent efforts by his former sergeant to relocate Unger and his wife to a milder climate in California, Unger occupies his time by guiding pheasant hunters on his property and is, to this day, a crack shot.

And, from these pages: George Patton, Omar Bradley, Dwight David Eisenhower, Gerd von Rundstedt, Winston Churchill, Bernard Montgomery, Adolf Hitler, and many more:

After the enormous struggles of 1944, these men must still confront the war, which will continue for nearly a year after the Normandy invasion. It is a different story, of heroes and horror and the bloody collapse of a madman's twisted dream. Another story for another time.

ABOUT THE AUTHOR

JEFF SHAARA is the author of seven bestselling novels, critically acclaimed historical epics that cover the American Revolution, Mexican War, Civil War, and World Wars One and Two. He has also penned a nonfiction guide to America's Civil War battlefields. Shaara was born into a family of Italian immigrants in New Brunswick, New Jersey, and grew up in Tallahassee, Florida, where he graduated from Florida State University. After many years in Montana and New York City, he now lives in Sarasota, Florida.

Contact the author at www.jeffshaara.com.

ABOUT THE TYPE

This book was set in Garamond, a typeface originally designed by the Parisian typecutter Claude Garamond (1480–1561). This version of Garamond was modeled on a 1592 specimen sheet from the Egenolff-Berner foundry, which was produced from types assumed to have been brought to Frankfurt by the punchcutter Jacques Sabon.

Claude Garamond's distinguished romans and italics first appeared in *Opera Ciceronis* in 1543–44. The Garamond types are clear, open, and elegant.